Y046080

LAURA PURCELL is a former bestseller and lives in Colchester with her husband. Her first novel for Raven Books, *The Silent Companions*, was a Radio 2 and Zoe Ball ITV Book Club pick and was the winner of the WHSmith Thumping Good Read Award, while her subsequent books – *The Corset* and *Bone China* – established Laura's reputation for spooky, page-turning fiction.

laurapurcell.com
@spookypurcell

D1581777

BY THE SAME AUTHOR

The Silent Companions
The Corset
Bone China

THE SHAPE OF DARKNESS

Laura Purcell

R A V E N B O O K S
LONDON · OXFORD · NEW YORK · NEW DELHI · SYDNEY

RAVEN BOOKS
Bloomsbury Publishing Plc
50 Bedford Square, London, WC1B 3DP, UK
29 Earlsfort Terrace, Dublin 2, Ireland

BLOOMSBURY, RAVEN BOOKS and the Raven Books logo are
trademarks of Bloomsbury Publishing Plc

First published in Great Britain 2021
This edition published 2021

A catalogue record for this book is available from the British Library

ISBN: HB: 978-1-5266-0258-9; TPB: 978-1-5266-0257-2; PB: 978-1-5266-0254-1;
EBOOK: 978-1-5266-0256-5; EPDF: 978-1-5266-4503-6;
WATERSTONES SPECIAL EDITION: 978-1-5266-5128-0

2 4 6 8 10 9 7 5 3 1

Typeset by Integra Software Services Pvt. Ltd
Printed and bound in Great Britain by CPI Group (UK) Ltd, Croydon CR0 4YY

To find out more about our authors and books visit www.bloomsbury.com
and sign up for our newsletters

For Kevin

'... we together called into being, a weird shadow which was neither of us, only an unshapen, unformed thing ... the ideas crossed each other as the lines of two wet drawings laid face to face become crossed, blotted, effaced and unrecognisable.'

Elizabeth d'Espérance, *Shadow Land or, Light from the Other Side*

Chapter 1

It is the cocked hat that draws her to him: the way it arches above the barricade of toppers. Its golden edges end low to the brow and gild the face beneath.

He stands talking with half a dozen other gentlemen under the dying bonfire of Sydney Gardens's autumn foliage, impeding the passage of walkers like a clot in the blood. As he extends a hand, emphasising a point to his nearest companion, Agnes sees it: the perfect pose for a full-length silhouette.

She reaches for the scissors in her reticule but her fingers are cold, fumbling. By the time she has hold of the handles and the sable paper gripped, ready to walk through her hand, the man has already turned and replaced his arm at his side.

She will have to cut him from memory.

There is the familiar slip in her stomach, the tangle of breath within her breast. Hope refuses to die. Never will she see the dark blue coat of the Royal Navy without a wild belief that somehow, *somehow* ...

1

But this man is not Montague. Even through her cataracts, Agnes can see enough of his features to dismiss that fantasy. If John Montague is still alive – and she has no guarantee of that – he will not be a slim, active man engaged in debate, but a seasoned sailor, even older than herself. Decades on deck will have weathered his skin and aged him beyond his years. There may be a paunch beneath his waistcoat, or a limp from a bullet wound. Her dashing lieutenant belongs only to the past.

She cuts the outline of his face in smooth, bold waves, sliding the paper between the pad of her thumb and the finger that still bears his ring.

The breeze picks up. Her paper flutters, objecting. It has grown damp on the walk and does not hold its form as it should, but Agnes persists.

Once she passes the neck, her work becomes easier. Bodies are a different language. Shoulders with epaulettes, the coat-tails, moving down to the breeches and the lead foot, always cut dead flat. This naval officer must be fresh home. He is not supposed to wear his uniform on furlough. It is a rare sighting, a gift; a glimpse, however tenuous, of a happier time.

Wind gusts. The trees cast their treasuries of gold and bronze down upon the men and an oak leaf, crisp and brown, sticks upright in the rim of the cocked hat. It would be a beautiful detail to include, if Agnes had not cut that shape already.

She moves on to the final curve, the one she must not rush, even though her knuckles are beginning to cramp and … there. The shade emerges from its background, triumphant. Another puff of wind snatches the waste sable paper and sends it, spiralling, into the leaden sky above.

Agnes frowns at her work, dissatisfied. She has overdone the nose and underplayed the chin. This is a nuance people rarely understand about her art: a shadow, an exact replica of the shade a person casts, possesses next to no likeness at all. It must be honed and exaggerated before they will recognise the profile as their own. But she does not have time to make changes. The group of gentlemen are taking their leave. Clouds pillow fast behind the limestone of the old Sydney Hotel.

For all her talent, Agnes cannot work in the rain. It is time to return home.

She plods these days, a legacy of the Accident. Or perhaps she is just getting old. Bath's streets seem harder to navigate, and the soles of her half-boots slip whenever there are cobbles underfoot. Umbrellas sprout, making the crossing at Pulteney Bridge an ordeal of twice its usual bustle. Damp woollen coats press against her. The kennels run fast in the rain, carrying the odours of horse muck and sewage.

Surely it never used to be like this?

The Bath of Agnes's childhood was a city of palaces. People came for the cure, of course, but they were not all invalids in Merlin chairs back then; the fashionable

3

paraded in the Pump Room by day and danced in the Assembly Rooms by night. There was always a play or a concert in some white stone mansion.

Now carbon deposits have stained the buildings, giving them a funeral aspect. Dirt bleeds into the river, into the sky. The soul of Bath has left and its body is decaying. Only the Somerset hills glow in the distance, preternaturally vivid.

A horsewhip cracks the air. Agnes pulls up short on the edge of the pavement, just in time. A great cart lumbers past, its wheels squeaking, and splashes her skirts.

By the time she has reached the abbey churchyard, the breath is grating painfully in her lungs. Really, it was foolish to wander as far as Sydney Gardens. Barely two years have passed since pneumonia nearly claimed her life. She had not been strong even before the fever, but when she became lucid again she noticed a profound physical change: her body felt like a stranger's, unwilling to obey her like it used to.

Take it slowly, Simon counsels her. But it seems, at times, that she has taken her whole life slowly: at the sedate pace of a minuet dance. A spell in the wing chair by the fire, reading *Varney the Vampire* with her nephew Cedric, will fix her. Illness might have left her frail, but she is not beaten yet.

The rain spits with malice. Mustering all of her energy, she launches herself across the churchyard and round the bulk of the abbey.

4

Her home cowers in the abbey's shadow, its walls discoloured by time and soot. Ivy-choked pillars support a portico above the front door. Magpies have taken to nesting here, although there is no sign of them at present. All day long they chitter and cackle, disturbing her work; mocking it, as others do, dismissing it as the vestige of a bygone age.

But to Agnes the black paper shapes in her windows still look as beautiful as ever. The conversation pieces she designed to lure the browsing customer: a group of ladies at tea, horses riding to hounds. Then there are the brighter ovals, painted in Etruscan red; spots of vivid colour on this dreary day.

She is not the only one to view her work with admiration. As she draws closer, she notices two men standing by her parlour window. One consults his pocket watch and then knocks at the front door. From his manner, it appears that he is not knocking for the first time.

Cannot Mamma hear? And where is Cedric – can he really be out playing, in weather like this? Shaking her head, she scurries forward, determined to reach the visitors before they turn away. A fine artist she will look – panting and half-drowned – but she cannot afford to lose even a whiff of business.

It is only as the clouds part, letting slip the tiniest ray of light, that she discerns the man rapping on her door is no usual visitor. Raindrops drip from the portico onto his tall, beaver hat.

The stovepipe hat of a policeman.

'Miss Darken! You see, Sergeant, I am a man of my word. I told you she would not venture far on a day like today.'

Before Agnes can gather her wits, she recognises Simon's voice; sees Simon's watery blue eyes reproaching her beneath the sodden brim of his hat.

Simon and a police officer, waiting on her.

'I ... needed some air,' she explains. 'I turned back as soon as it started to rain.' She sounds guilty, like a child caught.

'Miss Darken, I'm Sergeant Redmayne.' The policeman possesses a granite slab of a face, unmarked by any trace of a smile. He tips his head forward and water cascades from his hat, wetting her feet.

Agnes represses a sigh. Manners seem to be declining faster than the city itself. 'And how may I help you, Sergeant?'

'It's a tad delicate, miss. Might I come inside?'

Simon clears his throat and fidgets with his collar. No doubt he is thinking the same as Agnes: that the sight of a policeman might set Mamma off on another of her strange turns.

The sergeant's eyes sharpen at their hesitation.

'If you must,' she says begrudgingly. 'Please excuse the mess. I have been working this morning. I did not expect ...' she gestures at him, 'you.'

Fishing in her reticule, she produces a set of keys and clunks one awkwardly into the lock. She hopes

6

the sergeant does not notice the tarnished brass of the letterbox, or the magpie droppings plastered on the door panels. Perhaps it is just as well he is not a customer, after all.

Agnes leads them in. No call answers the sound of her footsteps, or the slam of the door behind Simon, who enters last. Cautiously, she peers into the parlour – a small chamber dominated by the fireplace and an old, oaken grandfather clock that wheezes as it ticks. Captain Darken maintained vehemently, until his dying day, that the clock was made with wood from HMS *Victory*, but Agnes entertains her doubts.

A teacup remains on the side table where she left it, the dregs leaching into the white bone china. Nothing but ash lies in the throat of the fireplace.

Thankfully, Mamma is nowhere to be seen.

'Here you are.' She ushers the visitors in, ashamed of the dust and the paintbrushes dotted about the room. Even the profiles framed on the wall seem to avert their faces, refusing to look upon her clutter. 'Will this take long? Shall I boil water for tea?'

'That won't be necessary, Miss Darken.' Sergeant Redmayne sits heavily in the wing chair.

Agnes would rather change her clothes, stoke up the fire and take some refreshment before he relates whatever he has to tell, but the sergeant's manner is so grave, so dampening, she can do nothing but take a seat and remove her bonnet, waiting dumbly for his words.

'I called earlier, but you were out. Instead I met your physician, here.' He throws Simon a look that would fell a slighter man. 'Strange enough, he turned up again, just as I came back for a second try.'

'Fortuitous.' Simon smiles, but Agnes senses he is not altogether easy. He has not yet sat down.

'If you say so, Doctor. Look miss, I won't beat about the bush. You had a Mr Boyle come here for his portrait last Saturday, the twenty-third?'

'Not quite a portrait, Sergeant. I did some preliminary sketches. He wants the shade painted onto glass and bronzed with detail for his wife. A remembrance for the anniversary of their wedding day, if I recall.' Agnes twists the limp ribbons on her bonnet. 'But ... how do you know of this?'

'Mr Boyle wrote the appointment in his engagement diary. *Darken, two o'clock.*'

'Yes, that was about the time ...'

She is at a loss. What has a police officer to do with her work? She tries to remember this Mr Boyle. An unassuming man, old-fashioned. Not much in the way of a profile, except for his plump lips. The kind of man her sister Constance would have scorned as a *fogram*.

'Is Mr Boyle in some kind of trouble?'

'You could say that, miss. He's dead.'

'*Dead*!'

Simon steps forward. 'Really, Sergeant, that is not the way to break news to a lady—'

8

But Sergeant Redmayne carries on regardless, his voice as devoid of emotion as his face. 'Murdered, in fact. Found the body in the Gravel Walk with the head smashed in. Looks like they did it with a mallet. No doubt the villain wanted to delay the identification of his victim for as long as possible.'

'Now look here ...' Simon objects.

Agnes is grateful for his bulky presence, and the salts he waves beneath her nose. Their tang acts as a lash, keeping her upright.

'How hideous,' she gasps. 'Who would want to—'

'That's what we're trying to establish. Boyle had a dinner engagement after he saw you, at seven o'clock. Didn't keep it. But you can confirm he was here?'

Simon finally seats himself at her side. The sofa sags with his weight. Helplessly, her body topples in his direction, leaving her propped against him, shoulder to shoulder, like a house of cards. She rights herself.

'Yes,' she replies tentatively. 'Our business did not take long. One can sketch very quickly, you know ...' To think that her eyes would have been amongst the last to see Mr Boyle alive! It is some consolation to think that she chronicled the lines of his face before they vanished. Or collapsed. A *mallet*, did the policeman say? 'We spent longer discussing the final product. I suppose he left me at ... a quarter to three?'

Sergeant Redmayne nods. Not once, in the duration of their interview, has Agnes seen him blink. 'And how did he seem? Agitated? Preoccupied?'

9

Agnes tries to cast her mind back. Truth be told, Mr Boyle was a forgettable sort of man. Had she been overrun with sitters, as in the old days, she would scarcely have remembered him. As it is, she has an image of his face, turned to the left, captured for the last time on paper. No features, just pencil outlines. Already fading from memory. She had cut him a shade on black paper, to show him how it would look, before he opted for the paint.

'Oh,' she breathes on a downward note. 'Oh, no. He did not pay me.'

'What?'

'Mr Boyle was to pay upon collection of the glass painting. It is practically finished. All that work!'

The sergeant clicks his tongue, irritated. 'I can't see *that* as the greater of the two evils, miss. Some would say he has paid the ultimate price.'

'I do not mean to sound unfeeling. But one cannot eat pity, I cannot heat a house through the winter on pity. I daresay if the police station failed to pay your weekly salary—'

Simon's elbow nudges her. Perhaps she *is* being unreasonable. It is the shock. She is not herself.

'If we might return to how Mr Boyle appeared on the afternoon in question?'

The magpies shuffle in their nest, their feet going tack-tack on the roof.

'He was … ordinary. So far as a person unacquainted with him can judge. We spoke of his wife and the commission, I believe. Nothing more … He seemed perfectly in spirits. Oh, yes! He made a jest, about a silhouette of my sister. So I did not think him troubled in the least.'

Sergeant Redmayne nods again. 'I see. Well, perhaps if you do think of anything else, Miss Darken, you'll wait upon me? I'll leave my name and direction.'

He produces a calling card from his pocket and pushes it across the side table with his finger.

'Yes, yes I will.'

'You may have been the last person to see Mr Boyle alive. Except for the killer, of course. You'd oblige me by remaining in the city.'

She gasps a laugh. 'Wherever would I go?'

He shrugs and rises to his feet, leaving a watery mark on the wing chair. 'People go all sorts of places when the police start asking questions.'

It is Simon's turn to stand. 'I will answer for Miss Darken staying in Bath. Her health is not currently strong enough to permit travel in any case. Now,' he gestures to the door, 'we have distressed the lady enough for one day.' The grandfather clock whirrs, preparing to strike the hour. 'I would be happy to show you out, Sergeant.'

They are finally moving, finally shuffling through the door to the hallway, taking their hard voices and awful tidings with them.

Agnes lets herself fall full-length upon the sofa. Only now does she realise how cold she is, her teeth chattering uncontrollably. She should change out of

11

these wretched, damp clothes, but she has no energy. Every part of her feels heavy.

By and by, Simon's hand lightly touches the back of her head. 'Forgive me, Miss Darken. I told that blasted fellow all this would make you ill again. Not that he heeded me. These newfangled police give false consequence to upstarts like him.'

'I would forgive his impertinence if he had not brought me such dreadful news.' She coughs. 'Poor Mr Boyle! My first customer in months!'

'Hush, now. Hush. You lie there. I will fix you something to drink.'

'Where is Cedric? Mamma? She must not hear of this—'

'No.' He pauses. 'All is … quiet upstairs.'

'Thank you, Simon.'

Exhausted, Agnes closes her eyes, but the lack of vision only heightens her aches and her pains. That burning in her chest. A drum pounding, deep in the sockets of her eyes. The sight of that policeman has brought the Accident back with a clarity she would not have supposed possible, after all these years.

The house stretches and pops. She sinks her face into a cushion, ignoring its demands.

When she returns to herself, there is a shawl draped over her. Flames caper in the fireplace. On the side table, a fresh cup of tea steams beside a slice of cake.

Simon sits watching her. He has removed his coat and rolled his shirtsleeves up his broad arms. His right hand nurses a glass containing a whisky-coloured liquid. Opiates, possibly.

'Tea first,' he instructs. 'Then a dose of this to help you sleep.'

Dear Simon. He has waited upon her like a hired hand – and she cannot even afford to pay him for the medicine.

'How is Mamma? Cedric will be expecting his supper, we always try to eat that together and read a story ...'

Simon takes a deep breath. 'They are asleep.'

No light shines through the paper silhouettes tacked to the window panes; their shapes blend into the black of the night outside. It is far later than she had reckoned.

'I have kept you too long, Simon. You have better things to do. Other patients ... and who will have fed your little dog?'

A thin smile. 'Morpheus will manage well enough without me. Come, drink your tea. I want to see you settled before I take my leave.'

Obediently, she reaches for the cup. The liquid is too hot, but she forces it down.

'Simon, if news of this murder gets out ... and no doubt it will ...' She takes another gulp. 'I worry it might lend a certain *notoriety* to my business.'

'There will be time enough to discuss that later.'

This is hardly comforting. Her mind teems with questions and worries – it would be a relief to talk them over with Simon, but she has known him for long enough to recognise the professional closure in his face. This man is no longer her ally but 'Dr Carfax', who absolutely forbids excitement.

Instead she swallows the last of the tea, tasting nothing but heat, and takes a bite of dry cake. Simon hands her the opiates and she drinks them down as a bitter final course.

'Now you must go straight to bed.' He looks as if he could use a long sleep himself. In the firelight, his eyes are bloodshot. 'Promise me.'

'I will. But first let me see you out.'

She lights a candle and they leave the parlour together.

A chill breeze rushes in the moment she opens the front door, forcing her to cup a hand around the flame of the candle. The rain has stopped, but its metallic scent lingers. The street lamps cast sulphur pools on the pavements.

It is horrible to think of Simon venturing out there alone, with a murderer on the loose.

'Be careful, Simon. Walk quickly.'

He bows – a proper bow, one leg slightly behind the other. Even with his girth, he has more grace than the police sergeant.

'Until tomorrow, Miss Darken.'

Placing his hat upon his head, he turns. Agnes watches him walk away, his shape articulated against the light of the street lamp.

Always 'Miss Darken'. They have known each other since childhood; he is practically a brother to her, yet still there is this constraint between them.

Damp air sneaks around the abbey and touches her cheek. As the sound of Simon's footsteps die out, she shuts the door and bolts it.

The walls exhale.

Quietly, she begins to climb the stairs. *Straight to bed*, Simon said, but practice has taught her she has ten minutes, at least, before the opiates begin to drag.

She must look. Just once.

The doors to Mamma's and Cedric's bedchambers are closed. Neither of them makes a sound in their sleep. Avoiding the creaky floorboard, Agnes creeps past the threshold leading to her own cold bed and enters her studio.

It is the only place in the house where the air feels alive. Even at night, lit by the wavering flame of her candle, her workplace emits a sort of radiance. Perhaps it is the brass glow of the various machines and apparatus she has acquired over the course of her labour: a physiognotrace with its long pole and a camera obscura amongst them. They were necessary purchases. The modern public want machines, not people: something more like a daguerreotype.

Agnes does not see the appeal. A copper plate, a bit of mercury and they call it *art*. She is one of a dying breed who would rather have something drawn with

15

soft pencils, or painted lovingly with the stroke of a brush.

So was Mr Boyle. But he will have had his image immortalised by now. Policemen always seem to be photographing crime scenes these days. She swallows against an ache in her throat, tries not to imagine Mr Boyle translated into chemical shades of silver and grey, his blood a vast, inky pool.

She places the candle on her battered desk. Pushing aside bladders of paint, moving stacks of paper, she finally locates the item she seeks: a great leather-bound book, as big as the family Bible. Her album of duplicates: a copy of all the shadows she has captured.

She does not begin at the start, where her early work resides. It embarrasses her to look upon those blunt cuts of Constance and acknowledge them as her own. Instead, she flips far to the back. On and on she turns. The little black figures flash before her eyes, seem to move. At last she finds a piece of paper pushed inside the album hurriedly, unstuck: the head and shoulders of Mr Boyle.

She holds the profile to the light.

She did not take enough care placing it inside the book. The weight of pages has squashed her work. Mr Boyle is creased. Crumpled. The outline of his face is bent, almost as if …

Her hand begins to shake.

It is too cruel. A barbarous coincidence. The lines of Mr Boyle, his forehead and his nose, are not preserved at all. His shade has suffered the fate of his mortal physiognomy.

It looks exactly as if it has been hit with a mallet.

CHAPTER 2

It's Pearl's first time.

She sits in the cabinet as usual, behind its black damask curtain, but already she feels like someone else. Tonight she hasn't got the floor-length veil over her face and there aren't any ashes smeared on her skin. She isn't playing a spirit guide now: she's the Main Event.

She worries about how it will feel when the ghosts take possession of her. Myrtle used to screw up her face and roll her eyes – but that was all for show. Myrtle freely admits it.

'I'm a Sensitive,' she told Pearl. 'I hear the voices. But that ain't enough for ladies and gents. They want a thrill. Tables rocking. Materialisation.'

The spirits have since whispered to Myrtle that her real power lies in manipulating auras and controlling the universal force: Myrtle is a mesmerist.

It's Pearl who possesses the Gift of Mediumship: she's the Genuine Article.

She closes her eyes and inhales the familiar scent of lilies – waxy, like the black candles that stand beside them in the parlour. It doesn't calm her nerves.

Myrtle's voice echoes in the hallway, tuned to the pitch of sympathy. A woman answers her. Pearl gleans what she can – she's in the habit of professional eaves-dropping – and gathers that there are two women coming in: Mrs Boyle and Mrs Parker. They've both lost a man.

Was he their husband and father? Son and brother? Either way, the bonds seem close. She hopes she can satisfy them. It would be dreadful to let the mourners down. But if she succeeds …

A man will possess her. Speak through her mouth, see through her eyes. What if he doesn't go away again? He might occupy her for the rest of her life, use her like some sort of devilish puppet.

Pearl swallows her bile.

She shouldn't fear the dead. She's tasted death, as Myrtle's fond of reminding her. 'You did the dying part, before you were even born,' she says. But Pearl doesn't remember that, any more than she remembers the mother who lost her life bringing her into this world.

Footsteps sound in the parlour, followed by the movement of chair legs. Pearl ventures to open her eyes. Myrtle's turned down the lamps. She doesn't need to squint from the pain of their light any longer.

'Mrs Boyle, Mrs Parker. I must ask you to take your seats and remain in perfect silence. She will come to us presently.'

It's that breathy way of speaking that Myrtle has perfected. She ought to have been on the stage.

'But how—'

'She'll know. Leave the glove upon the table. If she requires anything further of you, she'll ask.'

Upholstery squeaks as they sit down. A little shuffling, settling in. The candles will be lit by now, their fiery eyes reflected in the crystal ball.

Still, it's not time to go out there yet.

Pearl takes a deep breath, longs to run from the cabinet and never come back. But she's eleven now, no longer a child. She has to work for the family like everyone else. She clenches her hands into fists. Waits until the silence begins to crackle.

Now.

She rings the bell. It cuts through the hush like lightning.

'Ladies!' Myrtle announces, 'The White Sylph arrives.'

Slowly, slowly, Pearl eases the curtain aside and steps out into the darkness.

There's always that little shock, the intake of breath when the mourners see her. But today, respect mingles with their awe. She has the Power – they can see it flowing from her in waves. Beside her they're desolate things: pinched and tear-stained, their clothes blending into the false night of the parlour.

20

She takes her seat. No one can see how her knees tremble beneath the tablecloth.

'Please, join hands.' Pearl uses the gentle, fluting voice Myrtle made her practise. Already, she's given up a part of herself. She swallows some more, tries not to think of what will happen next.

Gingerly, the women stretch out their fingers and clasp hers.

'We'll begin with a hymn,' Myrtle sighs softly, like a girl in love.

Myrtle insists upon this, says hymns help convince people they aren't taking part in something sacrilegious. She opens her bow-shaped mouth and begins:

Behold, a Stranger at the door!
He gently knocks, has knocked before,

Mrs Boyle and Mrs Parker join her in a feeble contralto:

Has waited long, is waiting still:
You treat no other friend so ill.

Pearl doesn't take part but instead sits, staring into the crystal ball. She's always thought it's cruel to make mourners sing. If there's one thing she understands about grief, it's how it chokes: the fingers of death, squeezing the throats of the living.

At last, the hymn ends. The air grows taut.

What now?

Remembering Myrtle's instructions, Pearl releases the mourners' hands and takes up the gentleman's glove that's been left for her upon the table. It's made of kidskin; warm from the candlelight, slightly stained on the palm. Is that a rip, by the ring finger? Hard to see. Her vision is clouding, as if she's gazing through fog.

She opens her mouth, exhales. A luminous ribbon flows out of it, drawing gasps. Her pulse goes wild. This has never happened before.

The ghosts are coming. Her arms are glowing, her breath is glowing. She's being swallowed.

Myrtle says, 'He's here.'

Something whispers, soft in her ear. Then cool, feathery hands touch her: dozens of them stroking her hair, patting her arms. She wants to scream but there's a buzzing sensation in her jaw, holding it shut.

A figure rises up from the mist. He's trailing garments and has candle flames for eyes. Can Myrtle see him, too? She doesn't know; the others are invisible to her and she's alone in the dark with this – thing.

The spirit parts his lips, revealing a great void.

Pearl can't take any more. Her mind pulls the shutters down.

When she wakes up, the lamps are back on. Two black candlesticks stand before her on the table, smoking.

The younger mourner has her arm about the shoulders of the elder. Both are sobbing.

'He remembered!' The old lady cries. 'H-he always remembered.'

Myrtle practically hums with delight. 'Hmm. The message has significance for you?'

'Yes! Today is the anniversary of our marriage.'

A fresh burst of grief.

Pearl feels bruised, hollow, as if the spirits have taken her up and dropped her from a great height. She folds her arms on the table, rests her head upon them.

What happened? What did she say?

'But if that was Papa,' the younger woman reasons, furrowing her brow, 'if it truly *was* him ... He would have told us, would he not? That is the reason we *came* here.'

Myrtle soothes them. 'Ladies, please, speak softly. There's no cause for quarrel. The language of the spirits is no more under our control than another mortal's voice. Why, you might be in the same room as a person, but you can't force them to talk to you. And if they do, you can't compel them to tell the truth. The spirits keep their own secrets.'

'Do not doubt, Harriet,' the older lady chides her companion. 'How can you question it? Look at the Sylph, how she glows!'

'It's the ectoplasm,' Myrtle says wisely. 'Spirit matter.'

'A miracle. Truly a miracle.'

Softly, the door shuts.

Coins chink. Pearl hears the farewells; hears Mrs Boyle and Mrs Parker speaking through the window when they gain Walcot Street.

23

'She could have looked up the marriage,' Mrs Parker insists from the pavement. 'And the murder was in the papers.'

'I know you do not believe, Harriet, but it gives me comfort. I *felt* him, I am sure I did. Please do not pooh-pooh it.'

'All I am saying is that she could not solve the crime, could she? Is that not rather convenient? Papa would not omit to tell us who killed him. He would be calling out for justice.'

The footsteps peter out.

Only one word remains with Pearl. *Murder.*

Her mouth is dry. It feels sullied, unclean, like it's been used without her consent.

Myrtle returns and lowers the lamps back to a comfortable level. 'All right, then. Bit of supper?' The genteel accent assumed for customers slides away as easily as a cloak shrugged aside. 'Got to keep your strength up, you know. Them spirits take it out of you.'

A tumbler of whisky and water is thrust before her, followed by a slice of bread coated in blackcurrant jam. The objects flicker, double. Pearl blinks.

'Thanks,' she manages. 'What … what happened?'

Myrtle sits down and plucks at a lily in its vase. 'You did it. Told you so. Genuine medium. Channelled the spirit of one Mr Boyle.'

Pearl's stomach cramps. 'He was here? He spoke through *me*?'

24

'Of course he did.'

It would be less disturbing if she remembered this Mr Boyle, if she felt like she'd met him. But now she's left with the sensation that something appalling has happened, and she's the only person who didn't see it.

'D'you think it's true, what the ladies were saying, Myrtle? That the man who spoke through me was murdered?'

'I know it's true. Read it in the paper.'

'But you didn't tell *me* that!'

Myrtle shrugs. 'Didn't think I needed to. The dead talk to you, don't they?'

'Through me,' Pearl mutters. 'Not *to* me. I never heard a sound.'

'You will. Now you've started to bleed each month, the power will grow. You'll harness it.'

Pearl takes a steadying breath. Her ears tingle, the only parts of her left untouched.

'Will I hear *her*?' she asks quietly.

Myrtle doesn't like to speak of Mother. A spasm of pain crosses her face and she purses her lips. 'I haven't. But you might.'

It would be worth it. Worth this awful, dirty feeling, to hear Mother just the once.

She forces herself to sit up and nibble on the bread. 'And so no one's been scragged? For killing this Mr Boyle?'

'No. The bluebottles don't even have a suspect yet.'

25

She shivers. 'Then that means … There's a murderer on the loose. Here, in Bath.'

'Yes.' Myrtle pats her hand, gives a wink. 'That's good for business, ain't it?'

Chapter 3

For a sleepless night and half the next morning, Agnes debates taking Mr Boyle's silhouette to the police station. Absurd as it sounds, she feels guilty keeping the discovery to herself, as though she is concealing evidence. When she looks in the mirror to fasten her hair, it is the haunted face of a criminal she sees: an accessory to murder.

Of course they will tell her it is a coincidence. She could not have *caused* Mr Boyle's death by scrunching up his silhouette. But is it not uncanny? Something beyond the realms of an everyday occurrence. She has never squashed a piece of work before; she has never had a client die before. The two hang together with an ominous weight.

If not the police, then maybe she should seek out Mrs Boyle. Present her with the finished painting and include the ruined paper shade as an afterthought. Let the widow make the connection, determine some significance, if she can. Yes, perhaps that is the best course of action.

She puts on a lace collar and fastens it with a brooch. It has been so long since she paid a social call that she has forgotten the correct hours, and the form. Well, Mrs Boyle will probably be too deep in grief to notice if Agnes does not observe the niceties. All the clocks in her house will be stopped.

In the studio, Agnes wraps the glass oval and squashed silhouette in brown paper and string.

She checks the address in her ledger one last time before descending the stairs.

The grandfather clock ticks. Mamma dozes in the parlour with a rug spread across her knees. She has added fuel to the fire, again, wasting their scant resources while Agnes was upstairs. Cinders drop in the grate as if they are setting out to vex her, to show her how quickly it all turns to ash.

But there is another noise rising above that of the flames. A pathetic *peep*. It is so forlorn that it makes her heart clench.

Warily, she cracks open the front door.

'Cedric? There you are! I missed you at breakfast.'

Her nephew kneels beneath the portico, his breath misting the air. In his hand is the stick that he uses to propel his toy hoop. That hoop, however, is nowhere in sight. Instead he pokes tentatively at a magpie.

'Whatever are you doing? Be a good boy and leave that nasty thing alone.'

He carries on, regardless. 'Aunt Aggie, it's got a baby! Look!'

She bends down to his height and instantly recoils.

A pink, downy lump squirms on the ground, the stubs of its wings circling frantically. The eyes are sealed, bluish bumps; only the beak gapes wide.

Agnes glances at the magpie and realises it cannot be the chick's mother. It has plundered the nest of a wood pigeon.

'Oh! Well, you had better let it be. Do come inside, Cedric dear.'

'But I want—'

'This instant, young man.' Her upbraids never sound convincing. No wonder he often ignores them.

A couple strolling gaze in their direction. Agnes smiles tightly at them, attempting to appear in control of the situation.

'Do as you are told, there's a good boy.'

It is the magpie that moves, kicking the chick, making it scream.

'Why is it doing that?'

She seizes his arm. 'I must show you something, Cedric.'

'No, don't!'

Before he can fend her off, she pulls him inside the house. The stick clasped in his hand leaves a dirty scrape along the hallway wall.

She elbows the front door shut just in time. The next sound from outside is a terrible squelch.

Of course she has seen it before: the cannibalism of magpies. It never ceases to appal her. Cedric may love

29

his stories of monsters, but she does not want him to really see a bird turn on its own kind, picking off the young and weak with no compunction for its atrocity.

'Auntie Aggie, you're hurting me.'

She drops his arm at once. 'Do forgive me, Ced. But I would not have to pull you about if you heeded me when I speak to you. Those birds can spread all manner of disease and I want you far away from them. It is for your own good, dear.'

He cocks his fair head to consider this. Or perhaps he is listening to the disturbing, wet noises creeping through the door.

'Is the baby bird eating his breakfast?' he asks.

'Yes,' she says hurriedly. 'Yes, he is eating. Now you must go along to the kitchen and eat too. I have made your favourite: egg fritters. Chop-chop.' She shoos him with her hands.

Sighing, Cedric trudges towards the back of the house, dragging his stick on the floor behind him, as if she has denied him some unparalleled treat. A great knot of love and frustration tightens inside her chest.

Much as she enjoys seeing him play, he should be above games by now. They take boys into the navy at the age of twelve and can you *imagine* one of those little midshipmen disobeying an order or running around with a hoop and stick? It is partly her own fault. She has indulged him, bought him Penny Dreadfuls instead of sending him out to work as other families would do.

30

But she thought his father would have made plans for him by now.

Cedric should have an education. An apprenticeship. He is likely to get neither unless the widowed Mrs Boyle coughs up some coins.

She picks up her parcel, unfastens the front door and squeezes herself through the smallest opening, taking care to snap it shut behind her so Cedric does not see the magpie's gruesome work.

Yesterday's shower has left puddles on the streets. No rain yet this morning, but filthy rags of cloud strewn across the sky pose the threat. The abbey clock chimes ten. Already nurses are wheeling the crippled and infirm to the Pump Room. One man with a bald pate slides his vacant eyes in Agnes's direction and she feels a jolt of his confinement. To be trapped, in that manner. Unable to walk where you will. She remembers the days lying sick with pneumonia and quickens her pace, just to prove that she still can.

By Union Street she regrets it. Her lungs protest with a spasm and her heart gives that great swoop that often proceeds a fainting fit. Chastened, she relapses into her habitual dawdle and turns away from the shops of Milsom Street and Bond Street. A cart has spilled some of its vegetables into the road, where they lie, rotting; a heap of bulbous shapes so dirty that Agnes cannot identify them. The same might be said for all around her. Dull, hopelessly dull. Gritty ash in the air. Birds wheeling like charred scraps from a fire.

31

How can bright young Cedric find his future in a place like this?

Beneath her glove, she twists the ring on her finger. It is the only way she can believe that Montague ever walked these streets. Montague, that man of vivid and impossible colours. He carried something of the places he had seen: a certain spice that spoke of the West Indies, even Africa. He told her of an ocean like aquamarine, so clear you could see the fish swimming in its depths. Rocks where the coral grew orange and pink at the waterline. Miraculous things she would scarcely credit from another mouth, but they *are* real and they are still out there, somewhere. Beyond her reach, because Montague has left her; left her with nothing but black and white.

Queen Square is quiet. A few tortured-looking oaks occupy the garden at the centre. Wind has already stripped them, burying their roots in the brown compost of their own leaves. A squirrel watches her from a naked branch, so still it might be a taxidermy model.

Agnes finds the Boyles' residence almost at once. There is the telltale straw laid out before it to deaden the sound of wheels and the windows are shuttered fast. She adjusts her grip on the package. Perhaps this was not a wise notion, after all.

Black material swaddles the brass knocker. It makes a muted, pathetic sound as she lets it fall. Some moments later, the door opens like a tender wound. Behind it is a squat woman dressed in mourning, but the expression upon her face is one of harassment, not grief. Her hands show coarse and red – evidently, Mrs Boyle is comfortable enough to keep a servant.

'I am here to offer my condolences to your mistress.' Agnes inserts her calling card through the narrow opening before the domestic has a chance to demur. 'She will not recognise my name, but I was acquainted with her late husband.'

The woman frowns at it, as if the letters mean nothing to her, but the thick quality of the card must make some impression, for she bids Agnes step inside.

'Don't know if she's up to receiving,' she warns. 'I'll check.'

Still staring at Agnes's card, she walks through an inner door and shuts it behind her. Agnes can hear the servant's clomping footsteps and the rumble of voices in conversation.

She had forgotten all of this: the stale, oppressive atmosphere that follows a death. Unaired rooms, mirrors covered in black fabric. A clock hangs on the wall, but its hands are stopped at ten and she wonders where this time has come from. Mrs Boyle cannot know the minute her husband breathed his last. Is this the hour they discovered the body, or when she received the news?

It was a mad, half-baked scheme to come. What is she doing here, uninvited, trespassing on a stranger's grief? She is tempted to slip back outside when the domestic returns, this time without the card.

33

'She'll see you. This way.'

Queen Square has not been a fashionable address for many a year. No one would suspect the Boyles of being wealthy, but they exude respectability. Agnes eyes the covered shapes of paintings and the nap on the drawn curtains, feeling the contrast with her own home forcibly. It was not always so. When her father was alive ... But perhaps Mrs Boyle will find herself overcome by a similar onslaught of retrenchments and economies. Perhaps her days of keeping this dumpy servant are numbered.

The widow sits by the light of a spermaceti candle. What a profile she would make, with her aquiline nose and double chin! However, she is quick to cover it, flicking down her veil before standing and exchanging a formal curtsey with Agnes.

'Miss Darken. How kind of you to call.' Red cheeks burn beneath the netting of the veil; Mrs Boyle has evidently been crying.

'Forgive my intrusion, I ...' Agnes gazes helplessly at the maid, whose eyes are pinned to the floor.

'Leave us, Mary.'

Mary bobs a curtsey and trots away.

The forced darkness is unnerving. Mrs Boyle extends a black-gloved hand to gesture at a chair on the other side of the table, and for a moment she looks like one of Agnes's full-length shades come to life.

Warily, Agnes perches on the edge of the seat. Her parcel fills her lap and she worries at the string with her fingers. 'Thank you, Mrs Boyle. I shall not detain you for long. I simply heard what had happened and I …' She wets her lips. What can she say? What can anyone say to atone for this? 'I am so terribly sorry,' she supplies feebly.

The widow sits opposite her with slow, heavy movements. 'Thank you. You are in mourning yourself?'

Agnes glances down at her own black dress, momentarily bewildered. She has not worn a coloured garment in so long that she forgets how it must appear to others. But Mrs Boyle is unlikely to comprehend the general, lingering melancholy that causes her to prefer dark clothing. 'A distant relation,' she embellishes. 'God rest them.'

The veil wafts as Mrs Boyle nods. She has certainly gone all out on her weeds – she must have emptied Corbould's mourning establishment. Tassels, jet buttons, a ring already mounted with her husband's grey hair. But then, who would not do the same? This is not simply a bereavement: the affliction of murder calls for shades deeper than a warehouse can supply.

'I have not been receiving visitors,' Mrs Boyle admits. 'I have an abhorrence of their pity and their … questions.' She places a hand on her chest, as if to put her emotions in order before continuing. 'But I recognised your name. From the engagement diary. You … you saw him that day, didn't you?'

The string pings from Agnes's fingertips. She knows. Naturally, she knows. What a simpleton Agnes was

35

not to think of it before. The policemen would hardly requisition the engagement diary without keeping Mrs Boyle abreast of their investigations.

Rather than answering, she pushes the package across the table.

Mrs Boyle unfolds the paper with painful exactness. This low candlelight is the perfect illumination for Agnes's art. Little bronzed details glint – hair, a coat collar, the shell of an ear. Mrs Boyle draws in a breath.

'There was to be a second appointment. A collection. Alas ...'

The crumpled papercut is there too, on the widow's lap. She does not heed it. Instead she strokes at the glass, leaving smudges.

In paint, the line of the face is softer. There is something angelic about this black and gold rendition of Mr Boyle. He is a mate for the shadow bride behind her veil.

'Thank you,' Mrs Boyle croons. 'Thank you, Miss Darken. What a blessing. He said there was to be a surprise. That was his way.'

'For the anniversary of—'

'Yes.'

Without the package, Agnes's hands feel obtrusive, too large. She could let matters rest here; retreat and leave the poor widow with her memories.

But that squashed papercut is like a rotten tooth: she cannot help worrying at it, glancing out of the corner of her eye to see its black curl. Someone else needs to share the horror of this coincidence.

'I included my preliminary cut in paper, madam. You will find it there, loose in the package. I am afraid it became rather damaged, but ...' She trails off as Mrs Boyle picks up the shade and smooths it out.

Agnes watches intently, unable to close her mouth or breathe until the widow speaks.

'Yes. Thank you.'

That is all.

The anticlimax is so great that her shoulders drop. Can Mrs Boyle not see it?

'He told me to expect a surprise,' Mrs Boyle repeats. 'He must have known that you would come.'

'I do not understand.'

The widow's expression is opaque through her veil. 'I spoke to him, Miss Darken. Across the divide. The things that are possible, these days. When I think back to my youth, I would not have credited such discoveries. Railways, telegraph, spirit mediums like the White Sylph ... Why, the Abolition of the Trade was thought radical enough!'

Agnes shivers. This is not the first time she has heard of spiritualists, although she usually keeps such talk at a distance by saying she does not believe. A more honest statement would be that she does not *want* to believe. She wants the dead safely caged in Heaven or Hell, not wandering, watching her through the cloudy eyes of a corpse. But a small part of her

37

acknowledges it could be true. It feels true, when Mrs Boyle speaks it.

'And the … spirit …' Agnes gulps. 'He did not give any hint as to who ended his earthly life?'

Mrs Boyle shakes her head. 'He has moved beyond such concerns. He does not call for justice or vengeance. He is at peace, and I suppose I should be also. I shall endeavour to be. But it is very difficult. How can I forgive those brutes?' Sudden as a gust of wind, Mrs Boyle's composure blows apart. The paper on her lap begins to rustle. 'Heaven help me! Was it not enough to cut his throat and take his precious life? Why must they be so cruel as to obliterate his dear face too?'

Agnes cannot stop her ears pricking at this new intelligence. The sergeant never mentioned a cut to the throat. If that was the injury that killed Mr Boyle … well, it puts her artwork in a less sinister light. There is no incision *there*. Footpads slit Mr Boyle's throat and smashed his face for spite. Or, as the sergeant proposed, to delay identification of the body. She must have been beside herself to think otherwise. This was a fool's errand.

'I have trespassed on your grief long enough,' she begins.

Mrs Boyle bids her remain seated with a motion of her hand. 'No. No, I beg your pardon. I should not have become agitated.'

Agnes would rather leave this suffocating room, but perhaps the widow is lonely.

38

'You shall not want for anything, Mrs Boyle?' she asks gently. 'You have family?'

'Our daughter is married to an excellent man. My grandchildren will keep me occupied, no doubt. I shall be as comfortable as one can be, once the joy of her life is gone.'

Agnes swallows. 'I am glad to hear it. You are fortunate. When my own father died ...' She nods at the silhouette on Mrs Boyle's lap. 'Well, you can see. My pastime was obliged to become a trade.'

Mrs Boyle shuffles uncomfortably beneath the paper wrapping. She glances from the profile to Agnes and back again, as if it had not occurred to her that women of her class might fall into penury. It had not occurred to Mamma, either. If Agnes had not risen to the occasion, and Simon was not so kind, all three of the Darken women could have ended up in the workhouse.

Clearing her throat, Mrs Boyle reaches into the folds of her skirt. When she speaks again, the tone is more formal. 'And you are most competent, Miss Darken. Permit me to contribute a little something for your trouble.'

Agnes holds out her hand and a silver shilling drops into it. The Queen's profile, grimed in dirt, stares indifferently. One shilling for all this heartache. The charge for bronzing would usually be more, but Agnes would not dream of saying so.

'Thank you, madam.'

39

Mrs Boyle sniffs. 'I shall call for Mary to see you out.'

She closes her fingers over the coin. Was her hint so tactless? Surely she has done no wrong. She *does* care, she has not come purely for the money, but she needs it. She wants to be independent, not reliant on Simon for charity.

Of course, she will never be able to explain this to a woman like Mrs Boyle, who has coin to spare on frivolities such as spirit mediums. Patiently, she waits in silence for Mary to answer the bell and lead her through the gloom to the door.

'Good day,' she says with a curtsey.

Mrs Boyle nods.

Compared to the twilight of the widow's parlour, the autumn day in Queen Square now seems perfectly bright. Agnes dawdles homewards, glad to have put Mr Boyle's death to rest. Her art is innocent. She has done nothing amiss – although she has been made to feel like an impertinent beggar woman.

She pulls the brim of her bonnet low to shield her face from passers-by. After Mrs Boyle's cold look, she does not want to meet the eyes of the square's other haughty residents.

It is not often she misses Constance, but she feels as if she would take comfort in speaking to her sister now. Constance would tell Agnes how little store she should set by the opinion of such dullards as the Boyles. She might even claim that the murderers had done a public service by putting an end to Mr Boyle.

Horrible, unforgivable things like that.

Still, they would make Agnes feel better.

CHAPTER 4

Pearl doesn't remember living in London, and she doesn't see a lot of Bath either. There's the parlour, the kitchen and the hallway, plus three other small rooms, which they use as bedchambers.

Sometimes, lodgers arrive and live in the rooms upstairs, but they never stay for long. The landlord won't let Pearl and Myrtle up there. They've only paid to rent the ground floor of the house. He might be hiding treasure or caged tigers above them for all she knows. She ought to check, but she's too afraid.

Today is market day, when she ventures to the front door to get some air. Her chair rests just inside the threshold and an old coal-scuttle bonnet screens her eyes from the worst glare of the daylight.

Her glimpses of the world outside are slight, like a tongue darting between the lips and slipping back in again. She sees cows shambling over the cobbles, their tails swishing at flies. A mass of black bricks and chimney stacks. Wafts of steam from Ladymead Penitentiary, where Myrtle sends their washing.

It's the smells Pearl enjoys the most. Even the straw and the dung. There's something alive about the scents in the street. They make her sit up and take notice.

Myrtle's already been out into the throng and returned with a punnet of blackberries for their favourite jam. Now she stands in the kitchen, behind Pearl, pulling them apart and pulping them.

Pearl turns and watches her sister. It's at times like these she tries to imagine Myrtle's father, Private West. He'd be a tall man, definitely. Probably handsome too, because he was Mother's first husband, and she married him at sixteen. You wouldn't marry that young if it weren't for the wildest romance.

Pearl always wonders what would have happened if Private West hadn't been killed in action. With a different father, she might have been born with Myrtle's lustrous eyes and widow's peak. Or maybe not. Maybe Mother wouldn't have birthed a second child at all. She'd still be on this side of the veil and it would be Pearl's soul wandering in that mist, without a home.

'I'm not saying the séance weren't good.' Myrtle wipes her forehead with the back of her hand. She's rolled her sleeves to the elbow and there are purple splotches all down her forearm. 'She was pleased as you like, that Mrs Boyle. But we can make it better for when the Society come. Can't we?'

'I don't know,' Pearl mumbles.

'Well, we can. People want a show. Don't matter to them you've got a genuine gift. They won't believe us unless we dress it up in tinsel.'

'But I can't control it! How am I meant to make it better? I don't even know what's happening to me.'

Sighing, Myrtle drops a blackberry into a bowl and crushes it beneath her spoon. 'I'll rig something up, won't I? I've been reading *Missives from Summerland*. Some places in London have these things they called *apports*.'

A cow lows from the street. Pearl turns to look. It's a dun-coloured beast, objecting to a man running his fingers down her legs. Does he want her for milk, or food? She's surely too pretty to be made into beefsteak.

'Pearl? Are you listening?'

She blinks, draws her eyes away from Walcot Street. 'Yes. What's an apport?'

'You drop them from the ceiling. Fruit, feathers, petals. Like a gift from the spirits. I could make that happen.'

'You don't think ...' Pearl wobbles on her chair, struck by a terrible thought. 'It won't just *happen*, will it? They won't just start giving presents through *me*?'

Myrtle considers this while she inspects a blackberry. 'I dunno, Pearl. Don't think so. Seems to me real ghosts are more subtle than that.'

Pearl recalls the way the spirit matter flowed from her mouth and it makes her stomach cramp in panic.

44

What else might come on that luminous tide? She might vomit forth objects. Manifest limbs. Anything could spew from between her lips and she wouldn't be able to stop it. She wouldn't even know it had happened.

'What about the fire?' Myrtle pounds into the bowl again. 'I could toss some coloured dust into it. That would go down well.'

'I hate it when you do that! It hurts my eyes.'

A sound of irritation escapes her sister, a harsh *tssssk*. 'Well, work with me, then! Think up something you *can* stand.' She's pummelling the berries so hard that the bowl shifts. 'I've got enough on my plate trying to work on *my* gift. Mesmerism ain't easy, you know. Don't you want to help me? Don't you want your father to get better?'

This stings sharper than the firelight, and Myrtle knows it.

Pearl grits her teeth. 'Yes.'

'Then act like it. Cudgel your brains.'

'I'm trying, but it's hard. Lifting the veil makes me feel sick. Did it make you sick at the start?'

''Course it did,' Myrtle says, more kindly, putting her spoon down. 'But you don't see me whining, do you? Buck up, my love.'

She envies Myrtle's strength. The spirits are right: her sister is vital, magnetic. Even in their shabby kitchen, wearing an apron, she vibrates.

'Can't the almshouse help Father?' Pearl pleads. 'While you're learning to heal with Mesmerism?'

Myrtle looks as if she's bitten into rotten fruit. 'Told you, they're stuck up. Either you ain't destitute enough for their help, or you don't deserve it. Them do-gooders don't consider "spirit medium" a good trade. They think we're all atheists, hysterical women and lecherous men.'

Pearl watches the smoke drifting from the chimney stacks outside, dark and free. How must she appear to those charitable workers? She didn't choose this gift, any more than she chose her albinism, yet she's punished for both.

'The Dispensary, then. Don't they help no matter what your religion?'

Myrtle's face shuts. 'Blinkered ignoramuses. Poisoners. Do you want them touching him?'

These fancy words are straight from the penny spiritualist paper, *Missives from Summerland*. The Society of Bath Spiritual Adventurers echo them in other forms. Drugs alter the natural flow of energy, Pearl is told. It's the one topic she dares to nurse a different opinion on – but she keeps that to herself.

The sun peeks out from behind a cloud. Even its watery autumn rays cause pain. Pressure masses beneath her forehead. She's a terrible thirst upon her.

'Too much light.' Pushing up off her chair, she wobbles to the kitchen where a jug of water sits waiting. She drinks one glass, two. She'd gladly drink the whole thing.

But that would be selfish. She's being selfish, even now: not helping her sister make the jam, getting in

46

the way of her father's recovery. She gazes around the damp room and up to the sooty ceiling. Is Mother here somewhere, watching her disapprovingly?

Myrtle goes on smashing the berries.

Prodded by guilt, Pearl fills a fresh glass and totters down the narrow corridor to the sickroom. She can't recall it ever being anything else. Father has always been ill.

Not *this* ill, though. As she pushes the door ajar, a rotten stench twines out to greet her: bad milk, fly-blown ham. It takes studied effort to place one foot in front of the other and creep inside.

Father lies on his back, fever-bitten. His head doesn't rest on the pillow but twitches this way and that. Does he see her? She's never certain these days. Whether he's alone or in company, he produces the same jerky movements, the same liquid-choked moans.

The curtains are drawn and the light is kind. Pearl edges closer. He's thrown the sheet partially off his body, exposing his shoulders, chest and one atrophied leg. How thin he's grown. A tortured shape, slowly disappearing into the mattress. He can't take solid food any more. Instead, the disease feeds upon him.

'D'you want some water, Father?' she asks softly.

He flings his head in her direction. *Yes.* She hears his voice clear as a bell, even though he can't speak. Maybe this is part of the Gift. Maybe her spirit can commune with Father's and they'll have no need for words between them.

With an unsteady hand, she reaches for the funnel. Father attempts to open what's left of his lips for her, but he can't control that black jaw. She wedges the spout in as best she can.

Few teeth remain. They jut at impossible angles. The actual jawbone is dark and decaying. When he could talk, Father said he needed a surgeon to cut it out.

Myrtle called them all butchers.

Pearl tries to imagine how Father would look after such an operation: he'd be a strange, broken doll of a man. She shudders at the thought. Maybe Myrtle's right about the surgeons.

Carefully, she tips the glass. Water trickles slowly down the funnel. She sees it slide over his gums, and the flick of his poor tongue. Of course there are drops that run to wet the pillow, but she's practised at this. She knows how to administer the liquid without choking him.

Her own mouth is still dry, despite her earlier drink. Maybe it's because of the nausea. Pearl listens to the soft flow of the water in the funnel and it becomes all she can think about.

At last the glass is done, and she can remove the funnel. The end that sat in Father's mouth is coated in something phlegmy. Pearl closes her eyes momentarily, sways on her feet. If only she was strong like Myrtle. Myrtle wouldn't even flinch.

Father looks exhausted by the short ordeal, too. She watches his eyelids droop, whispers, 'Rest, now.'

48

Pity wars with revulsion. She tries to focus on the parts of him that still look normal. His hair. It's a sweaty tangle, turned grey from all his pain, but at least it still resembles hair.

As she stares at him, something seems to shift and lighten. Pearl tilts her head. There. Behind him. It looks like an aureole of light. A glow disturbingly familiar …

Spirit matter.

Spirit matter teasing at his edges, seeking to claim him.

With a muffled sob she turns and runs from the room, leaving the glass and funnel behind.

Myrtle was right; she's always right in the end, no matter how harsh she seems. Time is running out. Father's mortal life will end if they don't find a way to treat him.

She leans against the wall and slumps into it, letting her head rest on the faded paper. *Help me. Help me, Mother. Tell me what to do.* She closes her eyes, wills and strains with all her might.

But Mother keeps her silence. The only image that fills Pearl's mind is colourless, shifting water.

CHAPTER 5

'Agnes! Agnes!'

Her stockinged feet slide across the floorboards. Dread clamps her chest in place of the corset she has left off fastening to hurry to her mother's aid.

But although Mrs Darken's wail suggested fire or murder, the lady herself sits composed in the wing chair, a newspaper spread over her lap.

'What is it, Mamma? Are you ill?'

Mamma turns her face up to the firelight. Dropsy has made it rotund and ruddy-skinned, rather like the characters in the Gillray prints Papa used to collect. 'They've put your advertisement in the paper, dear.'

Agnes pants, out of breath from her dash. 'I do not understand you. What advertisement?' Now that she stops to consider, Mamma should not have a *Gazette* in her grasp at all. Only last Wednesday, she told the boy to end their subscriptions because she could not pay the bill. 'Where did you get that from? We cannot afford ...'

Her voice disappears. As she draws closer, the print becomes less blurred. *Murder in Gravel Walk.*

'If you can pay for an advertisement, you cannot begrudge me my papers,' Mamma huffs.

Agnes snatches the newspaper so fast that a corner rips off in Mamma's fingertips.

She holds it close to her face. It is just as she feared. Those insidious journalists have crept in like so many lice.

The victim, last seen alive at Darken's Silhouette Parlour, Orange Grove, was ostensibly killed by an incision at the throat, although he endured multiple injuries after death.

What need had they to mention her premises? As if her little business were not struggling enough! It is as though they are *trying* to take away the one employment that gives her satisfaction.

'Did you *read* this, Mamma?'

Mamma fidgets her shoulders. 'You did not give me the chance. I only saw our name and thought you would like to know ...'

While Mamma subsides into grumbles, Agnes tears the paper up, tossing the shreds onto the fire, where they twist and writhe.

'Well, I never did! Whatever has got into you, Agnes? I might have expected this behaviour from *Constance*, but not you.'

She closes her eyes, tries to fetch enough air into her lungs. It is not Mamma's fault.

'Forgive me, Mamma, but they really do print such trash these days. I will see if I can stretch to a magazine. *The World of Fashion* ... But first you should eat. Where' – she casts a quick, unhopeful look about the parlour – 'where is Cedric? I thought we were to play backgammon. He is not out and about this early, surely?'

Mamma plaits her fingers. 'Ah, little Cedric. He'll be begging ginger lemonade from the soda manufactory or spying on the girls in Mrs Box's seminary. A wandering spirit, that boy. Just like his father – aye, and his grandfather before him.'

Agnes flinches. Her mother does not observe it, for she is gazing into the past now, her eyes filmed over.

'Lord, how he did drag me about, that papa of yours! If it wasn't Gibraltar it was the West Indies, or some other godforsaken place at the ends of the earth. You are lucky he took his half pay after Constance was born. Who knows where we should have ended up otherwise?'

A burn at the core of her chest, which has nothing to do with her bad lungs. 'I should have liked to see the West Indies,' Agnes replies softly.

'Oh no you would not! That life would not suit *you* at all. The heat is like the bowels of Hell. It took all morning just to get a *hint* of curl in my hair. Then I could barely eat. I lost so much weight, I had to take in every one of my gowns, I remember.'

Strange how Mamma can recall details like this, but not the pain her daughter has endured; how all Agnes's hopes of happiness were once centred on a ship cutting through the surf and ports in foreign climes.

'Speaking of gowns, I had better put mine on. I shall be back presently.'

The stair treads yawn beneath her feet. Agnes echoes them, rubbing the grit from her eyes. As she stumbles onto the landing, her shoulder knocks against a frame hanging on the wall. There is a crash followed by the dreaded tinkle of broken glass.

'Agnes?'

'It is nothing, Mamma.'

Stooping down, she turns the oval frame face up. Shards of glass fall to the floor. Behind them, unmarked, rests the profile of Constance.

This is the only shade of her they keep on display in the house. It is blind, without the eyelash Agnes now cuts in as a matter of course, but it remains one of her best pieces. There is a depth to it that conjures up the woman herself.

Indeed, time has softened the memory of Constance's face to such an extent that these lines now seem to represent her entirely. A dark hole that you might stare into and accidentally fall down.

In her bedchamber Agnes rests the broken frame upon the dresser and takes a gown from the press. Its dark shade calms her. Black: always ordered and neutral.

Reliable.

She notices something misshapen lying at the base of the cupboard. Her reticule. She chucked it hastily aside after the policeman's visit, but it had rained that day; she ought to have turned the bag out in front of the fire. Bending, she tuts to see the material is pocked with water marks. When she untangles the strings and opens it, it is even worse; a mouldy smell assails her nostrils.

'No, no, no.' Flames of rust lick the blades of her scissors, still nestled inside. She owns another pair, but these ones are special instruments – they do not come cheap. As for the silhouette she cut of the naval officer in the park, it is utterly ruined: limp and turning to pulp at the bottom of the bag. She blows out her breath. At least it was not a good likeness to begin with.

Frustrated, she throws the bag to one side and continues to dress. Her old governess always accused her of being easily distracted, and here is the proof: a smashed frame, rusting scissors and a ruined silhouette – all in one morning. She never means to abandon tasks. But there is so much pressing upon her mind. More than it can possibly contain. It is only natural that certain things should … slip out. Since her spell of illness it has only become worse: sometimes a whole hour will pass by without her even noticing.

She fastens her hair. It is an unpleasant surprise to see the woman in the looking glass. The fine bone structure that Montague praised as 'delicate' now only serves to make her look drawn. And then there is that grey streak in her hair; a vivid shock down one side like the blue band in a magpie's wing. That came after the pneumonia, too. She has still not grown accustomed to it.

Her eyes dart to the broken frame and to Constance's shade. Her dead sister has smooth, unwrinkled skin and her hair colour is without variation. All the spikes and bristles of her character are concealed safely behind black lines. She looks almost *amenable* in this form. It goes to prove that the silhouette really is the kindest form of art.

Back down the staircase to the accompaniment of another mournful, weary sound from the treads. Mamma remains just as she left her, peering through her spectacles at the fire.

'I am afraid you will have to take your breakfast tea without milk, Mamma,' Agnes sighs. Her mother raises an ear trumpet to catch her words. 'I shall have to go and fetch some more later ...'

'Oh, Agnes. Do you never keep your wits about you, dear?'

'I did not *forget*,' she explains irritably. 'I used it all making Cedric—'

'We won't be able to afford milk or anything else, will we, if you carry on ignoring customers like that?'

'Ignoring ... ?'

Mamma jerks her head in the direction of the window.

55

Peering through the thicket of silhouettes tacked to the glass are the startlingly bright eyes of a young man.

'He's been there for at least five minutes, knocking.'

Agnes is aghast. Today is market day. The sound of his banging must have been swallowed by the general bustle from outside. 'Why did you not call me?' she demands as she dashes to the door.

Mamma does not reply, but drops her ear trumpet and picks up last week's newspaper.

―――――

Agnes is old enough to be this young man's mother.

She feels antiquated, foolish, sat before him in her studio with her spare pair of scissors. Will he go to a coffee house with his friends after this, and joke about the old maid in Orange Grove?

She can almost picture them: their checked waistcoats and greased hair. Laughing. Laughing like the magpies outside.

But she is spoiling the experience for herself. This is her first chance to do a real piece of work since Mr Boyle's appointment, and she should relish it. The youth has an attractive profile, worthy of a place in her duplicate book. She glances from the paper to his face, enjoying as she always does the crisp sound of that first cut.

'You seem rather a young man, to be having your shade cut,' she ventures. 'I thought it was all daguerreotypes with your generation.'

'Well—' He turns to face her. Remembers, too late, that he isn't meant to move. 'Oh. Sorry.'

'Never mind. Just look to the side again if you would, sir.'

'Ned, please. No need to stand upon ceremony with me.'

How strangely the young conduct themselves nowadays! He is asking her, a woman he has just met, to call him by his Christian name. Not even that, an abbreviation of the name. She pulls the paper towards the jaws of her scissors and works on his lips. It is a shame that she cannot capture the tentative beginnings of a moustache that sprout beneath his nose.

'Ned, then. What prompted you to come to me for a shade?'

'It's my gran. She has a whole wall full of silhouettes. Every family member you can think of. I *did* give her my photograph, but the old dear wasn't pleased with it.' He laughs. 'Bit of a blow to my pride, eh? She said it looked odd amongst all those shadows.'

Agnes pauses as she repositions her scissors and begins to tackle the chin. 'Well, your grandmother is correct,' she says proudly. 'The shade is the purest of all portraits. Beside it, a photograph would appear too ...'

'Too alive?' he supplies. 'Too *real*, perhaps. I don't know why, but when I see her wall of silhouettes ... To me, it looks like a display of death masks.'

'Oh, no, surely not?' This judgement dismays her. She has always managed to find beauty and purpose

57

in the clear lines of a silhouette, no matter what else is going on in her life.

'Yes, I'm afraid they look that way to me. Like shells of things with the souls snuffed out.'

The blade slips. Only a little way, a quarter of an inch at most, but with this nick under the chin, she will struggle to cut the throat and shoulders. Damn these second-rate scissors.

'A good profile *exposes* the soul of the sitter,' she explains, frowning at her work.

'Well, a photograph is a good deal quicker. I thought you had machines to do this silhouette business?'

It stings, but he is correct. At the height of her powers, she had been able to cut a shade freehand in – what – two minutes? Sometimes less. The memory is like a small death. Skill is forsaking her, too, contrary as any lover.

'There *are* machines, but I favour the personal touch …' Outside the window, the magpies beat their wings, squabbling. Agnes sighs and lays down her scissors. Here is a way out of her present difficulty with the nick, at least. 'I would be happy to show you my physiognotrace, if you prefer?'

Ned turns again, his brown eyes sparkling. 'Really? Could I see it? I wouldn't want to be a bother.'

Despite herself, Agnes smiles. His enthusiasm is infectious. In a few years, Cedric will be like this: fancying himself an engineer and championing progress. An odd turn of events, considering the workers of Mamma's generation did all they could to smash the machines that stole their livelihood. But such is humankind: hopelessly fickle.

'It is no trouble at all. I will clean the contraption and we will use it to take your profile. You will enjoy the experience. It's very clever, in its way.'

Bustling to the corner, she moves various pads and paint palettes off the machine. It is so webbed in dust that she coughs.

'Here,' says Ned, rising to his feet. 'Let me help.'

Piece by piece, they reveal a chipped wooden box with a hatch on the side. Agnes is startled to think how long it's been since she last used the instrument. What appeared then as the cutting edge of innovation now looks poor and dejected, its quaintness the only virtue left.

Without asking for permission, Ned reaches and opens the hatch. A small brass cylinder, topped with a metal hoop, protrudes from the bottom of the box. Opposite it, on the far 'wall' a piece of yellow paper is tacked.

'Smells a bit musty!' he laughs. 'Well, how does it work?'

'Let me change the paper first, and then we will fit the pole.'

The holders are a little corroded, but Agnes manages to work the old paper free. It is powdery in her hands, as insubstantial as the past. Casting it aside, she reloads the machine with something crisp and white. She is quite looking forward to trying this again.

The other lengthy pole belonging to the machine is propped in the corner beside a bookcase. One end still holds a pencil, miraculously hard and sharp after all this time, while the other tapers into a rod.

Ned guffaws. 'Bless me! You could take someone's eye out with that pole.'

He means it innocently. He is not to know that his words bring Mr Boyle bobbing to the surface of her mind. Smashed, broken ...

But she must put that behind her.

'I promise to be careful. If you would fetch the chair and position it ... yes, that will suffice.' She threads the pole through the metal hoop.

Ned sits, keen as a puppy. 'And what – the rod passes over my face, does it?'

'Yes.' She smiles at him. His zest seems to be infusing into her. 'You must remain very still, even if it tickles.'

'And the pencil on the other end draws it there, in the little box?'

'Indeed. The image will be small, and upside down. That is of no matter. I will use a pantograph to make it larger, and we will turn it into an artwork worthy of your grandmother.'

'Well, fancy that! Let's get underway, shall we?'

She starts the rod at the nape of his neck. Feels the heat of his body rise to her trembling hands. He smells of bergamot pomade.

It is all rather enchanting. She cannot remember the last time she stood this close to a man. Other than

60

Simon. And there is nothing thrilling about Simon's clammy fingers at her wrist, feeling her pulse.

She holds the rod steady with both hands and softly traces the top of Ned's crown. His greased locks ruffle out of place. One or two strands cling to the pole with static. She senses him tense, trying not to laugh.

He closes his eyes as the rod comes sweeping over his forehead and down his nose. It kisses his lips, dipping between them and departing with the slightest gleam of moisture.

She is disappointed when it ends.

'Is it done? Can I see?'

'Just a moment.' She opens the contraption and reveals his double, inverted and ever so faint.

'How clever! That is me, isn't it? You can see, even though it's so small. It's unmistakably me.'

Agnes glances from the drawing to Ned and back again. It hardly does him justice.

'Remarkable accuracy,' he enthuses. 'Just from a rod! The things they invent. So you'll make it bigger and then it's done?'

She can imagine him presenting this paltry shade to his grandmother with aplomb, singing the praises of the blasted physiognotrace. *See, Grandmamma, you don't even need a person to draw these now!* Is she really going to let a machine best her?

'The head is too wide and flat,' she decrees. 'It needs an artist's touch.'

61

Taking a piece of black foolscap, she makes a single vertical incision and begins to cut Ned's profile as a hole in the centre of it. A hollow-cut – she has not used the technique in years.

For a moment she worries she has outstretched herself. The twists and turns of his face are tight. Slivers of paper peel away as she works on the detail of his cravat, her tongue clamped between her teeth in concentration.

But at last it emerges. Stunning. Her best piece in a long time.

She mounts it on white stock card. A shade reversed. Ned's profile is a light in the darkness, glowing with the purity of fresh snow.

'Do you call that soulless, Ned?'

He snatches it up, delight written all over his face. 'Why, that's remarkable! You did it in white, just for me?'

She glows with pride. 'Now you can cut a figure on your grandmother's wall. It is enough like the others to fit in her collection, but you have your own flair.'

He shakes her hand. Does not notice that she retains his a little longer than necessary.

'I'm so pleased,' Ned rattles on as he gathers his coat. 'I hadn't planned to do this today. I was just passing and saw your display. Isn't it lucky I knocked?'

So he has not seen the *Gazette*.

'It is very fortunate for me.'

Coins exchange hands. Although she is glad of the money, she is sorry they must part. Soon the shilling will be spent and she will have precious little to remember him by, this sunny boy who has brightened her day.

He is too young for her, of course, but there is something about him that reminds her of Montague. That easy manner, the ability to make her smile.

'Good day,' says Ned.

'I hope we will see you here again.'

He grins but does not reply.

It was a silly thing for her to say. Ned has no reason to come back to this forlorn house: he is young and free. But there is comfort in the thought that she will go with him. Her name, signed in pencil, will never part from his profile.

In some small way, she has claimed him.

CHAPTER 6

The gas lamps are up. Not high, but enough to taunt her. By their light, the parlour looks shabbier: the wallpaper a weak and faded lilac chintz that depresses the spirits. Pearl's spirits, that is. She doesn't know about the ghosts. They haven't complained about the decoration as yet.

Myrtle's been buzzing around like a honeybee all day. It's tiring just to watch her buffing the chipped wooden furniture, arranging the doilies in a thousand different positions before settling on the right ones. She's managed to get a tea service, good stuff but not matching. The seedcake she baked earlier still flavours the air.

Pearl can only watch her sister in admiration, wondering if they're really related. It's not just Myrtle's energy that amazes her, it's her dogged patience.

That hairstyle alone must have taken hours. Fat, sausage ringlets fall over one shoulder. Pomade makes them look like meadow hay. It's a big improvement on their usual dirty blonde colour. Myrtle can't afford to dress in a crinoline, but the deep maroon gown

– which she sewed herself – has enough pleats in the skirt to swing full and fashionable.

Pearl has been decked out in dove grey, but she doesn't care what she looks like. The whole point of girls like her is to *not* be there; to subtract herself from the room.

'I'll introduce you to Mr Stadler and Mr Collins – he's the chap who takes the photographs,' Myrtle calls over her shoulder as she plumps cushions. 'Just a few of them tonight.' She smiles artificially and adopts her posh accent. 'A *private* gathering. Can't have them thinking we're putting on a show.'

'But you said the other day—'

'I know, but you can't have them *think* it, Pearl. The minute they see you actually want to get paid for your work, they'll call you vulgar. Who else? Oh, Mrs Lynch—'

'I've already met them,' Pearl points out. 'You don't need to introduce me to Mr Stadler. I've sat on his lap as Florence King.'

Myrtle releases a sound of exasperation. For a minute, Pearl fears she'll throw the cushion at her. 'For God's sake, don't act like it! Don't let on. You've been an invalid, confined to your bed, remember?'

Pearl shuffles in her seat. She's going to say something bad. It tickles in her chest, then bubbles in her mouth. Usually good sense would press it down again, but the gas lights make her peevish.

'Don't you feel guilty, lying to them?'

Myrtle's cheeks turn the colour of her gown. 'I never lied. I did hear a spirit called Florence King. I just got you to play her. There had to be *some* use in you being pale as a ghost.'

Pearl shrinks back into her seat. Why does she say things like that to Myrtle? It's always a mistake. Each time she questions her sister she's filled with this painful, searing shame.

There's a rap at the door.

In a second Myrtle's over, straightening Pearl's posture in the chair, wiping a smear of jam away from her cheek with spit and a threadbare handkerchief.

'You'll be fine,' she whispers. 'Just dandy.'

Pearl thinks she might be sick.

She remains frozen in place while Myrtle goes to the hallway and opens the door. The voices of the Society enter before their bodies do. A full bass, another with cut-glass vowels and one at a higher, chirpier octave.

For people intent on peering into the grave, they sound unusually jolly.

'A dusting of snow,' Mrs Lynch announces from the hallway. 'It caught me quite by surprise. Look at my cloak!'

'Do permit me to brush down your shoulders.' Pearl is not surprised to hear it's Mr Stadler saying these words. When she acted the part of Myrtle's spirit guide, she was forced to endure this man's caresses. Having summoned a ghost, all he wanted to do was dandle it upon his lap. She remembers him displaying

66

her to Mr Collins for the first time. 'She is quite real, Walter. Just feel these hipbones ...'

Pearl can't blame the spirits for wanting to talk through her, rather than showing up themselves and letting people manhandle them. The indignity of it all is breathtaking.

There's a thump as Mr Collins struggles inside with what must be his photographic equipment. 'Is she here?' he demands. 'Is she ready for our experiments?'

Myrtle laughs gaily. 'You're very eager, Mr Collins. Won't you let us drink some tea first?'

Pearl sighs inwardly, knowing the version of Myrtle that comes back into the parlour won't be the sister who raised her, but the theatrical counterfeit. And she's right. Myrtle marches at the head of the pack, her eyes sparkling. She waves her hand with a flourish and says, 'Ladies and gentlemen, may I present Miss Pearl Meers? Or, as those who have seen her powers have come to call her, the White Sylph.'

The four visitors, two men and two women, stare. Pearl opens her mouth and closes it. Ought she to stand? She's left it too late.

'Hello,' she offers.

No one says a word.

The clock ticks. It makes the visitors' silence seem even more profound. Pearl registers their blank, shocked expressions, and feels a stab of foreboding. Do they recognise her as Florence King? Myrtle took so much care to make her look different tonight, and they both presumed that no one had seen her face clearly behind Florence King's long veil. It would destroy Myrtle if the Society found out ...

But at last, Mrs Lynch finds her voice. 'How extraordinary! You did not tell me, my dear Miss West, that she was an albino child.'

A blush stings Pearl's cheeks.

'Didn't I? I must have forgotten,' shrugs Myrtle, who forgets nothing. 'But I did tell you she was always upstairs, ill, when we performed our previous séances here.' She flicks a curl over her shoulder and raises Pearl to her feet. 'Pearl's been delicate since birth. I thought it was because her body's different, but—'

'But now we know better,' Mrs Lynch finishes sagely. 'How often it has been remarked that the Gift manifests itself after a period of severe illness!'

'Indeed, indeed,' Mr Collins cuts in. 'The Power always follows sickness and frequently comes to the gentler sex. The lower in status they are, the stronger they seem to grow. Deprivation, frustration and discontent: these are the grounds in which mediumship breeds.'

Pearl sees the rictus set into Myrtle's cheeks. This prig insults them openly, in their own home. If she was braver, she would spark back. But she's saving her strength for more important things.

At the last séance, she knew the name of the person she was summoning: Mr Boyle. This time, any ghost might come through. She shivers, feeling like the skin is shrinking on her bones.

68

The other woman, who looks like a facsimile of Mrs Lynch, pushes forward and lifts a lock of Pearl's hair from the shoulder of her gown. 'Look! Pure white! Even paler than Florence's. She might have come from the spirit realm itself, Mamma.'

'Well,' Myrtle considers, 'maybe she did. She was born with the cord wrapped around her neck, you know. Not a whiff of breath in her. It were me what brought her back to life.'

They all gasp.

Myrtle's eagerness to share the tale breaks through her false voice. No one seems to care.

She tells them the story, but there's one part she leaves out: she doesn't mention how their mother slipped away while Myrtle was busy reviving Pearl. None of the Society will know that it was all Pearl's fault; that if she hadn't been a distraction, someone might have saved Mother.

But Pearl remembers. She's heard it enough times.

Myrtle pats her on the shoulder. 'Come on,' she says. 'Let's sit down and have some tea.'

She guides Pearl to the table, her hand in the small of her back. When they sit down, she's careful to perform the introductions again, more thoroughly, giving Pearl the names of Mr Stadler, Mr Collins, Mrs Lynch and Miss Lynch.

Although they've all come to consult Pearl, they don't seem to want her. Myrtle pulls their gaze like a giant magnet.

'Such a pity, Miss West, that Florence King had to leave us,' Mrs Lynch laments. 'I cannot step foot inside this house without recalling your dear spirit guide. That farewell séance! I will never forget how tenderly she clasped me. But my loss is nothing compared to yours. You must miss her most of all.'

Myrtle concentrates on pouring the tea, avoiding Mrs Lynch's eye. 'Of course I regret that dear Florence had to go,' she sighs. 'But I knew her guidance would only be given to me for a short time. She's happy in Summerland now, and I'm living out her message here on Earth. It was Florence, you recall, who told me what would happen to my sister, and that I should study Mesmerism.'

'I myself possess a great interest in the mesmeric force,' Mr Collins announces pompously. 'A magnetic fluid that flows through all creatures, ready to be manipulated and controlled, it is like a chemical, dear ladies. As a photographer, I have a vast knowledge of chemicals, and it is my opinion that spirit matter is just another such substance. I have high hopes of being able to photograph its fumes tonight.'

'Do *you* consider the mesmeric force to be like spirit matter?' Mr Stadler asks Myrtle, pointedly turning away from Mr Collins. 'Is it composed of the same material?'

'That's what I'm going to find out,' says Myrtle, flashing a confident smile.

Pearl listens with bemused interest. She only knows bits and bobs about this. All her knowledge comes

70

from the parts of *Missives from Summerland* that Myrtle decides to read out loud to her.

Myrtle learnt to read when she worked at the match factory with Father, but she hasn't taught Pearl.

'I have heard the drollest anecdotes about Mesmerism,' Mr Stadler says. 'Accounts of nice young ladies suddenly swearing and kicking up their skirts whilst in a trance! One mesmerist even made his patient think that the water she drank was sherry instead. They willed it with the power of their mind, and she actually tasted sherry!' He tips a wink. 'Makes you think twice about the Miracle at Cana, eh?'

Pearl doesn't like to hear him talk that way. The contributors to *Missives from Summerland* sound like good-hearted people, committed to the cause of truth, who want to use their supernatural learning to make the world a better place. They're as devout in their faith as any Jew or Methodist. But the Society of Bath Spiritual Adventurers seek phenomena, and nothing more. All Mr Stadler wants the sisters to do with their precious gifts is to make ladies dance!

'Myrtle's going to heal my father,' Pearl stammers. 'She's – she's going to help people with *her* Mesmerism.' All eyes turn towards her. Her palms sweat and she wipes them on her lap. 'He thought he needed a – a doctor, but—'

'Pshaw, my dear!' Mrs Lynch cries. 'You cannot trust a physician. These medical men seek to impose

71

their control on our bodies and souls with their drugs. They think to steer the course of our destiny.'

But why is that a problem? Pearl has never been in control of her own destiny.

She focuses on the centrepiece of the table, wishing she hadn't spoken.

Tonight, the crystal ball's been replaced with a large glass bowl, half full of water. On the surface, purple flower heads float.

She'd like to drink that water. The tea hasn't quenched her thirst at all. Ever since market day, she keeps thinking of water. Does it mean something? It feels like there might be water building inside of her: this heaviness across the chest and at the back of her neck. It's like the pressure of a river behind a dam, desperate to break through.

'Must we delay any longer?' Mr Collins gulps the remains of his tea and surges to his feet. 'I am eager to begin.'

Mr Stadler cocks an eyebrow. 'We had not guessed.'

Everyone except Pearl puts their napkins aside.

She doesn't know what to do with herself. The others seem to have tasks: Myrtle turns down the gas lamps; Mrs Lynch and her daughter unpack notebooks from their bags; the men begin to assemble some monstrous contraption with a single glass eye.

Pearl looks at the machine, unnerved. Can it ... *see* her? Maybe the glass part is just like the crystal ball: something for her to stare into and glimpse the

Other Side through. But whereas Pearl's crystal ball is a bubble of soft light, this shape is blind. She squints, trying to see into the big wooden box behind it. Only darkness lies within.

'Careful with that, careful!' Mr Collins scolds his companion.

She's so intent upon the men that she loses sight of the ladies. Pearl almost forgets that they're in the room – until one screams beside her ear.

She whips round to see what accident has happened, but Miss Lynch is standing still, unharmed, gaping at Pearl.

'Look,' she gasps. 'I can see it. I can see the spirit matter flowing from her.'

A reverent silence falls.

Pearl looks down at her pale hands. Gentle wisps rise from them like breath on a cold day. They are coming, then. Ready to claim her.

Her shoulders turn solid with fear.

'The plate,' Mr Collins urges. 'Quickly, man.'

Before Pearl can draw another breath, a flash of white-hot pain scorches across her vision. Stunned, she claps her hands over her eyes, but that burst of light keeps repeating and repeating.

'Myrtle!' she cries.

Myrtle runs to her, buries Pearl's face safely inside the folds of her new gown. It radiates her familiar scent of berries and violets.

'What d'you think you're doing?' she demands.

'The – the magnesium powder.' Mr Collins holds up a tray that smokes. 'Friends of mine have used it to great effect. Through spirit agency, the—'

'If you've read so much, why don't you know better? Mediumship takes a toll upon the Sensitive. She's fragile.'

Pearl feels it. But it soothes her to hear the rumble of Myrtle's voice through her bodice and sense her hand moving over her hair. Much as they squabble, Myrtle is the only mother she's ever known.

'Poor dear,' frets Mrs Lynch. 'Pass her this tea.' Pearl drinks it greedily, her eyes squeezed shut. 'I remember, Miss West, how Florence King weakened *you*. Those bad nights you spent with your nerves in tatters.' She sighs. 'Such is the price of great power.'

'But if we can *capture* this,' Mr Collins enthuses, undeterred, 'if we could prove with an image what we witness here with the naked eye, it would alter everything! You must understand that? Our enemies will be forced to eat their words!'

'No more flash powder tonight,' Myrtle rules. When Mr Collins puffs with frustration, she adds, 'Patience and care, sir. You don't catch spirits with stomping feet.'

Gradually, Pearl can sit upright again. When she opens her eyes they feel raw, as if she's peeled a layer of skin from the lids.

Mr Stadler crosses the room to take her hand. 'Tell us what you feel equal to, Miss Meers. We all wait upon your convenience. But surely you will not send us home so early in the evening?'

She wants to snatch her hand away from him, but she doesn't dare.

'Last time,' Myrtle tells them, 'some friends and I sat in a circle and a spirit spoke through Pearl. Actually possessed her and used her mouth! I never heard her talk in such a deep voice before.'

'What power,' he marvels. 'Most spirits, even the materialised ones, have no utterance.'

'*Can* she materialise a ghost?' Mrs Lynch pushes forward, brimming with excitement. 'We might get Florence King back, or someone else entirely. What is your guide's name, dear?'

Myrtle snaps upright. 'The White Sylph has no need of a spirit guide.'

'Do you remember, dear Miss West, how we used to blindfold you and tie you in the cabinet while you made Florence appear?' Myrtle's face says she remembers only too well. 'We proved, beyond a doubt, that your gift was real.'

'Are you proposing that we tie Miss Meers up also?' Mr Stadler's fingers tighten around Pearl's hand. They are damp, as if the idea excites him. 'In the name of experiment?'

'What do you think might happen?'

The Society remind Pearl of dogs about to fall upon a bone. It's too much; the volley of voices, the wide, eager eyes. She flings Myrtle a terrified glance.

'I won't have my sister bound like a criminal. She isn't in the penitentiary.' Myrtle pats her hair back into shape. 'But let her try the cabinet by all means. We might get a surprise.'

It's a reprieve, of sorts. Pearl should probably be grateful.

Standing up, she edges reluctantly towards the cabinet. It gapes at her like a giant mouth. She thought this would be like the last séance. Why aren't they sticking to what she knows?

At least it's dark inside. She pulls the black damask curtain across the rail, free for a blissful minute from the Society's scrutiny. A sigh escapes her as she sits down.

Now what?

Her spine presses hard against the loose panel in the back of the cabinet. That's where she used to wait, dressed up as Florence King, quiet as a mouse, while the others tied Myrtle with silk scarves and sealed the knots with wax.

One time, she remembers she felt a sneeze coming, and nearly bit through her lip trying to stifle it. But even that was easier than what's being asked of her tonight.

She hears the fizz of a match lighting a candle. The gas lamps go out. Chair legs shuffle, Mr Collins clears his throat.

There is an ominous, charged silence.

Then they begin to sing:

When the hours of day are numbered,
And the voices of the night
Wake the better soul, that slumbered,
To a holy, calm delight.

The table is just on the other side of the curtain, but the distance between Pearl and the others feels huge.

Ere the evening lamps are lighted,
And, like phantoms grim and tall,
Shadows from the fitful fire-light
Dance upon the parlour wall;

It's horrible to be trapped here, cut off from flesh and blood. The Society all get to sit with another person's warm hand in their own, but Pearl … She trembles, realising anew how small and thin she is.

Then the forms of the departed
Enter at the open door;
The beloved, the true-hearted,
Come to visit me once more;

Tears form. It never used to feel like this in the cabinet. Myrtle was always there. There's something different in the air behind the curtain tonight. It's … agitated.

He, the young and strong, who cherished
Noble longings for the strife,

By the roadside fell and perished,
Weary with the march of life!

She looks from the left to the right. There's nothing there, just black, but it feels, it *feels* ...

They, the holy ones and weakly,
Who the cross of suffering bore,
Folded their pale hands so meekly
Spake with us on earth no more!

A current of cool air lifts the hair from her neck.

What is it? A trapped bird, fluttering around her, stirring up the atmosphere? She can't move, she can't speak, but she knows there's something alive inside the cabinet.

And with them the Being Beauteous,
Who unto my youth was given,
More than all things else to love me,
And is now a saint in heaven.

Cobwebs. Itchy, sticky *cobwebs* are passing over her face. Frantically, she tries to bat them away.

It's only when she lowers her hands that she sees the cloud of downy white, floating before her.

With a slow and noiseless footstep
Comes that messenger divine,

Takes the vacant chair beside me,
Lays her gentle hand in mine.

The cloud expands.

The others keep on singing as something rises up from the middle like a head beneath a bridal veil.

And she sits and gazes at me
With those deep and tender eyes,
Like the stars, so still and saint-like,
Looking downward from the skies.

Shoulders emerge but it has no arms, no body, no legs.

Uttered not, yet comprehended,
Is the spirit's voiceless prayer
Soft rebukes, in blessings ended,
Breathing from her lips of air.

From behind, a freezing hand falls heavy on her shoulder.

Pearl screams.

The singing stops. Chairs scrape but Pearl is faster than them, flinging the curtain back on its rail so hard that it makes the rings clatter.

She runs.

'Pearl!'

Commotion erupts around the table. She can't stop to explain herself to the Society; she can barely breathe for sobs. Hands – mortal, this time – try to restrain her.

79

'No!' she cries, flinging them off. 'No, I won't do it!'

She darts for Father's room.

There's a shout behind her. A sudden *bang* and *splash*.

Pearl doesn't stop until she reaches the door, where she risks a quick glance back.

The fishbowl of flowers has exploded outwards, drenching the spiritualists in water and glass.

Mrs Lynch stands spluttering, her arms held out at her sides. The ends of Myrtle's curls drip.

Water, again.

Pearl races inside Father's room and locks the door.

CHAPTER 7

Every year it's the same. Agnes does not wait for the almanac to tell her that winter is approaching; she feels it in her knuckles and her wrists. They become burning, swollen lumps: the price she must pay for her decades spent cutting shades.

With difficulty, she coaxes her gloves from their stretchers and pulls them on to keep her hands warm. The cold season seems to be starting earlier and earlier – either that, or she is getting old. Perpetually chilly, like Mamma with her thin blood and eroded defences. Agnes shoves the thought away. *Not yet.*

As she goes to leave her bedroom, her skirt sweeps against something on the dressing table and sends it floating to the floor. Constance's silhouette. She forgot she had left it there.

She resents having to bend and pick it up, having to pack her sister tidily away yet again. Without looking at the shade, she marches to her studio and opens the book of duplicates. A musty perfume rises from the

81

pages. It always falls open at the same place, but she will *not* put Constance's shadow on this page beside *him*. If that is petty of her – well, she does not care.

Agnes flips to the very back of the book, pushes Constance in and slams it shut.

It all started with her birthday: that was the first thing Constance took. She arrived exactly five years from the day Agnes entered the world, and she did not even soften the blow by being the little boy Mamma had promised.

Constance was not a winsome infant; she was born with the colic. In those first weeks she was not so much a baby as a pink, shrieking ball of rage.

Agnes remembers sitting on the stairs with her hands pressed over her ears, hoping Papa would take Constance away when he boarded his next ship.

The grandfather clock pings the quarter hour. Agnes swallows down her memories. She will be late for morning prayers at the abbey.

Downstairs, Mamma is reading an old *Herald* before a fire that scratches and ticks. More coal is gone, but Agnes cannot really blame her mother for using it today. The temperature has shifted palpably; it is as if the air has whetted its teeth overnight.

Cedric crouches by the side table, idly spinning the top Agnes bought him from the toyshop in Morford Street.

She smiles at him. 'Would you care to accompany me, dear?'

'Where?'

'Church.'

82

He pulls a face.

Cedric means no harm, but it hurts her to be spurned like this. Everything is much more cheerful when he is with her.

'Do come,' she wheedles. 'Say a prayer, for your Mamma in Heaven?'

The top falls over. Cedric's green eyes meet hers.

'Is *that* where she is?'

Agnes bites her tongue. She is reminded of the phrase the pawnbroker used, when she tried to get a better price for Captain Darken's medals. *Not bloody likely.*

'Yes, of course it is. We have discussed this, Cedric. Listen, dear, if you come along to church with me, perhaps I will take you for a bun at Sally Lunn's afterwards. What do you say to that?'

'I'd rather stay here and read.'

'But we can read together *after* —'

'Let the boy alone.' Mamma wets her finger and turns the page of her newspaper. 'He's well enough here with me.'

Sighing, Agnes puts on her bonnet and makes for the door. Before she steps onto the mat, she is forced to pull up short. A torn piece of paper lies at her feet. It looks like it has been pushed underneath the door, rather than through the letterbox. She is forced to bend yet again, to the protestation of her knees.

The paper is of a good quality. Suitable for sketching, and indeed someone has used a pencil to write four faint words upon it.

83

Agnes peers, pulls it closer.

Did you miss me.

She frowns and turns the paper over. Just that. Not even a question mark.

Who on earth would write such a thing? She cannot imagine anyone sending her notes except Simon, and he called only the other day, after young Ned had left with his white silhouette. Besides, Simon's correspondence is always a template of formal elegance.

She takes a few steps back to the parlour. 'Cedric, have you been playing with my sketchbooks again?'

'No.' He has pulled *The String of Pearls* onto his lap and is already engrossed.

Perhaps the writing is too developed for his young hand. But it does look familiar ...

'Did you happen to see who delivered this note?'

The boy shrugs, still reading his book.

Well. How perplexing. She reads the words again, and they touch a chord deep inside her. For the answer is *yes*: she misses so many people.

One in particular.

He would write her notes. Play games. But it cannot be, not after all these years ...

She tucks the note inside her newly dried reticule and leaves the house.

The sharp air cools her flaming cheeks. Frosty cobbles skid beneath her feet, and she forces herself to walk carefully, head down, concentrating on not slipping.

But her mind is running wild.

The man in the naval coat. She had been sure, at the time, that he was *not* Montague, but she was at a distance, struggling against her encroaching cataracts. It *is* possible …

She begs herself to stay calm. This is not the first time hope has surfaced. She should not trust it, but it is intoxicating; she can almost taste it in her mouth, like a rich wine.

Maybe Montague read of the Accident abroad. News from home might have been delayed, and perhaps this is the first chance he has had to return since. She must find a way to check the Navy Lists. She must know where he is.

The anticipation is almost more than she can take.

The abbey is always beautiful, but today it is especially so. Inside, the colours he promised her spill in a cascade from the stained-glass windows, right across the floor. Walking over them feels akin to passing through a cleansing stream. She takes a pew in sight of the golden cross. Usually she views it not only as an emblem of Christ, but the crucifixion of her own dreams.

It does not appear so this morning.

A few of her acquaintances nod to her from their seats – other impecunious spinsters, with which the city is swelling to capacity. Agnes does not count many friends amongst the pale, tired faces peering out from beneath dark bonnets. Even her own kind brand her as rather *odd*. They use the word as a sort of armour; in truth they are shying away from the scandal, the poverty and, most of all, the legacy of the Accident. It saddens her, but she does partly understand. She would not know what to say to a woman like herself, either.

The bells toll eleven o'clock.

The Honourable Reverend Brodrick acquits himself admirably during the service. It is not his fault that Agnes cannot lose herself in the sweet unity of prayer. She blames the engagement ring, which today feels enormous and insistent when she clasps her hands together. She wants to settle, to give thanks, but her thoughts are ungovernable. They fly around the abbey like a flock of doves let loose.

Did you miss me.

What if it *is* him?

She remembers her father coming back to shore. How she would pitch into his arms and sob, overcome with the relief that she was no longer alone. It sounds foolish, because of course she had Mamma while he was away, but it was not the same, just as having Simon around is not the same as having Montague.

She has missed Montague more than anyone.

When she was so ill with pneumonia, Simon said it was a miracle that she survived, and maybe it was, maybe *this* is why: she has been granted a second chance to live the life that was stolen from her.

86

Montague will be different now. Older, wiser, less susceptible to temptation. She can forgive his past errors. In all honesty, she never fully blamed *him*, but he left before she had the opportunity to explain that. She imagines the joy of introducing him to Cedric and their future taking a different course, away from Bath. She sees them being able to afford holidays together. How she would love for the three of them to visit the Isle of Wight!

Left to her own devices, Agnes would have passed from the abbey and back home caught in her dreamy cloud. But half a dozen women are clustered in the aisle, blocking her way, their cloaks pulled high on their hunched shoulders. Although they lean forward and show all the indications of whispering, their voices echo.

'Drowned, they told me. Humane Society couldn't revive him.'

'Oh, how sad.'

'That's nonsense. He would have been able to swim.'

'Look, I'm just telling you what I heard.'

'Does anyone know who he is?'

She pretends not to heed their chatter, but she can feel herself growing cold. They seem to be talking of the River Avon, which always sends her into a panic. Whenever she thinks of it, her mind fills with black water, her mouth with a brackish taste.

Agnes clears her throat. 'Excuse me, please,' she requests loudly.

They draw aside to let her past.

Before she opens the door, a hand reaches out and touches her arm. She stops and sees Miss Grayson: a small, sweet-looking woman; a portrait painter by trade, almost as short on work as Agnes herself.

'Pardon me, Miss Darken,' she says, drawing her aside from the group. 'I wanted to tell you the news, in case you had not heard.'

'News?'

Miss Grayson offers a wistful smile. 'I felt for you so awfully when that man was killed, right after your appointment. It was all anyone talked about.' Her hand squeezes Agnes's arm gently. 'But that's done now.' She nods at a wide, red-faced woman holding forth to her companions. 'Miss Betts has something new to gossip about.'

Agnes knows the reassurance is kindly meant, but she feels belittled by it. 'How fortunate for Miss Betts,' she says tartly. 'Pray, what is the latest scandal the crows are feasting on?'

Miss Grayson shoots a glance over at her companions. They really do resemble carrion birds, and perhaps she sees this, for her mouth puckers.

'A dreadful tragedy, Miss Darken. I swear it does not bring anyone pleasure to hear of it, but for your sake. A body has been pulled from the river at Weston Lock.'

Although Agnes prickles with sweat to hear of it, the event itself is not uncommon, particularly amongst the poor wretches living down in the Avon Street slums. 'Another drunk,' she guesses. 'Or perhaps *felo de se*?'

'No, Miss Darken. That's just it.' Miss Grayson shakes her head sadly. 'The man was a naval officer. He drowned wearing his uniform.'

CHAPTER 8

There's an airless silence in the chamber as Myrtle stands over the bed. She looks at Father as if he offends her sense of order. Beside him she appears more vital than ever, her skin peaches and cream.

She takes a breath. Then she begins.

Crouched in the corner, Pearl watches, fascinated. Myrtle's hands move with a careful intensity. Up and down, side to side, in fluid motions. It's like hearing poetry.

Sometimes Myrtle's palms face downwards, magnetising the body. As she makes a pass from shoulder to shoulder, she flips her wrist, so that the backs of her hands are closer to Father's skin.

How does she know when to do that?

Myrtle says a good mesmerist can see inside their patient, like they're made of glass. Pearl wishes she could see, too. She'd rather that cold, clean image than the one actually before her eyes: the discharge and the wasted skin.

Between each pass, Myrtle shakes her hands, ridding herself of the diseased magnetism. Pearl studies the air for a hint of the force but it's invisible to her.

Why can't she get a glimpse of it? Myrtle says it has colours, a different one for each person. It sounds pretty.

Pearl shivers and wraps her shawl tighter around her shoulders. She's been freezing all day. She turns even colder when she remembers that the shivering started just after Myrtle came home, yesterday afternoon. Almost the exact minute her visions of water abruptly stopped.

She shakes her head like Myrtle shakes her hands; ridding herself, casting it off. No good. Bad energy might drip from Myrtle's fingers, but it remains firmly lodged in Pearl's mind.

The ceremony reaches its conclusion. Myrtle dips into her apron and produces a clean handkerchief.

'What's that for?' Pearl whispers.

She doesn't receive an answer.

Myrtle opens the handkerchief out and lays it gently over Father's face, like a shroud. It sticks to the ooze around his jaw. Myrtle leans over him. Then Pearl hears her breathe.

A heavy inhalation through the nose and out through the mouth, onto the handkerchief. Four, five times. The sound of air puffing through her sister's lips. She's reviving him. Trying to pass some of her own vigour to Father.

Pearl hunches into her shawl and closes her eyes. It's so cold. But only she can feel the chill, and that means

… After yesterday's discovery, she daren't think what it means.

Myrtle's hand latches on her shoulder. 'Come on. Let him rest now.'

Her sister bundles her out of the room, back into the darkened parlour. Pearl climbs into an easy chair and curls her feet up beneath her for warmth. The crystal ball is back in pride of place on the table opposite her. It took them ages to clean up the shattered fishbowl. All that glass and water, everywhere …

The kettle whistles.

When the teacup finally arrives, it's so hot that it burns. Pearl cradles it in both hands, nonetheless.

'Don't spill it,' Myrtle warns.

Pearl thinks she wouldn't mind being scalded by hot liquid today.

Myrtle sits down, takes a bite of the toast she's made them. She's given all the jam to Pearl. 'That went well, I think,' she says through her mouthful. 'I'll keep at it. Phew! Mesmerism don't half take it out of me.'

But she doesn't look depleted in any way. Her eyes still dazzle beneath the frame of her widow's peak.

'How can you be so calm?' Pearl marvels.

'What d'you mean? He weren't no worse than usual …'

'No! Not about Father. I mean after yesterday.'

'Oh.' Myrtle picks at the crust of her toast. 'That. It's sad, Pearl. But these things happen. And we both know death ain't the end.'

92

'But you found the body in the river! Touched him …' A tremor runs through her as she thinks of the cold, clammy skin.

'I don't know what you're getting so upset about. You were here, you didn't see nothing.'

'Yes I *did*!' Pearl insists. Tea slops from her cup onto her shawl. 'I kept seeing water in my head … And then the fishbowl exploded … Don't you follow? I predicted the death. All I could think about was water, and then you found a drowned man.'

Myrtle shrugs and takes a vicious bite of toast.

'You don't think that's weird?' Pearl prompts.

'You're a spirit medium, ain't you? 'Course you're going to see things. And you need to deal with them better than you did that one in the cabinet, if we're going to make any money out of you.' Pearl pouts at her. 'Well, what did you expect when you got the Power?'

Some acknowledgement, maybe, of how frightening it is. A sense of wonder, at the very least. But Myrtle's seen it all before. 'I didn't think it would be … like this,' Pearl says lamely.

She *wanted* to see Mother, to hear her voice for the first time. And maybe she'd hoped the ghosts would be like the friends she never had, making the house less lonely when Myrtle's out and about on her errands.

'It's different for everyone,' Myrtle reasons. 'You'll figure it out. Maybe we'll try and contact the drowned man at our next séance. See if he's all right over there. Would that make you feel better?'

It really wouldn't, but Pearl finds herself nodding. She drinks the tea, hoping it might dilute the power that's inside her body.

'Myrtle?'

'What?'

Pearl looks down at her cup. 'D'you think it was the same killer? Who murdered Mr Boyle then drowned that man? Because a sailor would've been able to swim ...'

'Might've been.' Myrtle considers. 'Or maybe the sailor was just drunk and hit his head before he fell in the river. You can ask him, can't you?'

'But Myrtle ...' Pearl's feet are growing numb beneath her. She adjusts her position in the chair. 'What if I'm ... *seeing* him? The murderer? Seeing the ways he's going to kill people. First it was water, when I was so thirsty, and now I'm cold. What if he's going to freeze someone to death next?'

Myrtle rolls her eyes. 'Don't be daft. You're just poorly.'

But Pearl can't stop talking now; she's opened the dam and her thoughts are spilling from her. 'Maybe that's it. *That*'s why I've got this Gift, and we can use it, use it to catch him—'

'Enough!'

Myrtle slams her plate down. It makes Pearl jump. 'Listen to me.' Myrtle's voice comes tight and low. It's how she speaks to the Society when she's angry but trying to sound polite. 'This is silly. You've got a fever and you're raving, Pearl. You'd better go to bed.'

'But I—' she starts.

Myrtle's eyes fix upon her, snuff out the rest of her sentence. 'Bed. And no more talk about stopping killers. You're a spirit medium. People getting knocked off is your bread and butter. Do you understand me?'

It's an awful thing to say. Pearl knows it deep down, and yet somehow … It makes sense.

All her arguments melt like sugar on the tongue before Myrtle's gaze. She touches her forehead, starts to feel that she's been the one in the wrong, this whole time. 'You're right. I think I've got a fever. I'd … better go to bed.'

CHAPTER 9

Walcot Street is not far away. About ten minutes by foot – or at least, it used to be. Even if it takes her failing body twice as long, Agnes would rather make the walk than face the ordeal of riding in a fly or an omnibus.

But although the physical distance is short, there is a great social divide between her home, flanked by the abbey and the banks, and this bustling area of commerce. Everyone hurries: to the dyers, to the locksmith, to the grocers, to the chophouses that issue a malodour of hot beef fat. She cannot keep pace. And none of the men emerging from their work at the brewery possess enough gallantry to grant a lady a wide berth on the pavement.

Coal dust flecks the atmosphere. Buildings are white, yellow and black, like a set of progressively mouldering teeth, some with clapboard fronts and papered windows.

Struggling against the throng, who jostle her, Agnes checks the address she has written down one last time.

She *could* travel further, to the coroner at Walcot Parade, or visit the men at the Humane Society, or even contact that boorish policeman, Redmayne, for information. But she feels that this Miss West, who found the body, will be more likely to give her assistance; the woman will probably have observed more than all of the men put together.

Only yesterday she walked to church trying to convince herself that the man she had seen in the cocked hat was indeed Montague. Now, she would give worlds to be certain he was *not*.

The house she seeks stands just short of Ladymead Penitentiary, beneath the stern gaze of Paragon Buildings, its windows shrouded in soot. Behind the black smudges, she makes out a card advertising something, but the words are indecipherable.

Pedestrians push on behind her and tut. Taking a deep breath, she screws up her courage and knocks.

No footsteps sound behind the door, but it is opened instantly by a striking young woman, comely and golden-haired, perhaps twenty years of age. She stares at Agnes, all piquant features and bright, questing eyes.

'Yes?'

A London accent.

Agnes feels absurd, and very, very old. 'I ... Good morning. Forgive me for disturbing you. I daresay this is going to seem a trifle odd, but ... Are you – by chance – the Miss West who found the drowned man?'

97

An eyebrow arches, its shape unnervingly reflected in Miss West's widow's peak. 'Knocked on this door *by chance*, did you?'

'N-no,' Agnes stutters, face aflame. 'Of course I discovered Miss West lived here, but I did not like to assume that you ... She might not be the only resident.'

Miss West stares at her.

'Pardon me for interrupting you,' Agnes repeats. 'It is only that ... They do not seem to have identified the body yet. I am anxious for a friend of mine and I wondered if I might ... ask you a few brief questions about what you found?'

'Why don't you just go to the mortuary chapel? Have a look at him?'

The mere concept sends Agnes dizzy. 'I cannot do that.'

Miss West sucks her teeth, looks Agnes up and down. 'Well, I suppose you'd better come in, then.'

The light is strangely muted inside, not unlike Mrs Boyle's house of mourning. Agnes has a dim impression of a thinning carpet and cracks in the ceiling. What strikes her most is the odour: sulphur and rot.

There is no obvious sign of its origin. The parlour Miss West leads her to is clean, if rather worn. Faded lilac paper peels at the edges of the walls. A black walnut cabinet skulks beside the fireplace. There are several chairs grouped together in dark communion, a sofa and a circular table covered in cheap red plush.

Rather than flowers, the table has a glass globe as the centrepiece. Agnes has never seen anything like it.

Miss West seats herself upon the sofa and flicks her eyes towards one of the chairs.

Agnes takes it. 'Thank you.'

'Keep your voice down,' Miss West warns. 'I've a sick man and child to look after.'

'We are alike, then.' Agnes jumps upon the common ground, grinning rather foolishly. 'Since my sister passed, I have been caring for my nephew and aged mother. It can be a trial to—'

'You said you've got questions.'

She was going to begin with a preamble, apologise for dredging up unpleasant scenes, but it seems Miss West was born without a sense of delicacy. She imagines this bold young woman touching Montague's drowned body and her stomach turns over. 'Yes. I-I wondered if you happened to see, from the coat of this naval man you found, whether he was an officer? And of which rank?'

Miss West cocks her head. 'My dad was a soldier. Dunno about the navy, though I should. Had an uncle in the service.' Agnes opens her mouth to speak, but Miss West cuts her off again. 'And it's no use you explaining all the stripes and whatnot now, ma'am. To be honest, the coat was that torn up, I didn't even realise what it was until later on.'

Agnes grips the arm of her chair. She must see this through, no matter how painful the details. 'Perhaps … the age of the man?'

99

A sigh. Miss West's expression softens, along with her voice. 'The thing is ... A drowned body ain't a pretty sight, ma'am. It swells something awful. Don't look like the person no more. Even the hair ... I mean it's darker when it's wet. Looked kind of sandy to me, but ...'

The girl speaks with her hands. Not nervously; these are no fluttering birds but swift, decisive motions that sweep Agnes with them. She is grateful to have them to focus upon. The words are a buzz in her ears, for she knows exactly what Miss West is talking about: she too has seen a corpse pulled from the water.

Softened, puffy. The flesh spreading out of its firm lines.

'... do you see what I mean? Ma'am?' Then, sharper, 'Ma'am?'

Strong arms catch her out of the swoon. Agnes has a vague sensation of being moved and having her feet elevated. The next thing she feels is water against her lips. Forcing its way in, as if she is back in the river ... She splutters.

'Easy, now,' Miss West croons. 'Take a drink. It'll bring you round.'

Reluctantly, Agnes does. Her vision returns. Miss West offers a teasing smile.

'I see, now, why you didn't go to the mortuary.'

She is not amused; she feels like a colossal fool. Why does she keep charging about on these mad errands, instead of following Simon's advice to stay home and rest? Perhaps he has been right all along. Perhaps she *does* need someone to care for her, to tell her what to do. She makes such a hash of things alone.

She tries to sit up, but Miss West pushes her back down. 'Not yet. Give it a minute.'

'Sorry,' Agnes murmurs. 'I must seem terribly weak.' Then, feeling some explanation is necessary, 'That was how she died, you see. My sister. She ... well. Her body was recovered from the Avon.'

She is surprised to see Miss West's face, which until now she thought rather sharp, melt into understanding. 'Terrible thing for you.' After watching her a moment, Miss West adds, 'I can see it. That dusky, ash of roses colour. Like a wound slowly bleeding in water. It left its mark on your aura, didn't it?'

Agnes is too astonished to reply.

Miss West chuckles. 'Ah. You didn't read the card in the window, then? This is a special house.'

Agnes sips at the water, giving herself time to think of a response. Either she has lost her wits, or Miss West has. Given her fainting fit, the former seems likely.

'Special how?'

Miss West considers. Just when Agnes thinks she will not answer, she says, 'Tell me, ma'am. Would you like to speak with your dead sister?'

'Good heavens, no.' She drops her cup. Miss West lurches forward to save it, her brilliant eyes widening.

'Careful. I didn't mean to scare you. I know it ain't for everyone.' She hands the glass back to Agnes. 'I was just trying to explain what we do here. I read auras. Cleanse and heal them with my Mesmerism. That's not much good to you. But the Sylph … I thought the Sylph might be able to help.'

Agnes struggles to get her bearings. *Sylph* … she has heard this somewhere before. But it does not help her make sense of the strange words this girl is saying. Mesmerism? Was that not proved to be quackery? She remembers Simon speaking of it once, after he attended a demonstration. He had been impressed by one aspect, although she is at a loss to remember what …

'The truth is, ma'am, that I can't help you identify your friend. You'll have to go see the corpse, or else wait until someone else does. That might take months. Or' – she looks straight into Agnes's eyes, unabashed – 'the other way. We ask the man himself.'

'I do not have the pleasure of understanding you.'

Miss West points. 'Behind that door, asleep, is the White Sylph. She can speak to the dead.'

Prickles run all over Agnes's skin. *The White Sylph*. She remembers now: Mrs Boyle. Mrs Boyle spoke of contacting her murdered husband through a spirit medium of the same name.

It all crashes together in her head: the large cabinet, the crystal ball on the table. Necromancy.

'I …' she begins, but it transpires there is no adequate response when people talk of communing with the dead.

Can it really be possible? *Can* it?

Agnes imagines skeletons, ghosts and ghouls. The pictures fill her with an abject, quivering dread, until she thinks of Papa and her heart stutters. If it was true … If she could actually *talk* to him, one last time …

She clears her throat, raises herself to a higher position. 'I thought you said that your sister was unwell, Miss West.'

'She is,' Miss West agrees. 'The Power comes after a spell of bad illness, and it can make you sick, too. That's the price you pay for the Gift. But in a few days I'm sure she could do a séance for you.'

'And – and your father? You said you had two people to care for. He was in the army … He is wounded from a battle, I daresay.'

Miss West's pretty lips set. 'The man in there ain't my father.'

'No?'

'No.' The harsh London accent returns. 'My dad bit it when I was seven. Cannon fodder. I pleaded with Mother not to marry again, but what could she do? There was no one to help us. Neither hide nor hair of my uncle. And you see how it's worked out for me. She's popped off and I'm stuck caring for everyone.'

Agnes pulls a wry expression. She knows exactly how that feels.

'And what afflicts the poor man?'

Miss West puffs out her breath. 'Matches.'

'I beg your pardon?'

'He got us into matches. The hours I spent, miss, in that stinking factory, dipping the lucifers. They're right, you know, to name them after Old Nick.' Her hands gain animation once again. 'That work don't do you no good. All them fumes, they eat away at you. He got sick. And of course they don't care, do they, factory owners? Just paid him off. They said they'd keep me on there if I wanted, but would you fancy it, after seeing the work take his face away like that?'

'Oh. I think I may have heard of this malady. The corrosive effects of the phosphorus ... Phossy jaw, do they call it?'

'They can call it what they like,' she scoffs. 'It's me what has to deal with it. I brought him all the way here to Bath because a doctor said the waters would cure him, but that's a cock and bull story, ain't it? Bloody doctors. They didn't help my mother and they can't help him.'

Poor Simon. For all his authority, she doubts he would fare well, pitted against this young woman.

Miss West seems to catch herself. 'I'm sorry. You didn't need to hear all that. I don't usually lose my temper, but it's been a trying week. That body and all ...'

'I quite understand.'

'Like I said, my uncle was a sailor too, and he left us. Thinking of them always makes me angry.'

Agnes feels ashamed of how silly she has been. Neither the waterlogged corpse nor the river are here;

they cannot touch her. And Miss West is not a wicked heretic, only a frustrated and poorly educated girl.

She drains her glass and, for want of a side table, places it on the carpet. The fibres are unpleasantly stiff and coarse, like sackcloth. 'Thank you so much for your kindness, Miss West.' Slowly, she sits up. 'I am sorry to have troubled you. Please accept my best wishes for your family's return to health.'

Miss West watches her stand, one hand outstretched to catch her in case she should fall again. 'That's all right. And what will you do, ma'am? About your friend?'

'I am not certain.'

She touches Agnes's shoulder. Her flesh feels startlingly warm through the black fabric of her gown. 'You should talk to the Sylph. Honestly, ma'am. Just to know for sure.'

Agnes gives a thin smile. 'And what is the price for a consultation with the dead, these days?'

'For you? I'd take sixpence. Just this once, mind.'

Half a shilling! Half the price of a shade, for a piece of mummery. But she must not be rude to Miss West in her own house.

'I will think upon it,' she says.

'Make sure you do. Miss … ?'

It surprises Agnes to realise she has come inside Miss West's home, heard her secrets, and not even given her own name. She was taught better manners than that.

For a second she considers inventing an alias, just in case the police come to hear of her visit, but her imagination fails her. 'Darken. My name is Agnes Darken.'

It is clear she has made a mistake.

Miss West removes her hand from Agnes's shoulder. A change comes over her, like a veil dropped across a bonnet.

Is the young woman literate? Could she have read the newspaper article describing Mr Boyle's murder?

'Well, you know where I am if you want me, Miss Darken,' she mutters.

Chastened, Agnes leaves the house. She thought she would enjoy being free of that close, stale air but the streets are as chaotic as ever: the rattle of wheels and the cries of the hawkers a rude awakening.

There was something soothing about that parlour which she cannot put her finger on. A feeling of being outside of herself, wrapped in Miss West's voice.

Agnes had thought that she was lying when she told the girl she would think about the séance. But she does.

She thinks about it all the way home.

CHAPTER 10

Most girls of Pearl's age and station share a bed with their sisters. She'd like that. But Myrtle's always reluctant for them to bunk together, even when Pearl is poorly. She says it's important that they each have their own space.

The problem is, Pearl's bedchamber isn't exactly a space to boast about. The wainscot is chipped, mould buds on the ceiling and a thick, dusty curtain covers the small window – Pearl's not sure it's ever been washed, or even drawn back. There's a dark wardrobe, which looks alarmingly like the cabinet in the parlour and is mostly full of Myrtle's belongings.

There's just one good thing about being alone in her twilit room: she can pray. Not like Father taught her, exactly; she doesn't know much about God other than His name. But she likes the idea of someone hovering beyond her sight, watching over her. Someone she can talk to who will maybe – maybe – talk back.

She sits on the bed, crosses her legs. This time it will work.

She can't stop the murderer or explain the shivering on her own, but there's a person on the Other Side who can help her: Mother. If she can contact Mother, they'll catch the killer together as a team. The idea fills her with a sweet glow. Not only the prospect of finally meeting her parent, but of being of use to the world outside for a change.

If she managed to call up that phantom in the cabinet and make the fishbowl explode, surely she's strong enough to find Mother now?

She closes her eyes. Waits.

Horseshoes clack distantly outside.

The colour behind Pearl's eyelids has a brownish tinge, it isn't as dark as it should be. Frustrated, she takes off her shawl and wraps it around her head. That's better. Warm, muffled. She can hear her own breath. It dampens the wool that presses to her face.

Where are you, Mother?

She tries to recreate that sensation of falling into an abyss that comes so easily in the parlour. Showers of light and stars usually spill from her, beyond her control, but now she actually wants to reach out and pluck something, there is ... emptiness. Just her hot breath and the terrifying blankness.

What would help? She hasn't anything that belonged to Mother. Doesn't even know what Mother looked like. But surely she'll know when she comes, she'll know instinctively.

Pearl holds out her arms like she's playing blind man's buff. She gropes into the darkness, concentrating with all her might.

'Please, Mother.'

Nothing happens.

'Where are you?'

Why can't she feel the ghosts? Normally, they scare her with their whispers and their butterfly touch, but in fact this void is worse. Calling out for help in a pitch-black cave and hearing nothing come back to her but her own voice.

The shawl itches her face.

Reluctantly, she unwinds it and tosses it aside, but keeps her eyes closed.

Maybe she's been too alert, too desperate? Myrtle says you don't catch ghosts with stomping feet. Pearl tries, tries so hard, to compose herself.

But still the blankness taunts her.

Slowly, she inches her eyelids open, hoping that by some miracle Mother will be standing before her, covered in a white shroud.

She isn't. There's only the wardrobe and the scuffed walls.

For the first time it strikes her that maybe Mother doesn't appear because she doesn't *want* to be seen. Not by Pearl.

'I didn't mean for you to die,' she whispers. 'I was only a baby. I didn't know. I couldn't help it.'

But it seems she is unforgiven.

Chapter 11

Agnes first met Montague over a table like this. Of course they went to Molland's in those days, but the essential layout of the refreshment room is the same here in Marlborough Lane: circular tables with sprigged cloths, pale green and white crockery, spiced steam in the air. They even have a similar bell over the door. It tinkles sporadically, making no impact on the chatter and clinking spoons.

When she thinks back, her memory is hazy. To tell the truth, she had no indication at that first meeting of what Montague would come to mean to her. She was more interested in sponge cake and cocoa than the two young men Captain Darken had rushed across the shop to shake hands with.

Bedford and Montague had served under him as midshipmen, her father explained. They were due promotion any day now, and he would put in a good word for them, if his word still meant anything to the navy. It had meant something to Agnes. When the engagement was finally formed, after Captain Darken's death, one of her chief pleasures had been the certainty that Papa would have approved of her match.

But on that day, John Montague was simply an agreeable young man who shared stories of life below deck. The only virtue to recommend him over his companion Bedford was the honour of his attention. For Bedford relished a challenge and had set out to engage Constance in conversation.

Although the sisters were similar in appearance, it was generally agreed that Constance's visage lacked the prettiness Agnes's possessed. Constance's chin was more pointed, her nose like a freshly sharpened pencil. Beside the rest of the family's brown eyes, her blue ones struck as particularly cold. But still there was something that drew gentlemen to Constance. That face: provocative, even at repose. Daring you to animate it.

Bedford did not succeed.

Was it that day, or later on, that she discovered Montague's fondness for marchpane? A box of it sits on Agnes's lap now, ready to take home for Cedric. It emanates a scent of almond that is almost unbearably sweet. Like her memories – one can only indulge in moderation. A surfeit is sure to cause rot, somewhere down the line.

The bell tinkles. Simon steps into the room, carrying his small black dog under one arm. The animal has a ribbon tied around his neck that matches Simon's best waistcoat.

She is oddly touched. He always remembers the day.

'Miss Darken!' He walks over, takes her hand and raises it to his lips. 'Many happy returns to you. Forgive my tardiness. A gentleman should never keep a lady waiting.'

'So why did you?' she enquires archly.

'A patient.' He sits opposite her, placing the dog upon his lap. 'This snow has caused a flare in all the rheumatic complaints.' The dog yawns. She suspects he would rather be home by the fire than trussed up for her benefit.

'Well, you see how extravagant I have been in your absence: a whole box of marchpane!'

'On the anniversary of your birth, I believe you may do whatever you wish.'

This is not something she often hears, especially from Simon. 'Anything?' she teases. 'You would let me order a cup of coffee without a warning that it excites my nerves?'

Concern flickers across his brow. He quickly wards it off with a smile. 'For today, I believe I would.'

But Agnes can be kind too, and she places an order she knows he will approve of: ginger tea and a small apple tart in honour of the occasion. If one can call it an *occasion*.

They amuse themselves by feeding sugar lumps to the dog while they wait for their refreshments. She wonders why it never seems to strike Simon that this is also the day that Constance was born. *That* would be reason

113

enough to dampen the celebrations. Yet each year they re-enact this charade: him, so desperate to treat her; she, trying to appear pleased for his sake, as if growing older were a privilege rather than the burden it feels.

She has stopped counting her age with any accuracy. Simon could probably tell her the exact figure, but his gallantry would never allow it.

'That is enough, now, Morpheus,' Simon finally says as the dog's tongue works busily at his fingers, trying to lick off every stray grain of sugar. 'We are both of us portly already.'

'But you are strong,' Agnes tells him. 'Whereas I do not think Morpheus can say the same.'

The dog answers with a burp. They laugh.

'It is true, of course,' Simon chuckles. 'I indulge him. He is a greedy, lazy little brute. But I do so enjoy seeing him content.'

Morpheus is content, she thinks, because he never met Simon's wife. His previous dogs were not so fortunate.

She gestures to the box beneath the tablecloth. 'Perhaps I am the same with Cedric. Taking home treats although he *never* remembers to wish me a happy birthday. And Mamma cannot remind him. You know how her mind wanders these days.'

He shifts uncomfortably, but is prevented from replying by the arrival of their victuals.

The aroma of her ginger tea is pleasantly warm. She has not drunk it in a while, but she remembers now it was always her sister's favourite. That kick of spice, just like the woman herself. Simon has ordered coffee, proving that physicians never follow their own advice. To be fair, he looks as if he requires a whole vat of the liquid. Despite his attempts to dress smartly and oil the remains of his hair, Agnes can see his fatigue. In the moment he pauses to lift his cup, the mask slips, and what she glimpses beneath is exhaustion.

It frightens her. She has become so reliant upon him.

Morpheus's round eyes grow large at the sight of the apple tart. Agnes pulls it to her side of the table.

'Simon,' she begins. She does not look directly at him but stirs her tea, round and round. 'I did wonder if … With it being my birthday … I might ask a favour from you?'

'As ever, I am at your service.'

Her heart flutters its wings inside her chest. It is only Simon; she should not be afraid to speak candidly before him. But the problem is, Simon knows her better than anyone; he sees the things she keeps hidden, even from herself.

'There was a man. He drowned in the Avon not long ago. You may have read of it.'

He clears his throat. 'I did, yes.'

Her spoon is moving very fast. Morpheus watches it, his eyes flicking forward and back. 'With your medical connections, I wondered if you might … make some enquiries for me. See if they are any closer to establishing his identity.'

The sound of cups and plates moving only exaggerates Simon's silence.

He is so quiet that she thinks he may have stopped breathing.

At last, he says, 'And may I ask why … ?'

She must concentrate. She cannot let either feature or voice betray her. 'He was a naval man, it seems. I very much doubt he ever served with Papa, but I should like to know if—'

'Miss Darken, it is not *him*.'

Her cheeks scald, as if he had thrown his coffee in her face.

'You mistake me,' she snaps.

'Do I?'

Morpheus whines.

Agnes lets go of her spoon. It chimes loudly against the cup. Without it to clench, she notices that her hand is unsteady. 'Yes. This is not about Montague, precisely. But I was not being wholly honest when I said it was about Papa, either. The truth is, Simon … Something very strange is happening. Do you remember when the policeman came around? Asking about Mr Boyle?'

'Naturally, I recall it.'

'That very same day, I took a study of a naval officer by Sydney Gardens. Do you understand? The silhouette – and then – the man – he drowned! What if it was *him*, Simon? What if it was the same man?'

She pants, short of breath.

Simon scrubs a hand over his chin. 'Well,' he says slowly. 'What if it were? What would that mean?'

She flicks a glance around the crowded tables. She must try to comport herself with more dignity; already an elderly lady is peering at them through her pince-nez.

She takes a sip of ginger tea, which lights a flame in the back of her throat. 'It would mean, Simon, that my sitters are dying. That may be a given in *your* profession, but it is rare in mine. What if people find out this death also had a connection to my business? The customers ... And that dreadful Sergeant Redmayne would come back, upsetting me.'

Simon draws his lips together, pats her hand awkwardly across the table. 'Do not fret. I would never allow that upstart to hurt you. And let us consider. You say this man was just a study you took? In the gardens? Then no one will ever know. He will have no appointment scheduled, nothing that links him to you.'

This is true, but she is not appeased.

'All the same, it makes me uneasy. I should like to know for sure whether it was the same officer. I know it sounds superstitious and dreadfully silly, but I shall be frightened to cut another shade in case the sitter is ... hurt ... again.'

A pause. Steam hisses.

'You could not ... retire from cutting silhouettes?' he suggests gently.

'We would starve!'

'I would never allow that to happen. Do you need more assistance? You have only to ask. Let me extend my surgery, shoulder more of the load. Given our relationship, it would not be improper …'

Her eyes begin to sting. When all else in life has been taken from her, does Simon really think she will surrender the one occupation that was ever truly hers? Her studio is the last room in the house where she feels *herself*; the only one that does not require Cedric's presence to enliven it. She will not relinquish her last means of independent joy.

Simon seems on the point of saying more, but Agnes pulls back in her chair.

'Use your money to help Cedric establish himself, Simon. That is all I ask of you.'

He hangs his head. Deep down, she thinks she knows what he was going to say next.

He has been not saying it these ten years at least.

'Thank you for the tea.' She pushes the plate away. 'I do not think I can manage the tart. I seem to have lost my appetite.'

Morpheus swoops in and gobbles it up.

———

Fresh snow has fallen outside. She is tempted to accept Simon's offer of a sedan chair home simply to avoid the awkwardness of walking by his side. But when it comes down to it, the enclosure and its movement are too similar to that of a carriage. Any social discomfort is preferable to being reminded of the Accident.

'We will walk slowly,' he decides, setting Morpheus down on the pavement.

The dog's stubby black legs disappear beneath the drift, which reaches his belly. He whines. Simon ignores him and holds out an arm for Agnes to lean on.

She takes it carefully. The friction of their disagreement seems to prickle through his coat.

'You are not cold, Miss Darken? I will not have you catch pneumonia again.'

Agnes assures him she is wearing her chest preserver and thickest boots. How does he suppose she managed to make her way to the tea shop in the first place?

'We used to enjoy weather like this,' she reminds him. 'When we were young. Let's wander up a little and see the gardens. They will look so pretty in the snow.'

She had hoped to soften Simon with the memory, but the muscles in his arm tense. 'Not the gardens. They are too far and perhaps treacherous. I would not wish for you to slip. In these low temperatures, we really should get you home as quickly as possible.'

'So much for pleasing myself on the day of my birth.'

The frown deepens on his face. 'Well … Perhaps just to Crescent Fields.'

Morpheus huffs and begins to push his way through the snow. It cuts a track for them to follow.

Bath is a different city in the snow. White smothers every soot-stained building, every dungheaped road and every skeletal tree. This is how it must have appeared when the limestone mansions were freshly built and full of promise: a dazzling expanse of unclaimed space.

Well, not quite unclaimed. Even in this enchanting tableau, the iron railings at the top of the Crescent ha-ha show dark against the glare. It is the divide between the private lawns of the rich and the public ground below. Everyone carefully contained and in their space.

Today, Agnes is content to be on her own side. Those braving the fields do so with genuine glee. Laughter peals through the frigid air. She smiles at the children, who pelt each other with snowballs. Nurses scold and run after them, but they are powerless to stop the fun.

'Do you remember …' she begins, turning towards Simon, but the sentence dies in her mouth. The tears shining in his eyes tell her he recalls only too well.

She lowers her head, chastened. Simon was born to a large family. Sometimes it seems impossible to believe that there is only him left. She pictures the little Carfaxes running in the snow as they used to do. Their faces live in her memory, but she cannot reach all of the names. Nancy, the eldest, who used to hold Constance's hand when Agnes would not. Edmund. Or was it Edward? There was certainly a Matthew.

Now they are only silhouettes hanging in Simon's hall.

Morpheus wades past a trio of men in knee-high boots, then another cluster of young people building walls out of snow. In vain, Agnes searches for Cedric amongst the red-cheeked revellers. He should be out, on a day like this, playing with children his own age. She wishes she had the energy to pull him on a sled or teach him how to skate.

The air smells pleasantly clean. While Simon is lost in thought, she steers him gently in the direction of the Victoria Obelisk. It wears a lace cap. She can almost make out the lions beneath, sprinkled as if with sugar. It gives her a strange satisfaction to see everything in chiaroscuro. She might have painted it herself.

Trudging through the snow *is* tiring her and the box of marchpane now seems full of rocks, but she is determined to reach Victoria Gardens ere her birthday is done.

Before they come within full view of the Victoria Gate, a sound snaps Simon from his reverie. Morpheus cocks his head and listens alongside his master. A man is calling Simon's name.

Releasing Agnes's arm, he turns. A gentleman of perhaps thirty years of age, ill-dressed for the weather, is stumbling towards them. 'Dr Carfax!'

Two women titter and clear themselves from his haphazard path.

The man sports a thin, dark beard which only serves to show the dreadful pallor of his face.

'Mr Oswald?' Simon cries.

He skids to a halt and nearly collapses, but Simon catches him under the elbows.

'Dr Carfax,' he pants. 'Thank heavens I have found you!'

'Calm yourself, sir. Whatever is the matter?'

'Mrs Oswald.'

Simon blanches. 'The child is not … Not already … It is so early …'

'I pray to God, no!' The man gasps, trying to catch his breath. 'But she slipped. She slipped on the ice and she fell.'

'Where?'

Mr Oswald throws out one arm. 'Just there, further down the Royal Avenue. I knew I saw you, in the distance. Thank God I *did* see you! Will you come to her?'

Simon hesitates. Glances at Agnes.

'Go, go,' she orders. 'I shall come to no harm waiting here.'

'But—'

'The dog will protect me.'

It is a bold claim to make on behalf of a fat pug, but Simon seems mollified.

'Please,' Mr Oswald urges, tugging at his sleeve.

Simon nods and takes off through the snow.

It is blissfully quiet after they have left. Agnes stands for a while, watching the breeze skim a fine layer from the top of the drifts. White specks wheel into shapes that abruptly collapse. If she listens hard enough, she can hear the snow melting in the tops of the evergreens, crackling against the leaves.

It seems the Royal Victoria Gardens are hers, after all.

She walks to the gate and pushes it open. Snow falls from the black iron bars as they swing on their hinges; Morpheus whuffs and grumbles at her feet.

No one else has braved the park. The lawns stretch pure as a freshly starched petticoat. There are no blemishes, no indication of where the footpaths and carriage drives lie buried. Agnes may choose her own route.

She sets off straight, towards the lake, hugging a belt of mature trees. The earth is uneven underfoot. Somewhere down there, life slumbers, waiting to burst forth again: green shoots, daffodils. They will be a long time coming. They have not even made it through October yet.

It is early, for snow, but then it has been a tumultuous year, what with the war breaking out and cholera in London over the summer. Everything is out of sorts. At least here there is beauty and peace.

Morpheus toddles on ahead, curly tail twitching. She watches him sniff and forage, following a pattern of twig-like bird tracks underneath the trees.

If she is reasonable – and she tries to be – she can understand why Simon grew prickly at the mention

123

of Montague. His objections against the man are probably just. Her own should be stronger. But the difference is, she forgives him. If that makes her despicable as a woman – well, she would rather be happy than prudent.

Let her assume Simon is right: the drowned man is somebody else entirely. It hardly makes circumstances much better. She is still faced with the question: why are her sitters dying?

Agnes regards the humped shapes of box, laurel and privet hedges. They look like furniture covered by dust sheets, or perhaps ghosts in their shrouds. Her mind returns to that strange, vibrant young woman in Walcot Street and her outlandish claims of seeing auras. What colour did she say Agnes's was? Ash of roses. She imagines the pink seeping out from the bottom of her skirts into the snow, a circle spreading to reach Morpheus who is digging beneath the trees. It must be interesting for Miss West to see everyone like that: tinged with their own hue. Agnes views them in lines of black and white.

You should talk to the Sylph. Just to know for sure.

It might be that Miss West's sister *could* contact the dead and tell Agnes what happened to her clients. But even if Spiritualism is real, it is wicked, a kind of devilry that should not be meddled with. She knows this. She tries to remind herself.

A pigeon breaks free of a group of conifers and takes wing.

When all is said and done, Agnes should trust Simon. Accept that both deaths were unfortunate mischances and no incidents like them will ever occur again.

Morpheus barks.

It is odd, because Morpheus is not usually a barking dog; he vocalises through grunts instead. Yet here he is, yowling over and over in distress. His paws scrabble wildly, flinging up powdery snow.

Agnes doesn't know what she is supposed to do.

'Bad dog,' she tries. 'Come here!'

He starts to obey but then dashes back yapping.

After four repeats of this charade, Agnes realises the dog wants her to follow him.

'For heaven's sake.'

She pulls up her skirts. The snow is deeper at the edge of the gardens. She will struggle to wade out there, and for what? A rabbit hole? A half-eaten squirrel? But she can hardly return to Simon without his precious dog.

'What is it, then?'

Morpheus is barking so hard that his feet seem to lift off the ground. She proffers the box of marchpane, hoping it will tempt him out to her. It doesn't.

Morpheus never refuses food.

Ducking beneath a snow-laden branch, she toils towards the dog. He looks half-frantic. His eyes roll.

There is a sharp, fungal smell. She glimpses the frozen earth Morpheus has uncovered and the pale tree roots writhing up from the ground.

'What—?'

She cannot finish her question.

The box of marchpane falls silently from her grip into the snow.

Erupting from the white hill in front of her are three grey-blue fingers of a human hand.

CHAPTER 12

Sergeant Redmayne has brought company to the house this time. His fellow officers are no more courteous than the man himself; their voices bray so loudly from the parlour that they carry up the stairs and through the open door of Agnes's bedchamber.

Morpheus has flattened himself against the landing, cowering with ears back, while Cedric pets and tries to comfort him.

'Fancy seeing you here, sir. Again,' she hears Sergeant Redmayne say drily to Simon downstairs. 'And you just *happened* to be in the park when the lady discovered the body, too?'

Chuckles from below. One of the other officers pipes up with: 'Quite the old beau, ain't you?'

Agnes is grateful they cannot see her angry blush. When Simon replies, his tone is dangerously polite. 'Yes, I was escorting my *sister-in-law* on a constitutional walk. And thank goodness I was. She took ill at the sight of the dead man, as any lady might.'

The police stop laughing. 'You didn't mention your relationship last time I called,' Redmayne points out. 'Said you were her physician.'

'I act in that capacity also. What does it signify?'

'Everything matters, sir. And where might your lady wife be?'

'Deceased. I am a widower.'

Snow drops down the chimney and makes the fire hiss.

Agnes lays her head carefully back on the pillow. She doesn't want to listen to the discussion taking place downstairs, but nor does she want time alone to think. Sleep is no relief. Each time she closes her eyes she sees again the frozen rictus of horror.

He must have been there since the early hours of the morning, at least. Maybe days. She cannot remember when it first started snowing. Someone must have dug in the drift to bury him, knowing that any later snowfall would further conceal their sin. Out there, on the edges of the park, he would not have been discovered until the thaw, were it not for one busy little dog.

The abbey bells toll.

Part of her is glad they found him. His poor remains did not deserve to lie alone in an icy grave for any longer. But she wishes she had not seen the face. How it had changed. The eyelashes and brows flared shockingly white. His hair had clumped into one semi-transparent shape, like wax that had melted and set. Patches of the skin showed black. Scorched by fire, she thought, until she realised: the cold can burn, too.

The floorboards creak. Simon's voice rumbles downstairs. 'I can answer for Miss Darken. Neither of us has seen the unfortunate gentleman before in our lives. Did he have nothing about his person to suggest his identity?'

'We've a lad reported missing. The family are on their way to view the body.'

'Well, then. We can hardly be of further assistance.'

'But if we could talk to Miss Darken herself—'

'Absolutely not. I made it clear to you that the lady is unwell.'

'It's a murder inquiry, sir. Can't stand upon niceties.'

Simon fumes: 'So you would have another death upon your hands, would you? I am telling you that as her physician, I advise against it. She very nearly died in '52. Can you not wait a few days until she is recovered?'

'We'd prefer to—'

'I see I will have to speak to your superior. But let me make this plain now: if you continue to harass my sister-in-law, I will not be answerable for the consequences to her health.'

Agnes's hand grips the bed sheet. Simon is exaggerating, but she really does feel ill. The walking, the cold and the shock have overwhelmed her. If Sergeant Redmayne appeared in her room, she thinks her heart would stop.

129

There is more movement downstairs. Cedric leaps up from his position beside Morpheus on the landing floor and scurries back inside his own chamber.

She hears some last, muffled words and the slam of the front door. The stairs groan. Morpheus's tail begins to thump as Simon makes his way up, a mug in hand.

He enters the bedchamber with eyes respectfully averted. Sweat beads his brow. She detects its slight tang beneath his usual scent of carbolic soap as he approaches the bed and offers the cup.

'Drink this. It is not laudanum, I promise, just hot flip. It will help you sleep, without the dreams.'

Agnes shuffles into a sitting position and takes it from him. His manner is odd, and she senses it is not just because he is inside her bedroom. She feels as if she has misbehaved, disappointed him in some way. 'I forgot to ask after Mrs Oswald.'

'Hmm?'

'The lady who fell.'

'Oh, she will recover. Merely a sprained ankle. Her child is unharmed.'

Agnes takes a sip of her drink, wincing at how alcoholic it is. 'Small mercies.'

He remains silent. Concentrating, although she does not know on what.

While she drinks, her eyes shy away from Simon to survey the room. It is in a bad state. She needs to dust the dressing table and pull the hair out of her brush.

Some pencils have found their way in here, and the silhouette of Constance …

She frowns.

The shade that fell from the broken frame is propped up, beside her mirror. She could have sworn she put it away in her book.

'I imagine the police will return,' Simon sighs. 'Especially if no one identifies the body.'

'Ned,' she whispers. 'His name was Ned.'

Now the moustache shading his upper lip will never grow. She remembers his self-effacing smile, even his pomade, and it is impossible to reconcile them with the *thing* they pulled from the snow. But Agnes was not mistaken. The body was certainly his.

'Why would you not let me tell them I had met him and knew his name, Simon?'

He bridles. 'You ask me *why*? What of the business you were so worried about at teatime? Do you think this news will help matters?'

He has rarely been this short with her before. A tear slips down her cheek as she takes another mouthful of drink. 'I just … I worry they will find out he was a client here anyway.'

Simon shakes his head. 'You said it was a drop-in appointment, unrecorded—'

'Unless he already gave the shade to his grandmother?'

'I doubt that is the case.'

She takes a shuddering breath. 'It was ... some of my best work, Simon. I was so proud of it. And now ...'

He places a hand on her shoulder and lets her cry.

'You must believe me *now*,' she sniffs. 'You must see.'

'See?'

'Three people, Simon. Three people have died after sitting for my art.'

Simon appears at a loss for words. He brings his watch out of his waistcoat pocket, puts it back again.

'It is ... true that three gentlemen have died,' he reasons. 'But I believe it was a mere coincidence that you happened to cut their profiles. Consider. How would this murderer have known about you? What motive would he have to interfere with your livelihood?'

She looks at her hands, swollen and arthritic around the cup. 'I cannot explain it, Simon. I feel somehow responsible. As if my gaze has cast a shadow over them.'

People did say, when photographs first appeared, that there was danger in having your image captured. Part of your soul would remain forever imprisoned in that glass lens. Sit for too many and you might be ... depleted. More alive in the photograph than in real life.

She never suspected the same could be true with art, until now. For isn't that what she has been trying to do: reduce someone to their essence, and capture it?

132

But Simon is staring at her with utter dismay. She has never seen him look so wretched, and she feels like a simpleton.

'Oh dear. I can see from your expression that it is Kingsdown Lunatic Asylum for me.'

'That is beneath you, Miss Darken.'

He *did* commit a patient to a madhouse once. A lady. He will not speak of it, he only tells her, darkly, *never again*. Whatever happened to her must have been terrible.

'Simon,' she says slowly. 'If you truly will not consider me mad … Can you tell me what you think of Mesmerism?'

He blinks. 'Mesmerism? Why?'

'Is there a science to it?'

He wets his lips, seems to think. 'Yes, I believe there may be. Not that it has been conclusively proven. They theorise that a vapour flows from every living thing, which a trained operator can manipulate. If he does so correctly, he may exert the power of his mind over another person's body. I have seen a mesmerist put a patient into a trance and tell them that they will feel no pain. The patient then underwent a surgical procedure without making a sound of protest. Before we had ether and chloroform, it could be useful. Not that I ever practised it myself.' A cloud passes over his face. 'It struck me as distasteful to see a patient under the power of a stranger's will. Entered and dominated, as if by a parasite …' His gaze sharpens.

'*Have* you been mesmerised, Miss Darken? Is that why you are asking me this?' He leans down towards her so quickly that it startles her. 'Is *that* what has happened? Tell me.'

'No! It was only a question, and I do not know why you should be so nettled by it.' She pulls away from him to the other side of the bed, spilling some of the flip. 'I saw an advertisement in someone's window, that's all.'

'Well, I' – he tries to gather himself – 'I am sorry. I spoke hastily. But you must understand that there are charlatans about. People who meddle with forces they should not. In the mesmeric trance, a person is subject to a lower and more automatic level of functioning. They are permitted – nay, encouraged – to renounce their consciousness and let their usual personality fade away. The brain is a powerful organ, Miss Darken, but delicate. One should not … tamper.'

'And I expect you feel the same about Spiritualism?'

'Good God! Is it possible you have been bitten by that nonsense?'

It is a relief to feel annoyed with him. Anger is something she can grip onto. 'Nothing has *bitten* me, Simon. I am considering possibilities, asking questions. If you cannot help me understand what happened to these men, I must find someone who will.'

He puts a hand to his forehead. 'Forgive me, forgive me. I *shall* help you. Only do not visit a spirit medium. I beg of you.'

'Well, perhaps I shan't. It is bad enough with the police coming here. I do not want you calling the alienists in on me, too.'

Simon flinches, turns from her. 'Do not try to provoke me. That was your sister's trick.'

'Simon ...' She was only being flippant, she did not mean it, but it is clear she has wounded him. 'I apologise.'

Without answering, he leaves the room.

She hears him plod downstairs. Morpheus thumps after him.

She casts the mug of flip aside and falls against her pillow, miserable. She has ruined everything, but it is not her fault, she is not well. The shock ... Her temples pound so fiercely she thinks that they will crack.

The bells chime again.

When their peal dies out, the hinges of her chamber door creak open. 'You mustn't worry, Aunt Aggie.'

Cedric stands at the threshold, watching her. He is the only person whose presence can bring her comfort. She opens her arms to him.

He trots over and pulls his gangly legs up on the bed. He is still wearing his shoes, but she does not scold; it's rare that she gets to cuddle him like this nowadays.

'My father's just scared,' he explains. 'People get cross when they're scared.'

'Really? And what makes a grown man like Simon afraid?'

'Spirit mediums,' Cedric replies simply. He raises his chin to look up at her. 'He never liked reading me ghost stories.'

'I daresay he didn't.' She winks at him. 'Penny Dreadfuls are *our* little indulgence, are they not?'

He chuckles. 'You read them much better, anyway. But do you know ... When we lived with Papa in Alfred Street, I found these great big hooks he kept in a box. They were really heavy. I couldn't lift even one of them.'

She is thrown by how suddenly he shifts topic. 'What – Cedric, I do not understand how hooks relate to spirit mediums ...'

'Listen! I'll explain. Papa told me he'd used the hooks when he was studying medicine in Edinburgh. He went fishing.'

'Again, how do fish have any bearing on—'

'Not for *real* fish!' he laughs. 'That's just what they *called* it. The medical students used to go fishing for coffins.'

She starts. 'Coffins?'

'They dug the earth at the head end. Then they inserted the hooks, you see, under the lid. Tied them to big ropes and hauled them up through the soil. They needed the bodies. You know, like Tidkins in *The Mysteries of London.*'

She never equated Simon with this diabolical practice. In a story, bodysnatching is horridly entertaining, but in real life ... She can only hope this is

136

an exaggeration Simon employed to quench the boy's thirst for gruesome tales.

'Papa didn't have a fresh supply of bodies for his anatomy classes, like students do today. He said everyone was forced to do it. He looked so sad when he told me. Poor Papa. He hated the time he spent away studying. That's why he didn't want me to learn to be a doctor too.'

Well, that was possibly one reason. Heaven knew the young Simon who went off to Scotland was a very different creature to the one who returned to find his entire family either dead or dying of cholera.

'He's scared,' Cedric repeats. 'Because he dug up dead people. So he doesn't want to believe they could come back and haunt him.'

How did this sweet, perceptive boy come from Constance? Agnes had been so afraid that the apple would not fall far from the tree. But Constance's vindictiveness has not been passed on. Her son has inherited nothing except her taste for the macabre.

'You are very wise, you know, Ced.'

He grins. 'I know. I'll probably be prime minister one day.'

She plants her lips on the top of his sandy head, wishing she could give him that chance.

CHAPTER 13

Pearl cries deep into her pillow. She's exhausted and would rather save her breath, but she can't seem to help the sobs. Myrtle's words go round in her head. *You're a spirit medium. What did you expect?*

She only knows what she *didn't* expect. She never bargained on feeling this ill. Being in pain every day is wearing her down, like the seams on the easy chair in the parlour. And what has it got her? She still hasn't met her mother, still hasn't been able to discover who is killing people around Bath.

They call what she has a gift, but Pearl doesn't want it any more. She doesn't want it at all.

Beneath her quiet snuffles, she can hear Father in his room, fighting for breath. Shame fills her to the brim. How dare she lie here thinking these selfish thoughts? Using the Power was never about *her*. It was about making money, so that Myrtle could concentrate on her Mesmerism and heal Father.

All her family want her to do is sit still in a dark room and give up control. It isn't so much to ask.

Except it is.

Some days it feels as if it's sapping her very soul.

She needs guidance. It's times like these that she really wishes Mother hadn't died. In stories, the mother characters are always kind, with words of wisdom to bestow. Myrtle's not like that much. She can be wise, but she has a limited supply of pity, and most of it is used up on the mourners.

As for Father … She misses the sound of his voice. They hardly communicate now, and while his presence still brings some comfort, it's also harrowing to look upon his face. Or what's left of it.

She scrubs the tears angrily from her eyes. She *should* look at his face, and remind herself why she's doing this. Her pain is bad, but it must be nothing compared to his.

Pearl stands up, opens her door and stumbles out, past Myrtle's room and towards the sick chamber. Already the stink is bubbling. She takes a deep breath and forces down her biliousness.

It's far too bright inside. Pearl yelps. 'Myrtle!'

Myrtle's sitting at his bedside, reading penny papers by the light of an open window.

'I was taking a rest,' she says defensively, clearing the papers away. 'See that water he's just drunk? I magnetised that.'

Pearl doesn't answer, just pulls at the curtains.

'Does him good to get some daylight. We don't all want to be shut up in the dark like you.'

In deference to her sister, Pearl only closes the curtains partially, leaving a sliver of burning sun. It doesn't *look* like it's done Father any good.

The hinge of the jaw is fully exposed, all gristle and string, but she takes care not to dwell upon that. She just kneels down on the opposite side of the bed from Myrtle and takes his hand in her own.

She must help him. She *must*.

'Don't look so glum,' Myrtle cajoles. 'We'll have punters knocking down our door for séances soon. They've just found another body.'

Pearl holds her tongue. She yearns to ask how, where, if it had anything to do with her uncontrollable shivering, but she remembers their previous argument.

Besides, the murderer doesn't seem important any more when she's kneeling here, listening to Father's struggling, gummy breath.

'When will you treat him again?' she asks.

'In a minute. With a new technique. I was just reading over it. Business has been that good, I've been buying *The Zoist*.' Myrtle flourishes one of the rustling sheets in her direction. 'I'll be a proper expert soon.'

'But ...' Pearl glances down, unwilling to meet her sister's eye. 'Will it *work*? Promise me it'll cure him.'

Myrtle tuts. 'Of course it will! Look at this. If Mesmerism weren't real, would they have opened a special hospital for it? The London Mesmeric Infirmary. Says right here. And the women, Pearl.' Her voice climbs a notch in excitement. 'They've got women mesmerists. Working right alongside the other doctors. Like equals. That'll be me, one day.'

Pearl can see it. She's never been in a hospital, but she can imagine a lot of beds lined up with people like Father in them, and Myrtle striding confidently down the aisle between them, waving her pretty hands.

The only problem is, there's no room for Pearl in this dream.

'You wouldn't just … leave me alone here, would you?'

Myrtle laughs. 'Don't be daft. When your dad's better, he'll look after you, won't he? Then I can go off and do what *I* want to do. That'll make a change!'

Father's hand squeezes Pearl's. She glances up and shrinks from the expression in his tortured eyes.

She wants to believe Myrtle. She *does* believe. Her sister can do anything.

But she knows that Father isn't so sure.

Father thinks he's going to die.

CHAPTER 14

Agnes makes the practice cuts in waves: peaks and troughs that roll smoothly like a black ocean. Papa and Montague would have seen the sea at night many a time during their travels – she wonders if it looked anything like this. They were brave men; Agnes would find such pitch-darkness utterly terrifying. It is true that she likes shadows – but even shadows need light to exist.

Today's light is sodden and pale. It seems to hesitate at the window, irresolute.

Her studio, on the top floor of the house, is not in the direct eyeline of any other residence, yet as she sits curving the sable paper with her second-best pair of scissors, she has the uncanny feeling of being watched. It is as if her work and her person are under scrutiny – and both have been found wanting.

She pauses, flexes her fingers. She is not used to feeling this way inside her studio, her refuge. Perhaps it is a magpie observing her from the window. The birds have been clattering away on the roof all morning; she dare not imagine how much of the property is infested with their nests.

She starts to cut again. None of her usual joy sparks. It must be these scissors – they are of no use. How did she manage to make Ned's hollow-cut with such a clumsy instrument? Poor, poor Ned. She sighs, shakes her aching hand. After all that has happened, maybe it is time she stuck to painted shades instead.

She is an accomplished painter: that is a fact, not a boast, but it was always the papercuts that were her real talent, even from a child. Must she relinquish them now? The stubborn part of her refuses; she expects that when her hands have given up entirely and she is physically unable to make a single snip, that portion of herself will still be there, clamouring to get out.

She puts the inferior scissors down, defeated by the burning in her fingers.

The woman she knew as Agnes is fading day by day. Determined to remember there is *something* of her left, she crosses the landing to her bedchamber, retrieves the shade of Constance from beside her dressing-table mirror and brings it back to the studio.

Yes, she captured it well: the curious way her sister's head sat upon her shoulders. You can see, even without bronzing, where the ears and eyes should be.

It would be wrong to consign such a good piece to the back of the duplicate book – although she could swear she had done so previously. Agnes opens it again, at the front this time, where her collection of earlier Constances live. Page by page they grow, become taller, the lines of their faces more defined.

Looking back, she realises how often Constance offered herself as a model. Was it a kindness, or was she just trying to keep Agnes's focus trained upon her? Constance never could endure competition for Agnes's attention; even her papercuts were viewed as rivals.

Perhaps she is judging too harshly. Constance *could* be agreeable at times, only ... there was an uncomfortable intensity to it. She was *too* nice, a person playing at being nice.

Then came the betrayal. It was hard to believe any good of her after *that*.

Agnes is still at a loss to say exactly why Constance did it. Was it spite, jealousy – or just to prove that she could? Somehow she would feel better if love were involved in the matter, but evidently it was not. The whole affair was about power, manipulation, ownership.

There is no use going over it again. Constance is dead now, and a dead person cannot control her any longer.

She slots the paper Constance amidst her twins and lets the book fall open to its wonted page.

Montague's shade faces to the right. Symbolically, this means he is looking forward to the future – and that was apt for the man – but now she wishes she had cut it facing the other way. Because the future, when it came, held only sorrow for them.

Montague is the one full-length in her collection with added colours. When he made first lieutenant, he showed her his uniform, and she recreated it from memory: a bold, blue coat with white breeches. Only the face remains shadowy and inscrutable. Agnes runs the tip of her finger over it.

'Where are you? Do you think of me?' she asks.

Forcing herself to turn the pages, Agnes leafs to the forlorn little physiognotrace Ned was so impressed by. Her throat tightens. Mr Boyle's death saddened her, but Ned's seems even worse: a boy full of promise, cut off in the bloom of his youth. She remembers thinking that Cedric might resemble him in another five years. Who could want to hurt such a nice young man?

Outside the abbey bells toll.

'Agnes!'

Mamma's usual screech. She closes the book gently and puts it away.

In the parlour, the grandfather clock falters on. It needs winding. She forgot to lay the fire too, but somehow Mamma has found a way. Agnes frowns at the blaze as she steps inside. It is sweltering, extravagant. All that precious, expensive coal …

'There you are!' Mamma's cheeks are alarmingly red above her newspaper. 'When were you going to tell me about the scrapes you've been getting yourself into?'

'I do not—'

'Right here!' Her eyes seem to bulge behind her spectacles. 'A body, Agnes? You found a *corpse*?'

145

'What is that? What are you reading?'

She wrests half the paper from her mother's grip.

There it is in black and white: every self-respecting lady's nightmare. Simon said he would keep her name out of print and make them use his instead, but evidently there is one reporter who has given both.

'Really, Mamma, it was nothing.' She quells the tremor in her voice. 'They do exaggerate in the newspapers. Simon's dog found something and we alerted the authorities. I am quite safe.'

Mamma's hot hand clamps on hers. 'My poor Agnes! Splashed all over the papers ... It is one thing to have an advertisement, but this! Whatever would your father say?'

'Hush, now. Papa would be pleased I have performed my duty in reporting the discovery. And you see, I appear next to Simon's name, which will always be respectable.'

How easy it is to lie to Mamma. The truth is, this article is a disaster, the death kiss for her business. She has not had a customer since Ned, and maybe she never will again.

Her eyes catch the price of the paper. Simon must have paid off her debt at the newsvendors without telling her. She should be thankful for his benevolence, but it only feels like another shackle preventing her from making her own way in the world.

Yes, that is the sensation: one of being chained or trapped. She has been feeling it ever since the killer started targeting her business. How can she countenance a future in which she has no money of her own, and no opportunity to practise the art that has been the pleasure of her life? She shudders to think of being a burden to Cedric in her old age, of him waiting upon her in the same way she is tending to Mamma.

'No more policemen will be coming here, will they?' Mamma continues to fret. 'Agnes, I don't think I could bear to see a policeman after—'

'No, no.'

She blesses her lucky stars that Mamma was in bed asleep when she and Simon arrived back from the gardens and the discovery of Ned's body. Quite how she managed to doze through the ruckus of Simon's argument with Redmayne is a mystery, but Agnes is not about to look a gift horse in the mouth.

Mamma's breath saws.

'Try to be calm, Mamma. *This* is why I did not tell you. It was a trifle, and I knew you would get upset. Sit there. I will fetch you some tea.'

She walks out of the heat into the coolness of the kitchen. A plague on those reporters, and the policemen too. As if she did not have enough trouble without them.

Locating the key, she unlocks the caddy. There is no tea.

Agnes slides down against the cupboard and sits on the floor.

It will not do. She cannot endure this any longer. Simon's promised help is not forthcoming: she must

147

take matters into her own hands and rescue her silhouette parlour.

But she can think of only one course of action.

———

Naturally, the event must take place in the evening; wicked deeds require the cover of darkness. The abbey bells toll seven as Agnes slinks out of the front door and locks it behind her.

She shivers from cold and fear. It is not exactly late, but at this time of year, seven o'clock might as well be the middle of the night.

Her senses sharpen. People she would scarcely notice crossing the churchyard by day now carry an air of menace. Do they regard her with disapproval? A lone woman out at this hour is unlikely to be virtuous, and Agnes feels that she is not: she is about to do something repugnant to her feelings and decency alike.

Twice, she nearly turns back. What is it that makes Bath so eerie when the sun goes down? It could be the mounds of snow, pale as flesh against the black sky, or it might be the buildings that tower over her, conspiratorial and worn. More likely it is the frightened whispers of her own conscience.

But what else can she do?

She listens to her heartbeat and her footsteps. Both strike too rapidly. The pointed spire of St Michael's looms up, making her feel helplessly small.

She tries to remind herself that this anxiety is simply a sign of her own weakness, not an indication that she is making an error. Attending a séance is the only way to obtain answers: the definitive identity of the drowned sailor, and the name and motive of the person who is killing her clients. The knowledge of the dead is useful beyond measure: that is why it is forbidden.

The house on Walcot Street is clothed in darkness, its parlour curtains drawn tight against the light of the street lamps. A mere passer-by would think all of the inhabitants were long asleep.

Agnes raises her fist to knock on the door, but she cannot quite bring herself to let it fall.

What if she peers beyond the veil and sees a sight she is not able to bear? It is not too late to turn back. She really *should*. But there is a nightmarish inevitability to her actions. Somehow she knew she was going to come here, from the moment she first heard Mrs Boyle mention the White Sylph.

Releasing her breath, she finally knocks.

As before, Miss West steals noiselessly to answer the door. That is the one aspect familiar to their last meeting. Tonight the young woman is dressed from head to toe in jet, her flaxen hair extinguished by something like a widow's cap. The only feature alive in her face are those simmering, witchy eyes. Their expression is far from friendly.

'Miss Darken. Good evening. Do step inside.'

This is not the woman Agnes spoke to about the corpse. She is a polished version with better diction. Speechless, Agnes follows her into the house, which is even darker than on her previous visit. A powdery, sickly aroma overlays the rot she detected.

As she turns into the parlour, she sees bunches of open lilies glowing like pale, white hands by candle-light. Lilies and wax – that explains the cloying scent.

'May I introduce the White Sylph?' Miss West gestures to the far side of the circular table, near the drawn curtains.

For a split second, Agnes thinks she has already glimpsed a ghost.

The child sits behind a flickering barrier of black candles. She is an albino, entirely without pigment. A white gown bleeds seamlessly into the alabaster of her skin and ivory hair falls loose over her shoulders. Her lips and brows must be powdered, for Agnes cannot make them out. Even the girl's eyes show clear as glass marbles.

'Come. Be seated.' Miss West has the air of a housekeeper revealing hidden rooms. She sweeps Agnes effortlessly towards a chair she does not want to take; there is no resisting her.

The White Sylph watches with uncanny serenity. She must be even younger than Cedric but there is an agelessness to her: it does not feel like sitting opposite a child.

Miss West takes the third chair, closing in the circle.

The Sylph reaches out and offers Agnes her bloodless palm. It is cold to the touch. By contrast, Miss West's feels warm and dry.

There is no escape. Agnes is in their power now.

'We'll start with a hymn,' says Miss West. She opens her mouth and sings.

> Jesus, full of truth and love,
> We thy kindest word obey;
> Faithful let thy mercies prove;
> Take our load of guilt away.

She has a beautiful singing voice. Agnes knows the words and tries to join in, but her vocal chords are taut.

> Weary of this war within,
> Weary of this endless strife,
> Weary of ourselves and sin,
> Weary of a wretched life.

The White Sylph does not sing. She stares into the candle flames, her pupils shrinking to pinpricks as she retracts, further and further inside herself.

> Lo, we come to thee for ease,
> True and gracious as thou art:
> Now our weary souls release,
> Write forgiveness on our heart.

151

The last notes of their hymn hang suspended for a moment, then everything falls still.

One of the candle flames silently dies.

Slowly, the Sylph lifts her chin. Material whispers as her head lolls backwards, strangely contorted. Her glassy eyes roll to the whites.

Agnes's hand twitches involuntarily.

'Yes, come,' Miss West murmurs.

And they do.

An invisible bell rings. Agnes's heart leaps into her throat. The Sylph's neck grows turgid, her white cheeks flush and she is glowing, actually glowing with light from the afterlife.

Her lips begin to move. Agnes leans forward, desperate for the words, but this is not language it is … bubbles. Kisses popping from a fish's mouth.

'Spirit.' Miss West's hushed tones are calm. 'Welcome. Have you heard Miss Darken's call?'

The Sylph's head jerks in a nod. Agnes did not realise it would be like this. She thought the spirit would speak to the child, not take possession of her.

'You are the man I found in the river?' Miss West confirms.

Agnes watches, transfixed, as the lips try to form a reply. All that comes is a heaving gasp.

He is drowning. He is still drowning after death.

The Sylph tosses her chin, trying to break above the surface. It is difficult to keep hold of her hand. Agnes feels something wet pool in her palm and hopes it is sweat. But why can she smell something brackish, like river water?

'It's him,' Miss West hisses. 'Ask your questions. We will not keep hold of him for long.'

Her tongue has never felt so dry. All she wants to do is reach out and help, to pull whatever suffers there from the water.

'His ... his name?' she croaks.

Fluid gurgles in the Sylph's throat as she struggles for air.

'H-h-h-harg ... reeeaves.'

'Hargreaves?' Miss West repeats.

The Sylph exhales like a load has been lifted from her. Then she keels forward, her head landing on the table with a smack.

Another candle puffs out.

Agnes breaks their circle of hands, reaching out to see if the child is hurt, but it is not over yet.

No sooner does one spirit discard the marionette than another picks it up. The Sylph's thin shoulders quake beneath her white gown and the table moves with her.

For the first time, Miss West looks afraid.

'Sp-spirit?' she ventures. 'Look at me.'

Trembling, the Sylph raises her head from the table. Her jawline is in constant motion and Agnes realises the girl's teeth are chattering.

The temperature plummets. Breath steams not just from the Sylph, but from all of them.

Miss West swallows audibly. 'Spirit, name yourself.'

Agnes does not need the answer.

'Dear God,' she breathes. 'It's Ned.'

The Sylph turns to face her. It is not the girl's physiognomy, nor even Ned's, but a death mask with staring eyes.

This is what Agnes wanted: to converse with the dead, yet she is speechless before their eternity. She tries desperately to remember the easy-going young man in her studio, what she would say to him if she still had the chance.

'Oh Ned, what happened to you? I am sorry, I am so, so sorry. You were so young, and—' The fixed, glassy eyes seem to look right through her. 'Was it my fault? Did someone murder you just to hurt me?' she whispers.

At first there is no reaction. The Sylph – or whatever moves the Sylph – seems to consider. Then it says in a low, creaking voice, 'Y-y-yes.'

She nearly sobs.

'Poor Ned! Stay a while. Are you so cold? If only I could warm you! Won't you tell us, dear? Tell us what monster did this?'

Abruptly, the eyes slide to the right. Agnes starts back. The Sylph is still shuddering, but she seems to be taking furtive glances about the room.

'A-f-f-fraid.'

Miss West flexes her fingers nervously, regarding her sister as if she has never seen her before. 'What of?'

she demands in her natural voice. 'Whoever killed you can't hurt you no more, can they?'

The Sylph's lips are turning a sickly shade of blue. She is losing the power to move them. 'S-s-s-sent Ag-agnes-m-m-message.'

Agnes gasps. 'The killer sent a message to me? What message?'

But the mouth is freezing up, too numb to speak. The Sylph distorts her face to no avail.

'Tell me the message!'

Agnes is trembling so fiercely that it takes her a moment to realise that the room is shaking too; the picture frames are rattling on the walls.

Miss West releases a strangled shriek.

The lips. She must focus on those dead lips and read the words, or all of this will have been for nothing. Straining with all her might, Agnes manages to catch the last word.

'… m-mine.'

All of the candles blow out.

As quickly as it dropped, the temperature returns to normal. A chair scuffs against the carpet and Miss West lights the gas. Her face is almost as pallid as her sister's.

'She's … never done that before.'

Both of them glance at the child, flung back in the chair with her arms hanging loosely by her sides. Cataleptic. Helpless. Is it Agnes's imagination, or has the Sylph physically shrunk? Her white gown seems loose upon her.

Tentatively, she leans forward and touches the ivory hand. It is cold as marble. An acrid smell breathes from the skin, a sort of tang that reminds her of the charnel house. She wrinkles her nose.

'Spirit smells.' Miss West brushes down her gown repeatedly, although nothing marks it. 'That ... that happens.'

Agnes watches, tensed, expecting the girl to snap up again any minute, possessed by another spirit. But she seems to be in a deep swoon. Miss West places cushions behind her, covers her with a blanket and wipes the disarrayed hair from her forehead. The young woman's mouth is set in a hard pout Agnes cannot interpret.

She completes a nervous survey of the room, wondering if ghosts are lurking in the dark corners. The few cheap prints hanging on the wall are all aslant and the table itself seems to have moved a full six inches to the left.

It is horrendous and evil, even worse than Cedric's books, and yet it is undeniably true: the dead walk. They have burst from the tomb.

She wants to laugh and to cry.

Here is all she sought: the drowned man's name – not Montague! – and a chance to speak with poor Ned. She has confirmation from his icy lips of what she knew from the start: that the murderer is hounding her, trying to send her a message through her clients.

But that knowledge is no relief.

156

'The séance is over,' Miss West says. 'She needs her rest now.'

Agnes's legs have turned to water. With great difficulty she rises from the chair and fishes in her reticule for the coins, all she has left from Ned's commission. Miss West snatches them.

This séance, she senses, was not like the others. The young woman is twitchy, on edge, as she leads her into the hallway and towards the front door.

Agnes hesitates. 'If ... I wanted to come back ...'

'Back?' Miss West repeats, her eyes wide and tinctured with loathing.

'To ... hear the rest of the message.'

Miss West shakes her head. 'It won't be cheap. Cost you one and six.'

Even after the horror of the evening, a laugh escapes her. 'A shilling and sixpence? Do you know how long it would take me to earn—'

'I don't care! Didn't you see the state of her? She'll be like that for days now and we won't make a penny. You're no good for us. I should never have asked you here.'

Miss West has dropped her act so completely that she is practically trying to push Agnes out through the door.

Perhaps it is a business tactic. Agnes doubts it, though. Reluctantly, she steps out onto the cold street. If she leaves now, she will be in a sorrier condition than the one she arrived in: knowing that she really is a target, but not what the killer wants from her.

'I do not have the money, but we could come to some arrangement,' she pleads, turning back. 'I am a silhouette artist. I could cut you a shade for payment. They usually cost a shilling apiece. I would do one of each of you. Two shades – that's worth even more than you asked for.'

Miss West shakes her head darkly. 'We've got enough shadows in this house.'

She shuts the door with a bang.

CHAPTER 15

It's coming again. Burning, corrosive. Myrtle holds back Pearl's hair as liquid fire spills from her lips into the chamber pot. There's no other pain like it. She's doubled up, squeezed together.

Wasn't she cold, a while back? She'd give anything to shiver now. The heat is unbearable, inside and out. Sweat pours from her skin as freely as the vomit issuing from her mouth. Why won't it stop?

Tears half-blind her. She's already felt the chill of the grave; maybe she's gone further still: deep in the ground – like those do-gooders warned Myrtle – into the fires of Hell.

Bile dribbles from her chin and Myrtle wipes it with a rag before crossing the room to push open the sash window.

Pearl's got a horrible compulsion to see what's come out of her. Struggling for breath, she opens her eyes and instantly wishes that she hadn't.

The chamber pot steams with white smoke, the same as the stuff that rises up from her during the séances. The ghosts have got right inside her. It's like she's eaten them for supper.

Myrtle hands her a glass of water. Pearl's mouth is parchment dry but she swallows slowly, carefully, afraid to set her stomach muscles heaving again. Drinking doesn't dull the scorch within. The flames are still there, simmering.

'Myrtle,' she wheezes.

Her sister clenches her free hand. 'Another mess I'll have to clean up,' she jokes.

Pearl tries to smile and holds on tight. Myrtle is one of the living. She needs to anchor herself to that.

'You gave me a scare,' Myrtle admits. 'Getting too powerful for your own good.'

'I don't feel powerful.'

Even speaking tires her. She's never been weaker in her life.

That's how it seems to work: the stronger the spirits get, the more listless she becomes. There's only room for one or the other.

She struggles to hold the glass upright in her feeble hand. This isn't a fair fight. The dead – they are legion. Pearl's all alone.

'I want us to try,' she bursts out.

'What?'

'If you think my powers are strong now. I want us to try and reach …' She bites her lip, waiting for courage

160

that never comes. It's almost as painful as pushing the vomit from her mouth. 'Mother,' she finishes in a whimper.

Myrtle lets go of her hand.

Why can't her sister understand? If Pearl could contact Mother, she'd have an ally, someone to protect her from the bad spirits and stop her getting sick like this. She longs to feel Mother's cool hand on her burning brow.

'I ain't stopping you from talking to her,' Myrtle says eventually. Her voice has gone gravelly and she's got that puffy look, as if she's about to cry.

'But you are. I need a circle. I can't do it alone. I never see ghosts when I'm on my own.'

'No. I won't do it, Pearl. Let her rest in peace.'

Pearl slumps. She's so exhausted and so hot, she hasn't the strength to fight, but she must. This is the only thing that really matters to her.

Mother's the only one who can help now.

'Please, Myrtle. Don't you think she'd want to meet me? She can be my spirit guide.'

'You don't need one.'

'But I never knew her!' Pearl bleats.

'No, you didn't,' Myrtle fires back. 'So you never had to lose her. You can't even imagine what it's like. Every day …' She glances away, trying to hide angry tears. 'Nobody suffered like I did.'

'Father lost her too.'

Myrtle scoffs. 'Right. Someone he was married to for a couple of years. That ain't the same as having

161

your Ma ripped from you. But what would you know?'

Pearl can't bear to have her father talked about like he doesn't count. 'He loved her,' she whispers.

'He *killed* her!' Myrtle erupts. Her eyes aren't beautiful now; they're frightening. 'If it wasn't for him putting a baby in her belly, she'd still be alive. And look what he's gone and done to himself. I *told* him we shouldn't work in a match factory. Now here we are. I'm the mug, busting my guts to cure the man who murdered my own mother.'

Pearl's still hot, but she's shaking, furious and heartbroken all at the same time. Maybe it's true: maybe she's the offspring of a feckless man and a mother who resents her every bit as much as Myrtle does. But Father didn't *mean* for it to happen. He'd never hurt anyone on purpose, and if he's done wrong, isn't he paying for it now?

She finds a thread of voice. 'It's not Father's fault. You have to help him, Myrtle. Don't take your anger out on him. Blame me instead.'

Myrtle's nostrils flare. She peers down at Pearl, still crumpled on the floor by the chamber pot. 'D'you know what? Sometimes I do.'

With that parting blow, she strides off and shuts herself in her bedroom.

Pearl's free hand grips at the carpet. It feels as though the floor is moving. She wants to cry, to really howl and weep, but her head's just too painful.

Everything hurts so much.

For a moment she sits swaying, utterly hollowed out by her sister's words.

Then she's sick again.

CHAPTER 16

'You should not be here!' Agnes cries once more, but the lady is impossible.

Her dome-shaped skirt takes up most of the studio. Wide, fringed sleeves send paintbrushes clattering to the floor as her busy hands explore every surface.

Her daughter, about sixteen years old, lurks on the landing with her arms crossed. Her expression carries all the disdain Agnes feels, but must not show.

'Is this where it happened? Where Mr Boyle sat?' The lady tries the chair for herself. 'And that young gentleman you found? Did you take his shade too?'

'No,' Agnes lies. 'That was an entirely separate matter. Please, Mrs …'

'Campbell. I already told you my name. I hope you observe better than you listen.'

'And I have told *you* that you must leave this place, Mrs Campbell. It is not safe for you to be here.'

The lady's eyes twinkle. 'Now, now, I know what you are about. I won't pay more. Two shillings apiece is a fair price for a silhouette from the *parlour of death*.'

'Please, stop calling it that!'

A magpie cackles.

Agnes had anticipated whispers and avoidance after the newspaper article, but not this. She had not reckoned on the ghoulish crawling out from their holes to revel in all the morbid detail.

'Look, Lavinia!' Mrs Campbell takes off, knocking over the chair she has just sat upon. 'Look at the Etruscan pieces. So classical. I am minded to have one of them.'

These are the silhouettes where either the profile or the background has been worked in terracotta to resemble ancient pottery. Agnes always thought it was a cheerful colour; now she looks at the specimens hanging on her walls, and it seems as if they have been smeared with blood.

'I will not do it!' she repeats. 'I cannot. I have reason to believe my customers are being persecuted and until I—'

'But then the bronzing is charmingly quaint,' Mrs Campbell rabbits on, moving to another frame. 'A nice ethereal, ghostly quality, don't you think?'

Like Mr Boyle's shade, these pieces are black profiles with little details, like the hair and the collar, sketched on in gold. Agnes remembers how these features glittered by candlelight in the house of mourning at Queen Square and her sense of foreboding deepens.

'Really, I must insist—'

Lavinia catches her eye from the doorway and shrugs her shoulders. 'You had better do as my mother says,' she tells her wearily.

'Do you not understand the danger?'

Mrs Campbell laughs. 'And do *you* not understand four shillings, my good woman? Come, you could use them. I see that you could. Get inside the room, Lavinia, for heaven's sake. Pick up that chair. Let the woman take your likeness with this nice machine here.'

Four shillings. It is blood money, and yet … they would certainly prove useful. Agnes needs to buy tea, and to make up for that sixpence she spent at the séance.

Can she in good conscience turn down four shillings, when poor Cedric has spent all morning complaining of hunger?

Mrs Campbell is not a pleasant woman, anyhow …

But the daughter. She sits where Ned sat, albeit far less eager. A pretty, sullen thing. Long, lace-trimmed bloomers show at her ankles and an innocent white ribbon threads through her hair.

Young Lavinia does not deserve to come to harm.

'I beg you to reconsider—'

'Do it!' Lavinia groans. 'I'll never hear the end of it if you do not.'

Agnes hesitates. She sees it now: she is a coward. Has always been. She might put up a fight, but eventually she will let others' actions control her own, just as she used to let Constance dictate their games.

166

'Four shillings?' she confirms.

Mrs Campbell beams. 'Let us say four and six if you sign them both nice and clear.'

Everyone has a price. Agnes honestly thought hers would be higher.

Hating herself, she loads the physiognotrace with paper.

It is a very different experience to tracing Ned. There are no smiles or suppressed giggles. Agnes holds herself stiff, not savouring every dip and hollow this time but moving the pole mechanically, as grave as a torturer turning the handle of a rack.

The abbey bells sound.

Could the murderer be watching her do this?

Working used to be a pleasure. Now some unknown person has found a way to turn it against her. It is as though they want her to have nothing of her own. Why? What threat could she, an impecunious spinster, pose to anyone?

'Done,' she announces shortly.

Lavinia heaves a sigh and vacates the chair. She shows no interest in the results, but Mrs Campbell already has her fingers on the box, trying to unfasten the hatch.

'Careful,' Agnes warns. 'Mind the pole. Let me—'

'I wish to see it!'

Agnes shoulders her out of the way. This lady might be paying twice what her art is worth, but by God she is making her earn it.

167

'There will be little to see at present,' she explains as she opens the instrument and reaches inside. The paper unclips easily. 'I will need to enlarge it with a pantograph before—'

She has barely withdrawn the sheet from the machine before Mrs Campbell snatches it.

As she inspects the tiny sketch, her smile rapidly subsides to a frown.

'Is there a … problem?' Agnes ventures.

Wings beat as the birds squabble on the roof.

'It looks nothing like her.'

'It will not, until I have—'

'Really, it might be a different person altogether. Do it again.'

She drops the page. Agnes lunges for it.

'I'm sure it's not so bad, Mamma,' Lavinia says languidly.

'It truly is. Look for yourself.'

Agnes turns the paper over for the girl to see. Freezes.

There is no mistake, small and faint as the profile is. Mrs Campbell was right: it is not Lavinia.

The physiognotrace has drawn Constance.

'That's adequate for me,' Lavinia yawns. Her perfectly manicured fingers tug at the paper but it is a moment before Agnes can force herself to let go.

What is happening? How is this possible?

'I will enlarge it, cut it out—' she starts but Lavinia waves her off.

168

'Really. Do not trouble yourself.'

Mrs Campbell sniffs. Her mouth has pinched, highlighting the wrinkles around it. 'I *did* have something better in mind. I take it you will not be using that incompetent contraption for my own shade.'

'No, no.' Agnes hurriedly pushes the physiognotrace aside, disengaging the pole and propping it up in the corner. 'I did not wish to use it in the first place. Please, have a seat. I will … Let us use paint! I will paint your silhouette onto plaster, how about that?'

She hopes her hand will be steady enough. The prospect of four and six seems to be drifting further and further away.

Why Constance?

She cannot begin to comprehend how a machine, an actual machine, could make this error. Her own hand might cut something from memory, yes, if she lost concentration. But the physiognotrace? She is tempted to take the paper from Lavinia and pore over it, see whether her eyes were mistaken.

It must be the séance – all that talk of ghosts is making her see them everywhere.

Mrs Campbell spreads her skirts and descends upon the chair.

Agnes gathers her apparatus: not really paint but India ink, water and soot blended together to make the perfect consistency of black, and a white oval of plaster for the background.

Her trembling fingers select a round, soft brush. Then she begins to work.

It is soothing. With scissors, she is forced to cut away from her body, but now she can pull the brush towards herself. The lines are soft, oily smears. There are two edges to her brushstroke and she focuses on the left, the clearer one, ignoring the other that encroaches into the white space she will later fill.

Forehead, nose, mouth, chin.

These are not Constance's features. She makes sure of that. But the machine's drawing still flashes before her. Impossible, as were the things she saw in Miss West's parlour on Walcot Street.

Perhaps this is what happens when you meddle with the natural order. She did not stop to fully consider the consequences before she called up spirits, but of course it makes sense: if *one* ghost can wander, surely they all may.

Constance always wanted to be her only sitter.

Agnes adds more water, makes the ink thinner and thinner as it reaches the back of Mrs Campbell's head. The woman appears to be falling through an empty, white space. She picks up a needle, ready to scrape in some finer detail.

'Are you nearly finished?' Mrs Campbell complains.

Maybe Constance has *actually* appeared to help defend her against this fussy customer. It amuses her to think of how icily her sister would have treated a woman like Mrs Campbell. Mamma once said: 'If

Constance loves anyone, it is you, Agnes.' But she is not sure if that was true. She only remembers feeling tied to her little sister. As if she were a doll Constance wanted to carry about with her everywhere: something to own and control.

On the day Montague left, Constance took her hand and said, 'Now he will never part us.' As if that were some kind of comfort.

Well, death has parted them. And although her ghost might be trying, Constance cannot *really* get back to her now.

Agnes is no spirit medium. She cannot be possessed.

'Is it ready?' Mrs Campbell persists.

'Almost.' Agnes lays the needle down and signs her work. It is charming, despite its subject. The painted woman is silent and without Mrs Campbell's haughty expression; she has even managed to capture the wispy lace in her hair. 'Here. Please be gentle with it. Some parts may still be wet.'

Mrs Campbell comes over to the table and beams down at her shadow self. 'Well! *That* is more like it. What do you think, Lavinia? Is not Mamma very handsome?'

Lavinia just blinks.

'A treasure,' Mrs Campbell continues, scooping it up. 'Wait until my friends see! An actual silhouette from the infamous Darken's Parlour. I will be the envy of Laura Place.'

Agnes grimaces. 'Allow me to show you out.'

When they gain the hallway, Mrs Campbell produces her purse. 'Make yourself useful, Lavinia, hold the shade.'

Her smooth, pale hands tell out the coins, four and six as promised, without the slightest demur about Lavinia's failed portrait. How rich she must be, to fritter money away like that.

Agnes closes her fist tight over the treasure.

'You should take a cab home,' she advises. 'The streets are filthy.'

Opening the front door illustrates her point. Greyish-brown mush heaps the pavements. What was beautiful and snowy has melted into formlessness once more. It smells, too, possibly the effect of thaw water running down the drains.

'Nothing like a walk for the constitution,' Mrs Campbell announces, striding out without a backwards glance.

Lavinia raises her eyes to heaven and mopes after her, still carrying the shade.

Agnes watches them nervously from the threshold. She ought to shut the cold out, but how can she? She must see her customers safe, at least until they have turned the corner. She has a dreadful feeling that she has just signed their death warrant.

Few people have ventured out into the dirt. The young girls stay firmly inside Mrs Box's seminary, yet there are still servants carrying packages from the butchers, and clerks scurrying around the banks.

Agnes hunches behind the door. Any one of them could be the killer, spying on her house.

Mrs Campbell has nearly disappeared from sight but Lavinia dawdles, no doubt enjoying a respite from her mother's company. She is drawing level with the abbey when Agnes glimpses something hurtling towards her from the opposite direction, throwing out spray as it goes.

Agnes rubs her eyes. The object is too small to be a cart, but part of it does resemble a wheel ...

It *is* a wheel – or to be exact, a hoop, Cedric's hoop, jouncing along while he dashes after it with his stick. In this slush! She represses a groan, foreseeing hours spent over the sink scrubbing his trousers.

He pays no heed to where he runs. People seem to miraculously sidestep out of his path and he does not falter, not even when he is nearly upon Lavinia.

The girl has not noticed him. Agnes raises a hand, lets it hover uselessly beside her mouth. She ought to call out but the last thing she wants to do is attract attention to her customer, to Cedric ...

Now it is too late.

Cedric weaves, skims past Lavinia with barely an inch to spare. The girl gives a violent start and drops the shade.

Even from this distance, Agnes can hear the *crack* of plaster splitting into a jigsaw.

'Whoops,' Lavinia says dispassionately.

Agnes casts about wildly to see who observed the accident – did that lady, wrapped in fur? No, she only gave the merest twitch of her head, but what if the killer is out there somewhere, and this has drawn their eye … ?

Cedric barrels in through the door. His clothes are wet against her skirts and she leaps back with a shriek.

'Cedric! Careful, dear! What are you running away from?'

'Have we got any food yet?' He makes to push past her into the kitchen.

'Wait just a moment, young man.' She grabs hold of his shoulder and snaps the door shut. 'You should have stopped to apologise to that lady in the street, and helped her pick up her parcel. You made her drop it and now it will be broken. It is not like you to forget your manners.'

He blinks up at her from under his sandy fringe. 'Sorry, Auntie Aggie.'

'You really *do* need to be more careful, Cedric. Watch where you are going, at the very least. There are dangerous people about. I often worry that you will—' She loses her train of thought, caught suddenly by the state of him. 'Goodness me. What on earth have you done to your coat?'

He looks down at his feet. They too are caked in grime. 'I fell over. Tore it.'

It must have been a prodigious fall. The material is blotched all over with dirt as if it has been trampled underfoot. One tear is a crescent shape and the other gapes wide at the shoulder; the sleeve is almost hanging off.

Her anger flicks quickly to worry.

'Darling! Are you hurt?'

He glances up as if it is a foolish question.

'Come here. Give me that. That's it dear, take it off.' She coaxes him out of the coat, both relieved and amazed that she cannot see any bruises on him. He is unharmed – that is the important part – but she cannot help grieving over the garment. She does not want to ask Simon to pay for another; she must sew it up as best she can.

She drapes the ruined coat over her arm and places a hand upon his head. 'This is precisely what I mean, my love. I do not scold to be cruel, but for your own good. Please be more careful. I do not know what I would do if something were to happen to you ...' A chilling possibility occurs to her. 'It *was* a fall, Cedric? No one pushed you, did they?'

He looks a little tearful. Her heart clenches. It is one thing for a killer to victimise her practice, but if they were to touch Cedric ...

'I'm sure it was my fault,' he whispers.

Please God, let him be right. For if this assailant really is trying to take the things that she loves, it makes sense that they would move on to her family after her art. The idea makes her feel like she is in the river again, fighting desperately for breath, but poor tattered Cedric gazes remorsefully at her and she does not want to give him further cause for fright. She dredges up a wobbly smile. 'Never mind,' she says. 'Look what I have for you here.'

'Food?'

'Almost as good, my dear: money.' She pretends to produce a coin from behind his ear. 'Why don't you run to the Cross Keys and see if they have any pork pies left? And could you pick up an ounce of tea from Mr Asprey for your grandmamma?'

His troubled face lights into a grin. When she sees that smile, nothing else in the world seems to matter.

'Thank you, Auntie Aggie.'

He seizes the coin but makes sure to leave the house more slowly than usual, showing her that he has heeded her warnings.

Agnes lets her false smile drop. Her lips purse in worry instead. At least she knows where Cedric is going, and he is familiar to the tradespeople he will be buying from: they will keep an eye on him. But if her fears are correct, she will not be able to let him gad about with his hoop and stick any longer. She must keep him indoors.

It feels wrong. He is too bright, too noisy and busy for this gloomy little house. He has already read all of his chapbooks; she will have to visit Milsom Street and see if she can get any more.

But first: the coat.

Her workbox is in the parlour. She opens the door and tiptoes inside. Mamma is slumped in the wing chair, snoring alongside the grandfather clock. Her poor swollen skin looks red, but perhaps that is a flush from the fire and not a result of the dropsy. If only Simon would examine her again. He is always so reluctant.

Agnes sits on the sofa, opens up her workbox and selects a spool: a dull brown. It does not match the colour of Cedric's coat exactly, but it will have to suffice. She spreads the garment out on her lap. All these torn, tangled threads look like the roots of a felled tree. She snips them into shape, threads her needle and begins to sew.

It is difficult to concentrate. There are too many concerns swirling around her head. Not just Cedric and Mamma, but the Campbells. Are they still safe, out there? Perhaps she did the wrong thing by giving into that overbearing woman's requests. Maybe she should have tried to remove them from her premises by force. She pricks her finger, curses under her breath. She cannot think of it. She simply must not allow herself to dwell upon anything but the stitches.

The crescent-shaped rip is finally repaired. As she picks up the coat and turns it over to reach the torn sleeve, something drops onto the floor. A piece of paper. It must have been tucked in Cedric's pocket.

She bends to scoop it up. The edges are rough; it was probably torn from a book and folded twice into this vague square. She hesitates. It belongs to Cedric. Young as he is, he deserves some privacy. She should put it back into his pocket and forget about it.

But she doesn't.

She sets down the needle and begins to tease apart the damp folds of paper.

Pencil, just like the note pushed under her door. The same handwriting, Agnes realises, as she opens the scrap in full, revealing a single word.

The same word she heard at the séance.

Mine.

Chapter 17

Agnes has locked Mamma and Cedric in the house. It is hardly a foolproof plan, but she can think of no alternative while she runs for help.

Her footsteps clack against the pavement. She is walking too fast, striding right through icy puddles. She wheezes, but carries on. Wet feet and shortness of breath do not signify; after receiving that note, the prospect of catching pneumonia again seems like the very least of her troubles.

She turns through alleys plastered with handbills for coach builders, boarding houses, and a lamp depot. Pasted fresh over the last is Ned – or *Edward Lewis*, as the police appeal for information calls him. There is a lifelike drawing of his face, clearly copied from a photograph. It seems the picture he had taken for his grandmother came in useful in the end.

Agnes averts her eyes from the poster with a fresh spurt of horror. If it were Cedric, in his place …

She has no good likeness of her nephew, nothing beyond a silhouette. She has always resisted daguerreotypes, but now she sees why a relative might pay good money for such a clear record. It is insurance against a failing memory. For if Cedric's face were not before her every day, she would lose not only his precious features, but those of someone else dear to her heart.

She would lose sight of the resemblance to his father, Montague.

It is mainly uphill to Alfred Street. Her lungs heave for breath. Simon has established himself in a good location, close to the Circus and the Assembly Rooms, where his rich patients recline on chaises longues and sip languidly at the Bath waters. She stumbles up to the black iron railings that surround his house, pausing to blot her brow with a handkerchief and pinch her cheeks so she looks less like a person on the verge of collapse.

The more reasonable and collected she appears, the greater chance she has of persuading Simon.

She knocks. The charwoman answers the door – or, rather, sees Agnes and shuffles away again, uninterested by such a regular visitor. Perhaps she was hoping for a gory injury to brighten her day.

Agnes wipes her feet, takes off her bonnet and gloves and lays them on the console table beside the door. This house always smells of herbs and carbolic soap. Impersonal, sanitised. The silhouettes of the dead Carfax children that line the staircase are the only decorative touch. It is the home of a man without substance, lacking flesh and blood.

Simon could surely afford to hire one or two live-in servants, but he seems to prefer his isolation. The charwoman, Mrs Muckle, comes in for a few hours each day to tackle the worst of the drudgery – everything else, he does himself.

She recalls what Cedric said about Simon's time in Edinburgh. Maybe it *was* digging up bodies and anatomising them that changed poor Simon from the eager, ambitious young man that he once was. She always assumed it was his marriage. That was certainly when he started to lose his hair.

His consulting room is on the lower floor, in concession to his less perambulatory patients. Agnes makes her own way there, collecting Morpheus as she goes. Simon's previous dogs would not walk confidently beside her skirts inside the house, but cringe in anticipation of a kick. The pitiful things did not have wit enough to distinguish one Darken sister from the other; all they heard in the rustle of a gown was danger.

She taps on the door in case a patient is within, but Morpheus headbutts it open before Simon can respond.

The consulting room is papered in a damask the colour of potatoes and beef. Walnut furniture houses inkwells, empty glass domes, a magnifying glass and piles of paper tied neatly with string. Beside a row of leather-bound books, a chipped phrenology bust gazes impassively down at them.

Simon's desk is lit by a brass lamp with a tall, glass chimney. He sits behind it, reading a newspaper, but her entrance raises him to his feet.

'Miss Darken! I did not expect you. Have you been walking in all this damp?'

He pulls out a chair for her and rings the bell for tea. Her prepared speech thickens on her tongue; it is not possible to be eloquent while he fusses about her. 'Simon – I must … I had to …'

'I suppose you have already seen,' he cuts in, as Morpheus settles down by her feet. He gestures at the newspaper. 'It has been a busy morning and I only just read it myself.'

She stiffens. 'Not another death?'

'No. Did you not hear? They have identified the man.'

'The killer?'

He shakes his head. 'Oh, no. The man who … drowned. The one you asked me about.'

She had almost forgotten. Looking back, her former worries seem insignificant.

Noting her silence, Simon speaks gently. 'It was not … Lieutenant Montague.'

'No.' She shudders, remembering the Sylph's frantic gasps. 'His name was Hargreaves.'

'So you *have* read it?'

The charwoman interrupts them, thumping inside with two cups of a questionable-looking beverage. Chagrined, Simon stops leaning over Agnes's chair and returns to his own seat.

182

'I put sugar in it, Doctor,' the woman informs her employer as she sets the cup down on his desk. 'Thought you might need it after this morning.'

'What happened this morning?' Agnes asks.

Simon waves the question away with a pained expression, but his charwoman is only too keen to elaborate. 'Suicide, weren't it, Doctor? Is that what you found?'

'Indeed, the contents of the stomach lining would seem to suggest it was not accidental. Now, please, Miss Darken is—'

'So he ate them? A whole box of matches?'

'It would appear so. That will be all, thank you, Mrs Muckle.'

Still she hovers. 'I'll be off home for the day, then?'

'Yes. Thank you.'

The charwoman raises her eyebrows at Agnes, as if she has revealed a great wonder to her, and makes her exit.

'My apologies.' Simon grimaces, sips at his tea and grimaces again. 'That was not intended for your ears.'

It is endearing how he still thinks to protect her. She saw things at the séance in Walcot Street that would make his hair stand up on end.

Death is not the conclusion, but the alternative she saw is hardly comforting. If Hargreaves is still drowning, and Ned is still cold, she dare not think how this other man, who died feasting on phosphorous, will linger through eternity.

183

'I am not so *very* fragile, Simon. I do encounter sad stories in my work, too. In fact, I lately met a woman who worked in a match factory.' She pauses, conscious she must not reveal the full circumstances of the meeting. 'She worked there with her stepfather, and he suffered terribly from the chemicals, even without ingesting them.'

'Ah. The jaw, was it?'

'Yes. What is the cure for that? Is there anything a physician can do for him?'

'Not a physician, but a surgeon.' He mimics with his index finger and thumb. 'Removing the mandible – the lower jawbone – is the only way to give the poor fellow a fighting chance. One must cut out the rot before it can contaminate the entire body.'

'Have you ever performed that operation, Simon?'

'I have,' he replies on a downward note, closing the topic. As with Edinburgh, as with the lady sent to the asylum, Simon does not speak of his surgical days. Sometimes Agnes wonders if that is why he has become so plump in recent years: he is swelling with all the words unsaid.

Feeling uncomfortable, she picks up her cup. The tea looks pale and insipid. Come to think of it, that is what has always troubled her about the atmosphere of this room and its dull decoration: it is like a cup of weak tea.

She pours some into a saucer and offers it to Morpheus, who laps it up without hesitation. His forebears would have been warier. Of course, there was no *proof* that Constance poisoned them …

It will be better if she does not mention Constance at all today.

'Simon,' she says, crafting his name carefully. 'I know you try your best to shield me from all delicate matters. But you see, I can talk to you quite composedly about a suicide and a jawbone extraction, so I hope you will realise there is no danger in being candid with me today. We must face a topic we have long been avoiding.' She draws in a breath. 'We must speak about Cedric.'

He blanches, reaches for a paper on his desk. 'This is not the best time to—'

'Listen, Simon. Please put that down and listen to me. I understand why you do not wish for him to inherit your practice – that would be, well, I understand your objections. You did him a great kindness in giving him your name. But you must give him something more!' He tries to screen his face with his hand but she sets her tea down by Morpheus and goes over to him. 'Please, Simon. Apprentice him to someone else, send him from Bath. I know you do not have a vast fortune …'

'His mother saw to that,' he laughs bitterly. 'Even before the separation.'

'I know, I know. But none of it is *his* fault. He is fond of you, he believes you are his parent, and you avoid the boy.'

Simon's watery blue eyes do not focus on her, kneeling beside his chair, but on the bookshelf, as if it were telling the story of his pain. 'It was difficult,' he croaks. 'His father ... I did try. But his father was stamped on his face the moment I delivered him.'

'You saved the whole family by marrying Constance. None of us are in danger of forgetting your goodness. The scandal she would have faced, the shame upon my mother ...' She takes his hand.

'I did it only for you.'

'Then do *this* for me too. Perhaps Cedric can train for the army? He needs to get away from here, some place safe. It is *better* if he goes. I can be brave, for him ...'

Finally, Simon regards her. 'Can you, Miss Darken? I am not convinced you can make up your mind to live without your nephew.'

She bites her lip.

'Come, now. Whatever has brought this talk on?'

'I am afraid, Simon! The killer is drawing closer to me. They will not stop at my clients, they will take the people I love next. They want me to be all alone.' Simon's hand turns rigid beneath hers. 'I have received a note – two notes in fact. One was pushed under my door and then I found one in Cedric's coat pocket! They want me to know how near they are, how easily they can destroy everything ... Should I go to the police?'

'No!' he exclaims. 'There is no call for that yet, I am sure, but ...' He pulls at the tiny flecks of stubble on

186

his chin, thinking. 'But what did these notes say? Was there any indication of who they were from?'

She rubs at her forehead, as if she could erase the image of that slanted writing. 'No, it was just pencil words ... One asking if I had missed someone, and the paper in Cedric's coat said *"Mine"*. As if they would claim our dear boy! I thought ...' She looks sheepishly at him. 'There was a moment when I thought it might be Lieutenant Montague. That somehow he had found out ... But he has no right, has he, no legal right? Nobody can prove ...'

'No, no,' he says distractedly. 'In the eyes of the law, Constance gave birth to my son. And much as I despise the man, I must do Lieutenant Montague the justice to say I do not consider him capable of *murder*.'

No. The pain he caused Agnes may have felt like death, but even his betrayal cannot convince her that he was a thoroughly bad man. He was young, easily swayed, far more equipped to navigate the ocean and the demands of a ship than the tempests of human relationships.

'Yet *someone* is capable of it, Simon, and now they have turned their eye upon my family! Please, find the boy some work safely away from Bath. I do not care about anything else, so long as Cedric is not harmed.'

Simon seems to realise he is squeezing her fingers. He lets go of her hand, pats it. 'Leave it with me. I will make enquiries.'

187

'Is that all? And what am I supposed to do in the meantime? You are sure I should not take these notes to the police?'

'On no account. That would only fuel gossip. Besides, a single word written in pencil cannot aid the investigation in any meaningful way.' Always the slow crawl of a snail with him. It drives Agnes distracted. 'Have some patience, Miss Darken,' he counsels. 'Wait for me to call upon you with more information.'

'*Wait*?' she echoes, indignant. 'When my clients are being killed and my nephew is in danger – you expect me to just wait?'

Simon burdens her with a sad, sad smile. 'You have waited all these years for Lieutenant Montague. You might at least give me a few days.'

CHAPTER 18

Pearl curls her fingers into her palms, fighting the urge to open her eyes. Just when she thought all her hope had tired, there's this: a patting, a tapping.

This is the moment everything will change. Mother's answering her at last. She just has to concentrate a little bit harder ... But she's already focusing so intently that it feels like her head will burst.

The tap comes again, in the same rhythm but louder, like the telegraph machine Myrtle told her about, beating out messages from important men in London to important men in India. Only this message is travelling further – not just across water but through the veil itself.

She hones in on the sound, leaning forward.

All at once there come three loud thuds.

A female voice calls. 'Hello?'

Pearl can't breathe.

'I say, hello?'

It isn't Mother. It's just someone at the front door.

Miserably, Pearl gets up from her cross-legged position on the bed and walks out into the hall. Myrtle's gone on an errand and she's not meant to make a peep while she's out. But the woman sounds so forlorn …

'Please, I am desperate for your help. It is wet out here and people are beginning to stare at me,' she wheedles.

Pearl dare not speak above a whisper. 'Who are you?'

'Miss Darken, dear,' the voice says. 'We met at the séance.'

A swell of giddiness overcomes her. Miss Darken must mean the séance that took place before she became so ill. Her body still hasn't fully recovered from that evening and what's worse, she remembers so little about what happened.

'My sister's out,' she stammers.

'I know that. I saw her leave.'

'You must go away,' Pearl calls. 'I'm not supposed to open the door.'

'But I need to speak with you.'

Nobody ever wants to talk to *her*; it's always Myrtle they're after. And if Myrtle finds out that she's spoken to someone at the door, she'll be in a whole heap of trouble.

'I'm not allowed.'

'Please.' The lady is taken by a cough.

Pearl's within an ace of turning back and running to Father's room for safety, but something stops her. Her hand grows cool and tingly, like it does when a spirit's about to come, and suddenly it's moving, sliding the bolts and turning the handle to open the door a crack.

'Ah! Thank you, my dear.'

Pearl squints. The lady standing outside does look vaguely familiar. She's petite and fine-boned. Her eyes are not big like Myrtle's, but they grab Pearl's attention because they're so lined and troubled. She must be nearly fifty years old.

'What d'you want?' she asks.

'Please let me inside. I am tired and rather cold.'

Pearl hesitates. She can smell the rain, and she doesn't want to be stuck here talking at the door where the light's too bright. Reluctantly, she steps back to let the slender lady and her carpet bag into the hallway.

'Thank you,' the visitor wheezes, shutting the door behind her. She removes her gloves and a drooping bonnet, revealing dull brown hair with a streak of brilliant white through it.

Pearl's fingers stray to her own loose tresses.

'May I sit down for a moment?'

'I suppose you'd better come to the parlour, ma'am.'

The lady clears her throat. 'I hope that we shall become friends, so I am happy for you to call me Agnes, dear. And you – well, I only know you as the White Sylph. I am certain that is not your real name.'

'It's Pearl,' she tells her shyly.

The lady smiles. Her teeth are clean but slightly crooked. 'How pretty.'

191

Pearl's not meant to be doing this. Walking to the parlour feels like running a race, because her heart beats so fast and her breath's all ragged. She subsides into her usual chair, while the lady who calls herself Agnes puts down her carpet bag and perches on the edge of the sofa.

'Pearl,' she begins. She folds her hands together on her lap and stares at them for a moment. 'Pearl, I need to talk to you about your Gift.'

'I don't remember,' she blurts out. Seeing Agnes's confused glance, she hurries on. 'I mean, I remember you a bit. But not the séance we had. When I contact the spirits, it's like … They possess me. Take over my body, make it do and say things, but I'm not there. I don't know where I go … It feels like a dream. A mad dream you have and then you wake up in the morning and parts of it are gone forever.'

'Yes, I understand,' Agnes replies seriously. 'I have those kind of dreams sometimes. Especially since I was ill. I forget an awful lot.'

Pearl notices the lady's sleeves. They're worn thin at the elbow, going from black to mackerel skin. For all her airs and manners, she can't be that wealthy.

'Maybe you have the Gift too.'

Agnes presses her lips into a closed-mouth smile. 'You jest. But no one else has a talent quite like yours, Pearl. When last we met, you performed an … extraordinary séance. It was remarkable. And what is more, I now have confirmation that your revelations were accurate. You correctly identified a man who had drowned – why, you must know this already. Your sister, Miss West, found his body.'

Pearl's ears prick. Myrtle *hasn't* told her that. She doesn't tell her anything important.

'Good. I'm always glad to help,' she murmurs.

'I hope that is true. For I need your assistance once again.'

'You'll have to make an appointment with Myrtle, I don't—'

Agnes holds up a hand. It is knobbly; all joints. 'I would. But since you became so unwell ...' She fidgets. 'Well, the truth is I cannot afford the price your sister is asking for a second sitting.'

Pearl's gripped by a sudden panic. 'I can't change her mind for you. Don't ask me to talk to her, because she won't do it. She never listens to me. And she'll kill me if she finds out I spoke to you or let you in the house—'

'Hush, now. Hush, dear child. I do not wish to cause you trouble. But you see, there was a message for me, from the beyond. You began to tell me at the séance, but unfortunately you were taken ill and I did not have the opportunity to hear it in full.'

'Sorry. I don't remember what that message was. It wasn't me speaking. I can't just turn it on and off like the gas. I wish I could ...' Her throat's closing up. What a failure she is. Don't let her cry. Not in front of this nice lady.

'Oh, come now. None of this!'

To Pearl's astonishment, Agnes gets up from the sofa and holds out a hand to her. She freezes, wanting but unable to accept it.

Her hesitation doesn't matter in the end, because the lady crouches down beside her chair anyway and wraps one arm around her shoulders.

'I imagine all these spirits must be rather frightening for you. I was scared of them myself, and I am ... well, a woman grown! You can only be about the age of my nephew. He is twelve years old.'

'I'm eleven,' Pearl snuffles.

'Eleven! My, oh my. And so accomplished already! Your father must be very proud of you.'

She worms a little closer to the lady who smells of faded paper and dry ink, like a well-thumbed book. 'Does he look like you? Your nephew?'

'Oh, no. Cedric is handsome, like his father. He was a naval officer and every bit as dashing as you can imagine.'

Pearl grins. She'd like to see this nephew. Young men rarely attend the séances, and none of them are comely. Mr Stadler thinks he is, but he's not. 'Just like my uncle. I never met him, but Myrtle says he was in the navy.'

'As was my papa. Many naval men settle in Bath.'

'Maybe all three of them were on the same ship, once upon a time. Where's Cedric's father stationed now?'

The muscles tighten in Agnes's face. It looks like she's about to say something, but then she just shakes her head. 'Cedric is an orphan. I look after him and his grandmamma. So you understand why I do not have a great deal of money …'

'Neither do we,' Pearl points out.

'However, I *can* offer you something. A useful service in exchange for your own. Altogether, it is probably worth far more than you can earn in a dozen séances.'

'You'd have to ask Myrtle …'

Agnes shakes her head. 'Oh, no, my dear. This would be just between us. Our own séance, in secret.'

Her chest constricts. She feels as scared as if Myrtle were sat opposite her, listening to this conversation. 'I can't—'

'I doubt Miss West would approve of my tender. She dislikes doctors. No doubt she means to treat your father in quite another way … Although I am sorry to say, her experiments will be doomed to failure.'

'My father?' Pearl echoes, confused.

'Yes. Miss West told me that the unfortunate man suffers from phossy jaw as a result of his work in a factory. A terrible, terrible condition.' She tuts sympathetically. 'But all is not lost. My brother-in-law is a renowned surgeon. At a word from me he could perform an operation, free of charge, to cure your father.'

It's like a ray of sun has come out from behind a cloud: beautiful – but terribly painful. Pearl flinches as she would from the real thing.

195

'You could … do that?'

'Together we could. It is the only way to help him, you know. He cannot be saved without an operation.'

A cure for Father.

A *cure*.

Myrtle's voice snaps in her ear: 'Butchers, the lot of 'em.' Yet Pearl's never believed that. Father was happy to see the doctor who sent them to Bath in the first place, and he told her, before he lost the ability to talk, that he wanted to consult a surgeon.

She's dizzy. An hour ago, she would have said she'd never dare to cross Myrtle for anything.

'How would we even …' she starts.

'The operation could not be performed here, of course,' Agnes acknowledges. 'We would wait for your sister to leave, like I did today, and then the doctor and I would come to take your father somewhere more …' She casts an eye around the parlour, searching for a word. 'Salubrious.'

Pearl doesn't know what that means, but she understands Father would be somewhere safe – maybe like a hospital – and Myrtle wouldn't be able to do a thing about it.

What a traitor she is. But Father …

It feels like she's being split in two.

'Won't Mesmerism cure him?' she asks hopefully. 'Myrtle says it can.'

Agnes turns down her mouth and shakes her head. 'Oh, my dear. Mesmerism is all very well in its way.

But diseases of this nature are rather more complicated than that.'

Are they? How would Pearl know? She's never felt so stupid in her life. She can't read, and Myrtle doesn't tell her everything. Even the ghosts say their piece while she's in a trance.

'Your sister is remarkably talented within her remit,' Agnes says kindly. 'Yet even you must admit that she has never studied medicine, or attended a university.'

'She taught herself.'

Agnes observes her with pity. What must she think? That Pearl's some poor simple girl with no brain between her ears?

How her head aches. It's hard to think straight. She can't believe she's even considering putting her faith in this stranger, rather than her own sister, but she finds herself asking, 'Your brother-in-law would really do the operation for no money? Just for one séance?'

Agnes removes her arm from Pearl's shoulders and sits back on her haunches. It looks like it hurts her to kneel down. 'Perhaps more than one; it all depends on our success. The truth is, I am trying to contact several of my clients. They are ... well, I suppose I do not need to mince words with a brave girl like you. They have been killed, Pearl. First Mr Boyle and then the sailor Hargreaves, drowned in the Avon. Last was poor Ned, whose body they found frozen in the snow.'

197

Mr Boyle. Wasn't that the very first spirit Pearl reached out to? And what did Agnes say, about the last man? *Frozen* after her shivers.

'I need to contact their sad murdered spirits,' Agnes continues to explain. 'Oh Pearl, I must. How else can I find the vile wretch who hurt them and put a stop to his crimes?' She presses one of Pearl's hands. Her touch is dry. 'And consider, my dear. Why would Providence bestow such a gift upon you unless it was to help your fellow men? Catching a killer, saving lives – why, I am sure that is the noblest action anyone can perform!'

They're her own words. Better words, obviously, but they mean the same thing. This is the argument Pearl had with Myrtle. She could use her power to stop the killer.

Everything's spinning. There's too much to think about, too much to hold in her head, so she grips on tight to Agnes's hand.

She wanted to hunt the murderer with Mother, but since she hasn't appeared ... Mightn't this nice lady do just as well for the time being?

'I saw water,' she gabbles. 'Before the drowned man. Then I was cold. Perishing with cold. Did they really find someone all frozen?'

Agnes nods, mouth slightly ajar.

So she was right. *She* was right, and Myrtle was wrong. Thank God she's holding on to Agnes. If she weren't, the force of that would sweep her away.

'Do you ... feel anything now?' Agnes probes.

Nothing she can put into language: just pain.

Pain, Pearl believes, should have its own vocabulary, because no one else seems to feel it like she does. Up until now her experience of pain has been mainly bodily hurt: her continual exhaustion and the sense that all her bones are on fire. But now she feels … shattered. Like her mind is cracking apart into jagged fragments.

If Myrtle was *wrong* …

Myrtle.

Oh, hell.

Pearl jerks her hand away and climbs speedily to her feet. The parlour wobbles. 'You need to leave,' she frets. 'She'll be back soon. She'll come home and find us.'

Agnes does not budge. 'The séance …'

'There's no time *now*! What will I do if Myrtle catches you here?'

'We could make up an excuse.'

Pearl doesn't think she could lie to save her life. The few times she tried, growing up, she bungled it terribly. Myrtle always caught her out.

She opens her mouth to explain, but then she hears a horribly familiar step.

'It's her!' Panic strangles her voice. '*Hide*!'

'I beg your pardon?'

'Shh!' She hears a jangle; Myrtle must be getting out her keys. Pearl thinks she's going to faint. 'Oh God, please hide, ma'am. I'll never, ever help you if you don't hide right now.'

199

Agnes purses her lips, but suddenly she moves. If she hadn't seen it, Pearl would never believe this lady could move fast, but she does, nipping quick as a bullet from the parlour to Pearl's bedchamber and shutting the door behind her.

A mere second later, Myrtle comes in. Her cheeks are flushed from walking. She looks impossibly tall and bright as she stands there in the hallway and removes her bonnet. 'All right?'

Pearl makes a squeak.

'What you looking all het up about?'

'Nothing.'

Myrtle narrows her eyes.

It's one thing to act a part when your face is painted in ashes and everyone thinks you're the spirit of Florence King. But here, in the light of day, dressed only as herself, Pearl can't do it. The secret's heavy in her chest, and she can practically taste her heartbeat.

'I did a bad thing.' The words spill out.

Slowly, Myrtle enters the parlour. Her presence is totally different to Agnes's – youthful and almost overpowering. 'What did you do?'

'I – I …' Pearl's gaze drifts to the carpet bag, still beside the sofa. Myrtle's follows. 'I went upstairs,' she invents. 'While you were out. I was nosing about upstairs and I found that bag.'

Myrtle sniffs. 'Well, what's in it?'

'I dunno. Haven't opened it yet.'

Myrtle herself once told Pearl that all the best tricks are based on truth.

Her sister glances at her, at the bag again, and laughs. 'You're a rum one, ain't you?'

'Sorry.'

'Well, you'd better put it back. *I* don't care if you want to poke around upstairs, but if the bloody landlord finds anything missing he'll chuck us out in a flea's breath.'

'Yes, Myrtle.'

Myrtle rakes her with one more searching look. Pearl's guilt shifts and stings.

'Guess I'll make us a bit of supper, then.'

Pearl tries her best to smile. 'Thanks.'

Her sister walks leisurely to the kitchen. Pearl closes her eyes, releases her breath. The danger isn't over, she can't relax.

She inspects the closed door of her bedroom. Agnes is hiding there, just like Pearl used to hide in the cabinet, unable to cough or sneeze.

But Pearl's no showman with hidden trapdoors.

How on earth is she going to get Agnes out?

CHAPTER 19

Time is a strange concept. Ticking clocks and the slow creep of their hands mean nothing in the dark, where you cannot see them.

At first, Agnes did not dare to bend her knees in case she made a noise, and now she is uncertain whether she still can. She thinks this must be how corpses feel in their coffins.

The wardrobe seemed the perfect hiding place. Hardly any clothes occupy the cavity and there are no shelves inside, but the wood smells musty and small chinks of light in the door show where worms have eaten through it. She dare not muse upon what manner of bugs make their home here, or upon the few garments that hang on pegs beside her. Her skin itches, yet she cannot scratch it.

She has no idea how long she has been standing here. It was past midday when she called upon Simon, and then she returned home to check on Cedric and fetch her carpet bag. It must be reasonably late. There is no timepiece in Pearl's bedchamber and in this part of the city she cannot even hear the toll of the abbey bells.

Of all the days to get stuck away from her family! She should be watching Cedric like a hawk, guarding him at every turn after finding that note, and instead she has left him in the care of his feeble grandmother. The doors to the house in Orange Grove are locked, but what does that matter? Someone determined could find a way in ...

She peeps through the holes in the wardrobe door. The tiny bedroom window is swathed in heavy curtains. Everything remains static and unchanged. Time is not passing. It is holding its breath, encapsulating her.

When the wardrobe door finally creaks open, she cannot trust that the sound is real. A flame wavers, releasing the scent of tallow. Finally an ashen face comes into focus behind it.

'She's asleep,' Pearl whispers. 'You can go now. I've fetched your bag for you. You left it in the parlour! Nearly got me in all kinds of trouble.'

Night has fallen. Agnes has been inside this wardrobe all afternoon! Her feet have forgotten how to move; she half-climbs, half-falls out.

'Shhh!' Pearl urges.

By daylight, it was easy to treat this girl as a regular child. Other than her pallor, there was no material difference between her and Cedric, or even someone like Lavinia Campbell. But there is something ethereal about Pearl's albinism at night. Her shape seems to be pinned against the darkness, the reverse of a shadow. Agnes could swear that she trails a fine mist as she moves.

'Can we do it now?' she asks. 'The séance?'

Pearl hesitates. 'I'm tired,' she replies softly. She does look it. 'And Myrtle might hear us.'

'Then you will have to come to me.'

'What?'

Agnes feels like a pressed flower, sapped of her essence, but she needs to recover her wits quickly. She'll be damned if she's spent hours in that worm-eaten wardrobe for nothing.

'Where did you say my carpet bag was, dear?'

Pearl moves the light and shows her where the bag sits, beside her narrow little excuse for a bed.

'Come and look.' Agnes gropes her way forwards, struggling to keep her movements quiet and her voice hushed. Now that she is out of captivity, she is aware of the rotting smell again: an odour somewhere between potato peelings and a spoiled egg.

Her carpet bag contains a set of Cedric's clothes and a large cap that belonged to Agnes's grandfather. One of Papa's greatcoats sits under the collection, still faintly speckled with tobacco.

'If you could not do a séance today, I was going to ask you to creep out and come to my house at a later date,' Agnes explains. 'I have drawn you a detailed map of the buildings, you see. You can understand where to go even if you cannot read the words. I thought that if you dressed as a boy, there would be less danger in walking alone ...' Only now does she realise how absurd this plan sounds. Hurriedly, she puts the map away. 'But tonight I can bring you there myself. If I wear the greatcoat, we will pass for a man and his son, no one will remark upon it. And our séance will not be disturbed at my house. My family sleep deeply, believe me.'

'I'm not going anywhere with you,' Pearl asserts.

Of course she isn't. The girl may be young, but she has a steady head on her shoulders, which is more than Agnes can say for herself. What was she *thinking*? Has she really grown desperate enough to come up with this half-baked scheme?

She nods, defeated. 'I understand.'

Pearl watches her repack. The small, white face shows reluctance, but there is something harder under there, pushing against it.

'We could ... go upstairs,' she suggests. 'Further away from Myrtle. Maybe we won't wake her.' The light is burning dangerously near to Pearl's fingers and she blows it out. 'But there's a condition,' her whisper continues from the pitch-blackness. 'I won't do any séances unless you agree to it.'

'Anything, my dear.'

'These circles won't just be for you. We'll talk to your dead men, but then I want to contact my mother.'

Agnes feels a flicker of annoyance; she does not see why the girl cannot do *that* in her own time, but in the grand scheme of things, what is one more ghost amongst so many? She does not hold the power here; she must remember that. 'Very well. I agree.'

Small, hot fingers thread themselves through her own. The little hand tugs at her, forces her to walk onwards into the dark.

The bedroom door opens softly. Pearl seems perfectly comfortable in this twilit world, pulling her down the hall and up the first few stairs with ease.

Agnes reaches out a hand for the bannister. She cannot see her feet.

'Shhh!' Pearl hushes her.

Shabby as the house is, the stairs are actually in better condition than the ones where Agnes lives; they have endured less use and the treads hold their tongues.

On the landing, Pearl loses some of her confidence. She does not seem to know which way to turn. Choosing a door on the left-hand side, she drags Agnes into a room that is bare of furniture and even carpet. Ash stains the maw of the fireplace. There is one bottle-glass casement, blinded by dirt, but it lets in a faint tint of lamplight from the streets.

Pearl scowls. 'I'd prefer it to be completely dark.'

'Oh, but we had candles at the séance. Surely this light is comparable? I am positive a talented girl like you can manage.'

Pearl shrugs and seats herself cross-legged on the floor. Apparently it does not occur to her that Agnes cannot do the same with ease.

She holds out two lily-white palms. 'Come on, then. Form the circle.'

Painfully, Agnes lowers herself onto her knees. Her dark skirts pool around her. She hopes there are no mouse droppings on the floorboards.

She reaches out, clasps the child's hands in hers.

There is a connection.

She remembers standing like this with Montague, ready to lead a dance.

'Do we … sing?'

Pearl shakes her head. Locks of hair pale as lint rustle. 'We're doing it my way tonight.'

Agnes attempts to concentrate, shut out the squalor and focus upon the little girl who, in another life, might have been her own. She notices there is a yellowish tinge to her, like the first rays of a rising sun.

'No talking through me,' Pearl orders whatever she sees in the darkness. 'I don't want to be possessed this time. You can speak *to* me with knocking. Three raps for yes, one for no. Two if you're not sure.'

Agnes feels a tremor in the small hands – or is it in her own?

Pearl closes her eyes and waits. Agnes does not feel comfortable doing the same. Whatever takes place here tonight, she needs to see it.

'Is anyone there?' Pearl calls softly.

Silence replies.

Time seems to stretch. The house groans, settling. Five, perhaps ten minutes pass.

Eventually, Agnes tires of staring at Pearl and begins to study the leprous walls of the room. They are misty, blurring together. She can just make out a faint outline where a cupboard must have stood, and dirty prints smeared across the floorboards.

Nothing in this abandoned chamber reminds her of the downstairs parlour with its theatrical paraphernalia, but there is a similar sensation: a current seething beneath the surface, just waiting for someone to tap into it.

Pearl's breath comes in gentle bursts.

The hours of standing in a wardrobe are beginning to take their toll. Agnes feels her own eyelids begin to close in spite of herself. She could, she *could* let them fall, ever so briefly …

But then the atmosphere shifts.

There is no sound, no movement, yet all at once it feels as though someone has stepped inside the room.

'Are you there?' Pearl asks again. This time, her voice shakes.

Knock. Knock. Knock.

They flinch so violently that they nearly break the circle. The sound comes from the wall behind Pearl and ripples out to where they sit; Agnes feels the vibrations in her knees.

'Mother?' Pearl gasps.

Knock.

Desperately, Agnes tries to gather her scattered thoughts. One rap meant *no*. It is not Pearl's mother. That can mean only one thing. She pushes words through the fear that congests her throat. 'You are here for me.'

Knock. Knock. Knock.

Each tap hits her like a physical blow. Her hands are drenched in sweat and slip within Pearl's.

'Ned—'

Knock.

'Mr Boyle?'

Knock.

'Please! I need your help. I need you to tell me who killed you and—'

Knock. Knock.

Pearl's glassy eyes shine out of the darkness, wide with amazement. 'Two knocks. That means they don't know.'

'You must know something! Anything. Why else would you be here?' Agnes is speaking too loudly but she cannot control herself; the words will either come with force or not at all. 'Please help me. Give me some clue! My nephew, my little nephew may be in terrible danger—'

The ash in the fireplace ignites.

Agnes's voice drains away. She can feel the heat from across the room as the flames leap and claw upwards.

'What's that?' Pearl twists around to see, pulling Agnes with her.

Shadows flee across the plaster like a fantascope.

Pearl squints and lowers her chin to protect her eyes. 'There's no kindling,' she squeaks. 'There's nothing in that fireplace.'

But they can hear it crackle and pop.

The dark patterns begin to take form: they flatten out, grow edges, spread into faces – no, profiles. They are shades; the shades Agnes has cut with her own hands. Astonished, she watches them flick past as quickly as the pages of her duplicate book.

The Carfax children, Montague, Mr Boyle, Ned – and other faces with names she has long forgotten. Was that Mrs Campbell, there? She cannot be sure, the images are cycling by so fast …

But the last shape she knows.

It flickers, suspended, as if held underwater.

'Constance?' she cries.

Soot rattles down the flue, raining black over the flames. Constance's profile breaks and scatters.

As quickly as the fire burned, it winks out.

The room falls into darkness and whoever it was – whatever it was, it has gone.

Pearl releases her hands. Without their support, Agnes topples.

'Careful!'

She catches herself just before she meets the floorboards. Her arms shake under the strain; her knees feel like they have had knitting needles driven through them.

'Here, let me help you stand up.'

Looking at the room, Agnes can barely credit that any of it really happened. The house around them seems tranquil. Their noise has not awoken Miss West or the neighbours.

Pearl steals up to the fireplace and pokes one of her fingers into the ash heap.

'It's cold,' she marvels. 'How can it be cold after that fire?'

The entire place feels cold to Agnes, even though she is slick with sweat. She keeps seeing the way those flames rippled, more like water than fire, and Constance's face beneath the river.

'Are you sick, ma'am? It's usually me what gets ill after a séance. Take a big breath. I'd give you a glass of water if I had any.'

At the mention of water, Agnes shakes her head.

'Who ...' Pearl starts cautiously. 'Who's Constance? You called out her name. Was that your sister?'

'Yes.'

'How did your sister die?' Pearl whispers.

Agnes closes her eyes. 'She ...' She is about to say *drowned*, but she bites the word back. That is only the socially acceptable version of the story. This girl who has hidden her all day and risked so much for her sake deserves honesty.

'No one was able to tell us exactly what killed her. Whether it was her injuries or ... You see, there was ... an accident. We were in a carriage when the horses bolted. It ended up in the river. They say my

211

friend Simon rescued me but I cannot recall that. I lost consciousness underwater. When I came to myself, I was safe and Constance was … gone.'

Pearl clutches her hand. 'I'm sorry.'

But here is the nub of it: *they* were not sorry. Simon was released from a loveless marriage that had led to embarrassment and financial loss. Cedric had always been closer to his aunt, anyhow. The family had been … relieved that Constance had died.

It eats her with shame to think of it now.

And yet death has not altered her sister. She is still enigmatic and infuriating, pushing in front of the other spirits to claim Agnes's attention. Why? It is next to no use for her to be popping up here, there and everywhere; if she truly wants to contact Agnes, why does she not use words?

She shakes herself. 'It does not do to dwell upon these tragedies. I must return home now, I have been away too long.'

'It's very late. Will it be dangerous out there?'

'I will wear the greatcoat in the carpet bag. I will pass for a man in the dark.'

Still, Pearl clings on to her hand. 'You'll come back?' she pleads.

Agnes wonders if it is worth the effort. She has learnt no more tonight than she did in the last séance, and that was precious little. Ghosts, it seems, are contrary creatures. Not the oracles she had hoped for but imps, out to tantalise and tease.

212

No wonder Constance fits in amongst them so well.

'I did not receive any answers,' she says, non-committal.

Pearl's teeth show as she smiles. They are discoloured, darker than her skin. 'Then you've got to come back, haven't you? We'll find your killer, and we'll talk to my mother. I can't ...' She sweeps an alabaster arm towards the fireplace. 'I can't do *that* alone.'

But Agnes is no longer looking down into the girl's eager face. A slice of lamplight near the window shows the dust on the floorboards has been disturbed.

'Are those mouse droppings, Pearl?'

'Where?'

'Or did you do that when you ...' She trails off, frowning. Pearl would not have passed across the area when she went to the fireplace, although she was near it.

Slowly, Pearl follows her gaze. Gasps.

'What is it, Pearl?'

'I ...' She finally lets go of Agnes and steps closer. 'I can't read, but they look like some kind of letters?'

Dread is a leaden ball behind Agnes's ribs. She wanted words, and now she has them. She ought to be more careful with her wishes.

She slinks up to the child, peers over her shoulder. It's the same writing. The very same as on the notes pushed under her door and hidden in Cedric's pocket, only this time a finger has traced the words in the dust.

'What does it say?' Pearl urges.

Agnes blinks. She would give worlds to believe that her cataracts have deceived her, and she read the wrong message.

But it is still there, defiant in the dust.

'Ma'am? What does it say?'

'Too late,' she croaks. 'The writing says: *Too late.*'

CHAPTER 20

Agnes does take the greatcoat in the end, for warmth more than anything else; being seen out alone, or accosted by a rough man no longer register as legitimate fears in her mind. The writing has warned her that something far worse waits ahead.

Too late.

Walcot Street lies deserted. Shutters cover the shops and night has dulled the cheerful gilt letters on their signs. A breeze slips down the road, flattening the lights in the street lamps. She hears her weary footsteps – just the one pair, stumbling along – and yet she has the peculiar feeling that she did not leave that house alone.

Shadows flee across the cobbles and climb up walls. Agnes has spent her life studying them, but she has not appreciated their sheer number until tonight. She sees shadows thrown by a dancing flame, the shadow of a tree branch, of an alley cat, shadows from nothing at all.

Twice she winces at the sight of a figure rising up a wall. Each time, it turns out to be her own. The shape of the greatcoat changes her silhouette, confuses the eyes. She curses herself for a coward. *Afraid of your own shadow* – that is how the saying goes. Cedric scoffs at this. He says the real monsters, like vampires, do not even cast a shade. You never see them coming.

Well, Agnes can certainly feel *something* approaching fast behind her: a terrible premonition that bites at her heels as she walks. She will not turn and examine it, will not let it develop into a clear thought until she is home.

Too late, too late.

Her mind has never felt so disjointed and febrile. A crescent moon curves behind tattered clouds and she finds herself absurdly grateful that it is not shining full – why should that be? A large moon would help her to see. She does not believe in Cedric's ghouls and lycanthropes.

But then, a few weeks ago, she did not believe in ghosts.

In another turn, she is greeted by the welcome sight of the abbey, a bulwark of protection. If she had the strength, she would run to it. No murderer or monster would dare attack her *there*.

Panting, she crosses the churchyard and looks up at the place of worship. Angels are carved either side of the great arched doorway, where they climb Jacob's Ladder. They seem to be leaning in, offering Agnes a

216

hand. Their stone faces are mottled the colour of decay; she notices for the first time how stern their features are. Perhaps they are not going up to Heaven at all. They might be spirits climbing *down*.

The house she has lived in nearly all of her life appears from the darkness, just the same as it always was: with its portico and sleeping magpies, its sightless windows locked secure, and the little whiskers of foliage that grow between the lintels. Nothing has been disturbed.

She breathes a sigh of relief.

Tiredness makes her all fingers and thumbs, but she finally manages to fit her key in the lock and turn it. She opens the door and steals inside.

What strikes her most about the house is not its lack of light but its silence, weighted and profound. She finds herself closing the door behind her with infinite care, so as not to disturb it.

Why does everything seem so airless and strange?

A smoky, charred smell breathes across her face as she passes the parlour door; Mamma must have doused the fire before going to bed. Agnes cocks her head, considers the stillness of the room. *That* is the anomaly: Papa's grandfather clock. It has stopped ticking.

She stifles a childish plunge of panic. She liked to hear the clock's steady rhythm, always in the background, as if dear Papa were there watching over her. Without that wheezing tick, it feels like the heart of her home has ceased to beat.

217

But there is no real cause for alarm; the clock may not be broken, she may simply have forgotten to wind it. She will investigate further in the morning.

Perhaps it *is* nearly morning already; she has lost all sense of time. Even her full bladder, hitherto so imperious, no longer complains.

Groping for the bannister, she pulls herself up the staircase. Each tread offers a feeble creak. Beneath this noise, another sound: Mamma's rumbling snore.

Proof at least that Mamma is safe and fast asleep. The nerves that have fluttered through Agnes like so many moths still their wings. Nothing is wrong, no one is hurt and she is certainly not *too late*.

Perhaps she has let her imagination run away with her. Seeing Constance's shadow again at Walcot Street flustered her. Maybe the words said something else entirely? They had *looked* the same as the handwriting on the notes, but it was dark, and Agnes's eyes struggle in poor light: there is a chance they were just incidental marks in the dust.

The door to her own chamber stands wide open. Tempting as it is to enter and fall straight upon the bed, she knows her mind will never settle to sleep unless she checks on Cedric first.

Carefully, she creeps past Mamma's room and edges the door of Cedric's bedchamber open. Dark shapes litter the floor: the toys and books she has bought him over the years. She is pierced by the contrast with the hovel that Pearl calls her *room*. Agnes suspects it was converted from a maid's cabinet. There were certainly no ornaments or trinkets there, no little touches of decoration to make a child feel loved.

At least Agnes has given Cedric *that*.

She steps inside and navigates her way towards the small brass bed. The boy does not snore; he always sleeps quiet as a lamb. Even as an infant, she does not recall him wailing in the night; perhaps he did not dare to, with Constance as his mother.

She never wants him to feel fear like that again, or to feel unwanted because of Simon's behaviour. Cedric may not have been conceived in wedlock, and his parents may have had no attachment to each other, but he is precious: the only gem snatched from all the misery.

Agnes reaches out a tender hand to place it upon the lump beneath the covers and watches it sink, slowly, to the mattress.

Nothing. There is nothing there.

The floor seems to pitch under her. Her hands tear at the covers, the pillow, even push the mattress from the frame as if her nephew might somehow be concealed beneath.

He is not.

'Cedric!'

She starts to rip the sheets, hoping to find him hidden inside.

'Cedric!' she screams. 'Ced!'

He could not have left the house: it is not possible, everything was locked up tight.

She drops to her knees with a cry. She can hardly see, can hardly breathe for tears, yet her hearing is not at fault for her ear catches a distinct rustle of paper as she pounds the shredded bedclothes.

Searching, she feels a torn page at the bottom of the mattress. A note.

She snatches it up and staggers over to the window. The note is rumpled and a little smudged, she cannot make out the words ... Moaning with frustration, she pulls the window shutter back and leans greedily into the light from the street.

She feared she would read *too late* again, but this is worse.

That slanting hand, now as familiar as her own, has written:

You both belong to me.

Chapter 21

Pearl thought she'd got off pretty lightly, all things considered. No spewing or fainting. She'd been tired when Agnes left, but not too tired to sleep, and after a few minutes tossing and turning feeling guilty about disobeying Myrtle, she'd drifted off.

This morning is different, though.

She feels queer, like the food she ate for breakfast was an ember that's tracked a fizzing path down her gullet, into her belly, where it's setting light to everything.

Myrtle eyes her across the table. 'You peaky?'

'A bit.' She still can't look Myrtle in the face. She's going to have to become an awful lot better at this lying business if she's really going to get Father out of here, to a real doctor …

Her innards lurch. It's not just the fear of getting caught that causes her stomach to ache; it feels as if there's something *alive* in there.

'Well, see you recover before tonight,' Myrtle orders. 'I'm not cancelling this séance. These ones have money, and connections. We'll clean up if we can impress them.'

Pearl stares at her jam-smeared plate. The crumbs on it seem to dance. 'I didn't sleep all that well,' she excuses herself.

'You still need to work. Christ! I don't ask a lot of you, Pearl. You're lucky you've got me for a sister. Others would be selling tickets to let people gawp at an albino like you. Maybe I should just bundle you off to the circus – you and your dad, both.'

Her stomach pitches and this time, there's no controlling it. Pearl crashes down from her chair and hurries into her room, where she manages to sit on the chamber pot with just a second to spare.

It's agony: ripping her body just like she rips away the veil to enter the land of the dead. Pearl folds in half, her head between her knees and her lips parted in a soundless scream.

The pain doesn't go away when she's done, but it does dull to a simmer. She's left with a brand of disgust and shame. Who would've thought her body was capable of making those sickening noises, those *smells*. The room stinks nearly as bad as Father's wound.

Nearly.

She uses the old copies of *Missives from Summerland* to scrub herself clean: it seems fitting. All those writers harp on about the beauty and the wonder of the spirit world. What's that word they use? *Ethereal*. Myrtle says it means pretty and airy, but there's nothing pretty about the ache pulsating deep in the pit of Pearl's belly, or the contents of this chamber pot. Contacting the Other Side isn't a pleasure cruise. If you want to talk to the dead, you have to go digging amongst the worms and maggots.

Grimacing, she manages to stand and holds the pot at arm's length by its handle. God forbid someone should walk down the street while she empties this out of the window. She couldn't bear the humiliation if anyone else were to see …

She blinks, her eyes watering. Is *she* really seeing this?

Fumes drift up from the pewter rim: spirit matter trying to make its way back to Summerland.

Every inch of her skin crawls. It was bad enough with the smoking vomit; now they're in her evacuations, too. Spirits and ghosts are tucked into her every nook and crevice, seeping through every pore. She's never felt so dirty.

She looks down at her slender trunk and wonders just how much of herself is left under the skin.

She twitches the curtain aside and raises the window sash, not even cringing from the daylight. She's so full of pain, her body simply won't absorb any more of it. Her waste sloshes out of the chamber pot onto the pavement outside and she shuts the window quickly, before the fumes can get back in.

Drained, Pearl staggers back to her bed and lies down. Even with her eyes shut the world is spinning.

Dimly, she hears Myrtle cleaning up crockery and padding softly to Father's room for another session of Mesmerism. Another waste of time, she adds mentally, before a bolt of pain erases the thought.

The fact of the matter is, she doesn't know who to believe. Myrtle says doctors are useless butchers; Agnes says Mesmerism won't help the sick – they can't both be right. The only sure way to save Father is to play both sides.

Everything depends on Pearl now. She must keep doing her regular séances so Myrtle doesn't suspect anything's afoot, and she must put in extra work for Agnes in secret so that the doctor will come and help Father.

But all that means she'll be giving herself over to the misty hands of the dead more and more each day, and her body's telling her, louder than the spirits ever speak, that it's too much.

If she keeps pushing herself, she can save Father's life. Maybe she'll save *lots* of lives, by catching the killer. But she has to be brave and accept the truth: that all this hard work might just claim her own.

Chapter 22

The police station waxes various shades of brown. Drab beige plaster coats the top of the walls; below the dado rail it darkens to umber. Someone has tacked up handbills announcing rewards, items lost and found, but these too have become parched, curled up like decaying leaves.

Behind a walnut structure that resembles the bar of a public house, a policeman stands, avoiding everyone's eyes, looking only to his vast, leather-bound book. A brass lamp shines on him; he has a brass bell at his side too, as if he might call for assistance, or tea.

Agnes thinks she may scream.

Some people do. They are all here: the dregs of Bath. Men with black eyes and cuts; guilty-looking, flea-ridden youths; women wrapped tight in their shawls, rocking back and forth. The din would be unbearable, if it were not in tune with Agnes's inner wail.

The police are too slow. Their station looks like it has been dipped in treacle and that is how they move:

painstakingly, with no comprehension of how urgent her errand is, even though she has impressed it upon them several times. No doubt everyone is here on important business. But Cedric—! A missing child! Why are the policemen not galvanised with horror?

Perhaps she has gone mad. It feels possible: she is living at a rate twenty times faster than their insipid pens can scratch. Where, oh where is Sergeant Redmayne? Anyone of importance is shut away from her, behind doors with panels of frosted glass.

This place sparks memories of the Accident. How different *that* was. Back then, the policemen seemed to be ricocheting around the room at speed, firing questions with the rapidity of a locomotive train. Even the kindly inspector with a moustache, who had tried to prepare Agnes for the sight of her sister's body, had spoken quickly. She only absorbed a handful of his words: *caught up ... dragged behind ... spokes ... axle ... velocity.* None of them were adequate to describe the smashed, skinned wreck she had finally identified.

Papa had once complained that Constance must be pure black inside. She was not. She was very, very red.

'Miss Darken?' Her head shoots up. Sergeant Redmayne has materialised from nowhere. His face is as large and stony as she remembers; it does, however, register a hint of surprise to see her. 'This way, please.'

She stands up so fast that she nearly trips over her skirts.

226

'My nephew,' she begins, before they have even reached the little room he is escorting her to. 'Sandy hair. About ... four feet, three inches tall?'

Now that she has someone to listen to her, the words come confused and garbled. She has not slept. It *must* have only been yesterday that she stood in the wardrobe, but it might as well have been years ago; she feels that she has died, come to life and died all over again.

Sergeant Redmayne ignores her rambling and opens a door. Nothing much lies inside: a deal table and two uncomfortable-looking chairs, plus a pair of iron cuffs on reserve in case conversations should grow too heated.

'You've remembered something about Boyle?' he enquires, showing manners at last by letting her enter the room first. 'Or Lewis? Your brother-in-law said he'd bring you down here for questions when you were feeling better.' He produces a pocket notebook and throws it on the table before closing the door behind them. 'There's a few things in there I want you to help me clear up.'

'Anything. I will tell you anything you like, only please send someone to search for him this minute! He could be in danger, he is all I—' Tears throttle her. She is so exhausted that she has no defence against them.

The sergeant catches her out of a swoon and guides her to a chair that creaks as it takes her dead weight.

'Dr Carfax told me you'd been seriously ill,' he says with a gruffness that is very nearly concern. 'I suppose he's right. Should you be back home, miss?'

She shakes her head. 'Cedric,' she gasps.

'Who?'

'It's my nephew. Sergeant, he has been taken. Abducted.' She raises her chin, gulps in breath. 'The killer was targeting me all along, I can prove that now.'

Were she not so wretched, she would triumph in the fact that she has finally managed to make the impassive sergeant blink.

'I'd better fetch the Inspector.' He stands, strides for the door and swings it open.

Simon is waiting there. Redmayne sighs. 'I was wondering when *you* were going to show up.'

'Where is she? Where is Miss Darken?' Simon pushes inside, red and sweaty. When he sees her, he picks up her hands and clasps them in his own. 'I have just this moment received your note.'

'Oh Simon! They took him. *Took* him. Why would you not listen to me?' For all her scolding, she is relieved to see him. Simon will take charge, he will make everything right, somehow. 'Dr Carfax is the child's father,' she tells Sergeant Redmayne. 'It was too late for letter carriers, so I sent him word by the first boy I could grab. I was not certain my message would get there.'

'All right. Good. The Inspector will want to talk to both of you.' He turns to leave, but Simon's imperious voice arrests him on the threshold.

228

'Wait!' More softly, he adds, 'A moment, Sergeant.' He pats Agnes's hands, returns them gently to her lap. 'Alone, if you please.'

The policeman's chest heaves beneath his uniform in another weary exhalation, but he gestures to the corridor, as if to say they may speak outside.

'But Simon—'

'I know, I know. Have no fear, Miss Darken, we shall return presently.' He has regained his poise. Smoothing back his scanty hair, he follows Sergeant Redmayne and shuts the door behind him.

Once more, Agnes finds herself on the wrong side of the frosted glass.

It would be enough to vex any woman. What can they be speaking of, if she must not hear it? Vague mumbles reach her: a droning she recognises as the base note of Simon's professional voice. Had she more strength, she would stand up and press her ear to the door.

She is Cedric's real blood relation. She has spent more time attending to his welfare than either of his parents ever did; she has earned the right to be involved in this conversation.

A conversation that is apparently going to take a long time.

She hears the words, 'terrible accident', and 'loss of mother', then 'dredged up old associations'. Simon is clearly explaining how Cedric came to be in her care, rather than his own.

229

She rests her elbows on the chipped table. Misery and guilt seem to be ingrained within the wood. She wonders how many people have sat here in utter despair. One of her predecessors has carved shapes with their fingernails; another has left a stain that looks like blood. She shudders, imagining the miscreants and blackguards who must have occupied this very same chair.

Her stomach growls. She cannot remember when she last ate. It is hard to focus on anything except Cedric. What is she going to tell Mamma? Anything but the truth. She shakes her head, unable to believe she has been such a colossal fool.

Each time she has an item or person of value, she loses it.

The door creaks, making her jump. Simon enters, alone.

'What is it, what did he say?'

Simon spreads his hands in that conciliating gesture of his. 'The police will do everything within their power. They have instructed me to take you home, in case the boy returns.'

Go *home*? That would feel as bad as giving up, resigning Cedric to his fate. 'But I have not told them—'

'I knew how upsetting it would be to explain the … circumstances surrounding Cedric. Consider the matter in hand. The police shall deal directly with me from now on.'

Her mouth falls open. She has never felt more impotent, more inconsequential. Does Simon really expect her to sit at home and do *nothing*? It was his reluctance to act that caused this mess in the first place! And he *cannot* have given Sergeant Redmayne the full story, because he does not know it himself. There is so much she has not told him.

Her shaking fingers fly to her reticule. 'But the proof! The notes. Surely they need this? It is evidence!'

Simon examines the heap of paper she has tipped out upon the table. His face turns white. 'Where – where did you find these?'

'I told you before: in Cedric's bed, in his pocket, under the door. I *told* you the murderer was writing me notes.'

He is holding himself remarkably stiff and still. His eyes do not leave the pieces of paper; it is as though they have turned him to stone. Agnes has a wild urge to slap him, spit at him, do *something* to shake him out of this lethargy. Any other man would be frantic with worry for his missing son, even if he is only a son by law.

'Do you recognise the writing, Simon? It is familiar to me, although I cannot place it … We both agreed it could not be Montague. He would not do such a thing.'

Simon draws out the other chair from under the table and sits down opposite her: she the culprit, he the interrogator. He even looks a little like Sergeant Redmayne now, with his frozen features.

'No, it cannot be Montague,' he says at last. 'I can assure you that he will never make a claim upon the boy now.'

'How can you possibly know that?'

He hesitates. 'I took the opportunity to consult the naval lists after our last conversation. I wanted to put your mind at ease on one score, at least.' A forlorn smile plays about his lips. 'You used to check them yourself, constantly. You were always looking for Lieutenant Montague … Tell me, when did you stop?'

She lowers her gaze to the table. 'I cannot recall. I suppose I listened to you, Simon. You said that it was not a healthy occupation for me.'

'Nor was it.' He drums his fingers upon the wooden table. They both stare at them, seeking answers in the rhythm. 'I have been considering how best to tell you this, Miss Darken. At times, I doubted whether I should tell you at all. But I think you have a right to know.'

Her breath catches. 'You found him?'

'I found a *Captain* Montague, of the HMS *Raptor*.'

He made captain! Why does that still cause Agnes's heart to swell with pride? 'Good God,' she gasps. 'You have really found him, after all these years. Where?'

She must write to him. Tell him that her nephew is missing – she need not explain the full truth. She could simply beg that he use his influence and put pressure upon the police. With a naval captain and an eminent physician demanding answers, surely they will make it a priority to find Cedric?

232

The man she knew would not hesitate to be of assistance. He had possessed a great regard for her father. He only went away because he thought it was best for the family, but now it is clear that Constance has gone and Agnes needs him ... Is she being too optimistic to believe that he might sail back?

But Simon is biting the peeling skin on his lower lip. He has not answered her question.

'Please tell me where he is stationed!' she urges.

'My dear Miss Darken ... I cannot.' Simon bows his head. 'He has recently ... passed from this world.'

All air leaves the room.

'H-he what?'

'I am afraid he succumbed to yellow fever.'

She can feel nothing, which makes no sense, for this is the most pain she has ever been in.

Montague is gone. Gone forever.

She cannot make herself believe it.

'Miss Darken? Do you need me to fetch your salts?'

Salts! She nearly bursts into laughter. What use are salts? Simon may be a doctor, but he cannot stitch up what is beyond repair. To lose Montague and Cedric both, in one day!

Wearily she leans down, places her forehead on the rough wood of the table.

'Let me take you home.' Simon's worried voice sounds far away. 'The shock has been too great. I should not have told you. You must rest ...'

As if she possibly can.

Everything is slipping through her fingers: each person or occupation that ever brought her cheer. She does not feel as if she is only fighting against a killer; it seems like a battle for her soul.

Who can she be without her art, without her dear nephew, or even the hope of being reunited with the man she once loved? She tries desperately to picture Montague as she knew him, to conjure the sound of Cedric's voice, but already they are fading away.

Soon, there will be only Simon left.

Thank heavens for his kindness, for his warm touch upon her arm. Her other joys are mere shadows, retreating into the darkness when the lamp is blown out.

CHAPTER 23

Days have passed and Agnes still hasn't come back.

But she left her carpet bag behind, and Pearl has hidden it inside her wardrobe as a kind of talisman: the only proof that Agnes *was* here and promised to help her. Most days it's easier to believe in the spirits than it is to believe that Agnes will return.

Pearl spends her hours fever hot, bone dry, thrown from one encounter to the next. It's getting difficult to tell all the séances apart. So many clients, so much money changing hands. Her ears ring with wails and sobs and some of them are her own.

She trawls through the carpet bag and pulls out the map; she's already memorised its twists and turns. Agnes was right, she doesn't need to read in order to follow its directions, but she needs another talent that she doesn't have: courage.

The paper shakes in her fingers. Her whole hand looks as if it might shake to pieces. It's been like that all the time since the ghosts started sucking her dry.

The only steady objects in her life are Myrtle's eyes, watching, watching.

She tucks the paper away, fastens the bag and closes it in the wardrobe. She'll give herself a few more days. If Agnes doesn't return by then, she'll put on the clothes and follow the map.

Maybe.

Her pulse beats so hard she can see it in her wrists.

Donning the green-glass spectacles Myrtle has brought her to help shut out the light, she ventures from her darkened room. Everything looks emerald-coloured, which doesn't help her sense of unreality. The house is prettier through the lenses, but it still smells the same and is smelling worse day by day. The stink plagues her wherever she goes, like someone's shoved a piece of bad meat up her nostrils.

Maybe *she*'s rotting, being pulled down among the dead.

Father definitely is. When she pushes open the door to his room, she can see a halo of spirit matter circling his sleeping head. She wonders if that's how the reaper plans to take him: if he will drag poor Father to the afterlife headfirst.

She has to stop it.

Myrtle sits in a chair beside the bed, not reading for once, or even doing her Mesmerism, just looking. Her face is sad when it's relaxed; you can see creases in it, lines she shouldn't even have at twenty. Her wide eyes are glazed over.

236

It scares Pearl, to see her like this.

'What you doing?' she asks loudly, hoping to snap her out of it.

Myrtle blinks and turns her head, but she doesn't look that much brighter. Her attempt at a smile is more like a grimace. 'I'm thinking of my dad.'

Pearl hovers near the door, irresolute. Myrtle doesn't often talk about her father, still less their mother, and if she shows too much interest, her sister might clam up again.

'D'you remember him much?' she asks softly.

''Course I do,' Myrtle huffs. 'I remember him better than anyone. Even …'

She trails off, but it's another one of those times when Pearl can hear the unspoken words inside people's heads. Myrtle was going to say that she remembers Private West better than she remembers Mother.

Pearl creeps forward, interested. 'What was he like?'

The grimace finally turns into a smile, but it's a sorry one, tinged with pain. 'He was brave. Wouldn't let anything stop him. Used to say he'd make major if ever a common man did.' She grits her teeth. 'And he would have. He *would*. Life just didn't give him enough time.'

You could say the same of pretty much anyone who died young, but if this soldier was like Myrtle, Pearl has to admit he'd stand a good chance of getting promoted somewhere along the line.

'Lord,' sighs Myrtle, 'I miss that way of life. Following the army. It was tough at times, but …'

237

She flicks her eyes over the room. It was built to be a second parlour; it's the largest bedchamber in the house, but she seems to view it like a cage.

'There were men who should've treated us better. My dad saved their lives. They should have helped us out when he bit it, or married Mother if it came to that. They'll all be in the Crimea now and it serves them bloody right.' She knots her fingers together. 'But it's my uncle who gets me most. I'd never *be* in this mess if my uncle had been around to look after us.'

Pearl glances at Father: his eyes flicking beneath their closed lids. She thinks he's just as brave as any soldier – more so, in fact. Surely it would be easier to be shot down by a cannon than to waste away like this?

'We're not in a mess,' she says quietly. 'Are we? I thought the séances were going really well.'

Myrtle makes a harsh guffaw. 'You don't know the half of it, do you? You just sit there and close your eyes and it all happens for you.'

'I'm trying, Myrtle—'

'D'you know, I've envied you every day of your life?'

Pearl stares. Myrtle, the astonishing Myrtle, is jealous of *her*? What for?

'You don't have to *do* anything, Pearl. Plan for what we're going to eat, or beat out carpets, or fetch coal and haggle over it, or keep a book of everything that goes out to the laundry, or cook, or charm the landlord

238

into giving you a few more days, or bloody anything except the séances, and I arrange those too!' Myrtle's angry voice pinches out, strained by the effort of trying to keep it at a low volume.

Pearl stands there, stunned. She didn't even notice that Myrtle did all those things. Wouldn't know that they *needed* to be done.

Father tosses his head on the pillow but he doesn't wake up.

Myrtle glares daggers at him. 'Maybe it's not your fault. Maybe you just inherited it from *him*. He's not helping me either.'

'He's so ill—'

'He's resisting me. The Mesmerism. I shouldn't be surprised. I've had it up to here, Pearl, I can't feel sorry for him any more. He doesn't *want* to get better. It's too much effort for him.'

Even in her weakened state, Pearl manages to snap at her sister, 'You take that back.'

'I can't. He lost his wife, but I lost my ma. And he went all to pieces. Didn't take charge of the house, the funeral, even the wet nurse for you. He expected a nine-year-old girl to do it all. And I did. I've been doing *everything*, ever since.'

Myrtle's always been capable. Pearl assumed that was her character. But now she imagines Myrtle at nine, two years younger than she is now: grieving, looking after a sickly baby, running a house and working in a match factory.

239

Myrtle has done her duty ten times over. It's *Pearl*'s responsibility to fix Father. She's his flesh and blood. She can't just leave it to Myrtle, like she has done everything else in her life.

She sits down on the edge of the bed, fighting for some strength. Just an inch of it will do. She feels utterly, utterly useless.

Myrtle watches, and her features fall slack. 'I wish,' she says raggedly. 'I wish I could just've been your sister, Pearl. I think I would've been much better at that.'

CHAPTER 24

It is the silence that wounds her.

No pattering feet, no half-whistled tunes. Cedric's hoop and stick stand propped up against the old grandfather clock, which still refuses to tick. Even the magpies have ceased their chatter on the roof. The whole house holds its breath.

Mamma raises the trumpet to her ear. For once, it is not her hearing that is at fault.

'*Why* should Cedric be with Simon?' she asks for the third time this morning. 'He was perfectly well here with us.'

'You know why, Mamma. He is a Carfax.'

'He is *not*.'

The perquisite of grief is that it dulls all other emotions, even the temper. Agnes finds she can lie to her mother again and again, without the slightest compunction. She will keep saying Cedric is staying at Simon's house until the police return him. And they *will* return him. If she repeats it often enough, she may even believe it herself.

'According to the baptismal records and the law of this land, Cedric is Simon's son.'

Mamma snorts. 'That may be so. But the child was to live with us, after the separation. We agreed to it.'

'And he has. Now he is almost a man. He needs an occupation and an education. Simon will provide him with both.'

Mamma lowers the ear trumpet, unsatisfied with its message. 'What I don't understand,' she mutters, 'is why my grandson would go away without saying goodbye to me. And he didn't even take his books with him!'

'Because he is not far away,' Agnes says to herself. 'He will be back soon.'

How dull the parlour feels without him; cluttered and poorly kept, occupied only by a spinster and a widow. Rather than providing a place to rest, it offers a crushing weight of banality.

Agnes remembers leaving the police station, and how Sergeant Redmayne watched her departure with an altered manner. No doubt Simon told him the whole sorry story to gain his assistance: how she lost her father and supported the family; how the man she loved jilted her; how her sister died in the Accident; how she nearly succumbed to pneumonia two years ago.

A failing business, two scrapes with death and a legacy of fragile health. Even the police would pity a person with this history.

Agnes finds it difficult not to pity herself.

'I am going upstairs to work,' she announces.

Mamma mumbles something incoherent and stares into the fire.

Agnes touches a hand to the grandfather clock as she leaves. Papa would have helped her through this mess. In fact, Papa would have stopped all of it from happening in the first place. He was the only one who could keep Constance in check. She would never have dared to seduce Montague while their father breathed.

The stairs wail like the miserable damned as she climbs them and goes not to her studio, as she said she would, but to her bedchamber. The curtains have not been drawn back in days and discarded linen lies in heaps upon the floor. It is starting to resemble the benighted little house on Walcot Street more every day.

Agnes closes the door, sits carefully upon the bed and smooths her skirts out around her. Only then does she allow herself the luxury of tears.

Her sorrow will not fit inside the small space she has allotted to it. It is not like a fish that grows to the size of its pond; the more she tries to squash it down, the more it threatens to burst out and consume everything.

243

How she wishes she had a confidant to talk to. Miss Grayson from church and even gossipy old Miss Betts circle through her desperate mind, but they cannot be trusted with secrets. Agnes enjoyed the company of her peers in her younger days – where have they all gone? It was not easy to keep friends, with Constance as a sister. Her jealousy became a problem. Agnes's playmates would suffer 'mishaps', mysterious nips and burns until they eventually stopped calling at the house altogether.

The only female Agnes has spoken to with something approaching honesty since the Accident is young Pearl. Constance would have been jealous of her, too.

Of course there is still Simon, infallible Simon, but she can hardly weep for Montague's fate in front of him.

The tears show no sign of abating. Her head throbs with the pressure of them. She places a handkerchief over her mouth to stifle the sound of her gulps. Did Montague ever think of her with regret? He died a lingering death overseas. There would have been enough time for him to write her a line and say goodbye – but of course, he had no guarantee that she was still living in Orange Grove. He did not know about Cedric, or about the Accident. He had been so ashamed of himself that he had cut off all connections. He seemed to believe that the only way for the family to carry on was if he disappeared entirely.

Agnes never had the chance to say that she forgave him. She was hurt, of course, and incandescent with rage for a time. But he was not the first person unable to fight against Constance's will. She had a way of making you do things.

For all his flaws, Montague was a good man at heart. Cedric is the last whisper of his name. But *where* is he? Who would take him?

Teardrops spot the dark material of her bodice, each a tiny, bloodless bullet hole. Agnes scrubs at her eyes with the handkerchief. She has gone through so many of them lately that she's been forced to use Constance's old ones; she has picked the initials out but the ghost of the letter C still marks the corner.

Throwing her used handkerchief onto the heap of dirtied linen, she stands and goes to the press to fetch a new gown.

Her press is far better appointed than Pearl's wardrobe: floral-scented with a variety of shelves and hooks. Neatly folded stacks of jet clothing line up before her. Though there is scarcely any change in the hue, the material alters: poplin, coarse wool, smooth bombazine. Her fingers trail over each, selecting none. Instead she bends to the bottom shelf.

Constance's dresses have not been disturbed in years. On top lies a royal blue gown made from Henrietta cloth. Dust has turned it the colour of the sky on a cloudy summer's day. Underneath, better preserved, is crimson silk trimmed with black braid. Agnes pulls it out, holds it up before her.

She can move the gown, make it sway as if inhabited, but she cannot imagine herself wearing it. Nothing about the dress says *Agnes*.

Yet if it comes to that … What in her life truly does feel like her own, these days? There is no point left in being Agnes; there is so little to her.

Mechanically, she removes her tear-stained mourning gown and fastens herself into the crimson. It fits. She is surprised: Constance's clothes always used to be too long and tight for her.

Before donning gloves, she considers her hands. Veins rise beneath the fragile skin. Her nails are overgrown. The only vestige of beauty left is the gold band on her third finger and the glint of its small gem.

After all this time, the ring is difficult to remove; it jams around her swollen knuckle, but Agnes tugs, ignoring the pain, until it slides free.

What a tiny item of jewellery it is, to hold all the promises and hopes she bound up in it. She takes her reticule off the dressing table and drops the ring gently inside. Technically, the ring belongs to her, but *he* chose it and purchased it. It shall have to suffice. She has nothing else.

Misery still hovers over her head, but at least she feels like a different, more collected woman as she heads downstairs and walks out of the front door without bidding farewell to her mother.

The churchyard heaves with sedan chairs and it does not take long to lose herself in the crowds. There is an array of hats: proud toppers, low caps that cover the eyebrows and an aviary of decorated bonnets. Beneath them, most of the faces look cold and frustrated by their lack of progress. Each individual has become absorbed into the swarm: moving slowly forward with one accord, like a colony of ants, none acting of their own volition.

As Agnes shuffles towards Cheap Street, the feet walking in front of her own slow and then come to a complete stop. Standing on tiptoes, she perceives some movement up ahead: dark plumes wafting to and fro. When the men remove their hats and hold them to their chests, the reason for all this congestion becomes apparent: a funeral cortege is slithering through the streets.

To meet a hearse is bad luck. Instinctively, Agnes's hand seeks a button to hold for protection, but this is not her own gown and she cannot find one.

Respectful silence falls across the crowd. Only the clop of hooves echoes, like the beat of a failing heart. The deceased must have been a person of some standing.

A tall, thin mute heads the procession carrying a staff swathed in crêpe. There are so many black hand-kerchiefs fluttering behind him that they resemble wings, wafting the creature along. But of course that is not the real means of impetus: each carriage is pulled

247

by a quartet of ebony horses crowned with ostrich feathers. On their backs, black-clad postilions ride without expression on the solemn road towards the grave.

The glass hearse displays a coffin suffocating in lilies. It travels feet first so that its occupant cannot look back and beckon others to follow.

Yet they *do* follow: mourners trail wearily behind on foot and the family creep along in their own elaborate carriage. They have not pulled the curtains for privacy. Each stricken and contorted countenance is on view.

Agnes knows she should lower her eyes in consideration of the family's pain, but she does not; no one does. Everybody peers into the carriage, eager to see the mark death has left on those it passed so closely by.

One of the passengers is an upright gentleman with salt-and-pepper hair. A moustache obscures his mouth, but she can tell he is clenching it tight in an effort to appear composed. It only serves to make him look like he is being throttled. His lost, dazed children stare at the streets, and an older girl …

Agnes's mouth falls open.

That girl.

The carriage crawls so slowly that she can take a second glance, and even a third, but none of them prove her wrong.

She knows those loose blonde curls and that habitual pout. The slope of the slender shoulders is not caused by dejection; it is there whether the girl sits in a chair or dawdles through the churchyard carrying a package, which she then drops.

The girl travelling in the funeral carriage is none other than Lavinia Campbell.

CHAPTER 25

Dusk falls earlier every day. They're pushing towards full winter now and Pearl yearns for it: the gentle gloaming against her eyes and hopefully more snow to soothe her heated limbs. Her skin prickles, seems to crackle with its fever.

Outside, wind slips between the limestone houses. She imagines stepping into it: feeling the cold currents strike her face and lift the hair from the back of her neck. This doesn't have to be a dream; it's possible. All she needs to do is don the outfit that rests upon her lap.

Pearl's started to do this every night: take out the carpet bag and sit waiting for bravery to possess her, like the ghosts do, so she can put on the boy's clothes and follow the map. But it turns out bravery is the hardest spirit of them all to catch. She calls and calls, yet it doesn't come.

Her body's so tired. Though it's ready to give up, her mind isn't. She hasn't forgotten Myrtle's words about how useless she is, and she's determined to prove her sister wrong eventually. She'll do *something* to help.

The clothes don't smell like they belong to a boy. The men who touched Florence King were scented with tobacco, wine and bear's grease, but Agnes's nephew has his own musty perfume.

Gingerly, she unfolds the shirt and unfastens a button.

Just that daring makes her head spin.

Not yet. Not quite yet ...

Something rattles against the window. Pearl gasps and draws the clothes towards her chest.

She knows who it is: the murderer. He's come for her at last.

Tap, tap.

It starts as a note played by one finger but then it is a hand, maybe two, patting the glass, seeking admittance.

The killer can't reach her, can he? He'd need to break through the glass. And if he did she could run into the next room, screaming for Myrtle.

She puts down the clothes and takes a deep, steadying breath. This is what Myrtle was talking about: she needs to face up to things, not run away.

She crawls on all fours, very slowly, towards the window. When she gets there, she sits on her haunches and reaches a shaking hand towards the curtain. He can't, he *can't* get to her through the window.

The frantic tapping carries on.

Here comes the faintest whisper of what she's been waiting for: courage. It allows her to clench her teeth and flick back the corner of the curtain.

A white face is pressed against the glass.

It takes her a moment to recognise the bird-like features of Agnes.

Agnes, come back to help her!

All at once Pearl is on her feet, pushing up the sash. The cool wind that she craved reaches in and strokes her forehead.

Agnes's small hand clamps on her wrist; even through her glove, it feels cold. 'Please let me in. Your neighbours will think me a housebreaker if they see me out here.' She really *does* look like a desperate woman, with strands of hair escaping from under her wind-blown hat and her papery, fluttering eyelids.

Pearl glances down the street to check no one is abroad and then helps Agnes scramble gracelessly over the sill.

'I thought you weren't coming back!'

'Forgive me, I ...' Agnes's voice cracks.

'Why are you so cold?' she whispers.

Agnes slides the sash closed. 'I have been walking the streets for hours. Searching ...' She swallows audibly. 'I have lost something very precious to me.'

Pearl doesn't know what to say. Her head's full of her own troubles. She so needs Agnes to be solid and comforting. 'I'm sorry. But my father's worse. Much worse. I nearly put these clothes on to come and find you.'

The carpet bag and Cedric's shirt lie on the floor. Agnes covers her mouth and stifles a sob at the sight of them.

'What is it?'

Agnes picks the shirt up tenderly. Pressing it to her face, she inhales, as Pearl has often done.

'Has … has something happened to your nephew?'

'I cannot find him. He is … Oh, sweet child! So many terrible events have occurred since last we spoke. It does me good to see your face.'

Pearl's taken aback. She doesn't know Agnes well enough for her to say these things, but she understands the lady's scared and grieving too. Mourners come out with some odd sentiments. It's not their fault, really.

'I need your help,' Pearl emphasises. 'I know we haven't found the killer yet, and I haven't got a chance to speak to my mother, but Father's that sick, I think we just need to—'

Agnes places a finger on her lips. 'One more. One more séance and you will have your reward.' Her mouth twists. 'How naïve we were. Believing we could track down a murderer with the help of ghosts. And what did we get? A few garbled messages and some shadows. Did we really think we were going to challenge the police with *that*?'

'We only tried the once,' Pearl says defensively. 'And I'm still new to this.'

'Hush, dear. I am not blaming you. Only myself. I was never strong enough to be trusted with so much,

253

alone.' She shakes her head. 'Papa should have known that.'

Pearl shifts uncomfortably. She thought seeing Agnes again would be a cause for joy, but there's something funny about her, like her attention's fixed on a tune no one else can hear. Why's she talking about her papa, now? It's *Pearl*'s father who needs help.

'Is that who you want to talk to? Your papa?'

Agnes reaches into her reticule and produces something shiny. It's gold: a ring.

'No,' she says. 'There's someone else I need to speak with, one last time.'

CHAPTER 26

They have barely seated themselves on the dirty floor-boards upstairs before Agnes starts to see hints of the celestial about Pearl. Undoubtedly, the girl's power is growing stronger.

Agnes has not yet mentioned how Montague died, but already the child has taken on a yellowish tinge that reaches to the whites of her eyes.

His spirit is surfacing beneath.

Will he be as the others were, caught in the moment of his death? He had his faults, but it is too cruel to imagine him suffering the sweats of yellow fever throughout eternity.

'Tell me about him,' Pearl says.

Agnes places her engagement ring on the floor between them. 'His name was Montague. John Augustus Montague. Captain of a ship called the *Raptor*. This ring was … was a gift he gave, once.'

Pearl picks up the ring and inspects it. She is frowning, as if she has heard these names somewhere before.

Even as Agnes gazes at her hungrily, waiting for something to emerge, she's conscious of nerves. She has dreamt of Montague, fixated upon him for so many years now. She ought to have prepared what she was going to say to him.

One thing she *does* know: 'Knocks on wood will not suffice for this séance. Montague must be able to answer me.'

Pearl turns the ring over. Her pupils fatten in the darkness. 'But I don't want him to possess me. I hate the spirits using my mouth.'

Once again Agnes sees the wisps of them, teasing at the girl's edges. She plays the only card she has. 'For your father, Pearl. Think of *his* mouth.'

Pearl screws up her face. When she breathes, it comes out like mist. 'A ghost called Florence King used to speak to Myrtle inside her head. Then she'd tell me what Florence had said. Would something like that do for you?'

A flush creeps into Agnes's cheeks. There is bound to be some mortifying content to this conversation; she would prefer if Pearl *was* possessed, absent, and heard nothing of it. She takes the ring back. 'I could go to other spirit mediums,' she bluffs.

Pearl's too sharp to fall for it. 'Not for free, you can't.'

Agnes sighs. What a pass she has come to when she is the lesser power, the weaker link, even when pitted against a child.

256

'Very well. We shall just have to see what Captain Montague chooses to do.'

There is a snag of tension as they join hands, neither of them fully satisfied with the other. Montague's ring is pressed between their palms.

Pearl closes her eyes. 'John Augustus Montague,' she repeats.

There is a pause.

Agnes cannot bear the suspense. 'Are you there?' she whispers, but silence reigns.

What if he does not come? What if he jilts her, again?

Her face begins to tingle. She has the strangest sensation, as if threads are being drawn out from the pores of her skin. Every jagged sound of the day, from the hoof beats of the funeral procession to her fruitless cries of Cedric's name, seems to build to a crescendo inside her head.

'Please, Montague. Please.'

Suddenly, the fireplace springs to life.

The flames burn higher than last time. She can taste their smoke, but there are no shapes dancing on the wall like before. Only a single patch of black appears upon the floorboards.

Pearl makes no movement; she looks cataleptic. Whatever is taking place, she is not a conscious agent in its production.

The dark blot stretches across the room and touches the skirts of their gowns. For a moment it wavers there, then the umbra spreads and begins to take form.

257

Agnes knows what it will be; she has stared at it often enough. The shadow is assuming the outline of Montague's silhouette.

'Pearl! Pearl, can you hear him?' she hisses.

Pearl gives no response.

She can't breathe. The shade is life-size. Bigger, perhaps. Growing. She closes her eyes.

'H-h-hello?' The voice is faint and close to her ear. It fizzes through her veins. But these are not the words of endearment he once muttered; he sounds confused and afraid. 'Hello?'

'Montague,' she breathes.

'Where … Who …'

She promised herself she would not cry, yet the tears are already flowing. 'Oh, Montague. Don't you recognise me?'

A pause. The fire cracks.

'Agnes?'

'Yes!'

There is no immediate response. All she can hear is the rustle and snap of flames. Carefully, she opens her eyes. The shadow remains on the floor. She wants to reach out and touch it, but that would break the circle and he might disappear.

'Will you not speak to me?' she pleads.

The words come muffled and incoherent. She can only catch at odd ones: '… must … not safe … She … watches you.'

This is how Mamma must feel, listening through her ear trumpet. Agnes groans in frustration.

'Montague, I have so much to tell you! You do not even know ...' She looks helplessly at Pearl, but the girl is clearly going to be of no use in communicating. She takes a breath, tries to focus on the most important thing. 'You had a son, John. A lovely boy. The spit of you.' Tears force her to break off. 'He is missing. I thought you could help me find him. I thought ...'

Something bumps downstairs. For an instant, she worries it might be Miss West, but then Montague fades in again.

'... here ... together ... We ... held ... but she ...' Nothing animates the silhouette; its lips do not move when Montague speaks. It is disconcerting, for the voice that comes through the interference is ardent; even panicked.

'I cannot understand you! What are you trying to say to me?'

Knock, knock.

Agnes flinches. It is the sound that came at the last séance, but what did it mean? Memory fails her; all that strikes her is how ominous it sounds.

Montague's voice pitches higher. 'Marry ... Carfax ... keep ... safe.'

'What?' She frowns. 'It was *Constance* who married Simon. She made the poor man miserable, but it was the only way to save our name. You cannot think that I would—'

'... takes over ... unaware ... But if Carfax ... husband ... protect you.'

259

She feels like a piece of sable paper, being snipped to pieces. It sounds as if he is telling her to *marry* Simon. A wave of hurt and rejection hits her. After so much time, can *that* be all he has to say?

Knock, knock.

The shadow flutters.

'Montague, are you still there?'

Knock.

'You cannot think I would marry another ... I never loved anyone but you!' The confession bursts out of her. 'Despite everything. If you had not run away like that, perhaps we ...'

His shape is quivering wildly now, threatening to break apart. Thin black lines creep like fingers across the image.

She shoots an anxious glance at the fireplace. The flames are dipping and swooping, roaring louder than ever; their spitting seems to fill her ears, censoring anything he might say.

Then a single, terrified sentence breaks through.

'She's coming.'

'Montague!' Agnes flings out her left hand to clutch at him; the ring flies with it, clatters somewhere.

Montague's shadow starts to trickle away.

She sees Pearl's empty fingers droop to her side and realises, too late, that she has broken the circle. She is losing him.

'No. No, come back!'

She snatches up Pearl's hand again, but it is no good: the damage is done. The flames dwindle faster every second.

'Montague!'

The fire sputters and dies.

The sudden darkness is like the shutting of an eye.

He is gone. Gone, again.

A painful moment passes, then Pearl comes back to life with a gasp. 'What? What happened, where am I?'

Agnes cannot even speak.

Behind her comes the creak of wood. Something approaches.

Pearl's face turns a paler shade of white. 'Oh, no.'

Still winded, Agnes peers warily over her shoulder. Recoils.

Two malignant eyes burn above the thin glow of a rushlight.

It is Miss West. Her fury radiates through the room.

'What the hell d'you think you're doing?'

CHAPTER 27

Now she's for it.

Pearl wishes she could sink into a trance, but Myrtle's already striding across the room, puffing up dust as she goes. She grabs her by the earlobe and jerks her to her feet.

It hurts. It really hurts.

'Miss West, let me explain ...' Agnes starts.

Myrtle thrusts the rushlight holder forward. She must recognise Agnes from the first séance, because she growls, '*You.*'

'Yes, it is me, Miss Darken. Forgive my audacity, I—' She breaks off, emotional. Her cheeks are already shining with tears. 'We can discuss this between us. The child is not to blame.'

Myrtle gives Pearl's ear a twist and makes her squawk.

'Please, do not hurt her,' Agnes cries. 'It was *I* who persuaded her to hold a séance—'

'Then you owe me a bob,' Myrtle cuts in.

'I beg your pardon?'

'A shilling,' Myrtle spits. 'You use a service, you've got to pay for it. Otherwise it's stealing.'

Agnes is aghast. 'I … I do not have it.'

'Guess I'd better call the constable, then.'

Myrtle hates the police almost as much as she hates doctors, Pearl knows she'll never do it, but Agnes starts to panic, pulls out a purse and offers odd pennies and farthings on an outstretched palm.

It makes Pearl feel better to see the older woman is helpless before her sister, too. She isn't the only weakling.

Myrtle glowers at the coins for a long time. Finally, she drops Pearl and grabs them. 'It'll have to do. Now get your arse off my property.'

Pearl gasps in relief. She raises a hand to cup her smarting ear.

'Yes, of course,' Agnes blusters. 'But please do remember, it was my fault entirely—'

'I won't tell you again.'

Shooting an apologetic glance at Pearl, Agnes hurries out of the door.

They hear her stumbling down the stairs in the dark.

Pearl looks at her feet; it seems the safest place. Panic's crashing inside her head, but maybe the money will calm Myrtle down, maybe she won't be furious enough to … what? She doesn't even know what Myrtle will do. She's never crossed her this badly before.

263

'You ungrateful little bitch,' she snarls.

Pearl can't utter a word.

'All I've done for you, and here you are, stealing bread out of my very mouth.' When Myrtle's in a good mood, her voice can cradle you. Right now it sounds like smashing crockery. 'Get down those stairs. Now.'

Pearl's legs are weaker than water. She lurches, rather than walks, but Myrtle comes up behind her and the motion of her sister's knees against her back seems to push her on.

She should've known it would turn out this way. She's never been good at lying or sneaking about. As she totters into the darkened hallway, she has an urge to follow in Agnes's steps and flee out of the front door. But she's not strong enough to run, and she can't leave Father.

Father …

'Go on, then,' Myrtle demands. 'Explain yourself.'

If ever there was a time Pearl wished a ghost would take over and speak for her, it's now. But of course they don't; they're never there when she needs them.

'It was just … She wanted to find the murderer. And I thought—'

Myrtle groans. 'We've talked about this before. Don't you want to earn your living?'

'We'd be popular if we caught a murderer,' she mumbles. 'It's not just ghosts that interest people.'

'No, that's right. People pay to see albinos too. Maybe I'll just put you in a cage, and we can have a menagerie instead of a séance? Is that what you want? Is it?'

Pearl shakes her head.

'How the hell did that woman even get in here?'

'I … It was when you were out …'

Myrtle's lustrous eyes spark in the shadows. 'You *opened* the door?'

It's useless. She hasn't got the words to defend herself; she doesn't even deserve them. She knew all along that she was being wicked and she did it anyway.

'I'm sorry,' she pleads.

Myrtle puffs out the rushlight. Neither of them need it. 'I should've known,' she seethes. 'You're just like your dad: out to spite me. Going under my nose, in my own house. I don't know why I bother with you. Maybe I should've left you with the cord tied around your neck.'

Pearl shrinks within herself. 'I'm sorry.'

'But *why*, Pearl? Why would you do this? Just to pull the wool over my eyes and punish me for saying I weren't going to mesmerise him no more?'

It's on the tip of her tongue to tell Myrtle about the doctor and the jawbone but something holds her back. She's in enough trouble already, without mentioning medicine.

Seeing Pearl isn't going to answer, Myrtle starts to mutter to herself. 'I didn't think you could do this. Didn't think you even *capable* of … I messed up. What did I do wrong?'

265

This stings worst of all. Myrtle's not just mad, she's ashamed of her; thinks she's raised a thankless wretch, but Pearl was never *trying* to hurt her sister – was she?

Leaning against the wall, she starts to cry.

'Save me the waterworks,' Myrtle tuts.

She can't. She's too weak and ill, and still so *hot*.

It's all right for Agnes, who can just peg it and get away. All Pearl's ever known is contained inside this house. Father and Myrtle. That's it. All she's got. One's dying, and the other one hates her.

'You wouldn't ...' she sobs. The words don't want to come out. 'I never would have ... But you wouldn't ... help ... me.'

'What are you on about now?'

'Mother!' she bursts out.

The fetid, stale air rings with her cry.

Myrtle grabs her wrist and pulls her away from the wall. 'Don't you dare.'

'I only ... did it because she ... she promised me ... She said we could try and ... talk to ... Mother.'

Myrtle's face twists into something cruel. 'And did you, Pearl? Did you and your little friend manage to call her back?'

Pearl catches her breath. She shakes her head miserably. 'We had to do her ghosts first. Both times. She never let me.'

'But you found the murderer, right?'

'No ... I don't think so. She wanted to talk to some sailor.'

Myrtle scoffs. 'Oh, I bet she did. Don't you see? That woman is trouble. She used you, you dolt.'

It bursts upon her like Mr Collins's powder: the same agonising flash.

Agnes only talked about her sister, her papa, and the man who gave her the ring. She brushed off Pearl's concerns about Father tonight and got all snotty when she mentioned the killer.

Agnes was never going to help anyone. It was all lies.

At last, her weak legs give out. Myrtle catches her, lets her sob against her nightgown.

Berries. She still smells of berries and violets.

'I told you,' Myrtle speaks hoarsely into her ear. 'You can't trust no one. Got it?'

Her head hurts too much to nod.

She's such an idiot. How could she *ever* think she knew better than Myrtle, strong Myrtle who lifts her up and carries her all the way to her room?

The curtains are still open from where Agnes climbed in. The carpet bag and shirt lie on the floor. Myrtle kicks them out of the way.

'Get some sleep.' She plonks Pearl ungracefully on the bed. 'You've got more work to do tomorrow. Proper work.'

The pillow is blissfully cool against her hot face. She feels like she could sleep for years. Never venture out of this bed or her place again.

Myrtle turns her back on her and crosses the small room. For a minute Pearl thinks she's going to close

267

the curtains and save her from the glare of the street lamp, but she doesn't; she picks up the pair of green glasses, which Pearl had taken off when it got dark.

'You'll get these back when you deserve them,' she says.

Then she leaves Pearl all alone.

CHAPTER 28

'Slow down, Miss Darken. Tell me again who is at risk?'

Simon spreads his hands on his desk and leans towards her. Agnes finds herself regarding him anew, after Montague's words. He was never *handsome*, even in his youth, but he does have a trustworthy, open face and real solicitude in his gaze.

She cannot see his blue eyes without calling to mind those of Constance. Hers were fringed with long lashes, intelligent in expression but cruel, savouring another's misery. Simon's could not be more different. They are lighter and small, yet there is a depth to them that few people possess.

'I have made such a muddle of everything,' she confesses. 'Worse than that. I have caused harm to others. But you see, I was not thinking straight. How could I, over these last few months?'

'Never mind that. I know better than anyone how severely you have been tried. Just tell me what happened. You know you can always talk to me.'

There is not much left of his brown hair. A belly protrudes beneath his waistcoat, but she must admit that both these signs of age rather suit him. *She* has altered physically, and he has never treated her the slightest bit differently.

'I am afraid you will be displeased with me.'

'I could never truly be displeased with *you*, Miss Darken.'

Dear Simon. Montague seemed to imply that he was the proper match for her. Can it be true? Simon is not the type of man she envisaged for herself, but perhaps real love is not all romance; perhaps it is friendship and a dogged devotion that stands the test of time.

'You are kind to say so, but I am conscious of doing wrong. You advised me as a physician and a friend, and I deliberately went against you.'

Despite his assurances of forgiveness, annoyance flits across his face. Perhaps annoyance is too strong a word; it is more like a shifting: Simon making room for some new disappointment he must deal with.

What an irritant she has been to him. She irritates *herself*, with her caprices and violent mood swings. Truly, this man has been a saint to endure her for so long.

'I am sorry, Simon. The uncertainty ate away at me. I needed to be *doing* something, and I ... I called upon a spirit medium.'

Rather than brave his gaze, she concentrates on the dark brown and beige damask on the walls. Under consideration, it is not so *very* dull a pattern; there is a stolid respectability to it, much like the occupant himself.

Simon's breath pours out. Morpheus, who is keeping aloof today, grunts from the corner.

'I see. I ...' Simon picks up a dry pen and fiddles nervously with it. She wonders if he is remembering those plundered Edinburgh graves. 'I advised you against that practice for some very specific reasons,' he says in his professional voice. 'Foremost, I consider it a trick, but that is not my only objection. It is the ... exposing of the mind, if you will. Those women give themselves over to a suspension of common sense. They encourage nervous agitation. No doubt there is a feeling of freedom to it all, but surrender of conscious control is not ... something I would wish for you. Your health has never recovered from the pneumonia. It should not be tested in any fashion.'

She considers telling him what she has seen at the séances and decides it is better not to. It is one of those phenomena a person must experience for themselves.

'You had my best interests at heart, as you always do, Simon. The elder of the women involved is indeed a grasping, mercenary thing, full of affectation. But the medium herself ... She's a child, an innocent child, and I have caused her such trouble.'

'How so?'

Her cheeks warm to recount the circumstances. She will exclude the part where she climbed in through the window, if she possibly can. 'Oh, Simon. You will hardly credit how foolish I have been. I could not afford the fee for a séance, but I thought I might get some clue, something to help me find Cedric ... So I persuaded the little medium to see me in private without her sister's knowledge. We were caught and I am so afraid that the girl will be treated unkindly for my error.'

'I see.' Simon turns the pen in his fingers. 'That is most ... regrettable. Yet I suppose the child *did* disobey her guardian, and must be punished as she sees fit. Distasteful to the feelings as it is, we have no right to interfere ...'

'The sister is *not* her legal guardian, though. The child has a father living. Do you recall me mentioning a man with phossy jaw?'

His forehead wrinkles. 'We ... spoke around the topic, I believe.'

'And that is another blunder I have made.' She makes a steeple of her hands and leans her nose against it. This whole conversation is an exercise in mortification. 'Forgive me, Simon. It is not only strangers I have caught up in this mess. I may have implied that ... you ... might operate upon him ... in return for the child's services.'

Simon presses his lips firmly together.

'It was rash of me, I know. I cannot defend it, Simon, I can only apologise. There are times when I am not ... collected. How can I be? The police do nothing, they have not even caught Mr Boyle's killer yet, and I am expected to trust them with finding poor Cedric! I hear of such clever detectives in London, but here they do not see what is right before their eyes. I *am* being watched, Simon. Just the other day I stumbled upon the funeral for another one of my clients.'

'No.' Simon shakes his head, lays the pen back on the desk. 'That is not being investigated as murder. The police believe Mrs Campbell tripped and fell onto the railway tracks in front of a train. There is no evidence of anyone pushing her.' Seeing her astonishment, he goes on: '*I* have been watching you, Miss Darken. Whatever you might think, I did take your claims seriously. I heard through a patient of mine that Mrs Campbell intended to have her silhouette painted by you, and I have made sure to keep an eye on the Campbell family ever since.' He folds one leg over the other, making his leather chair squeak. 'The police are not quite as dull as you esteem them. I have spent a good deal of time answering their questions on your behalf. The crime scenes were evidently left by a person of some intelligence. Sergeant Redmayne believes the culprit may have had practise with this sort of thing – concealing the time and method of death, and so on.'

'But the police do not know the full extent of my involvement: we never told them of my connection to Ned or Commander Hargreaves. They have no idea I took both men's silhouettes.'

'True. And it is advisable to keep them in ignorance. That information cannot reflect well upon you.'

She throws up her hands in frustration. 'But they might be able to discover *why* this killer targets people close to me, and why on earth they would take Cedric! I have thought it over and over and it makes no sense. The only *possible* person with a claim on him is ... well, you told me yourself, he is deceased. So unless we are proposing that a *ghost* is behind this ... Are you sure I should not give the sergeant the notes I came across?'

Simon bites a fingernail. 'No. No, I believe those notes may have been old, immaterial scraps that turned up by coincidence. You said that you found one in Cedric's coat?'

'You know I did, I showed it to you.'

'Yes. Well. The writing that *I* saw ... on the note you showed me ... That belonged to someone else. Someone we both knew, Miss Darken.'

'Who?'

'It was the hand of ... my wife.'

Constance.

He is right. Memory dawns on her, sickening but irrefutable. *That* is why she recognised the writing. Constance has been gone so long, she did not think to associate the notes with her. 'But how—'

'There was not much love lost between the pair, I grant you, but Constance *was* Cedric's mother. Do you not consider it feasible that he might have chosen to keep a small memento of her about his person?'

It seems unlikely. Cedric was mainly frightened of his mother. But then Agnes *had* suspected him of playing with her papers on the day she found the first scrap. Perhaps there is some vestige of feeling left inside the boy that she cannot understand. It makes more sense than any other explanation.

Simon is so overwhelmingly *reasonable*.

Yet Simon does not know about the writing in the dust at Walcot Street. *Too late.* Was that from Constance, too?

She shivers the thought away. Does not want to face the possibility that in trying to contact other spirits, she might have accidently let her sister back into her life.

Simon's theory is far more comforting.

'Yes,' she says forcefully. 'Cedric *might* have kept a token. Yes. I am sure everything is ... just as you say it is, Simon.'

'Then that is settled.' He musters a hairbreadth smile. 'Nothing more to trouble the police with for the present. Now, will you stay for dinner, or shall I walk you home?'

'You have done so much for me already. For all of us. It pains me to beg another favour, but do you think that you could take a look at this man? The one with phossy jaw?'

He hesitates.

'Please. I have failed to protect my nephew. It would be so nice to help just *one* young person, to put *something* right. I do not want the medium girl to be orphaned. When I think of what it cost me to lose my own father, I—'

Morpheus sits up and yawns. He is ready to leave the room; he seems to know what his master will decide to do.

'This man is not under the treatment of another physician?' Simon asks.

'No! The elder sister will not allow it. The poor soul is being kept from all aid.'

Simon gives a single nod.

She *does* love him then: his goodness and his justice, even his silly dog, who is regarding her judgementally.

'Just promise me,' he says as he stands, 'that this will be an end of your spiritual adventures. Have a care for your health. Stay away from newfangled concepts that you do not understand.'

Remembering Constance's writing in the dust, it is not hard to make the pledge.

'I will, Simon. I will do whatever you tell me to.'

He offers her his arm and they walk out of the consulting room together with Morpheus trailing behind them.

———

Rain lashes the pavements. A couple of young ladies without an umbrella shriek and run for the cover of the nearest awning. Morpheus stops on the doorstep, takes one look at the drops bouncing off the puddles and turns tail back inside.

'A wise choice, I think,' says Simon, closing the door on his dog. He erects their umbrella – one of the old sort, with cane ribs.

Agnes lifts her skirts from the damp. Cedric must be out here, somewhere. Is he sheltered and dry? She worries that her stitches in his coat might not hold, and if he gets wet, he will not be able to change his shoes and hose before a fire. He could catch pneumonia like she did.

She searches for his face under every dripping hat and in every saturated alley.

They walk slowly beneath their shared dome, the patter of rain upon oiled silk making up all their conversation. Simon takes the side of the pavement nearest the road and moves heavily, a man burdened with other people's secrets, while dray carts swish down Broad Street and splatter his leg with mud. Still, it is better to take this longer, more crowded route than brave the slippery hill.

The damp resurrects Agnes's old aches and pains. She will not, she *must* not think of the Accident. She squeezes Simon's arm – the same arm that lifted her from the river, all those years ago.

As they round St Michael's church and turn into Walcot Street, the fresh, moist smell of the rain takes its last breath. Here, the odour of hops rules the air.

Commerce does not stop for the weather. A determined organ grinder turns his crank, playing the shanty 'Little Billie'. Agnes pulls Simon towards a chemist's shop. The windows have steamed and the prices chalked on the slate board outside are washing away.

'It may be prudent to wait for the sister to leave the house,' she advises him, although she does not relish the prospect of waiting in the rain.

'How do you know she has not gone already?'

Agnes gestures to the waistcoat pocket in which Simon keeps his fob watch. He produces it, shows her the time. She shakes her head. She has observed this house, knows its routines.

'It needs some ten minutes more,' she decides.

Simon peers through the misty windows at the array of glass bottles the chemist has on offer. 'Perhaps I will call inside. If this man is as bad as you say, he will need something to alleviate his pain.'

Resisting his entreaties to join him, Agnes takes charge of the umbrella and keeps surveillance on the house.

From this distance it looks pedestrian, blending in seamlessly amongst its limestone companions. No passer-by would suspect that ghouls swarm inside. It is a kind of ossuary, she thinks, holding captive the bones of an albino child and a man with phossy jaw. This is what her beautiful city has come to: the beau monde and the dandies have fled, leaving only the spinsters, the soot and the ghosts behind.

She tucks a damp strand of hair behind her ear, and notices with a jolt that her left hand is bare of all jewellery. Of course, Montague's ring must still be on the floor where it fell in the upstairs room; she did not have time to collect it before Miss West threw her out. She has worn the ring on her finger for all these years; it seems strange that she did not miss it until now. Perhaps hearing Montague's voice at the séance is finally helping her to move on. But she would feel better if she knew what had made his spirit so afraid. Or who. What were his last words? *She's coming.* Was he referring to Miss West, on the stairs? Or was he trying to tell her that the killer is in fact a female?

Agnes cannot ask him now. She has promised Simon.

Finally, the front door opens. Agnes turns to the side, letting her bonnet shield her face, and dips the umbrella a little lower. She is right to do so. Miss West leans out, casting her suspicious eyes up and down the street.

Satisfied, she calls over her shoulder – probably a warning to Pearl – and leaves the house. But then she performs an action Agnes has not noticed her take before: she turns and locks the door behind her.

'Chestnuts all hot, penny a score!'

Miss West walks straight past the man hollering his wares and weaves effortlessly around a costermonger's barrow. She has only a bonnet to cover her, but she does not bow her head under the rain. This is a woman who knows where she is going and will not let anything stop her from getting there.

Agnes watches her stride off towards Cornwell Buildings, where she is swallowed in a forest of umbrellas.

The shop bell jangles behind her. Simon emerges from the chemist's with a bottle and a brown-paper parcel.

'The sister has departed,' she tells him. 'We must move quickly.'

A boy does his best to sweep a path for them across the road and Simon tosses him a penny.

The rain has failed to wash the sooty fingerprints from the window of Pearl's house, but Simon is able to read the advertising cards aloud.

New and scientific treatment
The Magnetic Touch for chronic disease
No medicine given
No pain caused

The White Sylph
Conductress of Spirits
Blessed with the gift of trance-mediumship
Enquire within

He raises an eyebrow at Agnes.

'It is hardly Pearl's doing,' she points out and knocks at the door.

There is no answer.

The rain intensifies, running out of the eaves in great torrents. Agnes knocks again and again.

'Pearl,' she calls. 'Pearl, it's me. Agnes. Do not be afraid, dear. I have brought the doctor.'

'Perhaps she does not wish to see us,' Simon surmises.

'She is afraid of her sister,' Agnes corrects him, knocking until her knuckles hurt. 'Either that or ... Oh, Simon, you do not suppose Miss West has beaten the child? Perhaps she *cannot* answer the door.'

Simon bites his lip. The crowd on the pavement has thinned; even the street sellers are seeking cover now. He glances around, then hands Agnes his medicines. She takes them awkwardly, juggling the umbrella.

'Stand back.'

Raising a foot, he kicks open the door.

It is a cheap thing with a paltry lock but all the same, Agnes is surprised by how quickly it yields. She hears a gasp from inside as the door bangs back against the inner wall.

No one on the street remarks or cares.

'After you, Miss Darken.'

She passes him the umbrella to disassemble and enters the house, where acrid fumes replace the damp street smells. If she had her hands free, she would pull out her handkerchief and cover her nose.

Her vision takes a moment to adjust to the unnatural gloom; it is only when Simon closes the front door and squelches in after her that she discerns Pearl, hovering at the end of the hallway with all the fragility of a moth.

281

Her pinched face is wary, unsure.

Agnes cannot make out any bruises, but the child does look ill-conditioned. Her once alabaster skin appears jaundiced and her wrists look thin enough to snap.

An arrow of guilt quivers in Agnes's heart.

'Look, dear,' she croons, holding up Simon's purchases. 'We have brought medicine.'

The girl regards them the same way Agnes inspected the cabinet and the crystal ball on her first visit.

'You're … not meant to be here,' Pearl croaks at last.

Simon comes forward, past Agnes, but still leaving a comfortable distance between himself and the girl. Puffing, he bends down to her height. If he is surprised to see an albino child, he does not show it.

'Forgive the intrusion, Miss …'

'Meers.'

'Miss Meers. My name is Dr Carfax. I understand that your father is very unwell and I should like to help him, if I can.'

Pearl looks at her feet, scuffs one against the floor. The struggle is plain on her face. The poor child wants to trust Simon, but all her education – or rather her indoctrination – tells her not to.

'Myrtle says your medicine's poison.'

'Phosphorus can be a poison,' Simon counters. He is trying to be amiable to gain Pearl's confidence, but Agnes knows him well and can hear the concern in his voice. He is grieved by the sight of this waif she has

282

produced. 'That is the substance your father used, to make matches for his employer. The phosphorus has hurt his mouth.'

'We give him magnetised water to drink. Myrtle's going to exchange his bad energy with hers. She's strong, she's got the vit – vite – *vitality*.'

'Good. That's good.' He balls a hand by his side, the only indication of his outrage. 'Miss Meers, I would like to take a look at your father and see how he gets along. I will not hurt him, I promise. I will not administer any medicine or even touch him, if you do not wish it.'

The little body retracts like a concertina. 'He did say ... he always wanted to see another doctor. But Myrtle wouldn't let him, after the first one sent us here to Bath ...'

Simon nods, rises awkwardly to his feet and offers her his hand. Pearl accepts it like something that might burn her.

Agnes trails them into a chamber at the end of the corridor, which is about the size of a small parlour – an innocent-looking room to be the source of the rot she has smelt since the first day she entered the house. The stink here is not just humming but festering, choking the breath from her.

'Miss Darken, this is not a sight that—' Simon begins.

She wonders what end he intended to put to that sentence, for there is not a word adequate to describe what lies before her. That is cruel; she should say *who* lies before her, but in all honesty she is struggling to identify the person on the narrow bed.

He is too horrible to concentrate on for any length of time. The wasted, skeletal body she can just about stomach, but the lower half of his face is dribble, corroded flesh and gaps where no gaps ought to be. Perhaps the worst circumstance is that his eyes, nose and forehead all look perfectly regular. It is only below them that he becomes a puppet with a wide, oozing grin, the teeth poking out at angles.

Has such a spectacle been a normal, everyday sight for a young girl like Pearl?

'I will help,' she murmurs, hardly knowing how.

Of course Simon is more practised. 'Mr Meers?' he asks, approaching the bed. 'My name is Dr Carfax. With your consent, I should like to examine your jaw.'

The man blinks, struggles to focus. When at last his brain registers who Simon is, he gives an approximation of a nod. One atrophied hand motions to his face. The gesture is crude, but understood. *Cut it out.*

Simon takes a breath. 'Miss Meers, it would help my inspection to clean the area a little. I will use only soda, perhaps a touch of alkaline if necessary. Is this acceptable to you?'

Pearl wavers but her Father's pleading eyes get the better of her.

'If he wants it.'

'Miss Darken?'

284

Agnes realises Simon is asking her for the packages, and she begins to unwrap them for him. Her hands shake. She has never seen anything quite equal to this.

'The necrosis is advanced,' Simon whispers to her as she hands him his apparatus. 'The abscesses on the gums have not even been lanced.' He turns to Pearl, in the corner. 'Miss Meers, it is conceivable this will cause your father some discomfort. Perhaps you might hold his hand?'

Pearl plaits the gaunt fingers between her own small, pale ones. 'You're brave, Father,' she says. 'You won't even feel it.'

Agnes does not want to watch. She just holds the bowl of water and soda, and passes fresh lint when Simon asks for it. She notices light, pea-sized balls fall from the jaw as Simon wipes, and realises they are bits of dead bone the body has cast out.

God above.

The man clenches Pearl's hand. 'That's it,' she whispers. 'It'll be better in no time.'

Although Pearl whispers words of encouragement to her father, she frequently breaks off to narrow her eyes at Simon. She appears to think he is a sort of dark magician who requires her constant supervision. Whatever her suspicions, she can be in no doubt that he is proving useful; when the abscesses are burst and everything is cleansed, Mr Meers looks much less swollen and discoloured.

He has proved astonishingly stoical, with fewer groans than Agnes expected. She is pleased with herself too, for not swooning. Constance always used to mock her squeamishness, but now she is stronger, capable of seeing gore like her sister was.

Simon gathers all the dirtied lint and places it into her bowl, making the water filthy. 'Could you dispose of that for me, Miss Darken?'

She cannot imagine where he intends for her to take the bowl; it is doubtful this house has its own privy and she does not know where to find the close stool. Carrying her stinking cargo out into the corridor, she dithers for a while before finally deciding on the scullery. She places the bowl beside a box of matches and walks away from it, shuddering.

How can this family bear to light a match, after all that they have done?

She re-enters the sickroom to see Simon administering drops of opium. Pearl has crept over to stand beside him.

'Agnes said you'd take Father to a hospital,' she ventures.

Simon concentrates on his task. 'It would not be advisable to move your father at present, Miss Meers.'

'Then you'll do it here? Cut the rotten bone out and cure him?'

He does not answer straight away but frowns, hands Pearl the drops and takes his patient's wrist to feel the pulse.

Mr Meers's eyes close and he seems to drift out of consciousness.

'Is it like a trance?' asks Pearl. 'Do you do it while he's sleeping?'

'Leave him to rest a while,' Simon sighs. 'We will discuss the matter outside.' He gestures to the bottle in her hands. 'Retain those for his pain, Miss Meers. I have given him five drops. I should keep it to … Forgive me, but can you count?'

Pearl nods proudly.

'Let us say a limit of twenty drops a day.'

After a moment of consideration, Pearl hides the bottle beneath the mattress. Her father moves in his sleep.

Simon nods and wearily trudges outside.

Agnes follows him. In the hallway, she touches his arm.

'What can be done?'

He only shakes his head.

Together, they pass into the parlour. A single black candle burns on the circular table, making a moon out of the crystal ball. Dark shapes flicker again; black claws running along the red plush tablecloth and swarming up the curtains.

Agnes wets her fingertips and pinches the wick out. She is sick of shadows.

'It has gone too long untreated,' Simon admits dejectedly, leaning against the sofa. 'I fear that the poison has entered his bloodstream.'

'Do not say so,' she begs.

'I am afraid it is true. He is beyond help, Miss Darken.'

She sits down heavily at the séance table. It feels like she has suffered a physical blow.

Pearl's father was meant to be her atonement. If *one* person could emerge from this turmoil happier than they began, Agnes would be – well, not content, but easier within herself.

Now Pearl will become fatherless.

The pain of Agnes's own bereavement comes roaring back. Not just the grief for Montague, but for dear Papa. She misses him so much. She was not there at his final breath and she will never conquer her remorse for that.

She pictures him on his deathbed, and a morbid instinct forces her to try and imagine her own. Who will be there to hold her hand at the end? Cedric? What if he is never found? She once worried about being a burden to her nephew in her old age, but she would rather that than face death alone.

From what she has seen of the Other Side, it does not seem to be a better place. How, then, can she offer comfort to little Pearl in this dire situation?

'I fear it is doubtful he would survive the ordeal, Miss Meers.'

She jerks out of her abstraction to see Pearl has entered the room and is talking to Simon. The girl looks very slight, very vulnerable.

'I don't understand, sir,' she stammers.

'What I am trying to say, Miss Meers, is that your father does not possess the strength to undergo an operation. Even with ether, the shock to his body would be more than he could stand.' He withdraws a handkerchief from his pocket and mops his brow. 'Putting that fact aside ... I believe the performance would be futile, anyhow. The disease has progressed too far for me – for anyone – to help.'

'But you'll cure him,' Pearl asserts. 'Agnes promised you'd cure him.'

Simon's throat bobs as he swallows. 'In this instance, Miss Meers, I regret to inform you that it is quite beyond my power.'

The hush that falls is agonising.

'Miss Meers, you are unwell—' Simon starts forward, but Pearl dodges away from him.

She is shaking so much that her features seem to blur in the shadows. 'Get out.'

Is she possessed of a spirit? Agnes would like to believe so, but the voice is entirely Pearl's own. The child's weakened form cannot contain the emotions that are blasting through it; she is forced to lean upon the wall.

'Get out of my house!' she shrieks.

Agnes rises to her feet. She can feel a faint rumbling through the floor.

'Indeed, I cannot, while you are so ill,' Simon protests. 'I have been observing you and your health appears much depleted. I would like—'

'Don't touch me! We don't need quacks! I don't need you at all.'

'Pearl—' Agnes tries, but the girl is beside herself.

'Myrtle will cure him,' she insists, ferociously. 'Myrtle's curing him with Mesmerism. She was right about you lot. You don't know nothing.'

On the table, two candles ignite.

'I can assure you—'

'Bunch of bleedin' tricksters!' Pearl cries, batting Simon away. 'Get out! Get ... out!'

A line forks through the crystal ball like a crack in ice.

'Simon,' Agnes whispers, 'I think that we had better go.'

He gives a defeated nod, but his eyes do not leave the child as they walk out of the parlour and towards the front door.

The girl slides all the way down the wall to the carpet where she sits, arms around her knees.

The last sight Agnes has before the door closes is Pearl's white face, drenched in tears.

Outside, it is still mizzling. Walcot Street goes on the same, as if it could possibly tempt them to eat sheep's trotters or buy a ballad, after what they have seen in that house.

Agnes looks into her friend's troubled eyes.

'That child is very ill, Miss Darken. Did she work at the match factory also?'

'I do not know. I am so ignorant!' She groans, hating herself. 'I did not even trouble to acquaint myself with

290

her properly, I have simply blundered into her life and caused all this distress!'

He wets his lips, nods. 'It was only natural that you should sympathise with Miss Meers. You know what it is to have a sister who controls ... I mean to say, you have been treated in a manner that ... You can easily put yourself in the child's position,' he finishes awkwardly.

She pictures Miss West and Constance, side by side. He is right. There are similarities there.

'Oh, Simon. Whatever have I done?'

CHAPTER 29

Nine chimes of the clock and the sickroom is already rank. It stinks like cabbage soup. Pearl's opened the window, even the curtains a little bit, but the cool morning air won't come in.

They're burning up, her and Father. If anything, the December wind only fans the flames.

What is she meant to do now? Looking at Father makes her as giddy as if she were staring into an abyss. Did that fat doctor hurt him yesterday? Make it worse? She'd almost be glad to believe that, for it would mean that Myrtle was right, and all the doctor's sad *hmphs* and shakes of the head would be proved as humbug.

But she's got eyes – even if it is harder to use them without her green spectacles. And those eyes can see that Father slept much easier with the magic drops.

Their spell must be wearing off now. He's fidgety again, making that dreadful bubbling moan. The wisps of the spirit world are closing in around him; daylight scares them off, but Pearl knows they're still there, reaching out in expectation of plucking a treat.

She crosses the room and bends down to the cheap tick mattress. The bottle's still hidden under there. She pulls it out and weighs it, heavy as sin in her hands. It's got a cork in the top and a label covered in writing on the side; she squints at the weird symbols, but they don't mean anything to her.

It doesn't *look* like poison, it looks like really strong tea. But then, how would she know? Didn't the doctor say that even matches could be poison?

She can't decide what she's meant to do; who to trust, who to believe.

Father starts to twitch.

She walks to the head of his bed, the bottle still in her hand. 'You want this?'

Maybe he does, but that's not the gesture he's making; it's the one he used when the doctor came.

Cut it out.

Her eyes fill with tears.

'He's coming back,' she lies. 'The doctor's coming back and he'll do it; he's just … busy.'

Father gurgles a relieved sigh. Very briefly, the creases leave his forehead. He points to the bottle.

'All right.'

She wipes the sweat away from her eyes and awkwardly pulls the cork stopper out. She hasn't got much strength, and nerves are making her dizzy. The doctor said she could give him up to twenty drops, but that's the biggest number she knows and she's going to have to concentrate hard on her counting.

She aims at Father's tongue.

The drops fall slowly, landing with a tiny pat.

She gets lost counting around sixteen, so adds two more for luck – that will have to do.

Father's breathing slows. He gives her what she has always taken for a smile, though it's only in the eyes.

Cut it out, he gestures again. Then he drifts off to sleep.

Pearl leaves the room, hollow.

The Bath Society of Spiritual Adventurers are due over again tonight. It feels like a direct punishment for the broken door, but of course Myrtle couldn't have known about that when she arranged the séance. In fact, Pearl's still waiting for the real cost to become clear. Myrtle obviously didn't believe her stupid story about an attempted robbery, but she didn't do anything either; just went to the kitchen and brought back a piece of bread loaded with jam, which she made Pearl eat. Her face looked nearly black with choked-up rage.

Today, Myrtle's making the parlour ready for their guests: dusting with an old rag, while the carpet is strewn with used tea leaves. A vinegar scent lingers from where she's been scrubbing at the crystal ball. There's a line on it that won't come off – she says that's Pearl's fault, too.

Myrtle has her back turned, but she seems to sense Pearl emerge from Father's room.

'Hope you're in top form,' she calls. 'Mr Stadler's going to write this one up as a piece. Who knows? We might be seeing our names in *Missives from Summerland* one of these days.'

Pearl can picture the leering, eager faces of the spirit-seekers. She wishes Myrtle would care less for the dead, and more about the man on his last legs in the very next room.

'Father's pretty bad,' she says.

'So? *He*'s not got to do the séance.'

Desperation seizes her. Someone needs to sit with Father, to nurse him. Anyone with a heart can see that. She knows she can't make Myrtle cancel the séance. But maybe if she appeals to her sister's vanity, she can get *something* for Father.

'Won't you mesmerise him again?' she pleads. 'It'd help me concentrate, to know you'd looked after him. He's been so much worse since you stopped the treatment, I've really noticed it.'

Myrtle shakes her head. 'He fights against me.'

'He won't. I promise. He's too weak now, and you're so strong …'

'Doesn't matter. I'm busy today. Someone's got to fix that front door, ain't they?'

'Please! This will just take a few minutes. I'd be so grateful. You're the best mesmerist there is. Only you can make him well again, Myrtle.'

'Is that so? I thought you knew better than me, these days.' She folds her rag over to find a clean bit.

'Why don't you ask your new *friend* Miss Darken to help you?'

So it's like that: she's still not forgiven.

Flaming with sorrow and outrage, she stomps into the kitchen. On the table is a jar of jam and an empty box of matches. There's no water to cool her forehead – they used it all yesterday cleaning Father's jaw. She can't quench her thirst either, because Myrtle hasn't fetched any ale from the Northgate Brewery. She's sure that's deliberate. Myrtle *wants* Pearl to suffer, and Father too. She still thinks they killed Mother on purpose.

Pearl tries to steady her breathing but fails. She can't take any more of this: closed doors everywhere she turns. If one more person tells her *no*, she will scream.

Father will get better. He *must*.

Myrtle and the doctor think they're so clever, with all their learning, but it's Pearl everyone comes crying to, wanting answers. *Pearl*'s the one with the power and she needs to use it. If she can talk for people who are dead, she can surely cure the 'fuzzy jaw'?

Her eyes range the surfaces, fall upon the biggest, sharpest kitchen knife.

And she knows what she has to do.

CHAPTER 30

Something has happened.

Agnes felt it the minute the crystal ball cracked. She does not know if Pearl has unleashed some dark entity in her distress, or whether this is the presence she has sensed building for so long: the one that follows her through the streets, teasing closer and closer at every séance.

But it is here now.

She sits in her studio, hugging the book of duplicates to her chest. The abbey bells throb, strong as a pulse, through the magpies' chitter and cackle.

One by one, the framed silhouettes drop from the wall to crash beside her feet. Bronzed work, painting on wax, hollow-cuts. No visible hand touches them. For years they have hung there, undisturbed, but now they smash onto the floor and hatch as the profiles break free of their glass.

There is a slow malevolence to the destruction; first one frame, then the next, each dislodged without a hurry. Whatever it is, it is working its way towards the centre of the room.

A trio of Etruscan silhouettes painted in vermillion hang directly in front of her chair. The frame to the left of them goes down, then the one to the right. *Thud, crack, thud, crack*, until only the three profiles remain: a man wearing a peruke and two ladies with feathers in their hats.

Agnes stares at them, her agitated brain trying to find meaning. There is no obvious connection between them other than their orange-red colour. She cranes back in her chair as the oval frames start to tremble, but they do not fall. Instead, the one of a man in the centre seems to … melt.

Livid drops trickle down the wall, slowly at first, and then they are streaking, gory, splattering onto her desk with the iron scent of blood.

Her work is being exsanguinated.

She surges to her feet, head rushing, and hurries from the room.

Dusk is blooming outside but still the abbey bells toll, on and on, relentless. The shadows of the bannisters waver across the landing like the bars of a cage. A female shadow flits behind; it does not look like her own.

She blunders down the staircase, still clutching the heavy duplicate book in her arms. The profiles hanging on the wall seem to turn and watch her as she goes.

Mamma sits in the darkened parlour with only the fire for company. There are shadows, more shadows,

298

massing around her hunched, shawl-covered frame. Agnes cries out and drops her book onto the wing chair. Picking up the pail of sand that stands beside the poker set, she uses it to douse the flames. The orange tongues hiss, crackle and die, until all that remains is a charred pile of sand and the grey smoke.

'Whatever did you do that for?' Mamma protests. 'It's cold in here.'

Agnes pants and places the empty bucket down. This must be why Pearl keeps it dark – shadows cannot haunt you in the dark.

'I told you, Mamma. No fires.'

'No fires, no papers, no Cedric,' Mamma grumbles, shuffling her swollen feet. 'Very high and mighty with your orders, miss. Who died and left you in charge?'

'Papa did!' she shouts, wheeling round to face her mother. 'Papa entreated me to take care of you all and I have …' She softens, ashamed of her outburst. 'I have *tried*. But I have failed. I was not strong enough.'

Mamma looks ancient in the dark; sadder, without the rosy-red hue of her cheeks. She scrunches her wrinkled hands together and glances down at them, contrite.

'Was I a bad mother to you, Agnes?'

This winds her. 'Bad?' She sits down on the sofa beside Mamma and touches her shoulder. 'Why would you think so?'

'Well. I can't help but question it, considering. I never found you a husband. And Constance …'

299

Yes, Constance.

What can Agnes say? This is her mother, she loves her. The last thing she would wish to do is hurt her. Yet what Mamma says is true. Papa never thought of extracting deathbed promises from his wife – he knew instinctively that she would not cope. And perhaps Constance *would* have turned out differently if their mother had not treated her with such open resentment and hostility. It was hardly Constance's fault that she was not born a boy, or that her infant sickness discouraged the usual bond. If Mamma had paid attention, if she had educated the girls herself, maybe Constance would not have developed her obsession with Agnes at all.

'I think,' she says slowly, 'that many mothers would have struggled with a daughter like Constance.'

Something creaks upstairs. Agnes stiffens. The presence must still be there, amongst the broken picture frames. It could not be ...

It is not Constance herself?

She tries to stifle the panic that wails inside her chest.

A ghost, even Constance's ghost, cannot actually *hurt* her, can it? None of the spirits she has witnessed at séances were physically threatening. Yet Pearl was afraid of them ... The girl feared to let them use her mouth. To her the spirits were predators, wanting to invade and take control.

Well, Agnes is not a spirit medium. She can only be haunted, not possessed. And thank heavens for that!

300

If it really were Constance … She would leap at the chance to control Agnes. Was that not what she always tried to do in life?

Agnes shakes the bitter thoughts away. 'Constance was a woman,' she reminds herself. 'Not a monster. She was a troubled woman …'

Mamma sighs. 'That she was. But it was not *you* who failed her, dear. I always wanted to tell you that. The fault was mine. I could never warm to her, like I did to you. Those ways she had! When she used to visit the butcher and just stand there, watching him work. How she would bring a dead cat home if she found it in the street. I took a … fear of her. Like she was something sent from above to punish me.'

'You made up for it with Constance's son,' Agnes consoles her mother. 'No one could accuse you of being an unaffectionate grandmother.'

'Hmph. Much good my love did Cedric.' The grey head shakes. 'She was jealous of him too, wasn't she? Jealous that we all adored him. And your father …' Agnes goes to speak, but Mamma talks over her. 'The truth is, Agnes, I should have risen to the occasion. It should have been me, not you, reining her in and earning money for this family.'

'You were grieving. And your heart …'

Mamma unclenches her hands and takes one of Agnes's. She experiences a twinge of guilt for dousing the fire; Mamma does feel very cold.

301

'You were always my good girl. You tried. No one can ask more of you than that. Just ... please don't hold it against me. I already blame myself more than you can know.'

She squeezes her mother's hand and says the only thing a daughter can. 'It was not your fault, Mamma. None of it was your fault.'

There's a thump in the hallway. Agnes jumps.

'Something through the letterbox,' Mamma says.

She is right: it was a soft sound, dulled by a mat; not the harsh crash of the frames upstairs. But it is late for post. Unbidden, that slanted writing comes to mind: Constance's hand.

A coincidence, Simon said.

Cautiously, Agnes rises and goes out to the hallway. An envelope lies in the centre of the doormat. She picks it up and takes it to the kitchen where she keeps her matches. Already she can feel that the envelope is of a good quality and not one of the scraps she so feared to find.

She breaks the wafer and unfolds the paper before striking her match. It hisses. A small bubble of light appears.

The writing it illuminates is Simon's:

Miss Darken,

I was sorry to leave you in distress following our visit to Walcot Street. It is my sincere hope that you have recovered from the disappointment of your unfortunate young friend.

302

My chief consideration remains your own health, and how it might best be improved. I cannot express half of what I would say upon paper, but I wish for your mind to be at rest as soon as possible. Therefore, I will convey only this: I know where Cedric is. Do not, I entreat you, run to the police upon receiving my communication: the cause of the boy's disappearance is of no concern to them. He was in fact embroiled in an accident, and I cannot bring you to his current location without peril to your health. However, rest assured that I have visited him, he is in a safe position and we are in no danger of losing him.

I will call upon you with further particulars very shortly and, if God is willing, take you to him when the risk of serious illness has diminished.

I am aware that inactivity at this moment will cause you pain, but I must crave your indulgence and ask you to trust me, as you have been so good as to trust me in many other instances. Believe me, madam, I am at all times anxious to prove myself your most humble and faithful servant,

Simon Carfax

'Thank God!' Her breath blows out the match.

Cedric is found. *Found*!

She clasps the letter against her heart. The poor boy must be in a hospital, where Simon will not let her tread for fear of infectious disease. She has half a mind to ignore him and make enquiries at Bellot's, the General and the United immediately. Cedric should not be there amongst the paupers, but treated at home by his family.

Did she not *tell* him that hoop and stick would lead him into an accident? To take more care, to look where he was going? Heaven only knows how he managed to sneak out and play when she had locked the house up tight ... But it does not signify. Nothing matters, so long as he is safe now. Whatever the injury, she and Simon can nurse him back to health between them. Everything will be different. After such a scare, Simon will no doubt realise how precious Cedric truly is. The rift will be repaired, and together they can watch him grow. It was wrong of her to despair. There will be a future for her, after all.

She must tell Mamma. Prepare her somehow for the prospect of an invalid boy returning home, without frightening the life out of her. She will soften the news. Tell her he has been taken a little unwell.

'Mamma!' she calls, running out into the passage-way. 'I have a letter from Simon.'

It is likely that Mamma has nodded off in the brief space of time she has been left alone, but as Agnes pushes the parlour door open, expecting to find her mother dozing, she is struck dumb by what she sees.

The fire is lit again. Not just sparking but blazing, as if it were made up and stirred by a careful hand. The shadows wheel, revelling in their freedom.

She wants to ask Mamma how she accomplished this so quickly; how she bent her arthritic body to relay the kindling and where she got the matches from.

She *would* ask her.

But Mamma is nowhere to be seen.

CHAPTER 31

There's more blood than Pearl reckoned on.

Some of it's red, some of it's black, there's even a little purple. All of it smells like copper coins.

Shuddering, Pearl steps back from the bed and wipes the tears from her eyes. Now she's got a new pair of spectacles, but these aren't green: everything she sees is streaked with red.

The pillow blooms deep claret. The stain keeps on growing, she can't stop it. All she's managed to slice off is a hunk of corrupted flesh.

She couldn't help him. There was too much badness for her to cut out.

The knife slips from her palm to the floor.

What has she done?

What has she done?

The magic drops kept him asleep, but he's not sleeping now. She knows it, yet she doesn't; the shock still has her in its grip. When he doesn't respond to her whispers and her shaking of his arm, she closes her eyes and tries to hear him inside her head.

Dead or alive, it doesn't matter, so long as she can reach him.

But she can't.

There's nothing.

She stares down at her trembling hands. Blood has soaked into the skin. Frantically, she rubs it off on her skirts, but it leaves a pinkish hue. Finally her white hands have a pigment.

'Help,' she whispers. 'Help.'

Who is she talking to?

She can't hide this. It's not something you can bundle in the wardrobe to make it go away. There's the knife, and the body, and the pillow, and the blood – so much blood.

Now it's on her clothes, as well as smeared onto her skin. She must look like she's walked through hell.

Myrtle's still cleaning in the parlour. She hums 'The Ratcatcher's Daughter'.

What's her sister going to say? What will she *do*? Will she send for the police? Myrtle was angry enough before, about the crystal ball and the broken door, but *this* …

Something pops inside Pearl's head. She sees the fishbowl of flowers exploding all over again and she's filled with a feeling more desperate than any she's ever known before: she has to get out.

She has to get out of here, *now*.

She gropes for the doorknob, leaving a gory handprint.

Myrtle keeps humming, brushing up the tea leaves, oblivious to everything but her own plans.

Pearl doesn't linger. Somehow her feet carry her straight into her own chamber. She doesn't even stop to turn her head and check that Myrtle hasn't spotted her.

Mechanically, she goes through the actions she's dreamed of a thousand times: she opens the wardrobe, pulls out the carpet bag and starts to change.

Trousers, shirt, cap. Her bloody dress and petticoats pool on the floor. It looks like the girl who inhabited their folds has melted away.

She takes one last look at the map. Then she creeps behind the curtains and opens the window.

Soft, cool air sweeps in. Her yearning for it fights against the reluctance of a long-caged thing. Does she really dare to leave her home? There will be no turning back.

Myrtle continues her tune in the parlour.

Pearl would pray for courage, but the last time she was courageous, she ended up with a knife in her hand.

There's no point in hesitation, no real choice. All she can do is escape.

It's easy to climb, wearing trousers. She clears the window ledge without difficulty. Only the harsh blast of daylight affects her, but it's not as bad as

308

she thought it would be; maybe the shock's softened that too.

Her feet touch the ground, she straightens up and for the first time in her life, she stands on the pavement outside her house.

What she sees rocks her back on her heels.

There's so *much* of it. More than she could ever glimpse from her station by the door. An omnibus clatters past; she feels the air whoosh with it, and through the window there are people, lots of people, squashed together and gaping out at her.

Light flashes off glass. She winces. It's mid-afternoon; the spiteful winter sun will soon go down and it's already throwing out shadows. Pearl spies her own: monstrous, stretched like a giant. She turns quickly and walks away.

She doesn't know what to do, where to look. How much space should she take up on the pavement? She tries to make herself smaller, but it's not small enough. Men pushing barrows elbow her in the ribs and she can scarcely move her feet without stepping on a lady's hem.

When she walked outside in her dreams, it was beautiful. The reality's quite different. It's scary.

Father, Father. She hears his name, sees his mutilated face with every step. Grief makes her too weak to struggle against the tide of people. She gives up, lets the crowd carry her along.

There's a turn she needs to make, somewhere up ahead. She has no concept of distance; some of the buildings look a bit like Agnes's drawing, but they're so much larger, so *stern*.

Her head pounds fit to split open. The cap only partially screens her tender eyes. At least her face feels cooler now. The wind blows and chills the tracks on her cheeks. She narrows her eyes, shuffles on.

Finally the crowd spews her out and she finds herself standing, small and insignificant before an enormous building that reaches right up into the clouds. It's the loveliest thing she's ever seen. There's shiny coloured glass, prettily carved pointy bits and a statue that looks like an angel, climbing the side.

She lays a palm against the rough stone. Maybe she'll just curl up on the ground here, safe under the gaze of the angels.

Something caws above her. Pearl flinches and peers cautiously up from beneath the peak of her cap.

It's a bird. He's perched on one of the lower roofs: a coal-black thing with a patch of white and one glorious streak of blue down his wing. He cocks his head at her, caws again, then takes flight.

Her watering eyes follow his swoop. Such a graceful, easy motion. Pearl wishes she could move like that.

Reluctant to lose sight of the bird, she starts to totter after him, but her energy's nearly all gone. In another few minutes, she'll faint.

With a last flap, the bird settles himself on a ledge supported by leafy pillars. That must be his home.

Half-dazed, Pearl inspects the building, wondering what type of house a bird would choose for its nest. That's when she sees the papercuts in the windows.

Agnes's papercuts.

It's the house from the map.

Relief nearly fells her.

She has no idea what she'll say to Agnes; she doesn't really care so long as there's somewhere to sit down and drink, where it's cool, and the shadow that's following her will go away.

Stumbling towards the door, she risks a glance over her shoulder. It's still there, attached at her ankles.

The door sits right underneath the bird's nest; she can hear him squabbling with his family above her as she raises a hand and knocks as hard as she can. Only a feeble, hollow sound comes back.

What will she do if Agnes doesn't answer, where will she go? Too late she remembers there's a murderer on the loose in Bath.

An image flashes across her vision: the knife, the jaw. Maybe she doesn't need to be afraid of killers any more; not now she's a killer herself.

The door creaks open a fraction, held back by a chain. Two beady eyes peer out from the darkness within.

Pearl bursts into tears.

'Cedric? Cedric!' The chain rattles off the door and Agnes is out in the street, gripping her by the shoulders, before she realises her mistake. 'Simon said you – Oh! Good God. Pearl, is that you?'

She gasps, choked by sobs.

'Pearl, is this *blood*?'

'Let me in,' she pleads. 'The light, it's too bright.'

Agnes's pointed face shows her astonishment, but she holds open the door and ushers Pearl inside without another word.

Pearl staggers into a narrow hallway with a staircase taking up the left-hand side. There are darker patches on the wall where pictures once hung. For some reason they're lying on the floor now. She sees some dead flowers in a vase upon a little pier table.

She thought Agnes would live in a house much fancier than this.

'What happened?' Agnes urges. 'Come here, into the parlour. Is it your sister? Did she beat you? I can send for Dr Carfax ...'

She goes wherever Agnes's hands push her. The parlour's blissfully dark, but it smells like the past has been bottled up inside and refuses to leave. Stacks of newspapers crowd the floor. Used plates and teacups litter the surfaces – one with paintbrushes sticking out of the top. She hears the low hum of a fly.

A sofa stretches before the unlit fireplace and Pearl collapses gratefully upon it.

'Dear child! You are worrying me to distraction. Are you ill?'

She's always ill these days, but this is worse, shredding the very inside of her. For the first time she understands why Myrtle's chary of talking about Mother. Grief hurts. It really, really hurts.

'He's dead,' she howls into the sofa. 'My father's dead.'

CHAPTER 32

The child sleeps deeply. If Agnes stands back from the sofa, she can easily imagine it is Cedric slumbering there. The oversized cap conceals the girl's shock of wintery hair, and her thin, pale limbs are tucked underneath her. Only the rise and fall of the slender chest gives Pearl away; it does not undulate gently, as Cedric's does, but jerks.

Is it safe to let her stay here? Mamma still hasn't returned, and although Agnes tells herself that her mother is her own woman, quite capable of leaving the house if she chooses, she does not truly believe it. In her mind, Mamma's disappearance is connected to the destructive presence that pushed her silhouettes from the wall. There is no evidence of it in the shady parlour at present. Is Pearl holding it at bay? She will keep everything dark. The darkness will protect them, somehow.

Yet ghosts are not the only thing Pearl needs saving from. Now that her father has succumbed to his disease, she will be living alone with Miss West. Could Agnes retain the child at Orange Grove, in secret, and give her a better life? She never told Miss West her address, the horrible woman would not know to come looking for her sister here ...

But it would only take one mention of 'Miss Darken' to the police and that odious Sergeant Redmayne would be banging on her door. Simon has endeavoured to clear her name of suspicion at the station, and this would undo all his good work. No. As much as Agnes would like the company, and to offer Pearl a refuge from her cruel sister, she cannot keep the girl hidden here.

As best she can in the scant light, she jots a note to Simon. He will be busy, visiting Cedric and running his usual practice, but she must tell him about Mamma, and she would like him to take a look at Pearl before sending her back home. No one can see the girl and suppose that she is healthy. They may have left it too late to act with poor Mr Meers, but Pearl is young. Perhaps she can still conquer her illness.

The difficulty will be securing her aid without Miss West noticing. The girl has no money of her own, and Agnes's purse is decidedly light. But what about Montague's ring? It must still be on the floor in the upstairs room at Walcot Street, where it fell during the séance. The pawnshop would pay for real gold – enough, she is sure, for Pearl to buy medicine in secret. After a brief internal struggle, Agnes decides. She will

315

tell Pearl where to look for the ring and ask her to keep it as payment for her services. Yes, that is the right course of action. Montague would understand. At least this way his token can deliver *some* of the good it once promised.

Agnes leaves the house quietly and passes the note to her usual carrier: a boy who sits in the churchyard awaiting errands. Mamma is nowhere to be seen, but she is struck by the number of people who are walking abroad at dusk. Everyone seems to have forgotten about the murderer already. Some men even have their wives linked on their arm, as if there is nothing to fear.

Were those lost lives insignificant in the grand scheme of things? She does not like to believe so. But if Simon has found Cedric, and those notes really were just relics of Constance somehow unearthed, it throws doubt on whether Agnes was ever being targeted at all. Maybe it *was* just coincidence that three men and a woman died.

This is Simon's way of thinking. She should have listened to Simon all along. It was folly to consult Pearl and bring the shadows of the past upon her home. What has she learnt, other than that ghosts *do* exist, and they are most of them frightened or in pain? That knowledge offers neither comfort nor earthly use.

She should have left well enough alone.

Now her elderly mother has wandered off, she has a phantom in the studio and a sickly child to nurse.

Gently, she unlocks the door and creeps back inside the house. She need not have taken such care. Pearl is awake and is standing in the doorway to the parlour, rubbing her eyes.

'I had hoped you would sleep a little longer. How do you feel?'

'Terrible,' Pearl whispers.

'Sit down again, dear. I will see if I can fetch you some refreshment—'

Pearl shakes her head vehemently.

'Perhaps my smelling salts?'

'That's not why I'm here.'

There is a mutinous expression on her small face. A streak of blood has dried on her cheek; Agnes wants to wipe it away, but she is worried to bring it to her attention.

'Then ... what may I do for you, Pearl? Why *are* you here?'

'I never got my séance.'

Agnes shoots a glance at the picture frames on the floor. 'I am not sure it is wise to—'

'You promised! We spoke to your people, now it's my turn.'

'Listen, dear, I have reason to believe there is an ... unwelcome spirit in this house, and rather than calling things up, it would be better if we tried to send her back—'

But something has snapped within Pearl, she has none of her usual timidity. '*When* I've had my séance,'

317

she cries. 'Or don't you mean to keep any of the promises you made to me?'

This hits home. Agnes hangs her head. 'I do regret that Dr Carfax was not able—'

'He's dead!' – Pearl is almost shrieking – 'You told me I'd be able to cure my father, and now he's dead. Does that sound like you've kept up your end of the deal?'

'No, but—'

'So either you're going to help me talk to him, or you're a bloody liar. Which is it?'

Misgiving wallows within her. What choice does she have? The poor girl is sick and half-mad with grief. Agnes must humour her, keep her occupied until Simon arrives. From the way she is breathing, she is very ill indeed.

'One séance,' Agnes concedes. 'Just one. And then we put the ghosts back, for good.'

Pearl sighs in relief. Then she throws up.

———

No candles burn this time. It is pitch-black, but Pearl is a faint, indefinite outline in the dark. She is propped up against pillows, determined to proceed no matter how eloquently Agnes entreats her not to.

The house still smells of vomit. If Agnes possessed better eyesight, she would have sworn that the liquid had *glowed*. She scents something acidic, corrosive, like the very reek of death.

318

'Give me your hands,' Pearl demands.

Agnes obeys. It is like holding a bunch of wet sticks. She closes her eyes and prays for Simon to arrive quickly.

The grandfather clock pings.

Her eyelids snap open. That clock has not made a sound in days. She waits for it to tick, but nothing happens; there is just a taut, expectant hush.

'Father,' Pearl whispers passionately. 'Father, come to me. I'm so sorry. I tried my best.'

A single flame crackles into life in the fireplace.

Agnes attempts to tug her hands back, but Pearl clings to them like a drowning girl.

This is wrong, it is all wrong. The flame is a light, however small, and light creates a doorway for the shadows to come slithering out.

'Father,' Pearl pleads. 'Don't be angry.'

Agnes holds her breath. There *is* anger in the air, palpable but invisible; it seems to pulse and thicken. They should stop, they really should stop.

'Talk to me!' Pearl cries.

The hands of the grandfather clock start to move; faster than any mechanism could push them. The pendulum begins to swing.

'Pearl—'

Sweat stands out on her ivory forehead. The girl is straining with all her might.

Agnes watches, helpless, as the fire climbs in the grate.

Papa once spoke of the French revolutionaries dancing 'La Carmagnole'. The way the shadows caper is like that: savage, with the inherent threat of violence.

A log bursts, spitting sparks.

'Pearl, stop!'

The girl opens her colourless eyes. The flames reflect in her pupils.

Round and round goes the clock; the fire burns higher and higher. Agnes yearns to run from the room, but she is held fast.

Where is Simon? Why hasn't he come?

Pearl's breath catches. Steam issues from between her lips; she is out of control. The entire séance is beyond her command.

Shadows close in around them like hungry wolves. Agnes gasps, tries again to yank her hands out of Pearl's slick hold, but it is impossible; it is as though the girl is focusing every last atom of her strength on this circle.

The grandfather clock chimes. Agnes's eyes flick towards it and she freezes.

There's something there. Unfolding in the corner.

The shadow of a woman rises to her feet. She is tall and slender in profile. Familiar.

Pearl's back is turned to the grandfather clock, she can have no conception of how the shadow raises its hands and stretches long, long fingers towards her.

Agnes tries to make a noise, but nothing comes out.

The hands are like twigs on a tree. The branches reach out, grow larger, longer. One of them touches the tip of Pearl's chin.

'Look!' Pearl exhales and her expression is beatific. 'Agnes! I ... I *see* her!'

With one final wrench, Agnes tears her hands away.

Pearl seems to come with them. She pitches forward, face first, onto the floor. The fire snaps out, the grandfather clock wheezes its last.

'Pearl? Pearl!'

Shakily, Agnes endeavours to prop her up again, but the girl's head lolls. It cannot be, it *should not* be ...

She touches a hand to the clammy flesh at her neck. Nothing pulses beneath.

Her translucent eyes are fixed open, staring at the image they so earnestly sought, and poor little Pearl is dead.

CHAPTER 33

The police call it the Dead Room. Agnes knows, because she has been there before: a space of cold white tiles and metal instruments. It is no place for a child.

Naturally, she is not allowed inside with Simon and the other doctors while they probe and examine. Instead she sits waiting outside on a bench, with a sympathetic clergyman keeping watch over her.

Occasionally Sergeant Redmayne checks up on them and offers cups of tea. All the previous suspicion has fled from his demeanour. Agnes does not think to ask *why*. She cannot think of much at all. She feels trapped inside a bell jar, the air stale and all sound muffled.

The death of a child is not a particularly rare event. Everyone knows that many tiny souls depart from this world before their fifth birthday, especially down in the slums. But it feels as if time should stop, or that at least the city should go about its business with more gentleness and decorum.

Nobody can quantify what has been lost. Pearl might have influenced many lives as she grew into womanhood, and now they will never know. Generations of possible children and grandchildren all perished with her last breath. There is nothing more tragic to Agnes's mind than the future that never was.

And where is Pearl now? Not in there, on a slab. She did not have the faith of a Christian, so Heaven is doubtful too. After the child's sufferings, it would be terrible to think of her wandering the earth, as lost as one of the spirits she so feared.

All Agnes can picture are those dark hands, reaching out.

I see her, Pearl had said. She looked happy. Agnes would like to believe it was the girl's deceased mother, come to claim her and take her home at last. But to her eyes, the figure had resembled someone else. Someone she last saw in the Dead Room.

A shouted curse shatters her torpor. The bell over the street door jangles wildly, and a chair crashes to the floor. Agnes looks up to see three policemen grappling with a young woman. She is all teeth and hair. Although her wrists have been shackled, she has not given up her attempts to escape. She jerks, feints, tries to bite.

'Steady,' one policeman warns the other.

A fourth officer comes forward with a leather truncheon. Clearly he has no compunction about striking a female. He cracks her hard on the shoulder; her head flies back, parting the curtain of her loose hair.

323

The face beneath belongs to Miss West.

'It weren't my knife,' she spits, 'I never—' But the truncheon swings again, and she is hustled into a side room out of view.

Agnes blinks. Were it not for the clergyman's pursed lips, she would doubt the scene had actually taken place.

What can Miss West stand accused of?

Of course Simon went to the police when he finally arrived and found Agnes with the lifeless body of Pearl. No doubt he told them where to find the child's next of kin. But she did not expect them to fetch Miss West to the station *bound*.

She said something about a knife. Agnes remembers the smear of blood she spotted on Pearl's cheek. She assumed that had rubbed off from her father's jaw as he lay dying, but perhaps not. Just what horrors was the girl fleeing from?

After another half hour of dismal uncertainty, a door opens at the opposite end of the corridor to the one Miss West was spirited down. The clergyman stands up.

Simon has returned to them.

His shoulders stoop low. He no longer wears a coat, and his shirtsleeves have been rolled back to the elbows. Carbolic soap has scrubbed his hands and arms clean, but Agnes knows exactly what they have been doing.

Her chest turns over.

She keeps her head bent while Simon exchanges a few words with the clergyman and takes a seat by her side. She cannot bear to think of his hands moving over Pearl, or of what substances lay embedded beneath his fingernails.

'Miss Darken,' he says softly.

'Is it done?'

She feels, rather than sees him nod.

'And do you know … ?'

Simon exhales heavily. 'The coroner found the cause of death I was anticipating. Miss Meers died of phosphorus poisoning.'

It makes little sense – yet what has of late? She is no doctor. For all she knows, being confined in that house with Mr Meers might have caused the infection to leach through into Pearl, like tea leaves colouring water.

'I suppose the miasma …' she begins dully.

'No,' Simon replies. He takes a moment, seems to be grappling with some powerful emotion. 'The phosphorus entered the body through the stomach.'

The stomach. Like that suicide weeks ago, the man who ate matches. 'But how —'

'I do not like to tell you this, Miss Darken. It will distress you, but I would rather you hear it from me than another source. You mentioned a glow around the young girl. An – what word do those numbskulls give it? – ectoplasm?'

She swallows. 'Yes.'

'That glow was manufactured. Miss West achieved it, it appears, by crushing match heads and concealing

325

them in jam to mask their unpleasant taste.' He takes a breath. 'She then fed the poisoned jam to her sister. Whole jars of the contaminated substance were found at the property on Walcot Street.'

Agnes sways.

Miss West killed her sister.

Poisoned her.

Can such wickedness exist in the world?

When Agnes thinks back, the clues were all there: Miss West's frustration and aversion to the obligations thrust upon her; her preoccupation with money; Pearl's strange, sickly glow. If she was clever like Simon, she would have realised.

She could have helped.

But as with her own sister, she did not spot the signs until it was too late.

'How could she do it?' she gasps. 'After seeing what phosphorus did to her stepfather ... How could Miss West feed her little sister matches?'

Simon places a hand on her shoulder, holds her steady. 'Miss West proved to be a very bitter young woman indeed.'

Footsteps sound on the tiles. Sergeant Redmayne paces towards them. 'Is she ...'

Simon assesses Agnes and nods to the policeman without saying a word.

'Well, I'll be brief, sir. I mentioned to you the like-lihood of a blade being used in the killings. We found one. In Walcot Street. She'd used it to ... ah ...' Agnes has never seen Sergeant Redmayne hesitant like this before. He keeps sliding her wary glances, as if he fears his words might capsize her. 'Miss West had another victim, sir. Her stepfather was discovered cut and … well. You can imagine.'

Mr Meers, *cut*? Just what happened before Pearl turned up at Orange Grove?

Agnes remembers the girl sobbing *I tried* and *I'm sorry* as she sought to contact her father. She presumed it was an apology for inadequate nursing, but this opens up a new possibility: that Mr Meers did not succumb to his illness at all. That what Pearl had *tried* to prevent was Miss West and her murderous intentions!

It is staggering. Even though she deemed Miss West malicious, she could not have imagined her poisoning a child and stabbing a man in cold blood.

'Is there another body requiring examination?' Simon asks wearily.

'No, there's no call for you to get involved. We don't need your help with—' Sergeant Redmayne breaks off and fiddles with a large brass button on his coat.

She can see him pushing words back. Evidently he did not believe they required Simon's help examining Pearl either, but Simon had still managed to insinuate himself into the post-mortem. She is glad he did. If she heard of Miss West's wicked deeds from another mouth, she would not have believed them.

'You had best get the lady home,' Sergeant Redmayne tries instead. 'This has been a shock to her.'

He is not wrong.

She wants to sleep. To lose time, as she sometimes does, while another person takes over the responsibilities.

'Yes,' she pleads. 'Yes, Simon, take me home. I have not spoken to Mamma since ...' Her memory turns blank. Where *is* Mamma?

'Gently, Miss Darken.'

'I must go,' she moans. 'I have so many chores to perform.'

Like tidying the parlour where Pearl dropped down lifeless. She thinks of the scattered cushions and the tang of vomit. The grandfather clock spinning. What will she do if the terrifying shadow still lingers there?

'I must ... I will ...' She attempts to stand, but her legs are fluid.

'Miss Darken!' Simon says from somewhere distant.

She slumps against him. His shirt smells bitter with carbolic and something else.

Dead flesh.

'Simon ...'

He guides her back to her own feet. She imagines that hand, touching Pearl's corpse, and the last candle in her mind winks out.

328

CHAPTER 34

It is a bright, crisp morning in Alfred Street. Not much traffic passes down towards the Assembly Rooms this early in the day, and if Agnes listens carefully, she can hear a robin sing. She swings gently in the rocking chair. Honeyed light dribbles through the window onto her lap, where Morpheus is curled up.

The dog resisted her caresses earlier, but he has a good sense of time and always reconsiders his allegiances around the hour the breakfast tray is due to arrive.

As the carriage clock chimes, Simon's charwoman shuffles in and sets down the food on a table. She tips Agnes a wink. 'Got it for you. Tucked under the egg plate. You make sure to give it back to me when you're done.'

Agnes thanks her. It is difficult not to betray the agitation that she feels, but Morpheus must sense it, for he stirs on her legs.

'That will be my reading for the train journey up to Gloucester,' the charwoman continues. 'Going to visit my brother in a couple of weeks for the holidays. Just as well this nasty business has come to a close before I leave, because I'd be loath to miss anything while I'm away.'

Of course, it is Advent already, and soon Christmas will come. She has lost track of time without attending church each week. Surely Cedric must be out of the hospital by now? She needs to convince Simon she is well enough to see him. Just one glimpse of his face would help her nerves to settle.

'I trust you will have a pleasant stay with your family, Mrs Muckle,' says Agnes, hoping she will soon be with her own. 'However shall we manage without you?'

The charwoman pinks with pride, but she brushes the compliment away. 'You'll get along well enough. Dr Carfax is a capable gent, much more orderly than most of them. Worth hanging on to,' she adds slyly.

Agnes pretends not to hear her.

When the domestic is safely out of the room, she reaches for the plate of coddled eggs and squeezes it onto her lap beside Morpheus. He starts to snaffle the food up at once.

Left behind on the tray is a newspaper, its pages ready-cut. A ring of grease marks the front.

Her heart pumps like a piston.

Simon has said that she requires absolute quiet and detachment from the outside world, and she has tried to be a good patient. But he cannot appreciate how much she frets while she does not know what is occurring in her absence. She has so many unanswered

330

questions niggling inside her. The solutions offered by the press will not be entirely trustworthy, but at least they will give her some idea.

Picking up the paper, she draws in a steadying breath. As she suspected, the story occupies pride of place. She begins to read:

The regular reader might be forgiven for supposing no further calamity could befall the beleaguered Darken's Silhouette Parlour, Orange Grove, following the twin misfortunes of a client's violent demise and the proprietor's discovery of a murdered body less than a month afterwards. Fate, however, proves capricious, and it is this paper's solemn duty to report the sad expiration of a female child upon the very premises.

It will be recalled that on the 23rd September this year Miss Darken, native to Bath, was the last known person to see the late Solomon Boyle, of Queen Square, alive. The unfortunate gentleman's remains were found mutilated in the Gravel Walk not one week later.

A further mistreated corpse was discovered buried beneath snow in Royal Victoria Park on 18th October. The body was later identified as belonging to one Edward Lewis of Weston. At the time, Sergeant Redmayne of the Central Police Station, Market Place, advised this paper that a connection between Boyle's and Lewis's killings was probable, given the identical method of execution, which was uncovered despite concerted efforts on the part of the murderer to conceal it. Each gentleman suffered a single, horizontal laceration to the throat.

The latest instalment in this serial of tragedy took place on 3rd December, when police were summoned to Orange Grove and later dispatched from thence to Walcot Street, in order to investigate the sudden death of eleven-year-old Miss Meers.

Miss Meers, a child known to Miss Darken, was a professed 'spirit medium', living and trading on Walcot Street in the company of her elder half-sister, Miss West. The observant reader will recognise Miss West's name in connection to yet another death: the drowning of Commander Hargreaves in mid-October. Miss West allegedly spotted the Commander's body in the water whilst crossing Dredge's Victoria Bridge and raised the alarm. She was present when the corpse was finally stopped and retrieved at Weston Lock.

However, the attractive appearance and outward virtue of Miss West proved to be a fallacy.

It transpired that on the afternoon of 3rd December, just hours before she was due to perform the mummery of another séance, Miss West assailed her invalid stepfather with a knife. The child Miss Meers, having witnessed this attack, fled from her family home to the misguided refuge of Darken's Silhouette Parlour. Before the night closed, Miss Meers would prove to be Miss West's second victim, falling prey not to the blade, but to the cowardly weapon of poison.

Miss Darken witnessed the collapse of her young guest around dusk and, unable to revive her, called upon the services of Dr Carfax of Alfred Street. As would be expected, the trained medical eye quickly spotted signs of foul play in the untimely death. A post-mortem examination revealed that the child had suffered from chronic phosphorus poisoning through the prolonged ingestion of match heads.

Prompted by motives of wickedness the reader will scarcely be able to credit, Miss West, herself a former match girl, had been crushing and concealing the toxic articles in her sister's victuals over the course of nearly four months. The aim was to produce a phosphorescent glow – or ectoplasm, to the credulous – which could fool the most ardent of ghost-grabbers. The murderess's success was equalled only by her rapacity. This paper can reveal that Miss West's name appears on the register of more than one Burial Club in the local area. Had her plans to kill Mr Meers and his child gone undetected, she would have stood to gain the substantial amount of £30 following their deaths – a sum more than sufficient to cover a simple child's funeral costed at approximately £2.

No further definite information has been obtained at the time of going to print, but this paper takes it upon itself to predict that the fair murderess will stand indicted for a number of additional charges. The deductive mind cannot help but remember that Mr Boyle and Mr Lewis received wounds consistent with a knife attack. Moreover, both gentlemen can be connected to Miss Darken – a lady whom, neighbours in Walcot Street report, Miss West nursed a peculiar antipathy towards and twice threw out of her premises.

Could it be that the bewitching but dangerous Miss West sought to cast suspicion on an enemy through her actions? This paper will offer no further speculation, but awaits with impatience the next official report from our city's esteemed Police Force.

By the time Agnes has finished reading, Morpheus has licked the plate clean.

She tosses the newspaper aside, praying Mamma does not read something similar. Simon has been so vague about how things stand at Orange Grove, simply assuring her that all the expected occupants are now present within the house and he is caring for them in her absence. But where did Mamma go, before? And how much do Agnes's family know about Pearl?

One thing is certain: Agnes's days as a profitable silhouette artist are well and truly over. Unless she means to set herself up as a museum for the ghoulish – and those are the only people who will come now – she must rely on Simon for financial support.

The realisation of this chafes, but not as much as she anticipated it would. She is bone-weary of depending

334

on her own resources. This spell of illness has made her appreciate having someone to care for her; she does not want to struggle alone any more.

There is a knock at the bedchamber door.

'Come in,' she calls.

Simon enters rather gingerly, as has become his custom while she stays in his house. She suspects his embarrassment is not *entirely* caused by her informal attire of a nightdress and a plaid dressing gown: some of it may be attributed to the fact that this was once Constance's room, Constance's rocking chair.

'Good morning, Miss Darken. I trust you slept well.'

Too late, she realises the newspaper is lying splayed on the floor in plain sight.

Simon sees her glance, follows it and offers a wry smile. 'There is no need to attempt concealment. I was already aware. Mrs Muckle is a very able charwoman, but her career as a smuggler requires some development in the area of stealth.'

'Poor woman. Do not blame her, for I am the culprit. Sorry, Simon. Do not be angry with me.'

'No, I am not angry.' He comes further into the room. Morpheus flumps off her lap to the floor, where he dawdles over towards his master. 'Your nervous complaint has shown much improvement. I believe you are ready to hear further particulars ...'

She leans forward and places the clean plate back on the breakfast tray. 'What is it? What has happened now? Has Cedric taken a turn for the worse?'

335

'No, no. Cedric is with your mother.' Simon comes over to the window and stands in a pool of light. Bath looks pleasant today. The golden limestone seems to sing. 'A request has arrived. I was inclined to turn it down immediately, but upon reflection I can see the benefits it may bring. It is plain that you need a definite resolution to this ... sad matter.'

'Whatever can you mean? You are speaking in riddles, Simon.'

'My apologies. I was attempting to introduce the idea gently. The fact is that Miss West has asked to see you at the gaol, before her trial in January.'

'Miss West!' Anger and disgust squirm within her. 'How dare that woman ask anything of me? She is a monster!'

He tilts his head, appraising her. 'A monster? Do you think so? I am wary of judging her as such. From what I can gather, she was deeply unhinged by grief. She lost her parents at a young age and was put under intolerable pressure caring for a newborn. It does not excuse her behaviour, precisely, but I have seen too many cases of imbalance not to feel a modicum of pity.'

Agnes always knew that Simon was a worthier person than her, and this only goes to prove it. She may have sympathised with Miss West on that first visit, long ago, but she certainly does not now. 'Her actions were calculated, Simon. She used the poison deliberately, to deceive and make money. Fools like me really believed ...'

336

'I have met at least one woman of a darker disposition,' he says sourly.

She chews her lip and considers. What strikes her is not his veiled reference to Constance, but the thought of the phosphorus. A sharper eye *may* have noticed that the glow surrounding Mr Meers and his daughter was suspiciously similar, but that is not all she founded her faith upon.

'You are right, in one respect, Simon: I do need answers. It does not make sense to me. Pearl was not party to the phosphorus deception, I am sure, yet she said remarkable things ... She manifested such believable symptoms ... There must have been *some* truth in her power. I do not think Miss West's abuse can explain Pearl's behaviour at the séances.'

'It can, though,' he says sadly, folding his hands behind his back. 'Miss West is a practitioner of Mesmerism. While that discipline is perfectly useless in curing physical ailments, it can readily supply a range of tricks. I have seen them myself in lectures. The mesmeric trance is a state of altered consciousness, Miss Darken, and it seems that your young friend was particularly susceptible to it. She was completely in her sister's power. All Miss West needed to do was put her in a trance each morning and instil the things she wanted Pearl to see, say and do. She may even have trained the girl's unconscious to respond to certain cues and stimuli. It is impressive, in its way. Beyond the powers of an ordinary match girl. It is a shame Miss West did not put her talents to better use.'

337

'But ...' Agnes stops and bites back her words. Simon sounds so certain that it was an elaborate hoax. No doubt parts of it were: Pearl's unearthly lustre, the rocking table, the information about Commander Hargreaves taken from the newspaper and gingered up with the imitation of drowning.

But she remembers how frightened Miss West looked when Ned manifested himself: her expressions were a little too good, even for an accomplished actress. And she was not present at the private séances. Miss West could have no influence upon the sights and sounds that reached Agnes then. She could not have staged the disturbing, incoherent exchange with Montague, or made the picture frames fall down at Orange Grove.

A memory of Pearl flashes through her mind. The child gesturing towards the fireplace upstairs in Walcot Street and saying, *I can't do* that *alone.*

'You are sure,' she asks cautiously, 'that the Mesmerism was the only viable power at play? Pearl's gift was all an utter humbug?'

Simon bends down to scratch behind Morpheus's ear. 'I would stake my honour on it. Pearl's colouration was albino and she suffered acutely from photosensitivity – but that is all. She was no different in any other respect from her peers.'

Agnes frowns. There was definitely *something* in that upstairs room, and in the parlour at Orange Grove.

If Pearl was not channelling the spirits ... then who was?

'This is the reason I did not reject the message outright,' Simon goes on. 'Speaking to Miss West may be your last chance to obtain the information you seek before she is hanged and takes her secrets with her.'

'You believe she will be found guilty, then?'

'Undoubtedly. And if you visit, you might take the opportunity to urge her towards confession of her other crimes. There can be little dispute that she was responsible for the deaths of your two unfortunate sitters.'

So the paper inferred, but Agnes is not convinced. Miss West could have no agenda against her at the time Mr Boyle and Ned died. She could not have set out to entrap Agnes: the animosity the newspaper wrote about came *afterwards*.

'As a matter of fact,' Simon continues, 'I would like to consult Miss West myself.'

'Oh?'

'I consider it only right to apprise her of an arrangement I have made. I hope you shall approve of it, also. I have paid for Pearl to be simply interred at Walcot Gate. She deserves a dignified resting place. There will be a modest remembrance with her name and the date of her birth, if I can obtain that from her sister.'

He is a good, good man. Her ribcage swells with the consciousness of it. 'Oh Simon, that is exactly what I would wish. I did so worry about what would become of her.'

'I am glad to have your approbation. Of course I shall attend the service myself, but I wonder ...' He

339

gives her a long assessment. 'I should never ask a lady of your constitution to witness a funeral. But I would welcome your company on a visit to the grave, if you think you would be equal to it. The unfortunate girl will have so few mourners …'

The cemetery rises up in her mind's eye, dismal and crowded with row upon row of stone slabs. She always fancied the gravestones looked like teeth in the maw of some hideous beast.

'The thought scares me,' she admits. 'And I am frightened of seeing Miss West, too. But I owe Pearl that much. I did not act well by that child, Simon. I used her for my own purposes.' Her face flushes with self-consciousness as she adds, 'I worry that perhaps … I have been using people like that my whole life: taking what I need and discarding them. It is my resolution to do better … much better, in the future. I mean to honour those who have always been so generous with me.'

Simon swallows and turns away to face the wall.

She is embarrassed. She had always assumed … But perhaps that is not the case. Maybe all his boyish passion is long since spent.

Trying to break the awkwardness, she resumes, 'I have not been a dutiful daughter these last few months. Mamma is one of the people I must try harder to please. I know you worry that seeing her will excite me, but do you think … I should so *like* to be reunited with my mother and Cedric for Christmas. Could they not

340

come here, if you think me too ill to travel? I must see how poor Cedric gets along. Is he quite recovered from his accident?'

Simon clears his throat. 'I … I am hoping to convey you to them both very soon.'

'Before Christmas, Simon?'

'If you wish it.'

Something has altered. He seems more melancholy than when their conversation first began.

His gaze is fixed upon a piece of needlework hanging on the wall: a sampler that Constance worked when she was young. There are the usual numbers, letters, trees and flowers, but the verse is idiosyncratic:

Behold this piece my hands have made
When I am dead and in my grave

Morpheus whuffs.

'Excuse me, Miss Darken,' Simon says, shaking himself out of his reverie and moving towards the door. 'I did not remark the time. I have patients I must attend to. Can I have anything else sent up to you?'

'No, thank you. Only remember: my family together at Christmas. I shall hold you to that promise, Simon.'

He gives her one last, pained smile. 'I am unlikely to forget.'

CHAPTER 35

Agnes still thinks of it as the 'new' gaol, built along the lines of Pentonville Prison. The turnpike road to Bristol is just visible on the horizon; in the other direction, beyond the high walls, steam puffs from engines on the railway tracks. It is cruel positioning. The convicts must watch the world go by without them, continually facing boundaries which they may never cross.

In the early years, there were rumbles about the prison management being too lenient to deter repeat offenders, but Agnes sees nothing of this. The gaol seems as cold and sterile as the interior of the Dead Room; from the morose demeanour of the staff to the harsh clang of metal doors that sets her teeth on edge.

It is fortunate that Simon accompanies her, because without him nothing about this miserable kingdom would feel real. She is painfully aware of her throat, and a blockage within it like a wad of cotton. Every instinct recoils and urges her to run. But this is the last place a person can fleé from.

The visiting room is packed with desperation. Coarse, rough-featured women cling to the chaplain and must be prised off; another, more genteel-looking creature sits listening to a lawyer with her head in her hands. There is no prevalent age group. Agnes is surprised by the number of women older than herself. Villainy, it seems, is not something one grows out of.

She thinks of little Pearl, who will never age now, and her empathy for the prisoners withers, replaced by a cool fury. If Agnes were to look in the mirror, she feels sure she would see the flinty expression of Constance staring back.

The warden makes them sit in front of a small desk. The chairs are battered and unsteady; Simon's squeals under his weight. She had hoped they would only be permitted to see the prisoners through bars; in this chamber, there seems so little standing between her and evil.

Boots crunch on the floor beside them. A turnkey with a heavy brow hauls a prisoner to the opposite side of the desk; it takes Agnes a moment to realise that it is Miss West.

Prison has sucked the glamour from her. Her flaxen hair is shorn and concealed beneath a cap; only a hint of her widow's peak shows at the brim. She wears a dingy prison uniform that dulls the lustre of her eyes.

'Strike me blind,' she laughs as she is pushed into a seat. 'You came.'

Agnes cannot speak; contempt almost chokes her. The way the young woman leans back in her chair and crosses her arms is not just insolent, it is heartless. She is still putting on a show: the unrepentant sinner.

'Miss Darken has called upon you, despite her ill-health, as an act of charity,' Simon announces sternly. 'And she hopes to encourage compassion in you likewise. Will you not admit to *all* your atrocities, Miss West? What about Mr Boyle, Mr Lewis and Commander Hargreaves?' He spreads his hands. 'Come, let us bring this awful matter to a conclusion. Give the bereaved families the comfort of knowing that justice has been served.'

Miss West smirks at him. They have not been feeding her well. She looks angular and raw-boned. 'Guess I might as well, eh? In for a penny, in for a pound. Seems better to hang for five bodies instead of two.'

'Confession is not about—' Simon begins.

'I always wanted to be in the papers,' she interrupts. 'If they're going to put me down as a killer, it should be a notorious one with loads of victims. What will they call me, d'you think?' She mimics an aristocratic drawl. '*The Mesmerising Murderess*. I'd like that.'

Finally, Agnes finds her voice. 'They will not credit you with any powers whatsoever. You could not mesmerise the guards into releasing you, could you?'

The pert expression is slapped from Miss West's face.

344

'Make sure to keep a civil tongue in your mouth,' the turnkey barks to the prisoner. 'I'll be watching you from over there.'

Keys chinking, she moves to a corner of the room. Her unflinching gaze swoops between the criminals, taking everything in. Those beady eyes have the authority here, not Miss West's. The prisoner must sense this, for the air around her sours.

'I wanted to talk to Miss Darken alone,' she gripes.

Simon straightens his posture. 'You are fortunate that Miss Darken condescended to visit you at all. Her health—'

Agnes lays a hand upon his arm. She needs Simon to remain nearby, but perhaps Miss West *would* come to the point sooner with him at a distance. Pearl always stressed how her sister hated medical men; much of this performance may be for his benefit.

'Be so kind as to fetch me a glass of water, Simon. It is very close in here,' she says, pressing his arm and giving him a meaningful look.

The floor shrieks as he pushes his chair back. 'I will ask the turnkey,' he says, eyeing Miss West. 'I will not let either of you out of my sight.'

Miss West gives him a sardonic smile.

As Simon paces out of earshot, Agnes feels her hatred bubbling up. There is no longer a need to appear ladylike and restrained.

She rounds on Miss West. 'How *could* you? What manner of depraved, filthy vermin are you? Pearl was

345

a child. Not a freak or a doll for you to play with. A *child*. Your mother would curse your name.'

The prisoner's chin juts out. 'You don't know what that girl cost me,' she says huskily. 'She ...' With an effort, she masters herself. 'She wasn't so bleedin' innocent. And she *killed* my mother. Killed her own father with a knife, too, before she ran away!'

Agnes rolls her eyes. 'More lies. You have good reason to believe me credulous, but it will not wash now. Come to the point. Why did you wish to see me?'

Miss West does not appear to hear her. Her lips twist and wobble. 'Tell me, was it ... bad, at the end? Did Pearl suffer an awful lot?'

Agnes remembers the rapt expression on the little face. She will not give Miss West that comfort; she does not deserve it.

'Of what consequence is it to you? You hated the child!'

'I did,' Miss West agrees tearfully. 'I did hate her! I wanted to get rid of her. But now she's gone ...' She swallows. 'I think maybe part of me loved her too. Just a bit. She was ... I felt ... Both. Love and hate. D'you see?'

Reluctantly, Agnes nods. 'Sisterhood can be like that.'

Miss West cocks her head and considers her. Very quietly, she says, 'I know what *your* sister did, Miss Darken.'

346

Agnes's flesh creeps.

This must be one of Miss West's tricks. Agnes reminds herself that the woman could have found an old newspaper report detailing the Accident, and decided to use it in one last desperate attempt to scare her.

It is all smoke and mirrors.

But it is working.

Miss West leans forward in her chair. Her face is so close that Agnes can smell the fetid confinement of the cells. 'I wish I'd been around when *that* scandal happened. My ma told me all about it. I could have blackmailed you about the boy – you and the quack both.'

Agnes's breath catches. 'Cedric?'

'The little bastard. Would have bled you dry trying to keep his origins secret. But what's the point now?'

She is too astonished to form words. How can Miss West *possibly* know about Cedric's true father? Not one of the family ever breathed a hint in public about the real reason Montague had left. As for Cedric, he was considered a little premature, given the date of his parents' wedding, but all records of birth and baptism clearly show Simon's name.

Yet somehow Miss West has managed to piece it all together. It would be dreadful if she revealed their shame now. Mamma's heart would not take it, Cedric's prospects would be blighted and Simon … Poor Simon would have married Constance for nothing.

347

'Please—' she starts.

'*That*'s why you're here, since you asked. I wanted to tell you all about my life, before I hang. I wanted you to know what you've brought me to.' She points a finger. 'Yes, you. You can sit there in your fancy clothes and call me vermin, but I wouldn't have done any of it if it weren't for you and your bloody sister.'

Agnes stares at her, bemused.

'Uncle John might've helped us. My ma wouldn't have married again if her brother were around to help. But he wasn't, was he? He ran off back to sea before I was born, all broken-hearted and never came back. Ma told me he left over a quarrel with some stupid hussy named Darken.'

'Your uncle …'

'D'you want to hear the funny thing? Do you?' Hysteria creeps into Miss West's tone. 'After all I did, trying to get that Burial Club money – guess what happened? He's only gone and snuffed it!' Her eyes blur and Agnes realises they are full of tears. 'Left me a legacy. *My beloved niece.* Beloved my eye! He never saw me in his life! Thought I was still in London and his lawmen couldn't find me, not until they saw my name in the papers.' She gasps a terrible laugh. 'It's a bit bloody late now, ain't it, Uncle John?'

'Good God,' Agnes grips the edge of the desk. 'Let me understand you correctly. Do you mean that your uncle was—'

348

'My uncle's name was John Augustus Montague.'

The visiting room spins.

He *did* mention a sister; only vaguely, the way he spoke of all his kin. She had married low, against her parents' wishes. By Montague's account, none of the family were ever close, which is why Agnes never sought them out.

'But this means that *you* ...' Agnes searches the wicked woman's face. There is nothing, no hint of the man she loved.

Then it hits her like a blow to the stomach: Pearl.

Pearl was Montague's niece, Cedric's cousin.

She thinks the knowledge will rip her in two.

Simon was right: Miss West has had a motive all along. That was why she tried to frame Agnes by murdering her clients.

'You're as useless and pathetic as Uncle John was,' she snarls as Agnes falters for words. 'You deserved each other. Shame your sister was such a whore.'

The reappearance of Simon with a glass of water stops her from responding. Concern furrows his brow.

'You look unwell, Miss Darken. I think perhaps it is time for us to leave.'

She snatches the water from him and gulps it down. Nothing would please her more than to get far away from this poorly lit prison and the deplorable souls within. But this is her last chance. There is so much she needs to know.

349

'Did you believe any of it?' she bursts out. 'The Spiritualism, the Mesmerism?'

Miss West blinks. 'Well the Mesmerism worked on Pearl, didn't it? It's a tool. The doctor can tell you – even *they* know that much.'

Before Simon can retort, Agnes carries on, 'But the ghosts?'

'Pah! I wanted to.' Miss West rubs at her jaw. 'Time was I would've given my right arm to talk to my parents again. I was desperate. So was Pearl's dad.' She shakes her head. 'But it didn't work. So I took that desperation, and I used it. Got to thinking how much other desperate people would pay for a show.' Her glance slides to Simon. 'Because people are stupid, aren't they, Doctor?'

A bell rings. Turnkeys come forward and the lawyers begin to shuffle their papers. Visiting time is over.

'Miss West, I am burying your sister,' Simon declares bluntly. 'I should like to know her date of birth before I leave.'

She remains silent. She looks tired, broken by the concept of a return to her solitary cell. Only when the turnkey comes and seizes her by the arm, ready to frogmarch her back to captivity, does she speak.

'Look up my mother's death in Bow. It's the same date.' She glowers at Agnes. 'I want you to read her name. My mother. Clara Meers, née West, née Montague.'

The last name lingers even through the clamour and the scraping chairs.

350

For the first time in her life, Miss West has produced a genuine ghost.

But before she can savour its effect she is gone, swallowed back into the dark bowels of the prison.

CHAPTER 36

Agnes expected Simon would speak to her as they made their way downhill towards the burial ground at Walcot Gate. She would welcome the distraction. It has been many years since she last visited a cemetery and her nerves are strung taught; she cannot decide whether it feels like she is approaching the gallows, or slipping out for an assignation with a lover.

But Simon descends Guinea Lane with solemn determination. There is nothing unkind in his silence: he still shows her the attentions of checking his pace and occupying the side of the pavement nearest to the road, yet he offers no words of reassurance. Occasionally he eyes her, as a horse that might spook.

Following the prison visit, he made Agnes spend more time cocooned inside Constance's room to 'collect herself'. She kept abreast of the news with Mrs Muckle's help. More speculation and dross surfaced around Miss West, and most of it wallowed in lurid detail: accounts of her soldier father's death, although they could not agree whether it was in China or Afghanistan; reports of the debts Mr Meers left behind him in London when the family relocated to Bath; the amount of compensation granted by Livingstone's Match Factory. Many conjectures were formed as to how Miss West could afford the residence on Walcot Street, none of which painted her in a chaste light.

To think that such a detestable woman would have become her niece, had Agnes's marriage to Montague gone ahead!

The weather remains dry, if overcast. Labourers are taking the opportunity to visit the Darby and Joan public house for a dose of the holiday spirit, even though the holidays have not officially begun yet. After her forced seclusion, the men strike Agnes as particularly brash and noisy. Even her nose is sensitive – she can smell sewage on the air.

'Are you well?' Simon asks as she cringes against him.

She nods, trying not to breathe in. He has told her she can see her family at last after they visit Pearl's grave, and she will not give him a reason to go back on that promise.

When they emerge near Somerset Buildings, the spire of St Swithin's church seems to pierce the mutton-coloured clouds. There is the low hum of organ music from within, and women singing carols. It is impossible to hear them and not recall Miss West's voice on

353

the night of the first séance. How sweetly she sang, for a fiend.

They round the church and progress further downhill through London Street. The place heaves and sparkles with the promise of Christmas. Holly, mistletoe and ivy please the eye through glass shopfronts; every man and his wife is trying to sell a turkey or a side of meat. There are wooden toys on display; hothouse oranges stuffed with cloves and the syrupy scents of a confectioner's shop replace the sewer's unpleasant odour.

It feels strange to see the world carrying on in this manner while Pearl lies beneath the soil. Flush-faced servants haggle as if their lives depended upon plum puddings. She wishes she could tell them how trivial it all appears beside the death of a child.

At last they turn left into Walcot Gate, where the air becomes cooler and more peaceful. The burial ground looms before them, its walls interspersed with black iron railings. Bald, ossified trees screen the view of the graves. Agnes tightens her grip upon Simon's arm.

'I have you,' he says.

It feels as though it is an imposter who enters through the gates and passes by the mortuary chapel. Surely Agnes would not be brave enough to countenance the lichen-grazed headstones that slope towards the river? Yet somehow she does; just as she stood before Mr Meers's terrible face without fainting. Perhaps this whole ordeal will end up changing her for the better.

354

The burial ground is shady, even though the trees have lost their leaves. There is a hush that feels gentle and kind. Gazing to the horizon, beyond the river that frightens her, she sees the roll of green hills.

There are no mawkish angel statues here. Simon leads her across some grass and down a line of identical markers constructed of grey stone. She does not read the simple engravings; does not want to know whose bones lie under her feet.

He stops before a headstone that is raw and unmarked by the weather. At its base, bare earth makes a mound four feet long.

Simon removes his hat.

So this is Pearl. Her last home looks pitifully small and narrow.

Agnes bends down and places the pansies she has brought with her carefully upon the soil. It occurs to her now that they were Constance's favourite flower.

'God rest you, sweet Pearl,' she whispers. 'Sleep tight.'

Her eyes skim the stone.

Pearl Meers
22 June 1843–3 December 1854

Her mind has a momentary blank. She wobbles, disorientated. Simon's arm slips around her waist.

'I am well,' she insists, 'I am ...'

Something troubles her; a general unease she cannot put her finger upon. But why should the dates upset her?

355

'I thought this was a peaceful spot.' Simon speaks as softly as the wind that moves between the graves. 'At dusk, the shadow of the chapel falls across it and it is most … serene.'

A blackbird sings. Agnes glances around. The place is pretty, with the church gazing down over them from above, and the river slipping effortlessly by. She thinks of little Pearl being shut away in the dark for so long, and how pleasant the girl would find this hillside with its shade and its foliage, and the city that she never managed to see spread out before her like a picture.

Her head begins to clear. 'It is perfect, Simon. You chose well.'

They stand for a long time, staring out into the distance. Simon does not remove his arm from her waist. From the corner of her eye, she notices him watching her tenderly. It is comfortable.

They observe a grey-haired couple and their adult daughter tending a grave. They are the only other mourners, which surprises her, given the crowded nature of the cemetery and the season.

Simon inhales deeply beside her. 'I must perform the duty of visiting another while I am here. Do you find yourself able to accompany me?'

It takes her a second to realise who he means. Constance is buried here, her grave woefully neglected.

'I … Yes. Yes, I will go with you, Simon.'

She turns to him, and sees that he has tears in his eyes. She never thought to see him weep for his wife.

356

He coaxes her hand into the crook of his arm. Slowly, they descend the slope, drawing ever closer to the river. A drake plunges his emerald head beneath the water in search of food. She can smell wet dirt and weeds.

'Just a little further,' he urges as she hangs back.

Wind soughs through the naked tree branches. The family of mourners turn and make as if to leave. Agnes wishes they would not. There is a safety in numbers.

Here, the headstones speak of wealth and respectability. They are clean and sturdy, and the engravings are more ornate. Most are white or pale grey in colour, but Simon comes to a halt before a marker made of black marble.

Constance Edith Carfax
18th October 1810–23rd September 1840
Respice Finem

Dark spots cloud her vision. This is worse than seeing Constance's shade appear at the séance. All her sister's complexity has been reduced to a collection of stern, unforgiving words.

When Constance died, Agnes vowed never to give her another thought, yet she has always been there, concealed, like an organ that cannot be removed. She remembers Miss West's description of sisterhood, and it is true: she feels love and hate, blended together. It is impossible to distinguish where one ends and the other begins.

357

Constance was controlling, and vicious, and grasping, yes. But her sole desire in life was to be with Agnes, always. In the grand scheme of things, in comparison with the abuse Pearl faced, that does not seem so very bad. For all her violent outbursts, Constance never once injured Agnes. Would never have poisoned her with matchsticks. In her own way, she loved her.

Maybe Agnes should have spoken to the shadow when it arose. If she had offered forgiveness then, it might have finally put Constance to rest.

'I should have thought,' she starts, but her voice croaks out. She swallows, tries again. 'I should have … brought more pansies.'

Somewhere, a bird calls.

Simon's eyes seem to peel beneath her skin. 'Look, Miss Darken,' he says, and it is a voice she has never heard him use before. 'Look closely. See … beside her.'

There are *three* slabs of black marble, she realises. They stand out like the sharps and flats on a piano, but they are in a line, clumped together.

Cedric Matthew Carfax
Agatha Darken

Shock holds her immobile.

Simon grips her arm. All she can think is that this is some kind of joke, a monstrous joke, but the names are carved … indelible.

'No. No, it cannot be.' Simon does not speak. 'You *promised* me. You told me that you knew where Cedric …'

Her legs give way.

Simon kneels with her. She feels his arm encircle her shoulders; inhales the aroma of carbolic soap.

'Who could … I don't … Was it Miss West? Did she kill them? *How? When?*'

'The dates.' Simon crafts his words with care. 'Please, Miss Darken. Observe the dates.'

Her eyes skate wildly over the shining black marble.

'I cannot …'

Simon waves a bottle of salts beneath her nose and then everything comes into terrible focus.

The date of death for all three is the same:

23rd September 1840

'They have been dead these fourteen years,' he breathes.

Memories crackle at the corners of her mind. Although the ground is firm beneath her knees, she feels herself being dragged down.

Simon reaches out and strokes her cheek. 'Come, Miss Darken. You *do* recall what happened that day.'

———

It had been a trip of mortification. Everyone knew about the matrimonial fracas, from the bucks who

359

turned their heads to watch them walk past, to the shop girls who sneered while they smiled. Whispers had followed the sisters like a cloud of flies. Agnes held herself tight and small, praying that no one would call out after them, but Constance had shown no embarrassment. If anything, she seemed to relish the attention.

Returning to the carriage provided no comfort. The day was unseasonably cold, which made the horses skittish. Dozens of parcels jolted against Agnes's legs while she tried her best to sit back from the window and the stares that raked through it.

Of course the horses were Constance's fault, too. She had insisted upon high-spirited beasts with an Arabian arch to their necks, delicate mouths and rolling eyes, ignoring the fact that they were unsuited to team a carriage.

The vehicle itself was ill-sprung, creaky and second-hand, yet Constance seemed determined to run it in the manner of a born lady, rather than a separated wife who should be comporting herself with discretion.

She wanted people to see her. Wanted to shame Simon as much as she could.

She was going about it the right way. Today's purchases alone would nearly ruin him. The latest and most extravagant was a swansdown tippet that looped around her throat and fell to the hem of her dusky rose dress. It had cost more than Agnes could earn in a month.

360

And was Constance satisfied, now? As always, it was impossible to tell. She sat composed with her hands folded on her lap, gazing out of the window as though she had nothing to be ashamed of.

Agnes wanted to pick up the nearest hat box and hurl it at her.

'I shall write to Miss Werrett and cancel that order,' Agnes threatened. 'I have no desire to wear matching gowns. The whole conceit strikes me as terribly affected.'

Constance offered no response. The horses skittered to the left, but she did not lose her balance. Agnes had to reach for the leather strap to brace herself.

'Do you hear me, Constance? I will not wear it.'

'Then I wonder,' Constance observed coolly, 'that you did not say so at the shop.'

'It was humiliating enough, with those gossiping widows peering at us. I did not want to cause a scene.'

Constance continued looking out of the window. 'No. *You* did not.'

How could she be so maddening? One would think her the picture of innocence sitting there in pink and white with a spray of flowers tucked behind her ear.

'I will write,' Agnes repeated.

'Then you must suffer the consequences.'

Anger flared, hot and impotent inside her chest. What would Constance do to punish her refusal to fall in line this time? Slash her other gowns? Take away Cedric's books again? 'Be reasonable,' she pleaded. 'I know you wish to make me a gift of the gown, but I do

361

not need it. How am I to face Simon this afternoon? Do you not consider that he must still pay your debts – even the ones you run up in presents for me?'

'Of course I consider it. I *want* him to pay.'

He could not afford to, Agnes was certain. His patients were numerous and wealthy, but not enough to justify the horses and their livery at Carter's, nor the many gowns, bonnets and necklaces Constance kept frittering away his money upon. Yet he would never refuse to honour a debt. An informal separation was one matter – the idea of *divorce* did not bear thinking about.

The horses spurted forward, eager to canter, while the coachman attempted to hold them at a trot. Agnes wished he would give them their heads. The sooner they were back at Orange Grove the better; Constance would alight with her infernal boxes and Simon, who was currently visiting Cedric, would take her place in the carriage.

Not that they would enjoy the pleasant afternoon tea she had envisaged. The whole time would be spent warning him of the bills to come. She and Simon never seemed to have anything except difficult conversations, these days. She remembered how they used to laugh together, and play with Cedric as a baby, but now a strain had been put on their friendship.

No doubt that was what Constance wanted.

Constance had taken Montague, she had taken Simon, and she had ruined them both.

'I wish you would leave Simon alone,' Agnes complained. 'He is a good man! He has given you everything: respectability, a name for your child and an income. I know he was always *my* friend, and you never warmed to him, but you are not even forced to endure his company now. What can you possibly hold against him?'

Constance's lips curved in a slow smile.

They were nearing home. Agnes knew her time was running short.

'Answer me, Constance. I will not let you leave this vehicle without you promising to be kinder to your husband.'

Constance breathed a laugh. 'Oh! You dear innocent. You know nothing about marriage!'

'And whose fault is that?'

The carriage jerked ungracefully to a stop. Constance leant forward to open the door; she never waited for the coachman to lower the steps. It was just as well, for he was cursing on the box as he struggled to hold the horses in check.

A cloud of jessamine scent engulfed Agnes as Constance climbed down. With one foot on the street, she fixed Agnes with a last, glacial look.

'Stop thinking about Simon all the time. He is not worth your consideration. No man is. You belong with *me*, sister. Do not forget it.'

Agnes slammed the door on her.

Just as she intended, the hem of Constance's ashy pink gown and one end of her tippet were trapped inside the carriage. They would be marked, ruined.

She heard a faint, strangled cry as Constance tried to walk away and was pulled back.

That would teach her a lesson, she thought.

Then everything happened at once.

There was a rolling, a rushing noise, and she heard Cedric calling her name. 'Auntie Aggie! Look what my father bought me!'

A horse reared, shrieking. The squabs slammed hard into her legs as she was jolted forward without warning, too late to grab the leather strap.

The world turned upside down as the carriage careered out of control. A box hit her in the head, another just beneath the ribs. She fought like a drowning woman reaching for the surface, but she could not tell which direction was up.

Blood filled her mouth.

Suddenly, they hit a bump. Agnes flew up in the air, screaming, and her scream seemed to be echoed outside. There was a sickening crunch as the wheels mounted and crushed whatever lay in their path.

Ribbons and gloves burst from their folds of tissue paper; boxes flew at her head like a flock of birds. She knew she was badly injured but could not tell where. Everything hurt; everything moved.

Clawing for purchase with her torn fingernails, she managed to snag something soft and silken. It was pink. Ashes of roses.

Constance's gown.

Bang.

A heavy weight crashed against the door and she realised Constance was still there, being dragged along with her.

She cried out for her sister, but there was no response except for the banging. She thought of the tippet, pulled taut around Constance's throat like a noose, and she began to choke. It could not be happening. None of this could be real.

Another object smacked her on the temple. Pinpricks danced before her eyes. She could hear screaming, endless screaming, and she yearned for it to stop …

All at once, it did.

There was a deafening crack. For a moment she felt weightless, free; and in the next her body smashed against what must have been the door.

She did not hear a splash; only glass fracturing beneath her. Ice-cold, turbid water gushed in around her legs.

'Constance!' she cried. 'Constance, are you still there?'

Then everything turned to black.

CHAPTER 37

After a long struggle, Agnes has reached a plateau. For the first time since her pneumonia, time does not pass in fits and starts; rather, it has become a paddle steamer that drifts gently, carrying her with it. Or perhaps that is Simon's medicine.

Her world has fallen apart, but it seems to go on perfectly well around her. Simon's charwoman, Mrs Muckle, departs for Gloucester, where she means to stay until Twelfth Night. Miss West is prevailed upon to confess, and she does it with aplomb: admitting not just to the murders of Mr Meers and Pearl, but to those of Mr Boyle, Ned and even Commander Hargreaves, despite the lack of evidence tying her to the crimes. She has the fame, if not the freedom, she always desired.

No one dubs her the Mesmerising Murderess.

The only transgression Miss West is not denounced for is the abduction of Cedric, for Cedric was never there to kidnap; he was trampled beneath the hooves

366

of the horses fourteen years ago. It was the brandishing of his new hoop and stick that caused them to bolt.

Agnes tries to accept this, tries to understand that her recent memories of the boy are entirely false. But sometimes she could swear she hears the *click, click* of his toy rolling down the street at night. Or perhaps it is the sound of a ghostly carriage, wheeling Constance to her doom over and over again.

'Am I quite mad, Simon?' she asks, as he sits up with her by the light of a single candle. 'Have I lost my mind entirely?'

He is always emphatic. 'No. You knew about their deaths and accepted them for over a decade. It was only the pneumonia of '52 that … unsteadied you. You were so very ill, Miss Darken. Near to death. I had half-steeled myself to lose you …' He breaks off, recovers himself. 'When you were past the danger, you seemed to … reset, somehow. You saw them. And you were so weak, I did not dare to retard your progress by breaking your heart all over again.'

She surveys Constance's bedroom. The red and yellow quatrefoil paper that her sister chose still hangs from the walls. Her four-poster bed remains, without curtains, as was her preference. The mahogany dressing table and mirror stand just as she left them. It seems Agnes is not the only person who has been afraid to confront the past.

But she *does* face it, in stages.

367

Simon pays the subscription for them to drink water from the Hetling Pump. It is still within sight of the abbey, but at least it is a little further away from her house at Orange Grove than the Grand Pump Room. She could not bear to be in such close proximity to the scene of the Accident – not yet.

She sips the tepid, mineral-tasting liquid, trying to make her peace with that element. The memory of the river rushing into the carriage, seeking to engulf her, is now painfully clear. It might not have succeeded in taking her life, but it certainly swept her old self away.

'Tell me, Simon,' she says quietly as they promenade the room arm in arm. 'What happened to Mamma? I do not recall that.'

There are ladies like Mamma here: stout and red in the face with slightly protruding eyes. They gossip, obliviously blocking the path of the wheelchairs. Old men lean on crutches for their gouty legs; someone complains of feeling bilious.

Simon hangs his head. 'Your mother ... saw everything. From the window in the parlour. She saw Cedric ... The shock was too great for her heart.'

Agnes winces. 'I expected as much.' She cannot decide who had it worst: Mamma forced to watch those she loved hurtle towards oblivion or herself; left to imagine the brutal scenes.

And what an imagination she owns. She recalls the conversations, the marks of affection; how she even conjured up Cedric in his torn and trampled clothing. She would not have believed her mind capable of such deceit, but Simon does.

'I have told you before that the brain is a powerful and delicate organ. That was why I wished for you to refrain from activities that might interfere with its natural workings, such as Mesmerism. You must view it from this perspective, Miss Darken: that what happened to you is not so very different from what befell poor Miss Meers. Your subconscious persuaded itself into seeing objects and people that were not there.'

His argument carries the benefit of logic, but Simon does not know what she and Pearl witnessed in their upstairs room at Walcot Street. Ghosts *do* exist.

She would rather believe that Mamma and Cedric were not hallucinations, but visitors. Her love called them up from beyond the grave. Did not Miss West say that the Gift often came after a long illness? It did *feel* like a gift: her short reunion with those she loved best.

But she must never confess her theory to Simon. He would not understand.

An orchestra tunes their instruments, ready to amuse the drinkers.

'Do you think my equilibrium will be restored, Simon?' She looks up at him, unsure of what she wants his answer to be. 'Will I be as I was, before the pneumonia?'

His smile does not waver. 'I am certain of it.'

He is so certain that over the course of the next week, he pays the two shillings for her to use the private baths. The famed healing springs are very different from the cold clutches of the River Avon. She descends into a cloud of fragrant steam, her shift billowing around her ankles, and when she is finally immersed the warm liquid feels like an embrace. She paddles her hands, watching her swollen fingers soften and flex. The mist makes her think of Pearl.

It is all very well for Simon to claim that the girl was being mesmerised. But how did she and Agnes see the *same* delusions? The shadows; the writing on the floor; the grandfather clock that whirred and the dark figure of a woman, reaching out her hands.

All of these spirits were definitely there.

Someone had the power to raise them. If it was not Pearl … could it possibly be Agnes?

She braves a chair back to Alfred Street. The jogging, jolting motion does not disturb her as much as she expects. It is not so very like a carriage after all. Stalwart men carry her along, instead of horses. They seem sturdy and reliable.

Just like Simon.

He has been so good to her. What must it have cost him to care for her these past two years? Few men would have acted with his devotion. He has saved her from death not once, but twice.

She has always reserved the word *hero* for men like Nelson, but it is conceivable that Simon may be one too.

She never thought them suited in temperament; could not imagine them living together. But as the chairmen set the sedan down on the pavement in Alfred Street, she realises that the house behind the black iron railings is already starting to feel like home.

Much of Bath has been a strange welding together. The Royal Crescent is orderly and geometric at the front, yet a jumble of different roof heights and depths at the back.

Perhaps it is the same for her and Simon. Perhaps they can meld, after all.

It may be that, given the right circumstances, two very different people can find a way to become one.

———

After attending the Octagon Chapel on Christmas Day, they set about preparing a feast. Naturally, the holiday will be a muted affair, but what they lack in spirits they make up for in food.

Simon knows how to cook a goose. They have chestnuts besides, butter-coated potatoes, a cranberry pie, ham and oysters which part at the merest touch of the knife.

371

It is pleasant to spend hours toiling in the kitchen, drinking wine as they work. Agnes finds she does not mind the sweat. While she is busy, she cannot dwell upon the family members she has lost.

It is only when the table is all laid out and she is sat at the end of it, facing Simon across the divide of two lit candlesticks, that she notices the empty spaces.

These gaps should be filled by Simon's siblings and parents. On previous Christmas days, Constance, Mamma and dear little Cedric occupied them. Now there are only two chairs and a dog who noses under the tablecloth, licking her ankles in expectation of dropped food.

Simon raises a crystal glass. He has drunk a touch too much wine and his nose is red. 'Your health, Miss Darken.'

She toasts it.

For a time the only sound is cutlery moving against china. The food is exquisite. Agnes has every reason to be content, yet somehow she is not.

It would be ridiculous to say she is lonely, while she is in the company of her closest friend. But there is something lacking. Perhaps it is the old adage that blood is thicker than water. She certainly felt a sense of fulfilment around her family which Simon cannot supply.

Her happiness should not be contingent upon another person, yet somehow, it has always been. She has clung to the memories of Papa, Montague and

Cedric in turn. Lived her life for others, never forming an independent identity outside of her art. Now that the silhouette parlour has gone too there is a flatness; a part of her is missing.

Simon swirls the wine in his glass. He, too, glances to the sides of the table and the piles of food they will never manage to eat between them. He seems to read Agnes's thoughts.

'We have both of us lost families.' The candlelight shines off the moisture in his eyes. 'The pain of that never fades. I miss them all, my brother Matthew especially. Every day. But if I am honest, Miss Darken ...' He puts his glass down, hesitates. 'The only companion I ever truly desired ... was you.'

These words have gone unsaid for many years. Simon must have waited most of his life to say them. But now that they are finally out ... nothing has really changed.

She knew. She knew before he went off to Scotland; she knew when she accepted Montague's offer; she even knew when he stood at the altar marrying Constance.

But she cannot tell him that. She dabs her mouth with a napkin. 'Your company is always a great pleasure to me, Simon.'

'Then you will ... stay here?' He touches the stem of his wine glass but cannot look at her.

'I do not know how much longer I am able to. I may be your sister-in-law, but people will start to talk about us.'

373

'I meant …' His throat works. 'Miss Darken. I must ask you, at last. Is there not any way you would consider staying … as my wife?'

It is all very restrained; nothing like Montague's ardent declarations and the kisses she showered on him. But Simon is so *good*, so kind, so assiduous for her health. Gratitude has done what affection alone could not.

She wants to accept.

'Could I?' she asks in a small voice. 'I mean to say … is it allowed?'

'Not by the laws of England's Church,' he admits. He glances up at last, and his blue eyes are imploring. 'Although Constance and I were never … It was not a marriage.'

A log pops on the fire. Somehow her sister still hovers between them.

'What is it you propose, then?'

Simon inhales. Clearly, he has been deliberating this for some time. 'It is a great deal to ask of you. I will understand if you object. But given the circumstances, perhaps it would be better for us both. A new leaf, without memories.'

She cannot think what he means. She blinks at him. The air smells of cooling meat.

'Our marriage would be possible on the Continent. I thought perhaps we could go to Switzerland, or Italy? The climate would be ideal for your lungs. It may even prevent your pneumonia from returning, and you know my work could continue without significant interruption. There are so many English families travelling in those parts that I would never want for patients.' His eyes slide away. 'I knew it was useless to ask while Captain Montague ... You were always adamant he would come back for you. But now he is truly gone, and I noticed ... you have stopped wearing your ring.'

'You want us to *leave* Bath?'

'I understand it is not a decision to be made in haste. You will require time to deliberate.'

Trepidation clutches at her. Bath is all she has ever known.

Can she really leave?

She always dreamed that she would one day; that she would stop living like one of her silhouettes, forever encased within its oval frame. She thinks of Pearl, who spent her whole life in the dark. It would be awful to end up like that.

'I do not want time, so much as courage, Simon. I have mastered the hot baths, but facing a sea voyage, after what happened to me ...'

'I would be there to protect you, as I was fourteen years ago.'

A spot at the centre of her glows. Simon *has* always been there, shielding her. And now he is offering her a version of the future she always wanted. She *will* be on board a ship, cutting across the sea towards new adventures, albeit in the opposite direction to the one Montague intended to take her.

'Would Morpheus be seasick, do you think?' she asks coyly.

She smiles at Simon and it works like a tonic. He has known her long enough to realise this is a tacit acceptance.

He throws his napkin down on the table. He appears handsomer, in his happiness, than she has ever seen him look before. 'Come to the tree, Miss Darken. Dinner can wait – I have a gift for you.'

Agnes obeys, feeling outrageously light and young. Was it really this simple, all along?

The fir tree stands in a pot upon a circular table, adorned with candles, silvered nuts and strings of scarlet berries. Two oranges sit beneath it for their dessert. There is a greasy-looking parcel which she knows is a pig's ear for Morpheus, and a small shagreen box she did not observe before.

Simon takes the box into his palm. 'It was not my intention for this to symbolise … I did not believe I would ever have the temerity to ask …' He laughs at his own awkwardness. She cannot recall the last time she heard a genuine laugh from him. 'I merely wanted you to have an item of jewellery in place of the one you have resigned.'

He hands her the box and she opens the lid straight away. Nestled inside is a milky opal. It takes the candlelight and splits it into a thousand colours: reds, yellows, purples and greens. These are the hues

376

Montague promised her, and more besides; Simon has provided an entire spectrum.

Reverently, she pulls the gem out and sees it is attached to a solid golden band; a ring of fractured colour and beauty. She slips it onto the third finger of her left hand.

Simon watches, enraptured.

She cannot help thinking of Constance's wedding ring. He did not smile when *that* was put in place. Nor did his bride.

A strange shiver runs through her. No, Constance would certainly not be smiling now.

'Do you like it?'

She glances up, basks in the warmth of his affection. The choice is hers now. Everyone else has gone; she is free.

'I will wear it always,' she says.

CHAPTER 38

The Feast of Epiphany approaches. They receive a letter from Mrs Muckle's brother, telling them that the charwoman has a putrid sore throat and must delay her return. In all honesty, they are happy to make do without her. There is plenty to eat, and Morpheus gobbles up any leftovers before they turn bad. The laundry can be sent out, so there is only the washing of plates and dishes to deal with for the moment.

Simon is adept at scouring. 'Cleanliness is paramount in medicine,' he tells her. 'A discipline no doctor should neglect.'

The charwoman will have to be given warning, anyhow, if they are to go abroad and wed this year. Simon anticipates being able to sail in late spring when the weather is calm. Any gossip that arises between now and then shall simply have to be borne. England may not accept a man who marries his dead wife's sister, but there are plenty of countries that will.

Agnes decides she will not return to Orange Grove in the interim. It is not just the memories of Mamma and Cedric that keep her away; she does not want to step into the parlour where Pearl died, or see the wreckage of her studio. She thinks of the shattered frames, of the presence hovering upstairs and it makes her shiver even when she is sitting before the fire.

In her dreams she sees the shadow woman rise again. Her black arms open in an embrace, stretching and extending around the walls, until their darkness encircles the room. *Could* it have been Constance, objecting to Agnes's friendship with Pearl? If she managed to call up her other family members, it is conceivable …

But it would be safer, Agnes decides, to never find out.

She will send Simon to go and pack the things she needs. He will look after her, always.

On Twelfth Night, Mrs Oswald, the pregnant lady who slipped on the ice back in October, is brought to bed. Simon is obliged to leave Agnes and attend the birth.

'I shall make all possible haste,' he says hurriedly, tucking the summons away and fetching his outdoor things. 'But confinements can be lengthy affairs. I am likely to be absent well into the evening.'

It is a disappointment to be left without company for the holiday, but she hoists a brave smile. 'You must

379

take as long as the lady needs. Do not fear, I shall save some wassail for you.'

He deliberates, slapping his gloves against his wrist. 'And you ... you will be quite well, on your own?'

'Oh, Simon, I am not alone.'

Morpheus grumbles his agreement. Simon gives the pug a long stare. 'Behave yourself, little beast. I am counting on you.'

At length, he is persuaded to depart. Agnes is strangely charmed to have the house to herself. It is clean and uncluttered, full of gentle sounds like the fire sifting and the dog's snorts. There are no magpies *here*.

'Well,' she says to Morpheus, 'it seems you are King of the Bean and I am Queen of the Pea. We will find a way to have a merry Twelfth Night of our own.'

Morpheus sits down and chews his foot.

Despite her cheerful prognostic, the novelty soon wears thin. She reads, she eats, she sews a little; there is not much else to do. Without Simon's conversation, the day drags. There are only so many times she can throw the ball for the dog.

Her hands itch to make a papercut, but she has given all that up. They have agreed between them that she will paint watercolour landscapes instead, when they go abroad; that will give her a creative outlet free from associations with Miss West and murder. Yet in the meantime ... Her fingers tug at her skirts. She really does miss the occupation.

But she promised Simon, and besides, she has no scissors. Although perhaps there is a surgical pair kept in the house for emergencies ... She brushes the thought aside.

As evening bruises the sky, she receives a hasty scribble from Simon, telling her there is a complication with Mrs Oswald and he will certainly not be home tonight. That decides her: she will retire to bed early. Morpheus can sleep by her feet if he likes; she is still not *quite* comfortable with the prospect of facing shadows alone.

She bars the street door, extinguishes the gas lamps and tamps down the fire. Deliberately not lighting a taper, she feels her way upstairs and climbs under the covers fully dressed. It is childish, she knows, but she does not want to give her fancy – or her power, whatever it is – a chance to stretch its legs. Imagine how pleased Simon will be if he comes home tomorrow to find she has managed to pass twenty-four hours with no illusions and no upsets.

Although she drank plenty of the cider-rich wassail, sleep evades her. She is not frightened, exactly; there is simply too much to occupy her mind. She tosses and turns, uncomfortable in her clothing. Morpheus does not share her problem. The dog snores, louder than Mamma ever did.

Somewhere down the street, perhaps in the Assembly Rooms, music is being played. There will be fun and games all over the city tonight, except for at the Oswalds' house, where all is fraught with tension, and at the gaol, where Miss West draws near to her sentence hearing and almost certain death.

She flips over the pillow. It does not feel like a night for ghosts. There is no sense of menace or oppression, nor can she hear Cedric's hoop, clacking over the cobbles.

So why can she not rest?

It is only when a firework explodes, waking Morpheus and prompting him to issue a single bark, that she remembers: Simon left in too much of a hurry to prepare her nightly opiate.

She sits up against the bolster. Morpheus pads around the chamber and she can sense people outside, celebrating. Nothing is eerie or strange. She is quite equal to venturing downstairs and finding a bottle of laudanum.

'Come along, then,' she sighs, throwing the covers back. 'I will not get a wink of sleep without it.'

Morpheus stands behind her legs as she fumbles the door open. There is a pier table on the landing – one that Simon's mother used to decorate with floral arrangements – but tonight it holds a lit beeswax candle, set into a silver holder.

Agnes frowns.

'Simon?' she calls.

Her voice echoes through the empty house.

She certainly did not bring that candle upstairs. Could it be a delusion? It burns like a genuine flame. She picks up the holder, tests its weight in her hands.

It *feels* real. The silver is slightly tarnished, engraved with a floral motif that matches the hairbrush on Constance's dressing table.

Morpheus sniffs.

'It comes in handy, anyhow,' she tells him and they set off together down the stairs.

She keeps her eyes trained straight ahead, reluctant to let them wander off and follow shadows. The music from the Assembly Rooms swells outside as she descends. It is sacred, choral, with the deep thrum of an organ beneath.

The consulting room door is unfastened. Agnes slips inside with ease. Her candle flame sparks on glass domes and slides over the gilt tooling on the spines of the books. She lights the lamp upon the desk, illuminating a circle of walnut wood.

Even now, the air is leavened with the scent of carbolic soap.

There are no bottles or medicines in sight. Where in this large room would Simon keep the keys to his cabinets and drawers?

She spies two inkpots standing on the left-hand corner of the desk. Picking each up in turn, she shakes them beside her ear. Metal tinkles in the second one. As she suspected, it is empty and washed out to hide a small brass key: a very simple ruse. Simon has become too used to living alone.

Down the street, the music soars. Morpheus tilts his head comically each time the organ surges into life. She listens, absent-mindedly unlocking the drawers one by one. The single key opens them all. How little Simon must have to hide.

She pulls out the first drawer. It reveals an almanac and newspaper clippings advertising vacancies for medical officers at the workhouse. Simon has scribbled names upon them – no doubt they are people he means to recommend for the positions. She sifts through orders to apothecaries. Under them is a glass vial with *Oil of Vitriol* written on the side.

In the second drawer she finds only a box of matches and some sticks of sealing wax. Where can the laudanum be? She opens another, finds a whole sheaf of letters tied up with string. Most are from other medical men, detailing cases and sharing news; she notices some from Scotland. They must be the doctors Simon studied with.

She gazes over the names. One occurs more frequently than the others: Tobias Dudfield.

The organ in the Assembly Rooms reaches a crescendo. Agnes yawns and a letter slides from the pile, landing directly beneath the light of the glass chimney.

Dear Carfax,

It gave me great pleasure to see you on Thursday – albeit a pleasure which I would rather have enjoyed under more auspicious circumstances. The difficulties of your situation inspire my deepest sympathy.

I undertook to write you my honest opinion, and so I shall set it out.

To gain an estimation of your wife's character on so short an acquaintance is next to impossible, and she is of the taciturn nature that yields precious little fruit even to the keenest observer. I could detect nothing of incipient insanity other than that she appeared to watch me suspiciously, and served me a peculiarly bony piece of fish.

I have no doubt in the veracity of your claims about her violence, nor in our ability to confine her, should we choose. However, we must question whether it is the best course of action for either you or Mrs Carfax's kin.

Your scruples, I fully comprehend, arise from what became of your patient Mrs B, and do you credit. I doubt there ever was such a regrettable case as hers, although I will maintain that none of the fault can lie at your door. Mrs Carfax does not strike me as similar in the slightest degree; I cannot comprehend her innocence being taken advantage of by unprincipled attendants, nor her refusing sustenance to the point of being force-fed. I could furnish you with details of two or three private establishments I have visited personally and found the inmates to be treated with the utmost respect. However, as you say, one is obliged to surrender a degree of control to another physician, and the fee for doing so is not inconsiderable.

My own inclination would be to agree to the proposed separation in an informal capacity. If Mrs Carfax has family who are willing to receive her and the boy, it is all to the good. Provide her with an ample allowance and wash your hands of the matter. Whatever high terms she proposes, you will in all likelihood still find yourself in a better position, both financially and with regards to your good name, than you would should you choose to commit her to an institution.

Having said thus much, I hope there is no need to assure you of my full support and assistance, whatever resolution you should arrive at. I remain, Carfax, your sincere well-wisher &c,

T Dudfield

A ripple passes over her, like wind moving across a lake. She puts the letter down.

She knew nothing of this. Simon never told her he had seriously contemplated having Constance *committed*.

Morpheus sighs and flumps down beside her feet.

What could have prompted it? What did Constance finally do, that was too much? She remembers the dead dogs, Simon's anguish.

Constance had a talent for cruelty, there was no doubt of that. But the idea of committing her to an asylum is somehow ... revolting. A primal, protective instinct flares inside Agnes's chest. She was her sister, after all.

386

Is there anything else? She turns the pile upside down, rummages through the later letters. There is another in the same hand, although not nearly so neat.

Carfax,

My distress on receiving your last you can well imagine. Embarrassment to oneself may be endured, but when threats are made to the safety of those dearest to us, urgent action is required.

The boy's reputation must undoubtedly suffer, yet better that than what you apprehend. I have fresh cause to lament you did not follow your heart and elect to save only the elder sister from the original scandal – it would leave you both now in a position to quietly adopt and raise the child. But I will not make you bitter with regrets.

Rest assured all shall be set in motion this end. I will send you word when you may expect the two inspecting physicians to assess the lady.

Yours &c

Dudfield

The note is dated about a week before Constance's death.

She drops it as if it has bitten her.

The room falls completely silent. Both the organ and the choir melt away; the concert must be over.

She sits glaring at the letters, shocked, astounded. Finally she separates them from the others and tucks

387

them down the front of her dress. She must keep them. Keep them and present them to Simon, to make sure that they are real, not a chimera.

He has betrayed her, though. It hurts to think he would contemplate something as serious as committal without even consulting her feelings. He has never mentioned it, in all these years. Perhaps he does not want to tell her about the awful thing her sister threatened, that inspired this letter from Dudfield? It is possible. But such a long silence suggests something else: it suggests concealment and guilt.

Constance must have known something of this. It must have been one of the reasons she hated Simon so much. Her determination to punish him, to ruin him financially, starts to make some sense.

Agnes cannot stop thinking about what would have happened, were it not for the Accident.

She will admit there were times in her life when she would have been glad to see Constance sent away. But the *reality* of it ... Agnes tries to imagine men putting her sister into a strait-waistcoat and hauling her out the door. Mamma would still have died. She would have died from shame instead.

She has a strange sensation of passing outside her body; of watching events unfold from her sister's point of view. What would Mr Dudfield have made of *Agnes*, had she sat at that table for dinner instead? If he had witnessed her delusions in action, watched her talking to the empty chairs that she thought housed Mamma and Cedric?

Two inspecting physicians.

A voice within whispers, 'How long before Simon turns on you?'

He would not. *Could* not; he loves her. He has tended to her in a deluded state for two years. He will have a good explanation for these letters – she will ask him as soon as he comes home.

Shakily, she returns the other correspondence to the drawer. Two silver items glint at the bottom of it. One is another key, tied upon a red ribbon; the other is a pair of surgical scissors.

Agnes takes them both.

Maybe she can calm herself by cutting practice waves in sable paper; rolling out onto that ocean of black …

But there is something else that will help her do that much more quickly: laudanum. She came here for laudanum. Everything will look better after she has drunk it, slept, and talked over the troubling letters with Simon.

She glances around the room, but it is still unclear where the medicine is kept. The key on the red ribbon must open something besides the desk; perhaps one of the various cabinets?

Her eyes fall upon a heavy leather trunk beside the window that she has not noticed before. It makes her feel … odd. The surface looks worn with much travelling. She imagines it tied to stagecoaches, trundling up the cold roads towards Edinburgh. The people and places it has seen have left their mark, and not just on the leather.

The trunk has an aura, like Miss West spoke of: a tension in the air around it.

Agnes does not want to go near it, but somehow she finds herself kneeling down, trying the key in the lock.

It clicks.

A low growl rumbles from Morpheus's chest.

He watches her intently as she pulls up the lid. The hinges creak like the timbers of a ship.

Inside are two large hooks.

She puts a hand to her forehead, trying to hold things in place. These are the hooks tied to ropes, which Simon used to fish coffins from their graves. Cedric told her about them.

But Cedric was dead.

She *imagined* that conversation. Unless it really was the ghost of her nephew ...

It feels like she is peering into a coffin now: she has the same sensation of fear and disgust. Her fiancé has robbed the dead, sliced up cadavers ... She endeavours to remember it was a duty of his employment a long time ago, and he was *forced* to do it.

There are other items in the box. Surgical tools – or perhaps implements for prising open coffins: a crowbar, a mallet, a saw. Her stomach sours.

She does not want to see any more.

It is only as she reaches to close the lid that she catches sight of a familiar face; or not precisely a face, but its outline, empty inside.

390

The monochrome shape she recognises as her own art.

Pushing rusty nails aside, she closes her fingers around the edge of the shade and pulls it out.

Ice pricks her skin.

The black foolscap has peeled a little at the corners. The white stock card is scuffed and tiny spatters of a dark liquid mark the chin. None of that matters. She would know this piece anywhere, even without her name emblazoned in the corner.

It is the hollow-cut of Ned.

CHAPTER 39

At dawn, Agnes unlocks the street door and takes down the iron bar. She puts Morpheus in the kitchen, sets out the remains of the ham beside his bowl and shuts him in the room.

Next, she returns to Simon's consulting room and sweeps everything off the desk. It makes a satisfying crash. In place of the lamp, the inkpots, the pens and Simon's various paperwork, she lays out four items: the two letters from Tobias Dudfield, Ned's silhouette and the pair of surgical scissors.

She waits.

There are a thousand conundrums that could be teasing her mind right now, but she finds herself oddly focused. All she thinks about is Pearl.

That little girl was kind of heart, and bright, in her way, but she was kept back; a seed never permitted to rise above the soil. Everything Pearl thought that she knew, her sister had told her, and she believed it. She believed it without question.

The clunk of the street door opening seems to fall right through her. Simon's voice calls out: 'Good news, at last! They are both safe. A healthy girl, named for the Queen.'

Morpheus's paws scrabble in the kitchen, but there is no other reply.

'Miss Darken?' A note of alarm. She hears his footsteps clipping across tiles. 'Agnes, are you there?'

He pounds up the stairs, throws doors open. By the time he returns to the ground floor and bursts into the consulting room, he looks half wild.

His face is drained of colour and shiny, like wax. The clothes he has worn since yesterday morning are crumpled, sweat-stained and smell faintly sour. In his arms he clutches an incongruous gift: a set of travelling paintbrushes and watercolours.

Prominent in the tired death mask of his countenance are his blue eyes. They knock from one object on the desk to another, settling on Ned's silhouette.

He does not move.

'Miss West did not kill my clients,' Agnes announces.

'No.'

She expected at least *some* denial. 'But you are going to let her hang for it. A crime she did not commit.'

He closes his eyes, takes a breath. 'I would gladly have put myself forward to die for the real culprit.'

And then he starts to cry.

393

Agnes stares, confused. She cannot recall him weeping like this, even when his family died. But she must not feel pity: this display in itself could be a manipulation.

'*You* did it, to scare me,' she asserts. 'To put me in your power. You wanted me to have no other choice but to marry you.'

He chokes. 'No! Miss Darken, I would never harm another soul—' Dropping the paint set, he starts forward, but stops when he sees her flinch back in the chair. 'I tried so hard to protect you.'

'From *whom*?' She concentrates on Ned's silhouette and the spots of blood that mark it; she cannot trust herself to look at her friend's face. 'I wonder you did not burn this. It is not like you to be sloppy, Simon. But I suppose you had your hands full.'

'You said it was your best work …' He breaks off, runs a hand across his sweating forehead. When he recommences, he sounds calmer, resigned. 'No, you are right. I should have burnt it. I should have dissolved the bodies, too, rather than hiding them, but I thought their families deserved something to bury. I did not have time to think it through … It all started to happen so quickly.'

She should feel frightened of him, but she is strangely numb. 'What did?'

He puts out his hands like he is trying to placate a rabid dog. 'Do not worry, Miss Darken. We will find help. We will stop these spells of disassociation

394

... I was wrong to attempt to handle them alone. My emotions got the better of me. I have a friend ...' He takes a step closer. 'It is not your fault. You were not in control. After the pneumonia ... there were times you were not *yourself*. You were more like ...' Another step. 'I thought that if I got you away from Bath, to Switzerland, it might stop.' His face seems to collapse. 'We were so close to being happy. I could have made you well.'

'*Me*?' she disputes. 'Do not try your trickery, Simon; do not try to turn this around on me, you are the one who has lied—'

'It must be in the blood,' he mutters to himself. He is so near now that she can smell the birthing chamber on him. 'A taint. I never thought you and your sister anything alike, but when it comes over you, I see her again ...'

Agnes scuffs her chair further away. 'Stop there. Right there.' She snatches up the letters and brandishes them at him. 'I am wise to your game. Now I know of your guilt, you will try to send me away, pretend that I am mad.'

'What have you ...' For the first time he seems to understand what the letters are. His eyes slide across the desk.

Stop on the scissors.

A chill runs over her skin. She remembers how Ned and Mr Boyle died: a single laceration to the throat.

Simon reaches out a hand.

395

'Stay back,' she snaps.

'Miss Darken, let me take those scissors.'

'I'm warning you, Simon!' Her voice rises, beyond her control.

Simon puts a foot forward. 'You cannot be trusted with them,' he explains. His blue eyes flick between her and the open blades. 'When it has possession of you—'

'You are lying! I could not hurt a fly!' She is screeching. It sounds like her vocal chords are being worked by someone else.

He wets his lips, inches closer. 'You can. You *do*. You lose hours, and I—'

'Stay *back*!'

Simon's pupils lock on hers.

They both lunge for the scissors at the same time.

———

There is a sense of retraction, of snapping back into herself. Her eyes pop open and she is standing alone in Constance's bedchamber, watching the sun set in a riot of pink and Etruscan red.

A pitiful whine comes from downstairs.

Perplexed, hollow, she wanders from the room. The carpet on the stairs is marked with paw prints; Agnes follows them to the kitchen where she finds Morpheus whimpering like a human child. At first, she thinks the dog is hurt, but when she picks up his little black feet to inspect them, they are uncut. His paws seem to be stained with a dark substance that is not his own blood.

'Silly boy,' she says.

He shies under the table.

The house has a comfortable hush. It is empty, yet occupied. She feels free, but not alone.

She finds a newspaper sitting on the doormat and has a quick leaf through the pages. The journalists speak of great wars abroad and plans for 1855; everywhere the old is being effaced and replaced with the new.

Leisurely, she strolls to the consulting room. Her feet kick against glass; more empty vials of oil of vitriol lie scattered across the carpet.

'What has happened here?'

The lamp upon the desk is lit. By the light of its chimney, she sees that someone has left her a piece of paper. A painting, in fact – a shade.

The sitter is Simon: there can be no doubt of that. His likeness has been taken as skilfully as if she had done it herself. But this profile has not been brushed with her usual blend of ink and soot; the paint is thicker, rusty in hue. She runs her finger over the bridge of Simon's nose. It feels like a crust.

Words are written beneath in the hand she recognises from the notes: *Now he will never part us.*

She turns her head. A shadow stretches up the wall, created by the failing sun: a slender woman wearing her hair in a chignon.

It is not Agnes, although it is similar.

She has no doubt now. She possesses the Gift.

The shadow holds out a hand.

'Oh, Constance,' she sighs, pressing her palm against the wallpaper. 'Whatever have you done?'

Acknowledgements

The first germs of this story came to me during the 2016 Jane Austen Festival in Bath. My friends and I attended a wonderful talk and workshop with silhouette artist Charles Burns, who was kind enough to let us loose on his own physiognotrace – with hilarious results! Charles Burns's instructive book, *Mastering Silhouettes* (Fil Rouge Press Ltd, 2012) also proved a key resource for me in writing about Agnes's work. I cannot thank him enough!

Pearl's experiences with spiritualism were largely inspired by the memoirs of Victorian-era spirit medium Elizabeth d'Espérance, quoted at the beginning of this book, but those conversant with the topic will recognise that the name of her 'spirit guide' Florence King is a nod to the famous medium Katie King, who supposedly 'materialised' the spirit of Florence Cook in the 1870s. *Missives from Summerland* is a fictional newspaper, very loosely based on the *Medium and Daybreak*. Similarly, the Bath Society of Spiritual Adventurers is my own invention: I did not wish to associate my fraudulent characters with real people of genuine spiritual belief.

I am indebted to Harriet Martineau's *Letters on Mesmerism* and Wendy Moore's biography *The Mesmerist* for helping me to create Myrtle's world. The Queen of Crime herself, Agatha Christie, must also be thanked for her novel *Dumb Witness*, which sparked the idea for phosphorus at a séance.

Pearl's physical appearance was inspired by Miss Millie Lamar, 'The White Fairy', who worked as a mind reader in 1890s America. In the Victorian era, it was sadly common for the unscrupulous to monetarise albinism, as is evidenced by the employment of a number of people with albinism in P. T. Barnum's travelling circus.

My version of Victorian Bath is based on the Cotterell map and Vivian's 'Street Directory' from 1852, plus local information discovered in the British Newspaper Archive. The characters' houses are of course fictional. Any mistakes are my own. The weather of 1854, I purposefully changed for my own devices.

I have borrowed some names from my mother's family for this tale; she had both an Auntie Aggie and a paternal cousin whose surname was Darken. I hope they will not mind me using them in this way – I must stress that the names are the only similarities!

On a personal note I would like to thank my husband, Kevin, to whom the book is dedicated. He came up with the title long before we had heard of the del Toro film! My agent, Juliet Mushens, who somehow still talks to me after reading my early drafts, and the wonderful team at Raven Books. My special thanks always go to Alison Hennessey, Lilidh Kendrick, Philippa Noar, Amy Donegan, Sara Helen Binney and David Mann, but I am sure there are many other silent heroes working behind the scenes who I never meet. My heartfelt gratitude to you all.

A Note on the Type

The text of this book is set in Linotype Stempel Garamond, a version of Garamond adapted and first used by the Stempel foundry in 1924. It is one of several versions of Garamond based on the designs of Claude Garamond. It is thought that Garamond based his font on Bembo, cut in 1495 by Francesco Griffo in collaboration with the Italian printer Aldus Manutius. Garamond types were first used in books printed in Paris around 1532. Many of the present-day versions of this type are based on the *Typi Academiae* of Jean Jannon cut in Sedan in 1615.

Claude Garamond was born in Paris in 1480. He learned how to cut type from his father and by the age of fifteen he was able to fashion steel punches the size of a pica with great precision. At the age of sixty he was commissioned by King Francis I to design a Greek alphabet, and for this he was given the honourable title of royal type founder. He died in 1561.

MISSIONARY WRITING AND EMPIRE, 1800–1860

Anna Johnston analyses missionary writing under the aegis of the British Empire. Johnston argues that missionaries occupied ambiguous positions in colonial cultures, caught between imperial and religious interests. She maps out this position through an examination of texts published by missionaries of the largest, most influential nineteenth-century evangelical institution, the London Missionary Society. These texts provide a fascinating commentary on nineteenth-century evangelism and colonialism, and illuminate complex relationships among white imperial subjects, white colonial subjects, and non-white colonial subjects. With their reformist and often prurient interest in sexual and familial relationships, missionary texts focussed imperial attention on gender and domesticity in colonial cultures. Johnston contends that in doing so, they re-wrote imperial expansion as a moral allegory and confronted British ideologies of gender, race, and class. Texts from Indian, Polynesian, and Australian missions are examined to highlight their representation of nineteenth-century evangelical activity in relation to gender, colonialism, and race.

ANNA JOHNSTON is Lecturer in Australian and Postcolonial Literature in the School of English, Journalism, and European Languages at the University of Tasmania. She is the co-editor of *In Transit: Travel, Text, Empire* (2002) with Helen Gilbert, and has published articles on missionary writing, postcolonial literature, and autobiography.

CAMBRIDGE STUDIES IN NINETEENTH-CENTURY
LITERATURE AND CULTURE

General editor
Gillian Beer, *University of Cambridge*

Editorial board
Isobel Armstrong, *Birkbeck College, London*
Leonore Davidoff, *University of Essex*
Terry Eagleton, *University of Manchester*
Catherine Gallagher, *University of California, Berkeley*
D. A. Miller, *Columbia University*
J. Hillis Miller, *University of California, Irvine*
Mary Poovey, *New York University*
Elaine Showalter, *Princeton University*

Nineteenth-century British literature and culture have been rich fields for interdisciplinary studies. Since the turn of the twentieth century, scholars and critics have tracked the intersections and tensions between Victorian literature and the visual arts, politics, social organisation, economic life, technical innovations, scientific thought – in short, culture in its broadest sense. In recent years, theoretical challenges and historiographical shifts have unsettled the assumptions of previous scholarly synthesis and called into question the terms of older debates. Whereas the tendency in much past literary critical interpretation was to use the metaphor of culture as 'background', feminist, Foucauldian, and other analyses have employed more dynamic models that raise questions of power and of circulation. Such developments have reanimated the field.

This series aims to accommodate and promote the most interesting work being undertaken on the frontiers of the field of nineteenth-century literary studies: work which intersects fruitfully with other fields of study such as history, or literary theory, or the history of science. Comparative as well as interdisciplinary approaches are welcomed.

A complete list of titles published will be found at the end of the book.

MISSIONARY WRITING AND EMPIRE, 1800–1860

ANNA JOHNSTON

CAMBRIDGE
UNIVERSITY PRESS

CAMBRIDGE UNIVERSITY PRESS
Cambridge, New York, Melbourne, Madrid, Cape Town, Singapore, São Paulo

Cambridge University Press
The Edinburgh Building, Cambridge CB2 8RU, UK

Published in the United States of America by Cambridge University Press, New York

www.cambridge.org
Information on this title: www.cambridge.org/9780521826990

First published 2003
This digitally printed version 2008

A catalogue record for this publication is available from the British Library

Library of Congress Cataloguing in Publication data
Johnston, Anna, 1972–
Missionary writing and empire, 1800–1860 / Anna Johnston.
p.   cm. – (Cambridge studies in nineteenth-century literature and culture; 38)
Includes bibliographical references and index.
ISBN 0 521 82699 3 (hardback)
1. London Missionary Society – History – 19th century.   2. Missions, English – India – History –
19th century.   3. Missions, English – Polynesia – History – 19th century.   4. Missions, English –
Australia – History – 19th century.   I. Title.   II. Series.
BV2361.L8J64   2003
266′.02341′009034 – dc21   2002041700

ISBN 978-0-521-82699-0 hardback
ISBN 978-0-521-04955-9 paperback

For Garth Tickle

Contents

Acknowledgements   *page* xi

Introduction: writing missionaries   1

PART ONE   THE MISSION STATEMENT

1. The British Empire, colonialism, and missionary activity   13

2. Gender, domesticity, and colonial evangelisation   38

PART TWO   THE LONDON MISSIONARY SOCIETY IN INDIA

3. Empire, India, and evangelisation   63

4. Missionary writing in India   79

5. Imperialism, suffragism, and nationalism   106

PART THREE   THE LONDON MISSIONARY SOCIETY IN POLYNESIA

6. Polynesian missions and the European imaginary   115

7. Missionary writing in Polynesia   136

PART FOUR   THE LONDON MISSIONARY SOCIETY IN AUSTRALIA

8. The Australian colonies and empire   167

9. Missionary writing in Australia   180

    Conclusion: missionary writing, the imperial archive and
    postcolonial politics   202

Notes   210
Bibliography   239
Index   253

Acknowledgements

This book has emerged over eight years. Across a range of cities, institutions, and social circles, I have been fortunate to be incredibly well supported. My acknowledgements here only begin to repay my debts of gratitude.

The University of Queensland's English Department provided a supportive and stimulating environment for my doctoral work. The Postcolonial Research Group provided crucial and ongoing feedback. Without Helen Gilbert's kind bossiness, my thesis would have lingered on the shelf. Alan Lawson, my associate supervisor, has always had a faith in me that I hope one day to believe myself, and taught me much. Above all, as supervisor and role model, Helen Tiffin kept me on track, inspired, and stimulated. Both her intellectual rigour and her generous friendship help me to conceptualise the kind of work it is worth doing.

Many people have read and commented on this work in various forms. Helen Tiffin and Alan Lawson provided valuable feedback from the start. Gareth Griffiths, Bart Moore-Gilbert, and Stephen Slemon each provided generous and motivating examiners' reports. After a day fence-building in Alberta, Stephen provided the impetus for my research on missionaries. His insightful, kind, and stimulating report on my thesis made me understand what it was I had been trying to do, and how to write this book. In their readers' reports for Cambridge University Press, Patrick Brantlinger and Robert J. C. Young provided me with extremely valuable ways of rethinking my original project. At Cambridge University Press, Linda Bree and Rachel de Wachter have been immensely helpful.

Colleagues and students at the University of Tasmania have been a supportive base for the past three years. Lucy Frost's advice, support, and research have been crucial. Without Tony Stagg, my research assistant, this book would not have emerged, and neither would I. Not only is he thorough, supportive, and indefatigable, but he also keeps me laughing and calm, and tells me wonderful stories about Tasmania.

Numerous institutions have supported my research. An Australian Post-graduate Research Award was crucial, and a University of Queensland Australian Studies scholarship funded vital archival research in London. The Centre for Cross-Cultural Research at Australian National University awarded me a scholarship for its visiting scholars programme in 1998, which changed the way I thought about my research and provided me with an ongoing network of friends and colleagues.

Archivists at the School of Oriental and African Studies, University of London, have always provided kind and useful advice about the London Missionary Society archives. I am grateful to librarians at the University of Queensland, the Australian National University, and the University of Tasmania.

Friends and colleagues have helped greatly. Carrie Dawson, Paul Newman, Kathryn Goldie, and Gil Woodley kept me company in the University of Queensland corridors and in postgraduate studies. Tseen Khoo is so reliable, emotionally and intellectually, that I take her advice without question. Linda Halsen, Lib and Craig Wheeley, Kate Douglas, and Ian Wilkins have been encouraging and supportive. Simone Coxall and Andrew Teverson coax me out of the archives and are such dear friends that they even listen to missionary stories. In Tasmania, Elle Leane, Sam Hardy, and Jeremy Whiteman have made me feel at home. Mitchell Rolls read part four, and makes me happy.

My family provides immense love and encouragement, which is all recip-rocated. My grandmothers, Patricia Tickle and Agnes Johnston, taught me in different ways to be independent but profoundly connected to the world. This book only exists because of my parents, Scott and Jenny Johnston, whose love, support, and confidence keeps me afloat. This book is for all my family, really, but it is dedicated with a special, undiminishing love to Garth Tickle, who would be proud if he could remember.

Different versions of material in parts three and four have been previously published: as articles in *Semeia* 88 (2001) and *New Literatures Review* 36 (Winter 2000); and as chapters in *In Transit: Travel, Text, Empire*, edited by Helen Gilbert and Anna Johnston (New York: Peter Lang, 2002) and *Colonial Frontiers: Indigenous-European Encounters in Settler Societies*, edited by Lynette Russell (Manchester: Manchester University Press, 2001).

Introduction: writing missionaries

On Wednesday, 14 May 1834, Reverend Robert Burns[1] preached before the London Missionary Society, at the Tabernacle, Moorfields. His sermon, entitled *The Indirect Benefits of the Missionary Enterprise*, sought to explain what he saw as five 'advantages' which had come about through nineteenth-century missionary activity. The first advantage, Burns states, is that 'Our views of man have been enlarged and rectified':[2]

Long did the Christian world remain very imperfectly informed of the real nature and effects of heathenism in regard to its blinded votaries. Misled by the theories of some over-refined speculators, and relying implicitly on the statements of certain interested voyagers or historians, we dreamed of the pagan tribes as pure in their manners, and refined in their enjoyments . . . It was not til the Christian world was awakened from its lethargy . . . that our mistakes regarding the actual state of man were rectified, and facts and illustrations, hitherto neglected, brought forward to view in all their revolting reality. A spirit of inquiry into the state of the world at large has been cherished. More accurate accounts of its real condition have been obtained. The causes of man's misery have been traced out. The theories of a false philosophy have been exploded. (7–8)

Burns positions evangelical philosophies and the lived experiences of missionaries in opposition to Orientalist attitudes of imperial and colonial elites. No longer should Europeans regard India's ancient civilisation as 'elegant' or 'wise' or 'venerable': missionary activity proved that India was simply 'heathen'. Nor should the Polynesian Islands be seen as utopian paradises untouched by industrialisation and inhabited by noble savages who lived close to nature: again, missionaries had shown that these were simply sites where the 'revolting reality' of heathenism could be witnessed. In a direct challenge to educated, liberal opinion, Burns posits the authority of evangelical philosophy and missionary zeal. The second advantage, Burns asserts, is that 'missionary enterprise has led to the successful culture of some important branches of intellectual and religious inquiry' (9), drawing attention to the vast amount of ethnographic, linguistic, and translation work missionaries carried out. Third, he argues, 'Missionary efforts have enriched the world with certain distinguished specimens of moral and religious excellence' (13). Missionary celebrities such as John Williams and David Livingstone had provided British evangelicals with figureheads of religious and national stature, men whom all should revere, and attempt to emulate. Fourthly, for Burns 'Missionary efforts have proved highly beneficial in securing the essential rights and liberties of mankind' (16); particularly, for evangelicals keenly interested in humanitarian issues, the abolition of slavery. Finally, Burns postulates, missionaries have been central in introducing the twin evangelical ideals of 'civilisation and christianisation' in Britain's 'heathen' colonies.

It is worthwhile bringing Robert Burns' comments to light again at the beginning of the twenty-first century. Having spent the past eight years researching missionaries, I am well aware that most people have an opinion about missionary work, particularly in colonial contexts. Generally, people are critical of missionaries' actions, seeing them as culturally insensitive and destructive. Some still celebrate them as introducing 'civilized', 'modern' practices to indigenous cultures. Others see them as the benign side of imperialism, providing a kind of moral justification for British expansion, and rightly argue that in some places they stood between the excessive violence of colonial expansion and indigenous peoples. All these images build on representations in histories, popular culture, film, and literature, where missionary figures are generally divested of agency and capacity for self-reflection. Burns' sermon reminds us that nineteenth-century missionaries were in fact highly conscious of the nature of their evangelical projects and their potential effect, both in colonial cultures and back in the imperial metropolis. Burns' five points make clear the pseudo-scientific, highly strategic nature of missionary interventions around the world. Importantly, he illuminates the contribution that evangelisation sought to make to imperial representation and ideology, to British self-fashioning on both an individual and a national scale, and to imperial reform of colonial cultures. Across the Empire, British missionary commentators sought, by their 'zeal', to remake colonial projects in the image of religious conversion. In doing so, missionaries constructed an ambiguous, ambivalent position for themselves within colonial cultures, a position negotiated in the many texts they produced: the 'more accurate accounts' which Burns promotes. This book maps this ambiguous position through the texts which constitute the London Missionary Society (henceforth LMS) archives, texts which provide a fascinating commentary on the complexities of colonial cultures and open up a place where the contradictory discourses of nineteenth-century colonialism can be clearly seen.

British Protestant missionaries were prolific writers. Diaries, reports, letters, memoirs, histories, ethnographies, novels, children's books, translations, grammars, and many more kinds of texts spilled from their pens. At a makeshift desk in some remote mission station, or in retirement amongst the comforts provided by their return 'home', the missionary at work was characterised by authorship as much as by daring deeds in foreign climes. The nineteenth century saw the vast expansion of archives filled with information about the world outside Britain, an expansion which grew exponentially alongside Britain's 'second' empire. Missionary texts were a foundational and influential part of this 'imperial archive',[3] and they are the focus of this book. Because missionaries inhabited such complex, ambivalent, and uncertain positions within colonial cultures I look closely and critically at the textual archive of missionary endeavours, in order to trace the ways these texts complicate traditional linear histories of imperial conquest and invasion. One of the instigations for this project was that such easy narratives co-exist in both old-fashioned history books and in the most cutting-edge postcolonial theory, as do the neat bifurcation of identities as either colonised or colonising. The LMS archive repeatedly proves that questions of history and identity under colonial conditions are much more complex than this.

Missionary texts are crucial to understanding cross-cultural encounters under the aegis of empire because they illuminate the formation of a mode of *mutual imbrication*[4] between white imperial subjects, white colonial subjects, and non-white colonial subjects. Through my discussion of mutual imbrication, I demonstrate that the ways in which colonial cultures enacted imperial philosophies were by no means straightforward – colonial experience profoundly altered imperial theories and policies, and had real effects on British ideas both about imperialism and about British domestic culture. More specifically, colonial missionary writing changed the ways in which crucial facets of nineteenth-century culture could be represented. For the LMS missionary archive, I argue that it was primarily through philosophies and practices relative to gender that this mutual imbrication was realised. The kinds of social relations and ideologies embedded in missionary texts introduced a concentration on gender and domesticity facilitating both moral allegorisation of imperial intervention and confrontation with British culture and its assumptions about femininity, masculinity, and domestic relations. By focussing on mutual imbrication, attention shifts from a top-down, colonised versus coloniser model of imperial cultural relations to one which reinstates the importance of colonial experience in the self-fashioning of British individuals and culture. In so doing, I aim to disrupt the monolithic logic of imperial history, but to do so from within, by bringing to bear textual and postcolonial theories on a closely bound set of historical relations.

The LMS and its archive form the basis of my analysis, because of the Society's interdenominational nature, its habit of sending married missionaries rather than single ones, and because it was one of the most influential missionary societies in the colonies in which I am particularly interested: India, Polynesia, and Australia. The kind of attention I pay to the texts emerging from the three sites of colonial evangelisation necessarily differs according to the context and nature of both missionary presence and textual history. In places where numerous missionary writers were prolific – notably India and Polynesia – a variety of texts are available for analysis, although volume does not necessarily produce diversity when one investigates the trite, recycled (if not plagiarised) narratives of colonial evangelisation. In Australia, by contrast, the LMS was represented by only a single missionary during this period – as controversial and textually productive as Lancelot Threlkeld was, the nature of that textual archive is obviously quite different. Inevitably, the LMS broad evangelical base produced a specific history differing considerably from that of other, comparable missionary societies: particularly, it speaks of a section of British society overwhelmingly concerned with class and identity. This specific history also produced a distinctive textual environment. Throughout this book, I distinguish the *particularity* of LMS representations, the construction of a discourse which arose because of the peculiar positionality of LMS missionaries in the colonial field and because of the characteristic contradictions inhabiting the assumptions they bear. But I will also trace the ways in which these highly particular representations circulated as 'general knowledge' both in the colonies and in Britain. Missionary representations were circulated strategically by the LMS, in ways which emphasised their universality rather than their particularity, and they were thus highly productive of imperial knowledge about the colonial world. Not only that, but they influenced how Britons saw themselves and their own cultural conditions.

I focus on the period from 1800 to 1860, because this was a critical time of social reform in Britain, when many cultural narratives central to British self-imagining were (re)invented. It is a period in which the evangelical Protestant revival, which had commenced in the late eighteenth century, found its full expression in a renewal of British religiosity, a range of philanthropic movements, and an attempt to dominate the moral agenda. It was also a time in which questions about race, class, and gender were important to a British community expanding its territory into, and acquiring knowledge about, other regions and cultures. The first sixty years of the century represented an intermediate stage before the aggressive high imperialism of the century's end, and, as a result, ideas about race, class, and gender were still under negotiation, and vulnerable to the sectional interests of groups like evangelical Protestants. In this time period, my three central colonial locations – India, Polynesia, and Australia – were formally brought under British rule. Britain was learning how to institute modern imperialism, which, as Jenny Sharpe argues, was 'guided by the moral imperative to bring the colonized into civil society' rather than earlier forms of territorial conquest.[5] The invidious philosophies of nineteenth-century imperialism ensured that morality and territory were intrinsically linked. Evangelical Protestant missionaries, keen proponents of what they termed 'Christianisation and civilisation', were extremely influential in both the material and intellectual realisation of modern colonial projects.[6]

I examine missionary texts about three quite different geographical locations of evangelical activity. My comparative approach enables an understanding of colonial evangelism as a broad-based, globalised project, but carried out in diverse ways in different colonies. These three locations are particularly interesting because missionaries were involved in substantially different types of cross-cultural relations, despite their shared interest in 'universal' issues such as gender. As a consequence, each individual geographical archive brings quite different ideas and influences to bear on both local missionary activity and on imperial philosophies of race, gender, and domesticity. They do not provide a neatly 'representative' survey of LMS writing in this period, nor do they make up a kind of composite synecdoche of colonial administrative/historical modes. Instead, they demonstrate that broader, ill-defined contemporary British ideas about these places informed the LMS textual industry, influencing the materiality of textual production from these sites and the conditions of its production, circulation, and control.

India was primarily an economic and trading interest for Britain, although by the 1860s Britain had added India to its imperial portfolio of colonies and had developed a keener sense of moral responsibility for its Indian subjects. Missionaries in India often battled as much with white colonial elites as with 'blinded votaries' of Hinduism.[7] The islands of the South Pacific constituted a kind of *de facto* colonial entity, though the British seem to have been reluctant to take any official responsibility for areas like Polynesia until competition with other imperial nations drove them to do so later in the nineteenth century. Indeed, for much of the nineteenth century missionaries were acting as surrogate imperialists, though under their own impetus rather than because of any directive to do so from Britain. Missionaries in Polynesia formed their own versions of colonial states. Arguably their interventions to some extent made possible the later wholesale colonisation of the region. Australia is always something of a unique case in colonial/postcolonial studies. As a penal colony, New South Wales was a particularly institutionalised colonial state, one not naturally conducive to evangelical activities. As Australia moved closer to settler colony status, conditions for missionary work were difficult – settlers were frequently more interested in moving Aborigines off valuable grazing land than converting them to Christianity – although missionaries made concerted efforts to evangelise the indigenous population from the 1820s onwards. Whilst there is continuing resistance to including settler colonies under the broad rubric of postcolonialism, careful attention to the localised experiences of imperial policy and colonial enactments of it is crucial to examining the different ways in which postcolonial and colonial discourse theories might assist in deconstructing the totalising potential of imperial histories. The particular politics of each location produced substantial differences in the ways in which missionary activity was carried out and, most importantly, to the manner in which missionaries, their proselytising, and their potential converts are represented in texts.

Although questions central to the practice of history contextualise this book, I concentrate throughout on issues of representation. This is not a history of imperial missionaries, except that it is a type of literary history of a particular archive central to Empire. It is also not a history of colonised peoples' personal or textual responses to evangelical intervention, because my concentration on close readings of British missionary texts provides a very filtered view of the *indigenous* history of missionary encounters. I focus instead on examining the public and institutional role of missionary work and its role within imperial projects, because it is this public, civic image that was crucial to the textual self-representation of imperial missionary enterprise in Britain and in the colonies. I examine only published missionary texts because of their authorised participation in this public discursive domain.

Published missionary texts have their own particular limitations. The first is one of genre. Most texts are the end result of a well-oiled and efficient production machine run by missionary societies and their supportive evangelical publishers. They are thus fundamentally and frankly propagandist in nature. Their aim was variously to inculcate public support for missionary endeavours; to ensure an on-going supply of donated funds from individuals, institutions, and governments; to cultivate a community of like-minded British citizens who would stand up for missionary interests in the face of more aggressive mercantile, industrial, or territorial interests; and to encourage a community of potential missionary recruits. As a result, missionary writing conforms to an identifiable set of generic regulations. Unsurprisingly, there is always an emphasis on positive evangelical achievements whilst limited successes or spectacular failures are rarely mentioned. Backsliding missionaries in the colonies – those whose faith was shattered in their confrontation with different cultures, or who abandoned missionary work because they formed attachments to local women or communities, or who left preaching for the rather more lucrative positions of colonial trader, planter, or merchant, for example – slide out of the public textual record. Missionary figures are almost exclusively heroic, long-suffering, and do not experience religious doubts, debilitating diseases, or personal crises. Native resistance is usually depicted as moral decay and intellectual depravity. Specific recurrent tropes of representation will be identified in my analyses of various missionary texts. Gaps between these tropes and the reality of experience become evident throughout my analysis. Identifying the 'truth' behind missionary representation is not my aim, but examining the means by which experience could be credibly and consistently narrated is.

The other major limitation of missionary writing is the relative uniformity of authorship – most texts discussed here were written by male missionaries. This is because in the period 1800 to 1860 the LMS was dominated by men, endorsing only male missionaries (with their wives as 'helpmeets'), and governed by male directors back in Britain. From about the 1860s, women began to be sent to colonial mission stations in their own right, and examining the colonial pressures which brought about this profound institutional change will be one of the major themes of the book. Texts by missionary women were also published, but proportionally few appear in the LMS archive for this period. Their production was dependent upon many factors, not the least of which were the circumstances of each mission location. My work on India can draw upon a range of texts produced by both women and men because the custom of separate women's apartments within homes (*zenanas*) precluded the entry of male missionaries, though their wives were able to gain some access. Missionary women in India therefore had a particular insight into the details of domestic arrangements and gender practices denied to their male partners and, as a result, they were encouraged to publish accounts of their experiences. But in Polynesia and Australia there were no comparable avenues of exclusively female evangelisation, and male missionaries, who were the only individuals formally invested with the authority of the societies in this period, mostly monopolised the textual archive and official publications. Though masculine authors tend to dominate missionary writing and therefore my primary material, questions of gender are important ones in these texts. Whilst remaining relatively silent about female missionary partners, male missionaries were rarely silent about gender, sexuality, and domesticity: in fact they were vociferous.

The role of missionary provided young men, frequently limited by class and education in England, opportunities for social advancement, community standing, and a challenging and exotic career. Intrinsically tied to the development of muscular Christianity, an ideal reaching its zenith in the latter half of the nineteenth century, missionary men both discovered and invented their masculinity through their encounter with other, colonised cultures. Vigorous but pious British manliness was contrasted with depraved native masculinity, and missionary texts anxiously but assertively represented the world in these terms. In parallel, the pious, domestic, British Christian woman was upheld as an embodiment of empire, a role model to which heathen women should aspire. Both of these emblematic figures in missionary texts hid the very recent, and highly contested, nature of such gendered roles within Britain itself.

But the gendered roles of colonised non-Christian men and women were intensely scrutinised. Missionaries are infamous examples of 'white men ... saving brown women from brown men', as Gayatri Spivak memorably wrote.[8] Both missionary societies and individual evangelists relied heavily on the figure of 'the native woman' as a means of justifying their colonial projects. They could do so because, throughout the mission field, images of the degradation of local women by traditional custom were graphically depicted and deplored. In so doing, the supposed deprivations of women became common knowledge in the colonies and in Britain. Gender was thus used as an additional justification of imperial missionary projects. The discourse of eighteenth- and nineteenth-century gender relations gave mission societies another language – both literally and figuratively – to legitimise their work by stressing the civility and integrity of colonial missionary evangelisation.

This book demonstrates that through evangelical projects, particularly through the discourses emerging from the missionary archive of this period, fundamental questions about gender, race, and civility were worked out in the colonies. I analyse a range of missionary writing to examine exactly how representations of gender worked to subsidise ongoing evangelisation and imperial intervention. Such missionary representations were not so much part of a unitary project, but rather, as Anne McClintock suggests of the dialectic between domesticity and empire in general, 'beset by contradiction, anomaly, and paradox'.[9] Simultaneously, missionary representations of colonial gender relations influenced debates about gender back in Britain. British suffragists used ideas about Indian women – figured as victims of Indian patriarchy – to make arguments about their struggle for equal rights. The 'licentiousness' of native women and the threat that such sexuality posed to the British social order provided authorities with both institutional models (lock hospitals) and ideological frameworks to regulate working-class prostitution.[10] The 'angel in the house' of the early Victorian period, once she realised the limitations of being a purely domestic figure, found in missionary work a wider sphere for her moral influence. In such ways I trace the mutual imbrication between imperial and colonial subjectivities, and their textual representation.

As an integral part of 'the philanthropic moralizing mission that defined bourgeois culture in the nineteenth century [and] cast a wide imperial net',[11] missionary figures are anomalous in a colonial environment. Always conscious of their liminality, missionaries sought to consolidate their precarious position in colonial cultures by mimicking stereotypical imperial practices, of racial superiority for example, and by rigidly enforcing and encouraging colonial versions of them in their 'heathen' charges. Like all colonial projects, these practices were only partially realised and unevenly enforced. Taking account of missionaries, though, pays serious attention to Johannes Fabian's call that not only 'the crooks and brutal exploiters, but the honest and intelligent agents of colonization need to be accounted for'.[12]

It is in missionary texts that the partial, provisional nature of these activities is most explicit. As Nicholas Thomas notes of colonial texts in general, 'even when colonizers surrounded themselves with the persuasive scenery of possession and rule, the gaps between projection and performance are frequently betrayed by the anxieties of their texts, which reveal the gestural character of efforts to govern, sanitize, convert, and reform'.[13] Missionary texts attempt to stabilise their potentially unsettling effect on empire and its supporting philosophies through their adherence to strictly authorised forms of genre. Inevitably, though, the disturbing nature of missionary work on cross-cultural borders leaks through. Missionary narratives often display ruptures in apparently seamless colonialist textual practices; they worry at potentially inappropriate mimicry by native 'heathens' and Christians; and they expose the instability of the missionary position on the colonial stage – an instability measured by its distance from both institutional imperial authority and from native cultures. Ann Laura Stoler argues that in colonial discourses of racialized sexuality, it is the 'cultural density' of these representations that is particularly interesting. Like Stoler, I am interested in unpacking this cultural density as it is manifested in the missionary archive, to trace, as Stoler does, the ways in which colonial discourse 'reverberated between metropole and colony to secure the tenuous distinctions of bourgeois rule'.[14] The density of missionary representations of class, race, and colonial power highlight not the hegemony of imperial systems of control, but 'their precarious vulnerabilities' (97).

PART ONE

The mission statement

CHAPTER ONE

The British Empire, colonialism, and missionary activity

Christian missionary activity was central to the work of European colonialism, providing British missionaries and their supporters with a sense of justice and moral authority. Throughout the history of imperial expansion, missionary proselytising offered the British public a model of 'civilised' expansionism and colonial community management, transforming imperial projects into moral allegories.[1] Missionary activity was, however, unavoidably implicated in either covert or explicit cultural change. It sought to transform indigenous communities into imperial archetypes of civility and modernity by remodelling the individual, the community, and the state through western, Christian philosophies. In the British Empire, and particularly in what is historically known as the 'second' era of British imperialism (approximately 1784–1867), missionary activity was frequently involved with the initial steps of imperial expansion. A heightened sense of religiosity in Britain at this time ensured that Christianisation was seen as a crucial part of the colonising and civilising projects of the eighteenth and nineteenth centuries. As Jamie Scott notes, 'by the middle of the nineteenth century, under the double aegis of "the bible and the flag", governments, merchants, explorers, and other adventurers were exploiting the aura of ethical responsibility lent by religion to every effort to carry British civilisation to a benighted world'.[2]

Whilst earlier European empires (such as the Spanish and Portuguese) had spread Catholicism, Protestant churches had traditionally been too deeply divided to make any commitment to overseas missions. Indeed, the historically strong regional church in German-based Protestantism ensured that mission activity prior to the seventeenth and eighteenth centuries was barely an issue. As Stephen Neill says, 'It is hardly possible for a Church so confined within the boundaries of a given geographical area ever to become missionary in any real sense of the term.'[3] The rise of Protestantism in the seventeenth and eighteenth centuries as a unified and less persecuted religious movement only benefited from imperial expansion into new

13

territories: 'In reality, it is only when the Dutch and the English began to push their commercial ventures to the ends of the earth that Protestantism begins to breathe a freer missionary air' (190).

The evangelical Protestant revival in Britain in the late eighteenth century provided the religious fervour and missionary impulse to ensure religious involvement in colonial projects. This revival coincided with complex social and economic changes, as well as more general philosophical shifts post-Enlightenment. Church historians of the time explained the rise of foreign missions as a direct response to anti-Christian public sentiment at home. The historian of the Baptist Missionary Society blames the disastrous effects of the French Revolution, where 'infidelity eclipsed the glory of truth, and spread its pestilential atmosphere amidst the moral darkness and confusion. The nation became warm in politics and cold in religion.'[4] C. Silvester Horne's stridently celebratory history of the LMS declares that 'Christianity itself had been challenged; the new missionary policy was a bold and trumpet-toned acceptance of that challenge.'[5]

The evangelical revival, with its roots firmly in the lower to middle social orders, was also a response to the growing industrialisation of British society and the resultant rise in power and status of the middle class. Individual denominations invested differently in various social communities – Baptists, for example, had a strongly artisanal constituency – but overwhelmingly the new Protestant churches were interested in ministering to 'the people', rather than the aristocracy. This is not to say that higher ranks were entirely absent from these congregations, but rather that they were emphatically not the focus of activity, nor did they constitute the congregations of most of these church groups.

The philanthropic impulse at the base of foreign mission societies had its roots in benevolent organisations which arose during the seventeenth and eighteenth centuries, when the idea of charity, ministering primarily to the poor and disadvantaged in Britain, became energised as an important social force. B. Kirkman Gray describes how early seventeenth-century philanthropy was based on a philosophy of individual benevolence, primarily in the form of financial contributions to those individuals or organisations who were committed to working with the poor.[6] The system of philanthropy was intrinsically tied in with a system of stratified class relations, where the wealthy were obliged to donate some of their time or money to support those less fortunate than themselves. As Gray notes, philanthropy became an integral part of upper-class success and self-image: 'The inducement is two-fold, in this world and the next. In the first place charity is a good investment... It is only by charity that rich men can cover their sins, escape oblivion, and gain immortality' (98). Economically sustained by the wealthy, charitable work became a respectable pastime for the middle class and for middle-class women in particular. However, as F. K. Prochaska also notes, whilst women were deemed to have a rightful and important place in the charitable world, the nature of their service was dictated by male leaders of the philanthropic societies. Foreign mission societies arose as an extension of these home missions when religious bodies began to encourage charitable organisations to extend their activities further afield. It is their subsequent expansion into the new colonial zones of the British Empire that is crucial for my study.

From the end of the eighteenth century, Protestant congregations began to establish missionary societies. Many of the earliest societies were established as inter-denominational (or nondenominational) institutions and thus demanded religious co-operation. As Stephen Neill describes it, this establishment of voluntary, inter-denominational societies was a peculiarly nineteenth-century phenomenon, caused by the Protestant churches' inability or unwillingness to take up the cause of missions institutionally (214). It was also a decision based on economics. Missionary societies were very expensive and relied heavily upon donations from British congregations, so nascent mission societies appear to have assessed the difficulties of competing for funds as well as souls. Prior to the late 1700s, only two British missionary societies existed – the Society for Promoting Christian Knowledge (SPCK, established 1698) and the Society for the Propagation of the Gospel (SPG, established 1701). However, as Jean Woolmington notes, 'these societies had concentrated largely on the dissemination of the Scriptures [in Britain] and on providing clergy for white settlers in colonial outposts, although the SPG sent missionaries to minister to Indians and Negroes in North America and the West Indies'.[7] The evangelical revival led to the establishment of the main Protestant missionary societies around the turn of the eighteenth century: the Baptist Missionary Society (1792); the LMS (1795); the Church Missionary Society (1799); and the Wesleyan Methodist Missionary Society (1813). These societies were established to intervene directly in the lives of native 'heathens' of the world – particularly those in the British colonies, where some level of colonial governmental support could be assumed.

British Protestant missions are especially interesting for a number of other reasons. Firstly, the historical conjunction of the evangelical revival and the second British Empire suggests certain cultural, intellectual, and ideological relations between the two. Secondly, evangelical Protestants operated the most successful and aggressive of British missions, and as such the relationships between Britain and her colonies, as well as the relations between missionaries, colonists, and indigenous populations, were complex and multi-faceted. Thirdly, my close readings of Indian, Polynesian, and Australian mission archives demonstrate that Protestant missions exhibited localised and specific examples of mutual imbrication in different places. They did so, in part, because Protestantism provided missionaries with rather more room for relative local autonomy than did Catholicism. Fourthly, Protestant missions were usually staffed by married couples and families, whereas Catholic and Anglican missions predominantly sent out single, sex-segregated religious personnel (nuns or priests). As the hopeful (but unsuccessful) missionary candidate G. H. Poole argued in 1835, 'My great distinction between the Popish and Protestant Churches is that of a married ministry, and it is easy to conceive that the usefullness [*sic*] of a missionary must greatly depend on his character standing above suspicion. Besides if such a help be needful for men in ordinary life how much more so in the case supposed.'[8] Protestant missions thus offer complex arenas for my investigations of gender relations and colonialism.

Part one discusses British missionary activities broadly, but with a particular focus on the LMS. The society was established with a specific charter, 'to spread the knowledge of Christ among heathen and other unenlightened nations'.[9] My decision to focus on a single society has been made for reasons of scope and comprehensiveness, as the sheer volume of missionary publications is overwhelming. I focus on the LMS because of its particularly inter-denominational character, too.[10] This means that its history is mostly free from the domestic strictures of a single home church, unlike the Church Missionary Society, for example, which was closely bound by the politics of the Church of England and its role in British society.[11] The LMS was also, as Anne McClintock wryly describes it, 'the largest evangelical institution peddling its spiritual wares in the arena of empire'.[12] Part one, then, provides a general perspective on colonial mission work during the period 1800 to 1860, with a particular focus on the LMS, as an introduction to the specific cultural and textual practices of the society which are analysed in detail in the rest of the book.

Class relationships within missionary societies mirror those of their philanthropic predecessors. Brian Holmes notes that one-third of the members of the inaugural Church Missionary Society committee were merchants, bankers, and brokers.[13] In contrast, the majority of early missionaries were of working-class or lower middle-class backgrounds, particularly in the LMS. These class distinctions came to cause significant trouble between the societies and their representatives and ensured that missionaries were profoundly conscious of class relations. Like the philanthropists, missionaries sought to 'raise up' those less fortunate – and both economic and religious upraising involved expectations of manners, labour, and gender relations. Early mission activity tended not to attract the highly educated or ambitious: indeed, many missionary societies deliberately recruited artisans and gave them theological training. LMS candidates' application papers reveal a prevalence of drapers or drapers' assistants amongst the expectant missionary candidates of this period (one wonders whether the literal 'men of the cloth' had a specific partiality for transforming their trade into the metaphysical realm).[14] Despite the lower-middle- and working-class background of some missionaries, middle-class expectations were integral to Protestant evangelising. For many missionaries, colonial service provided a substantially higher position in society than they ever could have aspired to in Britain because they were invested with the cultural authority of predominantly middle-class and prosperous mission societies. Upwardly mobile religious personnel often caused considerable friction between other members of white colonial communities and missionaries, who were regarded as acting 'above their station' and thus despised for their social aspirations. These class conflicts only contributed to the marginal position of missionaries in colonial communities, exacerbated by their willingness to criticise the behaviour and policies of white elites. Missionaries were acutely aware of class relations, both between themselves and their native populations, between mission communities and the surrounding white society, and between evangelical 'workers' in the field and the home society. They sought to consolidate and codify new, local social structures.

Different colonial enterprises, of course, entailed different levels of missionary involvement, but the centrality of religion in Europe in the late eighteenth and early nineteenth centuries ensured that religious personnel were usually provided for white colonists and frequently for colonised 'heathen' as well. Imperial expansion into America and other early locations of British colonial culture sparked the British public's interest in 'savage races' and foreign climes. Early imperial ideas about the 'noble savage' and the 'childlike' nature of the colonised races justified the posting of missionary personnel to those areas where native peoples were believed capable of 'raising up' to a civil, Christianised state. Colonial experience challenged many primarily theoretical imperial ideas about other races and their cultural practices, and, with the influence of more explicitly economic colonial interests, changed many of these philosophies. Missionary work was highly influential in altering nineteenth-century theories of race, as Robert Burns' sermon argued earlier.

Unfortunately for the missionaries, attitudes towards evangelising colonised people also changed during the nineteenth century. Events such as the Indian Mutiny (1857) and the Morant Bay Rebellion (1865) troubled earlier assumptions about the potential for the colonised to be 'civilised'. With the waning of religious zeal in the latter part of the century, smaller, more focussed missionary societies began to emerge. As a result of the sometimes violent resistance exhibited by potential (native) converts, the British public as a whole started to doubt the efficacy of evangelising them. Jeffrey Richards argues that 'as the evangelical impulse faltered, the religious thrust became secularised. Many of the feelings of crusading and commitment were transferred to the Empire, increasingly depicted as a vehicle for service and self-fulfilment. The army, with its image newly refurbished, became central to the myths and rituals of empire.'[15] Mission projects gradually became less theologically driven and more interested in 'good works' directed towards specific communities or problems.

Missionary involvement in British colonial policy and administration varied according to the impetus, funding, and intent of individual colonial projects. Early British involvement in India through the East India Company, for example, specifically prohibited the evangelising of the Indian public until the early 1800s, in line with the company's policy of cultural non-interference to facilitate commerce.[16] After this time missionaries flooded into many Indian provinces. Relations between the East India Company or British Army officials and missionaries were often troubled, primarily because the groups had profoundly different goals for the Indian public, as well as for the expatriate British role in the colonial community. Missionaries from Australia were proselytising to Maoris long before the official white colonisation of New Zealand; indeed many missionaries there resisted the incursion of white settlers because of their doubts about the success of a bi-racial community. In Australia, on the other hand, missionaries specifically contracted to evangelise Aborigines were not sent until 1821, after a considerable period of white settlement. On arrival, missionaries aggressively attempted to stop sexual relationships between white men and black women, which they believed degraded both parties. Unsurprisingly, such interventions were rarely welcomed by settlers or the colonial administration. In Polynesia, many missionaries formed a (semi-) permanent white population on islands which had previously been only periodically visited by European explorers, whalers, and traders. They frequently opposed any further contact between other, 'corrupting', Europeans and their potential converts.

Missionaries thus negotiated quite complex relations with colonial administrations and settlers: in different places they were in collusion, conflict, or strategic co-operation with various colonial structures. It is, of course, almost impossible to generalise about missionaries across the wide range of colonial environments, but it is possible to argue that, despite the missionary societies' sometimes good intentions, the processes of evangelisation inevitably assisted the subjugation and subjection of indigenous peoples and the consolidation of white institutions of colonial control.

MISSIONARY FICTIONS

Throughout different evangelical endeavours, the image of the missionary out in the colonial field functioned importantly (although differentially) for the British public. Public interest in missionaries was intense, particularly in the early nineteenth century, with many missionaries on furlough (or in retirement) undertaking extensive speaking tours; publishing a wide range of best-selling memoirs, histories, and other testimonies; and contributing to popular journals and newspapers. As Patrick Brantlinger notes of the popularity of LMS missionary David Livingstone's African writings,

> although such accounts of African explorations do not figure in standard histories of Victorian literature, they exerted an incalculable influence on British culture and the course of modern history. It would be difficult to find a clearer example of the Foucauldian concept of discourse as power, as 'a violence that we do to things'.[17]

The religious British public saw missionaries as representatives of their own religiosity and philanthropy and followed missionary 'adventures' with avid interest. Fictional texts, from novels to children's literature, included missionary characters and situations, particularly in the genre of adventure novels which took great interest in exotic corners of the empire.

Stuart Hannabuss analyses the numerous missionary characters in R. M. Ballantyne's novels, arguing that they figured largely in his 'message of Empire'.[18] In *Jarwin and Cuffy* (1878) the hero meets John Williams, the prominent LMS missionary. A missionary father and his (angelic) daughter are crucial figures in *Gascoyne, the Sandal-Wood Trader: A Tale of the Pacific* (1873), and missionaries also appear in *Man on the Ocean* (1863) and *The Ocean and its Wonders* (1874). Ballantyne's best-known novel, *The Coral Island* (1857), uses Reverend Michael Russell's *Polynesia: A History of the South Sea* (1842) as reference material, and graphically illustrates pagan and cannibal rites in Fiji. As Martin Green notes, we 'are told that only

Christianised natives are to be trusted in trade, and a pirate admits that anyone can see what Christianity does "for these black critters". When this pirate begins to repent his sins, Ralph consoles him with the evangelical texts, "Though your sins be red like crimson, they shall be white as snow", and "Only believe".[19] Ballantyne's *Black Ivory* (1875) also acknowledges the assistance of Edward Hutchison, Lay Secretary of the Church Missionary Society, and *The Fugitives, or, The Tyrant Queen of Madagascar* (1887) is a novel about the persecution of Christian converts in Madagascar following missionary involvement there. As Hannabuss argues, 'commerce, Christianity and civilisation, concepts often conjoined at the time, come together recurringly as a latent polemic underpinning his stories. Humanitarianism and evangelicalism were horses in the same stable: Ballantyne was one of many to work these issues and causes together and engage in political debate' (66).

Ballantyne was by no means the only author to be inspired by missionaries, though he was one of the few to be so congratulatory. The widespread interest in evangelical activity ensured that representations of their work were quite common. The colonial writings of Robert Louis Stevenson, Somerset Maugham, Charlotte Brontë, Herman Melville, Charles Kingsley, John Buchan, and Rider Haggard, to name only the most prominent, include missionary characters or scenes. Charles Dickens' criticism of colonial evangelism was indicative of increasingly cynical views of missionaries later in the nineteenth century. *Bleak House* (1853) famously condemns the foreign missionary enterprise for its neglect of urgent domestic need, typified by Mrs Jellyby's involvement in charitable missionary works in Africa which prevent her from carrying out her duties as a mother in London.[20] Dickens regarded missionaries as ' "perfect nuisances who leave every place worse than they find it". "Believe it, African Civilisation, Church of England Missionary, and all other Missionary Societies!... The work at home must be completed thoroughly, or there is no hope abroad." '[21] Whether missionary work was regarded with approbation or opprobrium, it is undeniable that it was central to the representation of imperial expansion.

Whilst imperial narratives of evangelical activity may have revolved around the heroic male missionary figure, missionary women were also seen to play a crucial, if secondary, role. Missionary wives were the *only* Protestant missionary women during the late eighteenth and early nineteenth centuries. Societies refused to employ single women until after the middle of the nineteenth century. These missionary wives, too, carried the burden of intense public interest. Although official histories and records paid women little attention, British belief in the supposedly natural piety of evangelical women and the assumed delicacy of women in general meant that sympathetic communities at home and abroad were very interested in missionary wives. The assumed harshness and potential danger of colonial environments (a danger embodied in both the landscape and the local population) was seen as a threat to the Englishwoman overseas, and the religious, self-sacrificing nature of the work of colonial missions enhanced the emotive appeal of the missionary wife to a British public eager for accounts of 'civilised' life on the 'uncivilised' frontier.

The important evangelical labour that these wives performed in colonial mission fields – notably their work with indigenous women – gradually convinced the societies that their initial policy of employing only men should be amended. First, though, women had to overcome prejudice about their capacity for, and commitment to, missionary work. Commentators in this early period fulminated about single women's tendency to marry male missionaries soon after arriving at their colonial postings, therefore technically leaving the employ of the societies. The Society for Promoting Female Education in the East (established 1834) was accused of being a 'Batchelor's [*sic*] Aid' society, given the number of women missionaries who married soon after being posted to India. The SPFEE then introduced clauses in their employment contracts requiring recompense of passage fares and initial support funds if women married within a specified time of their arrival.[22] Of course, the assumption that these religious women ceased evangelical work after marriage to a missionary was profoundly fallacious and based in conservative discourses on women's work. It also contradicted both the missionary societies' expectations that wives would be active partners of their husbands and the direct proof that they continually received of missionary wives' achievements. After the 1850s individual mission societies were established to proselytise directly to, for instance, Indian women in the *zenanas*, and women missionaries were finally considered suitable candidates for overseas service. From about 1860, the established societies began to send out female missionaries in their own right. The rise of the modern women's movement in the late nineteenth century ensured that British women demanded a field of service appropriate to their sex. Whilst there remained some controversy about the propriety of appointing single women missionaries, the success of women's proselytising meant that by the final thirty years of the nineteenth century, as Jane Haggis reminds us, 'what had been primarily a labour conducted by ordained men became one in which women predominated'.[23] The missionary experience of gender relations in the first part of century which led up to this significant change in policy will be traced throughout this book.

Questions of gender and colonial evangelism are discussed in further detail in chapter 2.

MISSIONARIES IN THE ACADEMY

Scholars in anthropology, history, comparative missiology, and women's studies have recently analysed missionary activity in the colonies. Until the early 1990s, most analyses tended to be historically recuperative rather than analytic. Niel Gunson's *Messengers of Grace* (1978) is a notable and exemplary exception. Gunson's meticulous historical work and evocative analyses have provided much of the impetus for my own thinking, and I am indebted to his work on missions in Polynesia and Australia. Recent work within women's studies, and particularly that which analyses 'Britishness' or imperial discourses in conjunction with studies of gender, provides me with material to support some of the foundational assumptions in this study. My focus on the changes wrought by colonial activity on the imperial state and citizenry follows the lead taken by those scholars, such as Simon Gikandi, Catherine Hall, and Homi Bhabha, whose work in part seeks to illuminate the effects of imperial policies and colonial experience on the British public.

Area studies of missions, such as T. O. Beidelman's *Colonial Evangelism: A Socio-Historical Study of an East African Mission at the Grassroots*, Jean and John Comaroff's *Of Revelation and Revolution: Christianity, Colonialism, and Consciousness in South Africa*, and Leon de Kock's *Civilising Barbarians: Missionary Narrative and African Textual Response in Nineteenth-Century South Africa*, provide key analytical models, and it is interesting that most work has been done on African missions. Central to my analysis is a consideration of both the congruence and the discontinuity between different mission locations, and so I will draw on these African studies but also distinguish my analysis from them at different, strategic points. Brian Stanley's *The Bible and the Flag: Protestant Missions and British Imperialism in the Nineteenth and Twentieth Centuries* is an historical study which addresses a similar time period in conjunction with the history of colonialism, though its Christian perspective ensures that it remains sympathetic to missionary ideology. Specific studies of evangelical activities in India, Polynesia, and Australia exist, but these accounts, such as Tony Swain and Deborah Bird Rose's *Aboriginal Australians and Christian Missions: Ethnographic and Historical Studies* (1988), are often more interested in the later implications of missionary evangelism for colonial populations, particularly in the late nineteenth and twentieth centuries, than in the initial establishment of missions.

Work by women's studies scholars has tended to concentrate on historical 'retrievals' of women's involvement in colonial relationships and policy, but some recent work here has tended to be unproblematically recuperative, particularly of white women's influence in colonial cultures. Such studies return white women's colonial experiences to the historical canon, but mostly without a critical assessment of the intricate negotiations of race, class, and gender in which their lives were enmeshed. As Haggis argues, 'the focus on the singular vision of white Women also confines and distorts the use of gender in... these studies, precisely through its eclipsing of colonialism, class, and race'.[24] Much of this recuperative feminism also fails to account for the entwined gender codes for both men and women, and in doing so provides only part of the complex picture that typifies colonial gender relations. Like Gillian Whitlock's *The Intimate Empire: Reading Women's Autobiography*, my interest in gender 'is not just [about] femininity; it is a discourse of femininity which is imagined in relation to a particular formulation of masculinity'.[25] A concentration on the negotiated codification of male *and* female gendered roles, both within white evangelical culture and between missionary and indigenous communities, allows a far greater understanding of the heterogeneity of colonial relations. Recent work on intersections of colonialism, race, and gender has critically influenced my thinking. Scholars such as Jane Haggis, Catherine Hall, and Ann Laura Stoler have produced much valuable work in this field, with an attention to specific colonial histories and cultural practices.

My analysis of the representation of missionary activity through mission narratives, histories, memoirs, reminiscences, and literary accounts brings to bear a close attention to the nexus of gender, colonialism, and representation. Three specific studies have been foundational to my thinking: Jean and John Comaroff's *Of Revelation and Revolution: Christianity, Colonialism, and Consciousness in South Africa* (1991); Susan Thorne's *Congregational Missions and the Making of an Imperial Culture in Nineteenth-Century England* (1999); and Catherine Hall's *Civilising Subjects: Metropole and Colony in the English Imagination, 1830–1867* (2002). My analysis in this book enters into a conversation with each of these earlier studies: a slightly different kind of conversation with each, respectively, as I shall explain.

The Comaroffs' *Of Revelation and Revolution* is a foundational text in critical analysis of colonial missionaries and their effects on colonial cultures and imperial policy. Positioned as a 'study of the colonization of consciousness and the consciousness of colonization in South Africa', *Of Revelation and Revolution* is an historical anthropology 'of cultural confrontation – of domination and reaction, struggle and innovation'.[26] Focussing on the period 1820–1920, it examines the interaction between Nonconformist missionaries (mostly the LMS, but also the Wesleyan Methodist Missionary Society) and the Southern Tswana, with a view to present-day concerns and to the experience of black South Africans more generally. Their study has in many respects brought about a rethinking of colonial contact and the complex forms of resistance and accommodation that missions engendered in colonised communities.

One of the many strengths of *Of Revelation and Revolution* is its focus on the struggle over symbolism, psychology, and social and individual subjectivity that characterised colonial evangelisation. This distinguishes their intervention into the vexed question 'Whose side were the Christians really on?' (7) by complicating and theorising this query. It is also this feature that is most useful for my analysis. Susan Thorne suggests that scholarly historical debate about the colonial expansion of British Protestantism has been split between 'Historians of colonized or formerly colonized societies [who] have typically viewed foreign missions as an expression of the exigencies of colonial rule, a theologically and politically undifferentiated agency of the British colonial state'[27] on the one hand, and metropolitan historians who 'have countered by emphasizing the metropolitan sources of missionary inspiration, among which theological developments figure prominently' (25) on the other. If this is so, then perhaps we need to change the questions being asked about missions.[28] The old questions have led, as the Comaroffs note, to the reduction of 'complex historical dynamics... to the crude calculus of interest and intention, and colonialism itself to a caricature' (7). Instead, *Of Revelation and Revolution* intends to show

that the evangelical encounter took place on an ever expanding subcontinental stage; that it was to have profound, unanticipated effects on both colonizer and colonized; and that, just as colonialism itself was not a coherent monolith, so colonial evangelism was not a simple matter of raw mastery, of British churchmen instilling in passive black South Africans the culture of European modernity or the forms of industrial capitalism. (12–13)

Jean and John Comaroff have well described the generic nature of missionary texts, drawing on Mary Louise Pratt's work on travel writing:

The epic accounts of missionary 'labours and scenes' had, by the late nineteenth century, become an established European genre, taking its place beside popular travel and exploration writings, with which it shared features of intent and style... This was a literature of the imperial frontier, a colonizing discourse that titillated the Western imagination with glimpses of radical otherness which it similarly brought under intellectual control. (9)

Whilst this description of missionary texts is integral to my understanding of these colonial artefacts, this is also the point at which my study departs from the Comaroffs' model. As I discuss later, I do not read missionary texts for signs of indigenous agency: the Comaroffs do. They argue that subtexts disrupt colonial missionary texts, in which 'the voice of the silent other is audible through disconcerted accounts of his "irrational" behavior, his mockery, or his resistance. Thus, while we have relatively few examples of direct Tswana speech in the archives, we do have ample indirect evidence of their reaction and conversations with the mission' (37). The Comaroffs do concede that

In all these cases...the Tswana speak through the European text; to the extent that 'the other' is a construction of an imperializing imagination, s/he will always dwell in the shadows of its dominant discourse. In this sense we anthropologists are still explorers who tell ourselves stories about savagery and civilization. (38)

Because I am a literary scholar rather than an anthropologist, I want to tell a slightly different story here: one that focusses on the texts of missionary encounter, but which *because* of its detailed attention to the nature of these texts means that I am profoundly sceptical about their capacity to tell indigenous stories.

More recently, Susan Thorne's astute historical analysis of the LMS and its location in British culture has been published. *Congregational Missions and the Making of an Imperial Culture in Nineteenth-Century England* (1999) has many connections with my book, but Thorne's focus is significantly different. Her precisely located reading of the LMS in its Congregation-alist, class, and cultural contexts argues for a tight connection between home and foreign missions – by extension, she argues that foreign missions provided a crucial site through which working-class and middle-class Britons experienced Empire. Most importantly, Thorne argues that close missionary ties between the colonies and the imperial centre significantly contributed to the ways in which domestic social power was constructed, negotiated, and represented, particularly for the middle class. 'The missionary imperial project was', she argues, 'central to the construction of Victorian middle-class identity, or at least to one influential version of it' (56).

Although Thorne is more ambivalent about the centrality of imperialism in understanding nineteenth-century missionary work than I am, she too states that 'Missionary propaganda claimed divine approval for the British colonial project' (38). Her interest is in reading foreign missionary work, and the work of its representation, back into British domestic concerns.

My analysis moves the other way: what happened to foreign missionary workers out in the field, who brought their ideological and religious assumptions out to the colonies? What happened, more particularly, to the modes of representation they brought with them? How did the language and form, both literal and metaphorical, of Protestant Britishness translate into new colonial environments and texts? Equally, how did the imperial environment inflect those colonial artefacts on their return to Britain?

Thorne provides important proof of an argument that runs throughout my book, albeit in a slightly different form: that colonial missionary experiences profoundly influenced parallel debates in Britain. My particular interest is in how gender and domesticity shifted the terms of representation, whilst Thorne's is more materially and politically based. Specifically, she is interested in the ways in which 'the imaginative relationship to empire encouraged by the missions contributed ... to some of the central developments of British social history in this period: class formation, gender relations, the rise and demise of English liberalism, and the role of organized religion therein' (7). Thorne argues that 'The local and the imperial were not mutually exclusive or even discrete frames of reference' (56), which correlates with what I discuss as mutual imbrication. This manifests itself in Thorne's work in textual ways too, though these are not her main focus. Principally, she analyses the ways in which missionary discourse was used to question the values of the Anglican establishment (or those attributed to them by evangelical Dissenters). She notes that missions 'provided a vivid canvas, biblical in its scope and reference, on which the virtues of the middle class could be promoted in the very process of condemning the sins of their social betters' (73).

In its second half, *Congregational Missions* moves to the latter half of the nineteenth century, which it characterises as a period of 'the feminization of foreign missions' (92). Here Thorne focusses on the period when women missionaries were recruited and sent to colonial stations, which brought about a profound change in the nature of LMS work, its ideological underpinnings, and its representation. The gender shift in missionary personnel, she argues, parallelled and, by implication, was related to the hardening of imperial attitudes to race. Missionaries' increasing enthusiasm for colonial expansion was also fostered, she suggests, by their increasing emphasis on women and children: 'this gendered split of the colonized targets of missionary intervention helped to reconcile the contradictions between missionary and more coercive imperial visions' (96). This argument is one from which my study differentiates itself. Thorne does not draw a direct causal connection between 'feminization' and the growth of 'missionary imperialism', but her argument has uncomfortable parallels with the kinds of claims made about British women's influence in India, for example, in the second half of the nineteenth century. In this 'mythology of empire',[29] race relations in India are seen as exemplary until white memsahibs arrived and, with their uptight Victorian morality, spoilt the natural, unaffected, intimate relationships that had flourished between the (homosocial) world of the colonial elite and Indians. Thus, as Hilary Callan tartly comments, 'may a post-colonial generation unload a little of its moral discomfort at the expense of its mothers and grandmothers'.[30] Hopefully such arguments are not taken seriously these days, based as they are on a sentimental, eroticised, boys-of-the-Raj imperial nostalgia,[31] and it seems unfair even to mention them in connection with Thorne's scrupulous study. But as Catherine Hall notes in her review of *Congregational Missions*, Thorne's periodisation seems a little too neat. For Thorne, gender appears to operate in making British identities only in the second half of the nineteenth century with the feminization of missions. As Hall notes, 'There is a curious chronology here since the debates about sati and about slavery, key sites of the British domestic encounter with colonialism in the 1810s, 20s, and 30s, were saturated with gendered assumptions and language.'[32] As my book will show, gender was in fact crucial to representation of LMS activity *throughout* the nineteenth century. My own argument about the hardening of racial attitudes within the LMS is somewhat different: that early missionary failures brought about this change, and that hardening attitudes to colonial women – when they were blamed for the resistance and recalcitrance of colonised cultures – specifically shifted the earlier missionary sympathy for their plight. Chapter 2 will discuss these issues in greater detail.

Catherine Hall's own comprehensive study of class, gender, and colonial missionary activity was published in 2002 as *Civilising Subjects: Metropole and Colony in the English Imagination, 1830–1867*. The recent publication date means that much of my reading of Hall's work has been though her earlier publication of this material. The new study, though, is adroit in its consideration of two different but linked sites of colonial culture: Jamaica, principally the Baptist missions there in the period 1830–67, and Birmingham, England, particularly its relation to both Jamaica and the empire. In doing so, Hall follows Frederick Cooper and Ann Stoler's call for placing colonial and metropole jointly in the analytical frame. Her study is an exemplary model for this kind of historical work.

Hall provides astute readings of various aspects of missionary culture in Jamaica, asking, in particular, 'What part did nonconformists play in the making of empire?'[33] Her answers to this question lead to an unravelling of a set of connected histories linking Jamaica with England, colonised with colonisers, enslaved men and women with Baptist missionaries, freed people with a wider public of abolitionists in the metropole. How did the 'embedded assumptions of racial language' work in the universalist speech of the missionaries and their supporters? (7–8)

The central argument of Hall's analysis is similar to that of Thorne's: 'that colony and metropole are terms which can be understood only in relation to each other, and that the identity of coloniser is a constitutive part of Englishness' (12). Hall's hypothesis here provides crucial buttressing of my argument about mutual imbrication in terms of missionary representation. Hall limits her focus to a particular moment in history, and to the ways in which a particular group of people, 'mainly Baptists and other varieties of nonconformists, constituted themselves as colonisers both in Jamaica and at home . . . I take the development of the missionary movement, one formative moment in the emergence of modern racial thinking, as my point of departure' (13). But she notes that this hypothesis could have been explored at many different sites, as I do here for India, Polynesia, and Australia. My argument focusses on texts across a geographical range, and it answers Hall's question 'Which forms of representation mattered?' (13)

Hall's work on Baptist missionaries in Jamaica has been highly influential. She is particularly interested in reading their texts as constituting a 'particular colonial discourse, not primarily to extricate the history of those "others" who the missionaries and their allies aimed to contain in their narrative strategies, but rather to investigate those English ethnicities which were in play'.[34] Nineteenth-century British national identity, she argues, was made up of interrelations between class, gender, and ethnicity as axes of power, and in the 1830s and 40s religion 'provided one of the key discursive terrains for the articulation of these axes and thus for the construction of a national identity' (241). Hall's perspicacious analyses of gender, family, race, and class in Jamaican Baptist missions will be referred to throughout this book.

All of these important studies, and other recent publications in the revitalised field of imperial history/colonial anthropology, make similar arguments to mine about mutual imbrication. Hall, through Frantz Fanon, seeks to explore 'the mutual constitution of coloniser and colonised',[35] so that she can trace 'how racial thinking was made and re-made across the span of colony and metropole' (27). Ann Laura Stoler, in *Race and the Education of Desire: Foucault's 'History of Sexuality' and the Colonial Order of Things* (1995), argues that the 'sexual discourse of empire and of the biopolitic state in Europe were mutually constitutive: their "targets" were broadly imperial, their regimes of power synthetically bound'.[36] Andrew Porter notes of missionary encounters between coloniser and colonised that 'All parties engaged, consciously and unconsciously, in a constant process of mutual engagement and two-way translation, even while unqualified dislike, conservatism, and incomprehension could easily be found on all sides.'[37] Thorne argues that the

> British public's engagement with missionary intelligence about the empire helped to shape social relations and political identities every bit as much as social relations and political identities influenced the reading of missionary texts. This was a mutually constitutive dynamic... [The] affects of missionary propaganda were not felt at the expense of more domestically inclined social identities, including those of class, but as their very precondition.[38]

It is at this juncture of missionary testimony, textuality, and the construction of the British reading public that my study enters. But it is also the point at which disciplinary differences come into play.[39] Historians such as Thorne and Hall, and anthropologists such as the Comaroffs, can make arguments about the material practices resulting from missionary colonialism. Literary critics like myself have to make more subtle, less directed arguments about texts and their relation to the social sphere. The strength of this kind of argumentation is that it draws much more detailed attention to the texts upon which other disciplinary studies have been drawing. Thus, despite the appeal of the idea of 'mutual constitution', I examine a different order of mutuality, one that Simon Gikandi has usefully called mutual imbrication.[40] Imbrication is a retreat from the larger (cross-disciplinary) claim about effectivity, but it is also a nuanced, specific reading of that argument. It implies inflection, influence, and effect. It also allows considerably more 'room for maneuver', in Ross Chambers' evocative phrase.[41] Unlike Chambers, though, I read for complicity in missionary narratives, rather than resistance. As I shall show, the discourses of gender/domesticity and evangelical missionary activity were co-dependent on each other. Missionary texts and the kinds of social relations they posited introduced a concentration on gender and domesticity ensuring that early imperial activity could be construed by the religious British public as an act of Christian generosity and aid, rather than aggressive annexation and commerce. It also provided a rationale for Christian missionary involvement in colonial states. Most importantly it introduced a particular kind of colonial discourse, one with strength and flexibility, and one continuing to inflect how we think about imperialism.

POSTCOLONIAL THEORY AND MISSIONARY TEXTS

A 'paper empire'[42]

My investigation of colonial missionary activity is situated within current theoretical debates in the field of postcolonial studies. Examining an historically bounded manifestation of colonialism facilitates an analysis heeding calls for a (re-)turn to specifically located historicism within postcolonial studies. This approach, as Stephen Slemon notes, complicates our understanding of colonial texts, and, as it does so, 'many of the usual pieties, and the obvious binaries, of the postcolonial master narrative become unglued. This in turn calls down the sense of obviousness over where the agents of colonial domination and anticolonialist resistance are to be found.'[43] The trend within postcolonial studies has been to respond to this call through detailed examination of precise historical 'moments', typified by some of Bhabha's articles, such as 'Signs Taken for Wonders: Questions of Ambivalence and Authority under a Tree Outside Delhi, May 1817' or 'By Bread Alone: Signs of Violence in the Mid-Nineteenth Century'. As Helen Tiffin describes it,

> there has also been a change in approach, with the 'marriage' between literary study and philosophy cooling a little in favour of a closer relationship with anthropology and history. This new liaison has helped to sharpen the trend towards located and specific studies, 'case-based' arguments that depend on detailed historical or anthropological research into particular periods and peoples.[44]

This historically based analysis is not only a recent phenomenon. The work of critics in allied fields, such as Peter Hulme or the Subaltern Studies group, has often been very mindful of historical contexts. However, the call for literary and textual studies to be carefully located, with the relation between texts and their historical locus central to any investigation, attempts to instil an historical imperative into the field as a whole.

Attention to missionary activity demands that a broad cultural dynamic be taken into account. My concern with the fashionable (re-)turn to colonial history within literary postcolonialism is that 'easy' historical points are sometimes made, without a fuller investigation of the cultural politics of the historical context. Missionaries are subject to numerous 'off-hand' asides and critiques throughout postcolonial discourses, be they fictional, historical, or theoretical. Bhabha's *The Location of Culture* collection, for example, contains no less than seventeen references to missionaries.[45] Bhabha is here being used as a scapegoat, but he is by no means the only critic to refer cursorily to colonial missionary activity. Most of these critics fail to contextualise missionary work in any meaningful way and instead rely on well-worn stereotypes. As Andrew Porter suggested in his 1985 article on commerce and Christianity, 'what is still required is an account of missionary expansion in the nineteenth century which will place it firmly within the context of both intellectual and material life'.[46]

This book in no way intends to offer an apologia for colonial missionary activity,[47] but it does seek to investigate missionaries with rather more historical and theoretical rigour than is evident in 'off the cuff' postcolonial references to them. Missionaries certainly did introduce inappropriate policies and destroyed local cultural practices, seemingly oblivious to the injurious nature of their interventions. At the same time, particularly in settler colonies like Australia and South Africa, some missionaries attempted to stand between the excesses of colonial behaviour and the humanitarian interests of indigenous people. In South Africa, missionary discourses provided the basis for a narrative of civil rights which was one of a wide range of factors which eventually enabled a concerted opposition to apartheid.[48]

Nicholas Thomas' *Colonialism's Culture* similarly argues against easy colonial stereotypes and simplistic binary constructions of colonial relations. As Thomas suggests, 'colonialism is not a unitary project but a fractured one, riddled with contradictions and exhausted as much by its own internal debates as by the resistance of the colonized'.[49] Missionary activity, whether at odds with more commercially minded forms of colonial intervention or in collusion with them, problematises simple hegemonic assumptions about colonial history and evangelisation. Colonial missionary activities do not constitute a singular evangelical project as opposed to other colonial projects, but *different kinds* of evangelical, colonial projects in each location they occurred. The complexity of colonial practices is made manifest in its representation in literary and historical discourses, as this book repeatedly demonstrates.

Thomas Richards' *The Imperial Archive* proposes that the nineteenth-century imperial imagination was obsessed with collating and controlling information about colonies. Much imperial history gives a fallacious impression of a unified British Empire, even though, as Richards suggests, 'most people during the nineteenth century were aware that their empire was something of a collective improvisation'.[50] A central tool for managing the often destabilising nature of colonial experience was this obsessive collation of information about the empire: 'they often could do little other than collect and collate information, for any exact civil control, of the kind possible in England, was out of the question' (3). Missionary textuality was profoundly implicated in this information gathering in an attempt to 'know' and thus to 'manage' the colonial heathen.

Published missionary texts are curious artefacts. They produce profoundly hybrid genres incorporating ethnography, linguistics, and geographical description and surveys, as well as detailed descriptions of evangelical work and native religious customs. These published accounts were drawn from the copious writings of missionaries in the field – their letters, journals, reports, and memoirs formed raw material that was then transformed into published texts. They were produced in prodigious quantities by missionary societies, keen to promote the evangelical work of their colonial representatives, in order to justify their ongoing involvement in colonial projects and to ensure continued funding. As Haggis describes it,

Not only did every Society have its periodicals, each aimed at a different audience: adults, women, 'juveniles' and children; but a constant stream of pamphlets, leaflets and the like were distributed, often free or for only nominal charge, as well as the more substantial literature of books about the work in the various mission fields and lives of well-known missionaries.[51]

Missionaries were required to provide an annual account of their work. Mostly these annual reports were written up from their own journals, sometimes as a direct transcription but more frequently as 'edited highlights'. In the case of the LMS, these reports were recycled in the society's quarterly *Missionary Sketches*, the quarterly *Chronicle*, and later in the annual *Reports to the Directors*. Each of these periodicals had a different intended audience and use, even though material was frequently recycled between publications. *Missionary Sketches*, designed 'for the Use of the Weekly and Monthly Contributors to the London Missionary Society', were slim four-page leaflets with a detailed engraving on the front cover, mostly of 'heathen' gods, artefacts, or mission buildings.[52] A sliding-subscription rate entitled individuals to different types of publication, in an economic structure typical of the LMS conflation of financial and spiritual value:

Each person who subscribes to the Missionary Society One Penny per week, or more, is entitled to one of the *Quarterly Sketches*, and each person who collects from his friends or neighbours the amount of One Shilling per week, or upwards, for the Society, is entitled to receive the *Quarterly Chronicle of the Society's Transactions*.[53]

Texts, fund-raising, and missionary propaganda were thus integrally related in maintaining the LMS domestic support-base.

In any discussion of missionary textuality it is important to maintain a kind of sceptical double-vision about the texts under examination. It becomes increasingly obvious when comparing original letters from missionaries, for example, with their recycled versions in society magazines or reports, that such texts rarely remained unexpurgated or unedited. Indeed, the chain of potential editors is such that the relationship between the missionary *ur*-text and its subsequent manifestations is always uncertain. This interference with original texts is not exactly hidden, although there is little attention drawn to the editing of primary texts in the printed versions.

Frequently, missionary accounts contain authorial comment on the nature of their own textuality, highlighting textual mediation from the very moment of production. In sending his journal back to the LMS in February 1813, Reverend Robert May notes that it 'has been copied for me by one of my young friends at Chinsurah'.[54] May's statement is ambiguous, but I am prepared to hazard a guess that May's 'young friend' is an Indian youth. The LMS deputation visiting Chinsurah reported that there were young Bengali boys with a 'strong desire to learn English; and in order to attain this object, they appear willing to read the Scriptures, or any other book'.[55] Chinsurah had a LMS presence since 1798 and Robert May was revered as 'an educationalist of no mean power'[56] with twenty schools and 1,651 students by 1815 (he had only arrived in 1812) – within this context an Indian student scribe seems feasible. Of course, the scholastic task of 'copying' ideally requires a precise replication of the original text, but it is interesting to speculate whether Bhabha's idea of 'colonial mimicry' – imitation with a crucial, potentially ironic, *difference* – could have operated here both materially and symbolically. If so, the possible textual presence of an Indian youth interestingly complicates issues of originality and authorship, allowing at least the potential for changes to the missionary's own words and ideas. Significantly, this incident also draws attention to the ways in which Christian converts were interpellated through pre-existing imperial missionary narratives, an issue which will be taken up in more detail in later chapters.

Another example of editing at the site of production is provided by George Mundy, a LMS schoolmaster and missionary at Chinsurah from 1820 onwards, in his reverential memoir of his wife Louisa written after her death in 1843.[57] In this text Mundy describes his wife's disapproval of anything bordering on exaggeration in his reports: 'My own official letters respecting the Mission at Chinsurah, generally passed under her eye before they were forwarded to England, and I have frequently thought her, in consequence of her suggestions to modify certain paragraphs, rather too particular.'[58] This kind of intimate and local editorial intervention is conspicuously absent in published accounts of the LMS, but it is fair to assume that these kinds of incidents did not only happen at Chinsurah.

For a contemporary archivist, the liberties taken by the societies with their representatives' documents are quite shocking. In examining the LMS archives, for example, one reads through ink and lead corrections, additions, and deletions to find the missionaries' handwritten accounts of annual reports, letters, and deputations. These 'corrections' by the society are often as fascinating in their own right as the original words of the missionary and just as ideologically laden.

Sections from the journal of James Robertson, a LMS missionary in Varanasi (1826–33), were republished by the society in the *Chronicle* (1829–32); and a comparison of the two versions demonstrates the editing process involved. Robertson wrote in his 1826–7 journal of a local festival, which he refused to let children and his native assistants attend. He writes: 'Next day, being the principal day of this infernal festival, on which every one that can creep out of doors disfigures himself in the most disgusting manner, and speaks things, that the lowest brothel in England would be ashamed of...' The *Chronicle* reprints Robertson's account almost in full but changes it to a '...disgraceful festival...' and deletes Robertson's improper brothel reference to a more polite '...speaks the most abominable things'.[59] Robertson certainly comes across as a 'hellfire and brimstone' evangelist, and it is obvious that the society intended to tone down his account before it reached a wider audience. It should not be assumed that this is the only instance of LMS modification of unseemly missionary writing. Numerous internal arguments between missionaries, personal remarks concerning missionaries and their wives made in the reports of deputations,[60] and an array of 'improper' comments were publicly circulated no further than the missionaries' initial accounts.

Missionaries also wrote up their experiences in fictional forms. Across the fiction/non-fiction divide, however, missionary textuality is typified by its reliance on stereotypic representations and the continual recirculation of European images of the 'other'. Bronwen Douglas suggests that these 'formulaic, pragmatic' portrayals were 'designed to titillate and encourage, not appal or dishearten the metropolitan faithful, on whose contributions the mission depended...Evidently missionary tropes for indigenous people should not be read literally, but neither should they simply be discarded for the evident offensiveness, nor taken only as signifiers in a racist, sexist colonial discourse.'[61] Such stereotypic characterisation and narrativisation closely connects missionary writing with broader imperial discourses. Brantlinger analyses Frederick Marryat's imperial adventure tales and notes that, as in the missionaries' trite narratives, 'character shrinks to a semaphore, a signal code of stereotypic traits, while action becomes paramount'.[62] For missionary writers the traits being semaphored are those of indigenous depravity – hence the urgent need for Christian intervention – and the action required is religious conversion by keen evangelicals.

My focus on three different colonial locations within the same historical period shows that British evangelists entered each mission field with similar sets of expectations about both imperial and indigenous gender relations. Historically located analysis of the texts surrounding these different locations illuminates both the shared cultural assumptions *and* the manner in which different cultures changed missionary practice. It is important to note that the imperial imagination had different expectations of each region, even though the universalising tendency of imperial discourses on gender produced disturbing elisions of cultural difference. Experience in colonial missions variously supported or undermined such totalising narratives of indigenous gender relations. This ambivalent participation in broader imperial discourses characterised the majority of missionary texts and ensured that missionary discourses both replicated and repudiated imperialist images, attitudes, and narratives at different times and in different places.

Through the examination of a diverse range of colonial texts, including missionary memoirs, histories, letters, and formal records, as well as literary representations of missionary activity, particular modes and tropes of missionary discourse reveal this ambiguous relationship with imperial discourses. It is clear that significant changes in imperial (missionary) policy resulted from early colonial experience. These institutional re-negotiations of relations between imperial and colonial orders expose the very provisional and negotiated nature of imperial policies from Britain at the colonial interface. Attention to specific colonial locations and local changes in imperial policy enables the mapping of the effects of colonial difference on the British psyche and polity. My focus on textual representation demonstrates that it was in the textualisation of this process that the operations of mutual imbrication are realised.

Ann Laura Stoler's discussion of the complexities of class relations in colonial contexts is particularly telling for any examination of early missionary texts. Stoler is insistent that 'colonialism was not a secure bourgeois project. It was not only about the importation of middle-class sensibilities to the colonies, but about the *making* of them.'[63] LMS missionaries are particularly interesting colonial agents to consider in this regard, being only *marginal* middle-class representatives though keen to assert themselves as such through their own behaviours and those they attempted to encourage in others. As Kenneth Ballhatchet suggests of missionaries in India,

Missionaries also played an ambiguous part on the imperial stage. Although most of them followed a European lifestyle, they were professionally involved in close relationships with Indians. Many proved to be uncomfortable members of the ruling race, criticizing British as well as Indian immorality. In this role they were strengthened by close ties with religious and reforming groups in Britain.[64]

It is only the European experience of evangelisation that emerges through my analysis, though it is continually tempting to read the voices and opinions of colonised subjects back into missionary texts. Rod Edmond rightly queries: 'Is it possible to get closer to the experience of contact from the native point of view? Can we, while still dependent on missionary texts, begin to construct a history of native subjects somehow distinct from colonial descriptions of them?'[65] The discomforting answer is that it is extremely difficult and highly problematic to read for native agency or resistance or history through such highly mediated discourses as those of colonial evangelisation. I will not attempt to read comprehensively for 'heathen' agency or resistance, because the ways of doing so would be so highly problematic and dependent on the postcolonial optimism of the analyst that the project of unravelling the text to assign a new colonial subject position[66] would be counter-productive.[67] Rather, my attention is trained on an exploration of what happened to the imperial-colonial psyche and textual archive in the process of colonial evangelisation. In doing so, like Edmond, I attempt

to ground these representations in the home cultures from which they derived, to read them back into the sponsoring institutions, publishing history and other cultural contexts in which, and for which, they were produced. Indigenous points of view are not forgotten but they are often out of reach ... [The danger of such an approach is that] to concentrate on the conventions through which a culture was textualized while ignoring the actuality of what was represented is to risk a second-order repetition of the images, typologies and projections under scrutiny. (20–1)

It is possible that this concentration on the artefacts of textual record limits the extent to which we can conceive of the complex picture of colonial encounters. In answer, I can only observe appropriate disciplinary protocols. Whilst anthropologist-historians like the Comaroffs or Greg Dening may possess the skills to 're-enact' past histories of cross-cultural encounter,[68] my study deals closely and carefully with the texts of colonial encounter, in order to map the ways in which imperial and colonial identities, knowledge, and history are represented in their confronting encounter with those of different religious and cultural inheritances. As Simon Gikandi argues, texts 'provided the medium through which the crisis of both colonial and domestic identities were mediated' (*Maps of Englishness*, xix).

Thomas Richards notes of the general imperial-colonial project of collating and cataloguing information that

The civil servants of Empire pulled together so much information and wrote so many books about their experiences that today we have only begun to scratch the surface of their archive. In a very real sense theirs was a paper empire: an empire built on a series of flimsy pretexts that were always becoming texts. The truth, of course, is that it was much easier to unify an archive composed of texts than to unify an empire made of territory.[69]

Missionary writers were, of course, very particular kinds of 'civil servants' of empire – indeed, as will become obvious in this study, they were the servants of God and civility as well as of empire.

CHAPTER TWO

Gender, domesticity, and colonial evangelisation

Anne McClintock's *Imperial Leather* offers 'a sustained quarrel with the project of imperialism, the cult of domesticity and the invention of industrial progress' (4) and suggests that 'imperialism cannot be understood without a theory of domestic space and its relations to the market' (17). In a passing reference to colonial missionary work, McClintock suggests that

the mission station became a threshold institution for transforming domesticity rooted in European gender and class roles into domesticity as controlling a colonized people. Through the rituals of domesticity . . . animals, women, and colonized peoples were wrested from their putatively 'natural' yet, ironically, 'unreasonable' state of 'savagery' and inducted through the domestic progress narrative into a hierarchical relation to white men. (34)

This book interrogates the coalition of imperialism, gender, domesticity, and colonial practice typified by nineteenth-century missionary experiences in colonial cultures. The later case studies in this book will examine the construction and maintenance of the colonial mission as a 'threshold institution' of both ideologies and practices through an examination of missionary texts and discourse. By way of introduction, this chapter examines the valency of gender in Protestant colonial missionary work, with specific reference to the LMS. I argue that missionaries' interventions into colonial gender and domesticity were productive of the 'domestic progress narrative' identified by McClintock, and discuss some of the ways in which missionary experiences were crucial in changing perceptions of gender and domesticity within Britain itself.

Gender and religion were important aspects of both individual and cultural British identity under negotiation in the early nineteenth century, and they were closely linked. Both these discourses were also critically bound to broader questions about race and class, equally contentious and important issues during the period. Critics such as John MacKenzie[1] and Patrick Brantlinger have identified the extent to which the central concerns

38

of nineteenth-century culture gradually shifted 'away from domestic class conflict toward racial and international conflict, suggesting how imperialism functioned as an ideological safety valve, deflecting both working-class radicalism and middle-class reformism into noncritical paths while preserving fantasies of aristocratic authority at home and abroad'.[2] Susan Thorne has astutely analysed the ways in which 'missionary imperial identities were not alternatives to but were the mediums through which domestic ideologies of class as well as gender were forged'.[3]

Gender was central to the ethos of evangelical Protestantism. Evangelicals 'nurtured the deep-seated conviction that Christianity sustained a high status for women; the place of women in pagan societies was portrayed, by contrast, as desperately degraded'.[4] Most evangelicals believed that their denominations in particular provided special respect and status for their female members. At the same time missionary work provided evangelical Protestant men with an exciting opportunity for self-development, where 'the action of combating sin, of enlisting in the army of God provided a worthy arena within which they could prove their manhood'.[5] Although women in the mission field were originally sent only as the wives of appointed missionaries, their work was essential to the success of individual missions, and their demonstrated skills in communicating with and converting native women led to the dispatching of single women missionaries by the 1860s in spite of earlier policies determinedly against this. Images of family were also crucial to the work of colonial missions. Gender proved a powerful tool of colonial evangelism.

GENDER, PATRIARCHY, AND MUSCULAR CHRISTIANITY

Evangelicals continued the traditional male domination of both hierarchy and parish practices from the established churches, but with an important modification in regard to female spirituality. Given the traditional gender roles endorsed by western Christianity, this dominance of masculine authority was not surprising. These formalised gender conventions, though, masked a highly constructed ideology of social and cultural relations that sustained evangelical religion in the British community and in foreign missions. Masculine activity in the public sphere was to be supported and complemented[6] by the pious woman at home: the 'angel in the house' described by Sandra M. Gilbert and Susan Gubar.[7] The new missionary societies of the late eighteenth and nineteenth centuries were founded by men of commerce and Christianity, men who had achieved sufficient financial success in the relatively new sphere of middle-class business to be able to donate both personal time and monetary support to establishing mission societies. For them, evangelical religion was important in maintaining middle-class respectability and they performed their civic responsibilities through the church and mission societies. The evangelical revival of this period also provided a language of religious and national confidence, as Catherine Hall notes: 'Religious belief provided a vocabulary of right – the right to know and to speak that knowledge, with the moral power that was attached to the speaking of God's word.'[8] That authoritative vocabulary was naturally associated with, and appropriated by, those men already awarded cultural leadership. Thus masculinity became intricately tied to the exercise of this authority. As Hall describes it, 'for evangelical Christians the action of combating sin, of enlisting in the army of God provided a worthy arena within which they could prove their manhood' (249).

'Muscular Christianity' ensured the inclusion of religious activity in the cultural construction of masculinity. Broadly, this concept 'represented a strategy for commending Christian virtue by linking it with more interesting secular notions of moral and physical prowess. "Manliness" in this context generously embraced all that was best and most vigorous in man.'[9] The term 'muscular Christianity' was coined in 1857,[10] but the review of Charles Kingsley's *Two Years Ago* which launched it clearly saw that the idea had been circulating prior to that date. Donald E. Hall notes: 'the broad divisions and broadly defined programs of the muscular Christians were their responses to complex contemporary questions on issues of class, nationality, and gender' (8). Norman Vance's study of 'Christian manliness' – *The Sinews of the Spirit* – links it closely with the nineteenth-century reformist agenda, noting that 'In the years between the two great reform bills, between 1832 and 1867, Kingsley and [Thomas] Hughes adapted this emerging sense of individual possibility, moral and political, to their own profoundly religious confidence in personal and social salvation through service and strenuousness' (2). Vance deliberately eschews the popular term, suggesting that it over-emphasises the muscular, athletic ideal at the expense of the inherent moral strength intended by nineteenth-century adherents of such principles. Hall's recent collection of essays uses 'muscular Christianity' for precisely that reason: its focus on the 'ideologically charged and aggressively poised male body' (9). Most importantly, however, this movement mobilised a liberal religious agenda imbuing British Christian practice with an urgent desire for ethical and spiritual action.

Jeffrey Richards suggests that evangelicals quite deliberately promoted muscular Christianity to provide an ideal more compatible with their ideologies than the eighteenth-century male model of physical prowess, aggression, and dominance of natural and human realms. New codes of masculinity also rewrote the potentially egalitarian aspects of previous models. Muscular Christianity was imbued with older ideas of chivalry, closely linked with (upper-) class ideologies. Broad Church liberals supported it with vigour, but muscular Christianity was not solely a preoccupation of the middle and upper classes. Indeed, 'raising up' working-class men was a central project, inculcating middle- and upper-class values across society. By the latter half of the century, as J. A. Mangan and James Walvin describe it,

the ideal of manliness [was] shaped and nurtured as a Victorian moral construct by influential and often over-lapping groups of nineteenth-century writers, educationalists and activists in both the old and the new worlds... Nor was proselytism restricted to the properties [*sic*] and the privileged: through school textbooks, children's literature, philanthropic organisations and the churches both the image and associated symbolic activities of both Christian and Darwinian 'manliness' filtered down to the proletariat through an unrelenting and self-assured process of social osmosis.[11]

The impact of such ideas on prospective missionary candidates during the period under investigation was undeniable, energising Christians demoralised by the early failures or compromises of missionary work. The role model developed through the early years of the century, in parallel with missionary expansion in the colonies. Potent exemplars such as the missionary in Ballantyne's novel *Gascoyne, the Sandal-Wood Trader* (1873) embodied this combination of Christian goodness and spiritual and physical toughness. Reverend Frederick Mason

was a man eminently fitted to fill the post which he had selected as his sphere of labour [as a missionary in the 'South Seas']. Bold and manly in the extreme, he was more like a soldier in outward aspect than a missionary.[12] Yet the gentleness of the lamb dwelt in his breast and beamed in his eye; and to a naturally indomitable and enthusiastic disposition was added burning zeal in the cause of his beloved Master.[13]

Muscular Christianity gave men a special role in both spiritual and cultural life by providing a masculine complement to the evangelical view of women's innate piety: it provided men with equal opportunity for religious sanctity.

The revival of chivalric ideals enabled a range of cultural manouevres advantageous to the British community. By the late nineteenth century, Thomas Hughes would announce that the 'least of the muscular Christians' should combine the 'muscularity' of Christian ideals with an imperial 'subduing of the earth' and 'protection of the weak'.[14] These ideas were also crucial to the textualisation of masculine missionary endeavour in the colonies. Jean and John Comaroff describe the gendered nature of missionary texts: 'What distinguished the reports of missionaries from more self-effacing travel narratives was their personalized, heroic form; for, as soldiers of the spiritual empire, their biographies – their battles with the forces of darkness – linked individual achievement to the conquests of civilization.'[15] Richards argues that muscular Christianity was 'deliberately promoted by key figures of the age in order to produce a ruling elite both for the nation and the expanding Empire which would be inspired by noble and selfless ideals' (6), an elite afforded dual authority by British class and religious systems. This sense of an imperial, masculine ruling class proved to be critical in the establishment and maintenance of a colonial culture of governance and command. Most colonies – including India, Polynesia, and Australia – were overwhelmingly masculine in their population demography, at least in the early years. As Dorothy Driver says, 'the place of women in the colonies was carefully defined and circumscribed within what was an avowedly masculine enterprise'.[16] A particular conception of imperial masculinity was therefore central to the implementation of colonial rule.

Applications completed by hopeful missionary candidates attest to the influence of earlier missionary celebrities on their desire to join colonial evangelical ranks. Later in life, too, missionaries like Joseph Bryant would explain how 'my interest in South Sea Missions dates from my boyhood, when in a Lincolnshire village, I listened, wide-eyed and spell-bound, to a missionary from Fiji. The proximity of my later home, Australia, to the Pacific Islands, has given me frequent touch with returned missionaries, and they have cast a further spell, less dramatic but not less moving, upon me.'[17] George Augustus Selwyn, the Anglican bishop of New Zealand[18] from 1841 onwards, was famous for his long hikes in the colonial wilderness. Graeme Kent reveals that Selwyn 'attracted a great deal of attention outside New Zealand and he became the epitome of muscular Christianity for many, even to the extent of having the author Charles Kingsley dedicate his book *Westward Ho!* to him'.[19] Indeed, *Westward Ho!* (1855) was jointly dedicated to Selwyn and 'the Rajah Sir James Brooke' of Sarawak,[20] and Kingsley lauded these two as possessing a

type of English virtue, at once manly and godly, practical and enthusiastic, prudent and self-sacrificing, which [the author] has tried to depict in these pages, [which] they have exhibited in a form even purer and more heroic than that in which he has drest it [*sic*], and than that in which it was exhibited by the worthies whom Elizabeth, without distinction of rank or age, gathered round her in the ever glorious wars of her great reign.[21]

Kingsley's linking of the colonial evangelist Selwyn and the private imperialist Brooke only serves to reinforce the importance of boyish adventurism and imperialism in the figuration of muscular Christianity. Figures like Selwyn, as Niel Gunson suggests, were crucial in the ongoing recruitment of young male missionary volunteers: 'Some of these men were 'idolized' by the young and impressionable... Paragons of moral virtue and physical beauty, they appeared like angels commissioned to call the young convert to the mission field.'[22] Gunson's description confirms the ways in which these missionary idols represented exemplary models of the muscular Christian ideal so revered by missionary candidates throughout the nineteenth century.[23] This is particularly noticeable with public figures such as John Williams, whose evangelical work in the Pacific was widely broadcast.

Juvenile literature was deeply implicated in the sanctification of missionary men and heroic ideals. In his 'Introduction' to *Imperialism and Juvenile Literature* Jeffrey Richards describes the genre as aiming for both entertainment and instruction, 'to inculcate approved value systems, to spread useful knowledge, to provide acceptable role models':

Evangelical organisations like the Religious Tract Society (RTS) and the Society for the Promoting of Christian Knowledge (SPCK) and, later, individual evangelical publishers like James Nisbet and Thomas Nelson published consciously didactic literature for children, seeking to instil obedience, duty, piety and hard work. The writers of evangelical fiction appropriated existing literary forms such as romance and allegory to expound their message. (3)

Later in the century, the Religious Tract Society launched one of the most influential and long-lived boys' magazines, *The Boy's Own Paper* (1879–), in which Empire was promoted as the ideal vehicle for the spread of Christian civilisation (5).

Given both the discourse of masculine authority and the LMS early policy of sending out only male missionaries (although usually accompanied by their wives), it was inevitable that missionary activity was seen as an essentially masculine endeavour. Women were involved in the evangelical community and missionary societies, but they were largely invisible in the official image and publications of the society. The transformation of mission activity into textuality played a major role in effecting this gendered 'disappearing act'. Christine Doran analyses the absence of women from accounts of the Malay Straits Settlement missions. She attributes this marginalisation to the genre of mission historiography, in which both church and imperial historians focused mainly on administrative, theological, and policy issues, where women's input was discouraged, rather than on the day-to-day work of mission stations, where missionary women were heavily involved.[24] The very nature of published historical sources also accounts for this marginalisation, since mission reports are 'official' documents tending to omit reference to female activities. As Jane Haggis notes, 'in the minutes of District Committee meetings, Annual Reports and letters to the Foreign Secretary for the South Travancore District [India], the role of missionary wives attains a visibility absent from the records of the Board and its Committees'.[25] Consequently, as Doran argues, 'missionary women have been stranded in something of an historiographical lacuna' ('Fine Sphere', 101). In tales of 'missionary adventure', too, women had little active place, except as passive victims awaiting salvation.

Missionary women did write about their own colonial experiences, but few women's texts were published by the LMS until later in the nineteenth century when women were employed in their own right. The notion that women's roles were complementary to their (ordained) husbands' ensured that their textual presence was similarly seen as merely adjunctive. Later missions, such as those recruiting educated middle- and upper-class British women, changed this perception of missionary women dramatically. They also changed the textual landscape. Many such women became strong, well-respected figures and public advocates for missionary work, and as such they published an influential body of work. Female writers dominated certain genres or subjects – particularly narratives about children, family life, or women – in the late nineteenth century. However, in the LMS archive up to about 1860, women's published writing is difficult to find. Given the strength of these women's vocations, some published works did appear, particularly from regions where women were given exclusive insight into local practices, such as *zenanas* in India. Missionary women's texts will be examined in this book, but their underrepresentation in the LMS archive in this period inevitably limits their inclusion. Missionary texts by both men and women, however, are rarely silent on questions of native women and gender relations, and through this unequal, though representative, combination of male and female missionary writers the spectre of colonial gender relations emerges.

EMBODIMENTS OF EMPIRE: EVANGELICALISM AND THE WOMAN QUESTION

In the homes, and schools, and hospitals of Christian, heathen, and Moslem lands, [the Christian woman] is to lift the Vision and fulfil the mission of the Incarnation and the Atonement to manhood, womanhood, and childhood, for the regeneration of the world, for the life, and teaching, and healing of the nations. Not in the ordained ministry of the Priesthood, but in the power of the HOLY GHOST of her Baptism and Confirmation – as the faithful handmaid of the Church – she is to take due part with her brothers in bearing CHRIST to the human race and winning the world to GOD.[26]

Laura Helen Sawbridge's *The Vision and the Mission of Womanhood* enthusiastically advocates women's involvement in colonial evangelisation. It is a text which knows its place in the world, dedicated as it is to 'my father John Sikes Sawbridge[27] and my eldest brother John Edward Bridgeman Sawbridge, Priests of God to whose love, sympathy, and inspirations this book mainly owes its origin'; and bearing a foreword by the Lord Bishop of London. The bishop commends Sawbridge's identification of 'the wonderful responsibility which falls upon Womanhood to-day to "lift the Holy Grail" before the men of their generation and also far away in the Indian and Moslem home' (ix). Such philosophies were developed in the intense coalition of ideas about gender, domesticity, and religiosity which had characterised missionary discourses since the late eighteenth century. To borrow Sawbridge's declamatory words, 'We are about to consider the Mission to which GOD has called Womanhood in the Empire and beyond, in this day of the world's supreme need' (xv).

Evangelical discourse ascribed women a special place because they were believed to be naturally 'more spiritual' than men, whose daily experience in the contaminating world of trade and the public sphere was believed to sully their religious purity. Discourses surrounding femininity in the eighteenth and nineteenth centuries imbued women with the moral authority of the modern nation, particularly those women involved in the evangelical Protestant churches. The ideal Christian woman was seen to embody both traditional morality *and* progressive modernity, in this way. This 'doubled time' of evangelical discourse proved to be profoundly important to missionary efforts to promote evangelical gender relations in colonial cultures. It meant that missionaries could represent their gendered interventions both as restoring a natural, Edenic state of relations between the sexes and as introducing the social relations characteristic of modern, Christian nations.

Antoinette Burton suggests that 'while Victorian sexual ideology cast woman as the weaker sex, it endowed her at the same time with unquestionable moral superiority, rooted in the ostensibly feminine virtues of nurturing, childcare, and purity'.[28] Peculiarly enabled by their moral superiority, many women took up social service in the name of nineteenth-century womanhood as an extension of their private moral authority. At the same time, women were induced to bear the responsibility for racial superiority through their roles as moral guardians and chaste wives,[29] in their capacity to bring racially pure, morally upright children into the imperial world.

The moral authority ceded to women was a complex investment in femininity from many different, sometimes contradictory, perspectives. Not simply a delegation of moral responsibility by men, it also functioned as a potentially empowering virtue for women. Burton makes the crucial point that 'liberal feminists, at any rate, enthusiastically *claimed* racial responsibility as part of their strategy to legitimise themselves as responsible and important imperial citizens' ('White Woman's Burden', 296). For the 'serious Christians' of the evangelical revival in Britain, the world of commerce and moral laxity was seen as a hindrance to true spirituality, as Leonore Davidoff and Catherine Hall explain: 'All were agreed that domestic seclusion gave a proper basis for a truly religious life and since women were seen as naturally occupying the domestic sphere this was one of the reasons why women were seen as more "naturally" religious than men.'[30] Through the circulation of such ideas about masculinity, femininity, and the proper division of the spheres of activity, women were represented as possessing a purer spiritual and moral authority. At the same time, as Felicity Nussbaum argues, the 'English nation came to represent its eighteenth-century [and nineteenth-century] woman as happier than women of the past, happier than the "savage", and happiest as mother.'[31]

The figure of British womanhood was already imbued with special significance before women left for overseas missions. In the colonies, feminine behaviour became even more important to the self-representation of British culture, because of imperial ideas about moral and racial degradation, and abhorrence of miscegenation. This was true of white women in colonial environments in general and was particularly the case with women in settler colonies, as the work of critics such as Dorothy Driver, Kay Schaffer, and Gillian Whitlock has demonstrated.

Evangelical wives were integral to the success of missions, and they bore the joint responsibilities of representing British and religious femininity. Few missionaries were allowed to leave for the field without wives, leading to a culture of quickly arranged, swiftly formalised marriages among religious couples.[32] Epitomising the expectations of mission societies, Horne's *Story of the LMS* states that

There will always be posts which it may be desirable to fill with unmarried missionaries; but no one can read the records of the LMS and not be convinced that the influence of a missionary's wife is simply incalculable, and the spectacle of a true Christian home the most powerful, concrete argument for Christianity, and the most easy of appreciation by the common people. The honour paid to women and the frank and full intercourse between man and wife carry their own lesson with inevitable effect.[33]

Horne's emphasis on the congruence of British womanhood and domesticity highlights the largely representative role expected of missionary wives, and elides their active involvement in evangelisation. His own identification of the importance of spectacle makes evident the ways in which missionary women were subject to the (masculine) gaze of missionary communities, the societies back home, and the reading public of evangelical Britons. Patricia Grimshaw notes the heavy strain of the performative role on American missionary wives in Hawaii:

The burden the wives had assumed . . . was a heavy one. They faced the challenge to become exemplary housewives of an exemplary household, which involved a continual struggle to survive materially in unaccustomed circumstances, with the weight of this responsibility and pressure upon them. Housewifery in the islands entailed an unending and unequal struggle for the dignified, acceptable subsistence they sought.[34]

Of course, many missionary wives actively ran Bible classes, schools, and basic medical clinics. Indeed, in 1832 Reverend David Abeel, an American Protestant minister, visited LMS stations in the British colonies of the Malay Straits and was especially impressed with the number of women working in education. On his return to London, Abeel promoted this work and sought funding for the expansion of this educational project, affirming 'that the mission schools of the Straits Settlements "afford a fine sphere for female usefuless" '.[35] It would also be a mistake to assume that these women were dragged to the colonies by their husband's vocation. As Grimshaw notes,

while almost all the mission women were married, their presence in foreign mission service was part of a separate female ambition for an important and independent career, the entry for which was marriage to a departing missionary. The women were imbued with notions of reform derived from the same religious and social impulses as other reforming crusades of the period. (*Paths of Duty*, xxi)

Ideologically, missionary texts tended to de-emphasise such active women.

LMS women were also restricted by moral propriety and the refusal of most societies to endorse them as missionaries in their own right. Marriage to a male missionary, with its attendant social attributes, was almost the only means Protestant women had for spreading the gospel overseas in the first half of the nineteenth century. This becomes evident in LMS candidates' applications to the Candidates' Committee, all of which remain unpublished and therefore contain intriguing and personal micro-narratives of evangelical women. On 22 July 1816, Robert Bourne attended the committee's meeting, bringing his wife, and expressed their desire to go to Taïti. Mrs Bourne spoke to the committee, and their minutes note that 'she also had been a member of Surry Chapel [*sic*] about 5 or 6 years – had regularly attended the School there – is desirous to go out with her husband as a missionary – and prefers Otaheite'.[36] On 26 August 1816, Mr Darling attended the meeting, and told them of his desire to marry Rebecca Woolston. Woolston accompanied him, and she told the committee that her parents were 'more reconciled than they were to her going' to the Pacific 'as the wife of Mr Darling and in the capacity of a Missionary'. She read the committee a paper she had written 'describing her early piety' and noting that her desire to devote herself to the missionary cause 'originated in a perusal of the publications of the Society about sixteen years ago'. The committee resolved 'that Rebecca Woolston be recommended to the board of Directors as a proper person to go out as a Missionary to Otaheite – and as the wife of W. Darling – and that the Sum of £50 be allowed for her equipment'.[37] C. J. Vanderschalk met the committee on 10 November 1840, and informed them that he was engaged. His (unnamed) fiancée, 'who in the earlier age of 11 years was brought to the knowledge of the Lord', had for a long time felt a 'fervent desire … to [be] personnally [*sic*] useful among the heathen for the extention [*sic*] of our Lord's Kingdom'. Vanderschalk explains how 'her unfeigned and sincere piety inspired in me for her the warmest Christian love', and describes his proposal:

After fervent prayer and meditation I proposed to her parents if I were accepted as a Missionary, to become my wife, and that also, if it were the Lord's will, she could fulfil her desire to be useful among the heathen. Her parents declared me that they considered my proposal as a call for their dear daughter, and that they did submit to the Lord's will.[38]

Clearly these (prospective) missionary wives and their husbands saw the involvement of women in colonial evangelising as part of a separate 'vocation' for Protestant women. Haggis suggests that such women 'undertook a missionary marriage not only to inspire their husband, his work, and any children to the missionary "cause", though they did all those; they also assumed a personal responsibility to be "useful" to God more directly'.[39]

Dorothy Driver argues that colonial environments provided white women with a new kind of emancipation in terms of their integration of the roles of domesticity and work outside the home, an integration for which suffragists in Britain would argue later in the century. She considers, though, that 'however much colonial women might have appeared to male observers to be the "models" of emancipation, they continued to act as the repositories of values shed by the male colonist as he played out his duty as frontiersman, aggressive, strong, confident and commanding'.[40] The dominance of missionary women's roles as domestic role-model and care-giver ensured that their activities in the public sphere were inevitably compromised. Activities such as 'Native Female Schools', Bible-reading groups with indigenous women, or medical clinics could afford to be neglected but domestic responsibilities (and all that they symbolised) could not.

Additionally, missionary wives and families were encouraged by the societies to remain at their husbands' sides because of their influence on morality. Vanderschalk preferred to be accompanied by a wife because 'I know by experience the carelessness of the heathen females. The means they set forth to attract the white man; and knowing that the devil go constantly round how he might devour a Soul. So I believe marriage necessary, lest a great blame should be cast on the Lake of our Redeemer.'[41] The many documented cases of missionaries leaving their stations for native women suggests that such moral monitoring was not always effective, even though missionary societies and administrations were vigilant in their attempts to limit liaisons between ministers and female members of their flocks. Reverend Samuel Marsden, highly influential in his advocacy and support for missionaries in both the South Pacific and Australia, was particularly concerned that wives accompany missionaries. Marsden's chief argument for the posting of women with their missionary husbands was that single men could not be expected to withstand sexual temptations, especially in Polynesia. He argued in 1801: 'Place a Young Man in a foreign Climate amongst Licentious Savages remove from his mind every other restraint, but that of Religion and even then we can but form a faint idea how much he will be exposed to the snares of the devil, and the Temptations held out to him by the Natives.'[42] Marsden's pragmatic view of missionaries' inability to contend with 'a Hot Climate the Vigour of Youth and the Most Alluring temptations' is indicative of the ways in which colonial LMS agents were aware of the disjunction between idealistic society policy and colonial practice. Marsden clearly believed that wives were crucial to maintaining a semblance of respectability in the missionary enterprise.[43] Similarly, Driver suggests that for settler gender relations in general it was considered essential for settlers to marry, for wives would stabilize British hold over the colonies and establish the colonial homestead: their presence, and with it the presence of children, would encourage the cultivation of the land and the production of agricultural surplus; wives would also produce their own 'surplus', bearing the children that would populate the British empire and swell the ranks of the white race, protecting the 'master' race from the 'blood' of those supposedly inferior to it.[44]

Throughout evangelical texts from various fields of mission activity the trope of missionary woman as role-model and as a civilised feminine icon recurs. Hilary Carey explains that missionary families were believed to assist evangelisation simply by carrying out their 'natural duties' as mothers and children in view of native members of the community.[45] In this manner colonial modes of performance and mimicry were seen to be crucial to effecting moral reform. Of course, the belief that missionary women innately personified such proper domestic and moral qualities masked the quite recent and contested 'cult of domestic maternity' in the eighteenth and nineteenth centuries.[46] It disguised the way that middle-class Englishwomen were encouraged to limit themselves in the emergent industrial system to producing life, even if 'the domestic woman gained power to shape the public realm, particularly the nation, through procreation and education of her children' (Nussbaum, *Torrid Zones*, 48).

But the colonial enterprise enabled (and arguably *required*) 'the domestic monogamous Englishwoman, who personifies chaste maternal womanhood, [to be] frequently contrast[ed] to the wanton polygamous Other' (*Torrid Zones*, 73). In the colonial world, British missionary women were not only invested with the weight of moral and domestic authority – they also came to embody the empire itself. Their highly symbolic role of bearing the responsibility of British home, children, and separate spheres meant that they became visible 'monuments of Empire'.[47] As McClintock argues, domesticity became central to British imperial identity: 'Imperialism suffused the Victorian cult of domesticity and the historic separation of the private and the public, which took shape around colonialism and the idea of race...As domestic space became racialized, colonial space became domesticated.'[48] The importance of these women was thus both physical and spiritual – Gillian Whitlock has highlighted the validation of women's reproductive labour inherent in ideas like 'The Uterus is to the Race what the heart is to the Individual: it is the organ of circulation to the species.'[49] Burton suggests that even feminist women tacitly supported this construction of British womanhood: 'feminists deliberately cultivated the civilizing responsibility as their own modern womanly burden because it affirmed an emancipated role for them in the imperial nation state. From their point of view empire was an integral and enabling part of the woman question.'[50] The emotive rhetoric of women as (physical and metaphoric) mothers of the nation and the imaging of Britain as the feminine figure of Britannia ensured that the moral investment in British womanhood was intense. The kind of righteous outrage invoked when British womanhood was perceived to be under attack – such as Nana Sahib's actions at Kanpur (then Cawnpore) in July 1857 which were instrumental to the British response to, and representation of, the Indian Mutiny – highlighted the symbolic importance of women in imperial self-imagining. Queen Victoria, writing to her uncle Leopold, King of Belgium, about the murder of British women at the Bibighar, notes that this 'engrosses all our attention. Troops cannot be raised fast or largely enough. And the horrors committed on the poor ladies – women and children – are unknown in these ages and make one's blood run cold.'[51] Jenny Sharpe's excellent *Allegories of Empire* points out that the colonial crisis in British authority in India was managed through the circulation of narratives about violated bodies of English women, which stood as a sign for the violation of colonialism.[52]

Missionary women also bore the historical symbolism of representative Christian women – the figures of the Virgin Mary, Joan of Arc, and numerous other suffering but holy Christian women. And, as Francis Cuningham points out in the preface to Mrs Mary Edwards Weitbrecht's *Female Missionaries in India: Letters from a Missionary's Wife Abroad to a Friend in England* (1843),

from the time when the sufferings of our Lord called forth the sympathy of the women who were about him, to this time, when females have been led to engage in the work of missions, we have seen the affectionate heart of the sex successfully occupied in communicating that sympathy which it has been peculiarly in their power to afford.[53]

THE 'FAMILY' OF CHRISTIAN MISSIONS

Protestant missionary activity was fundamentally based around the family. Davidoff and Hall argue that 'the linkage of Christianity, godliness and the family was crucial'.[54] Church structures privileged male authority, and were mimicked in the model British nuclear family. This model profoundly influenced missionary activity. As Catherine Hall argues, there was the 'clan' of the individual missionary societies and the 'family' of fellow missionaries, addressed affectionately in correspondence as 'brother' and 'sister'.

Evangelical families were utilised as models for indigenous 'Christianisation and civilisation', and the missionary himself filled multiple roles as 'father' of the congregation, the family, and the household.[55] Mission stations also formed a kind of 'extended family', where 'the family was defined not only by blood but also by religious brotherhood'.[56] Mission families were tied by a web of cross-relationships – many missionaries' families intermarried; they frequently named their children after evangelical friends or heroes; and they saw their children marry pious partners and become missionaries (or wives of missionaries) themselves (255). As Hall argues of the Baptist missionaries in Jamaica, family was a 'many-layered concept...for there was the family of origin, the family of marriage, the family of the chapel, the mission family, the family of Baptists at home; and the family-to-be in the skies – this last providing the key to the overarching spiritual nature of the Christian family' ('Missionary Stories', 254).

Importantly, the 'family of empire' provided a network of colonial colleagues and British benefactors. Helen Tiffin suggests that the phrase ' "I am your mother and your father" was the missionary rhetoric whose standard slippage in India, Africa, and the Caribbean was from God to Queen Victoria and [hence] the British Government.'[57] McClintock argues that 'the family as a *metaphor* offered a single genesis narrative for global history, while the family as an *institution* became void of history'.[58] She suggests that the power and importance of the family trope in colonial cultures in general is attributable to two factors. Firstly, because 'the subordination of woman to man and child to adult were deemed natural facts, other forms of social hierarchy could be depicted in familial terms to guarantee social *difference* as a category of nature'. Secondly, she suggests,

the family offered an invaluable trope for figuring *historical time*. Within the family metaphor, both social hierarchy (synchronic hierarchy) and historical change (diachronic hierarchy) could be portrayed as natural and inevitable, rather than as historically constructed and therefore subject to change...Imperial intervention could thus be figured as a linear, nonrevolutionary progression that naturally contained hierarchy within unity; paternal fathers ruling benignly over immature children. (*Imperial Leather*, 45)

'Family', in its many senses, was a fundamental way in which missionaries made sense of their world, and particularly when located in what seemed to them to be the moral vacuum of newly colonised places.

Widespread use of structures and images centred on family in colonial missions meant that gendered domestic relations were crucial to missionary endeavours promoting Christianity. Inescapably part of evangelising projects were the dual processes of 'Christianisation and civilisation'. Missionary activity in colonial cultures was deeply committed to these twin goals: in theory, they intended to 'raise up' native populations in standards of conduct, lifestyle, and industry at the same time as raising spiritual standards through the introduction of Christian principles. In practice, this meant that missionaries educated potential converts in ways that sought to reproduce, at the colonial periphery, middle-class British social structures and values. Missionaries encouraged the establishment of agrarian capitalist systems, and they promoted housing which replicated as closely as possible that found in English villages.

Gender roles and relations also proved a fertile field for such civilising practices. Missionaries attempted to install replicas of the patriarchal nuclear family in colonised communities, as it was widely believed that Christianisation was not possible without a change to a British-style nuclear family. Societies where women were afforded equal or dominant power in the cultural institutions of government, community, or religion – such as Polynesian societies where women of leading families could rule the community – were condemned by LMS missionaries, who believed that public power was definitely not women's 'natural' sphere. Cultures in which polygamy (or worse, polyandry) was practised horrified missionaries, who then had to confront the extreme social collapse that would occur should converts abandon all but one of their spouses. Missionaries also attempted to suppress overt female sexual power, and indeed most expressions of indigenous sexuality, in cultures whose practices differed from evangelical ideals.

But as Margaret Jolly and Martha Macintyre suggest, these domestic values 'were... idealised visions rather than realistic memories of the dominant modes of domesticity at home'.[59] In Jamaica, Baptist missionaries established idealistic 'free villages' – Hall explains these as

missionary utopias; designed and planned by them... [and] built around the church, mission house, and school. Free peasants could buy their plot of land, sometimes paying it off in installments, and thus securing their manhood, not only with the possession of property but also the vote it carried.[60]

Through such rose-tinted spectacles, missionaries measured civilisation and freedom by 'the cottager's comfortable home, by the wife's proper release from toil, [and] by the instructed child';[61] lifestyles by no means universal even in England.

Alongside their attempts to change religious practice, missionaries used the sphere of gender relations to effect real change in indigenous communities. The missionaries found their encounters with alternative systems of gender and family roles profoundly disturbing, for most had previously accepted the 'given' nature of gender roles. It is not surprising then that their interference in the arena of gender and domestic relations was one of the most troubling issues for both missionaries and indigenous populations. Missionaries took exception to many aspects of indigenous domestic life and saw reforms as necessary in each region. Missionary intervention in cultures such as India, Polynesia, and Australia brought to the fore crucial questions about gender, families, and social structures – questions which fascinated imperial audiences and underpinned colonial projects.

Alternative models of gender and sexuality fuelled the already exoticised (and eroticised) European view of indigenous cultures and women in particular, evident in popular colonial stereotypes of dusky, sexually available Polynesian women, or degraded Indian women as victims of Indian patriarchy. These stereotypes were extremely influential in the British public's perception of evangelical endeavours, and mission activity often came to be seen as 'rescuing' native women from their traditional travails – an emotive discourse which tapped into intense public sentiment about the role and importance of women as guardians of cultural integrity.

Missionaries shifted the prurient European interest in native sexuality into a new mode. In all three locations discussed in this study, colonised women had been stereotyped sexually, however missionaries brought a moralistic focus to bear on sexual practices. This ensured colonial attention was consequently focussed on local domestic practices and colonised bodies, especially on women's bodies. Missionaries also attempted to sanitise the opportunistic relations which had developed between colonising and colonised cultures, namely sexual relationships between white men and women of colour. Through the proliferation of missionary texts about the colonial 'heathen', evangelicals in Britain and the colonies sought to reform women's positions within both traditional and colonial cultures.

Significantly, missionaries scrutinised the practices of both the colonisers and colonised. It is particularly evident in the area of gender and sexuality that they were neither for nor against the imposition of colonial rule in any uncomplicated manner. Missionaries contradicted some of the more racist views of their colonial counterparts. In order to believe in the feasibility of their evangelical projects they had to maintain a belief in the potential of 'lower' heathen races to learn and 'improve' with Christian tuition. Many other colonists were violently opposed to such an idea, particularly in settler colonies where narratives of 'dying races' provided a justification of white dominance. Missionaries were instrumental in changing white understandings of cross-cultural encounters in colonial environment. They sought to domesticate the potentially subversive nature of colonial encounters between cultures by limiting cross-cultural relationships whether sexual or platonic; they instituted moral/religious frameworks of marriage and family life; and they lobbied for the legislation of civil procedures of authority, legislature, and religious responsibility. Gender was always central to the missionary agenda of reform, even though its early (male) proponents were mostly found wanting in their ability to cope with the intensity of gender differences and the difficulties which gender provided in effecting religious and social reform along Christian lines.

THE WORK OF GENDER IN COLONIAL MISSIONS

Both missionary societies and individual evangelists relied heavily on the figure of 'the native woman' as a means of justifying their colonial projects. Throughout the mission field, the alleged degradation of local women by traditional custom was graphically depicted and deplored, and the supposed deprivations of women became common knowledge in the colonies and in Britain. Horne's history of the LMS contains numerous typical references: 'Mr Murray describes the customs current on the island [of Aneityum, southern Vanuatu] thus: "War, murder, cannibalism, strangling of widows, murder of orphan children, polygamy, and the consequent degradation and oppression of the female sex" – a sufficiently appalling list.'[62] The pejorative tone of this quotation is not unusual – indeed, missionary accounts tend to assume female degradation in many different colonial locations. Details of local practice frequently appeared to bear little weight in missionary evaluations and representations.

In 'The White Woman's Burden' Antoinette Burton investigates representations of Indian women in mid- to late-nineteenth-century British feminist periodicals. She argues that they are always shown as singular, utterly foreign, and degraded, and are co-opted into universalising narratives of global womanhood (particularly in regards to maternity).[63] Indian women's experiences were seen as easily comparable to those of other women because of the common denominator of gender, in spite of differences in race, religion, caste, class, and social structure:

In light of this construct, the attention lavished on India and its women in periodicals... had the effect of stripping Indian women of their foreignness, their exoticism, thereby domesticating them for a British feminist audience... since Indian women rarely spoke for themselves in these controlled textual spaces, British feminists defined them even as they silenced them. In the process, they underscored their own moral purity and legitimized themselves as the authority on Indian womanhood. (303–4)

Feminist activists, like many other less radical British citizens, contrasted the image of Indian women with the moral standing of British women. The Indian woman represented a figure worthy of rescue: 'she became the embodiment of personal, social and political subjection in a decaying civilisation – the very symbol, in short, of what British feminists were struggling to progress away from in their own struggle for liberation' (305). It is interesting to parallel this with late-twentieth-century debates between white women and women of colour about the tendency of contemporary feminism to assume a similar global sisterhood. It would be productive to examine current political issues surrounding 'first' and 'third' worlds and gender, for example about clitoridectomy in Africa or veiling in Muslim cultures, within this context.

However, it was not solely feminist Britons who were fascinated with Indian women, nor was it only Indians who attracted such imperial moral outrage at their traditional roles. Indeed, missionary representation of degraded native women is so generic that the country of origin, the actual site of this destruction of 'natural womanhood', is virtually irrelevant. In missionary texts from around the world such representations recur with the familiarity of a well-worn trope. In these texts, from widely divergent geographical, social, and political locations, native women are represented as always subordinate to their male family members; they are inevitably unhappy, burdened by physical labour and domestic duties; their menfolk are usually lazy, aggressive, and abusive; the women inevitably die much younger than their British counterparts; and so on. *The Gospel Missionary for 1852* reported from the field:

The Indian women [in New Brunswick, Canada] are both wives and servants to their husbands. A traveler (Mr Gamer) says, 'It is no uncommon thing, even in the present day, to see a squaw bent down beneath a heavy burden, and her stately lord marching before her with nothing but a gun on his shoulder. The wife has to erect the hut or wigwam, cultivate the ground, make a canoe, catch fish, and provide for the children.'[64]

These representations focus on the native woman as victim, suffering because of her male relatives (be they fathers, husbands, or brothers) and, by extension, because of the native society itself. As Catherine and Ronald Berndt explain in their anthropological critique of nineteenth- and twentieth-century Australian missions, Aboriginal women too were regarded as being subordinate to their menfolk and badly treated by them. But, as the Berndts explain, the lurid stories of women's abuse were quite different from information obtained from Aborigines when questioned.[65] Representations of victimised women allowed the imperial imagination to assume a detailed critique of native society, providing what they considered to be a specific measure of the degradation of local cultures.[66] It also enabled a kind of 'divide and conquer' approach to missionary intervention, whereby women were encouraged to become aware of their 'oppression' in traditional societies and then to see that their enlightenment could only come about through the avenue of modern western Christianity. As McClintock argues, through Fanon, such interventions embodied the implementation of imperialism as a domestication of the colony: a 'reordering of the labor and sexual economy of the people, so as to divert female power into colonial hands and disrupt the patriarchal power of colonized men ... [Fanon's] insight here is that the dynamics of colonial power are fundamentally, though not solely, the dynamics of gender.'[67] In the mission field, particularly in Australia, this resulted in native women becoming the primary targets of concentrated Christian evangelising.

There is an equally large and well-rehearsed set of tropes regarding the native woman as 'unnatural', savage, and destructive. These tropes regularly revolve around representations of maternity – native women are invariably represented as 'bad' mothers. Lewis Hermon Gaunt's childrens' text, *School-Mates: Pictures of School-Time and Play-Time in the Mission Field* (1906), instilled the idea of bad native mothers in the British Sunday School children whose donations were funding mission schools:

In the mission field, at any rate, the reality is not always quite so picturesque. It is not usual, for instance, for the young Papuan to receive a mother's kiss as he skips away to school; and it may be doubted whether his hair is always so smooth and tidy as yours when he leaves home.[68]

Similarly Geraldine Forbes cites a songbook inspired by missionary tales – entitled *Songs for the Little Ones at Home* – that taught children that Indian mothers were capable of killing their own children.[69] In these negative representations of the Other woman, mothers commonly kill their children, particularly if those children are twins (especially common in texts about Africa), female, deformed, or unwanted; native women are overly powerful and therefore corrupt and dangerous; native women are sexually profligate, immoral, and therefore corrupting of male converts; and so on. The recurrence of these tropes, and the fervour with which even staid missionary texts emphasise such issues, indicates that local sociology is less at issue than homogenising imperial perceptions and constructions of the heathen Other.

In these ways, missionary discourse represented the 'rescue' of native women as a justification for evangelical intrusion into new areas. Native women gave the evangelical project added legitimacy – not only were missionaries carrying out the mission of Christ, but they were also performing essential philanthropic projects. Liberating colonised women was a humanitarian issue that even opponents of evangelical crusading could see was important, ensuring that saving women from themselves and their native societies was seen as a simple issue of social justice.

Gender was thus used as an additional justification of imperial missionary projects – not only through the salvation of native women but through a simultaneous reification of 'free' or uplifted *British* women as symbols of empire and Christian religious responsibility. It enabled the perpetuation of representations of passivity and submission – not just through stereotypical exploration tropes of virgin colonial land and imperial male penetration,[70] but through a rather more sophisticated discourse about vulnerability, moral restitution, and cultural amelioration.

Missionary discourse had an extremely uneasy and ambivalent relationship with other colonial discourses and their stereotypical figures, as these others simultaneously supported *and* disturbed the missionary project. Homi Bhabha declares of the stereotype that it is 'a complex, ambivalent, contradictory mode of representation, as anxious as it is assertive, and demands not only that we extend our critical and political objectives but that we change the object of analysis itself'.[71] Missionary discourse is caught in this complex and contradictory mode, unsure about its alliance with broader colonial political objectives, and in some circumstances directly opposed to them.

Bhabha notes that colonial discourse depended on the concept of 'fixity' – and the stereotype is its major discursive strategy. He describes the ways in which such stereotypes will 'vacillitate between what is always "in place", already known, and something that must be anxiously repeated' ('Other Question', 66). Missionary narratives, like other colonial texts, are dually invested with this already known yet anxiously uncertain perspective on colonised peoples and practices, yet these texts are precariously balanced on this fulcrum of stereotypical colonial representations. Missionary images of femininity inevitably see colonised women as degraded and as members of a lower 'chain of being'. However, ideologically they also sustain a notion of common humanity across race, in order to entertain the potential of Christian reform to transform and 'raise up' local populations to the standards set by British Christians. The use of gender as a justificatory trope thus assists the twin projects of 'Christianisation and civilisation' – missionaries firmly believed that Christianity could not be fully understood or established without also installing the civilised virtues of British society, in which gender played an integral role.

PART TWO

The London Missionary Society in India

Storming Satan's threshold[1]

CHAPTER THREE

Empire, India, and evangelisation

The Peculiar Claims of India as a Field of Missionary Enterprise

Reverend John Wilson, Church of Scotland missionary in Bombay and Honorary President of the Bombay Branch of the Royal Asiatic Society, lectured in 1844 on the 'Peculiar Claims of India as a Field of Missionary Enterprise'.[2] India should attract missionary attention because of its 'magnitude as a country, and the great extent of its population', he proposed. As a predominantly British colony, it is 'wholly accessible as a field of missionary operations', so that 'Through the whole of this vast country, the shield of Britain is held over the missionary for his protection'. Additionally, Wilson argues, 'we are placed as a nation under very great obligations to India', as a result of wars there. India also provides profitable employment for British men in both military and civil service; and commerce with India is the most advantageous in Asia: the 'conversion of India will be attended with great advantages to Britain, nay the whole of the civilized world'. More theologically, he suggests that 'there is a great deal of available Christian influence and co-operation in India, to be secured and directed in behalf of the cause of Christian missions', and, because 'India is either the fatherland or the asylum of the greatest systems of religious error and delusion, which now exist, or have ever existed, in the world', Britain should feel an evangelical duty to eradicate such religious systems. The evangelisation of India is also strategically useful, for the 'prevalence of Christianity every where marks the boundary which separates the civilized from the barbarous and semi-barbarous parts of the world; let but this boundary be extended, and the country included within its limits may be considered as redeemed from the waste, and prepared to receive the precious seeds of civilization and improvement'. In addition, the conversion of India 'will have a mighty effect on the other countries of Asia'. Finally, Wilson rather prematurely enthuses, 'We have great encouragement to prosecute and extend our missionary operations in India, from the remarkable success which

63

(through God's grace) has been experienced in that portion of the missionary field' (*Evangelization of India*, 216–56). Wilson's yoking together of commerce, colonisation, and Christianity typifies the acquisitive evangelical focus on India in the early nineteenth century, and reveals the competing demands of such colonial projects which came to trouble missionary efforts there.

The reform of both family and gender relations was a pivotal point in the evangelising projects of missionaries in India. However it was also an area of extreme complexity, one which proved to be resistant to missionary 'reform' and which came to destabilise the missionaries' own deeply held beliefs. Part two enlarges what can appear to be a straightforward linear evangelical history by interrogating recurring tropes in British missionary texts. In particular, I examine LMS missionary representations of Indian gender and domesticity, making clear the entanglements of gender relations across racial and class lines. In doing so, I reveal some of the blind spots of colonial historiography, as Ranajit Guha advocates, 'by having a close look at its constituting elements and examin[ing] those cuts, seams and stitches – those cobbling marks – which tell us about the material it is made of and the manner of its absorption into the fabric of writing'.3

This chapter provides an historical overview of the nature of evangelical work in India, detailing the proselytising practices of LMS missionaries. Their increasing attention to converting Indian women, and the cultural and political negotiations required to achieve this aim, will be viewed within the context of the society's work as a whole. Chapter 4 analyses issues of missionary textuality in India, looking closely at specific texts about domestic and gender relations. Chapter 5 concludes this Indian case study by briefly examining the effects of the period 1800 to 1860 on missionary policy, in particular the subsequent posting of women missionaries. It will signal the ways in which missionary discourses and narratives formulated during this early period continued to influence a range of groups interested in debates about gender, domesticity, and modern nationhood.

For most of the period 1800 to 1860, the East India Company embodied the interests of empire. Until 1858 the company administered India primarily in the interests of its industrial and trade enterprises and, in a *de facto* sense, of British government business in India. Whilst the company had control of British interests in India, British cultural and religious affairs had some local representation, although in a very limited, non-institutionalised manner. As an organisation, the company was highly suspicious of missionaries, predominantly because it feared that evangelising might disturb its commercial control. Scattered Catholic missionaries and some German

Protestants had infiltrated small communities in India, but their profile and success had necessarily been limited by the anti-missionary feeling within the company.

After the early 1800s missionaries gained better access to India. Although William Carey (1761–1834) is often described as the father of modern Indian missions, he was, in fact, one of a long line of missionaries. Nonetheless, his work is considered as representing a turning point in the evangelisation of the sub-continent. Stephen Neill argues that Carey 'marks the entry of the English-speaking world on a large scale into the missionary enterprise',[4] and, indeed, Carey's arrival in 1793 as the founder of the Baptist Missionary Society's mission in India represents the start of a significant influx of British Protestant missionaries. Both an historical and a discursive progenitor, Carey introduced the kind of colonial narratives which came to typify missionary writing about India. Even Stephen Neill's 1964 *History of Christian Missions* replicates such tropes. He describes how the Carey family necessarily 'disappeared' into 'the interior of the country', because they were effectively illegal immigrants, 'where the father worked as manager of an indigo plantation, but the mind of the mother became steadily more seriously unhinged and the children grew up as undisciplined ragamuffins' (262). This type of 'heart of darkness' trope, with its particular emphasis on the degradation of European women and children in the colonial environment, haunts many missionary narratives of India.

Up to 1833 most Protestant missionary work in India was carried out by the British societies (including the Baptist Missionary Society, the Church Missionary Society, the LMS, and the Wesleyan Methodists), but then many other nations entered the large Indian mission field. Carey had soon been joined by more missionaries, and together they established a mission station at the Danish settlement of Shrirampur where they could expect some protection from British and Indian resistance to Christian intervention. In 1798 the LMS sent its first missionary to India, Reverend Nathaniel Forsyth, and he settled in Calcutta and Hugli, where the Dutch seemed to promise similar protection.[5] Bengal,[6] the region around Calcutta, was a stronghold of LMS activity, and this area is the main geographical region under discussion here. In 1804 the LMS sent the Reverends Ringeltraube (a Prussian, previously working in India with the Society of the United Brethren), Des Granges, and Cran to Kerala;[7] and W. C. Loveless and John Taylor to Surat in the west. The region in the far south of the Indian peninsula, Kerala, was also a key location of LMS activity. These early postings began what was to become a well-worn missionary trail between the LMS headquarters and India.

India became one of the foremost LMS mission fields, as the size of the country and the expanding nature of British territories there increasingly consumed a large part of the LMS reserves of both financial and human capital. India proved to be a physically demanding posting. Lack of knowledge about tropical lifestyles and diseases resulted in a horrifying high attrition rate amongst the missionaries.[8] Gradually medical knowledge and local experience developed sufficiently to sustain them for longer periods of time, but there continued to be a significant number of deaths. The home society felt these losses greatly – the 1823 'Report' of the LMS began with an acknowledgement that it

would argue culpable insensibility, were we not to commence the present Report with adverting to the unprecedented mortality which has prevailed, during the past year, among the Societies [*sic*] Missionaries, chiefly in the East. Deeply do we lament to state, that, within this short period, no less than TEN of our brethren and sisters have been, in rapid succession, removed from the present world, and from the scenes of their useful labours.[9]

LMS narratives are consequently replete with sentimental images of the sacrificial deaths of missionaries and their families.

Due to the experimental and often ill-informed nature of Indian missions and intense local resistance to Christian evangelising, missionaries learnt to adapt their formal policies to local situations very rapidly. Education thus became a crucial feature, and Hindus were the main religious group targeted for conversion. The evangelists admitted that 'our object in conducting this [educational] institution is not to impart a very high intellectual training; but as much as possible to fit them for a better and more Christian-like exercise of those duties, which, will devolve upon them in their particular sphere of life'.[10] As Brian Holmes notes, 'the first and most important aim of education... was to make conversion possible. It could be done only if the Scriptures could be understood and preferably read. Bible study was the central aim of all Protestant mission education.'[11] In this way, literacy and the central and symbolic role of texts were fundamental to missionaries' educational and evangelical projects in India.

EDUCATION

A 'pure, enlightened, and active population will take the place of the myriads of its now deluded and wretched inhabitants'[12]

Small schools were established in villages near the missions and these schools were often supervised in part by the missionaries' wives. Education of Indian children became gender-segregated, leaving the missionary wife to attend to girl students whilst the male missionary would supervise boys. This segregation quickly evolved as the best solution to problems of gender arising out of local conditions, as missionaries were unprepared for the intense native resistance to European forms of education. As Reverend Edward Storrow, a LMS missionary in Calcutta from 1848 to 1866, describes it, 'the earliest mission schools were intended for both sexes and all castes and classes; but increased knowledge and experience convinced the missionaries that prejudice was far too strong for their good intentions'.[13] Partha Chatterjee suggests that middle-class Indian men saw missionary schools as representing a dual threat of both proselytisation and the exposure of women to harmful western influences.[14] Gradually, LMS missionaries discovered that there was much less resistance to female education when girls were educated within a female-only community, and that they would need to take education to the higher-caste women in their own homes rather than expect members of higher castes and classes to join the village schools.

It became virtually mandatory for LMS missionary wives to establish and/or superintend what were called 'Native Female Schools' – as Jane Haggis notes, 'wherever there was a missionary wife, a school for girls was established'.[15] The annual LMS 'Reports' approvingly note the establishment and development of missionary wives' educational efforts. The 1825 'Report', for example, comments that

The Directors observe, with satisfaction, the attention paid at the Calcutta stations to Native Female Instruction, convinced as they are, that the intellectual and moral improvement of this portion of the population is of the highest importance to the ultimate success of missionary efforts in all heathen countries, but more particularly in Hindoostan.[16]

Christine Doran describes very similar schools run by missionary women in the Malay Straits Settlements, and notes that there, like India, these schools 'commenced and collapsed with such frequency that it is virtually impossible to chart their histories in detail. At any one time most of the missionary women were involved in running at least one school, and often several'.[17] Nevertheless, as Haggis suggests, 'the responsibility for education given to wives was...a reflection of its supportive role in the "real" work of the missionary, a "work" that hinged on ordination, a qualification denied women. By the 1820s...male missionaries were placing much greater emphasis on boys' education as they sought to counter the resilience of Indian men to their preaching efforts' ('Professional Ladies', 129).

Pedagogic practice itself was highly gendered and details of the differences in curriculum in male and female schools reveal a great deal about the missionaries' expectations of their charges. Girls were predominantly educated to a level of basic literacy and numeracy, with an emphasis on domestic skills including housekeeping, sewing, and lace-making. These skills were seen as crucial to their future roles as wives and mothers of the modern Indian nation; like British women, Indian mothers were expected to fulfill their national duty by giving birth to the new generation of Christianised (and concomitantly Anglicised) Indians who would serve and support the British administration. Indeed, one girls' school in Kottayam in Kerala was known as the 'Husband Class', because it appeared to have been training girls solely for home life.[18] Girls were also instructed in decorative and productive craft industries, and LMS 'Reports' celebrated the success of this venture. The 1823 'Report' describes the Nagercoil Native Female School in Kerala where 'industry and learning go hand in hand. Besides the knowledge of the Christian Religion, the girls are taught lace-making, knitting, and sewing',[19] and the 1825 'Report' notes of the same school that 'the girls under instruction are taught reading and writing. They also learn to sew and knit, and to manufacture lace. The lace-making department of the school had already produced something considerable towards its support'.[20]

Boys, in contrast, were exposed to broader academic disciplines, including science and geography.[21] Importantly, they were also encouraged in a concomitant training of the physical body by proponents of muscular Christianity. Lewis Hermon Gaunt placed great importance on the place of school games in Christian schools in the colonies for boys. His description of school sports situated these activities squarely in the realm of disciplining native bodies and temperaments into appropriate imitations of Christian masculinity. He approvingly cites Mr Brown of a Berhmapur (Northern India) school, who believed that sport helped 'to build up a more manly character'.[22] Gaunt makes disparaging remarks about the zealous academic diligence of Indian scholars and their reluctance to play sport, in particular, football (107). Like the native female schools, boys' education in India served not only to educate their pupils academically but also to school them in European ideals of gender and Christian ethics. Later, Indian reformers specifically critiqued the notion of muscular Christianity that missionaries imported. Keshabchandra Sen, the Brahmo leader, told an imperial audience on his British lecture tour in 1870 that 'English Christianity appears too muscular and hard... It is not soft enough for the purposes of the human heart... Christian life in England is more materialistic and outward than spiritual and inward.'[23]

Christian texts were used as pedagogical tools across both curricula. Ralph Wardlaw Thompson and Arthur Johnson note disingenuously that 'the religious aim was in many mission fields helped by the fact that the only reading book available was a translation of one of the Gospels, or of some other portion of Scripture'.[24] In fact, as they later explain, this was hardly a matter of chance, because evangelicals believed that 'the puerility and impurity of Indian literature has made it impossible to adopt it for reading purposes in mission schools' (126). It is significant that Indian textuality was seen to embody the corruption of the Indian culture as a whole, a corruption which could only be eradicated by immersing Indian students in British, Christian texts. Texts became invested with crucial symbolic weight in missionary writing.[25]

Missionaries and their wives gradually realised the limitations of village-school style education as it accessed only a certain segment of the Indian population. James Kennedy, a LMS missionary in Varanasi, North India, from 1839 to 1877, notes with concern, 'we have had no girls of the higher classes in our schools, and only a small number of the lower classes, whose attendance has been brief and fitful, with the exception of that of orphan girls, who have been wholly under our charge'.[26] The public nature of this schooling practically excluded female students of higher caste/class, because of the high-caste custom of secluding women in *zenanas*, women-only apartments within homes.[27] During the first half of the nineteenth century, missionaries constantly lamented the lack of higher-class students in their schools and the prevalence of already marginalised members of the Indian community, but it was not until nearly mid century that they took practical steps to expand their potential conversion base. Indeed, the missionaries' ministrations to women and children of lower castes in some ways thwarted their own attempts to reach the more secluded higher castes. As Storrow describes it, 'Female education had evil associations, for were not harlots more generally trained than any other women [in Indian tradition]?... Since purdah ladies were untaught, what presumption was it for the poor and low caste to learn to read and write!'[28] Importantly, education appeared one of the most effective means of reaching the female Hindu population because of the caste and class restrictions which limited their participation in the public sphere.

THE *ZENANA*

... how vastly important, how incalculably beneficial is the influence of a cultivated female mind[29]

It took a surprisingly long time for it to be realised that if missionaries were to gain access to these potential students they would have to modify their methods. Storrow suggests that the delay in the development of a more appropriate method of proselytising was due to 'the intense reluctance of Hindus, even when educated and refined; and of Europeans, who were... wedded to the school system, and... impressed with the difficulty of reaching *zenana* ladies'.[30] He was convinced that 'the education of a *zenana* lady is far more important than that of a ryot's[31] child, for it may carry with it far-reaching issues' (218, n.1). Storrow's assumption of the greater importance of recruiting higher-class Indians would not have generated significant disagreement amongst any LMS missionaries.

Whilst, as I noted earlier, the class and status of many missionaries themselves was somewhat ambiguous, the desire to convert higher classes of Indian society to Christianity was certainly not. As Haggis argues,

to win a high caste (presumed higher class) convert fitted missionary notions both of contemporary Indian society and of that 'right society' they hoped to establish. Evangelising the high caste elite was the path to ultimate success, while Christianity alerted that same elite to its rightful duty: the moral and spiritual guidance of the 'labouring classes'.[32]

The disappointing experience of early village schools and missionaries' fervent desire to gain access to higher-caste Indians resulted in the development of what came to be known as '*zenana* visitation', when individual British women would visit small groups of Hindu women in their own compounds for the purposes of education and conversion. Missionary wives began this work early, but, as Haggis explains, it soon became a much more professionalised occupation for single women missionaries. Like many avenues of female evangelisation, though, the roots of the later public and vigorous '*zenana* Societies' were established in the earlier period with which this book is concerned. It is the work of these forerunners which forms the focus of this section.

Indian women of higher caste remained predominantly invisible to early male missionaries due to the restrictions of *zenana* seclusion – an avoidance of European surveillance which frustrated the missionaries' desire to bring light to the 'darkness' of heathen India. Reverend Alexander Duff, an advocate and pioneer of British-style education for Indian children, addressed the first annual meeting of the Church of Scotland's Ladies' Association in 1834 on the importance of gaining access to Indian mothers:

'In every country the infant mind receives its earliest impressions from the mother; that wherever the female sex is left in ignorance and degradation, the endearing and important duties of wife and mother cannot be duly discharged; and that no great progress in civilization and morals can, in such a state of things, be reasonably hoped for'... It can never be a question how vastly important, how incalculably beneficial is the influence of a cultivated female mind.[33]

The growing importance of *zenana* work was in part a result of the missionaries' (private) recognition that their early labours had not been successful, considering the quantities of funds and personal effort expended. One of the responses of missionaries in India and their British supporters was to place increasing importance on women's conversion and *zenana* work, and a range of vindicating literature encouraged the belief that this would be the locus of a real religious breakthrough into Indian society. As Geraldine Forbes suggests, documents about contact between British and Indian women increased after 1860, as 'the efforts of [missionary] women resulted in the penetration of foreign ideas into the *zenana*, the very centre of family life'.[34]

By the mid to late nineteenth century, evangelising the *zenana* came to be seen as an integral part of the Christianisation of India and, after the 1860s, the employment of single women missionaries was regarded as the most efficient method of infiltrating Indian households, because of the heavy demands that *zenana* work had proved to make of early missionary wives' time and labour. As a consequence of the important role of *zenana* work, the predominance of *female* missionaries by the end of the nineteenth century was particularly obvious in India. This significant shift in the gender of missionary personnel was mirrored by a growing British sense of responsibility for their Indian empire during the nineteenth century. At the same time, the cooling of evangelical fervour and an increasing trend within the British community (both at home and abroad) away from purely religious ministration towards a more secular aid-based philanthropy meant that the influence of missionaries in India towards the end of the century had waned. It is also likely that the very obvious lack of religious success (if measured by widespread conversion) and the rise of Indian nationalist movements ensured that Christian evangelisation seemed less important to both British mission supporters and potential Indian converts.

Evangelical belief in women's innate spirituality was sorely tested by the missionaries' inability to convert Indian women. Missionary attitudes changed from seeing Indian women as 'pure heathens',[35] victims of an Indian patriarchy, towards perceiving them, by the latter half of the nineteenth century, as recalcitrant harbourers of resistance to colonial rule and Christian conversion. Early European images of repressed Indian women continued to influence texts produced later in the century, through the circulation of stereotypical 'victim' representations. However, as the century progressed and the numbers of converts did not, missionaries and other social commentators began to question Indian women's complicity in their own oppression and attributed to them the ongoing strength of Hinduism in the face of Christian evangelising, particularly within families.

It is ironic that virtues ascribed by evangelicals to women in general – such as their 'natural' piety – were variously celebrated or condemned according to different cultural and colonial contexts. As noted in part one, British women's piety was revered and encouraged; by contrast Indian women's religiosity (because it was associated with Hinduism) was represented as treacherous and superstitious. The *zenana* was such a contradictory site of missionary attention because in many ways it replicated (with a cultural difference) the ideals of Christian gender and domesticity, and the missionaries recognised this. By this I do not mean that evangelical Protestants wanted to see the establishment of women-only compounds within British homes, but rather that key points of the fundamental principles supporting *zenanas* as domestic and cultural institutions coincided with evangelical ideology. For instance, the evangelical ideal of separate gendered spheres – the public world of commerce for men, the private, domestic, child-focussed sphere for women – was manifested in female apartments. Levels of modesty ensuring sexual exclusivity within marriage, guaranteed by restricting Indian women's movements outside the home, were mirrored by the evangelical emphasis on female modesty and the impropriety of sexual display. The notion of a household run by women, but under the ultimate authority of a patriarchal figure, too, was common to evangelical Britons and Indians. Missionary texts about *zenanas* disavow these similarities, but such parallels continually shadow these texts and account for an extraordinary level of intellectual inconsistency within them. Chapter 4 will expand further on the representation of *zenanas* and Indian women.

MISSIONARIES AND THE COLONIAL ADMINISTRATION

... by the merchant, the soldier, and the statesman, the Christian missionary was alike denounced and resisted[36]

The relationship between missionaries and the colonial state was one fraught with complications, ambiguity, and extreme provisionality. In different mission fields of the British Empire this relationship was variously mutually supportive, mutually antagonistic, or ambivalent – in short, it was highly contingent on local circumstances. It is necessary, however, to explain some aspects of the relationship between British missionaries and the colonial administration during the period under examination, in order to give some context for understanding the nature of evangelical work in India.

When Queen Victoria issued her proclamation assuming control of India from the East India Company in 1858, the company relinquished its administration to the British Crown. Prior to this period, relations between missionaries and the state had been fairly tenuous, although they had improved during the nineteenth century. In statements made in May 1793 the company had declared that 'the conversion of 50 000 or 100 000 natives of any degree of character would be the most serious disaster that could happen, and they thanked God it was impracticable'.[37] The LMS was perfectly capable of responding in kind: Lovett's 1899 history of the society still referred to the 'complacent paganism' of the company's rule.[38] Ramsey Muir's documentary history of the colony up to 1858 suggests that during the governance of Lord Minto and the Marquess of Hastings (the period from 1807 to 1823),[39] 'the chief worry of these years was the propagandist fervour of English missionaries, whose activity was due to the Evangelical Revival at that time stirring England. It sometimes took rather offensive forms which were sternly discouraged.'[40]

Indeed, the company had presented its policy in regard to Christian missions to the governor of Fort St George in 1807 thus:

it has been our known and declared principle to maintain a perfect toleration of the various religious systems which prevailed in them ... When we afforded our countenance and sanction to missionaries ... it was far from being in our contemplation to add the influence of our authority to any attempts they might make; for on the contrary we were perfectly aware that the progress of such conversion will be slow and gradual. (251)

Minto also advised company directors on a crucial point which missionaries either ignored or did not consider worthy of concern – that interference in the caste system would have the effect of destroying India's 'whole scheme of civil polity as well as their fondest and most rooted religious tenets'. Significantly, the company objected to the *textual* manifestations of missionary evangelising as much as their activities. Minto specifically condemned

the principal publications which have issued from the Serampore press, in the native languages, the sole effect of which was not to convert, but to alienate, the professors of both religions prevalent amongst the natives of this country. Pray read especially the miserable stuff addressed to the Hindus, in which ... without proof or argument of any kind, the pages are filled with hell fire, denounced against a whole race of men for believing in the religion which they were taught by their fathers and mothers. (251–2)

As will become evident in the next chapter, missionary textuality in India was indeed prolific and intended primarily to convince Indians and Britons of the urgency of Christian conversion.

In 1813 the company's charter was renewed, ushering in an era of change and making important shifts in relation to education and religion.[41] It was only then that missionaries were allowed to enter India without first obtaining a licence from the company,[42] although the 'good behaviour bond' of £500 – 'as a guarantee that nothing should be done to weaken British authority there'[43] – seems to have remained for a while. From the 1820s onwards, attitudes in Britain towards Indian subjects of empire began to change, stimulated by the Liberal movement in Europe. The 1833 Charter

threw open the whole continent of India as a place of residence for all subjects of His Majesty; it pronounced the doom of slavery; it ordained that no native of British territories in the East should, 'by reason only of his religion, place of birth, descent, or colour, be disabled from holding any place, office or employment'.[44]

This resulted in an increased imperial sense of obligation and responsibility for India, over earlier purely commercial interests. As Patrick Brantlinger notes, by the 1830s 'the idea had become paramount that Britain had acquired a special trust or obligation for civilizing India. The decade of reform at home – the 1830s – was also a decade of reform in India. And the chief reformers at home – the utilitarians and evangelicals – were also the chief reformers in India.'[45]

During this period, issues including the education of Indian girls and women, the suppression of *sati*, and the remarriage of Indian widows gained public prominence in both Britain and in India, fuelled by the reports of missionaries. As Kenneth Ballhatchet notes, missionaries used their allies in Britain to

bring pressure upon the Secretary of State: Liberal Governments, mindful of Nonconformist votes, were particularly sensitive to such matters. In general, however, the presence of missionaries of the ruling race encouraged the British to see themselves as more moral than the Indians and to think that the preservation of social distance was morally justifiable.[46]

Hence the work of missionaries was regarded with increased tolerance by the colonial state, particularly as missionaries were willing to assume responsibility for services which in other circumstances the state may have been expected to provide (such as education, health, and social welfare).

Legislation concerning the moral welfare of Indians began to be introduced from the 1830s onwards, beginning with Governor-General Lord William Cavendish-Bentinck's 1829 minute suppressing *sati*. Rajeswari Sunder Rajan argues that this first major piece of legislation by the company, 'like the series of laws that were subsequently enacted on behalf of women – served the moral pretext for intervention and the major justification for colonial rule itself'.[47] This kind of legislative action was, of course, firmly endorsed by missionaries working in India and their societies and supporters in England because to some extent such legislation justified their agitation on behalf of the 'degraded Indians' against the more materially minded early directors of the company. It tied missionary intervention closely to imperial achievements. Additionally, as I suggested in part one, such humanitarian projects helped to transform Britain's imperial history into a moral (and religious) allegory. As Storrow wrote, 'it is for the glory of God, the good of India, and the honour of England that this atrocity [*sati*] has come to an end...if England had done nothing more for India than suppressed suttee and greatly diminished infanticide, she could well claim the admiration and gratitude of the civilized world'.[48] Storrow's correlation of morality, gender, and empire reveals the influence that missionary representation sought to bear on imperial perception and policy.

For the missionaries it was highly gratifying when in 1858 Queen Victoria annexed India. Her *Proclamation* declares that

Firmly relying ourselves on the truth of Christianity, and acknowledging with gratitude the solace of religion, we disclaim alike the right and desire to impose our convictions on any of our subjects. We declare it to be our royal will and pleasure that none be in anywise favoured, none molested or disquieted, by reason of their religious faith or observances, but that all shall alike enjoy the equal and impartial protection of the law.[49]

This statement of religious intent, reportedly added personally by the Queen herself to the original draft,[50] was greeted with much enthusiasm by missionaries in India. As Haggis explains, they believed that 'here was additional support and vindication... for their arguments against the anti-missionary policies of the Company' (166–7). This supposedly new statement of intention (a fine piece of ambiguous writing that replicated at least the spirit of current company policy) was read by many missionaries as marking a new phase in their work in India and in relationships between the colonial state and the missionaries *in situ*. Coming at a time when the LMS had cemented their long-term commitment to their Indian missions, the proclamation seemed to reassure them that their work was a valued aspect of the British Empire.

If evangelicals in India were regarded with some ambivalence by both the colonial administration and the imperial centre, missionary attitudes towards various manifestations of the colonial state up to the 1860s were similarly complex and fluid. LMS missionaries were strongly advised by their society not to follow their own inclinations in their dealings with the administration but rather to follow the society's policy. In theory, the LMS provided them with strict guidelines for relations with the colonial government. The 'Admonitory Hints by the Directors of the London Missionary Society to its Missionaries in the East Indies' state that

for Missionaries to engage in political affairs or discussions would be to retard or endanger the success of their great object; and also be an intrusion into matters out of their proper sphere, and be incompatible with their sacred designation ... [Missionaries must be sure] of *manifesting in their own conduct, and promoting also in others, a sincere and affectionate respect to the Government and to the subordinate authorities which it appoints.*[51]

The LMS was intent upon their representatives obeying their strictures, so much so that 'any violation of it on their part, would be regarded as a ground of immediate dissolution of their connexion with the Society' (164–5). These policies, however, were being formulated by the society at a considerable distance from the nitty-gritty of Anglo-Indian relations, with the directors being both geographically and philosophically close to powerful institutions and personages of British imperial policy. Such official advice was often difficult for evangelists in the field to make any sense of locally. In addition, the early history of conflict between the colonial government and missionaries inevitably tainted later relations between the two, especially amongst a community where the experiences of older missionaries were part of many evangelical family histories. Thus at times missionaries lobbied strongly against the colonial administration. At the same time, however, they relied heavily on the government for support and protection, resulting in a curious double-vision about the relationship. As Guha describes it, ultimately the missionaries were 'symbiotically related to the Raj'.[52]

Missionary writers, no doubt encouraged by commentators in Britain, began to promulgate an intriguing discourse about British imperialism in India, simultaneously binding missions, empire, and the colonial state together, providing each with a justificatory discourse. This narrative proliferated in many different missionary texts and is perhaps best exemplified by the following example from Reverend John Wilson's *The Evangelization of India* (1844). Wilson represents the British colonisation of India as very passive – India's wealth had attracted many 'covetous' nations. However,

the English, alone, be it observed, at the commencement of their enterprize, disclaimed, and that sincerely, all idea of conquest. They were generally content, as a nation, with the commercial factories of chartered associations, and the gains which resulted from them. It was to protect these factories, and to avenge insults which had been perpetrated against them, that they first took up arms... [But the gradual 'evolution' of British rule in India] is a success, so unexpected, and brought about by so great a concurrence of events, and interpositions, that even the most indevout when reflecting upon it, must ascribe it to God himself. (195–8)

The discursive construction of British imperial annexation of India as 'an ordination of Providence, designed and adapted to become an inestimable blessing to the natives, by its becoming the means of the gradual introduction of Christianity',[53] recurs not only in missionary histories and discourses but also within histories of the period written by colonial elites involved in Indian administration. The rewriting of aggressive commerce and colonialism as a benign act of God effectively ties the two oppositional social groups together and provided a revisionist history of the British Empire in India which exonerated all. Wilson's reformist history explicitly yokes together the interests of acquisitive, aggressive colonialism and evangelical salvation. As Brantlinger argues, these revisionist histories and moral allegories contributed to a wider imperial discourse and culminated in comments such as Sir John Seeley's infamous statement in *The Expansion of England*: 'we seem... to have conquered and peopled half the world in a fit of absence of mind'.[54]

Crucially, however, both missionary societies and the colonial government were keen not to *appear* collusive to the Indian populace. Both believed that too much public alliance between the two institutions would thwart the aims of each. Mrs Mullen's novel *Faith and Victory*, which will be examined in detail in chapter 4, notes that 'notwithstanding all we may say to the contrary, there certainly is a floating idea among the people... *that Christianity progresses in India because it is the religion of the conquerors of the country and I think we ought to avoid any act which might tend to foster in the remotest degree an idea so inimical to vital Christianity*'.[55] So, whilst the LMS was adamant that it was 'of the utmost importance that [the Indians'] attachment to the English Government and nation should be promoted', they warned missionaries to do so in a manner which would not 'wound their feelings – produce a repulsive impression, or lead them to suspect, that it is the design of the English nation in the end to abolish their religion by force'.[56] The East India Company similarly warned that

if once they [Hindus] suspect that it is the intention of the British Government to abandon this hitherto inviolate principle of allowing the most complete toleration in matters of religion that there will arise in the minds of all so deep a distrust of our ulterior designs that they will no longer be tractable to any arrangement intended for their improvement.[57]

Later, however, the LMS was not reluctant to condemn the early British administration in India over the difficulties they had experienced in gaining access to 'heathens' in the early nineteenth century. The LMS 'Missionary Magazine and Chronicle for 1861' frankly stated that such obstructions

arose, not exclusively, nor even chiefly, from the opposition of the heathen themselves, but rather from the selfish and anti-Christian policy of their so-called Christian rulers. At that time, to the dishonour and shame of England, wherever her power prevailed in heathen lands, it was employed, legally and systematically, to exclude the Christian Missionary from the benighted multitudes who were subject to our sway.[58]

It is from such positions of ambiguity, and from within a language of ambivalence and multiple intentions, that the texts of missionary writers emerged. The next chapter analyses the work of representation and textuality in detail, through a focus on missionary representations of *zenanas*.

CHAPTER FOUR

Missionary writing in India

...the LITERARY LABOURS of missionaries in India[1]

In 1852, Reverend Joseph Mullens, a key LMS missionary in Calcutta who would later become the foreign secretary of the society, lauded the 'missionary literature' pouring out of India in the first half of the nineteenth century. Missionaries in India, he boasted, 'have done much towards drawing the attention of the Christian world to the claims of Hindustan upon their sympathies and prayers' (40). Such literature joined publications by other British personnel in India – the travel narratives, journals, letters, and histories written by East India Company officials and their dependents – but Mullens argues that

to missionaries we are indebted for full accounts of the religious systems professed by the people; of their religious rites, their religious errors, and their social condition; of the character of their priesthood, their caste system, their debasing idolatry, the ignorance and vice which every where prevail, and the great difficulties in the way of the peoples' conversion. (41)

Not only were these authors significant in Anglo-Indian literature, but they were exemplary in *missionary* literature: 'While but three or four such works describe the religious condition of China, or of the South Sea Islands, or South Africa, or the West Indies, we can name at least thirty works written about India by missionaries, or containing the lives of missionaries who have died in the country' (41).

Without doubt, textual representations of missionary work in India influenced both British imperial policy and missionary society practice. As Jane Haggis notes, 'the missionary account of India and its women was, if not the main, then undoubtedly a primary contributor to the public perceptions of India as an appropriate subject of British imperial rule'.[2] The colonial archive of the LMS in India provides an exemplary case of how evangelical texts were used to promote missionary activity to colonial and imperial audiences.

India was a highly productive field of missionary textual production for a variety of reasons. Firstly, early missionaries in India needed to feel that they had the support of the British public, given the sometimes precarious state of their relationship with the colonial administration. Vocal support from interested supporters 'back Home' provided them with protection against potential interference either from Indian or imperial governments. Secondly, the concentration of Protestant missionary activity in India in the early years of the nineteenth century coincided with a degree of intense religious interest in ministering to 'the heathen' among church and community groups within England, and these groups were eager for eye-witness accounts of colonial encounters. India proved to be a culture of such fascinating, although often abhorrent, difference from British experience that what could be defined as early 'ethnographic' narratives – accounts of customs and manners – were readily produced by missionary observers and widely circulated and sold to the British reading public. The conjunction of the missionary exposé of Indian women's 'oppression' with the growing British debate about women's place in the world also provided an impetus to produce texts on these subjects. As Patrick Brantlinger describes it, 'in one fashion or another most British writing about India between the 1830s and 1858 expresses utilitarian or evangelical concerns'.[3]

Thirdly, missionaries in India produced so many texts because they established printing presses at a relatively early stage and found these presses much easier to operate and maintain than LMS missionaries in Polynesia did, for instance. Of course, missionary texts were published both in India and back in Britain. However, the standard of printing and publishing done by the Methodist Press at Mysore, for example, was so high 'that for many years the Oxford University Press cut its costs by having many books printed in India'.[4] In addition, the superintendent of the printing press at Calcutta, Reverend Gogerly, was 'largely and liberally aided by the Religious Tract Society'.[5] The combination of these fortuitous conditions meant that the quantity of texts emanating from missionaries in India was extraordinary.

These texts were as diverse in their form as they were numerous. The LMS encouraged missionaries to produce diaries, annual reports, and formal correspondence. Missionaries also carried on an extensive private correspondence with family, friends, church congregations, and supporters back in Britain. As Valentine Cunningham notes in relation to his work on Micaiah and Mary Hill (Hill was a LMS missionary sent to India in 1822 with his wife), those who did not send back enough *publishable* news were castigated by their Society.[6] Publishable items could include autobiographies; biographies of individual missionaries, missionary wives, or Indian converts; local, regional, and colonial histories; and non-fictional (although often fanciful) accounts of Indian life and customs, education, women's place in society, to name only the most popular genres. Books about the plight of Indian women were common, though the missionaries' belated realisation of the central importance of *zenana* visitation meant that texts focussing solely on *zenanas* only emerged towards the end of the period up to 1860.

To a large extent, this proliferation of textual material concealed the fact that such texts relied on the endless re-circulation of tropes in a discourse condemning Indian customs and practices and in doing so often consulted only the accounts of other European witnesses and writers. Naturally this discourse was not completely monolithic; there were missionary accounts which, almost in spite of themselves, provided contradictory, ambiguous information about missionary work in India (see, for example, my discussion of William Buyers' writing later in this chapter). Initially, however, I want to identify the repetition of tropes within missionary textuality, with particular reference to the representation of native gender and sexuality in India, although I must preface this discussion with a cautionary note about the nature of the texts under examination here.

As discussed in chapter 1, missionary texts were subject to a series of editing processes. The confrontational nature of early missionary experiences in India seemed to require special attention in order to present an optimistic image of achievements. Additionally, given that this was only the second overseas incursion by the LMS, the society was still establishing the forms in which missionary discourses could and should be formulated and reproduced. Cunningham notes that there is little evidence of personal suffering in public versions of missionary experience: the 'British Christian public was clearly felt by the LMS's London administrators to need stories of spiritual triumph – distinct conversions of the heathen, pagan temples cast down, idol worship vanquished, positive missionary action and positive missionary thinking' (87). The usual breezy optimism expressed by the society's missionaries in public accounts is sometimes undermined by a sub-text of alternative and challenging narratives. In such a sea of Christian positivism, comments such as those emerging from the 'Third Report of the Mahí Kántha (Late Baroda) Mission' are startling and deeply disruptive: 'We are made to feel that we are in an enemy's country, and although our hand is against no man, we fear that, from these people, who are professional thieves, and fear not the shedding of blood, there are many whose hands is [*sic*] against us.'[7] Such admissions are, however, relatively rare in the LMS archive.

A different kind of textual mediation appears evident in the continual recirculation of narrative structures, phrases, patterns, and source material. It becomes obvious that there is a discernible Indian genre of missionary writing. Texts about Indian women usually provide an historical overview, a contemporary 'picture', and a plan of action for the future. As noted previously, substantial book-length treatments of *zenanas* did not emerge often before the 1860s, though shorter representations appeared consistently in LMS 'Reports' and in the private correspondence of missionary men, their wives, and daughters. From then onwards, however, *zenana* literature became extremely popular and widely published.

As Antoinette Burton explains, 'images of an enslaved Oriental womanhood were the common possessions of Victorian social reformers and exercised much of the rhetorical force behind humanitarian narratives of the Victorian period'.[8] These images were initially circulated by the missionary press and then, later, by the Victorian feminist press, which

effectively broadcast the cause of Indian women to the feminist reading public throughout the nineteenth and early twentieth centuries, showcasing the imperial activities of British women and, most significant, the ways in which they were devoting themselves 'to the glorious and blessed work of raising their Eastern sisters to fill that place in society for which the Creator has destined them'. (9)

My concentration on the period up to 1860, however, shifts the critical focus to an earlier period than that which has been (excellently) analysed by scholars such as Burton. My interest here is in a proto-discourse, the first germs of what would become something of an imperial media sensation. Crucially, *zenana* literature in this earlier form is almost entirely about 'white men...saving brown women from brown men', in Gayatri Spivak's terms.[9] Whilst *zenana* visitation (and associated work with or for Indian women) has rightly been explored as a crucial factor in the development of British feminist participation in empire *and* nascent feminist subjectivities, attention to the missionary progenitors of late-Victorian culture reveals the genealogy of this phenomenon, and its construction within evangelical discourses of gender and race. *Zenanas*, then, were a 'problem' for the male-dominated missionary movement, because they proved to be resistant to both masculine evangelical 'rescue' and imperial surveillance. To be obliged to concede the 'penetrat[ion of] the walls of the Hindu Zenana'[10] to women, and especially to feminist women, was really a profound measure of (male) missionary failure, a failure illuminating the intense challenge to missionary ideology posed by Indian women and the *zenanas*.

If missionaries lost the activist battle to feminist Britons, they tried very hard to win the textual battle. A great number of non-fictional texts were produced about British missionary experience with Indian women. These were pedagogical in intent, designed to inform the imperial public about the work of missionaries and the history and culture of their Indian subjects. Such works became formulaic: written by men or women who had substantial (and presumably diverse) experience in the mission field, nevertheless they followed a predictable discursive form. As Kate Teltscher notes of seventeenth- and eighteenth-century European accounts of India, these closely related texts 'constantly refer to, reproduce, counter and build on one another'.[11] These repetitive narratives of British ethnographic 'knowledge' about Indian culture and gender relations emanate from the complex negotiations of evangelical Christianity and acquisitive colonialism which mark missionary work in India. Missionary writers tended to focus on Hindu homes and practices, their limited commentary on Muslim practices tending to be derogatory and dismissive. The geographical and textual concentration on LMS work in Bengal also contributed to their particular focus on Hindu families. As Mrs Weitbrecht's *Women of India* noted, 'the valley of the Ganges is the stronghold of Hinduism, and it is there that the seclusion of the higher born females is complete. The system obtains more or less all over India, but in a modified way in the southern and western provinces.'[12]

A standard narrative pattern recurs throughout such texts and indeed different volumes are often almost interchangeable. In summary, these studies construct a historical narrative tracing the 'plight' of Indian women from ancient times to the nineteenth century: a narrative critically focussed on negative aspects of Indian women's lives. Writers frequently invoke an idealised time of equality and openness in the Vedic Age, thus establishing a kind of native precedent for Christian attempts to ameliorate the condition of Indian women. Reverend Edward Storrow writes: 'Contrasting the present with the past, it is clear that formerly women were then more respected and trusted... In those ancient records there is no evidence of the systematic and all-prevailing degradation to which the whole sex has been doomed for some centuries.'[13] Discursively and ideologically, this meant that missionary reform could be seen to be restoring an ideal Indian 'state of nature' – paradoxically by introducing a whole series of European domestic institutions and ideologies.

The 'Laws of Manu' are typically represented as having marked a profound change in Indian culture and to be responsible for the degradation of Indian women's rights and quality of life. Writers would quote extensively from Indian writings, highlighting their repressive, and, for them, reprehensible, aspects. Given that the ideological function of these works was fundamentally one re-configuring Hindu women within the discursive framework of evangelical Christianity, the representation of women in Indian texts was seen as evidence of their cultural oppression and degradation. Such a concentration on textuality and the belief in the potential of representation to effect real cultural change is characteristic of LMS philosophy.

My analysis now shifts from general representations of Indian women and *zenanas* to two specific books that are closely connected. These books, and the relationships between them and between their authors, provide a material example of those intimate links between missionaries and missionary texts that I have previously described. Edward Storrow's *The Eastern Lily Gathered: A Memoir of Bala Shoondoree Tagore* (1856) is the first text under examination. Storrow was sent to the LMS Calcutta mission in 1848, where he lived with Reverend Dr Joseph Mullens and his wife Hannah. Storrow venerated Dr Mullens as 'an ardent missionary, a zealous worker, and possessed of a rare amount of missionary information'.[14] Storrow declared that his interest in the condition of Hindu women commenced with this association with the Mullens, and led to his publication of a number of works on the topic. *The Eastern Lily Gathered* demonstrates his fascination with female conversion whilst working in India, and it is this text which forms the basis of the following discussion. Later, he published *Our Indian Sisters* (1898), a comprehensive study of the 'plight' of Indian women, and a clear example of how (male) missionaries sought to dominate the textual field of the *zenana* well after they had had to relinquish the field work to women. *Our Indian Sisters* is published outside the temporal limits of this study, and so I make only minor reference to it, though Storrow's service for the LMS from 1848 to 1866 clearly provides the basis for his book and his perspectives are rooted in the experiences and opinions of this period.

The second book under examination is Mrs Hannah Catherine Mullens' *Faith and Victory: A Story of the Progress of Christianity in Bengal.* Mrs Mullens came from a family deeply enmeshed in LMS culture – her father was Alphonse François Lacroix, a Swiss-born missionary originally sent to India by the Netherlands Missionary Society, who served with the LMS in Calcutta after the 1827 withdrawal of the NMS from India. Hannah Lacroix (1826–61) was born in Calcutta and grew up surrounded by both missionary activity and Bengali culture. She was apparently fluent in Bengali and, at the age of nineteen, married Joseph Mullens, a LMS missionary sent to India in 1843, whose argument about the significance of missionary 'literary labours' began this chapter. The Mullens were both hardworking stalwarts of the LMS. Hannah Mullens was crucially involved in the establishment and development of native female schools. She died aged thirty-five, by which time she had published several books including *Phulmani and Karuna: A Book for Native Christian Women* (apparently translated into twelve Indian languages); *The Missionary on the Ganges* (published both in English and in Bengali); and *Missionary Pictures; Or, Word-Painting of Scenes in India, for the Young*. She also wrote related magazine items. Because of her considerable achievements, the evangelical community in India and Britain regarded Hannah Mullens as an exemplary missionary wife. Her early demise only contributed to her saintly reputation. Mrs Weitbrecht's *Women of India* characterised her as possessing 'vigour of thought and imagination, deep religious feeling, and lofty, high-toned consecration'.[15] The Mullens and Lacroix families were pillars of the missionary community and their legacy pervaded nineteenth-century LMS history in India.

THE EASTERN LILY GATHERED

… the jungly marigold[16]

Storrow's *The Eastern Lily Gathered* serves as testimony to the potential for Indian women to convert to Christianity. Admittedly, the book tells of just one convert and promises no immediate flood of like women, but as a form of minor hagiography it was evidently positioned to work as an exemplum and an inspiration. Ostensibly the biography of Bala Shoondoree Tagore, the book is so full of introductory, explanatory, and authorising addenda that the memoir of Bala Tagore takes up only about forty pages of the 112-page publication. Instead, the bulk of the book is buttressed by the writing of male LMS missionaries, from Reverend James Kennedy's detailed 'Preface' to Storrow's lengthy contextualising chapters. Storrow's first chapter, 'On the Position and Prospects of Hindu Female Society', gives a general introduction to the 'plight' of Indian women. Subsequent to his brief memoir of Bala Tagore, his chapter 'Remarks suggested by the Preceding Memoir' positions the readers and attempts to regulate their response. The brevity of the biography suggests an absence at the heart of this publication, an absence due to the very brief period of Bala Tagore's Christian awakening (from 'glimpses' at the age of twelve when she went to live with her husband, to her death before nineteen years of age) and the lack of her voice in the text. Apparently, her story is told to Storrow by her grieving husband, Gyanendra Mohum Tagore, baptised a few weeks after his 'highly gifted' wife's death. The textual figure of Bala Tagore is so interpellated that it is impossible to feel any sense of the actual woman or her beliefs.

The missionary authors, however, have very clear voices. Their writings ring with the confidence of evangelical authority: an authority born less of experience (given the near impossibility of male missionaries gaining access to *zenana* women) than of the repetitive discursive stereotypes of missionary texts. In these prefaces and afterwords, Kennedy and Storrow rehearse the trite narratives of early LMS writing about Indian women and their place in the *zenana*. As such, this text will be used as a template for such recursive discursive manoeuvres, and its connections with other similar texts will be traced.

The litany of woes understood to have beset Indian women in traditional society were rehearsed endlessly in LMS missionary tracts. An outline of child marriage, infanticide (particularly female), *sati*, and widowhood was usual, and the repetition of these markers of cultural difference (read as depravity by missionaries) became formulaic. Storrow's first chapter maps all these positions, beginning with a statement that 'Mahomedan females are in a more degraded, humiliating position, than even their Hindu sisters are. The gross sensualism which is ever allied to their creed, polygamy, and the indifference with which the marriage tie is regarded, are the cause of this' (2). He catalogues the inferior status of female children – 'The birth of a son is always hailed with delight; that of a daughter, with disappointment, and often with sorrow' (3) – and then laments the lack of female education: 'The book of knowledge is as effectually closed upon her as the light of day is from the born-blind' (8). Storrow also condemns women's menial status within households, where 'the females of a Bengali's household are destined to perform all the offices which in a civilized society would devolve on menial servants' (8). He argues for the inhumanity of arranged marriages – 'Nothing, indeed, can be conceived more businesslike than the whole transaction' (10) – and against the harsh treatment of widows. Whilst Storrow is thankful that 'a loud and general voice of denunciation [was] lifted up by glorious England when it was known that hundreds of widows were annually sacrificed on the funeral pile of their deceased husbands... we question if that death, horrible as it appears, was not far preferable to the living death ... to which widows are now exposed' (15–16). Now, he argues, 'she is reduced to a yet more deplorable state... [where] almost everything in her domestic and social relations is of a nature to aggravate her sense of lonely desolation' (14), and it 'is not, therefore, to be wondered at that she becomes an easy prey to the tempter, and conceals her dishonour by the crimes of abortion and infanticide' (16). He lists the horrors of polygamy

(27), and the weakness of Indian women's character: 'they are generally fond of ornaments and finery, indolent, gossiping, capricious, and frail... but that these vices are the pernicious fruit of that social and religious system under which they live, we believe to be equally undeniable' (28).

All of these images are mobilised to represent the utter degradation of women's lives and the consequent degradation of Indian culture as a whole. Storrow's argument goes to the core of missionary philosophy about women's issues – that the treatment of women was a crucial marker of civilisation and advancement, and that until the Indian community reformed its treatment of women it could become neither a Christian community nor a modern nation. This linking of gender, modernity, and nationalism was not exclusive to missionaries, as Indian nationalist reformers were also interested in reforming gender relations.[17]

The formulaic exposition of women's woes generally concluded with a pitch for increased support of missions to the women of India. In the first half of the century this meant more financial support but, by the latter half of the century, writers targeted the employment of female *zenana* missionaries. Indeed, Storrow states that the purpose of his introductory chapter is to 'render the following narrative more intelligible, and excite a deeper interest, especially in the hearts of the favoured Christian ladies of Britain, in behalf of the women of Hindostan' (1). Only the intervention of British missionaries could guarantee real change in Indian culture, a change believed to be crucial to both Indian 'civilisation' and modernity. The locus of this change was domestic space, an area subject to particular attention by missionary writers, even though male authors could not literally scrutinise *zenanas* themselves.

It is Bala Tagore's upbringing in a *zenana* that Kennedy and Storrow mark as the crucial obstacle to her conversion. 'Brought up in the seclusion of a zenana, and among the abominations of idolatry', Kennedy notes her eager investigation of Christianity with surprise, because

the dwellers of the zenana [are] shut out from general intercourse, the sure victims of ennui, seldom privileged to see the fair face of nature, with uncultivated minds – if able to read at all, having in their possession only absurd and wicked legends – with untrained hands, unaccustomed even to the exercise and amusement of embroidery and similar gentle occupations.[18]

Here, Kennedy draws upon one of the dominant tropes of *zenana* representation: the prison. Storrow explicitly notes the 'prisonlike seclusion' of the *zenana* (6), detailing the 'high walls and grated windows [which]... do not admit of egress to the public streets' (5). The *zenana* woman 'lives in seclusion, and is narrowly watched, because she is regarded as incapable of self-control' (23). The *zenana* was an apparently influential site of Indian culture frustratingly beyond the grasp of earlier missionaries, one which fundamentally refused entrance to the male missionary profession. Miss Isabel Hart's later emotive description clearly expressed her frustration about the inaccessibility of these women, writing that they 'sit in darkness and silence and chains. No man's presence may peer into that darkness – no man's voice break that silence – no man's hands loose those chains.'[19] The opacity of the *zenana* convinced early missionaries that Indian women were prisoners in their own homes. Early missionary representations of Indian husbands enforcing the prison-like seclusion of women laid the blame squarely on a perceived masculinist Indian culture. John Wilson described how

among the higher classes of the natives, the wife is usually so secluded and confined, that she may be said to be a prisoner; and among the lower, among whom she has more liberty, she is so often overwrought, while the husband is spending his time in comparative idleness, that she may be said to be a slave, if not a beast of burden.[20]

Representations of Hindu households were typically programmatic and repetitive. The overwhelming motif was one of darkness and filth. These metaphors pervade representations of the *zenana* throughout British missionary texts and mimic the more general use of Manichean images of Christian 'light' and heathen 'darkness'. Intrinsically tied to Enlightenment philosophies of white, light virtue and dark, deceptive sin and depravity, these images provide the discursive and philosophic apparatus for missionaries to make sense of their Indian experiences. Mrs Mary Weitbrecht explains that, whilst the name may have changed in different parts of India,

everywhere it means the same thing, namely, that women are not to be trusted, but must be shut up as birds in a cage – must be hidden from the sight of all but their own husbands... Yet it is only lately that we have begun to realise, even in the faintest degree, the thickness of the gloom in which these poor women have been for so many long centuries simmered.[21]

Weitbrecht's description highlights the physical, literal gloom of *zenana* apartments as spiritually and psychologically indicative of the religious and cultural squalor of Indian women's lives. Storrow describes how 'the brightest things are soonest tarnished' in the literal and moral murkiness of the *zenana* (29). As Margaret Wilson, the wife of Reverend John Wilson, described it, 'India is dark, dark, but speedily will be light; God will most assuredly fulfil his promises, and give the heathen to His Son for an inheritance, and the uttermost parts of the earth for a possession.'[22] Education, exhorts Storrow, 'is of necessity the great instrument by which the zenana and the harem must be opened, that the light of the Gospel may enter in' (31).

Descriptions of Indian women's physical appearance similarly revolved around binary oppositions of darkness and light – Christian converts were inevitably described as being of fair complexion, whilst 'heathen' (and lower-class) women were represented as being of dark, deceitful colouring. Storrow's description of Bala Tagore is a good example:

In person she was extremely beautiful and dignified. She was slightly beyond the middle size, and thinly but elegantly formed. Her features were beautifully symmetrical, and finely chiseled; her eyes were large, black, and expressive of both modesty and intelligence; her complexion was of a light olive colour, and, like that of the higher classes generally, remarkably fair and pure. (75)

It is evident that this Christian convert conformed to evangelical European notions of beauty and femininity. As Inderpal Grewal argues, an aesthetics of transparency exemplifying beauty characterised much nineteenth-century thought. Representations of women, particularly indigenous women, emphasised the supposed opacity of female nature, unless rendered transparent by the light of Christian purity.[23]

Such transparency stood in opposition to the threatening opacity of the Gothic, or of the colonies, particularly signified by 'the East'. The imperial antidote to opacity was embodied in Bentham's panopticon, the 'instrument that would enable society to become transparent'.[24] In terms of architectural structures, as Grewal suggests, the panopticon stood in contrast to the dungeon-like gloom of the *zenana* or harem, and it reversed precolonial technologies of power based on the principle of visibility (26). Haggis notes that 'an urgent conquest of the forces of "darkness" by the "light" of Christian faith and civility gives a pungent immediacy to the descriptions'.[25] For Storrow, Bala Tagore's conversion is symbolically important: the 'least accessible of all who compose that mysterious compound – Hindu society – has been reached' (85). Here, the 'mysterious compound' of the *zenana* works explicitly as a metonym for Indian culture as a whole.

At the same time, some missionary writers also represented the *zenana* as far too *public* a sphere, in terms of its communal living arrangements, which prevented what the evangelicals believed to be the cohesion and privilege associated with the nuclear family. Hannah Mullens' novel *Faith and Victory*, for example, notes that Indian domestic arrangements, because of 'the number of people living together in a Hindu house, sometimes as many as thirty or forty, seemed to preclude life from being made a serious and earnest thing; so much of it was necessarily spent in idle talk or gossip; something in the fashion of life in a great passenger-ship during a long sea-voyage'.[26] Both heterosexual conjugality and the capacity for spiritual reflection were seen to be compromised by Indian domestic arrangements.

A sense that class compounds missionary outrage at the treatment of Indian women pervades these texts. Missionaries imply that the neglect of women's rights by lower-class Indians was understandable – after all, evangelical Christians had continuing experience of it in Britain whilst ministering to working-class communities.[27] However, the fact that middle-class and elite Indians participated in what missionaries regarded as 'degraded' practices seemed particularly shocking. Perhaps this was partially due to the mixed-class backgrounds of missionaries themselves – given that many came from lower-middle-class or working-class backgrounds they may have assumed that wealth and privilege carried with it more 'civilised' practices, at least in western eyes. Storrow admits his difficulty in gaining access to Indian women of rank, noting that it was only in rare cases that he had met any such women, 'and in these cases they are not fair examples of their countrywomen, since many of their habits and sentiments are the result of association with Europeans' (1–2). Bala Tagore's conversion is particularly significant, he argues, as 'the first instance of a *lady of wealth becoming a Christian in the zenana*' (85).

Indian women, kept in the dark and denied access to public affairs, education, and society, were believed to be in dire need of rescue, a deliverance they would embrace with gratitude. Storrow describes Bala Tagore's anxiety 'to break away from the bondage of her country's creed – like the bird, hung out into the open air, which hears the free songs of its fellows, and gazes on the leaves, and trees, and flowers, amongst which it once poured forth its happy song' (72). But Dr Thomas Smith's hyperbolic review for the *Calcutta Christian Observer* in 1840 suggests that few women possessed such agency:

does not the stronghold of female ignorance seem at present impregnable? Garrisoned by veteran hosts of prejudice and sin, – ruled over with strictest discipline and defended with craftiest policy by Satan himself, it raises its moss-clad battlements to the clouds, and scowls haughty defiance on the little band that threatens to beleaguer it.[28]

As Smith's polemic suggests, the metaphorisation of the *zenana* as an impregnable fortress enabled the discursive construction of missionary incursions as heroic rescues and made way for the increasing use of tropes of colonial adventure to represent the British 'salvation' of Indian women.

The unabashed use of colonialist images recurs in a number of texts concerned with *zenana* women. Storrow draws a metaphoric connection between the 'enlightenment and emancipation of the women of Hindostan' (31) and the foundational narratives of imperial incursion:

As Columbus and his companions . . . beheld the island which indicated that there *was* a mighty continent whose discovery would more than recompense the toils and sorrows of his life, and, amid the astonished awe of the aborigines, and the transport, chastened by glorious hope, of his followers, planted on the soil the cross, and called it San Salvador, – so may we rejoice over her who is one of the first fruits of India's daughters consecrated to God. (36–7)

Storrow's unfortunate metaphorisation equates the planting of a flag on South American soil with the body of Bala Tagore, making it explicit – if it has ever been in doubt – that the successful conversion of an Indian woman was a form of conquering, entering, and possessing, and that the masculinist rhetoric of colonial exploration and possession could be just as pertinent when used to explain the relationship between (male) missionaries and (female) Indian converts. In his later book *Our Indian Sisters*, Storrow uses similar devices to describe how 'custom, prejudice, and the strange immobility of native society barred [the early missionaries'] way, as a vast wall of ice the southward progress of the antarctic voyager',[29] representing the British 'emancipation of Indian women' in a similar way: 'We are as the Stanley expedition, resolved to rescue and free the Emin Pasha of Hindu womanhood, even in spite of its own apathy and helplessness' (182). Other missionary writers used related militaristic modes of representation. Reverend Alexander Duff explained that 'all females of respectability are shut up from the light and air of heaven, – being entrenched, as it were, *in castles which cannot be assailed*'.[30] Even Hannah Mullens informed the LMS about missionary women taking education into the *zenana* and confidently declared that 'as regards female education, we have nothing to do now but *to go up and possess the land*'.[31] Such militarist and colonialist metaphors contradict missionary denials of their implication in imperial activity, but such internal inconsistencies rarely seemed to bother them.

The continued resistance of *zenanas* to conversion increasingly turned missionary sympathies against Indian women. Alternative images of Indian women crept into some accounts of *zenanas*. James Kennedy warned that 'During my residence in India, I have been often struck with the powerful influence which I have known Native Women to exert. This influence has been, unhappily, hostile to the Gospel. The female mind is in India, as elsewhere, very susceptible of religious impression.'[32] Storrow cites 'an educated Hindu' who directly placed the blame for the survival of Hinduism within the walls of the *zenana*:

It is through the influence of women that reformation in India is so effectively opposed in its progress. Young Bengal is full of European ideas when abroad, but quite a Bengali when at home. He eats mutton chop and drinks champagne when he keeps out – within the walls of the zenana, he kneels before the image of stone which is the family idol. Half the amount of education that has spread over the land would have been sufficient for mighty changes, but for the influence of women. (47–8)

William Buyers, a LMS missionary in Northern India between 1833 and 1863, sought to correct other missionary representations of passive Indian women awaiting rescue:

Instead of the meek, abject creature that a Hindoo wife is often represented to be, I have often seen one of them firmly grasping her husband's hair with her left hand, while, with her right, she belaboured him about the ears; when, for fear of the disgrace of openly striking a woman, he has forborne to return a blow.[33]

He also argues that the usual representation of female seclusion, which 'is often, if not almost universally, spoken of in Europe, as one of an entirely involuntary nature of the part of the women, or as forced upon them, exclusively, by the jealousy of men', is quite erroneous:

There is no evidence...that men put any such restraint on their lawful, and honourable wives... To veil themselves, however, and shun the public gaze, even when no actual law was imposed on them by their husbands, or others, and to avoid general converse with the other sex, were...regarded as marks of modesty, and feminine gentility. (402–3)

Buyers' account did not seem to bring a recognition that, whilst the *zenana* system was not one which nineteenth-century philosophy (or, indeed, twenty-first-century feminism) would condone, it could be understood as a social system in which Indian women had made a real place for themselves, albeit in a very limited, private manner.[34] Such descriptions fed the missionaries' growing suspicions about the collusion of Indian women in their own oppression, and in the continual resistance of Indians in general to colonial and Christian change. These misgivings creep in through the guise of the abhorred 'degradation' of Indian women – Wilson wrote:

You must be chastened in your expectations from India's sons, whenever you advert to the incapacity and deprivations of India's mothers. In the degradation there of woman alone, you can account to a great extent for the degradation of the Hindú [*sic*] community. (*The Evangelization of India*, 427–8)

It was a short discursive step from commiserating with women's oppression to 'blaming the victim', a tendency starting to influence some writers by mid to late century when *zenana* women were continuing to resist missionary blandishments.

Evangelical concentration on the figure of the Christian woman, and particularly the mother, as the source of spiritual light fuelled statements such as 'the influence of females in all countries is great for good or evil – it is the chief means by which the chains of Satan are riveted on the minds of the young'.[35] The judgmental missionary writer could thus decide that Indian mothers' influence was more evil than good. Duff railed against female infanticide, writing that

Amid the retirements of home, amid the stillness of domestic privacy, have the thousand of hecatombs of helpless innocents been cruelly sacrificed! – sacrificed! massacred! butchered! Butchered by whom? – By the midnight assassin, wielding the Indian scalping knife and the savage tomahawk? No, no. Let humanity shudder! *They are the mothers, – the unhappy mothers, – who, in the name of false honour, and false religion, have no compassion on the fruit of their own womb, – who imbrue their hands in the blood of their new-born babes!*[36]

Duff apparently conflates all 'natives' (as 'Indians') in his image of the 'scalping knife and the savage tomahawk', a point telling in itself. Dr Thomas Smith writes of their condition somewhat more sympathetically: 'Shut up from the period when reason dawns in a zanána [*sic*] whose air is often tainted, and whose moral atmosphere is always impregnated with the seeds of poison, they arrive at the years of womanhood fit for nothing else (but eminently fitted for this) than to be the irrational ministers of their masters' lusts'.[37]

When the fight for converts became particularly fraught, though, frustrated missionaries were quick to blame the resistance of converts' wives and families.[38] The 'Second Report of the Mahí Kánthá (Late Baroda) Mission' reports in 1848:

In the cases of five converts, their wives have refused to join them. There is no subordination in families. The children will rail against the parent, and the wife will shut the door against her husband. Everything in their present social and domestic circumstances, is calculated to wear down the spirits of the converts, and drive them to despair.[39]

Such obvious examples of Indian women's resistance enabled missionaries to blame them fully when evangelical progress seemed troubled, principally because of their influence over younger generations of potential converts. Storrow approvingly quotes from 'an educated Hindu' on the 'inordinate' attachment of Hindu mothers to their children,[40] and in particular to their sons (19). He writes of Hindu mothers in Bengal:

The Bengali woman is not at all aware of the responsibility of her situation, and she carelessly puts into the young mind many unworthy ideas, which can with difficulty be eradicated in its maturer years. A Bengali's religious sentiments, his belief in the existence of ghosts and evil spirits, his piques and prejudices, are all owing to the lectures heard by him in the cradle from the lips of a doting mother. (21)

Within such a discursive framework, the missionaries believed that evangelising the *zenana* was imperative, for the sake of both Indian mothers and children. 'Opening' the *zenana* and converting Indian women was an efficient means of increasing numbers of Christian converts since they could then

return to their former sphere and as Christian wives and mothers, become, it may be unwittingly to themselves, centres of light to many a dark circle, sources of purity and refinement to many a degraded family and unconscious Missionaries and preachers of that pure Gospel with which their lives and thoughts are permeated.[41]

Mary Weitbrecht's letters, published in her book *Women of India*, continually emphasise the 'squalor' of Indian homes and endlessly describe the lack of windows in *zenanas* – this latter trope is a feature of most early accounts. I would suggest that this image of the window neatly encapsulates British missionaries' problem with *zenanas* – that *zenanas*, as native cultural institutions, explicitly denied the colonial specularity both missionaries and other colonial agents required. Malek Alloula's study of French representations of Algerian women under colonial occupation provides an interesting comparison to the role of *zenanas* in missionary discourses. Alloula writes:

Colonialism is, among other things, the perfect expression of the violence of the gaze, and not only in the metaphorical sense of the term. Colonialism imposes upon the colonized society the ever presence and omnipotence of a gaze to which everything must be transparent. The exercise of power, especially when the latter is arbitrary, cannot permit the maintenance of shadowy zones; it considers them equivalent to resistance.[42]

The *zenanas* in India were precisely these 'shadowy zones' for both missionaries and the colonial state. Alloula's study focusses on the Algerian 'harem' as figured in French imagination and representation and, whilst there are important differences between the harem and the *zenana*,[43] his identification of the colonist's 'scopic desire' being thwarted by the visual technologies of native institutions is equally pertinent to the *zenana*-missionary situation. Alloula describes how the phantasm[44] of the harem worked: 'a simple allusion to it is enough to open wide the floodgate of hallucination just as it is about to run dry' (3). Alloula's approach is fundamentally a psychoanalytic one and I would prefer to recast this statement as one about the 'floodgate of representation' rather than 'hallucination', in order to provide a reading of repetitive narrative descriptions and images in the numerous missionary texts about the *zenana*. Indeed, as Haggis suggests, 'Indian women are no longer the subjects of the narrative, but the textual device around which the missionary story turns.'[45] The textual figure of the *zenana* represented an intensification of colonialist interest in race, gender, and domesticity, functioning as a crucial narrative device around which missionary arguments were assembled.

Whilst missionaries in India condemned the apparent subjugation of *zenana* women to their husbands' control, evangelical texts advocate very similar practices for Christian conjugal relations. Reverend James Sherman, for example, exhorts:

'Wives, be in subjection to your own husbands, as the church is subject to Christ . . .' While he is the head of his wife, she becomes the crown of her husband, his ornament, his honour, and his glory. And thus the love of the husband makes amends for the subjection of the wife, and the subjection of the wife is an abundant recompense for the love of the husband.[46]

Storrow's condemnation of Indian conjugal relations seems remarkably similar, despite the very different values assigned. Indian women are 'assumed to be the inferiors of men, intellectually and morally; to be unfit for freedom; the subordinates of their husbands . . . Their condition must be lacking in some of the most rational, benignant, and desirable elements of domestic life.'[47] Similarly, John Wilson disapprovingly quoted from the Skanda Purána in order to condemn the over-dependence of Indian women on their husbands: 'Let a wife who wishes to perform sacred ablution, wash the feet of her lord, and drink the water; for a husband is to a wife greater than Shankara or Vishnu. The husband is her god, and priest, and religion; wherefore, abandoning every thing else, she ought chiefly to worship her husband.'[48] The parallels of masculinist authority across cultures are unmistakeable: only racial difference seems to have influenced missionary judgment of such practices.

The troubling nature of *zenanas* in missionary textuality, then, is attributable both to their 'foreign' nature *and* to their familiarity. As Grewal argues, 'certain discourses such as those of the "harem" become nodal points around which groups within colonizing and colonized cultures can formulate different and related hegemonic relations and their own subject positions'.[49] As I shall discuss in chapter 5, this ensured that the *zenana* and its sustaining network of ideas around class, domesticity, and gender were manipulated differently by a range of interested parties including British suffragists, male and female missionaries, and Indian nationalists.

FAITH AND VICTORY

...the garden rose[50]

Mrs Hannah Mullens' *Faith and Victory* was published posthumously in 1867, and, whilst the first seven chapters were written exclusively by her, the final three were completed by 'two ladies from her family' from her outlines (vii). Here again the mediated, multi-authored nature of many missionary texts is evident. The (unnamed) editor notes that 'many circumstances... contributed to delay the publication of the work till now' (viii), but Mullens' death in 1861 is proof that the novel rightfully belongs in the archival period addressed in this book. The novel was originally to be published only in the Bengalese language, and thus to 'penetrate the walls of the Hindu *Zenana*, and be the means of presenting the truth to its secluded inmates in a simple and attractive form' (v). However, the English language edition was produced first. Mullens explains that someone suggested that a British audience might well be equally interested in the novel, and 'it is with this view that this little book is presented to the public in an English dress' (vi). Mullens explicitly describes her attempts to appeal to her intended (Indian) audience – she

has endeavoured to draw a faithful picture of Indian life, which they should recognise, and in which they might claim special property. She has sought to lead her readers among their own rich meadows; to guide them through their own groves of date and acacia trees; to sail with them on their own majestic Ganges; and rest with them beneath the cool shade of their own giant tamarinds and banians. (v–vi)

This novel was thus directly intended to address, and effect, local Indian readers, and its author was keen to assert her right to speak to and for this colonial audience. Mullens sees her text as correcting some of the dubious narratives about Indian gender relations and *zenana* life which had previously circulated – she clearly disapproved of those 'Eastern Tales and

Indian Romances [which] have adorned our Drawing-room Albums for the last half century, describing incidents which never could have happened' (vi). Mullens makes a significant play for the veracity of *her* account, which, as she intimates, is in some ways validated simply by her gender, as well as her considerable experience in missionary work. Her editor spruiked the novel even more: 'as the judgement of those well acquainted with Indian Christian literature...no work has yet appeared so adapted to the special end it has in view, and so fitted to commend Christian truth to the educated young men of Bengal and to the members of their families' (viii).

Mullens strategically places herself as a humble Christian woman, but one who has exclusive access to the subjects of her narrative:

In penetrating into the secret recesses of a Hindu home, and lifting the veil of the *Zenana*, the writer is aware she is treading on dangerous ground. Nevertheless she feels humbly confident that her little work contains no glaring errors respecting Hindu life and manners. Unusual opportunities of direct intercourse with native families, the careful sifting of information supplied, and the kind aid of two native gentlemen who have examined these pages, afford some guarantee that her descriptions are in the main correct. (vi–vii)

It is notable that despite Mullens' strategic claim for authenticity through gender, her writing still draws on a masculinist rhetoric of 'penetration' and 'lifting the veil', images which mirror colonialist metaphors of the British 'emancipation' of *zenanas*. At such points, the pre-ordained nature of much missionary discourse is made obvious. Whilst British missionary women undoubtedly negotiated different relationships with Indians from those of their male counterparts, such appropriations of phallocentric imperial discourse highlight the extent to which 'women missionaries of the period were not only the helpmates of the imperialists but were themselves imperialists reenacting the drama of the coloniser and the colonised within the confines of the *zenana*'.[51] As Grewal notes of British women visiting harems,

in describing the harem which they could enter because they were of the same sex as the inhabitants, they used many of the stereotypes of the male empire builders... the object of the imperial, male gaze was somewhat different for the imperial European woman in its elimination of the erotic and the mysterious and the emphasis on the prosaic and unadmirable nature of the women behind *purdah* and their lives. (*Home and Harem*, 81)

Mullens' genuine experience of Indian evangelisation complicates accepted forms of missionary representation, and her perspective provides fascinating insights into British women's experiences of missionary zeal and *zenana* visitation.

In summary, *Faith and Victory* is a didactic novel presenting both missionary philosophy and Hannah Mullens' experience in fictionalised form (by extension, arguably, it also represents the experience of related missionaries such as her father, her husband, and Edward Storrow). The novel opens with a detailed account of Indian cultural knowledge concerning the Ganges (1–10), before introducing the first two generations of a wealthy Hindu family whose experience structures the narrative. Child sacrifice, one of the recurring tropes of missionary literature in India, provides the motor for the plot. An unnamed missionary intervenes in the intended sacrifice of a boy:

> The idea of the horrid crime they were about to perpetrate had just flashed across his mind with the most vivid reality... He knew that the Marquis Wellesley, the Governor-General of India, had ... enacted a regulation which interdicted the drowning of children at Saugor, under the severest penalties; but the law had never yet been enforced, and for him single-handed to insist on it... would have been madness itself. (13–14)

Luckily, he remembers that there should be 'armed sepoys which the Government had sent to the island for the prevention of this species of infanticide'. And so, after a tense scene juggling the child between a Brahmin priest, the 'agonised mother', the river, and the missionary, the baby Mohendro is saved from 'the jaws of some hungry alligator', and the 'insensible mother' gratefully accepts the child back and ambivalently accepts the missionary's 'own copy of the Bengalee New Testament' (18). The illustration from Storrow's later book, *Our Indian Sisters*, demonstrates how such narratives became part of the repetitive lexicon of missionary stories (see figure 1). The melodramatic opening sets the tone for the novel, and crucially introduces the book – the 'Bengalee New Testament' – that will literally and symbolically tear the family apart.

The novel shifts forwards forty years, and from this point onwards mostly focusses on Prosonno Kumár (Mohendro's third son), who converts to Christianity, thus risking the loss of his family, his young wife, and caste. 'Of a highly intellectual and reflective cast of mind', Prosonno had widely studied religion, rejected the old school Brahminism of his father 'as being a monstrous mixture of puerile absurdities, gross impurity, and soul-destroying falsehood', and embraced the modern form of Brahmism espoused by the Brahmo Samaj, though he still 'seemed restless

Figure 1 'Hindu Infanticide' from Reverend Edward Storrow's *Our Indian Sisters* (1898). (Reproduced from London Missionary Society/Council for World Mission Archives.)

and unhappy' (26–7). On visiting a Christian convert, Rám Doyal, he is given a copy of the Bible in Bengalese but his father Mohendro is 'enraged beyond measure': he dashes the book to the ground, and then orders it to be burnt (41). Prosonno's emotional response to the destruction of 'his highly prized volume', before he has a chance to read it, attracts the ire of most of his family but the sympathy of his grandmother. She gives him the old copy of the New Testament that she has been hiding for forty years. With the help of the 'good book', he converts. The family, violently opposed to his conversion and disbelieving his agency in this decision, kidnap him from the Christian community he has joined and imprison him, until his grandmother helps him to escape. Prosonno's wife, Kaminee, is represented as an intellectually curious young woman, and she eventually decides that Christianity holds appeal for her too. As a result she leaves her father-in-law's house (and the *zenana*) to rejoin her husband, accompanied by her widowed sister-in-law and her children. Naturally, the re-united couple live happily ever after in Christian harmony. The tone of the novel is moralistic and didactic, with unconvincingly staged set-pieces on various issues surrounding British missionary and colonial activity. To give Mullens her due, she does attempt to explain Indian resistance to Christian conversion within comparatively informed contexts of Indian religion and culture, although Christian ethics and ideals always emerge as superior. It is this negotiation and appropriation of Indian voices and resistances in these set-pieces that I want to consider in detail.

English as the preferred mode of education in India is raised as an issue of contention early in the novel. Prosonno's family is depicted as representing a spectrum of Indian opinion, from the traditionally Brahminical brother Surjo, to the somewhat more reasoned father, to the loving and potentially Christian grandmother, who is prevented from taking independent action by the strictures of female Hindu custom. The uncompromising Surjo takes a firm line on the role of English education in converting Prosonno: 'I hate your English education from the bottom of my heart. It is sapping the very foundation of Hinduism' (79). The father, by contrast, presents a much more negotiated view of education systems:

'I do not see that [English education] has anything in common with Christianity; besides we cannot get on without it in these days. See how well [Chondro, the other son], who have [*sic*] received an English education, have prospered in the world, compared to your poor brother Surjo... It cannot be helped, Surjo,' he continued, 'it would have been an injustice to the boys not to have had them taught English; besides, I again repeat it, the knowledge of English has not been the means of bringing Prosonno to abjure his father's faith.' (79–80)

The debate on English versus vernacular education had been played out not only in innumerable Indian households, but also in British and colonial forums. Heated arguments concerning the language in which Anglo-Indian education should be conducted had taken place throughout the early years of the century, with British participants divided on the issue. Early missionaries had either established 'vernacular' schools, where instruction was in the local languages, or English language schools, which required the teaching of English to Indian students. Missionary principles placed considerable value on the codification and use of vernacular languages – indeed, the first task of most early missionaries was to translate the Bible into the local language, although this practice waned somewhat during the nineteenth century. Joseph Mullens argued that missionary intervention even changed local languages:

To the missionaries, the languages of India owe a great deal. They found the higher range of terms appropriated by the learned, and they have brought them to the common people. They found many of the languages stiff; they made them flexible. They have brought down the high language of the Brahmin; they have elevated the patois of the Sudra, and thus formed a middle tongue, capable of being used with ease and elegance by the best educated classes.[52]

However, missionaries gradually realised that there were a prohibitive number of languages to be learned, and they believed that tuition in English had the potential to instil some essence of 'British-ness' through the language itself. Brian Holmes notes that language policy 'was incidental to their main purpose, conversion to Christianity. On the whole they received little direct support for this policy from the Home Government when political trouble was likely to result. To meet parental demand the missionaries opened English schools and inevitably introduced European ideas, attitudes and knowledge.'[53]

As Holmes describes it, from 1813 to 1833 there was a great debate over colonial education policies as to the relative emphasis given to English in schools. Macaulay's minute of 1835 was one of several official recommendations which advocated English language teaching in India. Even though Macaulay had no doubts about the superiority of western culture in the areas of ethics, aesthetics, politics, and science, he did wish to abstain 'from giving any public encouragement to those who are engaged in the work of converting the natives to Christianity'.[54] The East India Company's 1854 Educational Dispatch maintained a bifocal attitude towards English and vernacular language education: 'We have decided that our object is to extend European knowledge throughout all classes of the people. We have shown that this object must be effected by means of the English language in the higher branches of instruction, and by that of the vernacular languages of India to the great mass of the people.'[55] Hannah Mullens' staging of these discussions between Prosonno's father and brother, therefore, draws directly on these complex negotiations of British rule and missionary influence. It again highlights the central role played by language, literacy, and textuality in colonial evangelical projects in India: what Gauri Viswanathan has described as 'the imperial mission of educating and civilizing colonial subjects in the literature and thought of England, a mission that in the long run served to strengthen western cultural hegemony in enormously complex ways'.[56] When Prosonno is forcibly returned to his family, his own mother 'hardly knew her son again. His very phraseology was altered' (114).

Prosonno has long, detailed conversations with the missionary's wife on the finer points of English culture and Indian women's 'subjugation'. Prosonno's experience of living with a very different kind of (Christian) community is another central issue in the novel. The representations of his living 'outside caste' are particularly interesting. Mullens wrote:

He was treated like a man, and being a gentleman in character, education, and manners, he was treated like a gentleman also. But this was not on account of his brahminhood... All men are equal in the sight of God; all have originated from one common stock; and believing this, there was no one found among the Christians who would dare refuse to eat anything cooked by another person of different or even inferior caste. Well they knew that the insult was not so great to the man as to the God who made him. (177)

As noted in chapter 2, it was assumed that Christian men were 'naturally' gentlemen. As Mrinalini Sinha's study of colonial masculinity demonstrates, the processes and practices whereby British and Indian masculine elites were 'constituted respectively as the "manly Englishman" and the "effeminate Bengali"'[57] were closely linked to Anglo-Indian experience throughout the nineteenth century. Sinha argues: 'the consolidation in the schools and universities of a *national* representation of "English" masculinity for the British was itself tied to a strictly *provincial* representation of "native" masculinity for Indians' (9).

Two points are especially notable in Mullens' description of caste and class. Firstly, there is a distinct correlation drawn between English and Indian middle to upper classes and their attitudes towards masculinity. Secondly, Mullens makes the concurrent assumption that Christianity in itself would induce 'gentlemanly' virtues in Indian men. The congruencies between the upper classes of Britain and India were emphasised in a number of missionary texts. The impetus behind the expansion of *zenana* visitation later in the century was also primarily one of class. The introduction of single women *zenana* missionaries, who tended to be of respectable middle- or even upper-class backgrounds, relied heavily on the assumption that, as Haggis argues,

class serves to cement a sense of sisterhood between English ladies and their assumed counterparts in the (usually) upper class *zenanas* of India, whose members are acknowledged as ladies, or at least potential ladies, and thus as ideal recipients of lady missionaries' enlightening influence, and as the key to winning over to Christianity the influential male members of their class.[58]

This congruence of class and gender, across cultures, supported much *zenana* work. At the same time, many missionaries were dismayed to be thwarted in this neat corollary of class relations when upper-class *zenana* women continued to resist the spiritual ministrations of evangelical British gentlewomen.

Prosonno's comments on the representation of gender difference through clothing are particularly interesting, given that this topic is not frequently raised in missionary tracts about India and Christian conversion.[59] He decides that his new Christian clothes transform him almost as much as his new Christian beliefs:

These clothes were not made in the European fashion, as is supposed by most Hindus, but consisted of a tight-fitting long coat (termed chapkhan), and trousers, such as are worn already in the country by Mohammedan gentlemen. As Prosonno put off his two thin muslin wrappers, which, until now, had constituted his sole dress, and put on the new clothes, made of thick close calico, he could not but be struck, even in this trifling circumstance, with the strength that female influence exerted the moment a man came under its power: and his thoughts assumed a shape like this – 'If we, Hindu men, were accustomed to meet our ladies in society, we should soon be compelled to do away with our effeminate muslins, and adopt a decent costume[60] like this.' (154)

Prosonno's realisation that the very clothes of Hindu custom might contribute to the 'maladjustment' of the sexes and the 'oppression' of women places the issue of representation in the foreground of this text. The idea that a Hindu convert to Christianity would be made to wear clothes resembling those of a 'Mohammedan gentleman' is quite extraordinary. This deliberate confusion and conflation of Asian cultures and religions by missionaries at the point of physical representation perhaps begins to explain the intense Indian resistance to British cultural meddling (and muddling).

No wonder 'simple and attractive' (v) accounts of Indian Christians were needed to convince future converts, although it is likely that many *zenana* women and their Hindu husbands would have read Mullens' account with considerable confusion and mixed feelings.

Despite the fact that *Faith and Victory* constantly contrasts the image of secluded, insipid, Hindu women with fulfilled, active, Christian women, Prosonno's fellow conversationalist is never named – throughout the text she remains identified only as 'the missionary's wife'. For a writer such as Hannah Mullens, who in her own right was an accomplished and successful (female) evangelist, such an omission seems extraordinary. It highlights the way in which, as discussed in previous chapters, wives were expected to merge their missionary labours with those of their husbands. Regardless of how personal experience might have contradicted such rigid expectations, texts formed in the intellectual environment of early nineteenth-century mission policies continued to represent women's activities in the approved way, even if those texts are written by women. Then again, the (male) missionary who opened the novel by saving the baby Mohendro is similarly anonymous. Arguably, these features draw attention to the authority invested in the figure of 'the missionary' and 'the missionary wife', enabling the textual construction of a unitary, representative missionary figure. In addition, these typecast characters illuminate the extent to which *Faith and Victory* participates in constructing and maintaining a distinct genre of missionary discourse, one emphasising the universalised nature of missionary representation across local cultural differences and gender divides.

Prosonno's discussions with the missionary's wife are chatty, pedantic, and ideologically laden. The overarching message is that Prosonno, now that he possesses a real knowledge of Christian women, laments the position and treatment of Indian women in his traditional community. He constantly expresses evangelical ideas such as 'it was by raising the standard of female character that Christians had chiefly improved the ground-work of their society' (153). Prosonno wonderingly notes: Indian women 'are not wanting in beauty and sweetness, and even in intelligence; and yet they are as different from English women, as is the jungly marigold from the garden rose' (162). He exclaims: 'Why, ma'am . . . your English ladies do more in a day than ours do in a week' (172). This paradigm of femininity, contrasting the 'wild' Indian woman to the 'cultivated' British woman, is as crucial to *Faith and Victory* as is Prosonno's discovery of Christian masculinity. It also links this novel to Storrow's memoir of Bala Tagore. If *The Easten Lily Gathered* works as a minor hagiography of a female Indian convert, proving that 'jungly marigold[s]' could hope to achieve Christian 'cultivation', then

Hannah Mullens – the exemplary missionary wife – is the archetype of the English, Christian, 'garden rose'. The anonymous missionary wife in *Faith and Victory* can be read as the spectre of the book's author, the epitome of nineteenth-century Christian femininity to which Indian converts should aspire.

But the final issue raised in *Faith and Victory* of particular interest for this study is a passing remark made by the missionary wife to Prosonno. In explaining to Prosonno how 'lazy' Hindu ladies are in comparison with their English, Christian counterparts, she says, 'I was about to tell you . . . that I was born in England, where females are more independent than even our own country-women are in this land. Here the warm climate keeps us prisoners; and I fancy we have also unknowingly imbibed some of our neighbours' false notions about female delicacy and female reserve' (165). The admission that Indian experience significantly affects British women and perceptions of their behaviour and labour by the wider community is one made rarely in missionary texts, which tend to construct ahistorical monuments of ideal, European behaviour, whether of gender roles, educational standards, or Christian commitment. In fact, as such unguarded comments suggest, missionary texts *constructed* a hegemony out of multiple, dissonant Anglo-Indian and imperial British beliefs and experiences. As Haggis argues, representations of womanhood in Indian contexts were structured on two contrasting stereotypes:

the passive, pitiable Indian woman and the active, independent English lady missionary . . . There is an odd juxtaposition about the depth of difference constructed between Indian and British women . . . and a characterisation of a close, familial bond, that of sisterhood, surely based on a recognition of identity or similarity.[61]

Missionary representations of the contact zone of Indian gender reform evince the destabilising ways in which cultural difference might effect both Indian and British conceptions of identity. The missionary wife's admission is one about mutual imbrication, about how British femininity might have to be rethought in the aftermath of its encounter with Indian culture.

CHAPTER FIVE

Imperialism, suffragism, and nationalism

A Larger Way for Women[1]

The complex nexus of race, gender, class, and domesticity recurring throughout LMS missionary texts about India established a suggestive narrative which influenced other manifestly divergent discourses. A range of political groups adopted parts of this narrative, replaying it at different cultural sites. As such, missionary discourses of cultural and racial negotiation proved to be significant in ways unlikely to have been foreseen by their evangelical authors. In conclusion to part one, I want to trace some of the ways in which missionary focus on Indian women and native gender and domesticity issues affected broader imperialist, suffragist, and Indian nationalist discourses from the 1860s onwards.

British women discovered in *zenana* visitation a field in which their gendered skills and attributes were especially necessary. After the 1860s, religious and professional women flocked to the newly established missions for Indian women and the 'Ladies' Committees' of older institutions like the LMS. Jane Haggis' doctoral study 'Professional Ladies and Working Wives' examines the life of the 'Ladies' Committee' of the LMS, established in 1875 and dissolved in 1907. Her insights into the earlier period of missionary activity are invaluable, and her analysis of this later period is both critically astute and historically detailed. She suggests that the LMS moved to establish a separate 'Ladies' Committee' because of the expanding opportunities for female enterprise (which were often beyond the practical capacities of the already hard-working missionary wives), in addition to the availability of candidates and the proven willingness of the public 'at home' to finance such efforts. As Haggis notes, these rationales were 'reiterated again and again in the general literature [of the LMS] and that of the other major societies. Behind each one lay a range of social changes stretching from Britain to "the East" and back again.'[2]

The preceding chapters have already traced many of these social changes, including crucial renegotiations of British imperialism in India, a growing British sense of moral responsibility for Indian subjects of empire, and the broadening of earlier bifurcated communities of religious or commercial British interests. In addition, the growing British suffragist movement was influential in both establishing associations such as the Ladies' Committees and publicising Indian women's experiences. What is clearly evident in this marked change in institutional policy and practice is that early colonial experience led to a transformation of imperial philosophy. This mutual imbrication in terms of organisational structures was mirrored in imperial attitudes towards both British and Indian women, though neither universally nor unproblematically.

Support for women's entrance[3] into 'professional' mission work after 1860 was by no means global. Very early, missionary societies had discovered that women were extremely good at raising money for missionary enterprises. Women's and children's groups were continually entreated to raise more money for the support of the (predominantly male) missionaries because of their proven fund-raising abilities and they were encouraged to form 'auxiliary societies'. Missionary wives in the colonies, awarded no direct financial remuneration for their evangelical efforts, targeted their female friends and religious 'sisters' back in Britain for the funds which the societies did not provide. As Haggis describes it,

the Societies found themselves on the horns of a dilemma: it was beyond doubt that women were more successful fund raisers and enthusiastic contributors than their male membership, but grave doubts were harboured as to the propriety and consequences of such female activity...One way the Societies reconciled themselves to this organised female presence was to ensure they remained excluded from membership or office, in the parent organisation, while male 'managers' or 'organisers' exerted official authority over their activities. (133–4)

Following formal changes in their recruitment policies, societies were deluged by female volunteers whom they had previously dismissed without consideration. As the previous chapters have argued, early missionary work ensured that the image of Indian women was a familiar and emotive one for the British religious public. *Zenana* visitation was integral to these women's sense of mission. Most societies seemed to have one main requirement of their prospective female candidates: that they be 'ladies'. The LMS sought 'women of education and refinement', and considered an applicant's 'parentage and associations'.[4] As Geraldine Forbes and others note, these female missionaries disrupted established orders of evangelical work and its institutional structure. Whilst missionary women were often welcomed into Indian homes as teachers of reading, arithmetic, and needlework, 'they were thrown out when they went too far with religion'.[5] These women were uncomfortably placed, as they also challenged male bishops and missionaries by their insistence that *zenana* education was critically important and that women could organise, implement, and fund it without male interference. As Forbes notes, they clashed with male authority in both cultures. Additionally, many of the male missionaries

thought that women could make a valuable contribution by educating the children and womenfolk of native converts. But the women missionaries were not thrilled with the idea of teaching children from the lower castes and visiting the homes of poor women...In contrast, the *zenanas* were inaccessible to men, mysterious by reputation and filled with elite women whose conversions would be significant. (WS6)

These new women missionaries appear to have read their evangelical precursors carefully, so they maintained the early attention to class relations in their new spheres of influence.

Societies like the LMS did not easily accept women's role in evangelisation, nor indeed the institutionalisation of that role by the end of the nineteenth century. As Haggis notes, the history of the LMS Ladies' Committee was by no means mild or mannered – rather, the women were frequently in conflict with the society as a whole. By the 1890s, the members of the Ladies' Committee realised that whilst a special interest committee guaranteed their continued existence, it also excluded them from political power and influence in the larger institution. Specifically, they had no representation on the Directors' Committee, despite the growing importance and influence of their work. In response, they threatened to break with the LMS to form a separate '*zenana* society' if they were not granted representation. By the 1890s, the Ladies' Committee had been dissolved in favour of a 'Ladies Examination Committee' of nine women, who also sat on the board of directors. It is evident that the 'ladies' of the LMS learnt a great deal about institutional power, political influence, and the strategic use of the media and textuality through their connections with the society.

The development of 'women's missions' also conveniently provided a partial solution to social problems within Britain itself. As Forbes ('In Search of the "Pure Heathen" ', WS2) and Peter Williams ('The Missing Link', 56) both note, the foundation of a philanthropic and careerist category of female missionary solved part of the 'surplus women' problem in late nineteenth-century Britain, when the country found itself demographically out of balance with more women than men of a marriageable age.

Missionary discourses on gender, domesticity, and morality had repercussions in other colonial spheres as well. As Inderpal Grewal argues, it would be short-sighted to believe that what may have begun as an evangelical, European narrative about gender and domesticity remained the sole possession of evangelical Britons. Their prolific textuality ensured that such arguments were influential in many different forums. So whilst evangelicals were placing the (supposed paucity of the) Indian home at the centre of their reformist attention, nineteenth-century European discourses about binary oppositions of female and male spheres were 'recuperated within Indian nationalism, enabling the nationalist narrative of the "motherland" of India as an independent nation'.[6] Grewal maintains that the contentious question of Indian women's place within a modern, emergent, independent India was in part resolved through the nationalist construction of domestic space as a repository of the nation's culture, the embodiment of Indian spirituality. Such a construction was, of course, familiar from earlier missionary discourse, but nationalist discourses crucially reassigned positive value to the 'resistant' nature of *zenanas*, whereas missionaries had condemned them for the same reason. For nationalists, missionaries embodied the spiritually corrupt material world seeking to violate the intimate space of Indian womanhood and Indian cultural integrity. As Partha Chatterjee explains, the nationalist middle class brought about a new patriarchy, but one that strategically differentiated itself both from 'traditional' and 'western' models: 'The "new woman" was to be modern, but she would also have to display the signs of national tradition and therefore would be essentially different from the "Western" woman.'[7]

Similarly, nationalists used the image of British women in their own discourses to represent the dangers of western modernity. In nationalist texts, British women were condemned for openly consorting with men and the material world, abandoning the domestic sphere for public duties, and their apparent willingness to expose themselves to possible sexual temptation and/or danger as a result of their independence.[8] As Grewal argues,

Just as the discourse of the woman 'caged' in the harem, in *purdah*, becomes the necessary Other for the construction of the Englishwoman presumably free and happy in the home, the discourse of the Englishwoman's association with men and women becomes, for Indian nationalism, a sign of depravity. The '*purdah*' construct of the English imperialists becomes the 'home' of the Indian nationalists; Indian women's location in the women's part of the house becomes a symbol of what is sacred and private for Indian nationalist culture. (*Home and Harem*, 54)

Thus, across racial and cultural divides, masculinist interests continued to interrogate ideologically laden discourses of gender and domesticity and to align them with their own interests.

Equally, such gendered constructions of domesticity and women's place in society were mobilised by Indian women keen for change. For all the problematic aspects of British women entering *zenanas*, they did introduce new kinds of educational programmes informing Indian women about British cultural practices, knowledge that Indian women could then use to their own advantage. Missionary education supplied the intellectual background to many colonial independence movements in the late nineteenth and twentieth centuries. Brian Holmes notes that mission-educated young men generally went in two directions: either establishing national political parties or working as permanent officials in government agencies.[9] Whilst some mission-educated colonial subjects may have remained involved with institutions of colonial power, it is undeniable that many eventually used their education to bring about anti-colonial policies and eventually national independence.[10]

As Fiona Bowie argues, the presence of *zenana* missionaries, who often befriended their high-caste Indian charges, meant that 'with Independence there were women in the top echelons of society who had received a western education and who were poised to share in the government of their country'.[11] Access to powerfully emotive Christian discourses surrounding women (which constructed their treatment as indicative of the modernity of national cultures) also bolstered the arguments of Indian reform movements. Brahmo Samaj members advocating female education, Indian women activists such as Pandita Ramabai and Parvati Athavale, and women's reformist Hindu groups such as the Arya Mahila Samaj all mobilised debates about gender in India for their own purposes.[12] However, as Sinha suggests of the renegotiations of gender and morality arising out of the controversies surrounding the Ilbert Bill, Indian and British women understood and mobilised the politics of concepts such as 'pride of womanhood' very differently:

For British women, the pride of womanhood legitimated the participation of white women in the predominantly masculine colonial public sphere as well as confirmed the role of white women in a masculinist colonial society by stressing the need for the 'protection' of white women by white men ... To the middle-class Indian woman or *bhadramahila*, the pride of womanhood underscored their solidarity with Indian men of their class and opened up a space for the separate contributions of Indian women to a unified nationalist front against the British.[13]

Conversely, as I have noted, British suffragists used the example of Indian women to agitate for reform of the place of women within British society. Antoinette Burton's *Burdens of History* notes that British feminism came of age during the high period of British imperialism, and argues that 'In their quests for liberation and empowerment, Victorian and Edwardian feminists collaborated in the ideological work of empire, reproducing the moral discourse of imperialism and embedding feminist ideology within it.'[14] As I suggested earlier, this is a legacy continuing to bedevil contemporary feminist theory and practice.

Missionary work in India thus revolved around questions of gender, domesticity, and morality. As part one demonstrated, the sheer quantity of publications emanating from the LMS mission field in the first sixty years of the nineteenth century guaranteed that images of India (and specifically Indian women) were central to the imperial and evangelical imagination. Early LMS missionaries unquestionably saw India as an environment in which their superior masculinity would triumph over colonised men and where the 'chivalrous, delicate, and Christian sentiments we entertain for womanhood'[15] could find practical and commendable expression. The ever-changing nature of British presence in India, and the various ways Britain imagined its relationship with empire, ensured that such simplified narratives of masculine adventure were complicated and disturbed by early missionary experience in the field. Undeniably, missionary activity in India also provided specific opportunities for British women to prove their potential and their need for a separate, professional sphere of evangelisation. As will be evident in the next two parts of this study, such experiences were not common across the colonial continuum. The Indian experience was crucial to changes in institutional policies regarding women missionaries – in no other location was the case for female missionaries made so strongly.

PART THREE

The London Missionary Society in Polynesia

CHAPTER SIX

Polynesian missions and the European imaginary

We have discovered them, and in a sort have brought them into existence[1]

From the early European voyages of 'discovery' to South Pacific islands, interest in what were regarded as island paradises was intense. Romantic ideas about lost Edens, noble savages, and utopian island cultures pervaded European visions of the area, resulting in acute public attention and a subsequent demand for narrative accounts of these idealised locales. Within the British imagination, the South Pacific figured as a site of desire – desire for heroic discovery; desire for a prelapsarian state of nature; desire for the economic and strategic power which possession of the region promised; and desire for the social and sexual utopianism typifying European fantasies about the region and its people.[2] When the LMS deputation led by Reverend Daniel Tyerman and George Bennet reached Taïti in September 1821, they wrote: 'Tahiti, "the desire of our eyes", came upon us at sunrise, in all its grandeur and loveliness; – more grand in the height of its mountains, and more lovely in the luxuriance of its valleys, than our imaginations had ever pictured it from the descriptions of former visitors and Missionaries.'[3]

The South Pacific functioned as a very particular kind of colonial space. Whilst early European visitors went on to establish official colonies in places like Australia, European nations appeared reluctant to add the Pacific formally to their portfolio of overseas colonies. Later in the nineteenth century, competition between imperial nations increased, particularly between Britain and France, as the grab for Pacific colonies intensified. For most of the period 1800–60, however, islands in the Pacific operated under quasi-colonial status. Numerous Europeans moved into and around the region – missionaries, beachcombers, traders, escaped convicts, and the occasional private imperialist – yet missionaries usually formed the most stable and continuous white community. Missionaries generally behaved as if colonial status was imminent or even already in place – indeed, in many places, they introduced the signs and institutions of a colony regardless of the intentions of the imperial nation. In some ways, missionaries operated as founding settlers of a potential Pacific colony. As such, they were deeply implicated in European imperialist intervention into Pacific cultures.

Missions in the South Pacific have always held a special place within the history and memory of the LMS. The society's first overseas mission was to what was then called Otaheite,[4] and considerable personnel, funds, and interest were invested in this area during the nineteenth century. Part two focusses on the historical, cultural, and textual environment of LMS Polynesian missions. This chapter will outline a history of the LMS Polynesian missions in the period 1800–60, while chapter 7 examines three crucial sites of gender negotiations: sexuality, clothing, and the family.

Geographically, Polynesia commonly includes the islands of the central and eastern Pacific, including Hawaii, Samoa, Taïti, and Tonga, and excluding Micronesia and Melanesia. As Nicholas Thomas notes of the geographic entity Melanesia, such a grouping is 'an artifact of colonial ethnology',[5] but I use the term here to establish a sense of congruence across these islands' experiences of LMS missionaries. These missions were originally established in the society's first concerted move into the region at the end of the eighteenth century – in 1797 the LMS moved into Taïti, Tongatapu, and the Marquesas, and from 1817 to 1822 they extended their influence to the Leeward Islands. Whilst I do not want to conflate the very different cultures and often disparate missionary encounters across these islands, it is unquestionable that these locations felt the impact of the LMS, its policies, and representatives at a similar time and in comparable ways.

After the LMS formation in 1795, the directors sought to establish their first overseas mission. The choice of 'the South Seas'[6] as the inaugural site was somewhat contentious, with at least two dominant members of the directorial committee, the Reverend Drs Haweis and David Bogue, having strongly divergent opinions on the ideal location. Haweis' enthusiasm for the South Seas was due to his reading of Captain James Cook's published journals, whose description of an island paradise had caught the British public's imagination (Bogue preferred Bengal). In their 1899 history *British Foreign Missions*, Ralph Wardlaw Thompson and Arthur Johnson declared that the publication of Cook's journals was as the spark to tinder. The Rev. Dr Haweis, Rector of Aldwinkle, read the book, and immediately resolved to send a mission to the South Sea Islands... William Carey, an obscure Baptist minister in Northamptonshire,[7] read the book, and was stimulated to write, in 1789, his *Enquiry into the Obligations of Christians to Use Means for the Conversion of the Heathens. In which the Religious State of Different Nations of the World, and the Success of Former Undertakings are Considered*.[8]

Imperial textual representation was thus pivotal to LMS visions of the Pacific, influencing both how they thought about their Pacific missions and the ways in which they promulgated knowledge about their activities there. Cook's influence permeates many Pacific missionary narratives. In 1837, John Williams' *A Narrative of Missionary Enterprises in the South Sea Islands* lauded Cook as 'that truly great man, Captain Cook, whose name I never mention but with feelings of veneration and regret'.[9] These imperial narratives fostered and philosophically subsidised further colonial projects such as missionary ventures in Polynesia, allowing missionaries to draw a parallel between their role and that of more obviously aggressive imperial agents. Imperialist narratives of masculinist adventure and discovery clearly provided the template for the ways missionary writers experienced and represented their encounters with Polynesians.

Thomas Haweis had been warned by 'the worthy Admiral Bligh' that the major 'dangers and difficulties' encountered by missionaries in Polynesia would be those 'such as may arise from the fascination of beauty, and the seduction of appetite'.[10] Publications of European voyagers and adventurers constructed a utopian Pacific paradise where sexual licence and social freedom reigned. Hawkesworth's editions of the expedition journals of both Cook and Banks, for a long time the only versions available, certainly did not hide sexual dimensions of exploration, instead virtually foregrounding them.[11] Banks' suspected affair with the prominent Taïtian Purea (or 'Oborea' as she became known in Britain) was also relayed in Britain through the published journals and many more carnivalesque reenactments.[12] For a prurient European imagination with Orientalist views of the 'other's' voracious and deviant sexuality, Polynesian island cultures were almost solely defined by their sexuality. Evangelical missionaries too participated in this sexualised vision, though, strictly bound by Christian moral principles and their solid family ethic, they perceived such freedom to be detrimental to the islanders' immortal souls. Haweis laments the influence that European 'discovery' had had on island cultures:

We have discovered them, and in a sort have brought them into existence; but I read with *pity*, that we have hitherto only excited their curiosity to admire our ships, and the colour of our skin; with *grief*, that we have contaminated them with our vices, and with *indignation* behold them perishing with diseases communicated by those who bear the Christian name, without an effort to inform them of the truths which lead to salvation, or to impress them with a sense of moral obligation. ('The Very Probable Success', 263)

He thus promotes missions as a direct corrective to the corrupting influence of Europeans. Whilst many European adventurers went to the South Pacific to revel in expected sexual freedom, LMS missionaries in contrast went to stamp out such indigenous practices in the process of Christian conversion. Inevitably, this created tension between LMS missionaries and other Europeans in the region. Almost all missionaries were certainly very aware of the potential 'temptation' they were expected to resist – some responded with characteristic evangelical extremes of revulsion and irrational reform, whilst others found that the allure of indigenous lifestyles overcame their Christian beliefs.

The society procured a ship, the *Duff*, for their first voyage to the region and 'providentially' secured the services of Captain James Wilson. Through the ongoing process of mythologisation which characterises much of the LMS public discourse, both the *Duff* and Wilson came to assume iconic status: the ship because of its foundational (though short-lived) status in LMS history[13] and Wilson because he was not only a skilled captain but also an evangelical convert. The society, as Michael Cathcart notes, 'always loath to pass up a tale of providence',[14] endlessly retold the story that Wilson, before his conversion, had been the prisoner of an Indian prince (Hyder Ali) and had effected a miraculous escape in the tradition of adventure narratives. When he was recaptured, his Indian gaolers decided that his survival must mean he was 'God's man'. Wilson concurred and repented of his former heathenism (other sources suggest his conversion took place significantly later). He became such a devout Christian that he offered his maritime services free of charge to the society for this first voyage. Given the always constrained nature of the society's finances, one suspects that Wilson's offer to work voluntarily contributed significantly to his iconic status. On 10 August 1796, the *Duff* sailed to Polynesia, carrying a party of about thirty, including ordained missionaries, missionary artisans, and their wives. The *Duff* dropped successive groups of missionaries on various islands, leaving parties at Taïti (March 1797), Tonga (April 1797), and the Marquesas (June 1797).

Polynesia grew to fill a crucial role in LMS foreign activities. The choice of the region proved to be a shrewd public relations exercise because accounts of the society's experiences there built upon the already awakened public interest in the area. The *Duff* left only one year after the LMS inaugural and massively well-attended public meetings, and as Susan Thorne notes the 'expectation of immediate and miraculous divine intervention rendered these missionaries' departure an emotional event of unprecedented intensity'.[15] They were sent off with great fanfare and publicity but were strictly controlled by the directors, who were somewhat dismissive of their ill-educated missionary representatives and were eager for them not to be awarded hero status.[16] Later, more successful missionaries took hold of the public imagination and became folk heroes in their own right. To some extent, such popularity came to destabilise the society's authority over them. Missionary idols such as John Williams could effectively bypass the directors to gain funds or support. If the society opposed the wishes of individual missionaries (as occurred several times within this period), an appeal to the broader Christian public could shame them into acquiescence.

The first group of LMS missionaries to Polynesia were singularly unsuccessful evangelists. The 1796 mission was ill-conceived and, like much missionary work, fuelled more by religious zeal than informed planning. Whilst the society possessed some information about what their envoys might expect to encounter in the islands, individual missionaries were utterly confounded by the cultural differences and extreme isolation they encountered. Assertive female sexuality frightened one missionary from staying more than one night at his appointed mission station, whilst several missionaries of the first LMS party deserted their stations to live with Polynesian women and their communities. Others decamped to Sydney when civil unrest and political resistance in Polynesia appeared to threaten their safety. Within the first five years, almost all of the LMS Polynesian missions had failed and, by the end of the eighteenth century, only seven missionaries were left in the entire region.[17]

The second generation of LMS missionaries sent to Polynesia achieved considerably greater success. They built on the experiences of earlier evangelists, some of whom returned to the field and some of whom had managed to ride out the periods of unrest and remain in situ. John Williams was sent to Ra'iatea in 1817 and he came to be one of the most prominent LMS missionaries, a kind of David Livingstone of the Pacific.[18] Numerous other men in Polynesia became notable public figures, too. By the mid-1800s,

Polynesian LMS stations were held up as exemplars of missionary achievement and in 1830 Reverend James Sherman employed the region as an inspiration for further evangelical efforts. He exhorts a LMS meeting at Spa Field's Chapel to

Turn to the Islanders of the Southern Ocean, a people among whom were cherished every unhallowed passion, every debasing vice, and every species of cruelty; but by the preaching of the gospel their kings have become nursing fathers, and their queens nursing mothers, to the church – their judges peace, and their exactors righteousness... for the rectitude of their laws, the morality of their conduct, and the vigour of their efforts to spread the gospel around them, [they] are at this moment, perhaps, the most righteous and God-fearing nation on the face of the earth.[19]

The period up to the 1830s and 40s proved to be a halcyon one for Protestant evangelism in Polynesia. Soon after, religious zeal amongst the islanders waned (or the political advantage in, or compulsion for, conversion abated) and larger political and economic factors lessened the importance of missionaries within native communities. A survey of the annual LMS 'Reports' for the period 1800 to 1860 reveals that until about mid-century Polynesia held a central place in the society's very public success story as the subject of much self-congratulation and self-promotion. After this period a real sense of disappointment, if not betrayal, pervades representations of the region.

CHRISTIANISATION AND CIVILISATION

... remarkable evidence of the power of the gospel in promoting civilization[20]

In Polynesia, the philosophy of 'Christianisation and civilisation' was central to LMS missions from the very beginning. In some ways, early missionaries there focussed on 'civilisation' at the expense of 'Christianisation' – later evangelists were more successful at integrating the two. Central to the process of civilisation were reforms such as educating children; limiting Polynesian extended family groupings, particularly in terms of childcare and housing; abolishing gender-segregated cultural practices (other than those sanctioned by Christian ethics); establishing western methods of agriculture and industry; and constructing European-style housing.[21] Missionaries continually negotiated the competing demands of civilisation and Christianisation. Given the high degree of attention paid to this first mission by both their supporters and detractors, LMS representatives in Polynesia were vulnerable to criticism when the British public felt that they got that balance wrong. Textually, these tensions ensured that emblematic images – such as those of housing, Polynesian children and families, and agriculture – became invested with intense symbolic value, working metonymically for either Polynesian depravity or Protestant victory, depending on context. The image of newly built, white-walled, thatched cottages, for example, worked not just as a material symbol, but as one imbued with rich spiritual meaning.

Agricultural and economic reform problematised LMS efforts at introducing 'civilisation', as did the troubled questions of missionary remuneration, trade, and industry. Until 1819, LMS missionaries were financially supported by the society only in their passage to the mission field – no further salary or allowance was paid.[22] The society expected that their missionaries should rely on the generosity of their local indigenous 'congregations' or on their own labours for supplies of food, clothing, and shelter, an optimistic theory which assumed that Polynesians were interested in maintaining a foreign presence in their communities. In fact, missionary accounts, particularly early ones, routinely indicate the local market economy was manipulated politically. Supplies were withheld because they offended the local leader or his people, or because food was needed for local religious purposes, or because they were deliberately being made to feel unwelcome.

Missionaries resorted to bartering desirable European goods such as cloth; or trading, either selling produce grown by themselves or by acting as agents between island producers and Europeans; or establishing industries. This unavoidable conjunction between 'commerce and Christianity' proved extremely controversial and whilst some could easily justify using commercial means to effect religious reform, others found the idea repugnant. After investing material images of economy (such as European-style houses) with spiritual significance, missionaries could not easily recast their trade success as merely practical. John Orsmond, a LMS missionary at Taïti, wrote to the directors in 1837 that 'we are a set of trading priests, our closets are neglected, and our cloth disgraced'.[23]

The 1830 LMS 'Report' was ambivalent about whether or not trade was beneficial: it notes that the Polynesians'

former habits of indolence were incompatible with a consistent profession of Christianity. The rapidity with which the islanders are advancing in commercial enterprises; the eagerness with which many engage in trade; the increased number of ships visiting their ports; and the consequent influx of foreigners have also produced irregularities and occasional inconvenience to the missionaries... [although such commercial activities] are unequivocal marks of their industry and advancement in civilization.[24]

Williams energetically promoted this kind of commercial philosophy: 'wherever the Missionary goes, new channels are cut for the stream of commerce; and to me it is most surprising that any individual at all interested in the commercial prosperity of his country can be otherwise than a warm friend to the Missionary cause' (584). Williams established an entrepreneurial project of ship building, and by his initiative remade both the nature of missionary work there, and the nature of its representation. Gunson notes:

Williams changed the whole conception of the South Seas mission, as the mission ship was to become the focal point for missionary endeavour in the islands. The story of the *Messenger of Peace* [Williams' first ship] soon acquired legendary status and Williams became a popular hero during the remaining few years of his life. (*Messengers of Grace*, 118)

Ebenezer Prout's celebratory *Missionary Ships Connected with the London Missionary Society* (1865) made clear the symbolic capital represented by missionary ships, and encouraged children to donate their pennies to expanding the LMS fleet. By the 1850s the slogan 'commerce and Christianity' had great appeal. For many, as Andrew Porter explains, the influence of commerce within evangelisation was justified both for British and Pacific trade. He cites Bishop Samuel Wilberforce's 1860 argument that

Was it not meant that God had given us our commerce and our naval supremacy... that we might as the crowning work of all these blessings, be the instruments of spreading the truths of the Gospel from one end of the earth to the other?... Commerce... is intended to carry, even to all the world, the blessed message of salvation.[25]

Christian commerce would give 'value to life', 'dignity to labour', and 'security to possession', so that a Christian people, Wilberforce exhorts, would be 'a wealth-producing people, an exporting people and so a commercial people' (598).

Many critical observers of missionary endeavour saw the coalition of trade and Christianity as inimical. Hypatia Bonner's wholesale condemnation of British missionaries asks, with rhetorical indignation, 'is it justifiable... is it honest, to attribute to the confused and contradictory teachings of Christianity results which have been obtained by purely secular and material means – educational, medical, industrial, and economic?'[26] Others believed that LMS agents like Williams and George Pritchard were making 'unChristian' amounts of money out of their trade through their evangelical roles. It is unlikely that many missionary traders deliberately kept indigenous primary producers poor, but they certainly did not act aggressively to achieve good results for them. Indeed, in Rarotonga (and a number of other places) a European beachcomber told the local Taha'a islanders that 'the Missionaries, from interested motives, were keeping them in the dark upon these subjects; but that if they would allow *him* to manage their trade with the shipping, he would procure for them five or ten times as much'.[27]

Some missionaries attempted to establish industries including sugar, cotton, and coconut oil mills. These were largely unsuccessful, perhaps due to the missionaries' naïve assumption of Polynesian willingness to supply free labour, as well as significant political mistakes such as engaging a former West Indian slave overseer to manage the sugar mill.[28] A passing sea captain warned islanders of British industries' exploitation of indigenous labour in other parts of the world: 'should the sugar concern prosper, persons of property would come from beyond the seas, and establish themselves in the islands; that they would kill or make slaves of the people, and afterwards seize their lands'.[29] In consequence, labour and official Polynesian permission were often withheld from these doomed enterprises. Still, as Graeme Kent notes, 'a number of missionaries in the process became wealthy men, a fact seized upon by their adversaries, particularly by the traders with whom they came into competition' (*Company of Heaven*, 66).

Another crucial factor in the 'Christianisation and civilisation' process was the introduction of literacy and printed texts. The eminent LMS missionary William Ellis, a fully trained printer, arrived at Eimeo with a printing press in 1817, and the press was eventually established on the island of Mo'orea in that year. The arrival of the press was seen by the society as a seminal event in the development of Polynesian missions. Many missionary narratives, such as Horne's *The Story of the LMS*, celebrate the event when 'King Pomare set up the first types, and printed the first sheets, amid the most indescribable excitement and enthusiasm on the part of his subjects.'[30] Naturally, these first sheets were translated copies of Scripture. In both missionary narratives and, it would seem, in Polynesian cultures, books came to represent an artefact of modernity and western cultural capital in itself: particularly, for the missionaries, the Bible. In chapter 2 I argued that evangelical discourse constructed Christian femininity as embodying both traditional morality and progressive modernity. Similarly missionaries represented the introduction of the Bible into colonial cultures as both a symbol of modernity (brought into being by the machine of modern times, the printing press) *and* as a (colonial re-) instatement of the Bible's hallowed status as eternal, unchanging, and universal.[31]

Missionary educators in Polynesia relied on translated texts of Christian doctrine, after more practical basic reading and writing lessons. Prout's *Missionary Ships* mobilises a metaphor of 'freighting' missionary ships with religious texts. He writes that 'the *Camden* was freighted with five thousand Testaments in the language of the people – a gift more precious in their estimation than much fine gold'; and, later, that the *John Williams* was 'freighted with 5,000 Tahitian Bibles, 4,000 Pilgrim's Progress, and other useful books, an iron chapel, printing materials, and iron tanks to receive the oil which the natives so willingly contribute to the Society'.[32] Prout's metaphorisation of the Bible as a commodity was apposite – missionaries invested books with such significance that Polynesian communities recognised their importance as cultural signifiers and artefacts, though frequently without the biblical message which the missionaries intended. Prout described missionary Aaron Buzacott's arrival at Rarotonga with Bibles: 'So eager were [the local community] to possess the treasure, that Mr Buzacott could scarcely keep them from breaking open the boxes. And it was much the same at Mangaia and other islands, where all were ready, not merely to possess, but to purchase at its cost price the Sacred Word' (74). Significantly, Prout's message about the appeal of books was also intricately tied in with a message about missionary economics – the fact that local communities were prepared actually to pay for the Christian message seemed to imbue the project with particular success.[33] This was a recurrent theme across many mission fields.

MISSIONARY WRITING AND ETHNOGRAPHY

The trade in books was two-way. Given that the British reading public already had a taste for texts of European Pacific encounters, accounts from Polynesian missions had a ready-made audience. British evangelicals' intense interest in this first mission to 'the heathen' increased the size of this audience even further. Missionary publications were hugely popular. Williams' *Missionary Enterprises* and Ellis' *Polynesian Researches*[34] were extremely popular, best-selling publications. In 1840, one reviewer reported that *Missionary Enterprises* had sold 40 000 copies.[35] As their lengthy descriptive subtitles suggest, these books attempt an almost encyclopaedic overview of Polynesian culture. As such, they are generically hybrid, encompassing ethnographic, geographic, historic, and natural history modes, in addition to engaging with broader imperialist and exploration discourses. As Christopher Herbert argues, they demonstrate 'that obsessive minuteness of detail . . . [which] is in fact the stylistic signature of what we see emerging in these texts, the ethnographic concept of culture'.[36] Their entanglement with a wide range of other scientific and imperialist discourses will be considered in the next chapter.

Missionary encounters with Polynesian 'heathen' were significantly different from those experienced in India. On a basic level, missionaries did not regard underlying structures of Polynesian culture and religion as being in any way equivalent to those of western culture. In India, missionaries had recognized an ancient, complex culture bounded by intricate rules and practices (though they abhorred it). In Polynesia, whilst systems of *tapu*, religious rites, and community relations were evident to the missionaries, all these manifestations of Polynesian culture and polity were seen as being imbued with irreconcilable heathenism. As a consequence, they concertedly tried to dismantle them. The first body of LMS missionaries were so concerned with bare survival that few detailed accounts of Polynesian culture emerged – those that did usually condemned it as utterly depraved, and tended not to be published. However, later missionaries produced often the first, and sometimes the only, detailed studies of local culture; in India, by contrast, missionary accounts were preceded and contextualised by other European studies produced by administrators, Orientalist scholars, and travellers. A new ethos emerges, as Niel Gunson argues, with the second generation of LMS missionaries. This ' "new breed" . . . were supposedly better trained than their predecessors, more practical and less pietistic, more appreciative of knowledge for its own sake, more imbued with a sense of their own destiny'.[37] In addition, they introduced a new textual climate, one identifiable as missionary ethnography. Gunson astutely notes that to 'discover the writings of these men is to discover, as it were, the birth of new principles in the human sciences' (v). Christopher Herbert's excellent study of missionary ethnography – *Culture and Anomie* – provides suggestive ways to read these texts. He notes that missionaries had to collect and circulate evidence of the Polynesians' innate depravity in order to justify their aggressive incursions into native societies. But, Herbert suggests, in doing so they set up a self-contradictory task:

they were impelled to undertake a project of richly detailed scientific ethnography; [but] they were at the same time committed to a thesis of anarchic primitive passions which in effect rendered cultural particularities null and void . . . This contradiction chiefly expresses itself in their writings not as uncertainty about principles of research, however, but as a seemingly unresolvable moral and emotional predicament. (162)

Herbert convincingly argues that nineteenth-century missionaries developed the scientific method of ethnographic study – the particular mode of fieldwork and participant observation so beloved of early twentieth-century anthropologists such as Bronislaw Malinowski. But it is the 'seemingly unresolvable moral and emotional predicament' that particularly interests me here, for it provides a highly productive way in which to read the ambiguities and anxieties of missionary texts.

Lamont Lindstrom suggests that British colonial records (both images and texts) from the southwest Pacific

were mostly produced for and consumed by audiences 'at home' rather than in the colonies. As such, they served an internal system of social discrimination between cultured and uncultured, rich and poor, moral and immoral within European societies, as much as they regulated understandings of the European self and South Pacific other.[38]

As Lindstrom suggests, missionary representations heavily influenced evangelical understandings of the heathen 'other'. Encounters between missionaries and Polynesians, particularly around issues of gender and sexuality, would thus influence representations of cultural and gender relations in both Polynesia and Britain, as chapter 7 will demonstrate.

The transformation from missionary records to LMS publications was rarely direct. Niel Gunson describes how

although full accounts were received from the field, these were often misinterpreted, and as all the matter for publication was carefully edited, a false picture was built up which careful study of the original documents would have dispelled. Popular missionary propaganda directed at obtaining funds and recruits drew upon the South Seas of the poets and romancers as much as upon the annals of the missionaries.[39]

This 'deceptive' nature of published evangelical texts did not go unnoticed by new missionaries when they experienced Polynesian life and found the distance between society propaganda and colonial reality extreme and disturbing. Reverend George Platt wrote to his former colleague Ellis in 1840:

What wicked men *you officers* must be to deceive simple young people, and trepan them (for it cannot *be us* who have done it) into a service to which their hearts have no sympathy. You make them believe they are going to heaven. But when they arrive, instead of heaven, they find black men and fiends, and barbarized Missionaries and even the devil himself not cast out...Alas poor Williams! It appears he was the arch deceiver...O that we could soon behold his like in the work; And as fully devoted.[40]

Platt's remarks illustrate the credulity of hero-worshipping LMS believers, and this particular narrative of disillusionment begins to explain why missionaries were so utterly confounded by the cultural difference they encountered. By the time they reached their allocated stations and realized the distance between the society's representations (which they read avidly as preparation) and colonial realities it was too late for these young men to develop a method of critical reading of missionary rhetoric.

Platt's letter also illuminates the extent to which the LMS used missionary testimonies as raw material for their own purposes, regardless of the authors' wishes. To be fair to John Williams, who stands accused by Platt's letter, he too criticised evangelical texts for their unrealistic 'good news':

It appears to me that a work from the pen of a Missionary should not contain just what might be written by one who has never left his native country, but a plain statement of the perplexities with which he has been compelled to grapple, and the means adopted to overcome them...Should his measures in some cases have been less prudent than might have been desired, he has nothing to fear from the scrutiny of wise and good men, who will consider the situation in which he was placed, and the necessity under which he was laid of devising and executing measures in novel circumstances. (137–8)

Williams' accusation that many missionary texts could have been written 'by one who has never left his native country' was an explicit criticism of the society's highhanded reconstitution of writings from the field. His commentary also reveals the high level of effectivity that evangelical texts were assumed to have. Reading such texts would prevent the repetition of practical mistakes, it would inculcate the self-critical awareness required of Protestant missionaries, and it would bring about useful, judicious scrutiny by 'wise and good men' in Britain or other colonies.

Missionaries in Polynesia did not remain ignorant of the strategic use of texts, as evidenced by the comments of Platt and Williams. Rather, they were uncomfortably aware of the mediated nature of textuality as well as of its potential political usefulness. In order to remain a viable part of the society and to demonstrate commitment to its overall project of 'Christianisation and civilisation', missionaries had to accept a complicit role within the economy of texts and discourses stipulated by the society. There are a number of important points here. Firstly, the evangelicals' intense intellectual and emotional investment in the Bible meant that they placed great importance on the potential of biblical interpretation to effect religious conversion and provide a blueprint for an exemplary Christian life. Secondly, however, in the linguistic and cultural translation of the Bible, evangelical missionaries learnt that the Christian message was not necessarily universal nor easily explicable to those of different cultural backgrounds. Instead, as Homi Bhabha suggests, 'the process of translation is the opening up of another contentious political and cultural site at the heart of colonial representation'.[41]

LANGUAGE AND TRANSLATION

...the peculiar colouring of the Fijian idiom[42]

The act of translation made possible a variety of different interpretations, multiple meanings that were fundamentally uncontainable. As Bhabha describes the experience of translating works into Indian languages,

The written authority of the Bible was challenged and together with it a postenlightenment notion of the 'evidence of Christianity' and its historical priority, which was central to evangelical colonialism. The Word could no longer be trusted to carry the truth when written or spoken in the colonial world of the European missionary. ('Commitment to Theory', 33–4)[43]

To some degree at least, this *textual* crisis actually embodied the cultural and spiritual dislocation experienced by many LMS missionaries. It is easy to be wryly amused by the number of missionaries who defected to native communities and formed relationships with Polynesian women, but we must acknowledge that these men underwent a profound spiritual crisis in order to do so. Whilst they might not have been well educated, their piety had to be strong to withstand the society's demanding selection and training processes. I would argue that, particularly for the first evangelists in Polynesia, the linguistic and textual crisis was an integral part of missionaries' confrontation with themselves and the assumptions and expectations of their (religious, middle-class) culture. Inadvertently, Herbert argues, missionary authors were 'engaged collectively in a project amounting to the invention of a new subjectivity, the basis of which appears to be an impulse to experience a state of radical instability of value – or even the instability of selfhood itself' (*Culture and Anomie*, 157). When the supporting texts of their doctrine were found untenable or inexplicable and communication was felt to be so limited and culturally laden, evangelical reformers were forced to reconsider their basic criteria of civility, Christianity, and humanity in the context of cross-cultural encounters. As Bhabha suggests, 'the hybrid tongues of the colonial space made even the repetition of the *name* of God uncanny'.[44] The close attention that missionary texts paid to language collecting, learning, cataloguing, and interpreting revealed their deep investment in linguistic projects as a measure of their success or failure.

Missionaries spent many of their early years in the islands attempting to learn and transcribe Polynesian languages because they believed that 'there can hardly be education...where the language of the people has never been written down'.[45] Linguistic work in Polynesia was quite different to that in India – Indian languages already existed in written forms, whereas Polynesian languages were primarily oral. The type of linguistic work required in both Polynesia and Australia was distinctive, and consequently it was represented very differently in missionary texts. Missionaries aimed to teach local people Christianity in their own languages, an aim that was moderately successful, but not without problems. Early LMS missionaries to Polynesia were not particularly well-educated – whilst their linguistic achievements were considerable given their lack of expertise, they had little experience and basically had to invent an appropriate system as they went along. On arrival in 1797, they had some prior knowledge of Polynesian languages, supplied, somewhat ironically, by the *Bounty* mutineers, but early missionary narratives of the Pacific always included a section detailing the linguistic work in progress.[46] The missionaries' inexperience left them vulnerable to criticism from European travellers as well as from interested parties 'back Home'. Ellis defended the LMS work, arguing that

The Missionaries have been charged with affectation in their orthography, &c. but so far from this, they have studied nothing with more attention than simplicity and perspicuity. The declaration and the pronunciation of the natives formed their only rule in fixing the spelling of proper names, as well as other parts of the language.[47]

Ellis' emphasis on these issues demonstrates again that representation, language, and textuality were at the forefront of the missionaries' evaluation of their work in Polynesia. As Rod Edmond notes, 'a missionary's status, among both his own kind and the native population, depended heavily on his fluency in the local language' (*Representing the South Pacific*, 117).

Early LMS missionaries were often profoundly surprised at both the complexity of Polynesian languages and the difficulties experienced in learning them. Gunson notes that the directors' attempts to provide prior information to Polynesian-bound missionaries were well-intentioned but flawed and Reverend Samuel Greatheed's notes towards a 'Polynesian Grammar', which formed the primary linguistic preparation for the LMS missionaries before they left for the mission field, were 'naïve' (111–12). One suspects that missionaries had been encouraged to believe native language acquisition would be virtually effortless. By contrast, their narratives continually attest to the complexity of the languages and the trials of learning them. Tyerman and Bennet, travelling around the Pacific LMS stations in 1821–9 (after a considerable amount of LMS experience in the area), repeatedly note the sophistication of local languages. They write that 'the Tahitian tongue lacks neither nerve nor copiousness; nor are opportunities wanting to display all its excellencies on glorious themes and great occasions – as in courts of justice, national and religious assemblies, but especially on Missionary anniversaries'.[48] Elsewhere they admit their own linguistic difficulties:

We are daily learning for ourselves, from the lips of the natives, words and phrases of the language ... we often rehearse before our teachers of this class, who, sometimes seated in a circle about us, for hours together, exercise all their ingenuity and patience too, in giving us instructions, especially in the pronunciation, which is most difficult to catch, and delicate to use, there being a nicety and refinement in this, which our British friends would hardly believe could exist in a language of uncivilised men. (1: 85)

Herbert suggests that the missionaries' gradual recognition of the complexity and sophistication of Polynesian languages was highly significant, for at this point they realised that such languages were '*just like English*, equipped with a full range of expressive nuance and affective potency, and so perfectly attuned to the consciousness of native speakers that it seems almost to bring that consciousness into being'. He rightly queries: 'Given all this, how could an earnest British missionary fail to be at least subliminally aware that his deep immersion in Polynesian language tended to implicate him willy nilly in the whole vile array of "savage" things that he condemned?' (*Culture and Anomie*, 187). Language learning thus brought about a crisis in European self-confidence, and could threaten the previously impermeable boundaries between the missionary self and the heathen other.

Polynesian teachers, translators, and informants were always present in missionary accounts of language learning, though narrators continually attempt to discredit and downplay Polynesian agency. The following extracts from Ellis' *Polynesian Researches* demonstrate his ethnographic blindness when discussing Polynesians and Europeans learning each others' language. He condemns Taïtians for acquiring English phrases from Europeans, which

they apply almost indiscriminately, supposing they are thereby better understood, than they would be if they used only native words; yet these words are so changed in a native's mouth ... that no Englishman would recognize them as his own, but would write them down as native words ... It was not in words only, but also in their application, that the most ludicrous mistakes were made by the people. (1: 72)

Within a page of this comment, however, Ellis acknowledges the incompetence of European attempts to make themselves 'better understood' by using native words, and the tolerant education that Polynesians provided:

Although among themselves accustomed to hear critically, and to ridicule with great effect, any of their own countrymen who should use a wrong word, mispronounce or place the accent erroneously on the one they used, yet they seldom laughed at the mistakes of the newly arrived residents. They endeavoured to correct them in the most friendly manner, and were evidently desirous that the foreigners should be able to understand their language, and convey their own ideas to them with distinctness and perspicuity. (1: 73)

A kind of double-speak is evident at this site where, to borrow Bhabha's phrase, the 'discourse of post-Enlightenment colonialism ... speaks in a tongue that is forked, not false'.[49] These two narratives describe intrinsically similar events, but the predetermined nature of missionary discourses (and attitudes) ensured that each incident was read (and thus narrated) differently. Ellis' conclusion remains that indigenous people corrupt the English language by making it sound 'native', whilst European interlocutors could achieve a 'distinctness and perspicuity'. But as Herbert argues, Ellis placed considerable emphasis on language as a marker of native culture, eventually seeing it as 'a model for the representation of the whole range of social phenomena' (*Culture and Anomie*, 188). Europeans may well be able to achieve 'distinctness and perspicuity', but what are the consequences of doing so? Herbert suggests that using Polynesian language, and hence entering the culture's symbolic and material order, 'could not fail to throw in doubt the mythological premise that Polynesian life was based almost exclusively on "the gratification of monstrous lust," and to bring home to them the principle that even these licentious savages inhabited first and foremost a world of *meanings* and of articulated symbolic systems'. In learning language, missionaries discovered 'not at all the pandemonium of "unrestrained indulgence and excess" but symmetry, refinement, and flawless order. This discovery seems to have altered their perception of Polynesian life in a fundamental way, though the alteration was in good measure unconscious and never caused them to abandon the rhetoric of "unbridled passions" ' (185).

Language and its acquisition were complex and fraught issues for LMS missionaries in Polynesia. Apart from the practical difficulties they experienced learning local dialects, missionary accounts of language learning reverberate with the anxieties of cultural outsiders. Missionaries were often amazed by indigenous peoples' linguistic ability, particularly in the area of oral learning. Tyerman and Bennet's *Journal* notes that

it is surprising... with what diligence they commit to memory numerous chapters and whole gospels which have been rendered into their mother tongue. Some who cannot read themselves can repeat almost every text which they ever heard, and even large portions of the New Testament, which they have learned by hearkening to others, while these read aloud to little audiences which they sometimes collect in the open air, under a tree, or in their family circles. (1: 341)

This kind of bemused appreciation for Polynesian linguistic skills was quite common. In most texts, as here, the appreciation was tempered with scepticism and suspicion. That is, specifically, a scepticism that Polynesians were only learning the words, rather than the meaning, of the Christian message (that they were mimicking without understanding); and a suspicion that there were systems of Polynesian communication and educational networks which were beyond missionary control.

A European-style school system attempted to counteract these indigenous systems of language and information diffusion, though missionaries seem to be always aware that knowledge was being dispersed in different ways and for different purposes from those intended. LMS evangelists often report the desire of Polynesians for education and an awareness of its potential empowerment. Tyerman and Bennet write of an encounter with one of the Matavai (Taïti) chiefs on a day of baptism, where Upaparu 'addressed Mr Bourne in a very improper spirit, rudely demanding, "What are you teaching us? And why do you not instruct us in English, and other things besides religion?" ' (*Journal*, 1: 165). From reports like this it becomes evident that education was valued by local communities for their own purposes, and that they resented the narrowly evangelical curriculum endorsed by missionary educators.

Frequently, evangelists worried that their native informants were laughing at them, or misleading them, or not quite telling them the truth, or that perhaps they were actually using language to evade missionary intervention. Reverend Murray discussed the Samoan response to an early evangelical address:

Generally the address to us was couched in as soft and complimentary language as possible, but it was none the less decided on that account; though, till we became acquainted with Samoan politeness, we were apt to be misled by the first part of the speech, and fancy that we were about to gain our point. Sometimes we had almost a blunt refusal, but generally it was softened.[50]

Missionaries such as Murray were continually troubled by the fact that Polynesian people seemed to be saying one thing and meaning another. Frequently, they appeared to profess acceptance of Christian messages but then acted counter to them. At the same time, LMS missionaries expressed concerns about how local communities were adopting Christian teachings. As Steven Kaplan argues, 'translation of the Scriptures into local languages both created new questions of interpretation and placed the texts firmly in the hands of the local population'.[51] Converts from Mangaia, one of the large islands of the southern Cook group, were called *kai-parua* (bookeaters) because of the time they spent studying the word of God. Savage noted that the phrase meant 'literally ... to eat the words of instruction: denotes to receive religious instruction. A word introduced by the early missionaries from the Tahitian language'.[52] It is possible to see in these early missionary narratives the roots of strong, contemporary Pacific churches, as well as the millennial movements and cargo cults which came to characterise evangelised Pacific cultures.

Missionaries were also disconcerted by what they saw as the corruption of white children, in particular, by Polynesian languages. Tyerman and Bennet report discussions with missionaries regarding concerns they had about their children and their desire to protect them

from the moral contamination to which they are liable from their inevitable exposure to the society (occasionally at least) of native children of their own age, whose language they understand, and whose filthy talk they cannot but hear at times. The abominable conversation (if such it may be called) of infants as soon as they begin to lisp out words, is such a jargon of grossness and obscenity as could not be imagined by persons brought up even in those manufacturing towns of our country where manners are the most depraved. (*Journal*, 1: 465)

Missionaries believed language played a crucial role in maintaining and monitoring cultural values and integrity. The English language was seen to possess a kind of microcosmic essence of Britishness, characterised by Christianity and civility. As noted earlier in discussions of Ellis' bifurcated view of cross-cultural linguistic work, Polynesians were believed to contaminate English through their adaptations of it. In turn, European speakers could be corrupted by their adoption of indigenous languages, particularly the most 'vulnerable' representatives of the imperial race, white children. The image of the linguistically threatened missionary child manifests the central concern of LMS missionaries in Polynesia – that the European self, in its attempts to introduce the arts of Christianity and civility, would lose these virtues because of the contaminating colonial environment and contact with colonised 'others'. Language stood metaphorically for the transforming potential of many other cultural indicators, as evidenced by its centrality in their own attempts to produce cultural transformation in Polynesians.

It becomes obvious that the often over-wrought missionary insistence on depraved heathen customs carried a heavy load of Eurocentric fear of self-oblivion. When evangelists saw their children being profoundly transformed by their new, colonial environment in areas such as language, their reaction highlights the extent to which missionaries felt the need to resist categorically the *difference* of cross-cultural interactions. Herbert notes that 'hearing the language of cannibals issuing at last from their own lips, and even becoming, as John Williams declared, more familiar to them than their own native tongue' promised an existential and philosophical crisis for the missionaries (*Culture and Anomie*, 187), but the crisis intensified when the lips forming that language were those of a child. The figure of the threatened missionary child was a highly emotive and significant one, given the LMS investment in images of the Protestant nuclear family. Williams told an endearing, but ambiguous, story of the death of yet another of his children[53] which also demonstrated the fear of contamination of missionary children by Polynesian languages:

Just before the lid of the little coffin was fastened down, all assembled to take a last look, when our feelings were much excited by an expression of our then youngest child, who at that time was about five years of age. *Thinking in the native language, and speaking in English*, after looking intensely at the beauteous form of the lifeless babe, he burst into tears, and, in accents of sweet simplicity, cried out, 'Father, mother, why do you plant my little brother? don't plant him, I cannot bear to have him planted.' (400–1, emphasis added)

Williams' micro-narrative is highly suggestive of the profound challenge posed to European selfhood in Polynesia, which, as Herbert suggests, prefigures the modernist crisis of the self familiar from early twentieth-century literature. The image of a child thinking in indigenous language and having to translate concepts back into English foregrounds the way in which missionaries saw linguistic issues as crucial to the integrity of the European self. Indeed, it appears as if the child has been 'planted' from inside with native thoughts. This is one of those key points in missionary texts where we can see the 'almost hallucinatory crisis' of Europeans becoming aware that 'by becoming immersed in Polynesian culture as the missionaries' ethnographic code requires, and by relaxing one's grip on absolutist moral principles, one risks actually becoming infected with savagery one's self'.[54] If imperial policies of teaching natives English sought to inculcate a particular type of docile, civilised subjectivity, in the colonies missionaries learnt that acquisition of native languages might in turn alter their own subjectivity. Language, then, is a nodal point of mutual imbrication at the most personal, subjective level. Linguistic exchange threatens to destabilise foundational assumptions about selfhood and cultural integrity.

Williams' description of the 'planting' of another generation of missionary children in foreign, colonial soil metaphorises the ways in which missionaries were required to sacrifice themselves (and their families) to the work of colonial evangelisation. Margaret Atwood's poetic re-imaging of the journals of Canadian immigrant Susanna Moodie uses a similar image of settler children's deaths cementing their parents' commitment to the new colonial environment. Atwood suggests that interring European children in colonial soil creates a new 'archaeology' of colonial relations – one about which settler subjects were profoundly ambivalent. She imagines Moodie's response to her son's death by drowning: 'I planted him in this country / like a flag', a dead child who could 'set forth / on a voyage of discovery / into the land I floated on / but could not touch to claim.'[55] In Atwood's depiction, white children, because of their burial in colonial ground, partially resolve the troubled nature of settler identifications with and against the colonial environment in ways inaccessible to their parents, except through their grief and subsequent memorialisation of land in which white history has been interred.

The LMS experience with Polynesian cultures and peoples was characterised by a profound sense of unease at cross-cultural interactions. This unease was most explicitly at play at crucial points of *cultural permeability* – bodies, sexuality, language, and the family. It is at sites of encounter located between imperial philosophies and practices relevant to the maintenance of civility and modernity (such as manners, sexual mores, and verbal and textual interactions) and the (necessarily *different*) colonial enactment of these that the fissures in missionary texts are most evident. These are the themes which missionaries obviously struggle to recast within pre-existing imperial, evangelical discourses. The next chapter examines the ways in which missionary texts repeatedly mobilised images and narratives around three cultural issues – sexuality, clothing, and families – in order to describe and define their Christian encounters and reforms. In doing so, these texts reveal ways in which issues of gender and the mutual imbrication of colonial and domestic representations revolved around such negotiations between colonising and colonised communities.

CHAPTER SEVEN

Missionary writing in Polynesia

...that interesting class of any truthful narrative, however imperfect, of the trials and triumphs of Christian missionaries in Polynesia[1]

Truthful but imperfect narratives of missionary enterprises in Polynesia proliferated in the nineteenth century. This chapter looks closely at such texts, with rather more interest in their imperfections than in their truthfulness, specifically identifying key tropes within missionary writing. A variety of texts are analysed here, including the LMS 'Reports', but the two main publications from which I draw evidence of gender and cultural interactions are Daniel Tyerman and George Bennet's *Journal* (1831) and John Williams' *Missionary Enterprises* (1837). Before I discuss specific modes of missionary representation in Polynesia, however, I need to address issues of context, authorship, and structure in these textual interventions into Pacific cultures.

Tyerman and Bennet were engaged by the LMS in order to undertake a deputation to their mission stations 'in the South Sea Islands, China, India &c. between the years 1821 and 1829'. Daniel Tyerman was a clergyman associated with the LMS and George Bennet was a Sheffield businessman – their joint appointment exemplified the LMS home constituency of religious middle-class business-men.[2] The compiler of their *Journal* stated that they were engaged for the purposes of 'cheering the hearts and strengthening the hands of the Missionaries and, as representatives of the Christian community at home, to witness and report what great things the Lord had done for the heathen there'.[3] This was partly true, though in a broader, more politicised sense, the members of the deputation were sent as mediators and trouble-shooters for the society. The unsuccessful nature of the first Polynesian LMS missions, and the controversies which haunted them on issues such as commerce and trade, sexuality, and local politics, had created significant tensions between missionaries in the field and their directors. Tyerman and Bennet were appointed to investigate the state of

136

LMS missions and to assure missionaries that their work was valued by the society. The directors' circular required them

to suggest, and, if possible, carry into effect, such plans as shall appear to be requisite for the furtherance of the gospel, and for introducing among the natives the occupations and habits of civilized life. In order to [achieve] the attainment of these objects, it is proposed to form such arrangements as shall tend to the introduction of Christian Churches; the establishment and improvement of schools for the children of the Missionaries and of the natives, and, eventually, of trades; and a proper and constant attention to the cultivation of the ground.[4]

The many and diverse roles of the deputation – promoters of the success of Polynesian missions, informers for the directors, and soothers of the frayed tempers of LMS missionaries – ensured that it continually attempted to balance the often incompatible aspects of its tasks. As with many such compromised missionary ventures, this almost guaranteed that they would fulfil only part of their multiple charter and that they would inevitably be criticised for doing so. As Niel Gunson notes, Tyerman and Bennet 'were able to see for themselves some of the weak points of the missions, but their reports were written principally to boost the work of the missionaries, and little practical benefit – on a major policy level – seems to have been derived from this visitation'.[5] On a textual and historical level, however, the deputation's *Journal* of its voyages around the LMS Polynesian missions is intriguing. As relative outsiders schooled in the rhetoric pertaining to the early years of the LMS, the deputation's representations of Polynesian people and British missionaries are fascinating because they comment on the missionary figures who generally remain somewhat hidden behind their own texts. The deputation also represent themselves as explorers of the new 'contact zone'[6] of the Pacific. The loyal LMS constituents were encouraged to take a keen interest in the deputation's writings – the majority of LMS 'Reports' about the Pacific in the period 1822 to 1825 were dominated by edited versions of the deputation's reports back to the directors.

The textual 'authenticity' of the *Journal*, however, is compromised, due to both the contested nature of the deputation's experiences and the fact that the two-volume publication which emerged from their voyages was produced by neither of the travellers. Tyerman and Bennet seem to have had real difficulties working together from the very outset. As Gunson suggests, 'the ineffectualness of the "Deputation" was further highlighted by their own personal quarrels and disagreement over policy matters and the fact that Tyerman died on the way back to London' (*Messengers of Grace*, 124). Reverend Lancelot Threlkeld was one of the few (ex) Pacific missionaries prepared to discuss the dispute publicly,[7] and he complained of 'the difficulty of bringing the Deputation to act in concert, owing to the unhappy quarrel betwixt them...A Quarrel began by G. Bennett [*sic*] Esqr on their embarkation from England, continued through the voyage, rendered them unhappy in the Islands and ridiculed in this Colony.'[8] Threlkeld was always motivated by personal and/or political agendas – here he attempts to explain his heavy expenses in Sydney, later claimed from the society – but it is undeniable that Tyerman and Bennet were barely speaking to each other by the time they were in Sydney. Tyerman then died on the voyage home – when visiting LMS stations in Madagascar – and Bennet arrived back in England alone in 1829.

The text of their *Journal*, published in 1831, was compiled by James Montgomery from the joint journal of the deputation, in addition to Tyerman's private journal and Bennet's 'several interesting narratives and other valuable contributions' (1: vii). Because of the large amount of material available to him, Montgomery decided not to abridge or condense pre-existing sources, but 'to recompose the whole, in such a form as should enable him to bring forth...the most striking and curious facts relative to their personal adventures, or which came to their knowledge by the way'. Montgomery thus acts as amanuensis to his missionary sources, slipping into their subject positions:

He has, therefore, trod step by step after them, confining himself, as faithfully as practicable, to the order of subjects, under the original dates, after exercising his best discretion in the use of his materials, chiefly consisting of memoranda, generally rough and unshapen – the first thoughts, in the first words of the writers, at the time, and upon the spot, recording the actual impressions and feelings awakened or confirmed by the things themselves. (1: viii)

Montgomery was a minor, but prolific, nineteenth-century British poet and a close friend of Bennet. He addressed a long poem to the deputation when it left England,[9] and worked closely with Bennet editing the *Journal*. He was thus neither a distanced nor disinterested editor, and his representation of the deputation's voyage was carefully constructed. Nothing of the dispute between the deputation members entered Montgomery's version, because it is unlikely that Bennet wanted his high-handed behaviour publicised.

The *Journal* addressed other intertextual connections as part of its subject matter. In part, it was a reply to (and criticism of) a narrative published by Captain Kotzebue, a Russian voyager to the Pacific who, following his travels in the region, published a damning indictment of missionary intervention. Kotzebue claimed to be at Taïti when the deputation was there, though the *Journal* cast doubt upon his authority to comment, stating that he chose to assert 'as historical facts things which never happened under the sun, and to express sentiments, concerning the Missionaries and their converts, which no man could entertain who was not under strong prejudice, if not actual delusion' (1: x). The *Journal* also addresses, cites, or broadly incorporates other textual material. Appropriate religious poems are quoted, scientific descriptions of flora and fauna are given, whaling yarns and experiences are relayed, and prurient European accounts of the 'notorious' Polynesian 'lewdness' (1: 326) are condemned (though for their prurience rather than their content). The *Journal* is an intriguing narrative because it does not appear to be concerned by its lack of a single voice of authority (whereas many other LMS narratives continually assert such authority in response to perceived criticism) and because of its intertextual engagement with other writing of the time about the region.

John Williams' *Missionary Enterprises* is a text manifesting far greater degrees of internal coherence and authorial control than the deputation's *Journal*. Williams appears to have retained editorial control of his book and its central narrative voice is singular and controlled. His narrative aims at an encyclopaedic overview of a vast amount of information and experience collected since his posting to Polynesia in 1817. It makes an intriguing comparison with Ellis' *Polynesian Researches*, for both attempt similar projects, though, as Rod Edmond has argued, in significantly different ways.[10]

Williams' *Missionary Enterprises* was published in 1837 when Williams and his family were back in Britain, undertaking extensive lecture tours, meeting with interested supporters of missionary endeavours, and engaging in fund-raising projects. Rod Edmond rightly notes that the book 'aimed to sell the South Seas mission at home... [It] contained a number of direct addresses to the British reading public and ended with an appeal to the sons of noblemen to value missionary above military valour and become "soldiers of the cross" themselves.'[11] Williams was always a keen self-promoter as well as an effective salesman for evangelical work, and his success in Britain meant that Polynesian missions received additional interest and support.

Williams, like Montgomery, was keen to emphasise the specific structure and organisation of his text. For Williams, this is explicit in his description of the difficulties of condensing his experiences into a mere 590 pages. In Williams' favour, he did produce only one volume. Conciseness did not come easily to missionary writers and both Ellis and Tyerman and Bennet (or Montgomery) felt they required two lengthy volumes to convey their experiences. Williams instead emphasises the sheer amount of material he was forced to select from. He emphasises his experience as a 'witness', and seeks to convey the voices of Polynesians by preserving the dialogues, noting that he

has not spoken for the natives, but allowed them to speak for themselves. In doing this, he has carefully avoided the use of terms and phrases which are current among nations more advanced in the scale of intelligence and civilization, and the employment of which might lead the reader to form a higher estimate of the state of society in the South Sea Islands than facts would warrant; and he has been equally careful to convey native ideas in the phraseology and under the figurative garb in which they were expressed.[12]

Unlike the *Journal*, Williams' text stridently asserts its authoritative status. His emphasis on 'witnessing' attempts to preempt criticism about trite missionary discourses by inserting himself as the central observing eye.

Williams claims to let his native informants 'speak for themselves', a clear recognition of the complexities of gathering information about colonial subjects. Prefiguring the concerns of postcolonial theory over the right to speak for 'others', he strives for authenticity and authority in his narrative, characterising his study of heathen cultures as intimate and exhaustive. The text is validated both by the presence of the 'unmediated' voice of the native heathen, and by the ethnographic thoroughness of the European field worker. As Edmond notes in *Representing the South Pacific* of the use of dialogue in Ellis' *Polynesian Researches*, such claims for unmediated reportage are highly dubious: 'Ellis casts this in direct speech as if he is reporting verbatim. This is a common device, particularly in missionary accounts of the Pacific, designed to render the text authentic and allow the writer to put some unlikely-sounding speeches into the mouths of native informants' (43). Christopher Herbert reads this moment in *Missionary Enterprises* somewhat differently, arguing that 'This rule, again unpacked, can mean only one thing: that cultural meanings are to a significant degree untranslatable, expressible only in the semiological system in which they originate.'[13] Either way, Williams clearly regarded authority as a key part of his narrative.

Williams was very conscious of his reading audience. The seventh edition of *Missionary Enterprises* (from which I quote) notes that its revisions had taken account of earlier reviewers and critics (xii), and he states his goals as having 'aimed at nothing beyond furnishing a simple and unadorned narrative of the facts' (xi). *Missionary Enterprises* is nothing of the kind. It is a highly constructed, ideologically and politically conscious text seeking to inculcate certain attitudes towards LMS evangelising in the Pacific. As Edmond argues, this text had many different purposes: it was a 'campaigning work directly aimed at a missionary-supporting readership . . . a conversion narrative recording his energetic pursuit of lost souls across the Pacific . . . a kind of business report . . . [and] a providential narrative' (*Representing the South Pacific*, 114–15).

Herbert notes that 'Polynesian depravity expressed itself for British observers in such customs as cannibalism and systematic infanticide, but especially in the natives' promiscuous, glaringly dramatized sexual life and in their proneness to outbreaks of sadistic violence' (*Culture and Anomie*, 160). Here I want to unpack the arena of sexuality, by breaking it into three indicative spheres of gendered missionary intervention: sexuality, clothing, and the family. In doing so, I want to return questions of gender to the foreground, a place it occupied for nineteenth-century observers. Across a range of missionary texts, authors structured their writing around these themes both in terms of narrative content and evangelical, reformist metaphors. Such intense missionary attention to these critical issues brings into focus the specific textual negotiations of gender and mutual imbrication in Polynesian contexts.

SEX IN THE PACIFIC

. . . earthly, sensual, devils[14]

The vision of a sexualised Pacific was typically gendered female; as a consequence, homosocial masculinity also preoccupied missionaries' moral judgments. As Edmond argues,

gender was one of the most obvious and telling means of fixing the differences between Europeans and others. There is a long tradition of representing primitive cultures as feminine and child-like, with civilization as masculine and patriarchal. In . . . the Romantic tradition of South Pacific representation, Polynesian culture is coded feminine in quite particular ways. It is a culture of the body, of bathing and oiling and languid ease. The female Polynesian body becomes synonymous with a coral island paradise. (*Representing the South Pacific*, 74)

Most LMS missionaries were intensely disconcerted by Polynesian acceptance of female sexual curiosity and desire. William Pascoe Crook and Thomas Harris were the last of the *Duff* party to be deposited at their appointed mission in the Marquesas. After promising preliminary communications with islanders, the two missionaries spent their first night ashore and the local chief took Crook inland 'telling his wife to look after the remaining missionary'.[15] Graeme Kent's *Company of Heaven*, a twentieth-century history of South Pacific missionaries, continues the titillating narrative of his nineteenth-century forebears:

Unfortunately for Harris the chief's wife had put an over-generous interpretation on her husband's parting remark, and the scandalised missionary finally had to reject the woman's overtures. She had gone off in a huff, leaving Harris to sleep on the floor. But brooding on his brusque dismissal the woman had begun to entertain doubts as to his sex, and accompanied by other women of the village she had swooped on the sleeping man and conducted a practical examination in order to clear up the matter. (33)[16]

Missionaries like Harris, then, apparently encountered the (in)famous difference in sexual roles and freedom from their very first encounters with local inhabitants.

Historical accounts such as Kent's, which carry unmistakeable traces of earlier nineteenth-century narratives, mask and distort the possible meaning of such events within Polynesian communities. As Edmond suggests of Taïtians and Marquesans who swam out to meet with European ships and their crews, 'these counter-explorers were often native women who sometimes extended this tensile zone of contact much further by travelling on the strangers' ships to other islands' (*Representing the South Pacific*, 13). Eighteenth- and nineteenth-century missionaries read such experiences as signifying the utter degradation of social and sexual relations in Polynesia, confirming their expectations and fears. Nor was Harris' the only sexual drama of the first LMS group. During the first six months of the Taïtian mission, two single missionaries went to live in an adjoining valley, a few miles from the mission base. The remaining brethren were concerned, believing that the men were placing themselves in the way of temptation, and threatened to cut off supplies if the renegades did not return. Soon after they returned, one applied to marry a Taïtian woman – a serious issue for the brethren to consider and judge of the propriety of the matter. This first affair was treated leniently; but when another missionary applied similarly, he was told not to return to the main settlement at Matavai Bay and his supporters were ostracised.[17] Thus from the very first Polynesian mission, local women and social and sexual practices divided and challenged missionary expectations and experiences.

First encounters were often characterised by intimate exploration and missionary accounts foregrounded such interactions, as the account of Thomas Harris and Marquesan women illustrates. John and Jean Comaroff note this physical tendency of cross-cultural encounters, particularly relating to indigenous explorations of the European body. Encounters such as Harris' constituted a kind of playfulness across lines of gender and race that the politics of colonial hierarchy soon forbade,[18] even though such bodily curiosity recurred throughout early exploration narratives of the Pacific. Williams narrates an encounter with Samoan islanders at Savai'i, where the expatriated Christian convert Fauea introduced European visitors and their religion. Williams describes Fauea extolling the virtues of European superiority to the Samoans, specifically as it was revealed by their clothing. Williams writes:

Some of them then began to examine the different parts of our dress, when, not meeting with any repulse, one pulled off my shoe. Startled at the appearance of the foot with the stocking on, he whispered to Fauea, 'What extraordinary people these papalangis are; they have no toes as we have!' 'Oh!' said our facetious friend, 'did I not tell you that they had clothes upon their feet? feel them, and you will find out they have toes as well as ourselves'... All of them came round us, and in a moment the other shoe was off, and both my own feet, and those of my excellent brother underwent a thorough examination. (330)

As the Comaroffs argue, such bodily intimacy was only ever sanctioned at the originary moment, as it countered the later 'etiquette of the mission, with its deference to racial separation and the spatial discreteness of person and property'.[19]

Missionaries were also confronted by Taïtian acceptance of male homosexuality and repeatedly demonstrate a horrified interest in the role of *mahus*. Certain Taïtian men, *mahus*, played a transvestite role in which they dressed and behaved like women.[20] Pomare II, the young successor to the Taïtian throne during the initial LMS residence, was known to have his own *mahu*, increasing missionary dislike of him; they were already uncertain about his commitment to Christian principles and concerned that he would continue his father's resistance to Christian conversion. The added immorality of the son's *mahu* consolidated missionaries' lack of support for the new ruler.[21] Transvestite or homosexual masculinities were far from the muscular Christianity revered by missionaries, and such sexual and gender confusions seemed to them to exemplify the degraded, heathen nature of both Pomare II and Taïtian culture in general. It also represented additional evidence of what missionaries regarded as the overly 'feminised' nature of Polynesian culture.

Eighteenth- and nineteenth-century accounts were naturally reticent about discussing such scandalous issues, but coded representations of

Pomare II and his 'decadence' recurred in missionary narratives. Even contemporary accounts perpetuate snide, homophobic representations (and denigration) of Pomare II and other Taïtian men.[22] For evangelical reformers and their contemporary apologists, LMS missionaries had not only to teach Polynesian women how to be real, Christian women (that is, submissive, domestic, and appropriately focussed on their children) but also to teach Polynesian men to be real, Christian men (that is, monogamous, heterosexual, and authoritative heads of nuclear families). Most importantly, they felt the need to institute strict binary definitions of bifurcated gender roles: *mahus* were particularly disturbing to missionary attempts to categorise colonial cultures because they elided such differentiation.

The physical appeal of Polynesian people both repelled missionaries and attracted their attention. Exploration narratives conditioned Europeans to anticipate the allure of islanders[23] and missionary narratives of Polynesia continue this fetishisation of native bodies. Surprisingly, considering the homophobic *mahu* representations, men's bodies are almost equally admired as female Polynesian bodies by some missionary observers. John Williams describes the king of Rarotonga thus:

The king, whose name is Makea, is a handsome man, in the prime of life, about six feet high, and very stout; of noble appearance, and of truly commanding aspect. He is of a light complexion; his body is most beautifully tattooed, and was slightly coloured with a preparation of turmeric and ginger, which gave it a light orange tinge, and, in the estimation of the Rarotongans, added much to the beauty of his appearance. (101)

Women, too, were described in terms of their physical attractiveness:

Malietoa sent two of his own daughters to spread mats for us to sit upon. They were fine looking young women, about eighteen and twenty years of age, wearing a beautiful mat about the waist, a wreath of flowers as a head-dress, and a string of blue beads around the neck. The upper part of their person was uncovered, and anointed rather profusely with scented cocoa-nut oil. (344)

Overall, Williams described 'copper-coloured Polynesians' (i.e. of eastern Polynesia) as 'amongst the finest specimens of the human family...the form of many of the [Polynesian men] exhibits all that is perfect in proportion, and exquisite in symmetry...The women are inferior to the men; but yet they often present the most elegant models of the human figure' (514).[24]

Williams' admiring attention to both male and female Polynesian bodies was perhaps unusually even-handed and explicit. Given the predominantly heterosexual, male European observers in the area at this time, female bodies tended to attract the most admiring attention, though eighteenth-century images of noble savages ensured that some attention was paid to the physique of warrior-like men in texts of cross-cultural interactions.[25] The usually unclothed (or semi-clothed) female Polynesian body dominates missionary accounts as it did those of explorers and mariners, but missionaries usually aimed to cover up such 'states of nature'. As Lee Watts argues, Taïtian sexual practices

confronted the missionaries daily. They responded by rigidifying their rules of moral conduct as if they were guarantees of God's sacred power and protection. Those who were seen to deviate from these rules, be they missionary or Taïtian, were set apart from God's grace. The rules that the community invoked against transgressors both created and reinforced this moral order. ('Tahiti', 78)

Missionaries also could not countenance Polynesian women's social and sexual liberation. In different islands, different cultural practices attracted missionary condemnation. In Hawaii, they set out to reform women's 'idleness'; in Hawaii and the Marquesas, the power of women and particularly high-ranking women; and in the Marquesas, polyandry (which represented both female power and female sexual appetite).[26] Throughout Polynesia the pleasures of sexuality and procreation had to give way to Christian restraint and repression, and indigenous restrictions on sexuality and eating (*tapu*) were opposed by missionaries keen to effect Christian reform. As Margaret Jolly and Martha Macintyre explain, 'throughout the Pacific Christian missions took exception to the indigenous position of women and saw Christianity as improving their lot. Without exception these fine intentions were confounded by misunderstandings of the ancestral religion and by the patriarchal patterns of Christianity itself' (12).

Missionary wives in Polynesia, as in India and Australia, played important roles in religious conversion (particularly of women) and in maintaining the missionary household and community as a 'threshold institution'.[27] The *Duff* party left all five of its married members and their wives on Taïti, whilst the ten unmarried missionaries were left on Tonga and the Marquesas.[28] The presence of missionary wives in this first party certainly intensified missionaries' sense of vulnerability to violence and social unrest, and evangelical writers at home manipulated the image of endangered European women. Horne's polemical history of the LMS, for instance, continually invokes the trope of sacrificial, but brave, missionary women. He writes a seemingly endless eulogy that begins with the demise of Mrs Eyre and then laments the deaths of Mrs Henry, Mrs Davis, and Mrs Hayward.[29]

In official records, however, the society displayed little interest in missionary wives, except in their roles as 'helpmeets'. As Watts argues, 'the much discussed temptations that the Taïtian women posed to missionary men contrasted strongly with the silence surrounding the European wives. The Elysian myth, after all, was a male story, a projection of the male European imagination – in it, European women had no place.' In July 1801, though, when the second LMS party arrived in Polynesia, the existing group drew up guidelines for the newcomers, stipulating more missionaries in each mission station, and for the majority of them to be married ('Tahiti', 61, 69).

Missionary emphasis on transforming Polynesian sexuality and women's roles should not be seen as resulting solely from the European vision of the Pacific as a sexual utopia. As Sylvia Marcus notes of a very different group of missionaries, missionary enquirers also *produced* an excessive emphasis on native sexuality given the importance that their own religious consciences placed on it. Marcus discusses Catholic confession manuals used in colonial Spanish Mexico in the sixteenth and seventeenth centuries. She argues that the reliance in these manuals upon questions about sexuality (across manuals, 63 to 69 per cent of questions refer to sex) distorts real or probable indigenous responses: 'Such preoccupation with the sixth commandment, only one of ten, gives the appearance of an uncommon, obsessive interest on the part of the confessors and/or of the institutions whose beliefs they represented.'[30] Whilst the LMS practices did not resemble the formality of Catholic confession, they nevertheless relied heavily on native informants and interpreters to explain cultural practices. In particular, they depended on native Christian converts, who, like the newly Catholic Mexicans, had a vested interest in painting the blackness of heathen practices against their own (newly found) Christian purity.

In addition, the perceived moral degradation of Polynesian women facilitated the need for colonial missionary projects. Polynesian women could not be unproblematically represented as 'innocent victims' of native patriarchy as Indian women had been by early LMS personnel, because of their obvious assertiveness and power. As Felicity Nussbaum argues, establishing the native woman as sexually excessive was 'formative in imagining that a sexualized woman of empire was distinct from domestic English womanhood'.[31] European ideas based in natural histories about climatic variation and its effects on races, which portrayed warm climates as causing increased sexual activity, figured women's bodies as 'torrid zones' (8). Missionaries thus confirmed the sexual 'torridness' of tropical Polynesia, while simultaneously needing to prove that evangelical Protestantism could control such 'uncivilised', unChristian excess.

CLOTHING IN THE PACIFIC

...all of them, even to the lowest, aspired to the possession of a gown, a bonnet, and a shawl, that they might appear like Christian women[32]

The missionary obsession with sexuality and their attempts to construct nuclear, Christian families in Polynesian cultures resulted in concerted efforts to clothe islanders in ways replicating British evangelical fashion. Missionaries in the Pacific are justly (in)famous for their attempts to clothe indigenous populations. The stereotypical missionary figure in fiction, film, and television is represented as being inevitably obsessed with both exploring and controlling islanders' bodies, either exploiting Pacific sexualities or exposing their sinfulness. This section explores the missionaries' own nineteenth-century obsession with bodies and sexuality, concentrating on their representation of one item of European apparel which brought together gender and mutual imbrication – the bonnet.

LMS missionaries to Polynesia were profoundly interested in promoting civilised behaviour and dress reform became one of a constellation of methods for promoting such change. Modesty was a crucial component in the evangelical ideal of womanhood, and the missionaries' encouragement of bonnet-wearing became a crucial part of gender re-education. Margaret Maynard suggests that dress is a disturbing topic because of its relation to intimacy, physical bodies, and sexuality, and that questions of dress can be located within a number of current discourses, including those of 'beauty, sexuality, class, ethnicity, and economics'.[33] Nineteenth-century missionary narratives about bonnets in Polynesia address all these issues. On arrival in Polynesia, missionaries encouraged islanders to adopt European dress, tying issues of clothing to issues of Christian conversion. The 'Mother Hubbard', a loose-fitting smock for women still evident in contemporary Pacific cultures, was arguably 'the most famous style of mission-inspired clothing' and was developed in the Pacific in order to cover the female body modestly.[34] In numerous communities, the mark of Christian conversion was the wearing of European clothing, or particular parts of it. Thus, when Williams visited Aitutaki, he writes 'Finding, however, that we did not repose entire confidence in their assertions [of Christianity and peace], some held up their hats* (*the European shaped hat was worn only by the Christian party, the idolaters retaining their heathen head-dresses, war-caps, &c.) others their spelling-books, to convince us of the truth of what they stated' (59). In many places, wearing white clothing also signified Christian conversion.

Images of bonnets recur throughout missionary narratives of Polynesia – a survey of these texts suggests that there were bonnets throughout the region at this time. The 1822 'Report' notes approvingly that, in Taïti, 'Mrs Bourne and Mrs Darling [missionary wives] had taught the females to make themselves bonnets of a species of grass adapted to this purpose. Scarce a woman was to be seen in the congregation without a bonnet, or a man without a hat, of this simple manufacture.' In Eimeo, missionaries Henry and Platt report that

We were much pleased also to see so evident an improvement in the outward appearance of the people; most of the women having on very decent bonnets, made in the straw-bonnet fashion of the Purou bark, plaited, or sword grass, or some other plant or grass. The men also have got hats, like the common straw-hats, of the same materials, which make a very decent and respectable appearance.[35]

Williams also had a strong interest in bonnets. He notes that, when the travelling islanders reached Ra'iatea,

their astonishment was again excited; the Missionaries, their wives and families, the natives in European dresses, with hats and bonnets, their neat white cottages, together with the various useful arts which had been introduced amongst the people, filled the strangers with admiration and surprise. (41)

Williams later returned to Rarotonga where he remarks

compared with what they were when I first visited them, [the community] 'were clothed, and in their right mind'. All the females wore bonnets, and were dressed in white cloth, whilst the men wore clothes and hats of native manufacture. The change thus presented was peculiarly gratifying. (114)

Clearly, the bonnet came to assume some central significance for LMS missionaries.

My examination of missionary representations of bonnets teases out the importance of these artefacts of British femininity in a Polynesian landscape. I do not wish to recuperate the physical artefact itself, but rather to analyse what the image of the bonnet represented in missionary texts and discourses. Whilst it is obvious from reading these accounts that the bonnet represented something real and material to missionaries in the colonial field, the *image* of the bonnet in missionary discourses was clearly an important signifier to the British reading audience. In some senses, I use the image of the bonnet as LMS missionaries did, as a sign of much larger questions. Philippe Perrot notes that because (western) clothing is symbolically laden, its adoption or rejection, particularly in non-western cultures, is a politically and culturally charged action.[36] The bonnet in nineteenth-century Polynesia was metonymic of wider clothing practices, representative of the gender and body politics of Christianity. The introduction of European clothing to Polynesian mission communities was an attempt to bring converts into the worldwide Christian 'family', in order that missionaries (and other Europeans) could recognise and replicate classed Christian subjects in this new colonial environment.

The textual image of the bonnet focusses on an alliance of femininity, modesty, propriety, and self-presentation. It was such an effective signifier for missionaries and their British readers because it was an image deeply imbricated with European ideas regarding native bodies, women's bodies (both in the colonies and in the metropole), Christian propriety, and evangelical intervention. The bonnet signified a particular kind of preferred femininity, and a middle-class, modest, and controlled female subject was ideally wearing it.

Evangelical revivalists had always had a keen interest in questions of dress and they were eager to define what was the decent Christian way of presenting the body. Perrot argues that the devout nineteenth-century middle-class population valued 'conspicuous underconsumption, which churchgoing endowed with the new legitimacy of Christian humility, [and which] allowed one to distance oneself from showy costumes, which were very numerous according to fashionable sermon-writers' (99). John Wesley, the founder of Methodism, preached to his women constituents on appropriate Christian dress, telling them that his aim was to see a

Methodist congregation, full as plain dressed as a Quaker congregation ... Let your dress be cheap as well as plain. Otherwise you do but trifle with God, and me, and your own souls. I pray, let there be no costly silks among you, how grave soever they be. Let there be no Quaker linen, proverbially so called for its exquisite fineness; no Brussels lace, no Elephantine hats or bonnets, those scandals of Female Modesty. Be all of a piece, dressed from head to foot, as persons professing Godliness.[37]

Whilst few LMS missionaries were as sartorially strict as the Wesleyans, questions of clothing and morality remained central to most nineteenth-century evangelicals.

The bonnet was also implicated in European discourses concerning class and race. Women in Britain wore bonnets to protect themselves from the sun, to maintain (or imitate) the fashionable pale skin of the middle and upper classes. As Perrot notes, a cosmetic industry of 'electrifying baths' and 'freckle-removing milk' also developed in Europe in order 'to counter the dark pigmentation characteristic of the inferior dark races and the sun-burned skins of the lower classes (who worked outdoors)' (*Fashioning the Bourgeoisie*, 102). The pale skin of upper-class British women, therefore, signified both their ability to live a life of leisure within enclosed domestic spaces, and their husband's financial success in being able to maintain their wives in such a fashion. At the same time, to appear in public '*en cheveu*, or hatless, was lower-class' (103). Given the class consciousness of LMS missionaries, the role of bonnet wearing in preserving light facial skin and marking class differences from those who had to work out of doors was significant to the encouragement of bonnet-wearing in colonial environments. At this point the mutual imbrication of imperial and colonial gender and race representations becomes clear. White women in Britain wore bonnets to prevent 'contamination' by the environment, a contamination that was more than skin deep, for it could erode their racial and/or class superiority. Christianised Polynesian women, naturally 'corrupted' by their environment and race, were to wear bonnets to camouflage their debased femininity, and to signify their desire for (Christian) reformation.

Certainly white women in the antipodean colonies seem to have felt that the need to wear bonnets was intensified. Maynard discusses the disquiet expressed by a nineteenth-century woman, Rachel Henning, about sun-damage to her skin in the Australian bush: ' "we shall be taken for aborigines, I expect, when we present ourselves in the town". She was referring partly to her dilapidated clothes but more particularly to her skin, which had become deeply tanned as a result of the tropical sunshine' (*Fashioned from Penury*, 110). Clearly, Henning worried that her racial purity had been corrupted too.

Literally and morally, women were believed to require protection from colonial environments. Exposure to the sun, as well as the 'rough' nature of colonial society, seemed to threaten the feminine delicacy so prized by evangelical Protestants. However, evangelical inducements for Polynesians to wear bonnets raise questions about racial hierarchies. It may seem far-fetched to wonder whether missionaries truly believed that by encouraging Polynesian women to wear bonnets they might become physically 'whiter', though it certainly seems that the wearing of them was believed to make Polynesian women culturally and theologically 'whiter'. Missionaries, like other Europeans, certainly valued whiteness, or at least lightness of skin colour, in the indigenous peoples they encountered in the new colonial world. They noted approvingly those races whose skin colour approached their own. With a disturbing causal logic, the deputation noted of Huaheine that they

could hear of no crimes in this island, and the judges, as to criminal cases, were consequently without employment. They suppose a happier people than those of this island do not exist, and thus describe them and their island-: 'This little island is a beautiful spot, and abounds in all the fruits common to these climes. *The people are a fine race, well made, and of a remarkably light colour; many of them as fair as some of the English, especially the women, who are not much exposed to the sun.*'[38]

Whilst gradations of skin colour between different Polynesian cultures certainly existed, missionaries were deeply implicated in the racial politics discriminating between 'lighter' and 'darker' Pacific peoples, both between different racial groups *within* Polynesia and between Polynesian and Melanesian cultures. As Bronwen Douglas argues,

nineteenth-century evangelical missionaries mostly shared contemporary scientific and popular assumptions about the reality of a hierarchy of races ranged along a taxonomic continuum from savagery to civilization, though relatively few before the end of the century would countenance evolutionary theory . . . in normal scientific classifications 'Polynesians' ('Malays') were not only deemed more advanced than 'Melanesians', but superior to them in every respect.[39]

Bonnets, textually and materially, promised not just racial reform but labour reform also. Williams recounts a story of teaching Polynesian women bonnet-manufacturing skills: 'Rarotongans improved much in every respect during our residence among them . . . Mrs Pitman and Mrs Williams, who made some hundreds of bonnets . . . rendered many of the natives proficient in the art. They made also, for the chiefs' wives, European garments, and instructed them to use the needle, with which they were much delighted' (166). Richard Eves notes that 'the central locus of the retraining of [Papuan and New Guinean] women was the inculcation of various domestic and maternal arts, while for men it was through "industrial" means'.[40] Tropes of industry and idleness dominated evangelical representations of native women, and Polynesian women's labour in the manufacture of bonnets became a crucial indicator of success for LMS missionaries. Bonnet making was an appropriate domestic art – it required a disciplined, quiet body, which could be contained indoors, and produced an object that was specifically feminine, useful, and indicative of a preferred Christian subjectivity.

Bonnets, like the white cloth missionaries encouraged communities to weave for clothing, were very obvious, visual symbols of Christianisation and civilisation. Such symbols foreground the spectacular and performative nature of Christian conversion, potentially at the expense of genuine conversion. Williams' previously quoted descriptions of Aitutaki indicated that he did not believe the islanders' *verbal* testimony of their Christian status and intentions until they showed him the *physical* signs – hats and school books. Williams says that European dress 'was to the Aitutakians an ocular demonstration of the beneficial effects of Christianity' (62). It becomes increasingly obvious through evangelical narratives that issues of dress and Christianity were actually profound 'ocular demonstrations' sought by anxious and uncertain missionaries. Physical manifestations of Christian civility reassured missionaries that their converts were not merely mimicking their words, but actually adopting physical markers of European modernity, metonymically signified by books and clothes.

As Vanessa Smith has noted in her fine study *Literary Culture and the Pacific*, the language and communication difficulties experienced by early missionaries meant that reliance was placed on the material effects of 'Christianisation and civilisation' before a real spiritual change was felt to have taken place.[41] The intense missionary focus on bonnets, or on clothing more broadly, was another manifestation of this desire to read the indigenous adoption of western technologies as indicative of spiritual promise. Some missionary narratives also made explicit the economic and trade benefits of reforms such as Christianised islanders wearing European clothes. Perrot suggests that 'the monetary profit derived from commercializing Christian modesty, whether among the Africans or among the working class, went hand in hand with symbolic and political profits'.[42] As a strong advocate for trade in the Polynesian region, Williams made this point himself:

many thousands of persons are at this moment wearing and using articles of European manufacture, by whom, a few years ago, no such article had been seen: indeed, in the more advanced stations, there is scarcely an individual who is not attired in English clothing, which has been obtained in exchange for native produce. Thus we are benefited both in what we give and in what we receive. (583)

Gunson attests that 'in the wake of missionary expansion came the social attachments of Christianity... [When] the missionaries created spheres of British influence by introducing British institutions and concepts and a market for cotton cloth and other Western products, they assisted in stepping up the imperialistic process where other conditions were favourable' (*Messengers of Grace*, 146).

It should not be assumed that the bonnet had a significance only in missionary texts, nor that the proliferation of bonnets and other items of European clothing was due solely to missionary eagerness to implement them. Reading between the lines of evangelical narratives, it seems that Polynesian communities invested these artefacts with cultural meanings of their own, that they adapted local manufacturing techniques to these new products, and that they manipulated items such as bonnets with an awareness of their potential symbolic power. Missionary narratives often represent scenes where male converts castigated women for not 'living up' to new Christian standards. At a meeting held on 8 May 1822 by the Auxiliary Society at Ra'iatea, a member of the congregation, Atihuta, is reported to have said: 'Then, in [the time of false gods], our wives were almost entirely without clothing; now they have bonnets and gowns, and shoes and stockings, and soon we shall be all clothed, if diligent, and we obey our God.'[43] Tyerman and Bennet's *Journal* reports on a similar meeting at Ra'iatea in 1822, where another native Christian, Ahuriro, said: "It is a new year, let us have no more old heathen customs. Such women who in common go about without proper attire, and come here dressed because we are all assembled, let them remember that this is not right; God sees them always. It is not suitable to the word of God; it is no sign of their being born again" (1: 33). Clothing thus served as an internal marker of divisions within the Polynesian community.

Polynesian women, too, are represented as having incorporated some of the cultural and gender values of Christianity into their own systems of judgment and value. Tyerman and Bennet's *Journal* describes their arrival in Hawaii with a group of converted Taïtian women. Hawaiian women boarded the ship in order to visit the Taïtian women, who, the deputation states,

took the opportunity frankly to reprove them for appearing abroad with so little clothing on; assuring them that in the southern islands, no modest woman durst go out of doors so unbecomingly exposed. They added, moreover, *'and we will not acknowledge you to be women if you do not dress more decently'*. (1: 372–3, emphasis added)

These last two narratives of encounter between genders, on the one hand, and between different island cultures, on the other, suggest the complex politics which lie behind these evangelical representations. The missionary agenda of 'dividing and conquering', either in terms of gender or differing Polynesian cultures, was evidently at work at least in their accounts. At the same time, local motivations can also be glimpsed in such narratives. It becomes obvious that women in some places adopted clothing items such as bonnets with real enthusiasm for their value as cultural capital. The wife of an unconverted chief was thus described by Williams: she awakened our sympathy by stating that she had long wished to become a Christian, because, when she compared herself with the Christian females, she was much ashamed, for they had bonnets, and beautiful white garments, while she was dressed in 'Satan's clothes'; they could sing and read, while she was in ignorance. (258)

At the same time, missionary narratives reveal the subversive ways in which Polynesian communities may have thought about and manipulated the potential power and meaning of clothing. The undignified withdrawal of most of the first LMS party occurred when political unrest and resistance to missionary intervention threatened their security. Before leaving for New South Wales, Thomas Harris wrote of their precarious position: 'Our property has exposed us to much Danger from the Natives, but what our Brethren have left behind we mean to distribute among the Chiefs, and wear Otaheitean dress, for it is not safe to go far with European clothes. 'Tis a comfort to us they do not steal our books, pens or ink'.[44] The missionaries appeared finally to lose confidence in their situation when members of a missionary delegation to the chiefs were stripped of their clothes by rioting Taïtians.

Within pre-existing methods of indigenous manufacturing, too, local skills were employed and bonnets brought into local economies. When Tyerman and Bennet visited Ra'iatea they took particular interest in the local bonnets:

On every hand we remark increasing evidences of enterprize and industry, of peace and plenty, of social order and religious principle. Observing on the bonnets of many of the females' bows of ribbon, of different tints and curious patterns, some of which were exceedingly rich, we enquired how they had procured such ornaments, and were amusingly surprised to hear that these gay articles were nothing more than slips of the flexible inner bark of the purau-tree, stained with various brilliant colours. (*Journal*, 1: 516–17)

Such descriptions continually remark upon the ingenious use of Polynesian materials. It is clear from the deputation's account that it was a little disconcerted at the 'richness' of ornamentation, and it is possible to see here the subversive nature of the redeployment of Polynesian materials in the manufacture of European artefacts. In effect this redeployment served to transform these artefacts of European modernity and femininity into an entirely different Polynesian context. As Edmond argues, 'missionaries were eventually forced to recognize that nothing could cross the beach unchanged' (*Representing the South Pacific*, 122).

Such cultural and textual negotiations are clear examples of mutual imbrication. The final narrative of cross-cultural encounters over issues of clothing I examine is about the politics of dress in Samoa. Williams' *Missionary Enterprises* notes that native teachers' wives (converted Taïtian women) attempted to instruct Samoan women in the manufacture of 'white Tahitian cloth . . . but that the women were so idle that they could not be induced to learn the art, although the cloth was exceedingly admired'. More disturbingly, he continues,

We also found that they had unsuccessfully endeavoured to persuade them to cover the upper part of their persons, of which they were excessively vain. Indeed, they were continually entreating the teachers' wives to lay aside their European garments, and *faasamoa*, that is, adopt the Samoa fashions, which was to gird a shaggy mat around the loins, loop the corner of it on the right side, anoint themselves profusely with scented oil, tinge themselves with turmeric rouge, fasten a row of blue beads round the neck, and *faariaria*, strut about and show themselves; and they enforced their wishes by assuring them, that if they did so, all would admire them. (426–7)

Nicholas Thomas' citation of the source material for Williams' publication makes it clear that Samoan women were explicitly advocating the sexual attractiveness of traditional fashion: 'You will have, they say, all the *Manaia* the handsome young men of the town loving you then.'[45] Unsurprisingly, this particular formation is edited out of the published variant. Even in its sanitised form, this story is intriguing because of its total inversion of the power relationship that tends to dominate missionary narratives about clothing and sexuality. Clearly, Samoan women were taking pity on what they saw as their more dowdy Christian Taïtian 'sisters', and feeling they could help them become 'real women' by offering advice on their bodies and clothing.

FAMILIES IN THE PACIFIC

A 'species of domestic intercourse established, which was formerly unknown in the islands'[46]

Polynesian families were inevitably caught up in missionary attempts to re-form sexual practices and relationships. As was typical throughout the entire mission field, LMS evangelists in Polynesia sought to alter pre-existing family structures and gendered roles within families and they emphasised such projects in their reports. The 1820 LMS 'Report' canvasses the range of issues in which the society felt it necessary to intervene in Polynesia:

And not only is a species of domestic intercourse established, which was formerly unknown in the islands, but the members of the same family, generally speaking, dwell together in peace and harmony. The female, instead of being merely the slave of the man, is now raised to a level with him, as his companion ... And not only has the horrid practice of infanticide entirely ceased, but even mothers, who once destroyed their infants, now manifest towards their subsequent offspring a remarkable degree of tenderness and affection.[47]

In missionary narratives, these central concerns surrounded the family – gender relations, monogamous nuclear households, and maternity.

Missionaries objected to extended families living together, they abhorred the freedom which married spouses seemed to allow each other, they rejected the gender-based rules which structured Polynesian societies, and they believed that Polynesian children were maltreated by their parents and the wider community. As Jolly and Macintyre argue, missionaries heavily influenced the profound changes undergone by Pacific families after colonialism, perhaps more so than any other western group. Missionaries were self-conscious and deliberate agents of change: whilst 'other Europeans may have hoped for alterations in indigenous domesticities ... it was missionaries who articulated the need to reform the family and who actively intervened to promote such changes'.[48] Part of this active intervention was the reiteration of familial images in widely circulated missionary narratives.

Early missionary representations of Polynesian family relations emphasise the importance of gender in the division of labour, religiosity, and public life. Whilst missionaries were well-acquainted with gender-segregated spheres of labour and public life in Christian Britain, they portray equivalent Polynesian practices as impeding gender equity within both community and family. Missionary accounts remark disapprovingly on Polynesian gender rules regarding eating. The 1817 LMS 'Report' notes that 'women are not permitted to eat with the men, nor may they drink out of the same cup'.[49] Similarly, Williams explains that

Females at Rarotonga, like those of the Society Islands, were treated as inferiors. They were neither allowed certain kinds of food, which were reserved for the men and the gods, nor to dwell under the same roof with their tyrannical masters; but were compelled to eat their scanty meal of inferior provisions at a distance, while the 'lords of creation' feasted upon the 'fat of the land', and the 'abundance of the sea'. (214)

Images of sharing food recur throughout LMS narratives about Polynesia, perhaps because of the Christian principle of breaking bread as an act of communion signifying a shared commitment to certain (civilised, Christian) beliefs and community structures. As the 1819 'Report' notes, 'although this may not appear to be of much consequence, yet the former custom [of gender-segregated eating] led on to many and great evils'.[50] The 'many and great evils' attested to here relate to what missionaries saw as associated practices of gender-segregated households. Change to familial communal eating was seen as an early indicator of Christian success. In this spirit, the 1820 'Report' notes happily: 'Every woman now eats with her husband, and the family assemble together at the same meal: formerly the sexes ate separately.'[51]

Eating and food seemed both to fascinate and repel missionaries in Polynesia. Tyerman and Bennet note their desire to reform Polynesian dietary habits, stating that 'it is not to be imagined that a civilized people, whose habits, through cultivation of mind, and consequent personal delicacy, shall be proportionately raised above mere animal nature, could, under any circumstances, remain satisfied to subsist on bread-fruit and plantains, with occasional relishes of hogs' flesh' (1: 295). Exactly how the deputation logically connected diet and racial evolution within a religious framework is a little difficult to understand, but it perceived the benefits of this were firstly to encourage a system of agricultural reform and secondly, one suspects, to ensure that missionary visitors were fed in the manner to which they would like to have become accustomed. Pacific communities were very familiar with malnourished, scurvy-ridden sailors landing on their shores and devouring all the fresh produce they could obtain. The *Journal* hints at the ways that Polynesian communities interpreted such behaviour in their report of a meeting with elite Polynesians of Maiaoiti and Huahine: they

informed us that when our countrymen first visited their shores, they thought that England must be a poor hungry place, since the people sailed so far to obtain their abundant and delicious food; nay, they used to wonder much that king George had not long ago come hither himself, as he must have tasted or been told of their fine pork. (1: 208)

In some places missionaries seemed to have been so effective in tying diet to Christianity that each foodstuff was checked for its 'morality'. Williams includes a somewhat snide narrative about being questioned at Mangaia as to whether their local traditional practice of eating rats was sinful. He replies:

I informed them that we were in the habit of looking upon rats as exceedingly disgusting, but not perceiving any thing morally evil in the practice. I could do no more than recommend them to take great care of the pigs and goats I had brought, by which means they would speedily obtain an abundant supply of 'animal food', far superior to that which they esteemed so 'sweet and good'. (247)

Tyerman and Bennet also repeatedly note 'disgusting' eating practices, particularly in relation to Polynesian women (1: 469, 471–2). They were greatly impressed with the improvement in table manners that they believed Christian conversion introduced (1: 530–2), and also seemed pleased that Christianity had encouraged that crucial indicator of British civility, tea drinking (1: 533–4).

The role of table manners and food images in missionary texts is a suggestive one. Not merely a measure of civility and bodily discipline (though clearly this is a factor), these images inadvertently but inevitably drew attention to the very thing their authors did not intend to express: the homology between evangelical Protestant and Polynesian practices and beliefs. Food and its rituals, of course, were also crucial to Polynesian beliefs surrounding *tapu*. As Herbert saliently argues, through close contact with their 'heathen' charges, missionaries must have realised that 'Evangelicals and heathens alike lived under the constant sway of much the same panicky belief in processes of contamination by deadly metaphysical forces (conceptualized alternatively as moral evil or as the lethal sacredness called *mana*) through contact with unclean objects' (*Culture and Anomie*, 171). If *tapu* had certain rules pertaining to food and consumption, so too did missionary Christianity. Recognising these religious parallels allows us to read local anxiety about 'sinful' types of food quite differently: not as a marker of the collapse of indigenous food production/consumption practices, but as an extension of them and an appropriation of Christian dogma into pre-existing systems. Evangelical texts heavily imply, but never articulate, similarities between Polynesian *tapu* and British Christianity. Even though, as Herbert notes, their anxiety about contamination through exposure to Polynesian culture meant that 'they set up their own taboos to guard against such dangers', such parallels remain unspeakable within missionary discourse: 'yet they seem aware of it, indeed they almost compulsively hint at it...as though daring the reader to detect this scandalous secret' (171).

Another crucial signifier of domestic reform in LMS narratives was maternity and child welfare. LMS missionaries believed Polynesian women to be neglectful and abusive mothers and set out to reform maternity and the broader societal treatment of children. Infanticide figured largely in missionary representations of 'heathen Polynesia', as it did in similar representations of India. One of the early missionary goals was its elimination. I have earlier discussed the central figure of maternal women to British evangelicals: as Felicity Nussbaum argues, 'the cult of domestic maternity in the eighteenth century... encouraged the belief that females of every culture and species should be imagined as loving and nurturant mothers heavily invested in the care of their children' (*Torrid Zones*, 48). Nussbaum notes that the figure of the 'savage' colonial mother was opposed to the 'naturally' maternal British mother, in a discursive and ideological move naturalising British women's newly designated place within the domestic economy. Nussbaum suggests that the 'savage' mother serves this dual purpose; like the figure of the English mother, she is both revered and rendered incompetent, 'she is the worst and best of "nature," supposedly capable of eating, killing, or giving away her child' (51). Infanticide is the next trope upon which I base my analysis of missionary texts about families. It is a particularly suggestive trope, because it is a specifically gendered one, yet it also resonates with European fears about cannibalism and the 'other's' unnatural practices.

In the area of maternity, missionary writers were caught up in a contradictory mode of address characterising much evangelical philosophy. As Edmond suggests, evangelical texts about Polynesia were frequently discordant because they were influenced by other, competing discourses. These included ethnographic discourses of earlier Pacific explorers and early nineteenth-century British social theorists, as well as other missionary texts. Edmond argues that 'Ellis experienced Tahiti in the light of these narratives as well as in terms of some putative missionary writ; hence the competing generic models which shape his text, the clash of discourses and their complex interaction' (*Representing the South Pacific*, 108). However, missionaries had to believe in a kind of common humanity in order to justify Christian conversion, in opposition to the growing European belief that colonised peoples were 'degraded savages' and beyond redemption. In a similar contradictory mode, Williams condemns Polynesian mothers by stating

How striking the contrast between the feelings and wishes of the Christian and the heathen mother! The one devotes her babe to the God of love and mercy; the other dedicates hers to the god of murder, or of fraud; the one would give her infant a heart of stone; the other prays that it may receive a heart of flesh. Who hath made us to differ, and what thanks does He demand! (545–6)

Although he strongly contrasts 'heathen' and 'Christian' mothers, Williams is simultaneously obliged to draw attention to their similarities in spiritual education, arguing that if only Polynesian mothers devoted their children to the right (Christian) god they could be equivalent to British Christian mothers.

The LMS saw the 'abolition of infanticide'[52] as central to their early years in Polynesia. By 1819, the society was counting its discontinuation as indicative of reforms in Taïti. In missionary narratives, this was intimately tied in with the concurrent 'abolition' of 'the Arreoy Society* (*The Arreoy

Society, was distinguished for its barbarity and licentious manners, and restricted to people of the higher rank) which contributed so much to support this horrid custom.'[53] The question of relations between the 'Arreoy' or 'Areoi' society and missionaries is a large and complex one – members of this society formed a kind of indigenous elite and were central to religious practices, particularly those relating to Oro, one of the chief gods around the time of European arrival in Taïti.[54] Missionaries frequently refer to the Areoi in their narratives and the representation of them becomes fairly stereotypical, of which the following is typical: 'This society was composed of a privileged order, who indulged in extreme lewdness, and uniformly murdered the fruits of their licentious intercourse.'[55] Tyerman and Bennet describe them as 'those human harpies – the Areois, in whose character and habits all that is most loathsome – "earthly, sensual, devilish" – was combined' (*Journal*, 1: 254).

Missionaries regarded the Areoi adversely for a number of reasons that can be surmised from evangelical narratives. Firstly, they were members of an elite, considering themselves superior to missionaries, who were, as already suggested in this study, very sensitive to their social status. The Areoi were also deeply involved in 'pagan' religions, and as such needed to be discredited in missionary attempts at a Christian restructuring of Polynesian culture. They also played important parts in festivals of carnivalistic misrule which signalled key points in the Polynesian religious calendar, when the usual authorities were overturned and subjected to ridicule – practices which missionaries could ill afford to countenance. Significantly, though, Tyerman and Bennet describe a rather different role for the Areoi as travelling performers,

who went about the country, from one chief's district to another, reciting stories and singing songs for the entertainment of the people ... These compositions, we are told, frequently did credit to the talents of the authors, while the accuracy and liveliness with which they were repeated shewed considerable powers of memory as well as of imitation in the performances. But they were connected with unutterable abominations, and therefore have been entirely discontinued since purer manners have followed in the train of Christian principles. (*Journal*, 1: 94)

Missionary representations of the Areoi as a morally depraved elite attempt to elide their important role in Polynesian community life as conveyers of important cultural history and knowledge. Evangelical attempts to stamp out such practices were not only inspired by moral questions, but also by their desire to break down native structures of hierarchy, resistance, and cultural continuity.

The Areoi were also comparatively liberated in their sexual behaviour and it does seem that children were killed, though for reasons which missionaries failed to understand. As Watts explains,

if an *ari'i* gave birth to a child of a lower class, membership of the elite society was denied them. Thus, a principal Taïtian sanction against inter-class marriage was that children should not live to degrade the parents' rank. The missionaries' first rejection of Taïtian customs centred on this practice; it seemed to epitomise the dark, treacherous heathen. ('Tahiti', 59)

Missionary narratives resonate with images of infanticide. Tyerman and Bennet note: 'Till lately, multitudes of children were destroyed before or immediately after the birth, when the parents thought their families large enough... They were the absolute property of those who gave them life, and who might with impunity, any day, give them death' (*Journal*, 1: 449). They report, with a prurient interest, of learning

with horror, that it had been practised to an extent incredible except on such testimony and evidence as he, and the brethren on other stations, have had the means of accumulating. He assured us, that three-fourths of the children were wont to be murdered as soon as they were born, by one or other of the unnatural parents, or by some person employed for that purpose. (1: 71)

The fact that such 'depravity' was no marker of lower rank, but frequently the opposite, both shocked and satisfied LMS missionaries, much as indicators of elite 'degradation' had similarly affected missionaries in India. Initially, they believed that higher ranks were 'more civilised', tutored as they were in the hierarchical politics of the LMS and the British class system. The existence of what Europeans regarded as a Polynesian version of a monarchy had encouraged them in this belief. As Gunson suggests, at the time of the first LMS incursion

the social positions of the missionary and his South Sea subject were the reverse of what they would become by the mid nineteenth century... the missionary was thought of as a kind of tinker, who, as the Rev. Sydney Smith described him, could not look a gentleman in the face... On the other hand, although somewhat of a curiosity, the South Sea islander was regarded as the epitome of the natural man, a 'noble savage' and fit companion for a king. (*Messengers of Grace*, 31)

Missionaries often seem secretly pleased to find that Polynesian elites were at least as degraded as their lower-class converts. Tyerman and Bennet write of a 'prayer-meeting of a select association of females, principally the wives and daughters of chiefs, including the queen', who are asked whether, 'under the infuriating influence of idolatry', they had killed any of their children. Of course, the women confess:

Those present... declared that they often seem to have their murdered children before their eyes; and their own wickedness appears so great that they sometimes think it cannot be pardoned... They spoke with great humility, and, we had reason to believe, with sincere contrition, in respect to these sins of their heathen days; but their hearts and eyes overflowed with gratitude while they acknowledged the mercy of God in sending his faithful servants, and his word, to turn them from their evil ways, and shew them the path of life. (*Journal*, 1: 542–3)

Missionary views on infanticide were fed both by feelings of righteousness about gender and maternity and by a class-based attack on Polynesian customs. It was essential that missionaries indict practices of the socially powerful, in order to create the cultural vacuum into which Christianity could step. As some missionaries *almost* suggest, Polynesian infanticide really acted to control population growth and to maintain social stability – but such conclusions are literally unspeakable in missionary texts.

The missionaries' swiftness to claim the abolition of infanticide does make the contemporary reader question the supposedly widespread nature of the practice in Polynesia. Regardless of the cultural/historical reality, infanticide and its cessation were crucial signifiers in missionary discourses. The 1820 'Report' confirms that, in the Society Islands,

not only has the horrid practice of infanticide entirely ceased, but even mothers, who once destroyed their infants, now manifest towards their subsequent offspring a remarkable degree of tenderness and affection; and some of them deeply lament the loss of their little ones who formerly fell a sacrifice to this cruel and relentless custom.[56]

When missionaries could report that infanticide had stopped, they could then move on to 'improving' (i.e. intervening in) the ongoing treatment of Polynesian children. This intervention was not solely motivated by a universal concern for child welfare. Missionaries in Polynesia, as in many other mission fields, believed that children represented the easiest path to widespread Christianisation. As the 1820 'Report' makes clear, this intervention also promised to re-form Polynesian women into appropriate models of Christian maternity.

In hindsight, obsessive missionary focus on the state of Polynesian children seems ironic. As noted in chapter 6, LMS missionaries worried intensely about the effect of Polynesian people and landscape on their own children. Tyerman and Bennet reported on the numbers of children in early missionary families: the Crook family of nine children; the Henry family of eight; the Bicknell family of five; the Armitage, Platt, Threlkeld, Barff, and Wilson families of four; the Orsmond family of three; the Darling family of three; the Bourne family with only one child; and the childless Nott, Davies, and Jones families.[57] They noted that at Papeete, 'Mr and Mrs Crook have nine children; yet the comfort of their habitation, the order of it in-doors, and the behaviour of every member of the family, reflect the highest credit on their prudence and economy' (*Journal*, 1: 67). It is easy to sympathise with Australian journalist Beatrice Grimshaw's tart comment regarding Presbyterian missionary women in Vanuatu at the beginning of the twentieth century, when she 'speculates that the Presbyterian baby must be the principal product of the island, in advance of copra or coffee'.[58]

Though the number of missionary children was obviously high, their evangelical parents were intensely concerned about their welfare, to the extent that many missionary children were sent to Britain or Australia for their education and 'safety'. As Margaret Jolly points out in her article 'Colonizing Women', the 'maternal' construction of the relationship between missionary women and native women was a kind of surrogacy for their absent children (113).

Issues of maternity and childbirth were clearly important to LMS missionaries, and even narratives such as the deputation's *Journal* were surprisingly explicit about cross-cultural encounters in this arena. They note with some confusion the birthing practices common to the area. Whilst the following account attempts to query the wisdom of Polynesian practices, it concludes that in many ways these proved to be superior to European customs:

The shed stood within a few paces of the sea, and had been purposely chosen, according to the approved custom, for the benefit of free air, and to afford her an opportunity, as soon as she should be delivered, to plunge into the sea, and there sit in the water for half an hour. This strange, and we might deem perilous practice, to a woman in such delicate circumstances, is common here; and we are assured that, in most instances, it is the means of restoring strength and animation to the exhausted mother, who frequently goes about her ordinary household business an hour or two after she has come out of the purifying flood. (1: 352)

At the same time, however, they approvingly record that on the birth of a royal child by a Polynesian woman, Tarouarii, 'the wife of one of the Missionaries was sent for immediately, to dress the babe in the English fashion, as it has been determined, on every occasion, to conform as nearly as possible to the manners and customs of the nation which has sent them spiritual fathers and instructors in righteousness' (1: 358).

Such conflicting narratives of different cultural values repeatedly vex missionary narratives, particularly in the sphere of gender and sexuality. Whilst in some contexts missionaries were prepared to represent native practices as having positive attributes, their inculcation in ethnocentric imperial and evangelical discourses meant that they represented their experiences with cultural difference in highly contradictory ways. This tension within missionary narratives – between the potentially progressive nature of encounters with other cultures and the prescriptive discourse in which they were compelled to represent these – is particularly evident in Polynesian-based texts. This was in part because European understandings of racial hierarchies included a respect for Polynesian races which would never be accorded to Australian Aborigines. Missionaries here inherited pre-existing notions of 'noble savages' with which to temper their impressions and then their own representations of Polynesians. As will become evident in part four, European conceptions of racialised and sexualised orders of savagery profoundly influenced missionary practices and representations of different colonised peoples.

PART FOUR

The London Missionary Society in Australia

The dry bones in this wilderness[1]

CHAPTER EIGHT

The Australian colonies and empire

A 'country of civilized thieves and savage natives'[2]

It was the custom at this time for the Aborigines both male and female to parade the streets without a particle of clothing, and it struck me very forcibly, on my first landing in Sydney in 1817, to observe such scenes in the midst of what was called a civilized community, and when walking one day with some colonial Ladies, and meeting a mixed party of undressed natives of both sexes, no slight embarrassment was felt as to how dexterously to avoid the unseemly meeting, but this was speedily removed by their claiming old acquaintance privileges, and entering into a friendly conversation with our friends. It is astonishing how soon custom forms habits the most opposite to those esteemed in our native land.[3]

Reverend Lancelot Edward Threlkeld's narrative of black and white encounters in the colonial settlement of Sydney establishes the tone and sentiment of his *Reminiscences* and introduces the central concerns of part four, focussing on the LMS in Australia. Threlkeld's evidence about settler–Aboriginal encounters, his discussion of the place and behaviour of white and black women, and his comments about the unique nature of colonial manners were issues critical to the work of the LMS in early Australian colonies. Threlkeld's obvious social embarrassment at the potential difficulties involved when white 'colonial Ladies' interact with naked Aboriginal men and women is suggestive of the nexus of racial, cultural, and sexual issues which colonial Australia presented to white colonists and to arbiters of propriety and cross-cultural encounters such as Threlkeld.

Part four examines the cultural and textual environment of LMS work in Australia during the period 1800–60, focussing solely on New South Wales.[4] It is necessarily different in tone and form from the previous analyses of Indian and Polynesian missions, because of the very different nature of LMS commitment to the Australian mission field. LMS involvement in Australia was extremely limited and had few resources, both financially and in terms of personnel. The LMS supported only one Australian mission during this period, and only between 1824 and 1829. However, the termination of the

167

LMS support for Threlkeld and his mission was acrimonious, public, and well-documented in a variety of forums, and the disagreements between Threlkeld and his supporters on one hand, and the LMS and their supporters on the other, bring together an intriguing array of debates about the role and efficacy of missionary endeavour in this part of the world (and, by implication, others). This chapter sketches the historical and cultural tenor of New South Wales in this period, while chapter 9 examines Threlkeld's position in public discourse and textual culture.

The penal system ensured that questions of class, sexuality, and gender were crucial for early inhabitants. Such questions brought into focus ideas about the correlation between 'lower classes' and 'lower races' influencing contemporary European thought. As Ruth Teale notes, before 1850 men greatly outnumbered women in the colonies, because of the majority of male convict transportees, the preponderance of men in the colonial administration and their tendency to leave their families in Britain whilst they did their service in Australia, and the predominance of male-based industries (such as whaling and farming) in the early colonial economy.[5] During the period under investigation, the Australian colonies were characterised by a noticeable gender imbalance and hence by a social and sexual climate in which issues of gender and sexuality were particularly fraught.

The image of women in colonial Australia was a crucial indicator of the 'progress' of penal culture because of the common nineteenth-century belief that the treatment of women was a measure of cultural civility and modernity. However, colonies provided an environment in which imperial anxieties about gender and sexuality were worked out in explicit and often, for men like Threlkeld, disturbing ways. Threlkeld's self-conscious and uncomfortable description of indigenous nakedness in a 'civilized community' is crucial because it employs sexuality and gender to contrast the 'civilized' with the 'savage'. Threlkeld's deliberate characterisation of his companions as 'Ladies', too, signals specific negotiations of class and gender contextualising his anxiety. It is noticeable, however, that it is Threlkeld who sexualises (and thus problematises) the occasion – his description of the ease with which both black and white parties 'claim old acquaintance privileges' and carry on normal social interactions only highlights his *own* unease. His comment that 'it is astonishing how soon custom forms habits the most opposite to those esteemed in our native land' makes it clear that Threlkeld reads this occasion as being of wider social concern. His characterisation of the antipodal nature of British manners and values in the Australian colony is one which continually haunts his writings and his interactions with both black and white colonial subjects.

Australia's 'settlement' in 1788, marked by the arrival of the First Fleet in Sydney Cove, predated the real involvement of missionary evangelism in British colonising projects. As a result of this timing, and also arguably because of the hard-headed politics of a penal colony, Australia did not receive its first missionary specifically appointed to minister to the Aboriginal population until 1821. No mission society or missionary was connected with the arrival of the First Fleet and Governor Arthur Philip was not instructed to preach to the Aborigines. The first chaplain appointed was Richard Johnson, but his responsibilities were to minister to the white population, including convicts and white settlers, rather than to Aborigines. Samuel Marsden was the second chaplain sent to Australia, arriving in 1794. Joseph King describes him as 'a man cast in a different mould. He was a rugged man, full of energy and full of schemes, a censor with deep convictions, which he was not afraid to utter.'[6]

Marsden became a crucial player in religious and secular politics in the colony. His interest and central role in missionary affairs in both Australia and the South Pacific made him an influential figure in the politics and practice of evangelical work. In 1821 the Wesleyan Methodist Missionary Society's representative William Walker arrived in Australia to evangelise Aborigines. Walker was soon opposed by Marsden in his role as a member of the Native Institutions Committee, and these problems led to the Methodist Missionary Society severing their connection with Walker in 1826. Jean Woolmington notes that the 'only record of his success in his Christianising mission was the baptism of some Aboriginal children, one of them the son of Bennelong'.[7] Walker was one of many missionary figures to discover that Marsden was a fierce and influential opponent, who regularly thwarted the religious aspirations of other men. Like other white settlers, Marsden was sceptical about the potential for 'raising up' Aborigines.

Colonists in Australia were deeply ambivalent in their attitudes towards the establishment of Aboriginal missions. On the one hand, some believed that a Christianised and educated Aboriginal population would offer less resistance to the expansion of white settlement in Australia and that a 'civilised' Aboriginal community would ingest the tenets of British Christianity. Jean Woolmington suggests that educational schemes were introduced in a direct attempt to curb Aboriginal hostilities and that Governor Macquarie's prime motivation for establishing a school for Aboriginal children – the 'Native Institution' at Parramatta in 1814 – was to lessen resistance (78). At the same time, however, local support for missionary work amongst Aborigines was also a matter of conscience for some settlers, who saw Christianity as a viable solution to the difficult relationships between white settlers and Aborigines. As Woolmington describes it, some 'saw Christianity as a means of atoning for the wrongs done to Aborigines at the hands of whites. Indeed it would not be exaggerating to claim that some believed that the missionaries were appointed to act as the nation's conscience' (78). Ironically, it was the missionaries' tendency to take their role as conscience of the nation very seriously that alienated many white settlers and destabilised their position in colonial society.

Prior to the establishment of missions proper, a number of individuals had taken the opportunity to experiment with the potential for 'Christianisation and civilisation'. Niel Gunson argues that 'for perhaps the first fifty years of contact the most successful form of missionary endeavour was the "domestic experiment", the practice of raising orphaned Aboriginal children in the homes of pious citizens',[8] though he notes that 'a contrary view is taken by many historians who cite the much publicised "moral" failures and premature deaths' (104, n. 4). Marsden and other individuals conducted these 'domestic experiments', which involved not only orphans but also other Aboriginal children being deliberately removed from their parents, as an investigation of Aboriginal potential for 'upraising'. Gunson notes that 'it would be difficult to assess the success or otherwise of the "domestic experiment" in New South Wales as no public records were kept and Marsden denounced the practice' (105). Nonetheless, we do know that such experiments were largely unsuccessful, though from these more organised efforts at educational evangelisation emerged.[9]

LMS missionary William Shelley had been part of the first LMS group in Polynesia. In 1806 he and his family moved to New South Wales. Shelley too had brought Aboriginal children to live with his large family and he attempted to learn the local language from them. As a result, Shelley addressed Governor Macquarie 'on the practicability of civilizing' Aborigines, and the governor invited him to draw up plans.[10] In December 1814 Shelley was appointed as the superintendant and principal instructor of the Native Institution at Parramatta, but because of his death soon after (and despite his widow's best efforts at continuing the institution)[11] its success was limited.

These 'domestic experiments' are significant as the first instances of the domestic reforms which were as central to efforts to evangelise Aborigines as they were to the LMS attempts to convert other colonised peoples. Well-intentioned settlers like Shelley, Marsden, and Johnson strove to induce change in Aboriginal culture by bringing individual children into their homes, that is, into the European domestic sphere. I have discussed previously how missionary wives and children were believed to encourage

'Christianisation and civilisation' merely as examples of the Christian ideal. It is evident that these early domestic experiments in New South Wales were premised on a similar attempt at role modelling.

Significantly, the failure of this domestic method – especially for Marsden – reinforced colonialist ideas about Aboriginal resistance to conversion and 'civilisation'. The Marsdens had undertaken 'domestic experiments' themselves, taking young Aboriginal boys into their home. Gunson reports that Marsden took one child from his mother's breast ('Two Hundred Years', 10). These children were supposedly brought up alongside the family's children, and were taught to read, write, wait at table, and generally assimilate into settler society. A. T. Yarwood's biography of Marsden concludes, however, that the Marsdens' apparent goal was to fit 'their black protegé[s] for a menial role in white society. Its final failure, a decade later, would greatly influence the parson's assessment of the capacities of the Aborigines.'[12] One Aboriginal boy, named either Samuel Christian or Samuel Tristan (according to Gunson and Yarwood respectively), ran away from the Marsdens whilst travelling in Rio de Janeiro with them. Elizabeth Marsden noted that 'his master punished him [for drinking cheap Rio wine] and he went off'.[13] The other boy left the family to return to the bush and, presumably, his own people.

Whilst these evangelical individuals sought to effect Christianisation and civilisation through domestic role modelling, they did not accept Aboriginal children into their families as equals. Each 'domestic experiment' seems to have assumed that Aboriginal children would work as domestic servants in addition, and surely in contrast, to their supposed role as members of an evangelical family. As Yarwood remarks of Elizabeth Marsden's representation of Samuel Christian/Tristan's desertion, 'she reveals in the use of the term "master" a critical weakness in the boy's relationship with the family; in the last resort his colour had stood in the way of legal adoption and unreserved acceptance' (112). This ambiguous dual role of domestic servant and family member exposes missionary ambivalence in putting evangelical policies into action. Similar kinds of relationships between the charitable middle class and working-class orphans probably existed concurrently in Britain. The significant difference in the colonial context was that a discourse of Christian family values was used to construct these experiments as a concerted effort to cross (and effectively erase) racial boundaries. Whilst domestic and gendered role modelling was a core policy of mission work, the perceived threat posed by intimate encounters with indigenous people (even children) in colonial environments to those cherished symbols of British Christian civility – white women, children, and domestic spaces – reconfigured their implementation of imperial policies formulated in 'safer', European environments.

The disruption of Aboriginal families characterising colonialist (and missionary) intervention into Aboriginal lifestyles is evident from these 'domestic experiments'. Gunson's account of early missionary work claims that this practice 'was not consciously geared to racial assimilation, nor did the raising of black children in white households necessarily have the ugly features of some twentieth-century experiments when children were forcibly removed from parents'.[14] But researching missionary history and textuality in a period which has seen intense and emotional national debates about a 'politics of stolen time'[15] in regard to the later Stolen Generations in Australia clearly influences the way we understand such practices. In 1995, the Australian Attorney-General responded officially to Aboriginal concerns about the hidden history of forcible removal of Aboriginal children from their families, and the impact of this history on communities, and referred the issue to the Human Rights and Equal Opportunity Commission. The commission's report, *Bringing Them Home* (1997), sold in remarkable numbers, drawing the (contested) historical and contemporary practices of separating indigenous children from their families, and debates about white–Aboriginal relationships, to the forefront of public attention. Refocussing on early domestic experiments by evangelicals/humanitarians reminds us that, despite the contemporary church's moral support for Aboriginal causes, these colonialist policies not only had the full endorsement of the institutions and individuals of Christian benevolence, but were arguably introduced by them.

DIFFICULTIES OF COLONIAL MINISTRY[16]

The only formal LMS involvement in Australia in this period was the establishment of Reid's Mistake mission at Lake Macquarie, though their representatives and others loosely associated with the society had a continual, if informal, presence in other parts of Australia. As I noted in part three, LMS representatives, such as the first Polynesian mission, fled to Sydney when conditions in the islands deteriorated. As Joseph King's history of the LMS in Australia notes,

Early in the history of Australia the London Missionary Society was brought into contact with the official, social, and religious life of the Colonies. The earliest Australian historians . . . speak of the Society's missionaries. The connection is older and closer than is generally known . . . At a very early date, the Society found in Australia a new base or central outpost for its aggressive work.[17]

The LMS thus had an ongoing interest in Australia, even though it only ever maintained a single mission there for a short period. Furthermore, Australia functioned as a transit point for many missions to the Pacific. In 1803, for example, the (largely unsuccessful) missionary Thomas Harris, who had been in the Marquesas and Taïti, was employed at a school on the banks of the Hawkesbury River in New South Wales, where he also ministered.[18] In 1806 William Shelley had come to Sydney from Taïti, followed in 1807 by John Youl. Youl had been on the *Duff* when it was captured by pirates in 1799, after which he spent some time in the colony.[19] These and many other LMS representatives passed through Australia and frequently spent time in evangelical pursuits during their brief residences.

In 1801 Marsden became 'the recognised correspondent and adviser of the London Missionary Society in relation to its Tahitian mission',[20] a task to which he applied himself with his usual vigour and disregard for the aims and sensibilities of others. Marsden took his role as antipodean LMS representative seriously, policing the activities of missionaries both in Polynesia and Australia, and maintaining correspondence with brethren in the islands. As Hilary Carey notes, Marsden was a fervent supporter of the policy to provide and support missionaries with wives and families, supplying both the blessing and the financial support of the society. He arranged marriages, advised sending young women he knew in Sydney and London to Polynesia, and was very supportive of missionary wives. He followed the careers of missionary families closely.[21] As I noted in chapter 2, Marsden's support for a married ministry was based on his belief that men could not withstand the sexual temptations of Polynesia. Marsden's role in providing missionaries with wives sometimes seemed dangerously close to a kind of marital procuring and his interventions into intimate areas of missionaries' lives certainly rankled with some, though many isolated evangelists in the islands saw him as mentor and father-figure. For young, naïve men far from home and familial male advisors, Marsden represented the benevolent patriarchy that they both revered and sought to replicate.

In the early part of the nineteenth century five missions were established in eastern Australia by a variety of missionary societies and other religious institutions. The first, the Wellington Valley mission in New South Wales established by Walker for the Wesleyan Methodist Missionary Society (which seems to have been taken over by the Church Missionary Society), was quickly followed by missions at Nundah[22] (a northern New South Wales (now Queensland) Lutheran mission, under the control of John Dunmore Lang and the New South Wales Presbyterian synod); Stradbroke Island (a Roman Catholic mission in Moreton Bay (now Queensland), run by Italian and Swiss missionaries); Reid's Mistake near Newcastle (run by Threlkeld for the LMS); and in the Port Philip district (now Victoria) near contemporary Geelong (a subsequent Wesleyan effort, established in 1838).

Here I focus solely on the work of the LMS missionary at Lake Macquarie, Lancelot Threlkeld. Threlkeld's experiences were in many ways typical of all of these early missions. All experienced financial problems, troubles with sponsors, and internal quarrels; all fundamentally failed to change Aboriginal lifestyles and beliefs in the manner desired by mission supporters; and, by 1848, all of the first generation of missions in the Australian colonies had been abandoned as failures.[23] Threlkeld's mission is a particularly interesting case, nevertheless, because of his extensive use and manipulation of texts in order to vindicate his position within colonial society and leave a record of his endeavours in the colonial archive.

Threlkeld had had a substantial missionary career before he arrived in Australia. Trained as an actor in London,[24] the young Threlkeld experienced a religious conversion and volunteered for missionary service in Africa. Threlkeld's enthusiasm for the masculine testing ground of Africa was frustrated when the LMS chose instead to send him to Polynesia. Appointed to the recently re-established Taïti mission, Threlkeld married Martha Goss just prior to his departure overseas and she gave birth to their first son on the voyage to Rio de Janeiro. Threlkeld refused to leave Rio until the health of his sickly wife and child improved.[25] He set up a church and encouraged the white settlers to form a permanent congregation. His evident contentment dismayed the LMS, who were used to having their own way, and accounts of Threlkeld's departure from Rio for the Pacific suggest that considerable force had to be exerted on him in order for their wishes to be finally upheld. Nevertheless, Threlkeld and John Williams were appointed together to Ra'iatea in 1818 and were later joined by John Orsmond. In 1824 Martha died and Threlkeld left for Sydney to find a new wife, joining the ship carrying the LMS deputation of Tyerman and Bennet.

Tyerman and Bennet organised the Reid's Mistake[26] mission between October 1824 and June 1825, during their residence in Australia. It is surprising that they seriously considered the establishment of such a mission, given the appalling press other LMS figures had given the country and its indigenous inhabitants. Marsden had never been optimistic about the efficacy of Aboriginal missions, preferring to expend his energies on Polynesian and Maori 'heathen'. In 1813, William Pascoe Crook wrote from Sydney:

No means has ever been used to civilize [Aborigines]. They have been taught to swear and get drunk but no one has learned their language or attempted to teach them the knowledge of Christ. Indeed it requires one of 10 000 to be any way familiar with them as they are so filthy and smell so disagreeable they live naked in the weeds and embrace the rock for want of shelter and they frequently feed on maggots or grub worms.[27]

William Henry, a leading LMS missionary in the Pacific, condemned Aboriginal people as the 'most degraded' in a racial hierarchy:

I think the Greenlanders, Labradorians, or the inhabitants of Terra del Fuego, cannot be much more sunk to a level with the Brit Creation [*sic*] than they. O! Jesus, when shall thy Kingdom come with power amongst them? When shall the rays of thine Eternal gospel penitrate [*sic*] the gross darkness of their minds (well represented by their faces) & illumine their benighted souls.[28]

LMS missionaries evidently concurred with the racialist theories which saw Aborigines as inhabiting the farthest point away from European 'civilisation' – a view shared by many early colonists in Australia. Although missionaries obviously subscribed to the logic of nineteenth-century racial hierarchies, their evangelical ideologies also meant that they believed Aborigines to be especially in need of Christian salvation. Representations of relationships between missionaries and the indigenous populations of Polynesia and Australia, respectively, were quite different, because the two groups were believed to occupy very different levels of human development.[29] Even Threlkeld, whose personal experience with Aborigines in the colony led him to become more generous in his judgments than others, saw Aboriginal people as representing a kind of 'there but for the grace of God go we' existence. He writes: 'in the despised aborigines of New Holland we have a truthful picture of our fate if left by God to our own carnal propensities'.[30] This concentration on racial degeneracy, carnality, and sexuality came to typify evangelical attitudes to Aborigines.

Although the deputation was thoroughly advised by detractors of the mission about the unlikelihood of success, it persevered. In their *Journal* Tyerman and Bennet write of New South Wales that

all attempts to civilize the savage occupants have been fruitless; – it must be confessed, however, that those attempts have been few and feeble. Want of success, in such a case, is no argument to prove that the poor people are intractable ... From all that we can hear, the aborigines of New Holland are indeed the lowest class of human beings; but nevertheless, as human beings, there is 'hope for them concerning this matter'.[31]

Tyerman and Bennet's assertion that despite the supposed lowly stature of Aborigines, they were indeed human beings, makes clear the crucial differences in missionary attitudes from those of other white colonists. Despite the racial 'degradation' which appeared intractable to colonists, missionaries fundamentally had to believe in indigenous salvation and hence in a degree of common humanity. Whilst this did not prevent them from participating in racialist discourses remarkably similar to those of their less Christian or benevolent fellow colonists, it meant that missionary texts in Australia were always rent by the doubled discursive formation of the degraded, but salvageable, Aboriginal heathen. Tyerman's private letter to the directors of the LMS from New South Wales in 1825 admits: 'degraded as they are, they have souls whose powers, for all we know to the contrary, are as vigorous as our own'.[32]

The sections of Tyerman and Bennet's *Journal* relating to their Australian visit are particularly interesting as a record of colonial race relations and attitudes to evangelical work at the very beginning of Threlkeld's mission. Tyerman and Bennet were obviously confounded by their experiences in New South Wales, though they also saw the potential for this new colony to develop along appropriately Christian lines. The ideas they had picked up from missionaries in the Pacific and Christian settlers in Australia regarding the potential for *white* degradation in colonial environments were explored in their writings, and the unsettling nature of this knowledge influenced their texts. They note that white convicts were one of the 'striking but repulsive peculiarities' of the colony:

They are, for the most part, miserable creatures, and more basely branded with the looks of fallen beings on their countenances, than degraded by the symbols on their garments. How great is the change to us, in one respect! Among the South Seas Islanders we had no fear for our persons or our property, by day or night. Here we are surrounded with thieves and violent men of the worst character, and must look well to ourselves and our locks for security. (11: 143)

Tyerman and Bennet's recognition that they were less threatened by Pacific 'heathen' than by transported convicts is significant, because it challenges their other glib assessments of Aboriginal (and Polynesian) degradation. In colonial cultures such as Polynesia and Australia, such ideas about racial hierarchies and innate human depravity were both firmly, indeed obsessively, reinforced *and* fundamentally challenged. Their description of the 'servile condition' of convicts with the 'looks of fallen beings on their countenances' echoes precisely their descriptions of the degraded heathen of Australia and Polynesia. Like missionaries in the islands who found themselves physically and morally threatened by the presence of other, subversive, white people (usually traders, beachcombers, or sailors), Tyerman and Bennet found their presence of mind troubled more by the degradation of white society in colonial culture than by indigenous inhabitants. Of course, in Australia it was felt that white degradation would be exacerbated by the inhumane penal system.

Tyerman and Bennet encouraged future missionaries in Australia to make greater attempts to learn Aboriginal languages, as early linguistic efforts by chaplains and others had petered out with the colonial belief in the inevitable decline of the Aboriginal race. As Threlkeld himself pointed out, refusal to value Aboriginal languages and culture also meant that their destruction could be more easily justified. Tyerman and Bennet also argued that

it must be more rational for a few Missionaries to learn *their* language, and teach them knowledge of every kind in *it*, than to expect that, in mere common-place intercourse with Englishmen, three millions of barbarians, of the lowest order of intelligence, scattered over a wilderness, nearly as large as Europe, should learn *our* language, and listen to the hidden mysteries in *it*, without a motive to do so. (151)

Threlkeld thoroughly advanced these principles, writing the first versions of Aboriginal grammars transcribed by Europeans.[33]

Tyerman and Bennet in part justified their establishment of an Australian mission by focussing on what they believed to be the parlous treatment of women in traditional Aboriginal society. They write:

Like all savages, the New Hollanders use their women cruelly. They get their wives by violence, seizing them by storm, or springing upon them from ambush – when, if the unfortunate female makes any resistance, her uncourteous suitor knocks her down with his waddy (a tremendous cudgel) and carries her off, on his shoulders, in a state of insensibility, with the blood streaming from the love-tokens which he has inflicted on her. Ever afterwards she is his slave ... Their cross, deformed, and diseased children are often killed out of the way, but they are very fond of those whom they rear. (*Journal*, 11: 153–4)

This narrative about maltreatment of women and children was, as Tyerman and Bennet themselves implicitly note, typical of the complaints that missionaries and other white humanitarians around the colonial world made about indigenous cultures and gender relations ('like all savages'). The protection of women as a justification for missionary and colonial intervention was a familiar line of argument in India and Polynesia, so it is not surprising to find it replicated in Australia. Significantly, though, Tyerman and Bennet did not make mention of the complications of gender and sexuality experienced in the Australian colony *between* the races, though in private correspondence back to the society, Tyerman did note that 'those are the most debased who have been brought into contact with their *civilized* invaders!'.[34] This became an issue that their appointed representative, Threlkeld, would take up with vigour.

Tyerman and Bennet's letter appointing Threlkeld to the mission was published as a pamphlet in Australia and circulated as a public document. It is illuminating of the impetus behind this ill-fated mission, and makes clear the public and performative nature of Threlkeld's task (fortunately, perhaps, such performativity came easily to Threlkeld) as well as the colonising aspects. Tyerman and Bennet state:

The novelty of an undertaking which proposes the conversion of the debased Aborigines of this Country to Christianity, and their instruction in the arts of civilized life, will fix upon you the eyes of all in this Country especially, and the Christian world in general, and awaken at once a universal interest, and a peculiar curiosity in observing your operations, and in anticipating the results of the pending experiment.[35]

The deputation acknowledged the presence of ill-wishers towards the mission, though this did not seem to warn the LMS that Threlkeld would encounter strong resistance from white settlers, some of whom were happy to see the mission's later troubles.

The deputation's injunction to instruct Aborigines in the 'arts of civilized life' brings to the fore the critical role played by missionaries in irrevocably changing traditional lifestyles and cultural practices. In Australia, this was particularly pernicious. Clothing, body adornments, sexual and family practices, and education, for instance, were profoundly changed by missionary interventions, in ways devastating to the integrity and continuity of Aboriginal cultures.[36] Tyerman and Bennet explain in detail about the 'arts of civilized life' that they expected Threlkeld would encourage in the Aborigines, namely

instructing them in the arts of reading, writing, &c. and by communicating to them a knowledge of the doctrines and precepts of the Gospel, and the duties which they owe to the Government of this country, and mankind in general, you will at the same time endeavour to promote among them cleanliness, decency of dress, industry in cultivating land, and building themselves houses, and a regard to all the duties of domestic life.[37]

This endorsement of literacy, domesticity, bodily discipline, industry, and, significantly, colonial citizenship and its attendant 'duties' was critical to the 'Christianisation and civilisation' of indigenous Australians.

Threlkeld and his second wife Sarah Arndell[38] were both commissioned to undertake this massive evangelical campaign. Tyerman and Bennet wrote of the second Mrs Threlkeld:

We rejoice that Providence has directed you to a partner in life, like minded with yourself, we trust, as to Missionary views and feelings. Her intimate knowledge of the natives, will qualify her to take an active part with you in promoting their welfare, and especially the good of her sex, to which we are confident, to the extent of her domestic convenience, she will devote herself.[39]

Unfortunately, Sarah vanishes from the official record after this initial appointment, except as part of the substantial household that Threlkeld struggled to maintain on a missionary allowance, and so her 'active part' in the mission remains hidden. The Threlkelds were specifically instructed to convert Aborigines by encouraging imitation of their Christian virtues: 'a steady attention to these objects, together with a kind manner, a tender solicitude to promote their temporal happiness and comfort, and a glowing zeal to advance their eternal salvation, will not fail, we trust, to secure to you their love, confidence, and attachment. In you they will see what a Christian is, and be led to emulate his excellencies.'[40] As I have previously noted, such attempts to produce faithful mimicry usually failed. Whilst some missionaries may have hoped to encourage acute native imitators of Christian virtue, the sense that the 'heathen' colonised *could* hope to replicate the essence of white Christian modern subjectivity was ultimately inimical to and disruptive of the missionaries' sense of self and their relations with 'others'. It is tempting to speculate that the real cause for the unequivocal failure of early missionaries to convert or baptise any significant number of Aborigines was because Europeans could barely conceive of any degree of equivalence between themselves and those whom they regarded as 'aboriginal barbarians'.[41]

CHAPTER NINE

Missionary writing in Australia

... the most persevering and unabating zeal[1]

Situated on the borders of state governmentalities and evangelical concerns, both a 'man of God' and a man who frequented the colonial law courts, newspapers, and public forums, Lancelot Threlkeld's position within the colonial culture of early Australia makes him a particularly interesting figure. It is precisely Threlkeld's liminality, I suspect, which led to his estrangement from more conservative religious institutions and individuals. Yet it is a position which he evidently relished and encouraged. This chapter analyses Threlkeld's role in the colonial public sphere, and examines his writing and that of other LMS representatives, both in terms of their perceptions of local Aborigines and their interventions in broader debates about missionary practices, gender issues, and settler colonies.

Threlkeld appears in the colonial archives as an undoubtedly difficult and stubborn man – Ben Champion discusses the 'officiousness, self-opinionatedness and pessimism that tainted practically the whole of Threlkeld's missionary activities'[2] – yet his naïve assumption that colonial environments might allow such leeway in its public representatives is intriguing and, somehow, rather endearing. His liminality, and its inherent challenge to the colonial order in New South Wales, was especially evident in his writings. In textual debates surrounding Threlkeld, the LMS, Samuel Marsden, and other colonial and missionary figures, the highly provisional, improvisational nature of colonial missionary work was played out. Threlkeld's textual interventions into the excesses of colonial settler practices, namely in the arena of sexuality and gender relations, are significant in the history of race relations and colonial textuality in Australia.

Threlkeld's position on the interstices of various colonial institutions and communities was clearly shown in his own explanations of his work:

180

I have sustained a threefold office, arising out of my employment as a missionary, in which I have endeavoured to act conscientiously and justly towards my own countrymen as well as to the aborigines whenever I have been thereto called by duty. 1st. As protector, to which circumstances called me ever since 1825. 2nd. As interpreter, in many cases which unhappily occurred at the Supreme Court. 3rd. As evangelist, in making known the Gospel to the aborigines in their own tongue.[3]

It is possible to see, even in this sparse description of Threlkeld's roles, his potential to offend the politics of missionary, settler, and judicial communities. The letter of appointment by Tyerman and Bennet cited previously suggests that they would have expected at least the order and priority of Threlkeld's threefold responsibilities to be different, if not the content of his job description *per se*. It is also evident that Threlkeld's position as 'protector' and 'interpreter' placed him directly between the interests of settlers and Aborigines in judicial, land, and human rights issues. This triumvirate of cross-cultural issues was foundational to the new settler colony, and Threlkeld's interference in such affairs won him few white friends. He was thus embroiled in the complex colonial manoeuvring such issues necessarily generated, and his troublesome personality ensured inevitable conflict and controversy.

As Niel Gunson notes,

Threlkeld was the first person to get practical results, and that in a time when prevailing views regarding Aboriginal mission work were negative in the extreme. In reducing the 'barbaric sounds' of the Lake Macquarie tribe[4] to a written language and by writing down all he could find out about Aboriginal culture Threlkeld was essentially a pioneer.[5]

Such linguistic pioneering was probably the most notable achievement of all his involvements with Aboriginal peoples. Threlkeld writes in the introduction to his *Australian Grammar*:

To the mere Philosopher this grammar will afford abundant matter for speculation, in addition to which, the Christian will perceive another instance of the Providence of HIM who has said, 'I will draw all men to me.' For this object alone the laborious task has been undertaken, and must be considered only as the prelude to the attempt of bringing the Aborigines of New South Wales to the knowledge of God our Saviour.[6]

For Threlkeld, the process of transcribing Aboriginal languages was always one of both intellectual inquiry and religious import. His perspective on Aboriginal languages was surprisingly progressive for his time and his evangelical background, though like William Ellis he also notes with derision the pidgin 'Australian' language, combining both Aboriginal and Anglo-Celtic words:

It is necessary to notice certain Barbarisms which have crept into use, introduced by sailors, stockmen, and others who have paid no attention to the Aboriginal tongue, in the use of which both blacks and whites labour under the mistaken idea, that each one is conversing in the other's language. (xi)

Threlkeld's disapproval of this mixture of languages characterises his general distrust of other cross-cultural encounters, particularly in the areas of gender and sexuality. What recent postcolonial theory might regard as 'hybridity' and creative creolisation was seen by Threlkeld as linguistic miscegenation and he condemned it in the same moral tones he used regarding sexual miscegenation. His work on Aboriginal languages was also taken up in distinctly colonialist discourses. The 1892 edition of many of his early works was compiled by John Fraser, whose preface states that the volume was published by the New South Wales government

as a record of the language of native tribes that are rapidly disappearing from the coasts of Eastern Australia... The indigenes of the Sydney district are gone long ago, and some of the inland tribes are represented now only by a few families of wanderers. In all New South Wales, there are only five thousand full-blood blacks; only four or five hundred in Victoria; and in Tasmania the native race became extinct in 1876. They have decayed and are decaying in spite of the fostering care of our Colonial Governments. (*An Australian Language*, v)

Fraser's incorporation of Threlkeld's linguistic work into a broader colonial discourse about the 'dying' Aboriginal race and the ways in which the colonial government was 'smoothing the dying pillow' is ironic, given that Threlkeld had an intense local knowledge of the real problems of settler communities and their treatment of Aborigines, and knew that the government's attitude to Aborigines was rarely 'fostering'.

At the same time, though, and this is illustrative of his liminal position in the culture of New South Wales, Threlkeld forthrightly claimed the 'colonial' nature of his texts. His note prefacing the *Key to the Structure of the Aboriginal Language* (1850) remarks that this text had been initially intended as a paper for the Ethnological Society in London, but that it grew too large for that purpose.[7] Instead, he submitted the *Key* for the Royal National Exhibition in London, in 1851. Threlkeld affirms that his publication conforms to the Exhibition's requirement for a

'book, printed with colonial type, filled with colonial matter, and bound and ornamented with colonial materials'... The subject is purely colonial matter, namely, the language of the aborigines, now all but extinct; and the other conditions have been strictly adhered to, as far as the circumstances of the colony would allow, the paper alone being of English manufacture.[8]

His virtual celebration here of the intrinsically colonial nature of his research and writing is noticeable in a period in which intellectual work was not seen as one of Australia's natural exports. Indeed, Threlkeld's attempt at writing 'An Australian Anthem', albeit to the tune of 'Rule Britannia', suggests his personal identification with the development of the new colony.

Interestingly, though, Threlkeld does not endorse a celebratory colonial neonationalism because part of his identification with colonial identity includes a lamentation for white treatment of Aborigines. However, he both registers his disgust at aggressive colonial practices of land and population clearance, and participates in colonialist discursive modes. For example, in his translation of the Gospel of St Luke into Awabakal, Threlkeld's prefatory note endorses the 'dying race' trope, stating that

It is a matter of fact that the aborigines of these colonies and of the numerous islands of the Pacific Ocean are rapidly becoming extinct. The cause of their extinction is mysterious. Does it arise from the iniquity of this portion of the human race having become full? –, or that the times of these Gentiles are fulfilled? –, or, is it but the natural effects of iniquity producing its consequent ruin to the workers thereof in accordance with the natural order of God's government of the universe?[9]

Threlkeld's split colonial vision is particularly evident in his apparent blindness to acts of colonial violence, both physical and cultural, which he elsewhere documents as decimating Aboriginal populations. This double vision remains unresolved in Threlkeld's writing and complicates any easy categorisation of his place within colonial culture. It is overly simplistic to reclaim his work as a progressive part of a cross-cultural project – he was evidently equally pleased to be identified, though at different times and in different ways, with the authority and authenticity of both Aboriginal Australia and white colonial institutions.

However, Threlkeld explicitly recognised the political nature of his linguistic work. In his *Reminiscences*, he writes:

There were no other means of acquiring the language, but direct from the natives, and it was maintained by many in the colony that the Blacks had no language at all but were only a race of the monkey tribe! This was a convenient assumption, for if it could be proved that the Aborigines of New South Wales were only a species of wild beasts, there could be no guilt attributed to those who shot them off or poisoned them as cumberers of the earth.[10]

Threlkeld's deliberate interventions between aggressive white settlers and increasingly dispossessed Aborigines are made explicit in such provocative commentaries. It is significant, of course, that he had had previous experience in language acquisition in Polynesia, and made direct comparisons between the two regions. He argued that obtaining knowledge of Aboriginal languages is much more difficult than in Polynesia in part because of the nomadic nature of Aboriginal life occasioned by their necessity to move for subsistence, but he proposes that

The language is also much more complicated in its structure and peculiar in its idioms than that of the South Sea Islanders... What has hitherto been considered as the mere chatter of babboons [*sic*], is found to possess a completeness and extent, by the most simple combinations, that must eventually combat and defeat the bold yet groundless assertions of many who maintain, 'that the blacks of New South Wales are incapable of receiving instruction'. (42)

Threlkeld's confrontational nature is obvious here. His willingness to take on other early colonists and condemn their (presumed) actions and attitudes was also manifested in his libel case against John Dunmore Lang in 1836, and in the complaints about his annual 'Report' made by the first premier of New South Wales and future colonial treasurer Stuart Donaldson, who felt accused by Threlkeld's statement that some pastoralists were boasting of poisoning Aborigines in the New England district. Each of these inflammatory acts by Threlkeld involved the airing of colonial complaints and controversies in the textual domain.

Ironically, the acquisition of Aboriginal language could well have been the least political part of his work, for it could be justified by missionary policy as well as by a kind of scholarly good-will. Threlkeld did defend his work in this way, noting that the 'almost sovereign contempt with which the aboriginal language of New South Wales has been treated in this colony, and the indifference shown toward the attempts to gain information on the subject, are not highly indicative of the love of sciences in this part of the globe'.[11]

Threlkeld deliberately cultivated the political aspects of his linguistic work. With his growing skills in Aboriginal languages and translation, he volunteered to interpret for Aboriginal defendants and witnesses in the law courts. He consistently argued for Aboriginal witnesses to be heard in criminal cases and facilitated the airing of their testimony and perspectives through his translations.[12] James Backhouse and George Washington Walker, Quaker missionaries who travelled through Australia on a religious investigation of colonial culture, note Threlkeld's role as mediator between the government and Aborigines:

in various ways, through his influence with the Government, and knowledge of their language and customs, he has the means of assisting and befriending these poor people which he endeavours to exert for their benefit. This also gives him great weight and influence with the Blacks, which he does not fail to turn to good account, both as regards themselves and Europeans, whose mutual good understanding and peaceful intercourse, he anxiously seeks to promote.[13]

Threlkeld was also at pains to correct the negative views that many white colonists had of Aborigines' intellectual capacities. His previously cited criticism of colonialist beliefs that Aborigines were incapable of instruction recurs throughout his writings and he continually asserts their potential for education. He also believed that he could learn from Aborigines:

it afforded them much amusement to correct my blunders, point out my errors, not unfrequently ending with the unclassical reprimand of – 'What for you so stupid, you very stupid fellow.' The women and children were the most patient in hearing and answering questions, the females especially in persevering to make me understand the meaning of a phrase.[14]

Given that contemporaneous white settlers entirely dismissed Aboriginal learning abilities, Threlkeld's acknowledgement of Aboriginal assistance is significant. He is also forthcoming about the assistance he received from an Aboriginal man, variously named M'Gill (McGill) or Biraban. Threlkeld repeatedly acknowledged him formally in his publications, such as the following note in *An Australian Grammar*: 'An aboriginal of this part of the colony was my almost daily companion for many years, and to his intelligence I am principally indebted for much of my knowledge respecting the structure of the language.'[15] Threlkeld notes that 'M'Gill, a noble specimen of his race, my companion and teacher in the language for many years, but no more, could take a very good drawing of vessels especially.'[16]

Threlkeld's investment in promoting himself as the voice of dispossessed Aborigines is also evident. The pleasures of speaking for others, although always ambiguous and difficult in colonial contexts given the divided loyalties of white evangelicals, were evidently real. Catherine Hall discusses the evident pleasure of Baptist missionaries in Jamaica in speaking for the oppressed and argues that there was special satisfaction in speaking for the doubly-oppressed, colonised women,[17] because of a horrified fascination with sexual matters. In his defence, Threlkeld, though keen to intervene in questions of gender and sexuality, seems to have gained this dubious pleasure in a broader political context, rather than the narrowly prurient one often evident in Jamaica and India.

However, Threlkeld did see gender and sexual relations as particularly important arenas for him to bear witness to the evils of white influence on Aboriginal society. His *Reminiscences* frequently refer to the sexual abuse of Aboriginal women and, in particular, female children by white men; the drift of dispossessed Aboriginal women into prostitution; and the breakdown of Aboriginal familial and societal structures as a result of Aboriginal women's willing or unwilling co-option into white society. These issues form the basis for gendered LMS discourse about Australia, and they closely mirror those central tropes already identified in texts about India and Polynesia. It is clear that these tropes are universal and generic, with only slight alterations for their application in different colonial cultures.

COLONIAL DEGENERACY

... abandoned to vice[18]

Threlkeld's analysis of colonial society frequently blamed the treatment and place of the convicts (and freed convicts) for the ills of the young culture. He notes:

> It was a sad mistake of the first settlers in this country not to employ the natives and hold out encouragement to them for industry... *convictism, like slavery, destroyed the finer feelings of humanity, blasted the lovely spirit of Christianity and degraded the white to a lower degree than that of the despised aborigines of New South Wales...* The conduct of the convicts towards the aborigines tended much likewise to keep up a hostile feeling.[19]

The alliance of slavery with convictism is particularly interesting because of the role played by evangelical activism in the abolition of slavery. As Henry Reynolds and others have argued, the triumph of abolition in 1833 freed up humanitarian interests to focus on new subjects, such as the new-found concern for indigenous colonised people embodied by the 1835–38 Select Committee on Aborigines (British Settlements).[20] Gillian Whitlock argues that

> the struggle for anti-slavery is a site where we can pursue an historically specific set of ideas and practices about gender, race, class and ethnicity across Britain and its colonies. What was quite specific to the abolitionist campaign was the construction of an English identity in terms of discourses of domesticity, and the articulation of this as the style of a national, middle-class gendered subject.[21]

Threlkeld's deliberate yoking together of the two forms of imperialist and colonialist control – slavery and convictism – is indicative of the complex role of LMS missionaries in colonial cultures, and it enhances our understanding of the adversarial roles they were at times prepared to adopt. As Whitlock notes, much of the discussion around slavery focussed on its dehumanising effect – it is interesting that in Threlkeld's writing the potential for the 'barbarity' of lower classes was explicitly registered in racialised and classed labour relations. In unstable social spaces such as colonial New South Wales, such nineteenth-century British anxieties about class, race, and subjectivity could be articulated and explored in ways frequently unavailable in metropolitan culture. Slavery, convictism, and white degeneracy thus function as a nodal point of mutual imbrication in Threlkeld's texts: settler culture stands accused of (re)inhabiting the reviled subject position of the slave owner. It is worth noting that Threlkeld rarely represented white people as being contaminated by contact with black women or men – instead it was Aboriginal culture which was seen to be tainted (at least potentially) by the degeneracy of white convicts and settlers.

Threlkeld's condemnation of cross-cultural sexual relationships is thus partly a concern about the degeneracy of lower classes in colonial environments, additionally inflected by race and ethnicity. Certainly he notes exploitative relations between convicts or rural white labourers (frequently freed convicts) and Aboriginal women. Threlkeld's representation of shepherds finding sexual comfort 'irrespective of colour' mobilises dual discourses of race and class, highlighting similarities between working-class and heathen 'others'. Imperial and colonial discourses continually raise the unsettling thought that the state of colonial indigenes might be indicative of the potential for European degradation. The work of missionaries both in 'home missions' to the British underprivileged and in 'foreign missions' to the colonised heathen reinforced this comparison. By 1890, William Booth, leading light of the Salvation Army, had published his *In Darkest England and the Way Out*, the title paralleling Henry Morton Stanley's book about the African heathen *In Darkest Africa, or, The Quest, Rescue, and Retreat of Emin, Governor of Equatoria* (1890).

These anxieties became particularly acute in Australia for two reasons. Firstly, convicts and subsistence settlers formed the bulk of the population, and the presence of a large population of Irish immigrants (whether convict or free) meant that well-established English modes of representation of white degradation were transported and transplanted. From the medieval period onwards, the Irish served as the 'other' who had to be displaced to make place for English rule in Ireland: as a result, they were constructed in English colonising discourse through the tropes familiar to racialised others (degeneracy, barbarism, and pre-rationality, for example).[22] The peculiarity of this colonial discourse, of course, is that it is not skin colour that marks the boundaries between self and other, but a less visible ethnicity. As Luke Gibbons argues, 'it is clear that a native population which happened to be white was an affront to the very idea of the "white man's burden", and threw into disarray some of the constitutive categories of colonial discourse. The "otherness" and alien character of Irish experience was all the more disconcerting precisely because it did not lend itself to visible racial divisions.'[23] Irish convicts in Australia, already tainted in Threlkeld's mind because of the link he made between the subjectivities of convicts and slaves, were thus further contaminated by their ethnicity. Representations of degenerate West Indian planters were also common images in Britain, white colonials contaminated by their slave ownership. Given the battles between evangelical anti-slavery missionaries and pro-slavery planters and their supporters back in Britain (such as Thomas Carlyle),[24] Threlkeld's indictment of convictism as slavery strategically condemned white Australian elites as much as convicts.

Secondly, the colonial environment itself could, it was thought, cause degeneracy. Concern about whether white men could thrive in the harsh environment of Australia continually dogged settlement plans, particularly in the tropics but more generally throughout the country. Later treatises such as Raphael Cilento's *The White Man in the Tropics* (1925) both map the ways in which white men must adapt to 'master' the land and reinforce the anxiety that exotic environments were naturally inimical to white settlers. White bodies, and white minds, needed to protect themselves from the inhospitable antipodean environment. Such ideas were rooted in natural histories which constructed moral and racial geographies.[25] Later, they were fostered by Darwinian ideas of natural selection, and the subsequent Social Darwinism which led to hardening racial attitudes. Combined with anxieties about the otherness of colonial landscapes – the ways in which they resisted European efforts to belong, to see themselves reflected in nature, and to provide a textual landscape hospitable to pre-existing cultural traditions – this ensured that the Australian landscape was often figured as threatening to the white race, a source of physical, moral, and racial contamination. Thus Threlkeld makes the startling claim that convicts had become degraded 'to a lower degree than that of the despised aborigines'.[26]

At the same time, however, Threlkeld was prepared to note that 'there are also White Gentlemen whose taste, when in the Bush, leads them to keep Black Concubines: – no wonder that the unhappy convict, whose state of bondage generally precludes marriage, should readily follow the example of their betters, for whose conduct no such plea exists'.[27] Threlkeld's indictment of white elites in cross-cultural sexual relationships is significant, countering the suggestion of a class/race degeneracy that he elsewhere endorses, laying the blame fairly explicitly with race rather than conveniently subsuming it into a class hierarchy. Again, it is obvious here that Threlkeld's publicising of such encounters and their social consequences would alienate him from the powerful colonial elite.

Threlkeld repeatedly writes about white men's sexual relationships with Aboriginal women, and his micronarrative from the 1825–6 *Reminiscences* is worth analysing in detail. He writes:

Sometimes their daughters, and often their wives were either decoyed away, or, as I have witnessed, would have been taken by violence but for timely assistance. In the interior, the desolate Shepherd was glad to obtain by any means a female, irrespective of colour, to be his companion in his isolated position. This occassioned [*sic*] a reluctance in the frail dark-one to return to her sable lord, her treatment as a concubine being generally speaking far more humane than that which the Aboriginal wife received from her legal husband. The assigned servant thus placed himself in an awkward position, for the whole tribe would frequently visit his hut and expect entertainment, which pressed hard on the rations allowed for subsistence and quarrels were frequently the consequence of such intercourse.[28]

Threlkeld's characterisation of the Aboriginal woman as a 'frail dark-one' and as a victim of both 'her sable lord' and 'the desolate Shepherd' is significant. Like other LMS missionaries, Threlkeld continually realigns indigenous gender and marital relations within evangelical, European contexts. The representation of Aboriginal women as 'frail' seeks to locate Aboriginal femininity within evangelical discourses about women as the vulnerable sex, in need of protection from men and the masculine world of the public sphere. Naturally this protection was best provided by the domestic sphere of the (Christian) nuclear household. The representation of Aboriginal men as 'sable lords' – although ironic – similarly invokes evangelical ideals of masculinity, which attempt, contradictorily, to condemn authoritarian modes of gender relations whilst supporting the male dominance in the ideal (British) evangelical household. Threlkeld's argument that 'concubinage' was preferred by Aboriginal women over the traditional marriage relations of Aboriginal culture condemns both Aboriginal custom and colonial practice.

The sentiments Threlkeld expresses here, however, contradict other passages of the *Reminiscences* which deal with Aboriginal gender and marriage customs. Elsewhere, he notes: 'Blacks do love their wives. I have seen McGill, and Patty his wife, in all the playfulness of pure affection, like Abraham sporting with Sarah in the even-tide, and Patty like Sarah too, be as much displeased when another hand-maiden usurped her legitimate place in the affections of her lord.'[29] In these and other writings, Threlkeld frequently attests to the importance of mourning customs in Aboriginal culture, particularly for widows. Though he often disapproves of the physical manifestations of this mourning (notably scarification and finger amputation), he does not question its emotional sincerity or cultural importance. Here again, though, Threlkeld's narrative is torn between his remarkably clear-sighted ethnographic observations and the influence of missionary discourses which always had textual traditions for representing such cross-cultural experiences. Christopher Herbert astutely describes this kind of rupture in Polynesian missionary texts as a 'seemingly unresolvable moral and emotional predicament',[30] one brought about by the compromise of the missionary self in its intimacy with heathen others. It is a tension, as Herbert notes of William Ellis' *Polynesian Researches*, that missionary writers were acutely aware of, which can only be accommodated by allowing it to stand wholly unreconciled: the 'paradox in which all this literature is involved, in other words, is that it calls for the minute and sympathetic study, at the cost of arduous training, of social phenomena defined from the outset as worthless and marked out for the speediest possible forcible elimination' (166).

After his discussion about McGill/Biraban and Patty's obvious marital affection, Threlkeld continues: 'in general, the wives were what we call degraded, though themselves had no idea of such degradation. It is the gospel alone which raised woman, not only in her own estimation, but in that of the other sex, to her proper sphere, one with her husband.'[31] His general attitudes towards marriage and gender relations were of course directed by religious discourse, which firmly endorsed the belief that only evangelical Christianity could offer equality and respect to women. Threlkeld's suggestion that women may not recognise their 'degradation' is typical of the universalising nature of such ideologies. In anticipating resistance, evangelical tenets sought to neutralise it by insisting that once the unconverted embrace Christianity as the centre of their lives they would then (and possibly only then) realise that gender relations are deeply flawed outside the Christian paradigm. It is indicative of Threlkeld's comparatively enlightened view of racial hierarchies that he associates the Aboriginal and biblical couples of Abraham/Sarah and McGill/Patty. Many other colonists of the time would have seen this as heresy.

The final point raised by Threlkeld's narrative of relations between shepherds and Aborigines is the complex set of social and cultural relationships which such encounters established. His description of demands on white men for food and entertainment hint at ways in which Aboriginal communities viewed such liaisons and how they incorporated these newcomers and their interactions with them into a pre-existing system of Aboriginal sociality. In 'Bond-Slaves of Satan', Annette Hamilton saliently notes that white colonists were quick to read Aboriginal women's sexual assertiveness or male 'lending' of their wives as prostitution, when in fact examination of specific negotiations around sexuality (such as that detailed by Threlkeld) suggests that women may have initiated cross-racial contacts out of curiosity, desire, or to gain status or material benefit.[32] Threlkeld's narrative makes it clear that Aboriginal communities associated with individual women were often deeply involved in these transactions, and sought to gain advantage – here figured as 'entertainment' for 'the whole tribe' – from white men engaged in cross-cultural relationships.

Threlkeld also did not shrink from condemning settler ill-treatment of Aborigines. In December 1825 he wrote that 'it is not at all surprising that men are murdered in the Interior, when even in the vicinity of a town [Aboriginal men]...are grossly maltreated by the prisoners on account of the Black women'.[33] This comment was in response to a report of an incident when a white man beat local Aborigines because they prevented him from taking a ten year old Aboriginal girl. Threlkeld continues:

I...have heard at night the shrieks of Girls, about eight or nine years of age, taken by force by the vile men of Newcastle. One man came to me with his head broken by the butt-end of a musket because he would not give up his wife. There are now two government stockmen, that are every night annoying the Blacks by taking their little Girls... [but] the evidence of the Black cannot be admitted, and indeed they are really terrified to speak. (91)

His readiness to attest to the sexual and physical abuse of Aboriginal people, especially young girls, was conspicuous given that many other members of colonial society chose to ignore such incidents. His identification of these injustices as pertaining not only to questions about individuals and their human rights, but also to systemic judicial discrimination, is highly significant. Threlkeld thus condemns both the general inhumanity of the colonial system and its institutional biases. His comment about the inadmissibility of Aboriginal evidence and Aboriginal reluctance to attest to white colonial aggression reinforces the importance of his own work in translating and assisting Aboriginal defendants and complainants. Threlkeld's evangelical beliefs (and his desire to 'save' Aboriginal women from both white and Aboriginal men) clearly play a part in his emphasis on the vulnerability of women and children, but his willingness to bear public witness to colonial atrocities indicates how these beliefs could function simultaneously in conservative modes (reinforcing traditional gender roles) and in radical ones (as an humanitarian concern for the fate of indigenous peoples).

Threlkeld was clearly concerned about the degeneration of Aboriginal lifestyles as a result of interaction with white culture. He describes Aboriginal boys leaving his mission to go to Newcastle, 'where drunkenness is as common with the boys of seven or eight years of age, as prostitution is with the other sex of the same age, and all young or old, or either sex, are alike abandoned to vice' (96–7). Threlkeld's condemnation of the Aboriginal adoption of European vices parallels his disapproval of cross-cultural interactions in general. But his description of the degrading influence of European practices is also a testament to the deliberate destruction caused by colonial invaders, and represents an attempt to trace the real effects of this invasion on Aboriginal culture and society:

in this Colony, local circumstances have occasioned the total destruction of the Blacks within its limits... The un-matrimonial state of the thousands of male prisoners scattered throughout the country amidst females, though of another color, leads them by force, fraud, or bribery to withdraw the Aboriginal women from their own proper mates, and disease, and death are the usual consequences of such proceedings. The Official return from one district gives only two women to twenty eight men, two boys and no girls! (137)

Threlkeld thus identifies military laws and practices as resulting in the decimation of Aboriginal culture, as well as specific local practices of settlers. His acknowledgement that cross-cultural sexual relationships were not just 'sinful', in a religious context, but also highly destructive of Aboriginal cultures and laws, is relatively unusual both for white colonists in Australia and, indeed, for LMS missionaries anywhere in the colonial world. His recognition of the disturbance and destruction of Aboriginal gender and marriage relations did not prevent him from interfering in Aboriginal relations in order to instil Christian principles, but it is significant that Threlkeld, writing in the mid nineteenth century, could already recognise the destruction wrought upon Aboriginal culture by colonisation. Threlkeld was neither the first nor the only voice of humanitarian concern for, as Henry Reynolds suggests, major moral questions and qualms had been aired from the very beginning of Australian colonisation.[34] Nor, as Alan Lester makes clear, were these concerns uniquely Australian, being played out globally though a 'metropolitan sense of responsibility into new Asian, North American, African, and Australasian terrains'.[35] But Threlkeld's deliberate and thorough plan to reveal the ongoing effects of imperial incursion marks him, and particularly his voluminous textual output, for a special site within the colonial archive.

Threlkeld's Statement

The end of Threlkeld's Lake Macquarie mission came about from a combination of factors, predominantly financial, though his strained relations with influential members of the colonial society – particularly Samuel Marsden and John Dunmore Lang – certainly contributed. Although the deputation had initially advised him that 'the funds of the Society [would be] . . . responsible for the expences [*sic*]',[36] the LMS decided that Threlkeld was drawing far too much upon the society's coffers. It is difficult and probably unrewarding to judge the validity of their complaints, but it is obvious in perusing colonial records that the LMS reliance on Marsden as their intermediary in this affair would only inflame the matter. So too was Threlkeld's keen sense of personal entitlement. The combination of Threlkeld's feelings of slight and Marsden's unsupportive officiousness guaranteed that this affair became acrimonious and highly unpleasant. However, a fascinating aspect of the controversy was the way in which Threlkeld deliberately, thoroughly, and effectively manipulated publication and textual authority in an attempt to win, if not the argument as a whole, then certainly the public sentiment of the time *and* the authoritative historical 'voice'. As his official portrait suggests, he was keen to project himself as the voice of scholarship too – this image of Threlkeld with a copy of one of his many publications was staged for the camera on at least two different occasions (see Figure 2). In 1828 Threlkeld published *A Statement Chiefly Relating to the Formation and Abandonment of a Mission to the Aborigines of New South Wales; Addressed to the Serious Consideration of the Directors of the London Missionary Society*, a document which strategically manipulated texts surrounding this affair for the purpose of vindicating his activities.

Threlkeld published the *Statement* as a strategic, political act; he appeared to intentionally provoke the LMS and its local representative, Marsden. John Dunmore Lang described it as a 'pamphlet of crimination . . . against Mr Marsden'.[37] The 'note' at the beginning of the text claims that

Figure 2 Lancelot Edward Threlkeld (*c.* 1850). (Reproduced by permission of the Mitchell Library, State Library of New South Wales.)

this Statement being a communication to the Directors individually, which could not be effected in any other way than by the Press, even were the Writer in England, it is requested, that Persons who may accidentally obtain a perusal, will abstain from publishing its contents; the object desired being, that a more ingenious mode of conducting the general concerns of the Society be adopted in future. The serious consideration of the whole body of the Directors is most earnestly solicited to this statement, to prevent a more enlarged and general appeal becoming necessary.[38]

The obvious attention to issues of textual production, the propriety of public circulation of information, and the practical problems of colonial communication with the imperial metropolis express the central concerns of this very anxious document. These issues form both the subject and the textual form of the *Statement*. Whilst the LMS withdrew their support for Threlkeld primarily because they believed he was spending excessively on his Lake Macquarie mission, mail delays and confrontational communications between the Society, Threlkeld, and Marsden exacerbated the financial problems. These problems of communication, and of who had the authority to act for and on behalf of the LMS, recur throughout this text and others written by Threlkeld. His (over) emphasis on these matters and his continual self-justification suggest that profound personal (and typically colonial) anxieties are at play in and around this text. Indeed, Threlkeld's place on the margins of settler society are most evident here: it becomes obvious that he felt his position – one of 'the mortification of being at the Antipodes of our friends, abandoned to the mercy of whatever Mr Marsden might hazard to advance on his own responsibility, having no authority from the Society' (55) – to be a profoundly *un*settling one. His fears were real as well as psychological. Threlkeld was in fact arrested and briefly imprisoned because the LMS refused to pay the bills he had drawn.

Threlkeld tells his reader much about the necessity for producing this *Statement*. The prefatory note cited above opens the document; Threlkeld notes that 'the printing of this statement will supersede the necessity of my returning to Europe, in order, personally, to enter into explanations on the subject; by which much time will be saved, and the expenditure of several hundred pounds' (3); and he comments on the style of his text, explaining that

I could, if necessary, produce numerous testimonies as to my conduct, or shelter myself by a phalanx of witnesses, capable of forming a correct judgement, in this colony, on the business. But I feel persuaded, that the simple statement of the whole facts, as they really exist, will, to the unbiased mind, be sufficient to prevent unfavourable impressions against me. (65–6)

Such protestations at the necessity for publicly airing the controversy il-luminate the extent to which the *Statement* was a direct attack on the directors of the LMS and their policies, made in the form most dear to them, published missionary writing.

The issue of texts and authority, and of the appropriate address of mis-sionary writing, recurs throughout the *Statement*. Threlkeld complains that missionaries 'have little, if any, attention paid to their letters or representa-tions by the Committee' (4), and that 'the present communications [from the LMS to the missionaries] are more characteristic of the lordly masters, than of fellow labourers in the vineyard of Jesus Christ' (16). He aggressively accuses the directors: 'you treat your Missionaries in print as brethren, in your private communications as an inferior order of beings, hardly wor-thy of notice, or at least as the most suspicious characters. It is high time that a different feeling should exist' (27). It is evident that Threlkeld saw the problems of appropriate relationships between the directors and work-ing missionaries as being played out explicitly in the textual arena. His complaints about the gap between printed, public versions of the LMS communications and private correspondence make obvious the practical ways in which the society sought to control missionary textual production, in accordance with the production of an official discourse on evangelical ac-tivity which would consolidate their standing within colonial and imperial institutions.

This was not Threlkeld's first attempt to manipulate the public record. In his *Statement* he describes writing a letter addressed to the treasurer of the LMS (William Hankey) which he then had printed and circulated 'to each of the Directors in London, to many in the country, and to every person concerned in this Colony, on the same day as one was addressed to Mr Marsden' (37). This letter, obviously written in haste (and considerable anger) and concerning his incarceration, confronts the directors with the details of Threlkeld's situation:

I am detained a prisoner, obliged to state the facts of the case to exonerate my character as a Missionary to my friends; this becomes public, the Deputation and Directors are censured, and the cause of missions ultimately suffers through hasty acts of persons in authority, living 13,000 miles from the sphere of action ... [A]ll these things occasioned, not from any improper conduct on my part, but arising from that unaccountable policy which has driven so many Missionaries from the field, which is still grieving the hearts of those now engaged in the work, and which is tempting others to leave the Society in disgust. (38)

As Marsden disapprovingly suggested to Threlkeld, some of these observa-tions seemed 'only calculated to give offence to your superiors... It would have been more proper to have confined your remarks to your own particular case, and avoided all censure upon the conduct of the Directors towards other Missionaries.'[39]

Marsden was always prepared to criticise Threlkeld's writing in detail. In response to earlier correspondence, he rebuked Threlkeld: 'I cannot but observe your language in this letter is very strong; and I should apprehend, would give unnecessary pain and offence to the Society. It wants that meekness of wisdom which St Paul recommends.'[40] Marsden was also aware of the hierarchies of textual authority within the missionary community, adding that 'addressing such a letter to a public body, under whose authority you were acting, was very injudicious.'[41]

Threlkeld's reprinting of private letters – from the LMS, from Marsden, and from other missionaries, many of whom seemed to agree privately with his criticisms of the society – was in many ways outrageous, because it broke down the LMS policy of markedly differentiating between opinions expressed in personal correspondence and others which were appropriate in official, public documents. Threlkeld's actions probably alienated many of his correspondents, but he did manage to expose the society's obsessive control of missionary textual production and circulation.

The LMS mission in Australia was a colonial evangelical project raising many questions about missionary intervention in colonial cultures, about gender and sexuality, and about the particular politics of these issues in settler colonies. The level of acrimonious debate around Threlkeld and his Lake Macquarie mission, however, proves that these questions remained unanswered by the end of Threlkeld's missionary work for the LMS. The bitterness of elite colonial society towards Threlkeld's interventions in the legal system and in cross-cultural sexual relations, in particular, suggests that he managed to touch on precisely those issues which were integral to the maintenance and development of settler society in Australia.

The comparative lack of 'glamour' associated with the salvation of the Aboriginal heathen, too, had never helped Threlkeld's cause. Stories of *zenana* women and Polynesian 'noble savages' made better textual subjects for a British audience with a keen appetite for evangelical narratives of encounters with the 'heathen', as these neatly dramatised LMS work and mirrored earlier imperial discourses familiar from travel, ethnographic, and exploration narratives. Representations of Australian Aborigines, by contrast, specifically *because* they were perceived as embodying the 'basest savagery', were not as easily incorporated into appealing texts. In a telling omission, no images from Australia appear on the lurid covers of the *Missionary Sketches* pamphlet published monthly during this period, though illustrations from Polynesia and India frequently appear. Threlkeld himself notes that

it is to be feared that the high state of excitement to which the religious public have been accustomed, will render the appearance of this mission very unpromising, there being nothing here to encourage the feeble-minded; no moving on the tops of the mulberry-trees; no shaking of the bones; but all dry, dry, very dry scattered bones, in the midst of a waste howling wilderness. (29)

It is also interesting to note that the existential colonial crisis engendered in many writers and artists by the apparent 'otherness' of the Australian land-scape (Marcus Clarke's 'weird melancholy', for example)[42] is here evident in Threlkeld's writing too. For Threlkeld, of course, this was a dual crisis of colonial anxiety and religious isolation, where even within white colonial culture religious philosophies were open to ridicule.

The absence of a 'high state of excitement' about the Australian mission was also due, in part, to another rather different lack of *textual* opportunity. The Australian mission simply did not generate the same exciting sense of mass conversion that missions in Polynesia and India did and thus could not lend itself to quite the same textual grandiloquence. Arguably this was partly because of the very obvious lack of missionary success in Australia, but also because of the complicated politics and culture of a settler penal colony. Many of the criticisms of colonial missionary activity which would become dominant in later years within Britain itself were earlier voiced in settler opposition to the work of Threlkeld and other missionaries in colonial Australia. Of course, Threlkeld and his fellow brethren had a substantial local white community viewing their work and publicising their criticisms. For example, in the libel case brought by Threlkeld, John Dunmore Lang defended his publication of three volumes on the colony when he was last in England, and his contribution of

several articles on subjects of colonial interest, to a weekly periodical. Surely the subject of the aborigines was one which would be likely to claim the earliest attention of such a person, and it was natural, in treating of that subject, to point out the means that had been adopted for their spiritual and temporal wel-fare, and to direct attention to the degree of success which had attended those means.[43]

The participation of Australian colonial elites such as Lang and Archdea-con Broughton in British parliamentary committees, like Thomas Fowell Buxton's 1835 Select Committee on Aborigines (British Settlements), proves the influence that such 'imperial networks'[44] could have. In this way, too, missionaries in Australian colonies functioned quite differently from those in Polynesia, where they formed the majority white population and strongly encouraged other white inhabitants to move on if they disagreed with missionary reforms.

The presence of the white settler community also raised issues about class and colonial degeneracy. The implementation of European theories about racial (and classed) hierarchies and the potential of the environment to induce 'degradation' was central to many discussions about the Australian colony as a whole and particularly the work of religious personnel. Threlkeld's commitment to exposing the excesses of settler culture repeatedly mobilised such ideas, and evidently confused his own attempts to categorise or judge the black and white colonial inhabitants. His ability to move between these two communities meant that Threlkeld was the very embodiment of the ambivalent settler figured in postcolonial theory. His positioning on the boundaries of black and white Australia, and his willingness to mimic the authenticity and authority of either community at different, strategic moments of colonial encounters, mean that his texts, too, evince a doubled discursive positioning. His perspective on Aborigines as degraded but salvageable placed him in a curious position between two cultures – he neither accepted Aboriginal communities' integrity as survival cultures, nor advocated the (physical and discursive) displacement of those cultures by colonists. It is this double vision which makes Threlkeld's writings and position within colonial cultures so interesting, yet disturbing. The contradictions within his own texts mirror those of the LMS official discourse. Threlkeld's ability to see textual representation as a strategic, political affair (something of which he accused the society) perhaps meant that he could more easily accept the ambivalence of his own textual productions.

For this study it is significant that this ambivalence is most obvious in his discussions of gender and sexuality. Threlkeld's representation of himself as the 'saviour' of Aboriginal women from both Aboriginal and white men and, in evangelical terms, from themselves, was possibly his most controversial intervention into colonial affairs. His concern to eradicate cross-cultural sexual relationships was both evangelical and humanitarian in its motivation, even though in doing so he denied Aboriginal women any agency. As Annette Hamilton notes, whilst missionary figures such as Threlkeld were scandalised at the 'heathenism' of the Aboriginal population, they were 'among the very few who raised their voices to protest against the ruthless practices of settler colonists and to champion some kind of rights of indigenous people to survival and livelihood'.[45] Hamilton goes on to suggest that the real problem was that of sexual relations between white men and Aboriginal women, something which left visible and uncontestable signs within the colonial population in the form of venereal disease and part-European children. This was the terrible testimony of vice which the interaction between Aborigines and settlers produced everywhere, constituting a serious challenge to the bourgeois hegemony which was developing as the nineteenth century progressed. (251)

The complications of Threlkeld's position were that he was simultaneously an agent of publicising these 'visible and uncontestable signs' of sexual interactions *and* an agent promoting the practices and policies of bourgeois hegemony. This is the fundamentally unresolvable tension haunting Threlkeld's texts, writings that are, in this manner, characteristic of the tensions of missionary discourse as a genre. Located somewhere between the violently colonial and the humanitarian Christian, these texts trouble the easy categorisation of colonial cultures and the various agents of empire within them.

Crucially, Threlkeld and his texts not only troubled nineteenth-century arguments about the morality of colonisation, but continue to complicate contemporary debates about the same matter. Since the 1970s, Australian historians such as Henry Reynolds have been re-examining colonial history for evidence of what Bernard Smith has called the 'concerned conscience' of white Australians.[46] Some of these histories have examined the role of early missionaries in encouraging humanitarian relationships between black and white Australians in order to establish the complex and contested cultural politics of the early colonies. Reynolds' *This Whispering in Our Hearts* is the leading study, and it explores the history of white humanitarian concerns in Australia through a series of individuals and historical events. Reynolds uses Threlkeld's writing as evidence of nineteenth-century challenges to 'the ethics of colonial progress'.[47] Threlkeld's annual reports provide Reynolds with evidence about border wars, official and private punitive expeditions by white colonials, European attitudes towards Aborigines, and colonial atrocities, particularly Threlkeld's allegations about the Myall Creek massacre in 1838.

Published in 1998, *This Whispering in Our Hearts* contributed to the growing reassessment of the colonial past in postcolonial Australia. Coming one year after the Human Rights and Equal Opportunity Commission report, *Bringing Them Home*, the book appeared at a time when a profound and unsettling reassessment of national identity and personal culpability was beginning. On the one hand, this public self-examination led to stronger public calls for a national apology to the Aboriginal community by the Federal Government, a clear growth in public support for a national

'Sorry Day', and the extraordinarily well-supported 2000 Peoples' Walk for Reconciliation in Australian capital cities. On the other hand, Australian public discourse has experienced a concerted conservative backlash. A key part of this backlash has been the activism of right-wing intellectuals and commentators. In 2000, Keith Windschuttle published a series of articles in *Quadrant* magazine seeking to debunk claims made by Australian historians as to the nature and statistical significance of cross-cultural colonial violence: Reynolds is a favourite target. Windschuttle's third article specifically attacks 'Massacre Stories' and *This Whispering in Our Hearts*. Because Reynolds uses Threlkeld, Threlkeld himself becomes a target for Windschuttle's own revisionism. Their debate is, in part, about the reliability of Threlkeld's testimony as historical fact – an argument that is unsolvable in empirical terms, based as it is on subjective assessments of Threlkeld's textual authority and character. For Reynolds, Threlkeld is one of a number of 'disturbing and even dangerous agitators' (30), whose conviction and faith made them secure in their virtue and righteousness: 'tenacious, determined and often fearless opponents' (31), who, for their efforts, 'were seen as self-righteous, disturbing, dangerous, obsessive or mad' (xiv). For Windschuttle, Threlkeld had 'an obsessive desire'[48] to exaggerate colonial violence so as to ensure his continued employment: he was imaginative and may have 'intentionally exaggerated' the size of the pre-contact Aboriginal population to emphasise the decline after colonisation. He 'not only invented the notion of a "state of war" and "a war of extirpation" ' but was 'actually caught lying'. Windschuttle opines that Threlkeld's conscience 'must have been troubled at times by some of the gruesome details and inflated numbers he could not help himself adding to his tales'. 'The works of his imagination', Windschuttle complains, 'have coloured the whole record of Aboriginal–European relations in our early colonial history'.

This is not the place to analyse the debates between Reynolds and Windschuttle in the painstaking detail they require. Suffice to say, Windschuttle's methodology of unverified impugning of character and attribution of deceit hardly promises to advance the debate, but the dispute about Threlkeld (and others) makes clear the extent to which missionary texts continue to have essential cultural valency in postcolonial cultures such as Australia.

Conclusion: missionary writing, the imperial archive and postcolonial politics

This book has argued that missionary texts constitute a distinct genre of missionary discourse, a genre that has unmistakeable, though ambivalent, relationships with imperial discourses as a whole. To conclude, I want to trace some of the recurrent features of evangelical discourses in order both to map the overarching patterns of missionary textuality and to examine the ways in which different kinds of colonies produced different modes of representation. This chapter also addresses the complex relations between missionary and broader imperial discourses – particularly in terms of mutual imbrication and gender – to suggest the value of a focus on missionary textuality for postcolonial studies.

Across the colonial world, missionary representations of their evangelical activities amongst colonised 'heathen' introduced contradictory, conflicted knowledges into the imperial archive. For LMS missionaries, colonial experience provided a plethora of complex information, experiences, and narratives which could not always be aligned with imperial philosophies or society dictates. As such, almost every publication by a missionary with colonial experience was testimony to the obvious disjunction between metropolitan ideas and colonial practice. The texts analysed all bear evidence to this disjunction, though in a variety of ways. At the same time, however, these texts also promote colonial evangelical projects. This doubled discursive framework – simultaneously endorsing and challenging imperial institutions and ideas – continually troubled efforts to produce seamless representations of colonial evangelism.

Missionary writers could rarely maintain an innocent, unmediated view of textuality. Both the society's explicit manipulation of writings from the field and missionaries' own difficulties in structuring meaningful narratives ensured that writing and representation were issues with which they continually grappled. Missionary texts are thus characterised by both transparency and opacity. That is, these writings are highly explicit in both their mobilisation of pre-existing discursive practices and their dissatisfaction with such generic regulations. Missionary texts tend to be formulaic replications of their evangelical and imperial pretexts (recurring narratives about Indian women are a clear example). At the same time, their authors were highly conscious of the ways in which established modes actually failed to address complex issues at the colonial sites where they were written.

Missionary writing about race, for instance, is caught up in a number of different discursive domains. Firstly, as I have suggested, missionary discourses maintain a distinct position on racial difference which, although participating in racialist hierarchies, is nevertheless obliged to promote a 'common' humanity. Believing in the potential for Christian transformation, evangelical representations of the colonised 'heathen' stress not only their traditional degradation – which justified conversion and salvation – but also their productive response to encounters with British Christians. This aspect of racial 'improvement' was quite different from, on the one hand, the celebration of noble savagery characteristic of much eighteenth-century thought, and, on the other, the philosophy of racial degradation which sustained aggressive imperial destruction of indigenous cultures. Secondly, though, missionaries could not remain cocooned from these different views on race, and their texts frequently recite, revisit, or interrogate other imperial or colonial narratives. Thus, during the nineteenth century, missionary discourses gradually moved closer to these other racial ideologies, when evangelical belief in the transformative potential of colonised peoples was found unsustainable in negotiating specific local issues, because of native resistance to Christian and colonial intervention. This resistance could be manifested either passively (through a reluctance to convert to Christianity) or actively (such as the Indian Mutiny). In either case, representations of racial difference were fraught with tensions.

Whilst in some instances missionary writing glibly elides the difficulties of writing in European genres about non-western cultures (or the collision of British and 'other' cultures), it is frequently explicit about such issues. These difficulties are variously portrayed but with a common concern. Sometimes there is a frank discussion of the untrustworthy nature of other imperial/colonial texts, or a questioning of how to include the complexity of colonial experience within a narrative structure; in other cases texts simply fail to articulate adequately some crucial issues.

Because these texts are highly aware of both their formulaic nature and the difficulties of representing colonial experience, they are particularly valuable as sites upon which to explore contemporary critical questions about the nature of textuality, the politics of representation, and the possibility of recuperating historical traces through 'tainted' documents. These narratives are conscious of their selective and partial nature, and so the reader too becomes especially aware of his/her reading process. Reading such texts does not promise to decipher 'the truth' of cross-cultural evangelical encounters, but rather the issues which missionary writers failed to portray coherently.

Two issues in particular defeated missionary writers' attempts at coherent representation. The first is gender; and the second is the level of mutual imbrication characterising missionary experience. Representing gender was especially problematic for the predominantly male missionary profession in the first part of the nineteenth century: whilst evangelical men certainly profess to be able to represent and judge issues related to gender and domesticity, they are continually affronted by the very difference that they sought to realign with Christian paradigms. The *zenana*, as both a cultural institution and a representational trope, for example, remained fundamentally opaque to them, in spite of its repeated mobilisation within their texts. Infanticide, too, remained an issue that these writers simply could not resolve. Gender presented missionary authors with a range of cultural blind spots which even the most fervent reformers could not dismiss by simply reverting to imperial condemnation. Evangelical texts thus return again and again to such issues, yet they ultimately elude resolution into Christian, colonial paradigms.

Missionary texts are thus forced into issues of mutual imbrication. In grappling with the disjunctions between imperial theory and colonial practice, they highlight the ways in which colonial experience necessarily ameliorated missionary ideals. This is played out in a range of different textual realms: as a specific questioning of textuality and genre; as an explicit debate about the different values of British and native cultural practices; or as an adoption or recognition of the productive interface between cultures. Missionary texts continually refer to the ways in which they had to adapt evangelical practices to local conditions and they continually assess whether this accommodation is in fact a compromise. At the same time, they also report the various ways in which local communities incorporated parts of British, Christian culture. As the (often disapproving) discussions of linguistic hybridity demonstrate, such native adoptions of imperial/colonial culture were not always welcomed by missionaries, though in other contexts they were encouraged (such as the adoption of western dress).

The authors themselves perceived that this mutual imbrication was not only evident in their practical efforts in the field, but that it also influenced imperial culture within Britain. LMS missionaries constantly complain of feeling isolated, but it is evident that they felt this isolation, in part, because they very much identified themselves with broader imperial (missionary) projects. Either aggressively (like Lancelot Threlkeld) or more subtly (like John Williams), they sought to re-educate the imperial centre about colonial encounters and environments. They attempted to inform the British public through the publication of their ethnographic, encyclopaedic narratives, and to change imperial philosophies and policies. Their texts do so by ranging from unashamedly rhetorical propaganda to an explicit refutation of imperial arguments and criticisms of missionary work. Tyerman and Bennet's *Journal*, for example, specifically criticises poetry employing images of noble savages. They write: 'Alas! Such a race of "Indians" never existed any where on the face of this fallen world, in a state of nature – or rather, in that state of heathenism in which the best feelings of nature are incessantly and universally outraged.'[1] Missionary writers realise this mutual imbrication through a deliberate attempt to rewrite the imperial archive by introducing different knowledge about colonised peoples and cross-cultural encounters.

The process of mutual imbrication thus begins at the colonial periphery and is refracted to the metropole. The employment of women missionaries to India was a direct result of colonial experience. Significantly, it then led to the deployment of images of Indian women in the cause of British women's suffrage. Colonial missionary experience thus not only challenged the ways imperial people thought about colonised cultures, but also the ways in which they thought about themselves. Similarly, issues raised by white settlers in Australia both in support of and resistance to the placement of missionaries between Aboriginal and colonial interests were replayed in debates arising later in nineteenth-century Britain about the moral responsibility of imperial citizens for colonised subjects. Mutual imbrication is actualised in this dialogic relation between colonial (including both white and indigenous communities) and imperial cultures.

In terms of debates surrounding class, too, colonial experience profoundly influenced imperial attitudes in a variety of ways. Firstly, evangelical concentration on two specific constituencies – the British poor and the colonised 'heathen' – encouraged the correlation between them. Representations of both groups became increasingly similar. The 'dark' faces of the British urban poor resembled those of the 'benighted heathen'. Each group was simultaneously 'raised up' through the inculcation of the Christian work ethic, manners, domestic relations and, towards the end of the century, hygiene. Missionary experiences with each community reflected on their representation and treatment of the other, so that successful evangelical techniques with the working-class poor were used with the colonised, and vice versa. The underclass in Britain were also encouraged to take a religious interest in the welfare of their colonised counterparts as part of their own 'upraising', when LMS fundraising efforts specifically targeted working-class groups.

Secondly, missionaries were regular witnesses to instances of white degradation in colonial environments. This was specifically the case with LMS condemnation of beachcombers, traders, and naval personnel in the Pacific; and convicts and settlers in Australia. Tyerman and Bennet were particularly outspoken in regard to the negative effects of the white presence in Polynesia. In relation to local prostitution they write:

This is a subject on which we must not, we dare not, record 'what we have seen and do know'. The utter abolition of this infamy in the Christianized islands of the Southern Pacific is one of the signal triumphs of the gospel in the history of human wickedness, in any age or part of the world. It is painful to add... that for this very cause the gospel and its other triumphs are evil spoken of by many Christians (falsely so called) who visit these seas, and are filled with rage, disappointment, and malice, when they find that they cannot riot in licentiousness, as former voyagers did, on these once polluted shores. Therefore do they abhor the change, and calumniate those who have been instrumental in its production. (1: 383)

Such 'infamous' white behaviour in colonies, when European controls of social behaviour seemed to be absent and the 'degraded' nature of colonised cultures seemed prevalent, contributed to evangelical and imperial suspicion that colonial climates caused racial degeneracy. In such physical and moral environments, then, what seemed in metropolitan cultures to be differences attributable to class were complicated by the degraded behaviour of white communities. For individual groups like sailors or convicts this degradation could be subsumed within a paradigm of class, but Threlkeld's condemnation of white 'gentlemen' revelling in the sexual freedom apparent in New South Wales questions such tidy hierarchies. The readiness of missionaries to bear witness to the degeneration of white behaviour in the colonies, then, suggested that the categorisation (and reformation) of British communities in terms of class difference was not as coherent a programme as it might have appeared.

It was in the sphere of gender, however, that mutual imbrication was most effectively realised. Missionary personnel went to their colonial postings with highly prescriptive views on gender and domestic relations endorsed by the LMS and other societies. The experimental nature of their experience, however, meant that assumptions about gendered roles were almost immediately challenged, both by the new roles which missionaries and their wives assumed and by their exposure to alternate ways of demarcating gender. Whilst LMS missionaries continually reasserted their expectations of gendered differences both for native communities and their fellow evangelicals, they simultaneously acted counter to such traditional roles. Missionary wives, for instance, took on far greater public roles than they may have done in Britain, in areas such as education, healthcare, and community programmes. This was a natural extension of British philanthropy, but it was carried out on a substantially broader level by missionary wives in the colonies than it was 'at home'. Representations of missionary women, then, oscillate between their depiction as exemplary householders and domestic caregivers and their more public (and less subservient) roles in female evangelisation.

Male missionaries, too, found their conceptions of masculinity challenged by their confrontation with other cultural forms of masculinity. Missionaries in India, for example, demonstrate their uneasiness by representing Asian men as being both effeminate *and* a sexual threat to British women. Similarly, Polynesian men are condemned for their acceptance of male homosexuality *and* for their heterosexual 'licentiousness'. As Mrinalini Sinha argues of imperial British representations in general, 'the British demonstrated the Bengali's lack of "manly self-control" in arguments about the excessive sexual indulgence of the Bengali male, represented by the premature consummation of marriage as well as by the overtly sexual atmosphere of the Bengali home'.[2] However, such representations of the "other's" sexuality and gender roles profoundly influenced the reactionary formulation of British identity. Thus white colonial masculinity was necessarily constituted in opposition to native models and in so doing was substantially influenced by native practices. The tendency of male missionaries to regard themselves as heroic 'rescuers' of native women from their men and culture, for instance, was a direct manifestation of their self-representation as markedly different kinds of men from local husbands and fathers. Colonial missionary experience of gender relations not only introduced new ideas of 'other' conceptions of gender to British people, but through this exposure to gendered cultural difference influenced the ways in which colonial and imperial citizens understood and represented gender, domesticity, and sexuality.

This mutual imbrication was played out in specific ways in the three very different cultures of India, Polynesia, and Australia, and this was in part a result of profoundly different types of colonial relations. As a colony of occupation, India offers a case where relations between white officials, missionaries, and Indian people existed as a curious combination of military occupation, industrial and mercantile investment and, later, imperial moral guardianship. Missionaries brought about more ethical attitudes on the part of the British (both at home and in India) towards Indian subjects of empire. Their concentrated attention to social reform (particularly in relation to women's issues such as *sati*, *zenanas*, and female education) significantly influenced the ways in which the British conceived of their Indian imperial project. Missionaries brought about these changes primarily through the wealth of texts they wrote about India – their obsessive (if often inaccurate) codifying and cataloguing of Indian culture ensured that imperial attitudes were conditioned by missionary perspectives.

In Polynesia, LMS missionaries attempted to establish a kind of exemplary colony – as I noted in part three, mission stations there operated as a kind of *de facto* colonial administration. The vast number of publications emerging from their evangelical efforts manifest this quasi-colonial status in specific ways. Early missionary texts like those by Ellis and Williams are characterised by their encyclopaedic qualities. Rather like colonial explorers' narratives they codify and classify Polynesian cultures. Whilst they replicate early European narratives of 'discovery', they also attempt to construct missionary experience and the narrativisation of that experience in terms of 'first encounters'. That is, the narrative perspective generally suggests that missionaries were the first Europeans to observe Pacific customs, though this was rarely the case in Polynesia. In doing so, rather like other white settler writers in the eighteenth and nineteenth centuries, LMS missionaries seek to construct an originary role for themselves in new colonial cultures.

In New South Wales, missionaries occupied highly ambiguous, unsettled positions between colonial authorities, white settlers, and the increasingly dispossessed Aborigines. As is evident in the case of Lancelot Threlkeld, this role meant they were torn between identification with their own culture – as manifested by white society (despite its predominantly irreligious character) – and the culture to which they proselytised and often had to protect – the indigenous population. The incompatible interests of these two communities ensured that evangelicals were caught between them. Missionaries in Australia often had to choose on which side their own best interests lay. They rarely chose Aboriginal interests. The imperialist view of Aboriginal culture as fundamentally lacking any significant civilised traits ensured little attention was paid to gathering information or codifying cultural practices, compared with India and Polynesia.

Across a colonial continuum (which was also a divide), missionary interests repeatedly complicated tidy categorisations of colonial culture by their various investments and interventions into both indigenous and white cultures, and their desire to be part of both communities. Because of this ambivalence and mutual imbrication, missionary history and representation offer fruitful sites for a re-examination of a number of postcolonial paradigms. The role of the well-intentioned, but destructive, colonial agent, the place of humanitarian western Christian interventions into non-western cultures, and struggles over the control and maintenance of textual (and historical) records are all areas through which Manichaean binaries might be interrogated. Both postcolonialism and feminism have often focussed on either black women *or* white women in attempts to examine the links between these two academic disciplines, and such studies could only profit by examining the mutually constitutive nature of gender relations *across* racial and cultural divides. It is in a broad-based examination of this mutual imbrication that the hegemonic power relations which imperialism attempted to institute – albeit partially and unsuccessfully – can be deconstructed from within the residues of the imperial archive itself.

Notes

INTRODUCTION: WRITING MISSIONARIES

1. Reverend Robert Burns, DD (1789–1869), was a leading Presbyterian minister, who later emigrated to Canada where he was the minister at Knox Church, Toronto, and conducted missionary work throughout Ontario and the Maritime Provinces.

2. Robert Burns, *The Indirect Benefits of the Missionary Enterprise: A Sermon Preached before the London Missionary Society, at the Tabernacle, Moorfields, on Wednesday, May 14, 1834* (London: Frederick Westley and A. H. Davis, 1834), 5.

3. Thomas Richards, *The Imperial Archive: Knowledge and the Fantasy of Empire* (London and New York: Verso, 1993).

4. Simon Gikandi, *Maps of Englishness: Writing Identity in the Culture of Colonialism* (New York: Columbia University Press, 1996), xviii.

5. Jenny Sharpe, *Allegories of Empire: The Figure of Woman in the Colonial Text* (Minneapolis and London: University of Minnesota Press, 1993), 7.

6. Nicholas Thomas defines 'colonial projects' in a way that I am wanting to emphasise in this study: 'Colonial projects are construed, misconstrued, adapted and enacted by actors whose subjectivities are fractured – half here, half there, sometimes disloyal, sometimes almost "on the side" of the people they patronize and dominate, and against the interests of some metropolitan office'. Nicholas Thomas, *Colonialism's Culture: Anthropology, Travel and Government* (Carlton, Vic.: Melbourne University Press, 1994), 60.

7. Burns, *The Indirect Benefits*, 7.

8. Gayatri Spivak, *A Critique of Postcolonial Reason: Toward a History of the Vanishing Present* (Cambridge, Mass. and London: Harvard University Press, 1999), 284.

9. Anne McClintock, *Imperial Leather: Race, Gender, and Sexuality in the Colonial Contest* (New York and London: Routledge, 1995), 44.

10. See Judith R. Walkowitz, *Prostitution and Victorian Society: Women, Class and the State* (Cambridge: Cambridge University Press, 1980); Ratnabali Chatterjee, 'Indian Prostitute as a Colonial Subject, Bengal 1864–1883', *re/productions* 2 (April 1999).

210

11. Ann Laura Stoler, *Race and the Education of Desire: Foucault's 'History of Sexuality' and the Colonial Order of Things* (Durham and London: Duke University Press, 1995), 100.
12. Johannes Fabian, 'Religious and Secular Colonization: Common Ground', *History and Anthropology* 4 (1990), 339.
13. Nicholas Thomas, *Colonialism's Culture: Anthropology, Travel and Government* (Carlton, Vic.: Melbourne University Press, 1994), 16.
14. Stoler, *Race and the Education of Desire*, 97.

I THE BRITISH EMPIRE, COLONIALISM, AND MISSIONARY ACTIVITY

1. A note here on my use of the terms imperial and colonial. 'Imperial' is used to refer to the formal, institutionalised nature of Britain's expansionist policies and attitudes, whilst 'colonial' is used predominantly to refer to the practice of imperialism outside Britain, a usage that attempts to highlight the slippages between imperial policy and the colonial practice of that policy.
2. Jamie S. Scott, 'Introduction: "Onward, Christian Britons!" ', in *'And the Birds Began to Sing': Religion and Literature in Post-Colonial Cultures*, ed. Jamie [S.] Scott, Cross/Cultures: Readings in Post/Colonial Literatures in English Ser. 22 (Amsterdam and Atlanta: Rodopi, 1996), xvii.
3. Stephen Neill, *A History of Christian Missions* (Harmondsworth: Penguin, 1964), 188.
4. Quoted in Catherine Hall, 'Missionary Stories: Gender and Ethnicity in England in the 1830s and 1840s', in *Cultural Studies*, ed. Cary Neilson, Lawrence Grossberg, and Paula Treichler (New York and London: Routledge, 1992), 247.
5. C. Silvester Horne, *The Story of the LMS, 1795–1895* (London: LMS, 1894), 2.
6. B. Kirkman Gray, *A History of English Philanthropy: From the Dissolution of the Monasteries to the Taking of the First Census* (London: Frank Cass, 1905), 80–1.
7. Jean Woolmington, ' "Writing on the Sand": The First Missions to Aborigines in Eastern Australia', in *Aboriginal Australians and Christian Missions: Ethnographic and Historical Studies*, ed. Tony Swain and Deborah Bird Rose (Bedford Park, SA: Australian Association for the Study of Religions, South Australian College of Advanced Education Sturt Campus, 1988), 77.
8. 'Candidates' Papers: Answers to Printed Questions', in CWM: *Candidates' Papers Examination Committee* (1833–8).
9. LMS, 'Board Minutes', in CWM: *Minute Books 1795–1842* (1798–1801), 1.
10. Jane Haggis notes of the LMS and denomination: 'Always overtly non-denominational in principle, the Society rarely had doctrinal doubts in accepting candidates from low church Anglican, Presbyterian or Lutheran backgrounds. Baptists, however, were more problematic. A statement of belief in infant baptism – albeit qualified – was required on the Candidates' Questions

paper for both men and women' (Jane Haggis, 'Professional Ladies and Working Wives: Female Missionaries in the London Missionary Society and its South Travancore District, South India in the Nineteenth Century' (PhD diss., University of Manchester, 1991), 225 n. 1).

11. Susan Thorne's excellent *Congregational Missions and the Making of an Imperial Culture in Nineteenth-Century England* (Stanford: Stanford University Press, 1999) has been published since the manuscript of this book was initially written. Whilst I will discuss Thorne's work in detail later in this chapter, I have generally allowed my arguments to stand independently, without referring repeatedly to the similarities between Thorne's analysis and mine.

12. McClintock, *Imperial Leather*, 261.

13. B. Holmes, 'British Imperial Policy and the Mission Schools', in *Educational Policy and the Mission Schools: Case Studies from the British Empire*, ed. B. Holmes (London: Routledge, 1967), 12–13.

14. See, particularly, 'Candidates' Papers: Answers to Printed Questions', in CWM: *Candidates' Papers Examination Committee* (1839–47).

15. Jeffrey Richards, 'With Henty to Africa', in *Imperialism and Juvenile Literature*, ed. Jeffrey Richards, Studies in Imperialism (Manchester: Manchester University Press, 1989), 81.

16. There is some recent debate about the extent of the company's discouragement of missionaries – Kenneth Ballhatchet's article 'The East India Company and Roman Catholic Missionaries', *Journal of Ecclesiastical History* 44, 2 (1993), suggests that the company encouraged specific Roman Catholic missions from France and Italy in the eighteenth century.

17. Patrick Brantlinger, *Rule of Darkness: British Literature and Imperialism, 1830–1914* (Ithaca and London: Cornell University Press, 1988), 180.

18. Stuart Hannabuss, 'Ballantyne's Message of Empire', in *Imperialism and Juvenile Literature*, ed. Richards, 53.

19. Martin Green, 'The Robinson Crusoe Story', in *Imperialism and Juvenile Literature*, ed. Richards, 47–8.

20. Charles Dickens, *Bleak House*, ed. George Frost and Sylverre Monod (New York: Norton (1853) 1977).

21. Quoted in Brantlinger, *Rule of Darkness*, 178.

22. Haggis, 'Professional Ladies', 157.

23. *Ibid*., 14.

24. Jane Haggis, 'Gendering Colonialism or Colonising Gender?: Recent Women's Studies Approaches to White Women and the History of British Colonialism', *British Feminist Histories. Spec. issue of Women's Studies International Forum* 13, 1–2 (1990), 112.

25. Gillian Whitlock, *The Intimate Empire: Reading Women's Autobiography* (London: Cassell, 2000), 37.

26. Jean and John Comaroff, *Of Revelation and Revolution: Christianity, Colonialism, and Consciousness in South Africa*, 1 (Chicago and London: University of Chicago Press, 1991), xi.

27. Thorne, *Congregational Missions*, 25.

28. One of the few, and surprising, omissions from Thorne's study is any detailed consideration of the Comaroffs' work.
29. Hilary Callan, 'Introduction', in *The Incorporated Wife*, ed. Hilary Callan and Shirley Ardener (London: Croom Helm, in association with the Centre for Cross Cultural Research on Women, 1984), 5.
30. *Ibid*.
31. Many feminist scholars have critiqued this mythology: see Haggis 'Gendering Colonialism' (105); Margaret Jolly 'Colonizing Women: The Maternal Body and Empire', in *Feminism and the Politics of Difference*, ed. Sneja Gunew and Anna Yeatman (St Leonards, NSW: Allen & Unwin, 1993)' (105); for example. See Ronald Hyam's *Empire and Sexuality: The British Experience* (Manchester and New York: Manchester University Press, 1990) for a rehearsal of this mythology.
32. Catherine Hall, 'Review of *Congregational Missions and the Making of an Imperial Culture in Nineteenth-Century England* by Susan Thorne and *Good Citizens: British Missionaries and Imperial States, 1780–1918* by James M. Greenlee and Charles M. Johnston', *Victorian Studies* 43, no. 4 (2001), 696.
33. Catherine Hall, *Civilising Subjects: Metropole and Colony in the English Imagination, 1830–1867* (Cambridge: Polity, 2002), 7.
34. Hall, 'Missionary Stories', 243.
35. Hall, *Civilising Subjects*, 13.
36. Stoler, *Race and the Education of Desire*, 7.
37. Andrew Porter, 'Religion, Missionary Enthusiasm, and Empire', in *The Oxford History of the British Empire: The Nineteenth Century*, ed. Andrew Porter (Oxford and New York: Oxford University Press, 1999), 239.
38. Thorne, *Congregational Missions*, 14.
39. I am indebted to Stephen Slemon's rigorous and generous reading of an earlier version of this book for clarifying my thinking here.
40. Simon Gikandi, *Maps of Englishness: Writing Identity in the Culture of Colonialism* (New York: Columbia University Press, 1996), xviii.
41. Ross Chambers, *Room for Maneuver: Reading (the) Oppositional (in) Literature* (Chicago and London: University of Chicago Press, 1991).
42. Richards, *The Imperial Archive*, 4.
43. Stephen Slemon, 'Afterword: The English Side of the Lawn', *Testing the Limits: Postcolonial Theories and Canadian Literatures. Spec. issue of Essays in Canadian Writing* 56 (Fall 1995), 283.
44. Helen Tiffin, 'Introduction', in *Post-Colonial Literatures in English: General, Theoretical, and Comparative 1970–1993*, ed. Leigh Dale, Alan Lawson, Helen Tiffin, and Shane Rowlands (New York: G. K. Hall-Macmillan, 1997).
45. See my essay 'The Bookeaters' for a discussion of one particular way missionary anecdotes operate in Bhabha's work, and in a related series of academic texts.
46. Andrew Porter, ' "Commerce and Christianity": The Rise and Fall of a Nineteenth-Century Missionary Slogan', *Historical Journal* 28, 3 (1985), 621.

47. Such recent studies do exist – see, for example, John Harris' *One Blood: Two Hundred Years of Aboriginal Encounter with Christianity: A Story of Hope* (1994) and, to a lesser extent, Brian Stanley's *The Bible and the Flag: Protestant Missions and British Imperialism in the Nineteenth and Twentieth Centuries* (1990).

48. See *Of Revelation and Revolution* for the Comaroffs' slightly different assessment of this point. They argue, suggestively, that 'The situation of the mission between colonizer and colonized had another, related consequence. In mediating between the Boers and the indigenous peoples – and more generally in representing black and white to one another – the Nonconformists gave expression to emerging collective identities, identities at once political and cultural' (286).

49. Thomas, *Colonialism's Culture*, 51.

50. Richards, *The Imperial Archive*, 3.

51. Haggis, 'Professional Ladies', 90.

52. Many LMS illustrations were produced by George Baxter (1804–67), a lithographer and engraver who invented a process to produce colour prints from blocks and plates using oil-based inks. The 'Baxter process' made good, cheap prints available for mass sale for the first time. Baxter produced an entire range of missionary images, from the engravings which front the *Sketches* to a series of colour prints of heroes of the LMS, including the Reverends Knibb, Moffat, Pritchard, and Williams. Baxter's prints provide another fascinating example of the ways in which missionary endeavours entered nineteenth-century public culture, and were circulating as mass-market products. For information about Baxter's prints, see New Baxter Society, *George Baxter, Colour Picture Printer, and The New Baxter Society* (4 November 2001 [cited 16 August 2002]); available from http://www.rpsfamily.demon.co.uk.

53. LMS, 'Missionary Sketches' (London: F. Westley and A. H. Davis, 1820–).

54. Robert May, 'Letter to the Directors of the LMS', in CWM: *North India (Bengal) Incoming Letters*. Box 1. SOAS, London (Chinsurah), 1813.

55. LMS, 'Reports of the London Missionary Society: The Report of the Directors to the 27th General Meeting of the Missionary Society' (London: General Meeting of the LMS, 1821), 45.

56. Richard Lovett, *The History of the London Missionary Society, 1795–1895*, 2 vols. (London: Henry Frowde, 1899), II: 16.

57. Louisa Mundy (formerly Kemp) had an interesting missionary career. Widowed in her late forties, she was then approached to go as a missionary's wife to India; and arrived in 1833. In her ten years in India she established a number of Christian and native girls' schools at Chinsurah in Bengal (Mrs M[ary Edwards] Weitbrecht, *The Women of India and Christian Work in the Zenana* (London: James Nisbet, 1875), 186–8).

58. George Mundy, *Memoir of Mrs Louisa Mundy, of the London Missionary Society's Mission, at Chinsurah, Bengal. With Extracts from her Diary and Letters. By her Husband* (London: John Snow, 1845), 24.

59. J[ames] Robertson, 'Journal' in CWM: *North India Journals*. Box 1. SOAS, London (Benares: 1826–7); rpt. in the *Quarterly Chronicle of Transactions of*

the London Missionary Society, in the years 1829, 1830, 1831, and 1832. Vol. 4. (London: LMS, 1833), 22.

60. For example, Daniel Tyerman and George Bennet's snide remark about Mrs Nott in the Society Islands – 'we regret that we can say nothing in her praise' (letter to Reverend Burder 1824) – certainly does not reappear in the *Chronicle*'s lengthy reports of their journey, or in their later published *Journal*.

61. Bronwen Douglas, 'Recuperating Indigenous Women: Female Sexuality and Missionary Textuality in Melanesia', Paper to the Association for Social Anthropology in Oceania Annual Meeting, Auckland, New Zealand, unpublished (23 February 2002).

62. Brantlinger, *Rule of Darkness*, 50.

63. Stoler, *Race and the Education of Desire*, 99.

64. Kenneth Ballhatchet, *Race, Sex, and Class under the Raj: Imperial Attitudes and Policies and their Critics* (London: Weidenfeld and Nicolson, 1980), 4–5.

65. Rod Edmond, *Representing the South Pacific: Colonial Discourse from Cook to Gauguin* (Cambridge: Cambridge University Press, 1997), 123–4.

66. Gayatri Spivak, 'A Literary Representation of the Subaltern: A Woman's Text from the Third World', in *In Other Worlds: Essays in Cultural Politics* (New York and London: Methuen, 1987), 241.

67. Similarly, this book does not discuss the role of indigenous missionaries – converted colonised people who were employed by missionary societies to evangelise their own (or at least local) people – except in passing. The role of this indigenous ministry would form a fascinating area of investigation.

68. Greg Dening's admirable studies by no means claim this recuperative role easily or unproblematically. See *Mr Bligh's Bad Language: Passion, Power and Theatre on the Bounty* (Cambridge: Cambridge University Press, 1992), *Islands and Beaches: Discourses on a Silent Land: Marquesas, 1774–1880* (Chicago: Dorsey, 1980), and many of his published articles.

69. Richards, *The Imperial Archive*, 3–4.

2 GENDER, DOMESTICITY, AND COLONIAL EVANGELISATION

1. John MacKenzie, ed., *Imperialism and Popular Culture* (Manchester: Manchester University Press, 1986).

2. Brantlinger, *Rule of Darkness*, 35.

3. Thorne, *Congregational Missions*, 21.

4. Patricia Grimshaw, *Paths of Duty: American Missionary Wives in Nineteenth-Century Hawaii* (Honolulu: University of Honolulu Press, 1989), xiv.

5. Hall, 'Missionary Stories', 249.

6. Patricia Rooke notes that the 'paradigm of "complementariness" [was] basic to Christian assumptions about female and male natures and [was] mirrored in the social mores of sexual and marital relationships' (Patricia T. Rooke, ' "Ordinary Events of Nature and Providence": Reconstructing Female Missionary Experience in the British West Indies, 1800–45', *Journal of Religious History* 19, no. 2 (1995), 204).

7. See their *The Madwoman in the Attic: The Woman Writer and the Nineteenth-Century Literary Imagination* (New Haven and London: Yale University Press, 1979) for a history of the concept (17–27).
8. Hall, 'Missionary Stories', 241.
9. Norman Vance, *The Sinews of the Spirit: The Idea of Christian Manliness in Victorian Literature and Religious Thought* (Oxford and Cambridge, Mass.: Blackwell, 1997), 1.
10. Donald E. Hall, 'Muscular Christianity: Reading and Writing the Male Social Body', in *Muscular Christianity: Embodying the Victorian Age*, ed. Donald E. Hall (Cambridge: Cambridge University Press, 1994), 7.
11. J. A. Mangan and James Walvin, 'Introduction', in *Manliness and Morality: Middle-Class Masculinity in Britain and America, 1800–1940*, ed. J. A. Mangan and James Walvin (Manchester: Manchester University Press, 1987), 2.
12. Harrington notes that this seeming contradiction between battle and Christian goodness was typical of the muscular Christian ideal. He cites the ship's chaplain in *Westward Ho!* as an example: Jack Brindlecombe 'bears the Word of God to heathen South American Indians and in the next moment slays those same Indians – as well as some Spanish Catholics for good measure' (Henry Randolph Harrington, *Muscular Christianity: A Study of the Development of a Victorian Idea* (Ann Arbor: University Microfilms, 1976), 19).
13. R. M. Ballantyne, *Gascoyne, the Sandal-Wood Trader*, 24.
14. Quoted in Richards, 'Introduction', in *Imperialism and Juvenile Literature*, ed. Richards, 6.
15. Jean and John Comaroff, 'Through the Looking-Glass: Colonial Encounters of the First Kind', *Journal of Historical Sociology* 1, 1 (1989), 9.
16. Dorothy Driver, ' "Woman" as Sign in the South African Colonial Enterprise', *Journal of Literary Studies* 4, 1 (1988), 6.
17. Joseph Bryant, *Coral Reefs and Cannibals* (London: Epworth Press, 1925), 5.
18. Selwyn's 'New Zealand' diocese also included Melanesia – a geographic anomaly historically attributed to a clerical error in imperial administration (Graeme Kent, *Company of Heaven: Early Missionaries in the South Seas* (Wellington: A. H. & A. W. Reed, 1972), 140).
19. *Ibid.*, 208.
20. James Brooke, an English adventurer, instigated a colonial settlement in the 'Malayan Archipelago' in 1838 on political and religious grounds: Brooke was appointed Rajah of Sarawak in 1841 and in effect established a private imperial dynasty. See Graham Saunders' *Bishops and Brookes: The Anglican Mission and the Brooke Raj in Sarawak 1848–1941* for a detailed discussion of the interaction between the Brooke regime and missionaries; Cassandra Pybus' *White Rajah: A Dynastic Intrigue* for a recent popular history of Brooke; and Spenser St John's *Rajah Brooke: The Englishman as Ruler of an Eastern State* (1899) for an imperial history of Brooke's regime.
21. Charles Kingsley, *Westward Ho!: Or the Voyages and Adventures of Sir Amyas Leigh, Knight, of Burrough, in the County of Devon, in the Region of her Most Glorious Majesty Queen Elizabeth* (London and New York: Macmillan, 1855), vii.

22. Niel Gunson, *Messengers of Grace: Evangelical Missionaries in the South Seas, 1797–1860* (Melbourne: Oxford University Press, 1978), 60.

23. Gunson notes that this is a typical aspect of missionary textuality: 'There has also been a tendency amongst missionary societies to single out a few individuals whom they have decked up in great glory, not satisfied only in making the saints or martyrs, but in publishing many popular accounts of them and in endeavouring to perpetuate their memory in ships and institutions' (*Messengers*, 4).

24. Christine Doran, ' "A Fine Sphere for Female Usefulness": Missionary Women in the Straits Settlements, 1815–45', *Journal of the Malaysian Branch of the Royal Asiatic Society* 69, no. 1 (1996), 101.

25. Haggis, 'Professional Ladies', 78.

26. Laura Helen Sawbridge, *The Vision and the Mission of Womanhood in the Empire and Beyond* (London: Wells Gardner, Darton, 1917), xvi.

27. Sawbridge Senior was the Honourable Canon of St Edmundsbury and Ipswich.

28. Antoinette Burton, 'The White Woman's Burden: British Feminists and the Indian Woman, 1865–1915', *Western Women and Imperialism. Spec. issue of Women's Studies International Forum* 13, 4 (1990), 296.

29. Anna Davin, 'Imperialism and Motherhood', *History Workshop* 5 (Spring 1978), 10.

30. Leonore Davidoff and Catherine Hall, *Family Fortunes: Men and Women of the English Middle Class, 1780–1850* (London: Routledge, 1992), 90.

31. Felicity A. Nussbaum, *Torrid Zones: Maternity, Sexuality, and Empire in Eighteenth-Century English Novels* (Baltimore and London: Johns Hopkins University Press, 1995), 1.

32. Similarly, for South-African-bound American Protestant missionaries, Mount Holyoke College in the US became well-known as a 'rib factory' where theological students wanting missionary postings could rely on finding a suitable wife to accompany them (Norman Etherington, 'Recent Trends in the Historiography of Christianity in Southern Africa', *Journal of Southern African Studies* 22, 2 (1996), 208).

33. Horne, *The Story of the LMS, 1795–1895*, 431.

34. Grimshaw, *Paths of Duty*, 103.

35. Quoted in Doran, 'A Fine Sphere' (Taïti was formerly known as Tahiti.), 100.

36. LMS, 'Candidates Examination Committee', in CWM: *Candidates' Papers Examination Committee* (London: 1816–19).

37. *Ibid*.

38. 'Candidates' Papers: Answers to Printed Questions', in CWM: *Candidates' Papers Examination Committee* (1839–47).

39. Haggis, 'Professional Ladies', 126.

40. Driver, ' "Woman" as Sign', 8–9.

41. 'Candidates' Papers: Answers to Printed Questions', in CWM: *Candidates' Papers Examination Committee* (1839–47).

42. Quoted in Hilary Carey, 'Companions in the Wilderness?: Missionary Wives in Colonial Australia, 1788–1900', *Journal of Religious History* 19, 2 (1995), 230.

43. Marsden's role in providing wives for missionaries in Australia and the South Pacific will be discussed in further detail in the Australian section (part four) of this study.

44. Driver, ' "Woman" as Sign', 8.

45. Carey, 'Companions in the Wilderness?', 238.

46. Nussbaum, *Torrid Zones*, 48.

47. Stephen Slemon, 'Monuments of Empire: Allegory/Counter-Discourse/ Post-Colonial Writing', *Kunapipi* 9, 3 (1987).

48. McClintock, *Imperial Leather*, 36.

49. Quoted in Gillian Whitlock, 'A "White Souled State": Across the "South" with Lady Barker', in *Text, Theory, Space: Land, Literature, and History in South Africa and Australia*, ed. Liz Gunner, Kate Darian-Smith, and Sarah Nuttall (London: Routledge, 1996), 66.

50. Burton, 'The White Woman's Burden', 296.

51. Quoted in Joanna Trollope, *Britannia's Daughters: Women of the British Empire*, Cresset Women's Voices (London: Century Hutchinson, 1983), 14.

52. Sharpe, *Allegories of Empire*, 4.

53. Francis Cuningham, 'Preface', in *Female Missionaries in India: Letters from a Missionary's Wife Abroad to a Friend in England*, ed. Mrs M[ary Edwards] Weitbrecht (London: James Nisbet, 1843), vi.

54. Davidoff and Hall, *Family Fortunes*, 74.

55. Hall, *Civilising Subjects*, 93.

56. Hall, 'Missionary Stories', 254.

57. Helen Tiffin, 'The Body in the Library: Identity, Opposition, and the Settler-Invader Woman', in *The Contact and the Culmination*, ed. Marc Delrez and Benedicte Ledent (Liége: L3, 1997), 219.

58. McClintock, *Imperial Leather*, 44.

59. Margaret Jolly and Martha Macintyre, 'Introduction', in *Family and Gender in the Pacific: Domestic Contradictions and the Colonial Impact*, ed. Margaret Jolly and Martha Macintyre (Cambridge: Cambridge University Press, 1989), 9.

60. Hall, 'Missionary Stories', 264.

61. Reverend Knibb, quoted in Hall, 'Missionary Stories', 258.

62. Horne, *The Story of the LMS, 1795–1895*, 208.

63. Burton, 'The White Woman's Burden', 303.

64. *The Gospel Missionary for 1852* (published for the Society for the Propagation of the Gospel, 1852).

65. Ronald M. Berndt and Catherine H. Berndt, 'Body and Soul: More than an Episode!', in *Aboriginal Australians and Christian Missions: Ethnographic and Historical Studies*, ed. Tony Swain and Deborah Bird Rose (Bedford Park, SA: Australian Association for the Study of Religions, South Australian College of Advanced Education Sturt Campus, 1988), 54.

66. It is difficult to come to any neat resolution about the actual nature of indigenous women's treatment within traditional culture. In criticising the strategic use that missionaries made of gendered practices it may seem that inequalities not attributable to colonial violence were purely discursive constructions of

an imperial imagination, that traditional practices were somehow idyllic. This is not the intention of my argument here – rather, I want to highlight the ways in which missionary texts and discourses made use of gender in order to naturalise their implementation of evangelical and colonial practices.

67. McClintock, *Imperial Leather*, 364.

68. Lewis Hermon Gaunt, *School-Mates: Pictures of School-Time and Play-Time in the Mission Field* (London: LMS, 1906), 14.

69. One section of the songbook contains the following verse: 'See that heathen mother stand / Where the sacred current flows / With her own maternal hands, / Mid the waves her babe she throws. / Send, Oh send, the Bible there, / Let its precept reach the heart; / She may then her children spare– / Act the tender mother's part' (quoted in Geraldine H. Forbes, 'In Search of the "Pure Heathen": Missionary Women in Nineteenth-Century India', *Economic and Political Weekly* 21, 17 (1986), WS2). See my discussion in chapter 4 about other instances of this specific trope.

70. See Simon Ryan's *The Cartographic Eye: How Explorers Saw Australia* (Cambridge and New York: Cambridge University Press, 1996), for an analysis of gendered exploration discourses.

71. Homi K. Bhabha, 'The Other Question: Stereotype, Discrimination, and the Discourse of Colonialism', in *The Location of Culture* (London and New York: Routledge, 1994), 70.

3 EMPIRE, INDIA, AND EVANGELISATION

1. *Cannibalism Conquered: Mary Slessor, the Missionary Heroine; Pandita Ramabia, the Indian Orphans' Friend* (London: Pickering & Inglis, n.d.), 27.

2. John Wilson, *The Evangelisation of India: Considered with Reference to the Duties of the Christian Church at Home and of its Missionary Agents Abroad. In a Brief Series of Discourses, Addresses, &c* (Edinburgh: William Whyte, 1844), 213.

3. Ranajit Guha and Gayatri Chakravorty Spivak, eds., *Selected Subaltern Studies* (New York and Oxford: Oxford University Press, 1988), 47.

4. Neill, *A History of Christian Missions*, 261.

5. Stephen Neill, *A History of Christianity in India 1707–1858* (Cambridge: Cambridge University Press, 1985), 205–6.

6. Now known as West Bengal.

7. These three missionaries were supposed to gain information and experience here before proceeding to Sri Lanka, but they never reached their intended destination: Cran and Des Granges remained in South India; and Ringeltraube in Kerala.

8. Of the first twenty missionaries sent by the LMS to their mission stations in North India, for example, eight died at their stations in India within their first eight years in residence.

9. LMS, 'Reports of the London Missionary Society: The Report of the Directors to the 29th General Meeting of the Missionary Society' (London: General Meeting of the LMS, 1823), 1.

10. LMS, 'Third Report of the Mahí Kánthá (Late Baroda) Mission in connection with the London Missionary Society' (May 1851), 12.

11. Holmes, 'British Imperial Policy and the Mission Schools', 25.

12. LMS, 'Reports of the London Missionary Society: The Report of the Directors to the 35th General Meeting of the Missionary Society' (London: the General Meeting of the LMS, 1829), 32.

13. E[dward] Storrow, *Our Indian Sisters* (London: Religious Tract Society [1898]), 189.

14. Partha Chatterjee, *The Nation and its Fragments: Colonial and Postcolonial Histories* (Princeton, NJ: Princeton University Press, 1993), 128.

15. Haggis, 'Professional Ladies', 127.

16. LMS, 'Reports of the London Missionary Society: The Report of the Directors to the 31st General Meeting of the Missionary Society' (London: General Meeting of the LMS, 1825), 67.

17. Doran, 'A Fine Sphere', 104.

18. K. Nora Brockway, *A Larger Way for Women: Aspects of Christian Education for Girls in South India 1712–1948* (Madras: Geoffrey Cumberlege and Oxford University Press, 1949), 79. Brockway notes that Sir Henry Lawrence helped to finance this class. Lawrence (1806–57) was the Chief Commissioner of the Oudh district during the 1857 Mutiny and he died at Lucknow during the uprising. The connections between the army and the church in Anglo-Indian circles, as this case demonstrates, were multiple and unpredictable. See J. L. Morison's *Lawrence of Lucknow, 1806–1857* (London: Bell, 1934) for a celebratory imperial history of Lawrence.

19. LMS, 'Reports of the London Missionary Society (1823)', 70.

20. LMS, 'Reports of the London Missionary Society (1825)', 96. The LMS tended to assume financial custodianship for their converts' labour and produce throughout the colonial mission field. The voices of resistant primary producers emerge on rare occasions, though the society tended to dismiss accusations of profiteering by their conversion activities, arguing that any profits barely recompensed them for their outlay. Sometimes missionaries report native requests for payment for school attendance, another activity demanded by the evangelists of their converts. These issues emphasise the multifarious *economic* nature of colonial evangelism.

21. The relationship between science and evangelical religion was considerably closer at this time than contemporary experience might lead us to expect. Some missionaries saw scientific education as crucial to the conversion of Hindu youth. A number of different missionaries state that in 'proving' that scientific theories overrode previous religious explanations of the physical world, the young Indians' faith in their religion was severely dented. For example, W. J. Wilkins' publication, *Daily Life and Work in India*, noted this of his earlier experiences in northern India: 'As the Hindu youths study physical geography they see the errors with which their books abound, and naturally their faith in their divine origin is destroyed' (Wilkins, *Daily Life and Work in India* (London: LMS, 1888), 258).

22. Gaunt, *School-Mates*, 100.
23. Quoted in Chatterjee, *The Nation and its Fragments*, 39.
24. Ralph Wardlaw Thompson and Arthur N. Johnson, *British Foreign Missions 1837–1897* (London: Blackie, 1899), 118.
25. See my article 'The Bookeaters: Textuality, Modernity, and the London Missionary Society', *A Vanishing Mediator? The Presence/Absence of the Bible in Postcolonialism*. Special issue of *Semiea* 88 (2001), 13–40, for a detailed reading of the symbolic significance of the Bible as a text in colonial missionary contexts.
26. James Kennedy, 'Preface', in *The Eastern Lily Gathered: A Memoir of Bala Shoondoree Tagore. With Observations on the Position and Prospects of Hindu Female Society*, ed. Edward Storrow (London: Snow, 1856), vii.
27. Bernard Cohn notes that 'Upper-class Indian women in north India, both Hindu and Muslim, were rarely seen outside of their homes, and within their houses usually spent most of their time in their own quarters, the zanana. For these women there was an elaborate code of avoidances of certain male affines, and sharp separation of the domains of males and females… In the north, lower-class or lower-caste women would be seen in public, at times working the fields, assisting males in their work, or moving about on errands. In the south, except in areas of Muslim settlement, women tended to be less restricted in their movements and their appearances in public' (Bernard S. Cohn, *Colonialism and its Forms of Knowledge: The British in India* (Princeton, NJ: Princeton University Press, 1996), 137). Different names for *zenana*-like domestic arrangements were used in different parts of India. Mrs Mary Weitbrecht notes that *zenana* was not used all over India since, for example, it was rarely used in the south. Her list of terms includes *Purdah* in Delhi and the north; *gosha* in central districts; and *zenana* in Bengal even though, she notes, the real Bengali word is *anthakar* (Weitbrecht, *The Women of India and Christian Work in the Zenana* (London: James Nisbet, 1875), 104). I use *zenana* because of its aptness to Bengal and because it is the most common contemporary usage.
28. Storrow, *Our Indian Sisters*, 192–3.
29. Alexander Duff, *Female Education in India, Being the Substance of An Address Delivered at the First Annual Meeting of the Scottish Ladies' Association, in Connection with the Church of Scotland, for the Promotion of Female Education in India* (Edinburgh: John Johnstone, 1834), 18.
30. Storrow, *Our Indian Sisters*, 209.
31. A 'ryot' is a peasant, or a farming tenant.
32. Haggis, 'Professional Ladies', 322.
33. Duff, *Female Education in India*, 18–19.
34. Forbes, 'In Search of the "Pure Heathen"', WS3.
35. *Ibid*.
36. LMS, 'Brief Review of the London Missionary Society, from its formation, September 1795' (n.p.: LMS Annual Meeting, 1845), 5.
37. Quoted in Thompson, *British Foreign Missions 1837–1897*, 21.

38. Lovett, *The History of the London Missionary Society, 1795–1895*, II: 8.
39. Lord Minto (previously, as Sir Gilbert Elliot, one of Warren Hastings' prosecutors) assumed the governor-generalship of Bengal in 1807; Lord Moira, better known by his later title of Marquess of Hastings, succeeded him in 1814.
40. Ramsay Muir, ed., *The Making of British India 1756–1858: Described in a Series of Dispatches, Treaties, Statutes, and other Documents, Selected and Edited with Introductions and Notes* (Pakistan: Oxford University Press, 1915), 248.
41. Thompson, *British Foreign Missions 1837–1897*, 29.
42. Brockway, *A Larger Way for Women*, 16.
43. Lovett, *The History of the London Missionary Society, 1795–1895*, II: 48.
44. Thompson, *British Foreign Missions 1837–1897*, 30.
45. Brantlinger, *Rule of Darkness*, 76.
46. Ballhatchet, *Race, Sex, and Class under the Raj*, 4.
47. Rajeswari Sunder Rajan, *Real and Imagined Women: Gender, Culture, and Postcolonialism* (Routledge: London and New York, 1993), 42.
48. Storrow, *Our Indian Sisters*, 121.
49. Quoted in Muir, ed., *The Making of British India*, 382–3.
50. Haggis, 'Professional Ladies and Working Wives', 166.
51. LMS, 'Reports of the London Missionary Society: The Report of the Directors to the 30th General Meeting of the Missionary Society' (London: General Meeting of the LMS, 1824), 164–5, emphasis added.
52. Guha and Spivak, eds., *Selected Subaltern Studies*, 47.
53. LMS, 'Reports of the London Missionary Society (1824)', 165.
54. Sir John Seeley, *The Expansion of England: Two Courses of Lectures* (London: Macmillan, 1890), 8.
55. Mrs [Hannah Catherine] Mullens, *Faith and Victory: A Story of the Progress of Christianity in Bengal*, 2nd edn (London: James Nisbet, 1867), 105–6, emphasis added.
56. LMS, 'Reports of the London Missionary Society (1824)', 165.
57. Quoted in Muir, ed., *The Making of British India*, 294.
58. LMS, 'The Missionary Magazine and Chronicle: Chiefly Relating to the Missions of the London Missionary Society' (1861), 25.

4 MISSIONARY WRITING IN INDIA

1. Joseph Mullens, *The Results of Missionary Labour in India* (London: LMS, 1852), 38.
2. Haggis, 'Professional Ladies', 109.
3. Brantlinger, *Rule of Darkness*, 90.
4. Neill, *A History of Christian Missions*, 255.
5. Lovett, *The History of the London Missionary Society, 1795–1895*, II: 49.
6. Valentine Cunningham, ' "God and Nature Intended You for a Missionary's Wife": Mary Hill, Jane Eyre, and Other Missionary Women in the 1840s',

in *Women and Missions: Past and Present: Anthropological and Historical Perspectives*, ed. Deborah Kirkwood, Fiona Bowie, and Shirley Ardener (Providence, RI: Berg, 1993), 187–8.

7. LMS, 'Third Report of the Mahí Kánthá (Late Baroda) Mission', 21.

8. Burton, 'The White Woman's Burden', 8.

9. Gayatri Spivak, *A Critique of Postcolonial Reason: Toward a History of the Vanishing Present* (Cambridge, Mass.: Harvard University Press, 1999), 284.

10. Mullens, *Faith and Victory*, v.

11. Kate Teltscher, *India Inscribed: European and British Writing on India 1600–1800* (Delhi: Oxford University Press, 1995), 2–3.

12. Weitbrecht, *The Women of India*, 39.

13. Storrow, *Our Indian Sisters*, 35.

14. *Ibid.*, 5.

15. Weitbrecht, *The Women of India*, 194. Hannah Mullens and Mary Weitbrecht clearly held each other in mutual esteem. Indeed, the copy of Mrs Weitbrecht's *Female Missionaries in India: Letters from a Missionary's Wife Abroad to a Friend in England* held in the central LMS repository in the SOAS Library, London, is inscribed with the name of Hannah Catherine Lacroix, dated 5 October 1844.

16. Mullens, *Faith and Victory*, 162.

17. See my later discussion about the complicated politics of this issue in chapter 5.

18. Kennedy, 'Preface', *The Eastern Lily Gathered*, v.

19. Isabel Hart, 'Introduction', in *Historical Sketches of Woman's [sic] Missionary Societies in America and England*, ed. Mrs L. H. Daggett (Boston: Daggett, 1879), 9.

20. Wilson, *The Evangelisation of India*, 424.

21. Weitbrecht, *The Women of India*, 104–5.

22. Quoted in Weitbrecht, *The Women of India*, 182–3.

23. Inderpal Grewal notes that such ideas supported the belief that physiognomy gave a true indication of character; that prostitutes would become hideous in appearance; that black faces were opaque and therefore hiding their immoral character; and that the use of facial makeup was treacherous because it could hide intrinsic depravity (Grewal, *Home and Harem: Nation, Gender, Empire, and the Cultures of Travel* (London: Leicester University Press, 1996), 27).

24. *Ibid.*, 26.

25. Haggis, 'Professional Ladies and Working Wives', 98–9.

26. Mullens, *Faith and Victory*, 173.

27. See F. K. Prochaska, *Women and Philanthropy in Nineteenth-Century England* (Oxford: Clarendon Press, 1980), for a detailed discussion of the operation of class and Christian philanthropy in nineteenth-century Britain; further discussion of the missionaries' conflation of lower-class Britons and colonised subjects will be discussed in chapter 9.

28. Thomas Smith, 'Editorial and Review of *Hindu Female Education* by Priscila Chapman, and First Report of the Scottish Ladies' Association for the advancement of Female Education in India under the Superintendence of Missionaries in the Church of Scotland n.s.', *The Calcutta Christian Observer* 3 (March 1840), 118.

29. Storrow, *Our Indian Sisters*, 195.

30. Duff, *Female Education in India*, 19, emphasis added.

31. LMS, 'The Missionary Magazine and Chronicle (1861)', 235, emphasis added.

32. Kennedy, 'Preface', *The Eastern Lily Gathered*, vii–viii.

33. William Buyers, *Recollections of Northern India; With Observations on the Origin, Customs, and Moral Sentiments of the Hindoos, and Remarks on the Country, and Principal Places on the Ganges, &c.* (London: John Snow, 1848), 390.

34. It was not that other missionary writers had not read Buyers' account. Both Storrow (in *Eastern Lily*) and Mary Weitbrecht quoted from his *Recollections of Northern India* (1848), but they do so judiciously, omitting the sections which contradict their construction of stereotypical representations of the *zenana* and Indian women.

35. LMS, 'Report of the Ladies' Native Female School Society, in connection with the London Missionary Society, for 1839 and 1840' (Calcutta: 1841), 13.

36. Duff, *Female Education in India*, 16–17, emphasis added.

37. Smith, 'Editorial and Review', 121.

38. See the later discussion of family resistance in my analysis of Mullens, *Faith and Victory*.

39. LMS, 'Second Report of the Mahí Kánthá (Late Baroda) Mission in connection with the London Missionary Society' (1848), 16.

40. Providing an interesting contrast to missionary beliefs about Polynesian and Aboriginal maternity, as will be discussed in parts three and four.

41. Free Church of Scotland's India Mission, 'Report of the Female Orphanage and Schools of the Scottish Ladies' Association for Promoting Female Education in India (Madras Branch)' (1861–2), 3.

42. Malek Alloula, *The Colonial Harem*, trans. Myrna Godzich and Wlad Godzich, intro. Barbara Harlow (Minneapolis: University of Minnesota Press, 1986), 181 n. 27.

43. Differences which Alloula himself does not make explicit, even though he does refer to Indian *zenanas*.

44. Phantasms – 'an "imaginary scene in which the subject is a protagonist, representing the fulfilment of a wish ... in a manner that is distorted to a greater or lesser extent by defensive processes"' (quoted in Alloula, *The Colonial Harem*, 128 n. 2).

45. Haggis, 'Professional Ladies', 108.

46. James Sherman, *The Remembrance of Christ's Love a Stimulus to Missionary Exertion: A Sermon, Preached before the London Missionary Society, at Spa Field's Chapel, On Thursday, May 13th, 1830* (London: Fisher, Son, and Jackson, and James Nisbet, n.d.), 18.

47. Storrow, *Our Indian Sisters*, 67.
48. Quoted in Wilson, *The Evangelization of India*, 425.
49. Grewal, *Home and Harem*, 18.
50. Mullens, *Faith and Victory*, 162.
51. Forbes, 'In Search of the "Pure Heathen"', WS2.
52. Mullens, *The Results of Missionary Labour in India*, 38.
53. Holmes, 'British Imperial Policy', 22.
54. Quoted in Holmes, 'British Imperial Policy', 19.
55. Quoted in Brockway, *A Larger Way for Women*, 63.
56. Gauri Viswanathan, *Masks of Conquest: Literary Study and British Rule in India* (New York: Columbia University Press, 1989), 2.
57. Mrinalini Sinha, *Colonial Masculinity: The 'Manly Englishman' and the 'Effeminate Bengali' in the Late Nineteenth Century* (Manchester and New York: Manchester University Press, 1995), 1.
58. Haggis, 'Professional Ladies', 102.
59. In the South Pacific, by contrast, dress was a crucial issue of missionary control and its alteration was regarded as a measure of their success. However, dress was of little concern to missionaries in India. See Bernard S. Cohn's 'Cloth, Clothes, and Colonialism: India in the Nineteenth Century' (in his *Colonialism and Its Forms of Knowledge*) for a fascinating discussion of the colonial politics of dress in India and its manifestation in both Indian and British cultural practice. Cohn points out that the British in India were concerned that Indians should explicitly *look* Indian, and Britons British, particularly after the 1857 Mutiny (Cohn, *Colonialism and Its Forms of Knowledge*, 124–5).
60. Mullens' invocation of masculine 'decency' and appropriately masculine attire here may well be a response to sexual anxieties about such cross-cultural encounters. Cohn notes that British women newly arrived in India often 'recorded their shock not only at the semi-nakedness of lower-status Indian household servants... but also at their free access to the bedrooms of the memsahibs as if they were non-males' (Cohn, *Colonialism*, 130).
61. Haggis, 'Professional Ladies', 100.

5 IMPERIALISM, SUFFRAGISM, AND NATIONALISM

1. Brockway, *A Larger Way for Women*.
2. Haggis, 'Professional Ladies', 166.
3. It is important to keep in mind, as Haggis argues, that the process of formal inclusion of LMS women missionaries 'reflected less an innovation and break with the past than a process of incorporation and relocation' ('Professional Ladies', 330).
4. Quoted in Peter Williams, '"The Missing Link": The Recruitment of Women Missionaries in some English Evangelical Societies in the Nineteenth Century', in *Women and Missions: Past and Present: Anthropological and Historical Perspectives*, ed. Deborah Kirkwood, Fiona Bowie, and Shirley Ardener (Providence, RI: Berg, 1993), 57.

5. Forbes, 'In Search of the "Pure Heathen"', WS6.
6. Grewal, *Home and Harem*, 7.
7. Chatterjee, *The Nation and Its Fragments*, 9.
8. Conservative British commentators also noted the potential danger to British *zenana* visitors posed by their independent evangelical work. Ballhatchet cites an anonymous district judge who wrote to the *Friend of India* in the mid-1880s on the 'dangers' of *zenana* visitation: 'It was time that these missionary societies realized that they were putting their young ladies at the mercy of lascivious Hindu men ... The system of family life among the secluded females of a Hindoo household is quite inconsistent with the idea of any protection from familiarity or insult from the male members of the household being afforded by the ladies of the *zenana*' (quoted in Ballhatchet, *Race, Sex, and Class under the Raj*, 115). As Ballhatchet suggests, such speculation reinforced early imperial suspicions and stereotypes about Indian morals and sexuality and also served to detract from the on-going work of female missionaries (115).
9. Holmes, 'British Imperial Policy and the Mission Schools', 31.
10. However, it is also necessary to acknowledge the obviously disruptive nature of mission education. As Holmes argues, European-style education often maintained or widened the divisions within colonial societies, between literate and illiterate groups, and between Christians and non-Christians: 'mission education in particular tended to perpetuate and intensify the divisions among ethnic, regional and parochial groups. In short, the disintegrating effects of education in colonial areas are all too readily apparent' ('British Imperial Policy', 36).
11. Fiona Bowie, 'Introduction: Reclaiming Women's Presence', in *Women and Missions*, ed. Kirkwood, Bowie, and Ardener, 14.
12. See chapter 5 of Inderpal Grewal's *Home and Harem* for a discussion of Ramabai, Athavale, and their reform activities.
13. Sinha, *Colonial Masculinity*, 11–12.
14. Antoinette Burton, *Burdens of History: British Feminists, Indian Women, and Imperial Culture, 1865–1915* (Chapel Hill and London: University of North Carolina Press, 1994), 295.
15. Edward Storrow, 'Introduction', in *The Dawn of Light: A Story of the Zenana Mission*, ed. Mary E. Leslie (London: Snow, 1868), xix.

6 POLYNESIAN MISSIONS AND THE EUROPEAN IMAGINARY

1. T[homas] H[aweis], 'The Very Probable Success of a Proper Mission to the South Sea Islands', *The Evangelical Magazine* 3 (1795), 263.
2. Bernard Smith's *European Vision and the South Pacific, 1768–1850: A Study in the History of Art and Ideas* (London: Oxford University Press, 1960) establishes many of these tropes of European desire for the Pacific.
3. Daniel Tyerman and George Bennet, *Journal of Voyages and Travels by the Rev. Daniel Tyerman and George Bennet, Esq. Deputed from the London Missionary*

Society, to Visit their Various Stations in the South Sea Islands, China, India, &c., between the Years 1821 and 1829. Compiled from Original Documents by James Montgomery, 2 vols. (London: Frederick Westley and A. H. Davis, 1831), 1: 58.

4. Later Tahiti, now Taïti.
5. Nicholas Thomas, *Entangled Objects: Exchange, Material Culture, and Colonialism in the Pacific* (Cambridge, Mass.: Harvard University Press, 1991), 53.
6. Whilst I use the term 'Polynesia', the eighteenth- and nineteenth-century LMS tended to use the expression 'the South Seas' to refer to the same area, although terminology varied both among different authors and during the period 1800–60.
7. This deliberately disingenuous remark is intended to emphasise the importance and impact of Cook's journals – as noted in the previous section, William Carey established Indian mission work and was the venerated 'father' of Baptist missions to India.
8. Thompson, *British Foreign Missions 1837–1897*, 8–9.
9. John Williams, *A Narrative of Missionary Enterprises in the South Sea Islands: With Remarks upon the Natural History of the Islands, Origin, Languages, Traditions, and Usages of the Inhabitants*, 7th edn (London: J. Snow [1837] 1838), 4. (Hereafter cited in the text by page number alone.) His feelings of 'regret' are, of course, due to Cook's violent death. Ironically, Williams was murdered on the shores of Eromanga in 1839 in a *tableau* of death remarkably similar to Cook's. It was a scene of martyrdom which haunted the missionary imagination and archive – see Bernard Smith, *European Vision* (244–5) for an analysis of the various pictorial representations of Williams' death.
10. Haweis, 'The Very Probable Success', 261–2.
11. See Greg Dening's chapter 'Possessing Tahiti' in *Performances* (Carlton South, Vic.: Melbourne University Press, 1996) for a fuller discussion of this issue.
12. See Dening's *Performances* for a detailed examination of the British 'inventions' of Purea and the many ways her image and story were used in artistic/cultural productions.
13. The *Duff* was lost to French privateers on its second missionary voyage in 1800.
14. Michael Cathcart, 'Foundation of the Mission', in *Mission to the South Seas: The Voyages of the Duff, 1796–1799*, ed. Tom Griffiths, Michael Cathcart, Lee Watts, Vivian Anceschi, Greg Houghton, and David Goodman (Parkville, Vic.: History Department, University of Melbourne, 1990), 14.
15. Thorne, *Congregational Missions*, 60.
16. Thorne argues that the LMS leaders 'attributed their first missions' ignominious collapse to inadequate human agency rather than to divine disapproval, and they embarked on an ambitious program of organizational reform. There was more than a semblance of condescension toward the men and women, most of whom were skilled laborors, who comprised these early parties… Their London employers blamed their dismal performance in the foreign field on their "impure and inferior motives" and on the fact that their educational

background was not sufficient to secure them against heathenism's many temptations' (*Congregational Missions*, 61).

17. Neill, *A History of Christian Missions*, 252.
18. Reverend James J. Ellis' eulogistic description of Williams was, although excessive, typical of the ways in which missionary supporters portrayed him: 'The chastened sweetness of his disposition, which never degenerated into weakness, his ingenuity in devising expedients, and his resolute persistence in what often appeared to be labour in vain, together with the large heartedness that could "not be confined within the limits of a single reef", constitute him, in the writer's judgement, the very Prince of Missionaries, since the days of the Apostle of the Gentiles' (James J. Ellis, *John Williams: The Martyr Missionary of Polynesia* (London: S.W. Partridge, n.d.), ix).
19. Sherman, *The Rembrance of Christ's Love*, 21.
20. LMS, 'Reports of the London Missionary Society: The Report of the Directors to the 23rd General Meeting of the Missionary Society' (London: General Meeting of the LMS, 1817), 43.
21. See my essay 'Planting the Seeds of Christianity: Ecological Reform in Nineteenth-Century Polynesian LMS Stations', in *Empire and Environment Anthology*, ed. Helen Tiffin (Amsterdam: Rodopi, forthcoming, 2003) for further analysis of missionary interventions into the natural and built environments of Polynesian missions.
22. Gunson, *Messengers of Grace*, 119.
23. Quoted in Gunson, *Messengers of Grace*, 120.
24. LMS, 'Reports of the London Missionary Society: The Report of the Directors to the 36th General Meeting of the Missionary Society' (London: General Meeting of the LMS, 1830), 5.
25. Quoted in Porter, 'Commerce and Christianity', 597–8.
26. Hypatia Bradlaugh Bonner, for the Rationalist Press Association, *Christianizing the Heathen: First-Hand Information Concerning Overseas Missions* (London: Watts and Co., 1922), 2–3.
27. Williams, *Missionary Enterprises*, 224–5, emphasis added. See Vanessa Smith's *Literary Culture and the Pacific: Nineteenth-Century Textual Encounters* (Cambridge: Cambridge University Press, 1998) for a detailed discussion of the (fraught) relationship between European beachcombers and missionaries in the Pacific.
28. Kent, *Company of Heaven*, 54. Niel Gunson notes that John Gyles was sent to Taïti expressly to teach the agriculture of trade crops; formerly a plantation manager in the West Indies, he was not particularly effective at missionary work because he was used to the rather different social relations he had experienced with slave populations (Gunson, *Messengers of Grace*, 40).
29. LMS, 'Reports of the London Missionary Society (1821)', 5–6.
30. Horne, *The Story of the LMS, 1795–1895*, 42.
31. See my article 'The Bookeaters' for an in-depth analysis of the Bible as a colonial artefact.

32. Ebenezer Prout, *Missionary Ships Connected with the London Missionary Society* (London: LMS, 1865), 55, 70.

33. Of course, for LMS missionaries such apparent willingness to engage in these transactions did indeed represent a thorough success. It seemed to indicate that the local people had been converted both to Christianity and to the capitalist market system which missionaries endorsed. In contrast, Hannah Mullens notes of her *zenana* women in India that 'I would only mention that the best way of helping on zenana work, is to send us all the materials for fancy work, especially wools, canvass, patterns, and *needles*. The Native Ladies will gladly *buy* these of us, the proceeds of which could be applied to getting them Christian books, which they do not like to *buy* (though they read them willingly)' (quoted in LMS, 'The Missionary Magazine and Chronicle (1861)', 235). Here the negotiations of capital and Christianity are evidently quite different.

34. William Ellis, *Polynesian Researches. During a Residence of Nearly Six Years in the South Sea Islands...*, 2 vols. (London: Fisher, Son and Jackson, 1829).

35. J. M., 'Review of *Memoirs of the Life of the Rev. John Williams, Missionary to Polynesia*; by the Rev. E Prout of Halstead', in *Papers on Missions* (No Publisher: n.p., 1845), 129.

36. Christopher Herbert, *Culture and Anomie: Ethnographic Imagination in the Nineteenth Century* (Chicago: University of Chicago Press, 1991), 191–2.

37. Niel Gunson, 'Introduction', in *Australian Reminiscences and Papers of L. E. Threlkeld, Missionary to the Aborigines, 1824–1859* (Canberra: AIAS, 1974), v.

38. Lamont Lindstrom, 'Postcards from the Edge. Rev. of *Colonialism's Culture*, by Nicholas Thomas', *Meanjin* 53, 4 (1994), 744.

39. Gunson, *Messengers of Grace*, 111.

40. Quoted in *Messengers of Grace*, 61, original italics.

41. Homi K. Bhabha, 'The Commitment to Theory', in *The Location of Culture* (London and New York: Routledge, 1994), 33.

42. Joel Bulu, *Joel Bulu: The Autobiography of a Native Minister in the South Seas*, trans. by a missionary. Introduction by G. S. R. (London: Wesleyan Mission House, 1871), 3.

43. As Bhabha suggests, these linguistic problems in part led to the employment of native evangelists. Native catechists brought their own cultural and political ambivalences and contradictions, and were often under great pressure from their families and communities. In Polynesia, native catechists became important members of the missionary community, particularly in making the first forays into new communities. Indeed, they were used as a kind of cannon fodder, frequently assigned to places where white missionaries expected physical threats to their safety. As discussed in chapter 1, these indigenous catechists are not examined in detail in this book. However, a study of men like Ta'unga, Fauea, Joel Bulu, and others would provide a fascinating alternative viewpoint on the work of European missionaries during this period.

44. Homi K. Bhabha, 'Sly Civility', in *The Location of Culture* (London and New York: Routledge, 1994), 101.
45. Gaunt, *School-Mates*, 21.
46. See, for example, Ellis' *Polynesian Researches*, 1: 70–8; Tyerman and Bennet's *Journal*, 1: 338–9; and Williams' *Missionary Enterprises*, 524–31.
47. Ellis, *Polynesian Researches*, 1: 76.
48. Tyerman and Bennet, *Journal*, 1: 336.
49. Homi K. Bhabha, 'Of Mimicry and Man: The Ambivalence of Colonial Discourse', in *The Location of Culture* (London and New York: Routledge, 1994), 85.
50. A. W. Murray, *Forty Years' Mission Work in Polynesia and New Guinea, from 1835 to 1875* (London: James Nisbet, 1876), 52.
51. Steven Kaplan, ed, *Indigenous Responses to Western Christianity* (New York and London: New York University Press, 1995), 6.
52. Quoted in Sir Peter (Te Rangi Hiroa) Buck, *Mangaia and the Mission*, ed. and intro. by Rod Dixon and Teaea Parima (Suva: IPS, USP in association with B. P. Bishop Museum, 1993), 55.
53. This occasion was the death of the Williams' seventh child, clearly a severe trial to the family. Williams writes: 'we found it difficult to restrain the tear of parental affection; and even now, when we speak of our seven dear infants, whose little bodies are slumbering in different isles of the far distant seas, our tenderest emotions are enkindled' (Williams, *Missionary Enterprises*, 400). The poignancy of Williams' writing here highlights the personal devastation experienced by many missionary families whose children (and frequently their mothers, as well) appeared to be continually 'consumed' by the colonial environment.
54. Herbert, *Culture and Anomie*, 178–9.
55. Margaret Atwood, *The Journals of Susanna Moodie* (Toronto: Oxford University Press, 1970), 30–1.

7 MISSIONARY WRITING IN POLYNESIA

1. Prout, *Missionary Ships*, v.
2. However, Bennet was appointed first and had considerable input in the selection of his deputation partner. He objected to the initial candidate, Reverend R. MacLean, because MacLean insisted on taking his wife. In a manner which anticipated Bennet's limited sympathy for the specific problems of colonial missionary wives, he wrote: 'Of Mr MacLean's suitability I cannot judge further than that his proposing to take his wife on such an expedition is but an indifferent mark . . . I need not mention to you Sir the thousand ways and casualties by which a lady, being one of the Deputation (or, which is the same thing, being the wife of one of the Deputies) must lessen or greatly hazard the success of the Mission' (George Bennet, 'Letter to Rev George Burder', in CWM: *Home Odds Tyerman and Bennet's Deputation Letters 1821–1828* (Highfield: 1820)).

3. Tyerman and Bennet, *Journal*, 1: vi.
4. Quoted in Tyerman and Bennet, *Journal*, 1: vi–vii.
5. Gunson, *Messengers of Grace*, 123.
6. Mary Louise Pratt, *Imperial Eyes: Travel Writing and Transculturation* (London and New York: Routledge, 1992), 6–7.
7. Threlkeld is the main focus of the next section on LMS activity in New South Wales – his willing candour in discussing controversial LMS politics was typical of his general attitude, as will become evident in part three.
8. L. E. Threlkeld, *Australian Reminiscences and Papers of L. E. Threlkeld, Missionary to the Aborigines, 1824–1859*, ed. Niel Gunson, 2 vols. (Canberra: AIAS, 1974), 1: 111.
9. Joseph King, *Ten Decades: The Australian Centenary Story of the London Missionary Society: The Australasian Centenary History of the London Missionary Society* (London: John Snow, c. 1895), 66–7.
10. See chapter 4 of Edmond's *Representing the South Pacific* for an excellent comparative analysis of these volumes by Williams and Ellis; also Smith's *Literary Culture and the Pacific*.
11. Edmond, *Representing the South Pacific*, 113.
12. Williams, *Missionary Enterprises*, vii–viii.
13. Herbert, *Culture and Anomie*, 163–4.
14. Tyerman and Bennet, *Journal*, 1: 254.
15. Kent, *Company of Heaven*, 33.
16. Crook's stay, though significantly longer than Harris', was also notable for its lack of success: see Alex Calder's 'The Temptations of William Pascoe Crook: An Experience of Cultural Difference in the Marquesas, 1797–1988', *Journal of Pacific History* 31, 2 (1996), 144–61 and Greg Dening's discussion of Crook in *Islands and Beaches: Discourse on a Silent Land: Marquesas, 1774–1880* (Chicago: Dorsey, 1980).
17. Lee Watts, 'Tahiti', in *Mission to the South Seas: The Voyages of the Duff, 1796–1799*, ed. Tom Griffiths, Michael Cathcart, Lee Watts, Vivian Anceschi, Greg Houghton, and David Goodman (Parkville, Vic: History Department, University of Melbourne, 1990), 61–4.
18. Jean and John Comaroff, 'Through the Looking-Glass', 26.
19. Jean and John Comaroff, *Of Revelation and Revolution*, 18.
20. Edmond notes that male homosexuality appears to have been common in Polynesian cultures, as evident in the transvestism or social effeminacy of Taïtian *mahu*, the undifferentiated identity of the *tayo*, and the Hawaiian *aikane* (*Representing the South Pacific*, 69).
21. Watts, 'Tahiti', 60.
22. See Kent, *Company of Heaven*, 45, 48.
23. See Bernard Smith's *European Vision*, amongst others, for a discussion of this view of the Pacific.
24. Amongst the many differences accounting for the disjunction of Australian and Pacific mission experiences, this sense of a hierarchy of racial attributes

and, hence, status was crucial. Aboriginal people, in contrast to Polynesians, were usually depicted as physically degraded, inferior, and unattractive to Europeans.

25. Conversely, it appears that Polynesian men too paid sexual attention to the bodies of European travellers. Edmond admits that evidence is difficult to find 'but it is clear that young [European] sailors and officers were desired by native men' (69). As he notes, 'it needs to be remembered that the heterosexual aura around the Polynesian world was a European projection and that the homosexuality of Polynesian cultures had its own allure' (*Representing the South Pacific*, 70).

26. Jolly and Macintyre, 'Introduction', 9.

27. McClintock, *Imperial Leather*, 34.

28. Tom Griffiths, 'The Voyage', in *Mission to the South Seas: The Voyages of the Duff, 1796–1799*, ed. Tom Griffiths, Michael Cathcart, Lee Watts, Vivian Anceschi, Greg Houghton, and David Goodman (Parkville, Vic: History Department, University of Melbourne, 1990).

29. Horne, *The Story of the LMS, 1795–1895*, 31, 36.

30. Sylvia Marcus, 'Indigenous Eroticism and Colonial Morality in Mexico: The Confession Manuals of New Spain', trans. Jacqueline Mosio, *Numen* 39, 2 (1992), 163.

31. Nussbaum, *Torrid Zones*, 7.

32. Williams, *Missionary Enterprises*, 582.

33. Margaret Maynard, *Fashioned from Penury: Dress as Cultural Practice in Colonial Australia* (Cambridge: Cambridge University Press, 1994), 3.

34. Charles W. Forman, *The Island Churches of the South Pacific: Emergence in the Twentieth Century* (Maryknoll, NY: Orbis, with the American Society of Missiology, 1982), 1.

35. LMS, 'Reports of the London Missionary Society: The Report of the Directors to the 28th General Meeting of the Missionary Society' (London: General Meeting of the LMS, 1822), 8, 17.

36. Philippe Perrot, *Fashioning the Bourgeoisie: A History of Clothing in the Nineteenth Century*, trans. Richard Bienvenu (Princeton, NJ: Princeton University Press, 1994), 7.

37. Quoted in Aileen Ribeiro, *Dress and Morality* (New York: Holmes & Meier, 1986), 103.

38. Quoted in LMS, 'Reports of the London Missionary Society (1825)', 25; emphasis added.

39. Douglas, 'Recuperating Indigenous Women'.

40. Richard Eves, 'Colonialism, Corporeality, and Character: Methodist Missions and the Refashioning of Bodies in the Pacific', *History and Anthropology* 10, 1 (1996), 118.

41. Vanessa Smith, *Literary Culture and the Pacific*, 53.

42. *Fashioning the Bourgeoisie*, 79. Perrot quotes from Lemann's 1857 *De l'industrie des vêtements confectionnés en France, réponse aux questions de la commission*

permanente des valeurs relativement à cette industrie which notes 'All along the west coast of Africa the savages seek out our clothes. Who would have believed it? A firm in Marseilles, the Régis company, exchanges ready-to-wear clothes for the natural products of these countries' (78).

43. LMS, 'Reports of the London Missionary Society (1823)', 24.

44. Quoted in Gunson, *Messengers of Grace*, 151.

45. Nicholas Thomas, 'The Case of the Misplaced Ponchos: Speculations Concerning the History of Cloth in Polynesia', *Journal of Material Culture* 4, 1 (1999), 14.

46. LMS, 'Reports of the London Missionary Society: The Report of the Directors to the 26th General Meeting of the Missionary Society' (London: General Meeting of the LMS, 1820), 13.

47. LMS, 'Reports of the London Missionary Society: The Report of the Directors to the 26th General Meeting of the Missionary Society' (London: General Meeting of the LMS, 1820), 13–14.

48. Jolly and Macintyre, 'Introduction', 6–7.

49. LMS, 'Reports of the London Missionary Society (1817)', 43.

50. Mr Heyward quoted in LMS, 'Reports of the London Missionary Society (1819)', 15–16.

51. LMS, 'Reports of the London Missionary Society (1820)', 13.

52. LMS, 'Reports of the London Missionary Society (1819)', 15.

53. *Ibid*.

54. See Dening's *Performances* for insightful readings of ceremonies surrounding Oro and the arrival of Europeans in Polynesia.

55. LMS, 'Reports of the London Missionary Society: The Report of the Directors to the 24th General Meeting of the Missionary Society' (London: General Meeting of the LMS, 1818), 4.

56. LMS, 'Reports of the London Missionary Society (1820)', 13–14.

57. Daniel Tyerman and George Bennet, 'Letter to Rev. Mr Burder', in CWM: *Home Odds Tyerman and Bennet's Deputations 1821–1828*. Box 10. SOAS, London (1824).

58. Quoted in Margaret Jolly, 'Colonizing Women: The Maternal Body and Empire', in *Feminism and the Politics of Difference*, ed. Sneja Gunew and Anna Yeatman (St Leonards, NSW: Allen & Unwin, 1993), 118.

8 THE AUSTRALIAN COLONIES AND EMPIRE

1. Quotation from Lancelot Threlkeld's *Reminiscences* which describes 'evidences of motion amongst the dry bones in this wilderness' (118) in reference to Aboriginal interest in Christianity.

2. Samuel Marsden quoted in L. E. Threlkeld, *A Statement Chiefly Relating to the Formation and Abandonment of a Mission to the Aborigines of New South Wales; Addressed to the Serious Consideration of the Directors of the London Missionary Society* (Sydney: R. Howe, Government Printer, 1828), 17.

3. Threlkeld, *Reminiscences*, 44.
4. The colonial settlement of New South Wales at this time incorporated the regions of contemporary New South Wales, Queensland, and Tasmania.
5. Ruth Teale, ed., *Colonial Eve: Sources on Women in Australia, 1788–1924* (Melbourne: Oxford University Press, 1978), 3.
6. King, *Ten Decades*, 34.
7. Woolmington, ' "Writing on the Sand": The First Missions to Aborigines in Eastern Australia', in *Aboriginal Australians and Christian Missions*, ed. Tony Swain and Deborah Bird Rose (Bedford Park, SA: Australian Association for the Study of Religions, South Australian College of Advanced Education Sturt Campus, 1988), 79. Bennelong (*c.* 1764–1813) was the second Aboriginal man captured by Governor Philip in 1789, from whom Philip sought to learn language and customs. His son with his second wife Goroobarroobooloo, Thomas Talker Coke, was adopted by William Walker (*Encyclopaedia of Aboriginal Australia*, 117–18).
8. Niel Gunson, 'Two Hundred Years of Christianity', *Aboriginal History* 12, 1 (1988), 104.
9. Gunson, 'Introduction', *Reminiscences*, 11.
10. *Ibid*.
11. Elizabeth Shelley (neé Bean) was the daughter of a free settler. She continued the school after Shelley's death (in July 1815) until 1823 and she taught eleven boys and twelve girls, of three to fifteen years of age (Gunson, 'Introduction', *Reminiscences*, 11–12). Hilary Carey notes that the Shelleys advocated the joint education of boys and girls so that marriages between Christian Aborigines would be possible when their charges reached maturity (Carey, 'Companions in the Wilderness?', 232).
12. A. T. Yarwood, *Samuel Marsden: The Great Survivor* (Carlton, Vic.: Melbourne University Press, 1977), 52.
13. Quoted in Yarwood, *Marsden*, 112.
14. Gunson, 'Two Hundred Years', 105.
15. John Frow, 'A Politics of Stolen Time: In Memory of John Forbes', *Meanjin* 57 (1998), 351.
16. John Dunmore Lang, 'Australian Mission. To the Ministers and Elders of the Secession and Relief Churches; To the Colonial Committee of the Free Church of Scotland' (Edinburgh: 17 and 19 April 1847), 4.
17. King, *Ten Decades*, 17.
18. *Ibid.*, 37.
19. Youl then returned to Britain where he was ordained as a Church of England minister in 1813. He was later appointed senior chaplain in Van Diemen's Land, dying at Launceston in 1827. Youl's colonial/imperial career path is a fascinating example of the constant circulation of colonial agents throughout empire in the nineteenth century.
20. King, *Ten Decades*, 38.
21. Carey, 'Companions in the Wilderness?', 230–1.

22. See my article ' "God being, not in the bush": The Nundah Mission (Qld) and Colonialism', *Queensland Review*, 4, 1 (1997), for a discussion of the role of the Nundah mission in early colonial Australia.
23. Woolmington, 'Writing on the Sand', 89.
24. Threlkeld worked with the Royal Circus and later the Royalty Theatre prior to his missionary career (Gunson, *Messengers of Grace*, 40).
25. Sadly, but ironically, Threlkeld's son died in Rio after all, and his wife died in the Pacific within a few years of their arrival.
26. Given the somewhat disastrous nature of the LMS mission here, the naming of it seems fortuitous. In fact, however, it was apparently so named before Threlkeld's arrival 'in honor of its discoverer, whose name was Reid, being master of a colonial coasting vessel, and intending to run into Port Hunter, whither Colonial craft then resorted for coals, which were dug out of the cliff by their crews; instead of Port Hunter, this sagacious seaman took his bark into this opening, and thus, in memory of his error, the name has been given' (quoted in Ben W. Champion, 'Lancelot Edward Threlkeld: His Life and Work, 1788–1859. Part I.', *Royal Australian Historical Society Journal and Proceedings* 25 (1939), 313).
27. W. P. Crook, 'Letter', in CWM: Australia Box 1 (Sydney: 1813).
28. Quoted in Gunson, 'Introduction', *Reminiscences*, 11.
29. For further analysis of this differential representation of indigenous 'heathen' see my 'Antipodean Heathens: The London Missionary Society in Polynesia and Australia, 1800–1850', in *Colonial Frontiers: Indigenous-European Encounters in Settler Societies*, ed. Lynette Russell (Manchester: Manchester University Press, 2001).
30. Quoted in Threlkeld, *Reminiscences*, 53.
31. Tyerman and Bennet, *Journal*, II: 148.
32. Daniel Tyerman, 'Letter to the Directors of the LMS', in CWM: *Home Odds Tyerman and Bennet's Deputations 1821–1828*. Box 10. SOAS, London (NSW: 8 February 1825).
33. In terms of grammars, Threlkeld published widely: *Specimens of a Dialect of the Aborigines of New South Wales; Being the First Attempt to Form their Speech into a Written Language* (1827) (republished posthumously as *An Australian Language as Spoken by the Awabakal the People of Awaba or Lake Macquarie (Near Newcastle, New South Wales) Being an Account of their Language, Traditions, and Customs* (1892)); *An Australian Grammar, Comprehending the Principles and Natural Rules of the Language, as Spoken by the Aborigines, in the Vicinity of Hunter's River, Lake Macquarie, &c. New South Wales* (1834); *An Australian Spelling Book, in the Language as Spoken by the Aborigines, in the Vicinity of Hunter's River, Lake Macquarie, New South Wales* (1836); 'An Australian Grammar', published in *The Saturday Magazine* 8 (2 Jan. 1836), 9 (17 Dec. 1836), and 10 (14 Jan. 1837); *A Key to the Structure of the Aboriginal Language; Being an Analysis of the Particles used as Affixes, to Form the Various Modifications of the Verbs; Shewing the Essential Powers, Abstract Roots, and other Peculiarities*

of the Language spoken by the Aborigines in the Vicinity of Hunter River, Lake Macquarie, etc., New South Wales; Together with Comparisons of Polynesians and Other Dialects (1850) (republished posthumously as *An Australian Language* (1892)).

34. Tyerman, 'Letter to the Directors of the LMS'.

35. Daniel Tyerman, and George Bennet, 'Letter to Lancelot Threlkeld on his Appointment', in CWM: *Home Odds Tyerman and Bennet's Deputations 1821–1828*. Box 10. SOAS, London (Sydney: 1825).

36. Though again, like the Pacific, it is vital not to fall into a kind of 'fatal impact' theory about post-contact Aboriginal cultures. Indigenous appropriation, accommodation, and resistance figure strongly in 'missionised' communities – the importance of Christianity to many contemporary Aboriginal elders and their ongoing struggle to maintain (indigenous) culture provides a clear example of this.

37. Tyerman and Bennet, 'Letter to Lancelot Threlkeld on his Appointment'.

38. Sarah Arndell was the daughter of Dr Thomas Arndell, a former surgeon in the First Fleet who was then granted land at Pennant Hills, and became a settler with various interests – 'physician, magistrate, wool and wheat grower' (quoted in Champion, 'Lancelot Edward Threlkeld: His Life and Work, 1788–1859. Part I', 304).

39. Tyerman and Bennet, 'Letter to Lancelot Threlkeld on his Appointment'.

40. *Ibid*.

41. Threlkeld, *Reminiscences*, 136.

9 MISSIONARY WRITING IN AUSTRALIA

1. House of Commons, 'Copies of Instructions given by His Majesty's Secretary of State for the Colonies, for promoting the Moral and Religious Instruction of the Aboriginal Inhabitants of New Holland or Van Diemen's Land', in *British Parliamentary Papers: Colonies (Australia)* (Dublin: Irish University Press, 1831).

2. Champion, 'Lancelot Edward Threlkeld: His Life and Work, 1788–1859. Part I', 297.

3. Quoted in King, *Ten Decades*, 75.

4. John Ferry notes: 'Threlkeld's station at Lake Macquarie was situated within the boundaries of the Awabakal people, but Threlkeld failed to realise that the Awabakal were only a horde or sub-group of a tribe that extended right along the central coast from Tuggerah to Cape Hawke, and up the Hunter Valley' (John Ferry, 'The Failure of the New South Wales Missions to the Aborigines before 1845', *Aboriginal History* 3, 1–2 (1979), 30).

5. Gunson, 'Introduction', *Reminiscences*, 1.

6. Threlkeld, *An Australian Grammar*, iii.

7. Champion notes that Threlkeld was elected a Fellow of the Ethnological Society of London as a result of his work on the *Key* (Ben W. Champion, 'Lancelot Edward Threlkeld: His Life and Work, 1788–1859. Part II', *Royal Australian Historical Society Journal and Proceedings* 25 (1939), 390).

8. Threlkeld, *An Australian Language*, 87.

9. *Ibid.*, 125.

10. Threlkeld, *Reminiscences*, 46.

11. Threlkeld, *An Australian Language*, 90.

12. For example, the New South Wales Supreme Court cases R. *vs* Boatman (10 February 1832) and R. *vs* Wombarty (14 August 1837).

13. Quoted in Threlkeld, *Australian Reminiscences*, 126. See my article 'The Well-Intentioned Imperialists: Missionary Textuality and (Post)Colonial Politics', in *Resistance and Reconciliation: Writing in the Commonwealth*, ed. Susan Cowan Bruce Bennet, Jacqueline Lo, Satendra Nandan, and Jennifer Web (forthcoming, 2003) for an analysis of the influence of these Quakers on the early Australian colonies.

14. Threlkeld, *Reminiscences*, 46.

15. Threlkeld, *An Australian Language*, 88.

16. *Ibid.* Threlkeld noted that a drawing by Biraban was sent to the SPCK as proof of Aboriginal capabilities (Threlkeld, *Reminiscences*, 59). See my article 'Mission Statements: Textuality and Morality in the Colonial Archive', in *Australian Literary Studies in the 21st Century: Proceedings of the 2000 ASAL Conference*, edited by Philip Mead, Association for the Study of Australian Literature, 2001, for further analysis of Threlkeld and Biraban's relationship and the ways in which it has been memorialised in contemporary New South Wales.

17. Hall, 'Missionary Stories', 245.

18. Threlkeld, *Reminiscences*, 96–7.

19. *Ibid.*, 49, emphasis added. Again, the significance of colonial labour relations, and missionary interventions in this arena, is evident in Threlkeld's narrative here.

20. Henry Reynolds, *This Whispering in Our Hearts* (St Leonards, NSW: Allen & Unwin, 1998), 10; Alan Lester, 'Obtaining the "Due Observance of Justice": The Geographies of Colonial Humanitarianism', *Environment and Planning D: Society and Space* 20 (2002).

21. Gillian Whitlock, 'The Silent Scribe: Susanna and "Black Mary"', *International Journal of Canadian Studies* 11 (Spring 1995), 59.

22. David Cairns and Shaun Richards, *Writing Ireland: Colonialism, Nationalism, and Culture* (Manchester: Manchester University Press, 1988).

23. Luke Gibbons, 'Race Against Time: Racial Discourse and Irish History', *Neocolonialism*, edited by Robert Young. *Spec. issue of Oxford Literary Review* 13, 1–2 (1991), 96.

24. See his 'Occasional Discourse on the Nigger Question' (1849) for his polemical attack on abolitionists.

25. Nussbaum, *Torrid Zones*, 7.

26. Threlkeld, *Reminiscences*, 49.

27. *Ibid.*, 146.

28. *Ibid.*, 49.

29. *Ibid.*, 56.

30. Herbert, *Culture and Anomie*, 162.
31. Threlkeld, *Reminiscences*, 56.
32. Annette Hamilton, 'Bond-Slaves of Satan: Aboriginal Women and the Missionary Dilemma', in *Family and Gender in the Pacific: Domestic Contradictions and the Colonial Impact*, ed. Margaret Jolly and Martha Macintyre (Cambridge: Cambridge University Press, 1989), 252.
33. Threlkeld, *Reminiscences*, 91.
34. Reynolds, *This Whispering in Our Hearts*, xi.
35. Lester, 'Obtaining the "Due Observance of Justice" ', 278.
36. Tyerman and Bennet, 'Letter to Lancelot Threlkeld on his Appointment'.
37. 'Threlkeld v. Lang', in *Sydney Herald* (Supreme Court of New South Wales, 1836).
38. Threlkeld, *A Statement Chiefly Relating*, 2.
39. Quoted in Threlkeld, *A Statement Chiefly Relating*, 39.
40. *Ibid.*, 17.
41. *Ibid.*, 39.
42. Clarke's 1876 preface to a collection of Adam Lindsay Gordon's poems suggests that the dominant note of Australian scenery is like that of Edgar Allan Poe's poetry: 'Weird Melancholy' (Marcus Clarke, 'Adam Lindsay Gordon', in *Marcus Clarke*, ed. Michael Wilding (St Lucia, Qld: University of Queensland Press (1876) 1976) 645). Clarke's characteristic representation of the landscape is one of lack, the grotesque, and the gothic; as such, it is a landscape which is inimical to imported European aesthetics and white subjectivities.
43. Quoted in 'Threlkeld v. Lang'.
44. Alan Lester, *Imperial Networks: Creating Identities in Nineteenth-Century South Africa and Britain* (London and New York: Routledge, 2001).
45. Hamilton, 'Bond-Slaves of Satan', 238.
46. Bernard Smith, *The Spectre of Truganini: 1980 Boyer Lectures* (Sydney: Australian Broadcasting Commission, 1980), *passim*.
47. Reynolds, *This Whispering in Our Hearts*, xv.
48. Keith Windschuttle, 'The Myths of Frontier Massacres in Australian History. Part III: Massacre Stories and the Policy of Separatism', *Quadrant* 44, 12 (2000).

CONCLUSION: MISSIONARY WRITING, THE IMPERIAL ARCHIVE
AND POSTCOLONIAL POLITICS

1. Tyerman and Bennet, *Journal*, II: 8.
2. Sinha, *Colonial Masculinity*, 19.

Bibliography

Note: London Missionary Society (LMS) archives are held at the School of Oriental and African Studies, University of London. References to this collection are abbreviated as SOAS: the box numbers are catalogued under the Council for World Mission (CWM) numbers used here.

Alloula, Malek. *The Colonial Harem.* Trans. Myrna Godzich and Wlad Godzich. Intro. Barbara Harlow. Minneapolis: University of Minnesota Press, 1986.

Atwood, Margaret. *The Journals of Susanna Moodie.* Toronto: Oxford University Press, 1970.

Ballantyne, R. M. *Gascoyne, the Sandal-Wood Trader: A Tale of the Pacific.* London and Edinburgh: W. & R. Chambers, 1873.

Ballhatchet, Kenneth. *Race, Sex, and Class under the Raj: Imperial Attitudes and Policies and their Critics.* London: Weidenfeld and Nicolson, 1980.

'The East India Company and Roman Catholic Missionaries'. *Journal of Ecclesiastical History* 44, 2 (1993), 273–89.

Baxter Society, New. *George Baxter, Colour Picture Printer, and The New Baxter Society* 4 November 2001 [cited 16 August 2002]. Available from http://www.rpsfamily.demon.co.uk.

Bennet, George. 'Letter to Rev George Burder'. In CWM: *Home Odds Tyerman and Bennet's Deputation Letters 1821–1828.* Highfield, 1820.

Berndt, Ronald M. and Catherine H. Berndt. 'Body and Soul: More than an Episode!' In *Aboriginal Australians and Christian Missions: Ethnographic and Historical Studies,* edited by Tony Swain and Deborah Bird Rose. Bedford Park, SA: Australian Association for the Study of Religions, South Australian College of Advanced Education Sturt Campus, 1988, 45–59.

Bhabha, Homi K. 'The Commitment to Theory'. In *The Location of Culture.* London and New York: Routledge, 1994, 19–39.

'Of Mimicry and Man: The Ambivalence of Colonial Discourse'. In *The Location of Culture.* London and New York: Routledge, 1994, 85–92.

'The Other Question: Stereotype, Discrimination, and the Discourse of Colonialism'. In *The Location of Culture.* London and New York: Routledge, 1994, 66–84.

'Sly Civility'. In *The Location of Culture.* London and New York: Routledge, 1994, 93–101.

Bonner, Hypatia Bradlaugh, for the Rationalist Press Association. *Christianizing the Heathen: First-Hand Information Concerning Overseas Missions*. London: Watts and Co., 1922.

Booth, William. *In Darkest England, and the Way Out*. London: International Headquarters of the Salvation Army, 1890.

Bowie, Fiona. 'Introduction: Reclaiming Women's Presence'. In *Women and Missions: Past and Present: Anthropological and Historical Perspectives*, edited by Deborah Kirkwood, Fiona Bowie, and Shirley Ardener. Providence, RI: Berg, 1993, 1–9.

Brantlinger, Patrick. *Rule of Darkness: British Literature and Imperialism, 1830–1914*. Ithaca and London: Cornell University Press, 1988.

Brockway, K. Nora. *A Larger Way for Women: Aspects of Christian Education for Girls in South India 1712–1948*. Madras: Geoffrey Cumberlege and Oxford University Press, 1949.

Bryant, Joseph. *Coral Reefs and Cannibals*. London: Epworth Press, 1925.

Buck, Peter (Te Rangi Hiroa). *Mangaia and the Mission*, edited and introduction by Rod Dixon and Teaea Parima. Suva: IPS, USP in association with B. P. Bishop Museum, 1993.

Bulu, Joel. *Joel Bulu: The Autobiography of a Native Minister in the South Seas*, translated by a missionary. Introduction by G. S. R. London: Wesleyan Mission House, 1871.

Burns, Robert. *The Indirect Benefits of the Missionary Enterprise: A Sermon Preached before the London Missionary Society, at the Tabernacle, Moorfields, on Wednesday, May 14, 1834*. London: Frederick Westley and A. H. Davis, 1834.

Burton, Antoinette. 'The White Woman's Burden: British Feminists and the Indian Woman, 1865–1915'. *Western Women and Imperialism. Spec. issue of Women's Studies International Forum* 13, 4 (1990), 295–308.

— *Burdens of History: British Feminists, Indian Women, and Imperial Culture, 1865–1915*. Chapel Hill and London: University of North Carolina Press, 1994.

Buyers, William. *Recollections of Northern India; With Observations on the Origin, Customs, and Moral Sentiments of the Hindoos, and Remarks on the Country, and Principal Places on the Ganges, &c*. London: John Snow, 1848.

Cairns, David and Shaun Richards. *Writing Ireland: Colonialism, Nationalism, and Culture*. Manchester: Manchester University Press, 1988.

Calder, Alex, 'The Temptations of William Pascoe Crook: An Experience of Cultural Difference in Marquesas, 1797–1798'. *Journal of Pacific History* 31, 2 (1996), 144–61.

Callan, Hilary. 'Introduction'. In *The Incorporated Wife*, edited by Hilary Callan and Shirley Ardener. London: Croom Helm, in association with the Centre for Cross Cultural Research on Women, 1984, 1–26.

'Candidates' Papers: Answers to Printed Questions'. In CWM: *Candidates' Papers Examination Committee*, 1833–1838.

'Candidates' Papers: Answers to Printed Questions'. In CWM: *Candidates' Papers Examination Committee*, 1839–1847.

Cannibalism Conquered: Mary Slessor, the Missionary Heroine; Pandita Ramabai, the Indian Orphans' Friend. London: Pickering & Inglis, n.d.

Carey, Hilary. 'Companions in the Wilderness?: Missionary Wives in Colonial Australia, 1788–1900'. *Journal of Religious History* 19, 2 (1995), 227–48.

Cathcart, Michael. 'Foundation of the Mission'. In *Mission to the South Seas: The Voyages of the Duff, 1796–1799*, edited by Tom Griffiths, Michael Cathcart, Lee Watts, Vivian Anceschi, Greg Houghton, and David Goodman. Parkville, Vic: History Department, University of Melbourne, 1990, 11–29.

Chambers, Ross. *Room for Maneuver: Reading (the) Oppositional (in) Literature*. Chicago and London: University of Chicago Press, 1991.

Champion, Ben W. 'Lancelot Edward Threlkeld: His Life and Work, 1788–1859. Part I'. *Royal Australian Historical Society Journal and Proceedings* 25 (1939), 279–329.

Champion, Ben W. 'Lancelot Edward Threlkeld: His Life and Work, 1788–1859. Part II'. *Royal Australian Historical Society Journal and Proceedings* 25 (1939), 341–411.

Chatterjee, Partha. *The Nation and its Fragments: Colonial and Postcolonial Histories*. Princeton, NJ: Princeton University Press, 1993.

Chatterjee, Ratnabali. 'Indian Prostitute as a Colonial Subject, Bengal 1864–1883'. *re/productions* 2 (April 1999). Available from http://www.hsph.harvard.edu/ Organizations/healthnet/SAsia/repro2/Colonial_Subject.html.

Cilento, Raphael. *The White Man in the Tropics, with Especial Reference to Australia and its Dependencies*. Melbourne: H. J. Green, Government Printer, 1925.

Clarke, Marcus. 'Adam Lindsay Gordon'. In *Marcus Clarke*, edited by Michael Wilding. St Lucia, Qld: University of Queensland Press (1876), 1976, 643–7.

Cohn, Bernard S. *Colonialism and its Forms of Knowledge: The British in India*. Princeton, NJ: Princeton University Press, 1996.

Comaroff, Jean, and John. 'Through the Looking-Glass: Colonial Encounters of the First Kind'. *Journal of Historical Sociology* 1, 1 (1989), 6–32.

Of Revelation and Revolution: Christianity, Colonialism, and Consciousness in South Africa. Vol. 1. Chicago and London: University of Chicago Press, 1991.

Crook, W. P. 'Letter'. In CWM: Australia Box 1. Sydney, 1813.

Cuningham, Francis. 'Preface'. In *Female Missionaries in India: Letters from a Missionary's Wife Abroad to a Friend in England*, edited by Mrs M[ary Edwards] Weitbrecht. London: James Nisbet, 1843, v–ix.

Cunningham, Valentine. ' "God and Nature Intended You for a Missionary's Wife": Mary Hill, Jane Eyre, and Other Missionary Women in the 1840s'. In *Women and Missions: Past and Present: Anthropological and Historical Perspectives*, edited by Deborah Kirkwood, Fiona Bowie, and Shirley Ardener. Providence, RI: Berg, 1993, 85–105.

Davidoff, Leonore and Catherine Hall. *Family Fortunes: Men and Women of the English Middle Class, 1780–1850*. London: Routledge, 1992.

Davin, Anna. 'Imperialism and Motherhood'. *History Workshop* 5 (Spring 1978), 9–65.

Dening, Greg. *Islands and Beaches: Discourse on a Silent Land: Marquesas, 1774–1880.* Chicago: Dorsey, 1980.

Mr Bligh's Bad Language: Passion, Power, and Theatre on the Bounty. Cambridge: Cambridge University Press, 1992.

Performances. Carlton South, Vic.: Melbourne University Press, 1996.

Dickens, Charles. *Bleak House.* Edited by George Frost and Sylverre Monod. New York: Norton (1853), 1977.

Doran, Christine. '"A Fine Sphere for Female Usefulness": Missionary Women in the Straits Settlements, 1815–45'. *Journal of the Malaysian Branch of the Royal Asiatic Society* 69, 1 (1996), 100–11.

Douglas, Bronwen. 'Recuperating Indigenous Women: Female Sexuality and Missionary Textuality in Melanesia'. *Paper to the Association for Social Anthropology in Oceania Annual Meeting, Auckland, New Zealand* unpublished, 23 February (2002), n.p.

Driver, Dorothy. '"Woman" as Sign in the South African Colonial Enterprise'. *Journal of Literary Studies* 4, 1 (1988), 3–20.

Duff, Alexander. *Female Education in India, Being the Substance of An Address Delivered at the First Annual Meeting of the Scottish Ladies' Association, in Connection with the Church of Scotland, for the Promotion of Female Education in India.* Edinburgh: John Johnstone, 1834.

Edmond, Rod. *Representing the South Pacific: Colonial Discourse from Cook to Gauguin.* Cambridge: Cambridge University Press, 1997.

Ellis, James J. *John Williams: The Martyr Missionary of Polynesia.* London: S. W. Partridge, n.d.

Ellis, William. *Polynesian Researches, During a Residence of Nearly Six Years in the South Sea Islands; Including Descriptions of the Natural History and Scenery of the Islands – with Remarks on the History, Mythology, Traditions, Government, Arts, Manners, and Customs of the Inhabitants.* 2 vols. London: Fisher, Son and Jackson, 1829.

Etherington, Norman. 'Recent Trends in the Historiography of Christianity in Southern Africa'. *Journal of Southern African Studies* 22, 2 (1996), 201–19.

Eves, Richard. 'Colonialism, Corporeality, and Character: Methodist Missions and the Refashioning of Bodies in the Pacific'. *History and Anthropology* 10, 1 (1996), 83–138.

Fabian, Johannes. 'Religious and Secular Colonization: Common Ground'. *History and Anthropology* 4 (1990), 339–55.

Ferry, John. 'The Failure of the New South Wales Missions to the Aborigines before 1845'. *Aboriginal History* 3, 1–2 (1979), 25–36.

Forbes, Geraldine H. 'In Search of the "Pure Heathen": Missionary Women in Nineteenth-Century India'. *Economic and Political Weekly* 21, 17 (1986), WS2–WS8.

Forman, Charles W. *The Island Churches of the South Pacific: Emergence in the Twentieth Century.* Maryknoll, NY: Orbis, with the American Society of Missiology, 1982.

Free Church of Scotland's India Mission. 'Report of the Female Orphanage and Schools of the Scottish Ladies' Association for Promoting Female Education in India (Madras Branch)', 1861–2.

Frow, John. 'A Politics of Stolen Time: In Memory of John Forbes'. *Meanjin* 57 (1998), 351–67.

Gaunt, Lewis Hermon. *School-Mates: Pictures of School-Time and Play-Time in the Mission Field*. London: LMS, 1906.

Gibbons, Luke. 'Race Against Time: Racial Discourse and Irish History'. *Neocolonialism*, edited by Robert Young. *Spec. issue of Oxford Literary Review* 13, 1–2 (1991), 95–117.

Gilbert, Sandra M. and Susan Gubar. *The Madwoman in the Attic: The Woman Writer and the Nineteenth-Century Literary Imagination*. New Haven and London: Yale University Press, 1979.

Gikandi, Simon. *Maps of Englishness: Writing Identity in the Culture of Colonialism*. New York: Columbia University Press, 1996.

The Gospel Missionary for 1852. Published for the Society for the Propagation of the Gospel, 1852.

Gray, B. Kirkman. *A History of English Philanthropy: From the Dissolution of the Monasteries to the Taking of the First Census*. London: Frank Cass, 1905.

Green, Martin. 'The Robinson Crusoe Story'. In *Imperialism and Juvenile Literature*, edited by Jeffrey Richards. Manchester: Manchester University Press, 1989, 34–52.

Grewal, Inderpal. *Home and Harem: Nation, Gender, Empire, and the Cultures of Travel*. London: Leicester University Press, 1996.

Griffiths, Tom. 'The Voyage'. In *Mission to the South Seas: The Voyages of the Duff, 1796–1799*, edited by Tom Griffiths, Michael Cathcart, Lee Watts, Vivian Anceschi, Greg Houghton, and David Goodman. Parkville, Vic: History Department, University of Melbourne, 1990, 32–52.

Grimshaw, Patricia. *Paths of Duty: American Missionary Wives in Nineteenth-Century Hawaii*. Honolulu: University of Honolulu Press, 1989.

Guha, Ranajit and Gayatri Chakravorty Spivak, eds., *Selected Subaltern Studies*. New York and Oxford: Oxford University Press, 1988.

Gunson, Niel. 'Introduction'. In *Australian Reminiscences and Papers of L. E. Threlkeld, Missionary to the Aborigines, 1824–1859*. Canberra: AIAS, 1974, 1–40.

Messengers of Grace: Evangelical Missionaries in the South Seas, 1797–1860. Melbourne: Oxford University Press, 1978.

'Two Hundred Years of Christianity'. *Aboriginal History* 12, 1 (1988), 103–11.

Haggis, Jane. 'Gendering Colonialism or Colonising Gender?: Recent Women's Studies Approaches to White Women and the History of British Colonialism'. *British Feminist Histories. Spec. issue of Women's Studies International Forum* 13, 1–2 (1990), 105–15.

Haggis, Jane. 'Professional Ladies and Working Wives: Female Missionaries in the London Missionary Society and its South Travancore District, South India in the 19th Century'. PhD diss., University of Manchester, 1991.

Hall, Catherine. 'Missionary Stories: Gender and Ethnicity in England in the 1830s and 1840s'. In *Cultural Studies*, edited by Cary Neilson, Lawrence Grossberg, and Paula Treichler. New York and London: Routledge, 1992, 240–70.

 'Review of *Congregational Missions and the Making of an Imperial Culture in Nineteenth-Century England* by Susan Thorne and *Good Citizens: British Missionaries and Imperial States, 1780–1918* by James M. Greenlee and Charles M. Johnston'. *Victorian Studies* 43, 4 (2001), 695–7.

 Civilising Subjects: Metropole and Colony in the English Imagination, 1830–1867. Cambridge: Polity, 2002.

Hall, Donald E. 'Muscular Christianity: Reading and Writing the Male Social Body'. In *Muscular Christianity: Embodying the Victorian Age*, edited by Donald E. Hall. Cambridge: Cambridge University Press, 1994.

Hamilton, Annette. 'Bond-Slaves of Satan: Aboriginal Women and the Missionary Dilemma'. In *Family and Gender in the Pacific: Domestic Contradictions and the Colonial Impact*, edited by Margaret Jolly and Martha Macintyre. Cambridge: Cambridge University Press, 1989, 236–58.

Hannabuss, Stuart. 'Ballantyne's Message of Empire'. In *Imperialism and Juvenile Literature*, edited by Jeffrey Richards. Manchester: Manchester University Press, 1989, 53–71.

Harrington, Henry Randolph. *Muscular Christianity: A Study of the Development of a Victorian Idea*. Ann Arbor: University Microfilms, 1976.

Harris, John. *One Blood: Two Hundred Years of Aboriginal Encounter with Christianity: A Story of Hope*. 2nd edn. Sutherland, NSW: Albatross, 1994.

Hart, Miss Isabel. 'Introduction'. In *Historical Sketches of Woman's [sic] Missionary Societies in America and England*, edited by Mrs L. H. Daggett. Boston: Daggett, 1879, 7–12.

H[aweis], T[homas]. 'The Very Probable Success of a Proper Mission to the South Sea Islands'. *The Evangelical Magazine* 3 (1795), 261–70.

Herbert, Christopher. *Culture and Anomie: Ethnographic Imagination in the Nineteenth Century*. Chicago: University of Chicago Press, 1991.

Holmes, B. 'British Imperial Policy and the Mission Schools'. In *Educational Policy and the Mission Schools: Case Studies from the British Empire*, edited by B. Holmes. London: Routledge, 1967, 5–46.

Horne, C. Silvester. *The Story of the LMS, 1795–1895*. London: LMS, 1894.

House of Commons. 'Copies of Instructions given by His Majesty's Secretary of State for the Colonies, for promoting the Moral and Religious Instruction of the Aboriginal Inhabitants of New Holland or Van Diemen's Land'. In *British Parliamentary Papers: Colonies (Australia)*. Dublin: Irish University Press, 1831, 153–7.

Hyam, Ronald. *Empire and Sexuality: The British Experience*. Manchester and New York: Manchester University Press, 1990.

J. M. 'Review of *Memoirs of the Life of the Rev. John Williams, Missionary to Polynesia*; by the Rev. E. Prout of Halstead'. In *Papers on Missions*, unpaginated. No Publisher: n.p., 1845.

Johnston, Anna. ' "God being, not in the bush": The Nundah Mission (Qld) and Colonialism'. *Queensland Review* 4, 1 (1997), 71–80.

'Antipodean Heathens: The London Missionary Society in Polynesia and Australia, 1800–1850'. In *Colonial Frontiers: Indigenous–European Encounters in Settler Societies*, edited by Lynette Russell. Manchester: Manchester University Press, 2001, 68–81.

'The Bookeaters: Textuality, Modernity, and the London Missionary Society'. *A Vanishing Mediator? The Presence/Absence of the Bible in Postcolonialism. Spec. issue of Semiea* 88 (2001), 13–40.

'Mission Statements: Textuality and Morality in the Colonial Archive'. In *Australian Literary Studies in the 21st Century: Proceedings of the 2000 ASAL Conference*, edited by Philip Mead. Association for the Study of Australian Literature, 2001, 151–60.

'Planting the Seeds of Christianity: Ecological Reform in Nineteenth-Century Polynesian LMS Stations'. In *Empire and Environment Anthology*, edited by Helen Tiffin. Amsterdam: Rodopi (forthcoming, 2003).

'The Well-Intentioned Imperialists: Missionary Textuality and (Post)Colonial Politics'. In *Resistance and Reconciliation: Writing in the Commonwealth*, edited by Susan Cowan, Bruce Bennet, Jacqueline Lo, Satendra Nandan, and Jennifer Webb (forthcoming, 2003).

Jolly, Margaret. 'Colonizing Women: The Maternal Body and Empire'. In *Feminism and the Politics of Difference*, edited by Sneja Gunew and Anna Yeatman. St Leonards, NSW: Allen & Unwin, 1993, 103–27.

Jolly, Margaret, and Martha Macintyre. 'Introduction'. In *Family and Gender in the Pacific: Domestic Contradictions and the Colonial Impact*, edited by Margaret Jolly and Martha Macintyre. Cambridge: Cambridge University Press, 1989, 1–18.

Kaplan, Steven, ed. *Indigenous Responses to Western Christianity*. New York and London: New York University Press, 1995.

Kennedy, James. 'Preface'. In *The Eastern Lily Gathered: A Memoir of Bala Shoondoree Tagore. With Observations on the Position and Prospects of Hindu Female Society*, edited by E[dward] Storrow, iii–ix. London: Snow, 1856, iii–ix.

Kent, Graeme. *Company of Heaven: Early Missionaries in the South Seas*. Wellington: A.H. & A.W. Reed, 1972.

King, Joseph. *Ten Decades: The Australian Centenary Story of the London Missionary Society: The Australasian Centenary History of the London Missionary Society*. London: John Snow, *c.* 1895.

Kingsley, Charles. *Westward Ho!: Or the Voyages and Adventures of Sir Amyas Leigh, Knight, of Burrough, in the County of Devon, in the Region of her Most Glorious Majesty Queen Elizabeth*. London and New York: Macmillan, 1855.

Lang, John Dunmore. 'Australian Mission. To the Ministers and Elders of the Secession and Relief Churches; To the Colonial Committee of the Free Church of Scotland'. Edinburgh, 17 and 19 April 1847.

Lester, Alan. *Imperial Networks: Creating Identities in Nineteenth-Century South Africa and Britain*. London and New York: Routledge, 2001.

'Obtaining the "Due Observance of Justice": The Geographies of Colonial Humanitarianism'. *Environment and Planning D: Society and Space* 20 (2002), 277–93.

Lindstrom, Lamont. 'Postcards from the Edge. Rev. of *Colonialism's Culture*, by Nicholas Thomas'. *Meanjin* 53, 4 (1994), 743–6.

LMS. 'Board Minutes'. In CWM: *Minute Books 1795–1842*, 1798–1801.

'Candidates Examination Committee'. In CWM: *Candidate's Papers Examination Committee*. London, 1816–19.

'Reports of the London Missionary Society: The Report of the Directors to the 23rd General Meeting of the Missionary Society'. London: General Meeting of the LMS, 1817.

'Reports of the London Missionary Society: The Report of the Directors to the 24th General Meeting of the Missionary Society'. London: General Meeting of the LMS, 1818.

'Reports of the London Missionary Society: The Report of the Directors to the 25th General Meeting of the Missionary Society'. London: General Meeting of the LMS, 1819.

'Reports of the London Missionary Society: The Report of the Directors to the 26th General Meeting of the Missionary Society'. London: General Meeting of the LMS, 1820.

'Missionary Sketches'. London: F. Westley and A. H. Davis, 1820– .

'Reports of the London Missionary Society: The Report of the Directors to the 27th General Meeting of the Missionary Society'. London: General Meeting of the LMS, 1821.

'Reports of the London Missionary Society: The Report of the Directors to the 28th General Meeting of the Missionary Society'. London: General Meeting of the LMS, 1822.

'Reports of the London Missionary Society: The Report of the Directors to the 29th General Meeting of the Missionary Society'. London: General Meeting of the LMS, 1823.

'Reports of the London Missionary Society: The Report of the Directors to the 30th General Meeting of the Missionary Society'. London: General Meeting of the LMS, 1824.

'Reports of the London Missionary Society: The Report of the Directors to the 31st General Meeting of the Missionary Society'. London: General Meeting of the LMS, 1825.

'Reports of the London Missionary Society: The Report of the Directors to the 35th General Meeting of the Missionary Society'. London: General Meeting of the LMS, 1829.

'Reports of the London Missionary Society: The Report of the Directors to the 36th General Meeting of the Missionary Society'. London: General Meeting of the LMS, 1830.

'Report of the Ladies' Native Female School Society, in connection with the London Missionary Society for 1839 and 1840'. Calcutta, 1841.

'Brief Review of the London Missionary Society, from its formation, September 1795'. LMS Annual Meeting, 1845, 16.

'Second Report of the Mahí Kánthá (Late Baroda) Mission in connection with the London Missionary Society'. 1848.

'Third Report of the Mahí Kánthá (Late Baroda) Mission in connection with the London Missionary Society'. May 1851.

'Fourth Report of the Mahí Kánthá (Late Baroda) Mission in connection with the London Missionary Society'. August 1851.

'The Missionary Magazine and Chronicle: Chiefly Relating to the Missions of the London Missionary Society'. 1861.

Lovett, Richard. *The History of the London Missionary Society, 1795–1895*. 2 vols. London: Henry Frowde, 1899.

MacKenzie, John, ed., *Imperialism and Popular Culture*. Manchester: Manchester University Press, 1986.

Mangan, J. A., and James Walvin. 'Introduction'. In *Manliness and Morality: Middle-Class Masculinity in Britain and America, 1800–1940*, edited by J. A. Mangan and James Walvin, Manchester: Manchester University Press, 1987, 1–6.

Marcus, Sylvia, 'Indigenous Eroticism and Colonial Morality in Mexico: The Confession Manuals of New Spain', trans. Jacqueline Mosio. *Numen* 39, 2 (1992), 157–74.

May, Robert. 'Letter to the Directors of the LMS'. In CWM: *Candidates' Papers Examination Committee*. Chinsurah: CWM: North India (Bengal) Incoming Letters. Box 1. SOAS, London, 1813.

Maynard, Margaret. *Fashioned from Penury: Dress as Cultural Practice in Colonial Australia*. Cambridge: Cambridge University Press, 1994.

McClintock, Anne. *Imperial Leather: Race, Gender, and Sexuality in the Colonial Contest*. New York and London: Routledge, 1995.

Muir, Ramsay, ed. *The Making of British India 1756–1858: Described in a Series of Dispatches, Treaties, Statutes, and other Documents, Selected and Edited with Introductions and Notes*. Pakistan: Oxford University Press, 1915.

Mullens, Joseph. *The Results of Missionary Labour in India*. London: LMS, 1852.

Mullens, Mrs [Hannah Catherine]. *Faith and Victory: A Story of the Progress of Christianity in Bengal*. 2nd edn. London: James Nisbet, 1867.

Mundy, George. *Memoir of Mrs Louisa Mundy, of the London Missionary Society's Mission, at Chinsurah, Bengal. With Extracts from her Diary and Letters. By her Husband*. London: John Snow, 1845.

Murray, A. W. *Forty Years' Mission Work in Polynesia and New Guinea, from 1835 to 1875*. London: James Nisbet, 1876.

Neill, Stephen. *A History of Christian Missions*. Harmondsworth: Penguin, 1964.

A History of Christianity in India 1707–1858. Cambridge: Cambridge University Press, 1985.

Nussbaum, Felicity A. *Torrid Zones: Maternity, Sexuality, and Empire in Eighteenth-Century English Novels*. Baltimore and London: Johns Hopkins University Press, 1995.

Perrot, Philippe. *Fashioning the Bourgeoisie: A History of Clothing in the Nineteenth Century*, trans. Richard Bienvenu. Princeton, NJ: Princeton University Press, 1994.

Porter, Andrew. '"Commerce and Christianity": The Rise and Fall of a Nineteenth-Century Missionary Slogan'. *The Historical Journal* 28, 3 (1985), 597–621.

Porter, Andrew. 'Religion, Missionary Enthusiasm, and Empire'. In *The Oxford History of the British Empire: The Nineteenth Century*, edited by Andrew Porter. Oxford and New York: Oxford University Press, 1999, 222–46.

Pratt, Mary Louise. *Imperial Eyes: Travel Writing and Transculturation*. London and New York: Routledge, 1992.

Prochaska, F. K. *Women and Philanthropy in Nineteenth-Century England*. Oxford: Clarendon Press, 1980.

Prout, E. *Missionary Ships Connected with the London Missionary Society*. London: LMS, 1865.

Pybus, Cassandra. *White Rajah: A Dynastic Intrigue*. St Lucia, Qld: University of Queensland Press, 1996.

Rajan, Rajeswari Sunder. *Real and Imagined Women: Gender, Culture, and Postcolonialism*. Routledge: London and New York, 1993.

Reynolds, Henry. *This Whispering in Our Hearts*. St Leonards, NSW: Allen & Unwin, 1998.

Ribeiro, Aileen. *Dress and Morality*. New York: Holmes & Meier, 1986.

Richards, Jeffrey. 'Introduction'. In *Imperialism and Juvenile Literature*, edited by Jeffrey Richards. Manchester: Manchester University Press, 1989, 1–11.

'With Henty to Africa'. In *Imperialism and Juvenile Literature*, edited by Jeffrey Richards. Manchester: Manchester University Press, 1989, 72–106.

Richards, Thomas. *The Imperial Archive: Knowledge and the Fantasy of Empire*. London and New York: Verso, 1993.

Robertson, J[ames]. 'Journal' in CWM: *North India Journals*. Box 1, SOAS, London (Benares, 1826–7); rpt. in the *Quarterly Chronicle of Transactions of the London Missionary Society*, in the years 1829, 1830, 1831, and 1832. Vol. 4.

Rooke, Patricia T. ' "Ordinary Events of Nature and Providence": Reconstructing Female Missionary Experience in the British West Indies, 1800–45'. *Journal of Religious History* 19, 2 (1995), 204–6.

Ryan, Simon. *The Cartographic Eye: How Explorers Saw Australia*. Cambridge and New York: Cambridge University Press, 1996.

Saunders, Graham. *Bishops and Brookes: The Anglican Mission and the Brooke Raj in Sarawak 1848–1941*. Singapore: Oxford University Press, 1992.

Sawbridge, Laura Helen. *The Vision and the Mission of Womanhood in the Empire and Beyond*. London: Wells Gardner, Darton, 1917.

Scott, Jamie S. 'Introduction: "Onward, Christian Britons!"'. In *'And the Birds Began to Sing': Religion and Literature in Post-Colonial Cultures*, edited by Jamie [S.] Scott. Amsterdam and Atlanta: Rodopi, 1996, xv–xxvii.

Seeley, John. *The Expansion of England: Two Courses of Lectures*. London: Macmillan, 1890.

Sharpe, Jenny. *Allegories of Empire: The Figure of Woman in the Colonial Text*. Minneapolis and London: University of Minnesota Press, 1993.

Sherman, James. *The Remembrance of Christ's Love a Stimulus to Missionary Exertion: A Sermon, Preached before the London Missionary Society, at Spa Field's Chapel, On Thursday, May 13th, 1830*. London: Fisher, Son, and Jackson, and James Nisbet, n.d.

Sinha, Mrinalini. *Colonial Masculinity: The 'Manly Englishman' and the 'Effeminate Bengali' in the Late Nineteenth Century*. Manchester and New York: Manchester University Press, 1995.

Slemon, Stephen. 'Monuments of Empire: Allegory/Counter-Discourse/Post-Colonial Writing'. *Kunapipi* 9, 3 (1987), 1–16.

'Afterword: The English Side of the Lawn'. *Testing the Limits: Postcolonial Theories and Canadian Literatures. Spec. issue of Essays in Canadian Writing* 56 (Fall 1995), 274–86.

Smith, Bernard. *European Vision and the South Pacific, 1768–1850: A Study in the History of Art and Ideas*. London: Oxford University Press, 1960.

The Spectre of Truganini: 1980 Boyer Lectures. Sydney: Australian Broadcasting Commission (1980).

Smith, Thomas. 'Editorial and Review of *Hindu Female Education* by Priscila Chapman, and First Report of the Scottish Ladies' Association for the advancement of Female Education in India under the Superintendence of Missionaries in the Church of Scotland'. *The Calcutta Christian Observer*, n.s. 3 (March 1840), 117–30.

Smith, Vanessa. *Literary Culture and the Pacific: Nineteenth-Century Textual Encounters*. Cambridge: Cambridge University Press, 1998.

Spivak, Gayatri. 'A Literary Representation of the Subaltern: A Woman's Text from the Third World'. In *In Other Worlds: Essays in Cultural Politics*. New York and London: Methuen, 1987, 241–68.

A Critique of Postcolonial Reason: Toward a History of the Vanishing Present. Cambridge, Mass.: Harvard University Press, 1999.

Stanley, Brian. *The Bible and the Flag: Protestant Missions and British Imperialism in the Nineteenth and Twentieth Centuries*. Leicester: Apollos-Inter-Varsity Press, 1990.

Stanley, Henry Morton. *In Darkest Africa, or the Quest, Rescue, and Retreat of Emin, Governor of Equatoria*. London: Low, Marston, Searle and Rivington, 1890.

St John, Spenser. *Rajah Brooke: The Englishman as Ruler of an Eastern State*. London: T. Fisher Unwin, 1899.

Stoler, Ann Laura. *Race and the Education of Desire: Foucault's 'History of Sexuality' and the Colonial Order of Things*. Durham and London: Duke University Press, 1995.

Storrow, Edward. *The Eastern Lily Gathered: A Memoir of Bala Shoondoree Tagore. With Observations on the Position and Prospects of Hindu Female Society*. Preface by Reverend James Kennedy. 2nd edn. London: John Snow, 1856.

'Introduction'. In *The Dawn of Light: A Story of the Zenana Mission*, edited by Mary E. Leslie. London: Snow, 1868.

Storrow, E[dward]. *Our Indian Sisters*. London: Religious Tract Society, (1898).

Ta'unga. *The Works of Ta'unga: Records of a Polynesian Traveller in the South Seas, 1833–1896*, edited and preface by R. G. Crocombe and Marjorie Crocombe. Foreword by H. E. Maude. With annotations by Jean Guiart, Niel Gunson, and Dorothy Shineberg. Canberra: Australian National University Press, 1968.

Teale, Ruth, ed. *Colonial Eve: Sources on Women in Australia, 1788–1924*. Melbourne: Oxford University Press, 1978.

Teltscher, Kate. *India Inscribed: European and British Writing on India 1600–1800*. Delhi: Oxford University Press, 1995.

Thomas, Nicholas. *Entangled Objects: Exchange, Material Culture, and Colonialism in the Pacific*. Cambridge, Mass.: Harvard University Press, 1991.

Colonialism's Culture: Anthropology, Travel and Government. Carlton, Vic.: Melbourne University Press, 1994.

'The Case of the Misplaced Ponchos: Speculations Concerning the History of Cloth in Polynesia'. *Journal of Material Culture* 4, 1 (1999), 5–20.

Thompson, Ralph Wardlaw and Arthur N. Johnson. *British Foreign Missions 1837–1897*. London: Blackie, 1899.

Thorne, Susan. *Congregational Missions and the Making of an Imperial Culture in Nineteenth-Century England*. Stanford: Stanford University Press, 1999.

Threlkeld, L. E. *A Statement Chiefly Relating to the Formation and Abandonment of a Mission to the Aborigines of New South Wales; Addressed to the Serious Consideration of the Directors of the London Missionary Society*. Sydney: R. Howe, Government Printer, 1828.

An Australian Grammar, Comprehending the Principles and Natural Rules of the Language, as Spoken by the Aborigines, in the Vicinity of Hunter's River, Lake Macquarie, &c. New South Wales, Sydney. Sydney: printed by Stephens and Stokes, 'Herald Office', 1834.

An Australian Language as Spoken by the Awabakal the People of Awaba or Lake Macquarie (Near Newcastle, New South Wales) Being an Account of their Language, Traditions, and Customs, edited by John Fraser with an appendix. Sydney: Charles Potter, Government Printer, 1892.

Australian Reminiscences and Papers of L. E. Threlkeld, Missionary to the Aborigines, 1824–1859. Edited by Niel Gunson. 2 vols. Canberra: AIAS, 1974.

'Threlkeld v. Lang'. In *Sydney Herald*: Supreme Court of New South Wales, 1836.

Tiffin, Helen. 'The Body in the Library: Identity, Opposition, and the Settler-Invader Woman'. In *The Contact and the Culmination*, edited by Marc Delrez and Benedicte Ledent. Liége: L3, 1997, 213–28.

Tiffin, Helen. 'Introduction'. In *Post-Colonial Literatures in English: General, Theoretical, and Comparative 1970–1993*, edited by Leigh Dale, Alan Lawson, Helen Tiffin, and Shane Rowlands. New York: G. K. Hall–Macmillan, 1997.

Trollope, Joanna. *Britannia's Daughters: Women of the British Empire*, Cresset Women's Voices. London: Century Hutchinson, 1983.

Tyerman, Daniel. 'Letter to the directors of the LMS'. In CWM: *Home Odds Tyerman and Bennet's Deputations 1821–1828*. Box 10. SOAS, London. (NSW), 8 February 1825.

Tyerman, Daniel and George Bennet. 'Letter to Rev. Mr Bader'. In CWM: *Home Odds Tyerman and Bennet's Deputations 1821–1828*. Box 10. SOAS, London, 1824.

'Letter to Lancelot Threlkeld on his Appointment'. In CWM: *Home Odds Tyerman and Bennet's Deputations 1821–1828*. Box 10. SOAS, London (Sydney), 1825.

Journal of Voyages and Travels by the Rev. Daniel Tyerman and George Bennet, Esq. Deputed from the London Missionary Society, to Visit their Various Stations in the South Sea Islands, China, India, &c., between the Years 1821 and 1829. Compiled from Original Documents by James Montgomery. 2 vols. London: Frederick Westley and A. H. Davis, 1831.

Vance, Norman. *The Sinews of the Spirit: The Idea of Christian Manliness in Victorian Literature and Religious Thought*. Oxford and Cambridge, Mass.: Blackwell, 1997.

Viswanathan, Gauri. *Masks of Conquest: Literary Study and British Rule in India*. New York: Columbia University Press, 1989.

Walkowitz, Judith R. *Prostitution and Victorian Society: Women, Class and the State*. Cambridge: Cambridge University Press, 1980.

Watts, Lee. 'Tahiti'. In *Mission to the South Seas: The Voyages of the Duff, 1796–1799*, edited by Tom Griffiths, Michael Cathcart, Lee Watts, Vivian Anceschi, Greg Houghton, and David Goodman. Parkville, Vic: The History Department, the University of Melbourne, 1990, 54–78.

Weitbrecht, Mrs M[ary Edwards]. *The Women of India and Christian Work in the Zenana*. London: James Nisbet, 1875.

Whitlock, Gillian. 'The Silent Scribe: Susanna and "Black Mary"'. *International Journal of Canadian Studies* 11 (Spring 1995), 249–60.

'A "White Souled State": Across the "South" with Lady Barker'. In *Text, Theory, Space: Land, Literature, and History in South Africa and Australia*, edited by Liz Gunner, Kate Darian-Smith, and Sarah Nuttall. London: Routledge, 1996, 65–80.

The Intimate Empire: Reading Women's Autobiography. London: Cassell, 2000.

Wilkins, W. J. *Daily Life and Work in India*. London: LMS, 1888.

Williams, John. *A Narrative of Missionary Enterprises in the South Sea Islands: With Remarks upon the Natural History of the Islands, Origin, Languages, Traditions, and Usages of the Inhabitants*. 7th edn. London: J. Snow, (1837) 1838.

Williams, Peter. '"The Missing Link": The Recruitment of Women Missionaries in some English Evangelical Societies in the Nineteenth Century'. In *Women and Missions: Past and Present: Anthropological and Historical Perspectives*, edited by Deborah Kirkwood, Fiona Bowie, and Shirley Ardener. Providence, RI: Berg, 1993, 43–69.

Wilson, John. *The Evangelization of India: Considered with Reference to the Duties of the Christian Church at Home and of its Missionary Agents Abroad. In a Brief Series of Discourses, Addresses, &c*. Edinburgh: William Whyte, 1844.

Windschuttle, Keith. 'The Myths of Frontier Massacres in Australian History. Part III: Massacre Stories and the Policy of Separatism'. *Quadrant* 44, 12 (2000). Available from http://web3.infotrac.galegroup.com/itw/ifomark/200/228/44370939w3/purl = .

Woolmington, Jean. ' "Writing on the Sand": The First Missions to Aborigines in Eastern Australia'. In *Aboriginal Australians and Christian Missions: Ethnographic and Historical Studies*, edited by Tony Swain and Deborah Bird Rose. Bedford Park, SA: Australian Association for the Study of Religions, South Australian College of Advanced Education Sturt Campus, 1988, 77–92.

Yarwood, A. T. *Samuel Marsden: The Great Survivor*. Carlton, Vic.: Melbourne University Press, 1977.

Index

Abeel, Reverend David 47
Aborigine(s) 164, 201, 208
  and carnality 175
  debased by contact with Europeans 178, 192, 232
  destruction of culture 187, 193
  dying race 182
  evidence not admissible 191
  human despite degradation 176, 199
  'lending' of wives 191
  marital affection compared to biblical 190–1
  potential for 'raising up' 169
  and racial hierarchy 175, 197
  and sexuality 175
  unglamorous subject for missionary writing 197
abortion 86
Africa 19, 22, 52, 57, 174, *see also* South Africa
agricultural reform 120
aikane 231, *see also* homosexuality
Algeria 94
Alloula, Malek 94
America, North 15, 17
Anglican, *see* Church of England
anthakar 221, *see also* zenana
apartheid 31
Areoi 159–61
Armitage family 163
Arndell, Sarah (later Threlkeld) 179, 236
Arndell, Dr Thomas 236
Arya Mahila Samaj 110
Athavale, Parvati 110
Atwood, Margaret 135
Australia(n) 4, 5, 8, 22, 28, 42, 49, 54, 57, 167, 201, 205, 206, 207, 208, 233
  colonists: attitude to missionary activity 169, 178; degraded 206; violence towards Aborigines 183, 186, 191, 200–1
  colonisation 169

convicts: degraded 176, 188, 206; treatment of 186
missionaries in New Zealand 18

Backhouse, James 184
Bala Tagore 85–91
Ballantyne, R. M. 20
  Black Ivory 20
  Gascoyne, the Sandal-Wood Trader 19, 41
  Jarwin and Cuffy 19
  Man on the Ocean 19
  The Coral Island 19
  The Fugitives 20
  The Ocean and its Wonders 19
Ballhatchet, Kenneth 36, 74, 212, 226
Banks, Sir Joseph 117
Baptist
  compared to other Protestant denominations 14, 211
  missions, missionaries 27, 52, 53, 117, 185, 227
Baptist Missionary Society 14, 15, 65
Barff family 163
Baxter, George 214
beachcomber (European) 123, 206, 228
Beidelman, T. O. 22
Bennelong 169, 234
Bennet, George, *see* Tyerman, Reverend Daniel
Bentham's panopticon 89
Berndt, Ronald M. and Catherine H. 56, 218
Bhabha, Homi K. 22, 30, 33, 58, 128, 131, 213, 229
Bicknell family 163
Biraban (M'Gill) 185, 190, 237
Birmingham 27
Bligh, Admiral 117
body
  European, admired by Polynesians 232
  female, as torrid zone 146
  Polynesian, admired by missionaries 144
  point of cultural permeability 135
Bogue, Reverend Dr David 116
Bonner, Hypatia Bradlaugh 122

bonnet
  role in labour reform 151
  role in preserving light skin 149
  symbol of Christianisation 147–54
  symbolic role in missionary writing 148
  see also clothing
Booth family 163
Booth, William 187
Bourne, Mrs 48, 148
Bourne, Robert 48
Bowie, Fiona 110
Boy's Own Paper, The 43
Brahmo Samaj 68, 98, 110
Brantlinger, Patrick 19, 34, 38, 74, 77, 80, 212
British Army, attitude towards missionary
  activity 18
Brockway, K. Nora 220, 222, 225
Brontë, Charlotte 20
Brooke, Sir James 42, 216
Broughton, Archdeacon 198
Bryant, Joseph 42
Buchan, John 20
Buck, Sir Peter 230
Bulu, Joel 229
Burns, Reverend Robert 1–2, 17, 210
Burton, Antoinette 45, 50, 55, 82, 111
Buxton, Thomas Fowell 198
Buyers, William 81, 92, 224
Buzacott, Aaron 124

Cairns, David 237
Calder, Alex 231
Callan, Hilary 27
Canada 55
cannibalism 19, 55, 141
Carey, Hilary 50, 173, 217, 234
Carey, William 65, 117, 227
cargo cult 133
Carlyle, Thomas 188
caste, *see* class
Cathcart, Michael 118
Chambers, Ross 29
Champion, Ben W. 180, 236
charity, *see* philanthropy
Chatterjee, Partha 67, 109, 221
child(ren)
  Aboriginal, sexual abuse of 186, 191
  female, inferior status of 86
  forcible removal from parents 172
  marriage 86
  path to Christianisation 162
  sacrifice 98
  welfare 158–63
  see also family; infanticide; missionary children
childbirth 163

China 79
Christian, Samuel 171
Christianisation and civilisation 2, 120–4, 127
  missionary family as model 50, 52, 171
Church of England 16, 26, 211
Church Missionary Society 15, 16, 20, 65, 173
Church of Scotland, Ladies Association 70
Cilento, Raphael 188
civil rights 31
civility
  tea-drinking as measure of 158
  theories of 8
  treatment of women as measure of 168
Clarke, Marcus 198
class 14–15, 23, 38, 41, 42, 90, 96, 106, 168, 187,
  205
  aristocratic authority 39
  axis of power 28
  British poor 14, 205
  congruence across cultures 102
  correlation with degree of civilisation 161
  correlation with depravity 161
  and degeneracy, degradation 198, 206
  middle (British) 25–6, 39–40
  relations in colonial contexts 35
  relations within missionary societies 16–17
  representation in missionary writing 10
  and skin colour 149, 205
  status of missionaries 35, 70, 90
  studies of 27, 28
  theories of 5, 199
climate, *see* environment
clitoridectomy 56
clothing
  Christian, John Wesley's view on 149
  discourses of 147
  European: bartered in Africa 233;
    representation of civilisation 143; symbol
    of Christianisation 147, 148, 153
  missionary concern with 147–55, 167, 178, 225
  politics of in India 225
  representation of gender 103
  see also bonnet
Cohn, Bernard S. 221, 225
colonial
  anthropology, studies of 28
  degeneracy, degradation 198
  enactment of imperial policy 3, 6
  as opposed to imperial 211
  practice 38
  studies, discourse theories 6
colonialism 16, 23
Comaroff, Jean and John 22, 23–5, 29, 36, 42,
  142, 143, 214
concubinage 189

convict, *see* Australian
convictism 186
Cook, Captain James 116–17, 227
Cooper, Frederick 27
Cran, Reverend 65, 219
Crook, William Pascoe 141, 174, 231
  and family 162
cultural permeability, points of 135
Cunningham, Francis 51, 218
Cunningham, Valentine 80

darkness (opposed to light), *see* Manichean
Darling, David 48
  and family 163
Darling, Rebecca (formerly Woolston) 148
Darwinism
  natural selection 188
  Social 188
Davidoff, Lenore 46, 51
Davies family 163
Davin, Anna 217
Davis, Mrs 145
Dening, Greg 36, 215, 227, 231, 233
Des Granges, Reverend 65, 219
Dickens, Charles *Bleak House* 20
domestic
  reform 170
  relations 54, 206; British assumptions about 3
  social power 25
domesticity 38–59, 64, 87, 96, 106, 109, 110, 111
  cult of 50
  discourses of 186
  representation of 26, 29
  theories of 5, 38, 45
  topic of missionary writing 8
Donaldson, Stuart 184
Doran, Christine 43, 44, 67, 217
Douglas, Bronwen 34, 151
dress, *see* clothing
drink, *see* food and drink
Driver, Dorothy 42, 45, 48, 49
Duff (missionary ship) 118, 141, 145, 173, 227
Duff, Reverend Alexander 70, 91, 93, 221

East India Company, attitude towards
  education 101
  missionary activity 18, 64, 72–5, 212
eating, *see* food and drink
economic reform 121
Edmond, Rod 36, 129, 139, 140, 142, 154, 159, 231
education 33, 47, 66–70, 178, *see also* Native
    Female School; Native Institution
  disruptive nature of 226
  English as the preferred language of 100–2, 132
  of females 67–70, 74, 208

gendered 66–8
and independence movements 110
of males 68
means of civilization 120
means of curbing Aboriginal hostility 169
means of evangelism 66
valued by Polynesians 132
Elliot, Sir Gilbert, *see* Lord Minto
Ellis, Reverend James J. 228
Ellis, William 123, 124, 129–31, 133, 139–40, 159,
    190, 208, 230, 231
empire, *see* imperialism
English, *see* British; education; language
environment, climate
  potential to cause degradation 188, 199, 206
  threat to British women 21
Etherington, Norman 217
ethnicity 187, *see also* race
  axis of power 28
ethnography, *see* missionary writing,
    ethnographic
Ethnological Society of London 182, 236
European(s)
  corrupting influence of 118
  degeneracy, degradation of 176, 187, 188, 189,
    206
  subversive to missionary activity 177
evangelical revival, *see* evangelism, Protestant
evangelism, *see also* missionary activity
  American 47
  Anglican 16
  Catholic 13, 16, 64, 146, 173, 212
  colonial 5
  French 212
  German 64
  Italian 174, 212
  London Missionary Society 4
  Protestant 4, 5, 13–14, 15, 38, 65, 73, 147,
    158
  scholarly debate about 24
  and science 220
  Swiss 174
Eves, Richard 151
Eyre, Mrs 145

Fabian, Johannes 9
family 51–5, 155–8, 178
  mission as extended 52
  nuclear (as Christian ideal) 53, 120, 147, 156
  point of cultural permeability 135
  relations 64
  studies of 28
  see also Christianisation and civilisation
Fanon, Frantz 28, 57
Fauea 229

femininity, British assumptions about 3,
    see also womanhood
feminist
    activism, British 56
    activism, Indian 110
    participation in Empire 82
    press, Victorian 82
    suffragist 9, 49, 96, 106, 107, 111, 205
    theory 92, 111
    see also women's studies
Ferry, John 236
Fiji 19, 42
food and drink 156–8
    dietary reform 157
    and gender segregation 156
    morality of particular foodstuffs 157
    sharing of 156
    table manners 158
    and *tapu* 158
    tea-drinking 158
Forbes, Geraldine H. 57, 71, 107, 108, 225
Forman, Charles W. 232
Forsyth, Reverend Nathaniel 65
Fraser, John 182
French Revolution 14
Frow, John 234

Gaunt, Lewis Hermon 68, 230
gender 23, 38–59, 96, 106, 109, 110, 111, 126, 147,
    164, 168, 197, 199, *see also* clothing;
    manliness; woman/women
    axis of power 28
    congruence across cultures 103
    equity 156
    imbalance in Australia 168
    in missionary writing 8–9, 204
    justification for missionary activity 8
    missionary intervention 141
    representation of 26–7, 29, 81
    roles, relations 16, 21, 23, 35, 44, 45–51, 53–9,
        64, 87, 155, 190, 206: complementarity of
        39, 41, 72, 109, 215
    segregation 120, 156, *see also* education; food
    studies of 27, 28
    theories of 5, 8, 38
geography, *see* missionary writing, geographic
Gibbons, Luke 188
Gikandi, Simon 22, 29, 38, 210
Gilbert, Sandra M. 39
Gogerly, Reverend 80
Gordon, Adam Lindsay 238
gosha 221, *see also* zenana
Goss, Martha (later Threlkeld) 174
Gray, B. Kirkman 14
Greatheed, Reverend Samuel 129

Green, Martin 19
Grewal, Inderpal 89, 96, 97, 109, 223, 226
Griffiths, Tom 232
Grimshaw, Beatrice 163
Grimshaw, Patricia 47, 215
Gubar, Susan 39
Guha, Ranajit 64, 76, 219
Gunson, Niel 22, 43, 122, 125, 129, 137, 152, 161,
    170–2, 181, 217, 228, 235
Gyles, John 228

Haggard, Rider 20
Haggis, Jane 21, 23, 32, 44, 48, 67, 70, 79, 95,
    103, 105, 106–8, 211, 213, 222, 225
Hall, Catherine 22, 23, 27, 29, 40–3, 46, 51, 185,
    211
Hall, Donald E. 40, 216
Hamilton, Annette 191, 199
Hannabuss, Stuart 19, 20
Harrington, Henry Randolph 216
Harris, John 214
Harris, Thomas 141–2, 154, 173, 231
Hart, Miss Isabel 88
Hastings, Marquess of (formerly Lord Moira)
    73, 222
Haweis, Reverend Thomas 116, 117, 226
Hayward, Mrs 145
heathen, *see* native/indigenous
Henning, Rachel 150
Henry: family 162; Mrs 145; Reverend 148
Herbert, Christopher 124–6, 128, 130, 131, 134,
    140, 141, 158, 190
Hill, Micaiah and Mary 80
Hinduism 72, 83, 92
Hindus
    as focus of writing 83
    as target of evangelism 66
Holmes, Brian 16, 66, 101, 110
homosexuality, male 143–4, 207, 231, 232,
    see also body, sexuality
Horne, C. Silvester 14, 46, 55, 145
    The Story of the LMS 123
housing reform 120
Hughes, Thomas 40, 41
Hulme, Peter 30
Human Rights and Equal Opportunity
    Commission, *Bringing Them Home* 172,
    200
Husband Class 68
Hutchinson, Edward 20
Hyam, Ronald 213

imbrication, *see* mutual imbrication
imperial
    archive 3, 31–7

discourses 35
history 28, 31
ideology, policy 2, 3, 6, 17
  as opposed to colonial 211
  see also colonial
imperialism 38, 106
  British 14, 31, 107: 'second' era of 3, 13, 15;
    as moral allegory 13
  colonial projects 5, 31, 210
  Dutch 14
  Portuguese 13
  Spanish 13
India(n) 1, 4, 5, 7, 22, 28, 33, 36, 42, 52, 54, 63,
    205, 207, 227, *see also* East India Company
  colonial status 5
  London Missionary Society missions in 65
  Mutiny 18, 51, 203
industrial reform 120
infanticide 55, 57, 86, 93, 141, 156, 158–62, 177,
    204, *see also* child(ren); maternity
Irish, as the Other 187

Jamaica 27, 52, 53, 185
Johnson, Arthur N. 68, 116
Johnson, Richard 169, 170
Johnston, Anna 213, 221, 228, 235, 237
Jolly, Margaret 53, 145, 163, 213, 232,
    233
Jones family 163

Kaplan, Steven 133
Kennedy, Reverend James 69, 85, 87, 91,
    221
Kent, Graeme 42, 123, 142, 228, 231
King, Reverend Joseph 169, 172, 231, 234,
    236
Kingsley, Charles 20
  Two Years Ago 40
  Westward Ho! 42, 216
Knibb, Reverend 214, 218
Kock, Leon de 22
Kotzebue, Captain Otto van 138

Lacroix, Alphonse Françoise 84
  and family 84, 85
Lacroix, Hannah Catherine (later Mullens) 84
Ladies' Committees, *see also* London Missionary
    Society
Lang, John Dunmore 173, 184, 193, 198, 234
language(s)
  capacity to corrupt white children 133–5
  altered by missionary presence 101
  indigenous: analysis, recording, learning of 1,
    32, 129–35, 181–5; medium of evangelism
    177; translation into 1, 128–33

linguistic skills of Polynesians 132
pidgin, as miscegenation 182
point of cultural permeability 135
role in representing cultural values 133
Lawrence, Sir Henry 220
Lester, Alan 193, 238
Liberal movement 74
light (opposed to darkness), *see* Manichean
Lindstrom, Lamont 126, 229
literacy 123, *see also* education
literature
  adventure novels 19
  juvenile 19, 43
  travel writing 24
  zenana 82–4
  see also missionary writing
Livingstone, David 2, 19, 119
London Missionary Society (LMS) 1, 15, 16, 44,
    47, 49, 53, 64, 65–7, 76, 83, 136–7, 141
  in Africa 24
  archive (texts) 2–5
  in Australia 167, 172, 193–7, 198
  and British culture 25
  Candidates' Committee 48
  and denomination 211
  Directors' Committee, Board 108, 116
  first overseas mission 116
  in India 65
  Ladies' Committee 106, 108
  Ladies Examination Committee 108
  missionaries (names of) 19, 170
  periodical publications 32–4
  policy regarding gender of missionaries 7, 47
  in Polynesia 116, 118, 119
  Polynesia, initial lack of success 119, 227
  remuneration of missionaries 121
  Story of the LMS 14, 46, 55
  Tyerman and Bennet's deputation 115,
    136
Loveless, Reverend W. C. 65
Lovett, Richard 73, 214, 222
Lutheran
  and London Missionary Society 211
  mission 173

Macintyre, Martha 53, 145
MacKenzie, John 38
MacLean, Reverend R. 230
Macquarie, Governor Lachlan 169, 170
Madagascar 20
mahu 231, *see also* homosexuality 231
Malay Straits Settlements 43, 47, 67
Malinowski, Bronislaw 126
Mangan, J. A. 41
Manichean binaries 88–9

manliness
  assumptions about 3
  and authority 40
  Bengali effeminacy 102, 207
  British 8, 39, 42, 102, 207
  Elizabethan 42
  evangelical ideals of 189, 207
  representation of 40
  see also muscular Christianity
Manu, Laws of 83
Maori(s) 18, 174
Marcus, Sylvia 146
marriage
  arranged 86
  child 86
  customs 190
  see also domesticity
Marryat, Frederick 34
Marsden, Elizabeth 171
Marsden, Reverend Samuel 49, 169–71, 193–7,
    217, 233
  representative of London Missionary Society
    173–4
masculinity, *see* manliness; muscular Christianity
maternity 46, 50, 57, 70, 86, 94, 156, 158–63, 219,
    224, *see also* infanticide
Maugham, Somerset 20
May, Robert 33
Maynard, Margaret 147, 150
McClintock, Anne 9, 16, 38, 50, 52, 57,
    232
McGill, M'Gill, *see* Biraban
Melanesia 116
Melville, Herman 20
Messenger of Peace (missionary ship) 122
Methodist Press 80
Mexico 146
Micronesia 116
millennial movement 133
mimicry, colonial 33, *see also* Bhabha
Minto, Lord (formerly Sir Gilbert Elliot) 73, 222
miscegenation, *see* race; sexual relationships
mission station as threshold institution 38, 145
missionaries, *see also* women missionaries
  in fiction 19
  imperial, colonial role 2, 6, 13, 18–19, 24, 25,
    26, 27, 35, 37, 75, 79, 97, 116, 184, 208
  marriage to Polynesian women 142
  as nations' conscience 170
  native/indigenous 215, 229
  relationship to colonial state 72–8
  rescuers of native women 207
  speaking for the oppressed 185
missionary activity
  affecting local languages 101

commencement in Australia 169
commercial, economic 121–3, 152, 220, 229
'domestic experiment' 170, 172
evangelical 29
linguistic, *see* language(s)
perceived opportunity for 63–4
portrayal to British public 19
purpose 1
textual manifestation of 73
  see also Christianisation and civilisation;
    evangelism; printing press
missionary children 162–3
missionary experience, influence on parallel
    debates in Britain 26
missionary heroes 2, 7, 43, 118, 119, 122, 214,
    217
missionary ship, *see also Duff; Messenger of Peace*
  as icon 118, 122
missionary societies 15
  Auxiliary Societies 107
  Free Church of Scotland's India Mission 224
  Ladies' Committees 106
  Missionary Society
    Baptist 14, 15, 65
    Church 15, 16, 20, 65
    Netherlands 84
    Wesleyan Methodist 15, 24, 65, 169, 173
    see also London Missionary Society
missionary wives 20, 21, 39, 46–51, 107, 145–6,
    170–2
  domestic role model 49
  embodiment of Empire 50–1
  marginalisation in texts 43
  protecting against sexual temptation 49,
    173
  representation of 207
  vocation 48
missionary women, *see* missionary wives; women
    missionaries
missionary writing 2, 79–105
  audience(s) for 32, 96, 124, 126
  based on field reports etc. 32
  editing of 33–4, 81, 126–7, 138–9, 196–7
  ethnographic 1, 32, 125, 208
  fictional 34
  gendered nature of 42
  genre of 6, 9, 24, 32, 80–3, 104, 124, 202, 203
  geographic 32
  influence on imperial attitudes 208
  influence on missionary society practice 79
  London Missionary Society archive 3–5
  manipulation of 202
  masculine authorship of 7–8
  printing of, *see* printing press
  as propaganda 6, 25, 29, 32, 126–8

re-circulation of tropes 7, 34, 81, 82, 88, 203
as source of knowledge 4, 32
women writers 7, 44: masculinist rhetoric 91, 97
Moffat, Reverend 214
Moira, Lord, *see* Marquess of Hastings
Montgomery, James 138, 140
Moodie, Susanna 135
morality 109, 111
theories of 188
Morant Bay Rebellion 18
Mount Holyoke College 217
mourning customs 190
Muir, Ramsay 222
Mullens family 85
Mullens, Hannah Catherine (formerly Lacroix) 84, 91, 223, 229
Faith and Victory 77, 84, 89, 96–105
Mullens, Reverend Joseph 79, 84, 101, 222
Mundy, Reverend George 33
Mundy, Louisa 33, 214
Murray, Reverend A. W. 132
muscular Christianity 8, 39–43, 68, 143, 216
Muslims (ignored in missionary writing) 83
mutual constitution 28, 29, *see also* mutual imbrication
mutual engagement, *see* mutual imbrication
mutual imbrication 3, 9, 16, 26, 28, 29, 35, 105, 107, 135, 141, 147, 149, 150, 154, 187, 202–9
Myall Creek massacre 200

nationalism, Indian 96, 106, 109
Native Female School 67, 68, 85, *see also* education
Native Institution 169, 170, *see also* education
Native Institutions Committee 169
native/indigenous
agency 25, 36
childlike 17
degraded 159, 203
heathen Other 19, 58, 187, 197, 205
history of missionary encounter 6
noble savage 1, 17, 115, 145, 164, 197, 203
resistance to European intervention 203
see also Aborigine; Hindu; Maori; Polynesian; women; missionaries
Neill, Stephen 13, 15, 65, 219, 222, 228
Nelson, Thomas 43
New South Wales, *see* Australia
New Zealand 18, 42, 216
see also Maori
Nisbet, James 43
nonconformist 27

Norman, Vance 40, 216
Nott, Mrs A. 215
and family 163
Nussbaum, Felicity 46, 146, 158, 218, 237

Oborea 117
Orientalism 1, 117
Orsmond, John 174
and family 163
Oxford University Press 80

Pacific Islands, *see* Polynesia
pagan, *see* native/indigenous
patriarchy 39–43
pedagogy, *see* education
Perrot, Philippe 149, 150, 152
phantasm 95, 224
philanthropy 14, 16, 71, 223
role of women in 15
Philip, Governor Arthur 169
physiognomy (indicating character) 223
Platt, Reverend George 126–7, 148
and family 163
Poe, Edgar Allan 238
polyandry 53, 145
polygamy 53, 55, 86
Polynesia(n) 1, 4, 5, 8, 22, 28, 42, 43, 47, 48, 49, 53, 54, 79, 80, 115, 164, 174, 206, 207, 208, 228
colonial status 5, 115
culture 55: feminised nature of 143
geographical definition 116
London Missionary Society missions in 116
and racial hierarchy 175, 232
sexual licence 117
social freedom 117
white population 18
Porter, Andrew 29, 31, 122, 228
postcolonial theory, studies 3, 4, 6, 140, 182
and historicism 30–1
Australia 6
settler 6, 199
Pratt, Mary Louise 24, 231
Presbyterian
and London Missionary Society 211
missions, missionaries 163, 173
printing press 73, 80, 123
Pritchard, Reverend George 122, 214
Prochaska, F. K. 15, 223
Prout, Ebenezer 122, 124, 229, 230
purdah 221, *see also* zenana
Purea 117
Pybus, Cassandra 216

Quaker missionaries 184

race 23, 38, 106, 167, 187, *see also* Aborigine;
    Australian; European; ethnicity; Hindu;
    Irish; Maori; Polynesian;
    native/indigenous; missionaries; women
  imperial attitudes to 26
  miscegenation (abhorrence of) 45, 182
  and missionary writing 10, 203
  racial hierarchy 150, 164, 175, 199,
    231
  relations in India 27
  and skin colour 150–1, 205
  studies of 28
  theories of 5, 8, 9, 17, 45, 54, 188
Rajan, Rajeswari Sunder 74
Ramabai, Pandita 110
religiosity 13
  theories of 45
Religious Tract Society 43, 80
Reynolds, Henry 186, 192, 200–1
Ribeiro, Aileen 232
Richards, Jeffrey 18, 40, 42, 43, 216
Richards, Shaun 237
Richards, Thomas 31, 38, 210, 213
Ringeltraube, Reverend 65, 219
Robertson, James 34
Rooke, Patricia T. 215
Rose, Deborah Bird 22
Royal National Exhibition 182
Russell, Reverend Michael 19
Ryan, Simon 219

Salvation Army 187
Sarawak 42, 216
sati, *see* widows
Saunders, Graham 216
savage, *see* native/indigenous
Sawbridge, Laura Helen 45
Schaffer, Kay 45
school, *see* education; Native Female School;
    Native Institution
Scott, Jamie S. 13
Seeley, Sir John 77
Select Committee on Aborigines (British
    Settlements) 186, 198
Selwyn, George Augustus 42–3
Serampore Press 73
sexual
  abuse, *see* child(ren); women
  power, female 53
  relationships, cross-cultural 18, 54, 180,
    187–92, 199, 206
  threat: Bengali men as 207; Polynesian
    women as 49, 173

sexuality 54–5, 126, 164, 167–8, 178, 197, 199,
    see also body; homosexuality
  in Catholic confession manuals 146
  licentious 141, 207
  monogamy as Christian ideal 156
  point of cultural permeability 135
  Polynesian 117, 141–7; gendered female 141–2
  representation of 28, 81
  topic of missionary writing 8
Sharpe, Jenny 5, 51
Shelley, Elizabeth (formerly Bean) 234
Shelley, William 170, 173
Sherman, Reverend James 95, 120
Sinha, Mrinalini 102, 110, 207
Skanda Purána 95
skin colour *see* class; race
slavery 27, 74, 186
  abolition of 2, 186
Slemon, Stephen 30, 213, 218
Smith, Bernard 200, 226, 231
Smith, Reverend Sydney 161
Smith, Dr Thomas 90, 93
Smith, Vanessa 152, 228, 231
social
  difference as a category of nature 52
  reform 208
Society for Promoting Christian Knowledge
    (SPCK) 15, 43, 237
Society for Promoting Female Education in
    the East 21
Society for the Propagation of the Gospel
    (SPG) 15
Society of the United Brethren 65
South Africa 23, 31, 79
South Pacific, South Seas, South Sea Islands,
    see Polynesia
Spivak, Gayatri 8, 82, 215, 219
St John, Sir Spenser 216
Stanley, Brian 22, 214
Stanley, Henry Morton 187
stereotype(s)
  as discursive strategy 58
  in colonial discourse 58
  of colonized 54
  of missionaries 30
  see also missionary writing, re-circulation of
    tropes
Stevenson, Robert Louis 20
Stolen Generations 172
Stoler, Ann Laura 10, 23, 27, 28, 35, 211
Storrow, Reverend Edward 67, 69, 75, 83, 220,
    224, 226
  Our Indian Sisters 84, 91–5, 98
  The Eastern Lily Gathered 84–91, 104
Subaltern Studies group 30

subjectivity 187
suffragist, *see* feminist
Swain, Tony 22

tapu, see food and drink
Ta'unga 229
Taylor, Reverend John 65
tayo, 231, *see also* homosexuality
Te Rangi Hiroa, *see* Buck, Sir Peter
Teale, Ruth 168
Telscher, Kate 83
texts
    Bible as a commodity 124
    symbolic role in missionary activity 66, 69,
        123–4
    see also literature; missionary writing
textual representation
    imperial 117
    power to effect conversion 84, 127
Thomas, Nicholas 9, 31, 155, 210, 233
Thompson, Ralph Wardlaw 68, 116, 221, 222
Thorne, Susan 23, 24, 25–8, 29, 39, 119, 212, 213,
    227
Threlkeld, Reverend Lancelot 4, 137, 167–8, 174,
    201, 205, 206, 233, 235, 236
    colonial nature of writings 182
    contradictions in writings 199
    dispute with LMS 193–7
    and family 163, 235
    grammars of Aboriginal languages 235
    imperial/colonial role 180–201
    manipulation of texts 174, 193–7
    role as interpreter 181, 184
    role as protector 181
Threlkeld, Martha (formerly Goss) 174
Threlkeld, Sarah (formerly Arndell) 179, 236
threshold institution, mission station as 38,
    145
Tiffin, Helen 30, 52
trader (European) 206
translation
    problems of representation 128–33
    see also language
transvestite, *see* homosexuality
Tristan, Samuel 171
Trollope, Joanna 218
Tyerman, Reverend Daniel 235
    and George Bennet 115, 130, 132–3, 136–9, 153,
        154, 157, 160–2, 174–9, 181, 205, 206, 215,
        230, 231, 233, 235, 236, 238

utopia 53, 115, 117, *see also* native/indigenous

Vanderschalk, C. J. 48–9
Vedic Age (idealisation of) 83

violence of the gaze 94
Viswanathan, Gauri 102

Walker, George Washington 184
Walker, William 169
Walkowitz, Judith A. 210
Walvin, James 41
Watts, Lee 146, 231
Weitbrecht, Mrs Mary Edwards 51, 83, 85, 88, 94,
    224
Wellesley, Marquis 98
Wesley, John, Reverend 149
Wesleyan Methodist Missionary Society 15, 24,
    65, 169, 173
    and mission, missionaries 174
West Indies 15, 52, 79, 188
white man's burden 188
Whitlock, Gillian 23, 45, 186, 218
widows
    mourning customs 190
    treatment of 27, 55, 74–5, 86, 208
Wilberforce, Bishop Samuel 122
Williams, John 2, 19, 43, 117, 119, 122, 124,
    126–7, 134, 144, 147, 148, 151, 152,
    153, 155, 174, 205, 208, 214, 228, 231,
    232
    and family 230
    Missionary Enterprises 136, 139–41
Williams, Peter 108, 225
Wilson,
    family 163
Wilson, Captain James 118
Wilson, Reverend John 63, 76, 77, 88, 92, 95,
    219, 225
Wilson, Margaret 88
Windschuttle, Keith 201
woman/women
    Aboriginal: co-option into white society 186;
        frail 189; needing rescue 177; oppressed 57,
        177; sexual abuse of 186, 191
    Algerian 94
    'angel in the house' 39
    Christian: embodiment of Empire 8, 58;
        embodiment of progressive modernity 45;
        embodiment of traditional morality 45–6;
        fulfilled 104; role in evangelisation 44;
        status of 39; subject to husband 95
    Hindu, domestic arrangements 221
    Indian: degraded 86, 92; insipid 104; invisible
        to male missionaries 70; needing rescue
        55–6; oppressed 71, 80, 82, 102; resistant to
        missionary effort 71, 92–4; target of
        evangelism 64, 69; weak in character 87
    influence on children 70
    morally superior 45

woman/women (*cont.*)
  Muslim: degraded 86; domestic arrangements 221; veiling 56
  native/indigenous: actual nature of treatment 218; bad mothers 57; degraded 39, 54, 70, 190; justifying missionary activity 8, 55–8; lazy 105; oppressed 55–7; overly powerful 57; sexually profligate 49, 54, 57, 145; target of evangelism 21, 44
  naturally spiritual 45, 71, 72
  Polynesian: bad mothers 159; lazy 145; oppressed 146; overly powerful 145; sexually assertive 119; sexually profligate 141–7
  representation of British culture 46
  weaker sex 45
  see also feminist; gender; missionary wives; native/indigenous; sexuality, zenana
womanhood
  and domesticity 47
  pride of 110
  see also femininity
women missionaries 20–1, 26–7, 39, 44, 70, 71, 87, 106–9, 111, 205, 225
  clash with male authority 108

women's studies 22, 23, *see also* feminism
Woolmington, Jean 15, 169, 235
Woolston, Rebecca (later Darling) 48
writing, *see* missionary writing; literature; texts

Yarwood, A. T. 171
Youl, John 173, 234

zenana 7, 21, 44, 69–72, 81, 87–96, 97, 197, 204, 208, 221, 229
  dark and dirty 94
  denying specularity 94
  as fortress 90
  as home 109
  literature 82–4
  as prison 87, 109
  resistant to missionary effort 109
  Society 70
  source of danger to missionary women 226
  too public 89
  visitation 70

CAMBRIDGE STUDIES IN NINETEENTH-CENTURY
LITERATURE AND CULTURE

General editor
Gillian Beer, *University of Cambridge*

Titles published

1. The Sickroom in Victorian Fiction: The Art of Being Ill
by Miriam Bailin, *Washington University*

2. Muscular Christianity: Embodying the Victorian Age
edited by Donald E. Hall, *California State University, Northridge*

3. Victorian Masculinities: Manhood and Masculine Poetics in Early Victorian
Literature and Art
by Herbert Sussman, *Northeastern University, Boston*

4. Byron and the Victorians
by Andrew Elfenbein, *University of Minnesota*

5. Literature in the Marketplace: Nineteenth-Century British Publishing
and the Circulation of Books
edited by John O. Jordan, *University of California, Santa Cruz* and
Robert L. Patten, *Rice University, Houston*

6. Victorian Photography, Painting and Poetry
by Lindsay Smith, *University of Sussex*

7. Charlotte Brontë and Victorian Psychology
by Sally Shuttleworth, *University of Sheffield*

8. The Gothic Body: Sexuality, Materialism and Degeneration at the *Fin de Siècle*
by Kelly Hurley, *University of Colorado at Boulder*

9. Rereading Walter Pater
by William F. Shuter, *Eastern Michigan University*

10. Remaking Queen Victoria
edited by Margaret Homans, *Yale University* and Adrienne Munich, *State
University of New York, Stony Brook*

11. Disease, Desire, and the Body in Victorian Women's Popular Novels
by Pamela K. Gilbert, *University of Florida*

12. Realism, Representation, and the Arts in Nineteenth-Century Literature
by Alison Byerly, *Middlebury College, Vermont*

13. Literary Culture and the Pacific
by Vanessa Smith, *University of Sydney*

14. Professional Domesticity in the Victorian Novel Women, Work and Home
by Monica F. Cohen

15. Victorian Renovations of the Novel: Narrative Annexes and the
Boundaries of Representation
by Suzanne Keen, *Washington and Lee University, Virginia*

16. Actresses on the Victorian Stage: Feminine Performance and the Galatea Myth
by Gail Marshall, *University of Leeds*

17. Death and the Mother from Dickens to Freud: Victorian Fiction and
the Anxiety of Origin
by Carolyn Dever, *Vanderbilt University, Tennessee*

18. Ancestry and Narrative in Nineteenth-Century British Literature: Blood
Relations from Edgeworth to Hardy
by Sophie Gilmartin, *Royal Holloway, University of London*

19. Dickens, Novel Reading, and the Victorian Popular Theatre
by Deborah Vlock

20. After Dickens: Reading, Adaptation and Performance
by John Glavin, *Georgetown University, Washington DC*

21. Victorian Women Writers and the Woman Question
edited by Nicola Diane Thompson, *Kingston University, London*

22. Rhythm and Will in Victorian Poetry
by Matthew Campbell, *University of Sheffield*

23. Gender, Race, and the Writing of Empire:
Public Discourse and the Boer War
by Paula M. Krebs, *Wheaton College, Massachusetts*

24. Ruskin's God
by Michael Wheeler, *University of Southampton*

25. Dickens and the Daughter of the House
by Hilary M. Schor, *University of Southern California*

26. Detective Fiction and the Rise of Forensic Science
by Ronald R. Thomas, *Trinity College, Hartford, Connecticut*

27. Testimony and Advocacy in Victorian Law, Literature, and Theology
by Jan-Melissa Schramm, *Trinity Hall, Cambridge*

28. Victorian Writing about Risk:
Imagining a Safe England in a Dangerous World
by Elaine Freedgood, *University of Pennsylvania*

29. Physiognomy and the Meaning of Expression in
Nineteenth-Century Culture
by Lucy Hartley, *University of Southampton*

30. The Victorian Parlour: A Cultural Study
by Thad Logan, *Rice University, Houston*

31. Aestheticism and Sexual Parody 1840–1940
by Dennis Denisoff, *Ryerson University, Toronto*

32. Literature, Technology and Magical Thinking, 1880–1920
by Pamela Thurschwell, *University College London*

33. Fairies in Nineteenth-Century Art and Literature
by Nicola Bown, *Birkbeck College, London*

34. George Eliot and the British Empire
by Nancy Henry, *The State University of New York, Binghamton*

35. Women's Poetry and Religion in Victorian England: Jewish Identity
and Christian Culture
by Cynthia Scheinberg, *Mills College, California*

36. Victorian Literature and the Anorexic Body
by Anna Krugovoy Silver, *Mercer University, Georgia*

37. Eavesdropping in the Novel from Austen to Proust
by Ann Gaylin, *Yale University, Connecticut*

38. Missionary Writing and Empire, 1800–1860
by Anna Johnston, *University of Tasmania*